Kings and Pawns

A Novel of Viking Age Ireland

Book Nine of The Norsemen Saga

James L. Nelson

Fore Topsail Press
64 Ash Point Road
Harpswell, Maine, 04079

ISBN-13: 978-0-578-51510-6
ISBN-10: 0-578-51510-5

To Elizabeth Page, who made me feel welcome from the get-go, with love and gratitude for all your kindness over the years.

PLATE 1

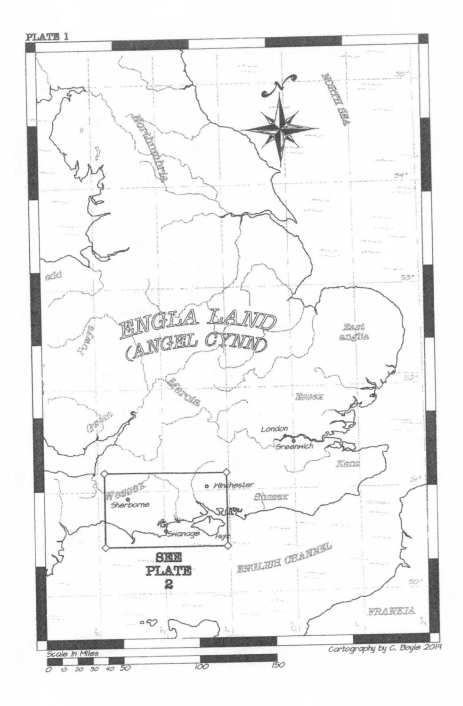

Cartography by C. Boyle 2019

PLATE 2

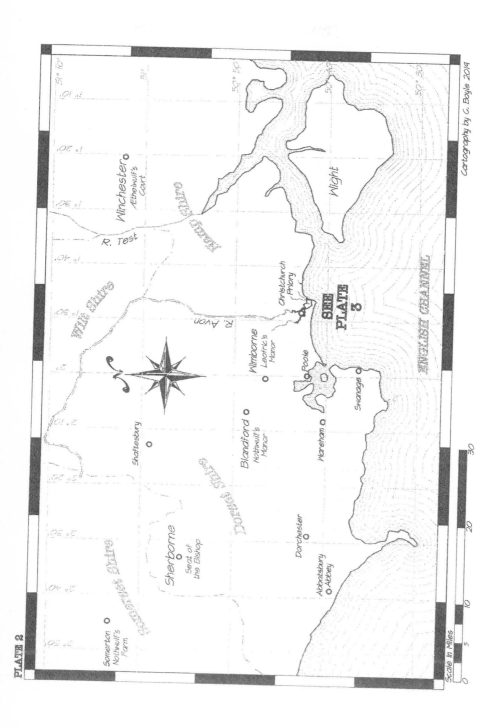

Somerton
Nothwulf's Farm

SOMERSET SHIRE

Sherborne
Seat of
the Bishop

Shaftesbury

WILTSHIRE

DORSETSHIRE

Abbotsbury
Abbey

Dorchester

Blandford
Nothwulf's
Manor

Wimborne
Leofric's
Manor

R. Avon

Wareham

Poole

Swanage

Christchurch
Priory

HANTSHIRE

R. Test

Winchester
Ætheiwulf's
Court

Wight

ENGLISH CHANNEL

SEE
PLATE
3

Scale in Miles
0   5   10   20   30

Cartography by C. Boyle 2014

51° 10'
51°
50° 50'
50° 30'

3° 10'
3°
2° 50'
2° 40'
3° 20'
3° 30'

PLATE 3

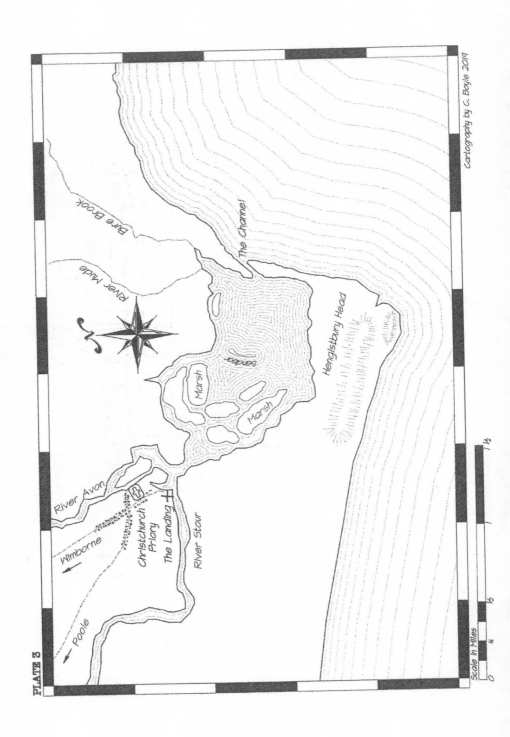

River Avon

Wimborne

Poole

Christchurch Priory

The Landing

River Stour

Burn Brook

River Mude

Marsh

Marsh

Sandbar

The Channel

Hengistbury Head

Cartography by C. Boyle 2019

Scale in Miles

0   ¼   ½   1   1½

The Viking Longship

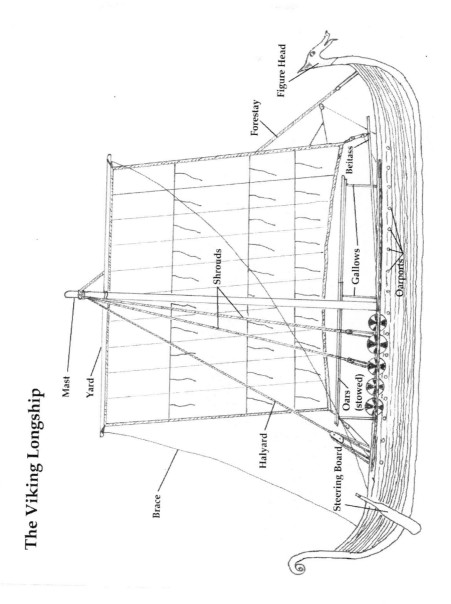

Mast
Yard
Brace
Halyard
Shrouds
Forestay
Figure Head
Beitass
Gallows
Oarports
Oars (stowed)
Steering Board

For terminology, see Glossary, page 350

Prologue

There was a man named Thorgrim Ulfsson, known as Thorgrim Night Wolf, who lived in Vik, which is in East Agder. As a young man he had gone raiding to the west with a local jarl named Ornolf Hrafnsson who was called Ornolf the Restless because he did not like to remain long at home. Thorgrim was one of Ornolf's men, but soon he became the leader of the other men and served as Ornolf's second. They had great success in their raiding and after some time returned to their farms in Norway where they enjoyed great wealth and fame.

Soon after returning to their homes, Ornolf offered the hand of his daughter, Hallbera, to Thorgrim in marriage. It was an arrangement that was agreeable to all, most of all to the two who were to be married. Thorgrim gave Ornolf fifty silver coins as his bride-price. Ornolf was also generous, as he loved both Thorgrim and his daughter. For a dowry Ornolf gave them a farm which was several miles north of Vik, in a place called Fevik. Though this was a very fine farm indeed, still Thorgrim decided to remain on his own land, and hired a free man as overseer of the second farm. But Thorgrim kept close watch on what was done at the farm in Fevik, and because he was as skilled at farming as he was at shipbuilding and raiding, the farm prospered and the land was bountiful.

Thorgrim and Hallbera were married for ten years, and in that time Hallbera bore Thorgrim Night Wolf three children. The first two were sons named Odd and Harald, and the third a girl, who they called Hild. Their farm prospered and Thorgrim's wealth and fame continued to grow until he was considered one of the leading men of that region, second only to the jarl Ornolf, who was Thorgrim's father-in-law. Thorgrim and Hallbera and their children were very happy on the farm.

When Odd became a man he wed a woman named Signy Olafsdottir whose father also had a farm in Vik. The wedding was a great affair. Thorgrim and Hallbera threw a wedding feast in Thorgrim's hall, and the people who lived in the countryside all around were invited. The feast lasted for three days and it was spoken of for many years after.

As a wedding gift, Thorgrim gave Odd and Signy the farm in Fevik that Ornolf had given him and Hallbera at their own wedding. Odd and his wife moved to the farm and Odd took over the running of it. Like Thorgrim, Odd was an intelligent man and had learned much about farming from his father, and soon the prosperous farm was more prosperous still, until it nearly rivaled Thorgrim's own land. Odd made many improvements in the land and the buildings. He expanded the longhouse into a great hall so that he could entertain neighbors and men of importance who were traveling there.

In the first years of their marriage Signy gave Odd three children: a son they named Ornolf, a daughter Thorgid, and another daughter they called Hallbera after Odd's mother.

Odd's mother, however, did not live to see her namesake. Soon after Odd and Signy were married, Hallbera conceived another child. Hallbera was not a young woman by then, and she died in childbirth, though the child lived. It was a daughter, and so great was the love that Thorgrim bore for his wife he named the child Hallbera as well.

Around this time Ornolf the Restless was once again eager to go raiding. The Northmen had just begun to plunder the country of Ireland, and to build longphorts there, and Ornolf, who had heard the tales, wished to go and see for himself, and he asked Thorgrim to accompany him. Now, Ornolf had asked Thorgrim many times over the years to go raiding once again, but Thorgrim was happy with his life on the farm and did not care to leave. But the death of Hallbera made it hard for him to stay, and so he agreed to join Ornolf for the summer's raiding to the west.

In Vik, and in all that country, young men were raised to be farmers and warriors both, and that was also true of Harald and Odd. When Thorgrim decided to sail with Ornolf, both were eager to go raiding with him. A young man like Odd did not understand how great were his joys at home, with a fine wife and children, but

Thorgrim understood that, even more with the death of his own wife. He knew as well how hard it would be on Signy and the children if Odd were to leave them to go a'viking and so he convinced Odd to remain at home.

Finally, Thorgrim and Harald joined Ornolf and his crew aboard the longship *Red Dragon* and they sailed to Ireland where they met with many adventures and won and lost several fortunes. They had meant to stay in Ireland for one season only, but the gods willed that they should not leave so easily and so they were several years in that country. Ornolf was struck down in battle at a place called Vík-ló and Thorgrim became the leader of his men. For a while he was lord of the longphort of Vík-ló and his men called him Lord Thorgrim. But finally he and his men grew tired of that place and decided to go a'viking once again, and see if perhaps the gods would allow them to return to their homes in Norway.

They came at last to a place the Irish called Loch Garman and built a longphort where they could repair their sea-damaged ships and build new sails from cloth bought from the Irish at a monastery called Ferns. While they were there, their company was joined by another band of Northmen, and soon Thorgrim had eight ships and more than three hundred men under his command.

Thorgrim had decided at that time that he would not leave Ireland, but rather would return to Vík-ló and once again be lord of that place. But before he could sail, the Irish, led by a monk named Brother Bécc, attacked the longphort and caused great slaughter. Thorgrim and his men got their ships underway with the thought of crossing the bay to the far shore, but a storm came up and it blew them out into the open sea. For three days the storm raged and the Northmen could do nothing but hunker down and ask the gods to deliver them.

And the gods did just that, save for the smallest ship of the fleet, named *Falcon*, which was not to be found when the storm ended. The Northmen found themselves in the middle of the ocean, with no idea where they were. Thorgrim chose a course by his best guess, and several days later they landed at a place they did not know, but soon found it was the country Engla-land where Thorgrim had raided with Ornolf as a young man.

Engla-land was a country of great wealth, as Thorgrim knew, and soon they found a rich monastery and captured it, finding considerable plunder and nearly two hundred English men-at-arms. The prisoners they meant to sell as slaves, but soon an Englishman named Oswin arrived and said that his lord would be willing to pay ransom for the men-at-arms and the priests as well. Thorgrim and his lead men decided that they would wait long enough to see if Oswin would make good on that offer.

Here is what happened.

Chapter One

*Now of thy wolves take
one from out the stall;
let him now
with my hog run.*

The Poetic Edda

It was dark and Thorgrim Night Wolf was running. The ground was moving swiftly under his feet, a fine sensation, odd and familiar at the same time, the tall grass brushing against him as he raced through it. He felt his body moving in a smooth, easy, nearly effortless way. The stiff elbows and knees were no more, the tight pull of the old wound in his back, the sharp stab of pain he often felt from the spear he had recently taken in side, all gone. It was the motion of power, and youth.

He was aware of the scents in the air. They, too, were both familiar and strange. He could smell wood smoke and the scent of animals, the odor of wet grass and the salty tang of the sea, not so far off. He could smell men. A lot of men. And they, too, were not so far off.

The ground rose up before him and he slowed, not because he was growing tired—he wasn't—but because he knew the men were very near now. It was no longer time for speed, it was time for stealth.

He paused in the dark and let the scents and the sounds settle over him. It was mostly men now, their smell overpowering the smell of horses and smoldering fires and leather and iron and cooked food. He could hear them moving about, but just barely. A shuffle and then silence, a muted cough. A few words spoken in a harsh, low

5

voice. Many men, being as quiet as they could be, which was not very quiet at all. At least not for Thorgrim's sharp ears.

He moved again, slowly, and even he could not hear the sounds of his own footfalls on the soft ground. He came to the top of the rise and bent low as he passed the crest and peered over. There was nothing below that surprised him. He had seen this sight before, many times.

There were tents. Rows of them, dull white, like old, exposed bones in the light of the sliver of moon overhead. Here and there a torch guttered or a small fire still burned, but Thorgrim did not look at them. He knew the light would impair his vision in the dark. And he knew it impaired the vision of the few men still awake in the camp, and that would make it harder yet for them to see him. Impossible, really.

He moved down the hill. He could see the shapes of men silhouetted against the flames in the camp, sentries posted beyond the throw of the light, armed men staring out into the blackness, looking for any threat approaching from the dark country beyond. But Thorgrim knew they would see nothing. There were no threats out there, save for him, and they would not see him.

The camp was laid out in a rough circle and Thorgrim moved around the perimeter. No clear thoughts came to his mind, no conclusions or observations. Nothing that could be articulated. Just impressions, senses, amorphous notions, but he took them all in, let them swirl like mist in his head.

The big tents were near the far end of the camp, large, round, pavilion-style tents that seemed to glow from inside. There were candles burning in there, men still at work or men who feared the dark. But there were only two of them, set up twenty feet apart. Guards stood outside the flaps of each. They looked bored and drowsy. Thorgrim could not tell if they were paying any attention to anything around them. If something happened they looked like they would be dead before they raised the butts of their spears off the trampled ground.

He moved on, coming to the far side of the camp. He had smelled the horses from a long distance away, long before he had seen the tents. Now the smell was growing more powerful, and with it he heard the animals shuffle nervously. The guards used their eyes to look out for danger, though sight was all but useless on that dark night. The horses used their hearing and their sense of smell, and even Thorgrim could not hide from that.

He paused and he heard the shuffling continue and he knew if he approached any closer the shuffling would turn to whinnying and that would attract the attention of the guards. For a moment he remained motionless and he heard the sound of the horses settling back down. Then he turned and moved back the way he had come. None of the sentries cried out or gave any indication that they were aware at all of his presence.

Then he was running again, the ground flying by, his muscles strong and tireless.

And then he was awake. His joints ached and the wound in his side throbbed and he felt as if he had been beaten with a heavy stick.

He opened his eyes, slowly. It was dark still, with just a hint of the dawn at the edge of the sky. He was lying on the ground. There was no fur or blanket over him, Failend was not by his side. Against the growing light in the east he could see the outline of a man, and even though he could not see anything beyond that, he knew it was Starri Deathless. Thorgrim moaned softly, involuntarily.

"Night Wolf," Starri said. It was a statement.

Thorgrim pushed himself up on one elbow and looked around. He thought he was somewhere near the south wall of the monastery. The one they had captured and plundered the week before. Where they had fought with English men-at-arms who had been there for some reason. Thorgrim could not recall the name of the place. He did not know if he ever knew the name. Or cared.

"Wolf dream?" Starri asked.

Thorgrim groaned again as he pushed himself up to a sitting position. He nodded his head, then realized that in the dark Starri probably could not see the gesture.

"Yes," he said. *Wolf dream.* He had had them since he was a young man. In the evening his temper would grow short and a black mood would consume him and he would have to stagger off and be by himself. He could not stand the presence of others, and in truth they could not stand him because they were afraid of him when he was like that. And after some time he would fall asleep and in his dreams he would travel over the countryside. He would see things. Things that would often turn out to be real.

It was how he earned his name. Kveldulf. Night Wolf. The older he grew, the more infrequently the wolf dreams came, but he was not free of them yet. Some said that they were not dreams, that his soul took on the form of a wolf and ran over the land as truly as a real wolf would. Thorgrim had no idea if this was true, but he doubted it. Mostly.

He looked over at Starri and he could see him more clearly now. Starri was fingering the charm he wore around his neck, a familiar gesture. It was the head of an arrow that had, in one of those odd occurrences that sometimes happen, struck the edge of Thorgrim's sword in the moments before battle and stuck there, split perfectly down the center. It was when Starri and Thorgrim had first met.

Thorgrim had pulled the arrow free and tossed it aside, but Starri took it as a sign that Thorgrim was blessed by the gods. He retrieved the arrowhead and had worn it on a cord around his neck ever since. And ever since he had rarely left Thorgrim's side.

That was particularly true when the dark mood came on, the precursor to a wolf dream. Since their first meeting Starri had always sat at Thorgrim's side during those times. And, for reasons Thorgrim never understood, Starri was the one person he could stand to have near him then. Even his son Harald, whom he loved more than anyone alive, was intolerable to him. But not Starri.

They had never spoken of it. Thorgrim did not know why Starri insisted on keeping him company, but he guessed the reasons were twofold. Starri wanted to make certain that Thorgrim's physical form was safe in those times when his soul was wandering far afield. And Starri felt that when Thorgrim was having a wolf dream the gods were close at hand, and Starri wanted to be there, too.

"What did you see?" Starri asked. He sounded like a calm and reasonable man. Starri always sounded that way when Thorgrim woke from a wolf dream. It was one of the only times he did.

Thorgrim made a grunting sound, but he did not answer at first. He thought back over the dream, the things that had appeared to him.

"I saw men," he said at last. "A camp of warriors. Not too far from here."

"The ones that Jorund's man Ofeig reported?"

"I guess so," Thorgrim said. "The army that this Oswin, shire reeve or whatever he's called, did not know about."

When they had captured that monastery, Thorgrim sent out scouts in all directions to see what threats might be approaching. Ofeig had come across an army, which he guessed was about two hundred men strong, moving their way.

Soon after, a fellow named Oswin had arrived at the gate, wishing to talk. He claimed to speak for the man who employed the men-at-arms Thorgrim's men had taken when they took the monastery. He claimed he could arrange ransom for those men. He claimed he did not know about this other army, but he said it was a threat to him and to Thorgrim as well.

I guess we'll find out the truth of this, soon enough, Thorgrim had thought as the fellow Oswin rode away, claiming that he was off to arrange for the ransom.

"Not a big army, no great force," Thorgrim continued. "Maybe two hundred men, like Ofeig said, maybe a few less. Horses. But not many."

"So, nothing for us to worry ourselves about?" Starri asked.

"As soon as we stop worrying, we're dead," Thorgrim said. "But this doesn't look like an army we can't beat."

"Good," Starri said. "Then we wait for them here, and when they attack us we'll crush them like the serpents they are."

In the dark Thorgrim smiled. Starri was a berserker, imbued with fighting madness that made him crave battle as if it were all that sustained him. It led him to take actions that more prudent men might shun. It also made him forget that such decisions as when and where to fight were not his to make.

"If it were mine to say, I would stay here and let you kill them all single-handed when they came," Thorgrim said. He put his hands on the cool, hard-packed dirt and pushed himself to his feet, awake enough now to stifle the groan growing in his throat. Starri stood as well, in that way of his that seemed more as if he was unfolding his lanky body.

"But it's not mine to say. I'll call a meeting of the lead men," Thorgrim said, though he knew the words were not true. It was his to say. He was the leader of these men, Lord Thorgrim, and what he said, they did. He would have it no other way.

At the same time, he wanted to show respect for the men who followed him. Jorund had joined with Thorgrim at Loch Garman, putting himself, his four ships and near two hundred men under

Thorgrim's command. He deserved a say in what they would do next. So did Godi and Harald, who had been with Thorgrim through so much, as well as the captains of the other ships.

"Very well, Night Wolf, do as you wish," Starri said, acquiescence which Thorgrim found surprising.

"That's very...reasonable of you, Starri."

In the dawn light he saw Starri shrug. "It's no matter," he said. "The others will just do as you say whether you ask for their opinions or not. And whatever you say always seems to lead to fighting. Enough fighting even for me."

It was still dark when Failend woke, the heavy furs under which she slept pressing her down into the straw pallet that made little crackling noises when she moved. She did not sense Thorgrim's presence in the bed with her. She reached out her hand, sliding it between the fur and the rough linen that covered the straw, but she could not feel him there. She rolled over and felt in the other direction. He was not there either.

Wolf dream...she thought. She had seen the dark mood coming on Thorgrim the night before, the furrowed brow and the downturned mouth, the expression that looked like barely contained and inexplicable rage. She had seen that before, on a few occasions since she had known him. She knew what the heathens thought it was, that his soul took on the form of a wolf and roamed the dark.

Under the fur she made the sign of the cross.

Failend did not believe such things. She did not believe what the pagans believed. But she also knew that there were many strange things out there, that God was not alone in His works in man's world, that Satan also had a hand in what happened in the night. She did not like to think that Thorgrim was a tool of Satan. But again, she had been raised to believe that all the heathens were.

Then another thought came to her. *Maybe he's sharing a bed with another woman.* That notion gave her more pause than the idea of the wolf dream. In part because it was more plausible. And like the idea of Thorgrim's soul turning into a wolf, it was not the first time the thought had crossed her mind.

"Who would he be sharing his bed with?" she asked herself in a whisper. There were women among the captives they had taken when they took the monastery, but they were the wives of the men who worked there, tradesmen or laborers or fishermen. The women were ugly, near toothless, hands and faces leathered, bodies misshapen and stooped from years of labor and childbirth.

"He would have none of them," Failend said, once more speaking softly but out loud, and in her mind added, *Not when he could have me.*

The wives of the working men were the only women at the monastery; there were no others. There had been nuns, apparently, judging from the garments they had found in one of the dormitories, but those women were gone by the time the heathens had arrived.

Every time that Failend wondered if Thorgrim was sharing another woman's bed, it led to the same string of thoughts. She figured he would not lie with another woman because there were no other women with whom he might want to couple. He would not be faithful because he loved her, or because he felt any loyalty toward her, but simply because she was the only desirable woman to be had.

"You don't know that," she said. And that was true. She didn't know, had no real notion of what Thorgrim Night Wolf thought or felt. She never spoke to him about those things. The very idea of talking to him about love and faithfulness seemed absurd.

Thorgrim loved Harald. He had apparently loved his late wife. He had three other children: a son named Odd and two daughters, Hild and Hallbera. He had told Failend a little about them, and she had the impression he loved them too, though he had not been in their company for several years now.

She did not know if Thorgrim loved anyone else.

"Well, it's not as if you're in love with him, either," she said, and then she closed her eyes and began to cry.

Chapter Two

It grew up, and well throve;
learned to tame oxen, make a plough,
houses build, and barns construct,
make carts, and the plough drive.

The Poetic Edda

Odd Thorgrimson stood poised, alert, muscles taut, sure of what would come next and ready for it. The ground was soft and he worked his toes into the dirt so that his feet would not slip when it was time for him to make his move. He was crouched low, his arms out on either side.

The enemy was close, no more than twenty feet away. *Not enemy...opponent*, Odd thought. He had no quarrel with the one he faced off with, no enmity, though he knew the other felt differently on that point.

Odd was outmatched, there was no question. The other was faster and outweighed Odd by a considerable amount. More powerful than Odd could ever hope to be. But he was angry, grunting with rage, and Odd was not, and that, Odd knew, was a significant advantage.

The crowd had been murmuring just seconds before, but now they were silent, anticipating the coming violence. Wagers were being made, Odd knew it, but it did not bother him. He hoped some had bet against him so that they would learn what a mistake that was.

Then, in an instant, the waiting was over and the combat begun. It was not Odd who initiated it, it was the other, digging his feet into the earth and launching himself forward in snarling, frothy rage, four hundred pounds of anger hurtling toward Odd, who stood his ground and waited.

It's just a pig, just a pig, Odd thought as he tensed his legs and watched the massive animal bearing down on him. It had no teeth or claws to speak of, but if it managed to slam itself into Odd at full speed—a thing it was trying very hard to do—then it could knock him flat or break bones or both. And once Odd was down, the boar would be in charge. But he had been doing this for years, and so far no hog had ever got the better of him, and only a few times had one even come close.

Ten feet, then five. Odd put his right hand straight out. It was all timing and sureness of foot now. The pig was not dumb. Once it came to understand that Odd had plans, plans to render it into some edible form, which the hog felt would not be to its advantage, then it had become enraged, the battle joined.

Two feet. Odd's hand came down hard on the pig's head and he leapt as straight up as he could. He felt his toes dig in and not slip and he felt a wave of relief even as the hog passed under him.

He landed on the far side of the pig and staggered, off balance, just for a step. The jump was the most dangerous moment, the place where he had nearly been bested by earlier hogs, but this next moment was the second most dangerous. Maybe third. Either way, he had to keep his footing, to turn and be ready before the hog was. And the hog, for all its size, was very quick.

Odd spun around, crouching again as he did, and the hog spun around as well, furious, grunting, unsure where its quarry had gone.

You're not the smartest I've faced, are you? Odd thought. He wondered if the onlookers would notice, if they would think this contest not so impressive as the earlier ones. Then the pig spotted him and launched into its second charge.

The pig's speed built, and Odd saw the next few seconds unfold in his mind, just the way it would happen if it happened right. He would not try that same trick again, in case the hog had figured it out. He didn't know if a hog was capable of such a thing, but reckoned it was not worth the risk to find out.

Again his right hand went out, ready to connect with the pig's head, when suddenly the pig did the unexpected. Just as Odd's hand brushed the tough hide, the pig swerved, and rather than coming straight on, it swung the great bulk of its body right into Odd's crouching form.

The impact sent Odd sprawling back and he was aware of the roar from the onlookers and his mind was filled with the half-formed thought that he had to get clear, had to regain his feet and his orientation before the huge animal was on him.

He hit the ground with his shoulder and rolled, and as he rolled he swung his legs around and let the last bit of momentum carry him back onto his feet. He came up facing the pig and he thanked the gods, because the boar had also found his footing and was charging again. The roar from the crowd, which had not stopped, grew louder still as the outcome seemed more in doubt. Odd wondered who they were cheering for. Most were for him, he was certain. Nearly certain. His wife and children, for sure, and at least a majority of the others.

It took the hog all of three seconds to reach Odd, but that was time enough. Odd guessed the beast would swerve again, since that had worked so well the first time, and he guessed it would swerve in the same direction for the same reason. Odd, therefore, dodged in the other direction, just as the hog swerved the way it had before, and this time its great flank met only air.

Odd leapt again. He launched off his right foot, left leg up, and came down on the hog's back as if he were mounting a horse. The hog screamed in rage and kicked its back legs and Odd felt the bristles on its back poking through his linen trousers. He leaned forward and put his arm around the hog's neck, hanging tight as the hog twisted and kicked and thrashed its head. He got a grip on the animal's jaw and pulled even as he slipped off the hog's back, twisting its head and toppling it over on its side.

A fathom of thin rope hung doubled around Odd's neck. He whipped it off and straddled the hog again as the animal squealed and bucked and tried to regain its feet. He grabbed the animal's two front legs and whipped the rope around them, low down, near the feet. It was a practiced move, one that his arms and hands did with no conscious thought. He pulled the end of the rope between the animal's legs, once, twice, cinching the loops tight, then grabbed for a hind leg next. The boar was kicking frantically now, its hind legs flailing with its front legs bound, but Odd managed to catch one in mid-flail and he lashed it quick with the tail end of the rope.

He paused for a second, took a deep breath, and then jumped to his feet, smiling wide. The cheers doubled and he saw men and women smiling at him and raising fists and he smiled back and bowed deep. There was laughter now, and shouts of "Well done!" and "Odd wins again!" Odd saw silver armbands and brooches being passed hand to hand, the winners' wagers being paid, and he noted who was paying whom, and who had bet against him.

Odd's wife, Signy, broke from the crowd and ran towards him. The beads that hung in a bight between the brooches on her dress bounced and the keys and scissors and knife that hung from thin chains from her right brooch jingled like little bells. Her yellow hair and her smile seemed to glow in the summer's early morning sun. In her arms she held Hallbera, their daughter, three months old and quite confused by the goings on.

Signy shifted the baby to one side, put her free arm around Odd's neck, kissed him. She whispered in his ear, "That one nearly had you, old man."

Odd grinned. "Not close, not even close."

He felt arms around his legs, cries of "Papa, papa!" The other little ones, Ornolf and Thorgrid, were holding him tight, proud of Papa, pleased that he had not been crushed to death by the hog.

Vermund Jurundsson approached next, a big smile on his weathered face, gaps where several of his teeth once stood. "Well done, Odd, well done, as usual!" Vermund was the overseer of Odd's farm, the one who helped Odd in the laborious task of seeing every one of a thousand tasks done and done correctly. Vermund had been born to farming, was intimate with every aspect of the work. He had done it all and he was not shy about jumping in with both hands and working still. It was why Odd paid him well and valued him so.

"Signy thinks the hog nearly killed me this time," Odd said.

The three of them turned reflexively and looked at the pig. It had stopped thrashing and was lying still now, breathing hard. The men who would do the work that followed Odd's subduing the animal, killing, gutting, bleeding and butchering it, stood off to the side as the crowd dispersed. It was not as if anyone on the farm had not seen animals slaughtered many times, but still it seemed as if a bit of discretion was called for. The pig had been a good sport, after all.

"That beastie get the best of you?" Vermund said. "Never in life! You're still young and quick! Get to be my age, maybe, but you've got too much experience now to lose to a hog!"

Odd did have experience, that was true. Pigs were something of a luxury in that country; few men raised them and they were food for the better sort. Odd had raised his first pigs five years back, soon after taking over the farm. The first time he had tried to butcher a hog it had not gone well when the hog decided to not placidly accept its fate. It had turned into a wrestling match, Odd versus the pig, and that had ended as a great entertainment for all of Odd's people. Enough so that the contest of Odd versus pig had become a regular event, generally played out once or twice a year, whenever a boar was ready to be butchered.

There were easier ways to subdue and bind a pig, but none so amusing, and it was not long before Odd felt obligated to put on the show, it being so popular among the folk.

Vermund slapped Odd on the back. "Your name will be Odd Pig-binder!" he said.

Odd smiled, an obligatory smile. "I hope we can come up with better than that," he said, his tone cheerful, Vermund's words like a dagger in the gut.

My father is Thorgrim Night Wolf, he thought, *my brother is known as Harald Broadarm. I am Odd Pig-binder.*

"Tell me, Vermund," Signy chimed in, she alone aware of Odd's discomfort. "How goes the haymaking in the south field?"

"Cut down, my lady, all but the southeast corner. But still too wet to bale. Another day or two such as this and we'll be quite ready."

"And the flock?" Odd said.

"Galti just come down from the hills for more victuals and he says all is well. Two ewes lost to a wolf, but the boys hunted the thing down and killed it."

Odd nodded. In the spring the farm's flock of sheep, a considerable flock, along with the milch cows and bulls, were driven up into the hills where the grazing was good. A dozen of Odd's men went with them as sheep herders, and a handful of women as well. They lived in a small house there called a *shielding*, and tended the animals while the weather was good.

The pigs remained behind, where they were transformed into bacon and salt pork.

"I'll join you with the haying, Vermund," Odd said. "I just have to see to a few things first."

Vermund nodded, made his goodbyes. Little Ornolf and Thorgrid had moved on to other pursuits, leaving Odd's legs free.

"May I walk with you, husband?" Signy asked.

"Of course, wife, of course," Odd said. He stepped off across the fields of low grass that ringed the farmhouse and the outbuildings, moderating his pace in consideration of his wife whose legs were not as long as his and who was carrying their youngest child.

He breathed deep. The air was good, just warming up as the sun rose higher, a tinge of salt water from the deep fiord that formed the southern boundary of his land. When his father had given him the farm as a wedding present six years earlier it had been a good place, a good fertile land, a small farmhouse and well-built outbuildings: a barn, a byre, a stable with half a dozen stalls.

In the years since, Odd had turned it into something much more substantial than that. He had expanded the barn and the byre to accommodate his growing herds. He had hired good men and women and bought strong slaves and made them work hard, and encouraged them by working hard himself. He was a clever man and had learned many things from his father, both about farming and selling produce in the most advantageous way and about leading men, and all those things served him well.

And Odd had one other advantage. When Thorgrim and Harald had gone off a'viking with Odd's grandfather, Ornolf the Restless, Thorgrim had asked Odd to look after his farm as well. There was an overseer, a man named Skafti who Thorgrim trusted with the daily running of the place, but Thorgrim asked that Odd take the overall responsibility. Any profit that the farm made was to be put back into improvements and generous payment to the people who worked Thorgrim's land. Anything surplus beyond that was to go to Odd for his trouble.

And there was quite a bit of surplus. Thorgrim had built up his farm over the years, acquiring as much of the land around as he could. He had a long hall and quite a few other buildings, and fields and herds of sheep and cows, flocks of chickens, and pigs as well. With Thorgrim gone the household was free from the great expense of hosting banquets for neighbors and men of consequence passing through, and that meant more silver all around.

The summer before, Odd had made his latest and grandest improvement to his own farm, one that brought it nearly to the level of Thorgrim's own. He had built a proper longhouse, a great, towering timber structure with walls of turf and stone. The original farmhouse had become the entrance hall to the new home, and to it

Odd had added a great hall one hundred and twenty feet long with a stone fire pit running down the middle. At the far end of the hall was the main room with its own fire pit, a place where the family might gather when there was no call to use the great space of the main hall. Two smaller rooms came off the back of the hall, one for storing food and sundry household goods, the other a latrine to be used when the harsh weather made using the outhouses less inviting.

Odd took great and justifiable pride in what he had accomplished with his farm. And he wondered why it was still not enough, though he kept that question to himself.

He and Signy passed the farm and continued down the worn trail through a stand of pines that led to another stretch of open ground rolling down to the water's edge. They could hear the dull sound of axes and adzes slicing into thick beams of wood, and the soft grind of saws. This was Odd's latest venture, a shipyard where he could build fishing boats for his own use and other boats and small ships that he might sell at considerable profit.

"I had an idea you were coming here," Signy said, her tone teasing.

"Ari is fitting the fourth strake today, and that will give us the shape of her at the turn of the bilge," Odd said. Ari was the shipwright Odd had hired to oversee the work. As with farming, Odd had learned quite a bit about shipbuilding from his father—it was one of Thorgrim's great passions—and he could certainly have built the vessel himself. But he had no time, with the myriad other duties that fell to him.

As he and Signy came through the trees they could see the trampled earth of the shipyard, the piles of timber drying, the small shed where the tools were stored, and, in the middle of it all, the long, half-built hull of the ship that was rising up from the wood shavings.

Ari saw them coming and he put his hammer and chisel down and stepped over to them, giving Signy a shallow bow and Hallbera's cheek a soft pinch. Ari was an older man, in his forties at least, his beard and long hair white, his hands and fingers gnarled and strong, his face in a seemingly permanent squint.

"Odd, well timed," Ari said. "We've fit the new strake on the starboard side and will have the larboard on by sundown, I would think."

"Good, good," Odd said, but his eyes were on the ship. Sixty feet long, her stem and sternpost standing high above the keel, the long sweep of her hull becoming more defined with each strake that was added. When the latest plank was fitted in place the lovely shape of the hull would start to emerge.

"Well?" Ari said.

"Lovely. Lovely." Odd ran his hand along the upper edge of the strake. He could feel the taper cut in the wood to accommodate the next plank to be fit above.

"She's very narrow, isn't she?" Signy asked. "For a fishing boat she is very narrow." The farm on which Signy was raised, like most farms in that country, was close by the sea, and like all such farms the folk there engaged in nearly as much fishing as they did farming. Signy knew ships as well as most.

"Narrow...I suppose," Odd said in a noncommittal way. "She'll be faster. More time to fish, less time rowing in and out."

"Might end up selling her, too," Ari offered. "Better to make her useful for a lot of different jobs, you know."

Signy nodded. She did not reply. But Odd had a good notion of what was playing out in her mind. They had had discussions about this. Sometimes heated discussions. Signy did not entirely trust Odd's motivation in building this ship. But in truth Odd did not really understand his own motivation.

Fishing, certainly, but he knew there was something else lurking behind that, barely seen, and he made a real effort to not look too close. He told Signy, when they discussed this, not to be concerned. He had no intention of going anywhere. What he did not tell her was that like all intentions, his could change.

Odd was about to say something further when a new sound inserted itself, far off but insistent. Horses' hooves, a common enough sound, but this was a horse moving fast, moving at a full gallop, and that was not so common. The three of them turned their heads toward the sound and Odd found himself tensing. A rider in a great hurry: it could be good news or bad news, but it was certainly one of the two and it was certainly something of importance.

The sound grew louder, hooves beating on the soft earth path that led from the farmyard to the shipyard. And then the rider appeared and Odd recognized him immediately. Skafti Hrappsson, the man who ran Thorgrim's farm in Thorgrim's absence. Odd felt a sick feeling in his gut.

Skafti pulled the reins in sharp and the horse stopped with a flourish and Odd noticed that Skafti had not taken the time to saddle the animal.

"Skafti, what..." Odd said, taking a step toward the man.

"Master Odd, down at the farm..." Skafti said, then paused to gulp air and Odd waited until he could speak again.

"Down at the farm, there's men come...a dozen or so, dressed fine, good horses and saddles. They rounded up the slaves and the servants, put the lot of them in the stable. Started going through the house, acted like the rutting masters of the place..."

"Men?" Odd said. He was trying to make sense of all this. "What men? Who sent them? What was there business?"

Skafti just shook his head as the questions came. "I don't rightly know, I'm sorry. I rode off as quick as I could. Don't know what they wanted, but whatever it is, I can say it ain't of no benefit to your father. And by all the gods it surely will be of no benefit to you."

Chapter Three

All the ways of this world are as fickle and unstable as a sudden storm at sea.

Venerable Bede

Cynewise was in a foul mood even before Oswin was ushered in. The affairs of the day, and Bishop Ealhstan in particular, had seen to that.

She was in the long hall, sitting on the big chair in the center of the dais. Her physical stature was not particularly impressive: five foot four and somewhere around seven stone. A mere eighteen years old. But she was also the ealdorman of Dorsetshire, a powerful office, and she understood that she needed such grand surroundings as the hall and the ealdorman's high seat to reinforce the idea that Dorsetshire and the fyrd and the thegns and all else were hers to command.

Bishop Ealhstan was seated beside her, in a less impressive chair, its legs a few inches shorter than her own. He was, physically, as near Cynewise's opposite as one could be. While she was a young woman, slightly built with long, blond hair, he was an old man, nearly bald, corpulent and red-faced. If not for his brilliant white linen cassock and cope trimmed out with an intricate gold lace, and the equally ornate biretta perched on his head, he might have been mistaken for an aging tavern-keeper.

It was a deceptive look, one that masked a sharp and strategic mind. He had been a bishop for thirty years, and in that time had expanded his diocese to include the shires of Dorset, Somerset, Devon and Cornwall. He was a good friend of Æthelwulf, king of Wessex and of Cynewise's father, Ceorle, the powerful ealdorman of Devonshire. Indeed, he was good friends with all of the important men of Wessex, and the less powerful as well. Or those men at least feigned friendship with Ealhstan, knowing how dangerous it could be to oppose him.

"Now, see, that brutal storm of last month has done great damage to the shire, great damage," Ealhstan was saying, the third point of bad news he had raised so far, and the morning was young. "Crops are ruined, the folks' houses torn apart. Many of my parishes have suffered great harm."

Cynewise nodded. "The storm would seem an act of God. Surely that would be your business, and not that of the ealdorman," Cynewise said.

"The Church is in the business of showing men the light, so that they may not incur the wrath of God," Ealhstan explained patiently. "The business of putting things to rights when the people's lack of faith brings on God's wrath would fall to the ealdorman."

Well, a bloody poor job you've done of it, Cynewise thought, but she knew better than to say such a thing. A storm had come through the shire weeks before, a freakish display of rain and wind such as none could recall. It had torn up trees, tossed heavy carts around like leaves, taken the roofs off well-made houses and knocked those less well-made flat. Crops had been ruined, just as Ealhstan said, and the people were growing desperate.

"I am not in the very best circumstance, financially," Cynewise said. "My late husband was most profligate, you know. What little taxes he brought in he spent just as quickly."

That was only partially true, of course. Merewald, Cynewise's late husband, had only been ealdorman for a year before his death. He had only been Cynewise's husband, officially, in the eyes of God and the law, for the better part of a minute before an assassin had cut him down at the altar, leaving his young bride both a grieving widow and ealdorman of the shire.

He had certainly been profligate, but that was not the real reason that Cynewise's treasury was nearly empty. Her financial straits had more to do with seeing that her posterior remained firmly in place in the ealdorman's chair than it did with Merewald's spending.

Cynewise had reason to fear that she might not be able to hang on to her office. Merewald had a younger brother named Nothwulf who understandably laid claim to the title. Nothwulf had assumed, on Merewald's death, that he would step in as ealdorman and send Cynewise packing back to Devon, or perhaps marry her. Nothwulf never had time to make his preference known before Cynewise began to solidify her hold on the ealdormanship.

Which she had done, mostly. Unfortunately her efforts to remove Nothwulf completely from the field of battle had been less than successful. So far.

Remaining ealdorman was an expensive business. The thegns, the men who controlled the land and whose collective men-at-arms would make the largest fighting force available in the shire, held great sway over matters of government. Not any one thegn alone, but a majority of them, depending on whom they chose to back, could practically dictate what happened in Sherborne, seat of the ealdorman and of the bishop. Their loyalty came at a great price: land, gifts, banquets.

Worse, King Æthelwulf had come to visit on his annual tour of Wessex, and with him courtiers, servants, men-at-arms, women, horses. They all had to be fed and housed with varying degrees of opulence. It had nearly drained Cynewise's coffers.

"Nonetheless…" Bishop Ealhstan continued when a servant entered from the far end of the hall, stepping with purpose toward the dais.

Now what? Cynewise thought. Part of her was relieved to have this unpleasant conversation with the bishop interrupted. Another part was deeply concerned about what this interruption could mean.

The servant bowed. "Shire Reeve Oswin, ma'am, returned and wishes a word."

Cynewise stifled a sigh. "Very well, send him in." She watched the servant turn smartly and head back for the door. Oswin, the shire reeve. The man who made the ealdorman's orders, wishes, and desires become reality, as far as the administration of the shire went. Now Oswin was returning from dealing with a new problem, one that had seemingly dropped out of the sky. Or more correctly washed up on the beach. Northmen.

"Has Oswin been to the south? Seeing about these Northmen?" Ealhstan asked. Cynewise wondered how he had heard about them. She had not told him, and their presence was not well known in Sherborne. But of course, little happened in that shire, or anywhere in Wessex, that Ealhstan did not hear of.

Oswin entered where the servant had gone out and walked with long strides across the hall. He stepped up onto the dais, kissed

Ealhstan's ring and bowed to Cynewise. Up close Cynewise could see that his boots and tunic were splattered with mud and there was a tear in his cape. His face had a weary look.

"Yes, Oswin?" Cynewise said.

"The Northmen, ma'am, they've taken Christchurch Priory," he said.

"Oh, Lord save us," Ealhstan said and made the sign of the cross and Cynewise and Oswin did likewise.

"Taken it?" Cynewise asked. "Plundered it?"

"Plundered it, I would imagine," Oswin said. "That's what they do. But I couldn't inspect it as they're still there. They didn't leave."

"Still there?" Ealhstan exclaimed. "Defiling that holy place?"

"Yes, your Grace, I fear so."

Cynewise was likewise troubled, though not so much by the notion of the filthy Northmen invading a holy place. Two hundred of her father's best men-at-arms had been sent by sea to Christchurch, where they were quartered in secret. Cynewise and her father meant to march those men to Sherborne, to cement her place as ealdorman and to crush Nothwulf if need be. It had all been falling into place. Until the damned Northmen had arrived.

"They have taken Christchurch Priory?" Cynewise asked again. "Taken...all the people there?" Oswin, she was certain, would understand her meaning.

"Yes, ma'am," Oswin said. "All the people. The holy people and all else who were there."

"How do you know that?" Cynewise asked.

"I spoke with them, ma'am. I rode to the priory gate and they let me in and I spoke with them."

"You were in the priory?" Ealhstan asked. "Was it sacked, was it much damaged?"

"Not that I could see, your Grace. None of the building burned down, nothing destroyed. But I suppose they wouldn't do that if they had a mind to stay awhile."

"How many of the devils were there?" Ealhstan asked next.

"I couldn't say. They weren't all gathered as one. But a lot, I would imagine. Their leader is a man called Thorgrim. I did count seven ships."

"Seven ships," Ealhstan said. "Could be three, four hundred men."

"Seven ships," Cynewise said. "Nothwulf said he saw seven ships at Swanage. It's likely the same pack of wolves."

"Likely," Oswin agreed. "So at least we have only one fleet of heathens to deal with, and not two. Peace will come at half the cost."

"Cost?" Cynewise asked.

"*Danegeld*, ma'am. They've demanded danegeld. One hundred and fifty pounds of silver."

If Cynewise had had a mouthful of wine she would have spit it all over the dais. "One hundred and fifty pounds?"

"But there's another thing to consider," Oswin continued. "Nothwulf and Leofric and their men are near Christchurch. I had the impression they were going to fight the Northmen, as you instructed them to do. It might be to the shire's benefit if they do."

Cynewise frowned as she studied Oswin. The shire reeve was a clever one. He understood the nuances of what was taking place, and his only concern, Cynewise knew, was to see that he, Oswin, was in league with whoever would come out on top. So far it looked as if that one would be Cynewise. But that could change.

There were many pieces on the board, and each move was critical. If she paid the danegeld then she would be considerably poorer, and she was already poor enough. But if she let Nothwulf fight the Northmen and he drove them off, then he would be the hero of the shire, and her hold on the ealdormanship would become that much more precarious.

The best outcome would be for Nothwulf to fight the heathens and lose. He might weaken them enough that Cynewise's forces could sweep in and stamp the remnants out. But there was no certain way to make that happen. The only thing that she could control for certain was paying the tribute, painful as that might be.

But it was not a bad option. Paying would mean being rid of the Northmen and freeing her father's men-at-arms, hopefully before her father ever got word of what had happened. She would rather the old man never know. The coming of the Northmen might have nothing to do with her, but her father would still find some way to fault her for it.

"Here's what we shall do," Cynewise said. "I'll find the one hundred and fifty pounds of silver, somewhere. I'm sure, your Grace, that the church would be willing to contribute a goodly share, since it's the church's priory we mean to liberate."

"Hmm," the bishop said. "We're not in a good way, you know, with our treasury. The folk have little to tithe, what with the great storm, and we're spending a considerable sum in helping the poor and the destitute."

Helping the poor, my arse, Cynewise thought. *Helping yourself to living like a king.* But once again she did not voice her real thoughts, but rather said, "It's my hope, your Grace, that we'll neither of us have to give over any of the silver to the Northmen. Nothwulf is near Christchurch with his men and Leofric's men and a good number of the fyrd. We'll collect the money, but I hope to see Nothwulf drive the Northmen from Christchurch before we must hand over the danegeld. Then we might get the silver back, and you can distribute it to the poor, to your heart's content."

"A good plan, as far as it goes," Ealhstan said. "But it seems to me that it might be best to apply to your father for aid in the military line. He has men-at-arms a' plenty, good men who could help you in driving these vermin out. And Ceorle is certainly no stranger to these things."

Cynewise nodded as if considering this, but she did not need to consider it, because she had rejected the idea even as Ealhstan was speaking. The last thing she needed was her father there in Dorset, bowling everyone over like a dray rolling down a steep hill, out of control. Ceorle might have figured that if Cynewise was ealdorman of Dorset it meant that he would be *de facto* ruler, along with being ealdormen of Devon, but that was not Cynewise's plan.

"What you say about my father is correct, Bishop Ealhstan," Cynewise said. "But he has more than enough on his mind now. Damage from the storm, for instance. Dorsetshire was not the only place to feel the brunt of that. And trouble with the thegns. Honestly, I think it would be a favor to the man if he were to not even hear about our problems with the Northmen."

"Well, I'm not sure I agree," the bishop said. "And as to him hearing about this, I have no doubt he will, and soon. I sent word to him, you see, just yesterday."

Chapter Four

I sing to thee the fourth.
If foes assail thee ready
on the dangerous road,
their hearts shall fail them,
and to thee be power,
and their minds to peace be turned.

The Poetic Edda

The building at the center of the priory at Christchurch was, unsurprisingly, a church. It consisted of a long hall that extended out to the east from the base of a tall, square tower. Thorgrim knew the Christ men called it something other than a hall, but he could not recall what, and was not sure he ever knew.

The whole thing was stone-built, in the manner of the Irish and English churches. His own people back home in Norway did not build in that manner, but he had to admit it was impressive. There was a permanence to it that was lacking in the timber, plank and sod construction in his native country.

Why they built the tower Thorgrim did not know either. A place from which archers could fire down on an enemy? Perhaps, but it was really too high for that purpose. A lookout post? Maybe. If so it was not well used, as the English seemed to have had little warning when Thorgrim's fleet arrived. The men-at-arms who were quartered there were caught in their nightshirts, and fought Thorgrim's men with only the weapons they had managed to snatch up. The great wealth of the church had not been carried off or hidden.

Thorgrim at least was grateful for the tower. From the top he could see for miles over the low country all around. He could see out over the wide, shallow bay they had crossed to reach the priory. He could see little columns of smoke that marked where hearth fires burned in farmhouses. He could see the thatched roofs of the houses that surrounded the monastery and the places where roofs had been torn away and weaker structures blown flat by the same frightful gale that had driven them clear across the open water from Ireland to Engla-land.

It was weeks before that he and his men had taken the priory and they had remained there since, happily ensconced. The folk of that town might have been near starving, but the priory's storehouse was crammed with barrels of salt pork and beef and dried fish and ale. His men had eaten well, a luxury they did not always enjoy.

A few days after they had taken the place, the first of the locals who had fled in terror returned. Thorgrim watched them from the high tower as they moved warily around the wall that surrounded the monastery, expecting no doubt to be set upon by the heathens. But there was nothing that those poor people had that Thorgrim and his men might want, and no reason for the Northmen to leave the luxury of the church. After a while the people realized as much, and more and more of them returned to their homes.

Thorgrim could see the people of the town struggling to set things to rights. He could watch them from on high as they poked through what remained of their pitiful possessions and rowed their boats out to sea to catch what they could, which was not a great deal as far as Thorgrim could tell.

And, most pleasing of all, Thorgrim could see the seven ships of his fleet pulled up on the muddy shore. They looked like toys from so high up, perfect little toy ships with their yards lowered and sails furled and oars stowed. Thorgrim had no concern that any harm would come to them. The people of that village would be too afraid of retribution to try any such thing, nor did they want to discourage the Northmen from leaving.

On that particular morning Thorgrim was not alone at the top of the tower. Harald and Godi were there, as were Jorund and Halldor and Hardbein and the others who commanded their own crews. As fine as it was at Christchurch Priory, they all knew they could not stay there for very much longer.

Thorgrim pulled his eyes from the view of the bay and the blue sea beyond and turned to the others. The roof was flat, about twenty feet on each side, with a stone wall, waist height, encircling it. It was a fine place to be on a warm, sunny day such as it was.

"Well?" he said.

The others glanced at one another. No one much cared to be the first to offer a thought. But Jorund was the oldest of them, and had commanded half the men who were now with Thorgrim. He was a leader, and as such not afraid to speak his mind.

"That fellow that came on the horse, the Englishman," Jorund said.

"Oswin," Harald supplied.

"Him," Jorund said. "He didn't blink when Thorgrim told him a hundred pounds of silver. So either such a price is no trouble to him, or he's lying, to give him time to raise an army."

"There is an army," Halldor said. "Ofeig saw them when he was sent scouting." Heads nodded.

"Don't know why they haven't come to fight us yet," Godi said.

"It's not a big army," Thorgrim said. "Two, three hundred men. But only a small number are men-at-arms. The rest are farmers with spears, such as we saw often enough in Ireland. I don't think they care to attack us."

There was quiet for a moment, and then Fostolf of *Dragon* asked the obvious question.

"How do you know that, Lord Thorgrim?"

"He knows," Starri chimed in. Starri always attended such meetings, whether or not it was his business to do so, which it never was. "Trust me, Thorgrim knows."

Heads nodded again. The men who had been with Thorgrim for some time all knew about the wolf dreams. Most of the others had heard rumors. No one really wanted to query Thorgrim on the point, and when they understood that Thorgrim's knowledge came from some place not of this world, they did not care to hear any more.

"The one thing we cannot do is be taken by surprise," Godi said and that was followed by a murmur of agreement.

"You're right, Godi," Thorgrim said. "We're getting fat and lazy here in all this luxury. We'll send scouts out in every direction, keep them out, rotate them between all the men. We'll send our best to keep an eye on the army that's coming near."

"That Oswin fellow," Harald said, "he told us the army was an enemy to him as well as us. Two English armies, and they are enemies of each other?"

"I don't know what we're in the middle of here, and I don't much care," Thorgrim said. "If this Engla-land is at all like Ireland, then they're all fighting each other, and we want no part of it. They can give us the silver, we'll give them the prisoners and then we'll sail away."

More nodding, then Halldor asked, "What if there is no silver?"

"Then it's the slave market for these men," Thorgrim said. "I'm not eager to do that. It's a lot of trouble. I'd rather have the silver. You don't have to feed silver or try to keep it alive. But we won't leave these bastards behind, either, not when they're worth so much."

"This Oswin's been gone for days," Jorund said. "How long do we wait?"

"We don't know how far away his jarl...or whatever he's called..."

"Ealdorman," Harald supplied and Thorgrim looked over at the boy. Back in Ireland, motivated to speak to a girl whom he loved, Harald had picked up the language very quickly. But now he was learning English quickly as well, and Thorgrim wondered if his son had some gift from the gods for such things.

"Right, what Harald said," Thorgrim continued. "We don't know how far away he is, how long Oswin had to ride to bring word. Or how long it will take them to collect the silver."

"Or how long to raise an army against us," Starri said, but he did not sound worried. Just the opposite, in fact.

"That, too," Thorgrim agreed. "But with scouts a'field we'll have fair warning of any army coming our way."

"Scouts will be a good thing," Jorund said, "but they can be tricked, and it's a fool who's taken by surprise. This monastery is as fine a place as any dwelling I've had, but it's right in the middle of this town. It's protected by a stone wall that a crippled man could climb over with ease. Not exactly made to defend."

Thorgrim looked down at the monastery below. The low wall encircling the place was, as Jorund said, not much of a barrier. Nor was it meant to be. As Thorgrim understood from Louis the Frank it was more of a symbolic thing. It was easily half a mile in circumference and Thorgrim did not have enough men to defend every part of it, or even half of it. An enemy could attack from any direction, or from several directions if they were clever, and they could swarm over the wall. He nodded his head.

"You're right about that, Jorund," he said. "There's no defending this place. You are most certainly right about that."

Nothwulf waited for word from Leofric, and when he was told the thegn was just a few miles away he sent the poachers out.

His army had been in camp, within a day or two march of Christchurch, for more than a week. He and Leofric had tried to catch the Northmen at Swanage, soon after they first came ashore, but that had been a failure. Despite their clever plan and stealthy execution—hiding their men in the abandoned town at night with the intention of a dawn assault—the Northmen had escaped. It might have been luck, or they might have known that the English were lying in wait, but either way the sun came up to reveal the seven longships gone.

It had sparked panic in Nothwulf's heart. King Æthelwulf was at Sherborne, and Cynewise was frothing to find some means of making him, Nothwulf, appear incompetent and feckless. How better than to order him, as if she had that authority, and in the company of the king, to drive the heathens out, only to see him fail. And he had indeed failed at Swanage. He could not fail again. If he did he would lose his seat as ealdorman, and perhaps even his life, and he did not know which he feared most.

They were still in Swanage when they learned that the Northmen had gone to Christchurch Priory, plundered the place and settled in, and Nothwulf saw his chance at redemption. He and Leofric had an army nearly three hundred men strong, and they began the march to Christchurch Priory as soon as they had word.

And then Nothwulf began to wonder if three hundred was enough.

The Northmen were a powerful force. They had seven longships, which could have been nearly four hundred men. And they would be fighting men, warriors bred to the work and well experienced with blood-letting, while at least half of his own army was made up of the fyrd, those common folk called to bear arms when needed. In battle they were not likely to stand up long to the heathens.

He talked it over with Leofric. Leofric was one of the thegns, one of the wealthiest, powerful and influential thegns, and Christchurch Priory was on his land, so he had good reason to want to see the Northmen gone. They agreed that Leofric would go to the halls of the other thegns within two days' ride, round up the men-at-arms who were sworn to them. They would augment their army with more fighting men, real fighting men, and then they would march for Christchurch. If the heathens made ready to leave before that, then Nothwulf would attack with what he had.

And now Leofric had returned. Nothwulf was informed that he and three other thegns and two hundred men-at-arms were half a day's march away. Nothwulf called for Bryning, captain of his hearth-guard, his second in command.

Bryning appeared moments after being summoned. "Lord Nothwulf?" he said.

"The heathen scouts, they're still out there?"

"Yes, sir," Bryning said. The heathens had been sending men to keep an eye on the English army, as Nothwulf would expect them to do. The men moved with care and stealth, but they were not as careful or stealthy as they thought they were.

Nothwulf had stealthy men of his own, in particular two brothers from Shaftesbury who were notoriously good at moving unseen across country. They were known to be poachers, but they were good enough at the business that they had never been caught, which was why they had never been hanged. They were part of the fyrd and Leofric saw to it that they were always called up when needed.

Soon the two men were standing nervously in front of Nothwulf. They were young men, lean, with arms and legs that seemed too long for the rest of them. Nothwulf guessed they did not like standing in front of a man who could sentence them to death, and that was good. It would assure their diligence.

"The Northmen's scouts, they're still out there?" Nothwulf asked.

"New ones come this morning, Lord," the older of the two said. "Two of the bastards, beg pardon."

"They're hiding in the tall brush just to the south of us, Lord," the other said.

"Good," Nothwulf said. "Time to bring them in. Will you need help with that?"

The brothers looked at one another. They looked back at Nothwulf. They shook their heads.

When they were gone there was little left for Nothwulf to do but wait: wait for them, wait for Leofric, wait for word from the men he had watching Christchurch Priory.

It was midafternoon when Leofric arrived. He rode in at the head of a column of men-at-arms, the other thegns riding beside him and the warriors strung out along the road. Some were on horseback but most were on foot, and all of them looked like good men. Some wore mail and others wore leather, but they all had armor of some sort, and shields and seaxes and swords and spears. These were the men that the thegns counted on to protect their homes and their persons and their families, to enforce their instructions and see that the common folk did not get any radical notions. It was in the thegns' best interest to see that these men had the best weapons and training that their treasuries could bear.

Nothwulf greeted Leofric with a hug and called for wine and bread, meat and cheese, while Bryning saw to the refreshment of the other new arrivals.

"Well?" Leofric asked after he had drained one cup of wine and held it out for Nothwulf's servant to refill.

"Heathens are still in Christchurch Priory," Nothwulf reported. "No change."

"When did you last get word from your scouts?"

"Yesterday. Midday. But the Northmen must still be there because their scouts are still here."

Leofric nodded. "Should we send the poachers out for them?"

"I already have," Nothwulf said. "One of the heathens was killed in the taking, but the other is mostly alive."

"Let's have a look at him," Leofric said.

Word was passed and soon Nothwulf's man Tilmund and another approached, half carrying the Northman between them. His hands were bound behind his back though he seemed to lack the strength even to lift his arms. Tilmund was a great brute of a man, and Nothwulf relied on him to extract information from captives, and other such work.

They pushed the man to his knees in front of Nothwulf and Leofric. He had long blond hair with a single braid hanging down one side. He was not particularly big, built more for running than fighting it seemed. A natural scout. He wore a green tunic, now ripped and blood-stained, leggings and soft leather shoes. One eye was swollen shut, his lip was lacerated and twin streams of blood ran from his nostrils down into his yellow beard.

"What did he say?" Nothwulf asked.

The man next to Tilmund, one of the few in the camp who could speak the Northmen's language, replied. "He said their leader is a man named Thorgrim Night Wolf. He says there are six hundred warriors under him there at Christchurch Priory."

Nothwulf snorted and Leofric chuckled. "Here's the problem with getting information Tilmund's way," Leofric said. "These sons of whores will say anything after a while."

"Anything else?" Nothwulf asked.

"Nothing of use," the translator replied. "He said they had near two hundred English men-at-arms captive, along with the folk from the priory. He said if we attacked the priory they'd start killing them."

"Ha! English men-at-arms in a priory! What an imagination the dog has!" Nothwulf said. He looked into the Northman's face. The Northman was staring back, tight-lipped and defiant. "Very well, take him out some ways from here and kill him."

Nothwulf and Leofric stood as the Northman was half-dragged away. Leofric stretched muscles made stiff and sore by many hours in the saddle. "What now, Lord Nothwulf?" he said.

Nothwulf had been thinking on this question all day. "The heathens will miss their scouts soon enough and that might make them wary."

"Of course," Leofric said. "There's no good can come from our waiting to move against them, I don't think."

"No," Nothwulf agreed. "There's no call to wait."

He looked up toward the sun, which was well past its zenith and heading toward the western hills. "The men you brought with you are weary from the march. Let them eat and rest. We'll have a half moon tonight, enough for the men to start for Christchurch. We'll go part of the way tonight, the rest of the way the night after. We'll enter the village after dark, lie in wait, and attack the heathens at dawn. Catch them asleep and unawares."

"Good," Leofric said nodding. The two men were silent for a moment. Then Nothwulf spoke.

"I know what you're thinking, Leofric," he said.

"You do, lord?"

"Yes. You're thinking that this is just what we did at Swanage, and the heathens slipped through our fingers."

Leofric nodded. "That thought might have occurred to me," he said.

"Well, that will not happen again, I can assure you," Nothwulf said.

"I'm sure not, lord," Leofric said.

Nothwulf looked away. He looked back at Leofric. He was about to offer his reason for believing that would not happen again, but even as he opened his mouth he realized that he had no reason to believe that, no reason at all.

Chapter Five

Go now ever where calamity may be,
and no harm shall
obstruct thy wishes.

The Poetic Edda

Odd could not quite fathom what Skafti was saying about the men at Thorgrim's farm, but he could tell that Skafti did not really know himself what was happening. Men had appeared, they had begun to order the people around, to demand food and ale and that their horses be attended to. They were men of means, the sort who were accustomed to having their orders followed, and so the farm people had followed their orders.

All but Skafti. Skafti at least had the presence of mind to slip away unseen, to bring word to Odd.

"Very well," Odd said. "Let's ride back and see what this is about."

"You won't go alone?" Signy said. "Maybe you had best get some of the neighbors, go with some force."

"No, no. No time for that," Odd said, his tone sharper than he meant it to be. The neighboring farms were miles away in all directions. It would take the bulk of the day to round up the men who owned those farms, and any able freemen who worked for them. It was ridiculous to think of it.

Signy, of course, was worried about Odd's safety, her first concern in such matters. She was Odd's wife, mother of his three children. There were two farms to oversee, probably a hundred or more people besides his family depending on him, it was no wonder that she wished him to take care of himself in all things. It was a function of his importance in Fevik, and her love for him, which was why he felt a flush of guilt that her concern should annoy him so.

"Come, Skafti, let's get some men together and go. Your horse is blown, I'll get you another. Do you have any weapons with you?"

"No, Odd, I have none." That was testament to how quickly Skafti had raced away from Thorgrim's farm. No man in Norway would venture far from home unarmed unless he had absolutely no opportunity to arm himself first.

"We'll get you a sword then. Signy, see to Skafti's horse. Come along." Odd walked back up the path, his pace just short of a run, with Skafti right behind and Signy left to deal with the baby and the panting horse. The two men raced up the path through the trees until they came out in the open ground that surrounded the outbuildings and the hall.

Work had stopped. The people had seen Skafti come riding in at a gallop, asking in a loud and urgent voice where he might find Odd. That had raised their curiosity enough that no one could do anything but wait to hear what was going on.

You'll have to wait longer still, Odd thought. He called out the names of the freemen who worked the farm, those he knew were within earshot.

"Get arms and horses! We're riding out this moment!" Odd shouted. The men paused, just for a heartbeat, then turned and ran off in various directions. Odd continued on and his pace did not slow until he reached the oak door of the entrance hall and threw it open.

The hall was dark, with the long fire mostly embers, waiting to be stoked up again for cooking the *náttmál,* the night-meal, and only a few torches mounted on the walls casting light. The high thatched roof and the raised platforms that lined the walls of the long hall were mostly lost in the gloom, but that did not matter to Odd. He moved quickly across the familiar floor to where his and Signy's bed closet was built against the wall.

His weapons were hanging from pegs on one side of the bed closet. He reached up and grabbed his sword, which was called Blood-letter, and with a practiced motion he whipped the belt around his waist and buckled it.

Thorgrim had given him the blade many years before. It had belonged to Thorgrim's father, Ulf, whose prowess in battle the skalds still honored in their poems. Blood had washed over that blade like the seas washing over the beach.

Odd wore Blood-letter whenever he went any distance from the farm, but despite its name it had only let blood seven times while in Odd's hands, and only three of those it touched had died. Odd thought of Ulf, and of his father, Thorgrim. He thought of his brother, Harald, and he felt a flush of shame, as he often did when the weapon was at his side. A farmer such as him carrying a blade such as Blood-letter.

A half dozen servants came rushing through the door, fearful of Odd's disapproval for having abandoned their work to watch the excitement of Skafti's arrival. Excitement was one thing that did not grow in abundance on the farm.

"Get a sword and a cloak for Skafti, and be quick!" Odd said, once again speaking sharper than he had intended. Servants scattered and he said to the one left standing there, "Are the horses ready?"

"Yes, Master Odd," the man said. "Near so. The boys are getting the saddles on now. The men you called, they're waiting on you in the stable yard."

A sword and cloak were handed to Skafti, and Odd tossed his own cloak over his shoulders as he rushed out the door, adjusting it so the brooch was positioned just at the right shoulder. He moved quickly across the open ground to the stable yard where a half dozen horses, sensing something was amiss, stood stamping and shaking their heads. Odd wondered if he was making too much of this, if perhaps the news that Skafti had brought did not really warrant such a reaction.

Too late now, Odd thought. He would look a bigger fool if he suddenly decided this thing was not so important after all.

One of the boys held the reins of his horse as Odd put his foot in the stirrup and swung himself up. He looked over his shoulder and saw the others were doing likewise. He took the reins from the boy and kicked his horse to a trot and heard the sound of the twenty hooves behind him likewise thumping on the soft ground.

They rode south and a little west. It was five or six miles from Odd's farm to Thorgrim's, through mostly open country of low, rolling hills, carpeted in green at the height of the summer. Ledges of blue granite poked through the knee-high grass here and there, and in some places the hard-packed dirt road ran though stands of oak, maple, and birch, and the ubiquitous pine and spruce.

After a mile or so of trotting Odd slowed his pace and turned to Skafti who was riding to his side and a little behind. Odd gave a nod of his head and Skafti moved his horse up to Odd's side.

"Tell me more of what happened," Odd said.

"We were at our work, just a day like any. Making hay, mostly, with the fine weather. Some of the women was up in the barn. The milch cows have been giving a lot, and they was eager to get butter and cheese made..."

"I'm sure they were," Odd said. "But about the men who came?"

"Oh, yes, right," Skafti said. "So they just came riding in, about a dozen I should think. No one saw them coming until they was riding into the house yard. Good horses, like I said, good hindquarters, good top line, nice length of neck. Not straight shouldered."

"And the men?" Odd interrupted.

"Ah, yes, the men. They wore fine capes and silver-hilted swords. Mostly. Some were not so fine. Anyway, they just started saying, "you go here, you go there, you fetch this for us," and the folk at the farm, they did like they were told, because these men, they seemed like they must be obeyed. And me, I fled, because I thought you should know, and I figured they wouldn't let me go if they saw me."

Odd nodded. "That's good, Skafti. You did the right thing. But no idea of what they wanted?"

"No," Skafti said.

"Not robbers? Bandits?"

"Not dressed like any bandits I ever seen," Skafti said. "And they seemed too...orderly for folk coming to rob."

They continued on over that familiar road, which Odd had traveled probably once a week since Thorgrim and Harald had sailed off. How long ago? Two and a half, maybe three years? Thorgrim had never met his new granddaughter, Hallbera, named after his wife, Odd's mother. Harald had never held his youngest niece.

Three years, and never a word. No, that was not true. It was about two years back, a man who had sailed with Thorgrim and Ornolf aboard *Red Dragon* returned to Vik. He had tired of raiding and so worked his way home as a sailor aboard a knarr from Dubh-linn. He traveled to Odd's farm and gave Odd word that his grandfather, Ornolf the Restless, had been killed in a fight at an Irish longphort called Vík-ló. The man told Odd that when he left Ireland Thorgrim Night Wolf and Harald were still alive.

That was two years ago. Since then there had been no word.

Your father wants very much to return home, the man had said, *but the gods it seems do not want him to. He's been pushed back to Ireland time and again.*

The thought made Odd feel anxious, near panic. It made him feel impudent and pathetic. His father, his brother, out there beyond the western horizon, tormented by the gods, and him safe on his farm, with no greater danger than wolves among his sheep to concern him. He pressed his lips together and spurred his horse back to a trot, and the men behind him did likewise.

They were half a mile from Thorgrim's farm when Odd slowed his horse again. The farm itself was hidden from view by a ridge of low hills. Odd's eyes were fixed on the stretch of blue sky just above where he knew the farm to be. He could see a few thin columns of smoke, and that was good. They were from cooking fires, or the blacksmith's forge. They were not the great, rolling black clouds of a hall or a barn put to the torch.

They came to the top of the hill and Odd held up his hand in a signal for the men to stop. Thorgrim's farm was not much different from his own, if perhaps a bit more extensive. From the vantage of the horse's back Odd looked down at the grand hall, the stables and byre and workshops. The shipyard down by the water. Or at least the place where the shipyard had been. There had been no sort of shipbuilding since Thorgrim had sailed to the west.

Nothing seemed out of place, as far as Odd could see, but still it seemed strange, something amiss. And then he knew what it was: there was no one around. Normally when he came up over the crest of the hill he was looking down at a bustle of activity, animals being driven here or there, women walking with purpose between the hall and the outbuildings, the smith or the carpenter working at some task, children running about. Now there was nothing. No one to be seen.

"Come," Odd said. He flicked his reins and walked his horse down the far side of the hill to the farm below. His eyes moved from north to south, scanning the grounds and the buildings, alert for any surprise, but still there was no one to be seen.

Their approach was being watched, of that Odd had no doubt. The men who had come to the farm would have to be fools to allow themselves to be taken by surprise. Still, it was not until they reached the flat land at the base of the hill and had approached to within a hundred feet of the hall before they saw any sign that they were not entirely alone.

The door to the hall was a great oak affair, carved with delicate, intertwined serpents and hung from massive iron hinges. It swung open and the motion caught Odd's eye, the first thing he had seen moving since cresting the hill. He did not slow his horse as the first of the men stepped out into the light. He did not slow as the next stepped out behind him, and the next and the next.

Fourteen in all, standing in a rough line just outside the open door. Odd approached slowly, watching for some move on their part, running his eyes over them, evaluating. They left no doubt as to the hierarchy among them.

One man stood in the center of the line and a few paces ahead of the rest He wore a cape that was dark green on the outside, lined with red, and a tunic of the same green cloth. His dark hair was neat and bound in a long queue, and he wore a thick moustache which ran down either side of his mouth and terminated at his chin, as smooth and orderly as a cat's fur.

A seax hung horizontal from his belt, and a sword at his side. The pommels of the seax and sword glinted in the sun. Even if Odd had not recognized him, which he did, he would have known he was the leader of that band of warriors.

Behind this man stood five others. Some wore beards, some did not, some had long hair and some had heads shaved, but all were in the fine clothes of wealthy men. Behind them stood the rest, rougher looking men with clothes and weapons not so fine. They were not impoverished looking men, not homeless vagabonds by any means. The fact that they each carried swords was proof enough of that. On their own they would have seemed like any other men. It was only in contrast to the others that they seemed shabby at all.

The man with the moustache spoke. "Odd Thorgrimson," he said. It was a statement, not a question.

"Yes," Odd said.

The man took a step forward. "I am Einar. Einar Sigurdsson."

"I know who you are," Odd said. Einar was the *sœlumadr* who served Halfdan, the one who administered the king's holdings, who saw that taxes and duties on imports were paid, and land distributed as it should be. Odd had met Einar twice, but it had been a few years and Einar apparently did not recall. In the past there had been little intercourse between the sœlumadr and landholders such as Odd.

Einar smiled. "Of course." He stepped forward again and extended a hand. Odd sat on his horse for a moment and regarded Einar and the hand and debated what to do. To shake his hand could send this meeting down one path, to refuse could send it down another. There was an arrogance to Einar that put Odd on notice and made him dislike the man. On the other hand, he had no idea what Einar's business might be.

Odd slipped down from his horse and shook Einar's hand, and the rest of Odd's men also dismounted. They had seemed a formidable force riding together toward Thorgrim's farm, but now, next to Einar's men, they seemed a weak company.

"What business do you have here?" Odd asked.

Einar spread his hands as if to indicate that his business was all-encompassing. "We're here to take inventory, mostly," he said, and gestured to the man beside him. Odd saw that the man held a slate on which he had written runes and made marks, a thing Odd had not noticed before.

Odd looked around, not sure which of the dozen questions would come out of his mouth next. "Where are the people?" he asked. "The people who work the farm?"

"They're in the byre," Einar said. "Some of my men are watching over them. Better that way. If they're kept from doing anything stupid then there's less chance anyone will get hurt. And trust me, it's not my men I fear for."

Odd shook his head, the only gesture that seemed appropriate in this bizarre chain of events. "I'm still waiting to hear what business you have here."

"Inventory, as I said," Einar said. "By order of King Halfdan."

"And what business does King Halfdan have here?" Odd asked. Halfdan was the king of that region, and had been for ten years or so. Odd had met him a few times, twice at least at feasts put on by Ornolf in Halfdan's honor, and a few times when Halfdan had visited Thorgrim at this very farm. Halfdan was ambitious, Odd knew, but other than the taxes he collected every year, his presence was not much felt in East Agder. Or Fevik.

"This is part of the land King Halfdan rules," Einar said. "Of course he has business here." Rather than simply explaining, he was making Odd drag the information out, bit by bit, and it was making Odd increasingly angry. He folded his arms and stared at Einar, frowning, and did not speak. The men behind Einar shuffled nervously and Odd heard his own men do the same. At last Einar continued.

"It doesn't please me to say this, but it's been three years since your father was heard from and at this point we must consider that he will not return."

"Two years," Odd said.

"What?"

"Two years. A year after Thorgrim sailed we had word of Ornolf's death, and with it word that my father and brother were still alive."

"Very well, two years then," Einar said. "It's still a long time. I know that he and Ornolf had intended to raid for one season only. So now we must assume that he is dead. Like Ornolf."

"I'll assume no such thing," Odd said, "but even if he is, what business is it of yours? Or Halfdan's?"

"Your father owed taxes when he left, and he owes taxes still. Quite a debt that has gone unpaid."

"Nonsense," Odd said, struggling with only partial success to keep the anger from his voice. "My father owed nothing when he left, and I have been paying the taxes on this farm in his absence. If you don't know that, then Halfdan certainly does."

Einar gave a look that suggested pity for Odd's ignorance. "Perhaps you are unaware of this," he said. "But the king keeps track of such things, and his men, me among them, do too. Thorgrim owes taxes and we're here to take an inventory to see nothing is removed before King Halfdan takes possession of this property."

The words were like a slap across Odd's face, just as shocking and sudden and unforgivable.

Take possession of this property?

He could hardly believe what he had heard. Grandson of Ornolf the Restless, son of Thorgrim Night Wolf, his first instinct was to draw Blood-letter and drive it through Einar's heart. But he was not his father or grandfather. He was Odd Thorgrimson and he held his passion in check. He could drive his sword through Einar's body, but he would be dead before he managed to pull it free, and the men with him as well.

And if he was dead he could not prevent this atrocity from taking place. Which he would do.

"Yes," Einar said. "We've been patient. Halfdan knew your grandfather and your father and he had great respect for them. But now it's time. The farm must be given up for the taxes owed."

You will not have this farm, Odd thought. *I swear on my sword you will not have it.* He was resolved and it felt good, gave him some relief, but still the fury, the humiliation and the helplessness burned like flames in his chest.

Chapter Six

Bravery in the world
against the enmity of fiends,
daring deeds
against devils,
thus the sons of men
will praise him afterwards

The Seafarer
Early Anglo-Saxon Poem

It took Nothwulf two days to move his army to Christchurch, just as he thought it would, and he was glad for it. Nothwulf did not want his men tired out before the fighting began. What's more, the heathens were living like kings in the priory, he imagined, and they would be stuffed and dull with the food they had plundered. And drunk as well. That could only help.

Nothwulf's men, and Leofric's, and the men-at-arms under the command of the lesser thegns and the men of the fyrd, broke camp on the same evening that Leofric returned. Then when the sun was down and the moon made its appearance, enough to allow them to see the road, they moved out in a column half a mile long. With Nothwulf and Leofric at the head they tramped down the road, making surprisingly little noise for so many. The creak of the wagons, the soft thump of the horses' hooves, the jingle of mail and weapons were the only sounds, and even they sounded muted in the dark.

There was an open field just short of halfway to Christchurch, mostly surrounded by trees, and they made camp there at first light, hoping the woods would be enough to hide their presence from the Northmen. They were still too far from Christchurch Priory to see the top of the church tower there, so Nothwulf knew that the heathens could not see them. But he would expect even those lazy buggers to send out scouts, if for no other reason than to see what had become of the last scouts.

Or maybe the heathens did not care enough, or worry enough to do so. He could only hope and pray to God that that was the case.

The soldiers, having spent the day before training and preparing, and then having marched all night, were exhausted, and Nothwulf gave leave for them to pass the day sleeping. They would move again when the sun was down, closing with Christchurch Priory in the dark, resting some there, and then attacking at dawn. He wanted his men as fresh as they could be, he wanted the heathens to be dead asleep and he wanted complete surprise if such a thing was possible. And thus far it seemed it might be.

Nothwulf did not feel the need for rest. His every nerve seemed to be firing like sparks from a blacksmith's hammer. He told Leofric that he would ride for Christchurch Priory, get as close as he dared, and see what he could see. To his surprise Leofric asked if he could go as well. The old man had to be twice Nothwulf's age, but he had stamina that even Nothwulf could envy.

They mounted up. "Should we bring a guard?" Leofric asked. "Half a dozen of my best men? It wouldn't do for the ealdorman to come to harm at such a time."

"No," Nothwulf said. "Two mounted men might go unremarked, but eight would surely be noticed. Surprise, my dear Leofric, it's all about surprise."

They rode out of camp with the sun a few hours above the horizon, the light flowing over the green fields and the darker brush and the road stretched out before them, now dried to a light brown color after the unusually long stretch of fine weather.

"It's good we move at night," Leofric said. "The army moving on this road will raise a cloud of dust they could see in Winchester. Even drunken Northmen would not miss it."

"I pray the Northmen don't know we're coming," Nothwulf said, "and I pray we can keep it that way. I'm sure our numbers are well superior to theirs, but the fyrd makes up a good portion of our men, and I wouldn't necessarily credit them with standing up to the heathens."

"That's why we send them in first," Leofric said. "Let them beat up on the heathens a bit, tire them out, and then the heathens will trip over their bodies when they try to get to our men-at-arms."

They rode on in silence for some time longer, until the tip of the church tower at Christchurch Priory began to poke above the trees in the distance. The smell of salt water was more noticeable now, and gulls, rather than hawks, wheeled above them.

"Nothing seems amiss," Leofric said at last.

"No," Nothwulf said. There were no columns of smoke rising from the priory, no townsfolk streaming down the road to escape the savage Northmen, no screaming or clatter of weapons. But in truth neither man had expected that. The Northmen had been there for nearly two weeks now. Even they could not continue to terrorize for that long.

The road came at last to the cluster of small homes and shops that lay scattered, seemingly at random, around the low walls of the priory. They were deserted, as far as Nothwulf and Leofric could see. They stopped at the first, a blacksmith's home judging by the forge and tools hanging from a makeshift shelter on the side of the thatched home. They dismounted and approached the house, moving with caution. Not that caution was necessarily called for; it just seemed the thing to do.

"Anyone there?" Nothwulf called, but he got no response. He stepped closer. The door to the house was open and he stepped in.

The interior, dark and smoky, was just what he would have expected. A crude wooden table and benches, a hearth on the floor at the far end of the house, a wide pallet for a bed, some tattered wool blanket tossed over it. All seemed in place. But no one was there.

They mounted again and rode on, closer to the priory, but still they could see nothing amiss, save for the fact that the village seemed quite deserted.

"Have they all fled?" Nothwulf asked.

"Could be," Leofric said. "If so, they've found someplace to go. We haven't encountered a one of them on the road."

They were a quarter mile from the wall of the priory when they stopped again. "I'm loath to go any farther," Nothwulf said. "If there were folk here we could mix in with them, but as it is we stand out a bit, being the only living things in the village."

Even if there had been folk there, the two would have stood out with their fine horses and mail and cloaks. Nothwulf did not want to risk having the Northmen know that men-at-arms were near, and he could see no benefit that could be had from getting closer. Still, they had seen no sign of the Northmen, and that worried him.

"Come with me," Nothwulf said and turned his horse down a road that ran roughly parallel to the priory wall. The houses blocked their view of the priory, except for those few times that the space opened to give them an unobstructed look, and then they saw no one, and Nothwulf hoped it meant no one saw them. But every time he looked at that seemingly deserted place he grew more and more concerned.

The road continued to follow the curve of the priory wall, running around to the south, toward the bank of the River Stour which led to the shallow bay and then to the sea. Soon the houses grew more sparse as the village ended and the river bank and the place where the fishing boats were pulled up on shore met.

Nothwulf slipped down from his horse and Leofric did the same. They moved slowly toward the edge of the village and the open space beyond. They kept close to the line of small, shabby, abandoned cottages where the fishermen lived. Or did.

Finally they came to a place where Nothwulf could see what he wanted to see. He stopped and he felt the tension ease and realized he'd been clenching his shoulders as if he were bracing against a bitter cold wind. There, a hundred yards away, pulled up on the shore, were seven longships. The heathens had not yet left.

"Hmm, our friends are still here," Leofric said in a soft voice.

"Yes. Seven. Must be the bastards from Swanage. Do they look as if they're making ready to sail?"

The two studied the ships for some time. There were men working on them, Northmen presumably, but it was too far to tell what they were doing. There were not very many men, however, and they seemed in no hurry. There was no sense that anything important was about to happen.

"I know little of such things," Leofric said. "But it doesn't look to me as if they plan to leave any time soon."

"I agree," Nothwulf said, still feeling that sense of relief. If he fought the Northmen and lost, that would be bad enough, but if they managed to slip though his fingers one more time, that would be a disaster. There would be whispers of cowardice, or gross stupidity. Cynewise would take full advantage of his bungling. But it seemed he would be spared that. They returned to their horses and headed back the way they had come.

They rode on in silence for some time, Nothwulf working himself up to ask Leofric the thing he most wanted to ask. Finally he cleared his throat and said, "Tell me, Leofric, do you hear anything of that pretender Cynewise? What she's been up to?"

Leofric was one of the most informed men Nothwulf knew, and he had just made the round of the thegns in an effort to gather men-at-arms, so Nothwulf imagined he had a good notion of what was going on in Sherborne. But he could also be tight-lipped at times, discreet to a fault, and Nothwulf knew he might have to do a bit of prying to get him to speak.

"Mmm, I hear this and that," Leofric said. They rode on in silence, but Nothwulf knew his friend well enough to know that he had only to wait to hear more.

"The thegns are pretty well divided," Leofric continued after some length. "Some side with her, some with you. The most of them, you know…their loyalty lies with whomever they think will end up in the ealdorman's seat. Whoever can do them the most good. And they don't much care who that is."

"Is there…do most of them lean one way or another?" Nothwulf asked. If he had been at Sherborne, or anyplace of importance, then he would hear these things for himself. But he felt like he was in exile, living in the wilderness, banished. And that was not so far from the truth of it.

"That's hard to say," Leofric said. "But there's another twist in this odd tale. There's word that Cynewise's father, Ceorle, intends to come from Devonshire to Dorset with a few hundred of his best men. To shore Cynewise up, apparently."

"Really?" Nothwulf said and he could not keep the genuine surprise and concern from his voice. Nor could he stop himself before he said, "You might have told me about that, you know, without me having to pry it from you."

Leofric shrugged. "It's mere rumor at this point. Gossip I picked up. I don't know if it's true. If it is, it's likely a mistake on the part of Cynewise and Ceorle. The thegns are not in love with the idea of Devon's men-at-arms marching around Dorset. They don't care for

Ceorle having such influence here. Better for Cynewise to be entirely independent of her father, as far as they're concerned."

Nothwulf fell silent, thinking about that as they rode. It gave him the first bit of hope he had felt in some time. *The little bitch might have made a grave error this time,* he thought. *Tried to be a bit too clever, shown that she doesn't have the mettle to be ealdorman without her father's help.*

Then his thoughts moved off in another direction. He thought of the silver chalices lined up like soldiers on Bishop Ealhstan's table, Ceorle's coat of arms etched in the side, an image that often returned to his mind. He thought of the influence that Ceorle had with his old friend, King Æthelwulf. If the thegns were looking to back the one with the most power in Dorsetshire, that one might well be Cynewise, with the backing of the bishop and her father. Nothwulf felt his hope snuffed out as quickly as it had been kindled.

It was just after noon when the two men returned to the camp. They had been challenged by pickets long before they arrived, several times in fact, and Nothwulf was glad of it. Had they been able to approach the camp unnoticed then he would have given Bryning a significant tongue lashing, but he knew it was only his ill-humor that made him think Bryning could ever be so negligent. There was a reason he trusted Bryning so.

The camp was quiet, most of the men asleep, as Nothwulf wished them to be. For now, rest was the thing, since, with God's grace, they were looking at a long night ahead with a bloody and victorious battle in the morning. He and Leofric ate, and then they slept as well.

The sun was nearly down when Nothwulf's servant gently shook his shoulder to wake him from a less than restful slumber. Nothwulf stood and stretched and stepped out of his tent. The camp, nearly lost from sight in the growing dark, was already bustling, the captains getting their men ready to move again, issuing orders in harsh but soft tones. There was no reason for quiet, really. They were miles from the enemy. But still, the secrecy of a night march seemed to call for a minimum of noise.

It was well past dark by the time the column snaked its way out of the clearing and back onto the road to Christchurch Priory, the one Nothwulf and Leofric had traveled that morning. They moved in near silence, just as they had the night before, and the miles dropped off quickly. The wagons with the tents and the food and the camp supplies had been left back at the clearing. They would not be needed over the next few days. That, at least, was Nothwulf's intention.

They had been on the road for a few hours when the scouts returned to say the village encircling the priory was just another mile or so ahead. Had it been daytime, Nothwulf was sure they would have been able to see the church tower from where they were, but the moon, now low in the sky, did not provide light enough for that.

An hour later they reached the edge of the village and those men who had horses dismounted, including Nothwulf and Leofric. The boys who marched with the army led the animals away, and the lesser thegns and the captains got their men organized into four columns.

Nothwulf and the others had discussed this all, how the four columns would each move through the village and position themselves at the four cardinal directions in relation to the wall surrounding the priory. When they attacked, it would be from four directions. The heathens could not possibly have enough men to defend each point of the wall.

Nothwulf spoke a few words to the thegns, reiterating the plan, and then he let each of the columns move off through the dark. When at last there was only the column led by him and Leofric, he waved his arm over his head, unsure if the men could actually see the gesture. He stepped off, gratified to hear the sound of nearly a hundred men behind him, walking as stealthily as they might.

The village seemed to have a different quality now than it had when he and Leofric had scouted the place the day before. Then it had seemed abandoned, but now it did not, despite the fact that there was no one to be seen. He could smell the smoke from cooking fires, and he thought he heard the sounds of snoring from a few of the hovels they passed. A dog barked at them as they moved down the dark road, and it did not stop until one of the men behind Nothwulf silenced it for good with his spear. Nothwulf thought he saw a face peer out from the doorway, but it disappeared before he could be certain.

Then the priory was just ahead, just across a stretch of open ground, a beaten road that circled the monastery wall. Nothwulf held up his hand and stopped and he heard the men behind him stop, too. They were still in the shadows of the village houses, hidden in the dark places where the tall peaked thatch roofs blocked off the moon's weak light. He felt something brush his arm and he saw Leofric step up beside him.

"Looks to be fires burning," Leofric said in a whisper.

Nothwulf nodded. He had seen the same thing, a soft glow of light that left the top of the wall easily distinguished from the rest of the priory behind. It probably meant small fires burning in the yard on the other side, which probably meant the Northmen were there.

Leofric turned to the man behind him. "Stand easy, pass it down the line," he whispered and the instructions made their way from man to man. There was some time yet until dawn. As soon as there was light enough to see the wall clearly they would move forward, and when the other columns saw them they would move as well. But until then, they had only to wait.

Nothwulf felt his uncertainty clawing at him.

This will not be a repeat of Swanage, he thought, which was his foremost worry. The Northmen had landed at Swanage, and there he and Leofric had moved their men-at-arms into the village, hidden in the dark, waiting for a dawn attack, just as they were doing now. But when the sun came up it revealed that the Northmen had gone, sailed away during the night.

But that would not happen this time.

The hours of darkness dragged on, and Nothwulf knew enough of this sort of waiting to know that every minute would seem an hour. It was torment, really, a taste of what eternity must be like, and a good reminder of why you did not want to spend it in the pits of Hell. He sat on a barrel pushed up against the house behind which they were hiding and tried to relax.

Sometime later he felt his shoulder jostled, saw the odd images floating in his head dissolve away and he realized with a flush that he had fallen asleep. It was Leofric who had jostled him, just the subtlest of touches. Nothwulf looked left and right, collecting himself before he spoke.

It was getting light. He could see the dull shape of the wall across the open ground, and the buildings around them were more distinct. Not long now, not long at all. He could hear from the soft sounds in the shadows behind, the rustle of mail, the soft scrape of weapons being drawn, the shuffle of shoes on the soft ground, that the men were making ready. They all knew. Not long now.

Nothwulf stepped out into the open, nothing between him and the far wall. He looked left and right but could see nothing. He stepped back.

"Soon, soon," he said to Leofric, and Leofric nodded. Nothwulf picked up the shield he had leaned against the wall of the hut and slung it over his back. He looked out over the open ground. The light had spread enough for them to see a hundred yards in any direction. Not sunrise yet, but close enough. Time to move.

Nothwulf moved out of the shadow of the hovel where they had been sheltering and Leofric and the others followed behind. He moved slowly, looking left and right. He was halfway to the wall and still had seen nothing and was just considering sending messengers when he saw the other columns, to the north and the south, also emerging from their concealed places. The thegns had been watching, and now they were moving as they had been told.

The wall was not high, about five feet, but Nothwulf did not want the delay that even a short wall could cause. He waved his arm and a dozen men behind him came running past carrying short barrels, crates, stools, whatever they had found to assist in getting the men over the top. They ran to the wall and placed the makeshift steps against the stone, then stepped aside.

Nothwulf was first up and over. He put his foot on a crate, his palms down on the top of the wall and swung his leg up. He twisted onto the top of the wall and then hopped down the other side. His feet hit the dirt and he swung the shield around and grabbed the handle on the inside of the boss and with his right hand he drew his sword.

Only then did he look around. He saw the smoldering remains of half a dozen small fires scattered around the priory grounds. That was it. There was no one to be seen. Nothwulf felt a twist in his stomach, the taste of panic in his mouth.

Heathens are asleep...drunk and asleep... he assured himself. He stepped away from the wall as more and more of his men came over, and he could see the other columns also climbing over the wall, unopposed. They were also slinging shields over their arms, spreading out in defensive lines. They had all been instructed back in the clearing to defend against a surprise attack. If they came over the wall and the Northmen did not attack, it did not mean that the Northmen were gone. It could well mean they were asleep. Or setting a trap. And either one of those would be fine with Nothwulf.

The three lines of men advanced inward toward the big church that formed the center of the priory, and presumably the column to the south was doing so as well. It was rapidly getting lighter, and the buildings and the spaces between were no longer hidden by shadow and still there was no one to see. Nothwulf felt the tension mount, waiting for a sudden attack, waiting for a terrific disappointment, he didn't know which to expect, or which would be worse.

Some time passed and still there was nothing. The thegns leading the north and south columns came jogging over, and they and Nothwulf and Leofric stood in a little cluster, away from the men.

"Don't see anything, lord," one of the thegns said. "No sign of the Northmen, or anyone at all." The others nodded.

"We saw their ships just yesterday morning," Nothwulf said. "They didn't look ready to sail, and the heathens sure as damnation did not leave without their ships. Each of you, pick four or five men and have them start searching the buildings. Tell them to be quiet. If they find the Northmen sleeping, don't wake them. If we can kill them in their sleep we will."

The thegns nodded and hurried off, and moments later handfuls of men from each column trotted off toward the cluster of buildings that made up the Christchurch Priory.

"If there are as many of the bastards as we think," Leofric said, "then we should find them soon enough. Then the church is about the only building big enough to hold all of them at once."

Nothwulf nodded. He saw a handful of his men push open the church door and step warily inside. He waited for shouting, a clash of weapons, anything. Soon the men came out again having apparently found no Northmen.

"Could they have sailed last night?" Nothwulf asked Leofric. He spoke softly, did not want to be overheard.

Leofric shook his head. "I wouldn't think so. The bay here, it's very tricky. Mudflats, sandbars, and they're always shifting. And the channel to the sea is narrow. I don't think they could have felt their way out at night."

That was a small relief, a very small one. The two men continued to watch as the buildings were searched, the searchers going in one after another, and then emerging again with nothing to report.

Nothwulf felt his spirits sink with each moment that passed, each building that was explored.

The sun came up over the edge of the wall and the light like the grace of God fell over the priory. The men searching the buildings were lost from sight, but soon they appeared again, heading back toward Nothwulf and Leofric. They moved slow, the weary steps of men who had marched through half the night, then had been keyed up to a fighting pitch, and then let down again.

Nothwulf closed his eyes. He would hear what they had to say, but it was hardly necessary. He knew already what they had found. Once again, the Northmen were gone.

Chapter Seven

[F]rom thy shoulders cast
what to thee seems irksome:
let thyself thyself direct...

The Poetic Edda

Thorgrim Night Wolf stood on top of the makeshift wall and watched the light slowly spread over the fishing village and the priory beyond. He knew the priory's name, had heard it spoken a few times, but he knew he would hopelessly bungle it if he tried to say it. It had the name "Christ" in it, he knew.

English... he thought. The language was similar to his own in many ways. He could hear it when one of those English fellows was speaking to Gudrid, and occasionally he could pick out a word or two, but that was it.

Harald seemed to be picking up the language quickly, in part, Thorgrim guessed, because it was not so different from his own. The boy went out of his way to speak with the women who had been taken with the priory, the wives of the laborers and craftsmen, though none were at all young or pretty. Harald must have been motivated to learn the language just for the sake of learning it.

He forced his attention back to the church. It was a half a mile away and just starting to emerge from the gloom of the pre-dawn. They had heard no obvious sign of an attack, just a few noises in the dark that might have been anything. Still, Thorgrim felt certain the men-at-arms had come. He felt it in his bones, in his gut, and he had learned to trust those signs. He had seen them, in the wolf dream.

"Nothing yet, Night Wolf!" Starri Deathless cried out. He was at *Sea Hammer*'s masthead, the highest lookout spot around. It was even a few feet higher than normal, since the ship's bow was still pulled up on the beach, along with six of the other seven vessels.

It had been a long night, and Thorgrim could feel it in his aching back and sore muscles, and the throbbing in the still unhealed wound in his side. In the wolf dream he had seen the soldiers.

He had no doubt they were coming to liberate the church and kill the hated heathens, or drive them off. Thorgrim and his men were outnumbered, but that was no great concern. Most of the army sent against them would be farmers, not true warriors with the strength to fight the Northmen.

The church and its grounds, however, were a concern. Too big, too exposed for his men to defend.

Two days before, Thorgrim had held his council on the top of the church tower, and they had all agreed with him. The priory was vulnerable and the ships, half a mile away, were undefended.

Thorgrim looked out over the shabby village clustered against the stone walls of Christchurch as he considered those problems. The fishermen were pulling slowly back to the shore with their catch. Men and women shambled through the streets at their various tasks. Life went on.

The people had fled when the fleet first pulled up on the shore, which was no surprise. What else would reasonable folk do in the face of the heathens coming from the sea? But it was not long before they started coming back.

Perhaps they understood, correctly, that the Northmen would not plunder their pathetic hovels because they were hardly worth the bother. That they themselves, worn down from lifetimes of labor, were of little value on the slave market. Maybe they resented those truths. But whatever their thoughts, or lack thereof, a few had returned, and then more, and then when it seemed clear the Northmen were minding their own business, the rest had come as well.

"We must abandon this place, the church," Thorgrim announced to his chief men, there on the roof of the church tower.

"Without the silver Oswin was supposed to bring?" Harald asked.

"We're not leaving this village," Thorgrim corrected. "Just the church. We must build a small ship fort, a longphort, down by the water, where the ships are pulled up. It will be easier to defend, and it will protect the ships. And if we can't defend it, we can take to the sea."

Heads nodded, but faces looked uncertain. "Build a longphort?" Godi asked.

"Yes," Thorgrim said. The dam was breached now, the ideas pouring through. "No great thing. We'll use timbers from these buildings," he said, gesturing toward the houses spread out past the walls of the church grounds. "Easy enough to pull down. We'll build a half-moon wall to enclose the ships, enough to cover, say, two hundred feet of the shore. That should do us. The water will protect our backs, and with so short a wall to defend we can hold off any who come."

Heads were still nodding, and with a bit more enthusiasm now.

"There's another thing," Thorgrim went on. "Whoever's leading this army, he must have men watching us. We can't let them catch us in the middle of building this new defense. We'll be in a bad place to defend ourselves if they do. We'll be spread out, disorganized. It must be done quick, built before they have a chance to react."

No heads were nodding anymore. "What are you thinking, Father?" Harald asked, the only one among them who would dare. "How fast do you want it done?"

"One night," Thorgrim said. "We make ready today, and then tomorrow, when the sun is down, we build it. And it's done when the sun comes up."

Still no heads were nodding. "Yes, I know what you're thinking," Thorgrim said. "I can practically hear it. Our numbers are not so great, and we have two hundred men-at-arms to guard. But they're not men-at-arms now. They're laborers. And they'll labor for us. The priests, too."

Now heads began to nod. "We can make them work, sure," Starri said. "But they'll malinger as much as they can. You know how these English are. Malingerers."

Thorgrim did not in fact know these English—he had been in Engla-land for just a few weeks, and the time before that had been many years ago. He wondered if Starri actually did know the English any better. He doubted it.

"It's a problem, getting forced men to work hard, that's true," Thorgrim said. "But they're not the only ones we have." He swept his arm in a half circle to indicate the village at their feet. "We have all these men here, and I reckon they're hard workers. And I reckon we can motivate them quite well."

He was right about that, and he was right about what the folk of the village would find most irresistible. Not silver or gold; they had little experience with such things, and if they tried to spend it, anyone in authority would know it had come from the Northmen, the only possible source, other than stealing it themselves. And trading with the Northmen or stealing could cost them their lives.

But there were other things to be found in the priory. The storehouses were filled with sacks of barley, wheat and rye, barrels of salted fish and pork, cured hams, barrels of ale, onions and carrots, butter, cheese, a bounty of food. Louis explained to Thorgrim that the people around had to pay a sort of tax to the church, and they often paid it in the produce of their farms, and the food in turn fed the people at the priory and the many wealthy travelers who passed through. This, Thorgrim knew, would be far more tempting than gold or silver.

He took Gudrid and Harald and a small guard and they left the walls of the priory and began spreading the word, telling anyone who stayed around long enough to listen that the priory's storehouses would be open for all who would come and give a few day's work. In the course of doing that they met with a few men, old sailors, who could speak the Norse tongue well enough, and they sent them off to further spread the word.

The villagers, several hundred of them, arrived at the priory gate the next morning. Thorgrim ordered the gates open and the people streamed in, and if any of them were reluctant to enter, the sight of the barrels and sacks of food stacked up on the grounds convinced them. Food was distributed, enough to make their breakfast and to demonstrate that there was indeed food to be had and that the Northmen were willing to give it out.

The people were still eating when Gellir came hurrying over. Gellir, a man with good eyes and quick wit, had been posted on the wall with instructions to watch for anyone in the town, but to not be seen himself.

"Lord Thorgrim? Two men, lord, sneaking through the town, trying to not be seen."

"Townsfolk? Thieves?" Thorgrim asked.

"Hard to say, lord, they're keeping their distance. But they don't seem like they're dressed like townsfolk. They might be wearing mail, I can't see for certain."

Thorgrim nodded. Not townsfolk, and not the sort of man who would be sent scouting. The commanders of this approaching army then, who wanted to see for themselves what they faced. Which meant he would have to wait until they were gone before moving ahead with his plans.

"Keep an eye on them. Let me know if they leave, or if they're still around when the people here are done with their breakfast."

Gellir nodded and left. It was not long before he was back again. "They're gone, lord. Saw them walk off, and later I could see them riding away."

"Good, Gellir, well done," Thorgrim said. So the commanders had left, no doubt satisfied that nothing of import was going on. Time to get to work.

The first order of business was collecting up the materials to make the walls. "Logs, beams, planks, whatever can be had," he told them, using one of the sailors as a translator. "Anything heavy enough that it would take two or three men to carry. Bring it all to the beach where the longships are pulled on shore."

Even Thorgrim, who was certain this would work, was surprised at the eagerness with which the local men, and women and children, set to the task assigned. The locals knew, of course, where such material would be found, and they began rounding it up. Others began to tear down houses nearby, houses that might have been abandoned, but more likely, Thorgrim guessed, owned by their fellow townspeople who had not returned with the others. Thorgrim wondered how many minor offenses and long-standing grudges were being avenged as certain houses were pulled down and broken into their component parts.

By end of day a substantial pile of beams and such had been deposited in a heap on the beach. There the men-at-arms and the priests who had been captured when the priory was taken were encouraged, at spear-point, to begin sorting the lumber out and stacking it neatly in various piles. That was as far as Thorgrim wanted to go in the light of day.

The two men whom Gellir had seen scouting that morning had left, but Thorgrim assumed that others from the nearby army had been sent to watch, men who were better at hiding themselves. If that was the case, then Thorgrim did not want to make it obvious what they were up to. They might be collecting wood to repair their ships or build new ones, or getting rollers to haul the vessels further out, or to build a shelter of some sort. Uncertainty would buy them time, but if their enemy knew what they were about, and if they had any competence at all, then they would attack before he and his men were ready.

The Northmen returned to the priory with the villagers who were herded warily in through the main gate. Once inside, the captive men-at-arms were made to distribute more food to them. Thorgrim climbed up on the back of a wagon and spoke to them, and the sailor translated.

"You did good work today, and you'll be paid. Some of it now, and the rest when the work is done. You've already seen the fine food and ale that's to be had here. More to come."

The villagers watched in silence as he spoke, but he could see they were not afraid, and that he had given them enough food already that they believed what he said, so he went on.

"But hear this," Thorgrim continued. "We have little time to do what we need to do. In fact, it must all be done by sunrise tomorrow. So eat your fill, and then rest yourselves, and then when it's fully dark we'll set to work again. Oh, and you must remain within the walls of the priory until we're done."

The villagers looked less pleased about this, but Thorgrim figured that they would understand that getting more food meant cooperating, and there was not much they could do to resist anyway. So, in the way of folk who had always lived lives that were not entirely their own, they accepted their fate and found places to bed down.

Thorgrim's reasons for keeping the folk there were threefold. Keeping the townsfolk penned in the monastery would reduce the chance of word getting back to whoever commanded the army coming for them, and it would make it much easier to assemble them for the night's work. And if the enemy did attack in the night, several hundred terrified villagers filling the grounds would create enough confusion that Thorgrim and his men could get clean away.

Once all was settled, Thorgrim went wearily off to the small house by the church that he had taken for his own, hoping for a few hours rest before a long and tiring night. A candle was burning on the table and giving off enough light in the dark interior that he could just see the pile of furs that covered his bed.

He had given word that all should rest and he had expected to see Failend there, in their bed or near it, but she was not. He took off his sword and lay down on top of the furs. He wondered if Failend would come and take her rest with him. She had not been in his bed the night before, either. He had seen her that day, working with the rest, standing guard over the prisoners, but he had been too busy to speak with her. He wondered where she was, if her absence had any significance, but before he could think much more on it he was asleep.

It was dark when he woke sometime later. Groggy with sleep, it took him a moment to realize someone was knocking on the door. He reached over and laid his hand on Iron-tooth's hilt and thought, *Murderers don't knock, you fool.*

"Come," he called and the door opened and there was light enough from the still-burning candle for him to recognize Harald's shape.

"Father?"

"Yes, Harald, what is it?" Thorgrim groaned and propped himself on his elbow.

"Sun's just set. We were expecting the scouts back before dark, but they never arrived."

"Who are the scouts?"

"Vandrad from *Blood Hawk*'s crew was one. The other was one of Jorund's men I don't know well."

"Humph," Thorgrim said. "Vandrad's a good man. If he didn't return, that's an ill sign." If Vandrad didn't return then it was likely because he and the other man had been taken. That, and the appearance of the two men who had been scouting the village earlier, probably meant the enemy was closing in fast.

He stood and said, "Let's get food and ale out to the folk sleeping on the grounds out there, and the prisoners as well. Just bread and cold meat. No time for anything more. Then we get to work."

The grounds of the priory were quiet and dark when Thorgrim left his quarters and walked over toward the mountain of barrels of meat and ale and sacks of grain, where a half dozen of his men stood guard. The quiet did not last long. With a few words Thorgrim had his men moving among the sleeping townsfolk and the prisoners, rousing them, getting them on their feet. They were not harsh about it, but they were not particularly considerate, either. There was much work to do, and Thorgrim's men at least understood that their lives might depend on getting it done.

Food and ale were served out, but the people were given little time to eat before the gates were open and the small army of laborers, willing and otherwise, marched down to the waterfront, where they had earlier stacked the beams and logs and such. Starri Deathless and a few others were sent in the other direction, out into the deserted village to see what visitors, if any, arrived in the night.

Thorgrim Night Wolf was no stranger to building fortifications. He had taken part in the construction of many. Some had worked, some had failed, but he had learned a lesson from each of them. And he knew what he wanted now.

He gathered Godi and Harald and Gudrid, Jorund and Halldor and Asmund to him. "You'll each of you take a section of the wall and oversee its building," he said. "The material is mostly sorted out, but we'll see that it's where it should be."

The others nodded as he spoke. He had already explained, in some detail, how he wanted this work done, and now it was only a matter of doing it.

From end to end the wall would cover two hundred feet of the shoreline, and bow inland in a near half-circle. The timbers would be set in a zigzag pattern, with one length of logs and beams meeting the next at a near right angle, the ends of the two stacked alternately one on top of the other so that each of the sections would support the next. Built with substantial baulks of wood, Thorgrim knew it would be strong enough to hold an enemy back when defended by a solid line of spears, axes, swords and arrows.

They worked for hours in the dark: Northmen and Englishmen and grumbling, angry men-at-arms. Layer by layer the walls rose up from the soft earth, irregular and ugly, but strong enough to do what they needed them to do. It was brutal work and would have taken considerable time if they did not have so great a hoard of men at work.

As it was, the night was less than half over when the wall stood six feet tall along its whole length, with timbers laid along the perimeter inside on which Thorgrim's warriors could stand and fight. All the leftover logs, and the branches and other detritus were strewn around the approaches to hinder any attempt to rush the walls.

Thorgrim and his chief men walked the length of the fortification and Thorgrim inspected it and saw it was good. He ordered the townspeople herded back into the priory where the last of the food was distributed. Then the tired folk were allowed to return to their homes, carrying sacks and rolling barrels, their pay for a hard night's work.

The English men-at-arms and priests, who had been demoted to unwilling laborers, were crammed aboard *Blood Hawk* and the ship anchored one hundred feet off the beach. The anchor cable was rigged in such a way that it could not be untied, only cut, and the prisoners had no means of doing that. If any of them thought they could swim to freedom Thorgrim was happy to let them try, but he did not think that many would.

Starri and the other scouts returned and they reported that there had been no enemy that they could see, but Thorgrim was certain they would come. He posted guards on the walls and sent the rest to sleep. He himself paced for a while, then sat on a barrel of salted fish. Later, as dawn approached, he climbed up on the wall himself. He looked behind him, scanning the grounds of the longphort, and he gave a half smile at what they had accomplished in one night.

The sky to the east grew lighter and Starri Deathless scrambled up *Sea Hammer*'s shrouds to the top of the mast where he might get the most advantageous view. "Nothing yet, Night Wolf!" he cried out once he was settled. Thorgrim nodded. He knew they would come.

And then they did. The sun was still below the horizon, the church still all but lost in the dark, when Thorgrim heard a sound. It was not clear what the sound was—a shield dropped as a man scaled the wall, something overturned by warriors stumbling around—but Thorgrim heard it, and in the same instant Starri cried out, "There they are! Ha! The sneaking dogs, they've gone over the wall!"

Thorgrim could not imagine how Starri could see them in that light, and he wondered if he really could, but Starri's eyesight had often proved more than surprising. Men who had been sleeping behind the longphort's walls stirred and stood and every ear was cocked toward the priory, but it was too far for anyone to hear anything over the buzz of insects and the lap of water on the beach.

So they peered over the wall and they waited. Soon enough the sun broke over the horizon and the church and the tower and the wall and the sorry little village were all lit up golden and looked almost magical in that light. And even Thorgrim could see them now.

The English were standing on the low wall surrounding the church. Thorgrim imagined they were staring off at the longphort, something that had not been there when the sun set the day before, and cursing an enemy who had slipped away from them.

Harald and Godi were flanking Thorgrim on the wall and the three of them looked out toward the church. "You recall, at that first village we landed at, right after the storm?" Thorgrim asked. "There was an army there that came to drive us off."

"We sailed in the dark," Harald said. "Left them scratching their asses when the sun came up."

"Exactly," Thorgrim said. "I wonder if this is the same army, come to fight us again."

Godi chuckled. "If so, they're cursing us up and down now."

They watched for a while more, but there did not seem to be much happening at the church. "So, what now, Father?" Harald asked.

"We wait," Thorgrim said. "We wait to see what these bastards bring us. Tribute, battle, we'll take either one."

Chapter Eight

Now let us reckon
up the ancient families,
and the kin's
of exalted men

The Poetic Edda

There were ten men in attendance, and they listened with polite and at times genuine attention, but Odd still had the notion that they had come mostly for the food and drink. They were seated in Odd's hall, a fire of moderate size burning in the hearth and torches throwing their light over the big space. Food was spread out before them, mostly the remains of the more popular fare: pork and mutton, vegetables from the first harvest, white bread and butter. Servants darted back and forth, refilling cups with mead.

Odd had started talking as the eating began to taper off, figuring no one was going to listen to him until they had had their fill. Now he was getting to the end of what he wished to say, the important point.

"King Halfdan does not want my father's farm because he needs another farm or more land or taxes or any such thing. He wants it to prove that he can take it. And he wants it to further enrich himself. And no doubt give it as a gift to the man who can do him the most good."

The ten nodded, nearly in unison. Odd never doubted they would believe him. He was not so sure they would agree with him on what needed to be done.

They were his nearest neighbors, though spread out as they were it had taken a day and a half to get word of this feast to all of them, and then another day for them all to gather here. They were the *hauldar,* the most prosperous of the men who owned land scattered around Fevic and Vik, holders of the largest tracts, and their status was well above that of the general yeoman farmers.

Though all had farms that were substantial, they varied in size: some respectable if not terribly impressive, and some larger even than Odd's own farm in the size of their fields, the number of head of cattle, the production of ale and mead and butter and cheese, ironwork and woodwork.

None had farms as grand as Thorgrim's.

"Halfdan is ambitious, there's no doubt on that score," said the man on Odd's right hand. His name was Amundi Thorsteinsson and his property, perhaps the largest of all those there, actually shared a boundary with Thorgrim's. He was near Thorgrim's age and the two men were friends and had been for many years. They had gone a'viking together in the younger days, before they had given that life up and turned to the less brutal work of farming. But Amundi was also a clever and practical man, and when he spoke, everyone listened.

"He's a powerful man, is Halfdan," Amundi continued. "But I've known him to be fair as well. Thorgrim did not owe taxes?"

"He did not," Odd said. "I have kept the farm running, as you know, and I've paid Halfdan everything that he was due. Just as you all have paid your share."

Heads nodded once again. Everyone there paid Halfdan the Black, King of Agder, what they owed him, an amount which Halfdan himself set. In exchange, Halfdan pretty much left everyone alone, and did not much interfere with what the people of Agder were doing. On occasion the king made a tour of his kingdom, forcing each of the jarls and wealthy landowners to host an expensive banquet in his honor and house the royal procession for as long as they wished to stay, but only rarely.

But that could be changing, and every man there knew it.

"Don't want to upset anyone here," said the man halfway down on Odd's left, looking at Odd as he spoke. He was Ulfkel Ospaksson who owned a small farm to the north of Odd's. He was heavy-set—fat, really—and he had consumed more food and drink than any other two men had. But as a young man he had gone a'viking, and it was said he had been an impressive warrior in his day.

Ulfkel took a drink and then continued. "And forgive me for saying this, but Odd, do you have reason to believe that your father is still alive?"

"I have no reason not to believe it," Odd said, and he felt himself flair at the question. He did not like to consider that his father might be dead. He did not like to think of Thorgrim and Harald dying in some distant land while he wrestled pigs in Fevik.

But he calmed himself, and added, "I haven't had word from my father in two years," which the other men there knew full well to be the case. "And even if he's dead, Halfdan has no right to take his farm with just a wave of his hand."

That comment was met with silence around the table. It was a tricky point. Certainly Halfdan did not have the right to take the farm. If Thorgrim was dead, then the farm belonged to Odd. But if Odd inherited the farm, it would make him the biggest and wealthiest landowner in all of Fevik, and most of Agder. Perhaps all of Agder. He knew that not everyone cared to see him thus elevated in an instant.

"Halfdan is taking a lot," said Vifil, who owned a farm to the south. "His appetite for land grows by the day."

"It is as bad as Ulfkel's appetite for meat and ale," said Amundi, and that drew a laugh and the tension in the hall dissipated.

Odd started in once more. "I've lived under Halfdan's rule all my life," he said. "He was a friend to my father, a guest in his hall many times. He's been a guest in my hall, and all of yours. And I won't fault a man for ambition. But if my land, or my father's land, becomes the object of his ambition, then it becomes a problem."

"This problem doesn't live in Agder alone," said Thorgeir Herjolfsson, whose farm certainly outstripped Odd's in land and produce, buildings, servants and slaves. "All of the kings and chiefs, all over, seem to be grabbing more and more power. A man used to be free to do as he wished, now there's always some king or other trying to put you under his heel."

"And Halfdan's among the worst of them," Vifil offered to more nodding heads.

"When your grandfather, Ornolf the Restless, was jarl here, it was different," Amundi Thorsteinsson said, turning to Odd. "Halfdan respected him. Even feared him, a bit, I think, because Ornolf was so loved by the people. Halfdan didn't dare cross him. Now? There's no jarl here. Who could take Ornolf's place?" He left the question hanging.

There was muttering around the table. "Very well, what do we do about this problem?" asked another, Ragi Oleifsson, who owned the smallest farm of the lot of them. He, too, had gone a'viking as a younger man and gained much wealth and reputation, though he had lost his left hand in the winning of it. The wealth might have been turned into a more prosperous farm if Ragi had much interest in farming, which he did not.

"We go to see Halfdan. We go as one," Odd said. "It's the only way he'll listen. One man can do nothing, but the most prosperous farmers in this part of the land? He must see we won't stand for having our farms taken."

That led to more silence. Odd had thought the point was obvious: if Halfdan was allowed to take one farm, there was nothing to stop him from taking any that he wished. They could only push back if they all pushed together.

But he could see that his ideas were not necessarily universal. Halfdan had been growing more powerful year by year, slowly enough that it had gone unnoticed, and now he was very powerful indeed. But still, he was a threat to Odd alone, not to the others. At least not yet.

"I agree," Amundi said. "We should go and speak to Halfdan. Let him know that we're not happy about him taking Thorgrim's farm. We don't know if Thorgrim is alive or dead, but it's only right we presume him to be alive. Tell Halfdan if taxes are owed, then Odd will see them paid."

At that last he looked over at Odd with a pointed expression. They would help him defend his father's land, even at the risk of setting him up as the most powerful landowner in the region, but they would do no more. Certainly nothing that would cost them silver, or part of their own farms' yield.

The others nodded their agreement, with various degrees of enthusiasm.

"Very well," Odd said. "Well said, Amundi. And thank you all."

It was a day's ride to Grømstad, where Halfdan the Black kept his great hall, his chief home, though he had several, but the guests at Odd's table were not prepared for such a trip, or an audience with the king. Odd knew that.

"You'll want to send to your farms for men and for your fine clothes and weapons. I know you didn't wear your best to come see me in my simple home. We'll have more ale and mead, and then I'll let you crawl off to your beds, then I'll send riders out in the morning. I hope we can ride for Grømstad the day after."

That was agreed from the others, and then the talk turned to weather and crops and the likelihood of a harsh winter, all subjects more agreeable to the farmers there than kings and politics. It took a couple more hours, and considerably more mead, before Odd's neighbors finally crawled off to their beds, arranged on the raised platforms that ran the length of the walls.

Odd, who had been ready for bed an hour past, stood and made his way to the bed closet that he and Signy shared. He stripped off his clothes and climbed under the covers. He stretched his arm out and Signy shuffled over and lay in the crook of his arm, her head on his chest, as she had done nearly every night since their wedding.

"Well?" Odd asked in a soft voice. During the men's discussion over dinner, Signy had been sitting inconspicuously off to the side, listening in on the talk.

"They all sound like they'll stand with you," Signy said, her voice slightly muffled by Odd's chest.

"'Sound?'" Odd asked. "You don't think they will?" Signy was his wife and his friend. They had known little of each other when they were wed, and it had taken Odd at least a year to fully appreciate how clever and insightful Signy was. But he had at last come to understand, and now she was his most trusted advisor as well.

Signy was quiet as she considered the question. "They'll stand with you," she said. "At first, anyway. They said they would ride with you to Grømstad, meet with Halfdan. I don't think they could refuse."

"How could they not refuse? Some of them…most of them…are richer and more powerful than I am. Amundi for certain. Amundi wouldn't feel compelled to go just because I asked it."

"No…" Signy said. "But they're not fools. They know Halfdan is trying to consolidate power. He's taken control of much of the West Agder and he probably wants to push north into Vestfold. They know he's a danger. But they know that standing by you could be even more dangerous."

Odd thought about that for a while, but he could not divine the deeper meaning Signy implied. "How do you mean?" he asked.

Signy rolled over and propped herself up on Odd's chest so that she could look in his eyes. There were still torches burning in the hall and light enough leaking into the sleeping closet that Odd could see her face, which was lovely, fine-featured and unlined. Despite the gravity of their conversation he could not resist reaching up and stroking her cheek with his fingertips.

"I don't know," Signy said. "I don't know any more than you, or anyone. Probably less. But I don't think it's just taxes that makes Halfdan come after your father's farm. He would like it, certainly. Who wouldn't? But even more, I think he doesn't want you to have it. He doesn't want you to become the richest man in this part of the country."

Odd thought about that. "The others, the men here today, they might be jealous if I were to have my farm and my father's too, but why would Halfdan care?" he asked. "Even with two farms I won't be as wealthy as he is, nor would I be in five lifetimes."

"Maybe not as wealthy. But it's your power he fears."

At that Odd laughed out loud, a soft but genuine laugh. "My power?" he said. "I have yet to meet the boar who's my match, but beyond that I have no power."

"You have more than you think, but you won't allow yourself to see it," Signy said. "You're Odd Thorgrimson. Son of Thorgrim Night Wolf, grandson of Ornolf the Restless and Ulf of the Battle Song, whose sword you carry."

Odd felt a flush sweep over him at the naming of his bold ancestors and he hoped it was dark enough that Signy could not see it. It made him feel vaguely ill, that such a line should come down to him. Odd Pig-binder. Maybe him alone, if Harald had died in glorious battle, which seemed increasingly likely.

"I'm not my father, nor my grandfather," Odd said and his voice sounded small to him.

"No," Signy said. "No, you're not. You're your own man, as smart and brave as any whose blood runs through you."

They were kind words, and Odd appreciated them. But he did not necessarily believe them, so they only served to make him more ill at ease. "That may be true or not," Odd said, "but I don't think the memory of men now dead would be enough to frighten Halfdan."

"It's you that frightens him," Signy said. "Because he knows who you are, and what you come from, and what you are capable of. He knows that the people here have always looked on your family as leaders. Your grandfather was the most loved of jarls, your father stood out like a stone tower. Halfdan knows that you could just as easily become a leader to these people. More so if you had all the wealth that's due you, and he fears it. You could be jarl if you wished it. You are a shieldwall in the way of his ambition."

Odd grunted and fell silent, thinking about those words. Finally he said, "Do you think I should push my claim the be jarl of Vik and Fevik?"

"No," Signy said without hesitation. "You've made Halfdan mad, and if you and the others go see him, it will make him madder still. The gods have given you luck, but only they know when it will be taken away."

"I must go see Halfdan," Odd said. "I must ride at the head of these men who've agreed to come. I would shame myself and my family if I didn't, and give Halfdan leave to feel he can take whatever he wants."

"I know, my beloved one, I know," Signy said with a resigned tone and laid her head down on his chest again. "Just promise me you'll take care. Genuinely take care."

Signy was his most trusted advisor, but she was not a disinterested one. She was his wife, mother of his children. Anything that happened to Odd would have an enormous effect on their lives, and not for the better. Odd knew her advice was colored by those considerations.

"I will," Odd said, but already he was moving the pieces on the board, thinking of what he would say in the presence of Halfdan the Black, and what Halfdan might do in response.

Chapter Nine

If a man sits long enough, sorrowful and anxious,
bereft of joy, his mind constantly darkening,
soon it seems to him that his troubles are limitless.

Deor's Lament
Early Anglo-Saxon Poem

For three days, from Sherborne to just north of Christchurch Priory, Cynewise and her father, Ceorle, had ridden side by side. The bishop, Ealhstan, rode just behind them, and behind him was a gaggle of thegns of varying importance. Behind them all marched an army, a rather impressive army, five hundred men strong.

The bulk of the men, about three hundred of them, were Ceorle's men-at-arms, his house guard and some of his more trusted warriors. They had marched with him from Devonshire to Dorset, arriving the day after Ealhstan had told Cynewise they may be coming.

The rest were Cynewise's men, or men-at-arms supplied by the thegns, or part of the fyrd who had not been dispatched to aid Nothwulf in his attempt to drive the heathens out. What she imagined was his ill-fated attempt to drive the heathens out. She had not had word of Nothwulf in a week or more.

The communication between Cynewise and her father during the ride had been varied and largely volatile, ranging from tense silences to outright verbal conflict, which always started in sharp but hushed voices, so that the others would not hear, but soon escalated to outright shouting.

They were in a period of silence as they covered the last mile to the place where the army would bed down for the night, just a few miles from Christchurch Priory. They had not spoken in an hour at least.

Ceorle was the first to break the silence. "You look ridiculous," he said. "Absurd. You'll impress no one."

Cynewise clenched her teeth. She had to do great emotional violence to herself to keep from speaking, but she knew it would be better that way, so she remained silent.

They had carried this fight from Sherborne. Cynewise was wearing mail, tailored for her slight form, and a red cloak over that. She wore a sword on her belt and had a shield hanging from her saddle. She knew that she looked like a child with toy weapons and costume armor. She only weighed about seven stone, how could she look otherwise?

At the same time, she knew she had to be seen as a leader, a leader in every way: politically, militarily, legally. If Nothwulf had been ealdorman then he would certainly have led the army to battle with the heathens, and so must she. It was the only way she could cement her hold on that office. The last thing she wanted was for her father, Ceorle, to ride to Dorset's aide and assume that mantle for himself.

The notion of her marrying Merewald and becoming ealdorman of Dorsetshire if some tragedy were to befall her husband had not been hers alone, of course. She and her father had discussed it at length, speculated about the power that the two shires might wield in Wessex if the ealdormen's houses were joined by blood. It seemed such a good idea that Cynewise had internalized any misgivings she had. But they would not stay internalized forever.

It was back in Sherborne, just a few hours after her father's arrival, riding at the head of his army, that those misgivings burst like a bloated corpse.

There had been the usual joyful reunion, father and daughter embracing, tears and enquiries. Ceorle had not seen his daughter since she left Devon, had not been at the wedding, sending word of an illness that prevented his travel. They dined together. It was only when the dishes and the servants and the sundry guests had been cleared away that things began to fall apart.

"Tell me of my army," Ceorle said, sitting alone with Cynewise in the empty great hall. "My other army. The one I sent to Christchurch Priory, that it might help you solidify your position here."

Cynewise frowned, but kept the expression as subtle as she could. "You already know, do you not? Surely the good Bishop Ealhstan, that holy man of God, has kept you informed?"

"I hear things," Ceorle said. "From many people, because I have many friends. Now I wish to hear it from you."

"The men-at-arms…"

"*My* men-at-arms," Ceorle corrected.

"The men-at-arms were at Christchurch," Cynewise continued. "I had all things in readiness. Food, horses, wagons. It was a great secret, no one knew. But then the Northmen came, the way Northmen come, out of the sea, no warning. It was something I could not predict."

"Taken by surprise," Ceorle said. "I guess all was not in readiness."

"I presumed your men would be able to defend themselves, that they would have the mettle to stand up to the Northmen. Apparently not."

It was Cynewise's best thrust, but it failed to strike any vulnerable spot her father might have. He was like a massive stone wall around a city: no matter how hard she flung herself against it, no matter what her approach, she always bounced off. Cynewise could manipulate any man—fool him, seduce him, frighten him—but she could not reach her father.

"So what do you intend? How will you correct this blunder and have my men set free?" Ceorle asked, and Cynewise knew the old man did not know himself what to do in this situation. If he did, then he would never have asked, he would have just issued instructions. Instead he was letting her make the decision so that she would take any blame that might come along. Meanwhile, he would criticize every step she took.

"The Northmen are not our concern," Cynewise said. "They're a distraction when we need to solidify my place as ealdorman. We'll pay them off so that they go away, and then we can attend to business."

"*We* will pay them off?" Ceorle sounded incredulous. "What amount of danegeld did you offer these swine?"

"Two hundred pounds of silver," Cynewise said.

"Two hundred pounds…are you mad?" Ceorle sputtered. "Just to make a handful of heathens go away?"

"That, and to keep two hundred of your incompetent men-at-arms from the slave markets of Frisia," Cynewise said. "My treasury is in poor shape. My late husband was a spendthrift and Æthelwulf's visit cost me dearly. If I'm to buy the freedom of your men, then I need some of your silver to do it."

"Not likely," Ceorle said. "Not likely I'll pay for your incompetence and poor judgment. You collect up the men you have, whatever excuses for soldiers you can find, and I'll lead my own men—good warriors, all—and we'll march to Christchurch and we'll see about these heathen whore's sons."

There was a note of finality in his voice, and Cynewise had long ago learned that it was pointless to continue arguing when her father adopted that tone. She stood and said, "I have much to attend to, so I must be off. It's a pleasure, as always, to see you, my dear father." She gave him the most meaningless of kisses on the cheek and then swept out of the hall, leaving her father sitting at table alone.

Cynewise climbed the steep stairs to her bed chamber. Guards with spears flanked the door and on seeing her approach one of them turned and opened the door and held it open for her. She stepped through without acknowledging either man's existence and the guard shut the door softly behind her.

The bed chamber had a comforting look, lit by candles on tall stands scattered around the room and a low fire burning in the fireplace, but there was little that was going to comfort Cynewise now, not after an interview with her father. A heavy silver cross on a chain hung around her neck and she ripped it off and flung it against the wall.

Aelfwyn, Cynewise's lady's maid, stepped out from the small room off to the left, which held a bathtub and a table and chair for dressing Cynewise's hair. She gave a quick bow and said, "M'lady. Will you be retiring?"

But Cynewise was in too great a rage to consider retiring. She looked at Aelfwyn. The girl was younger than she was by a year or so, very pretty with thick wavy brown hair. Aelfwyn was pretty in a robust way, not in the frail and delicate way that Cynewise was pretty. It was another thing that irritated Cynewise to distraction.

She had made use of Aelfwyn's looks on a few occasions by whoring her out to men from whom she needed something, information, mostly. The last was Nothwulf, and Aelfwyn had garnered some important intelligence before Nothwulf had sussed her out and taken her captive to his country manor. Aelfwyn had escaped—how, Cynewise did not ask—and the bruising she had suffered in that adventure had mostly healed now.

Cynewise took her eyes off her lady's maid and looked around the room, looked at her bed. "Where is my mail? My sword?" she asked.

"Still with the armorer, m'lady," Aelfwyn said. Cynewise could hear the edge of fear in the girl's voice. Aelfwyn knew how her mistress could get.

"The armorer?" Cynewise snapped. "I told you to have it here. Now." She had a good idea of how her father was going to react to her donning mail and a sword, and any mention of those items further inflamed her.

"Yes, ma'am, but the armorer said…"

Aelfwyn got no further. In two steps Cynewise was across the room. She swung her open hand as she moved and hit Aelfwyn on the side of the head. Aelfwyn was knocked to the floor, falling sideways, her clothes like a heap of linen and silk, and Cynewise kicked her.

"Damn the armorer, you stupid whore! You do as I say, not the bloody armorer!" Cynewise shouted and then kicked her again, but not so hard that time.

This was the true worth of servants, Cynewise knew. She could arrange her own hair or get herself dressed; she didn't need a lady's maid for that. But she was no monk; she did not care for self-flagellation, not when she had a pretty thing like Aelfwyn to beat.

Cynewise breathed deep. She looked down at Aelfwyn, whose mass of thick hair obscured her face as she lay on the floor, half propped up on one elbow, unsure if she should stand or remain as she was. Cynewise felt some of the tension drain away.

"I'll retire now," she said. "Once you've helped me to bed, then rouse the armorer and get my mail and sword or there'll be more of that."

The thegns and the men-at-arms and the fyrd were gathered at dawn the next day for the march to Christchurch Priory. Cynewise appeared in her mail, her sword at her side, a red cloak pinned to her shoulders. She carried a leather bag with her, in which she had packed various things that she felt she might need, items to deal with a variety of contingencies. Her father reacted to the mail and sword just as she knew he would, and their muted antagonism just blossomed from there.

When they reached the open ground where the army was to camp, after three long days of travel from Sherborne, they could see the thin columns of smoke rising up from Christchurch Priory a few miles off. Cynewise and Ceorle rode their horses to the top of the hill that commanded the fields around. From that place they could see the top of the church tower in the distance, indiscernible unless one knew what to look for.

"That's not the smoke of a city that's been sacked," observed one of the thegns, a man wealthy and powerful enough that he felt justified in riding to the hilltop with the two ealdormen. There were only a handful who enjoyed that status.

"Not sacked," Ceorle agreed. "Damned heathens have settled in, made themselves at home. They're not going to burn the damned place."

They watched for a few moments more until it was clear there was nothing to be learned from that distance. Cynewise turned to the thegns, her mouth open, ready to tell them to get their men set up in camp, when Ceorle said, "You lot, get your men to set up their camp. Men-at-arms there" he pointed to a place to the left—"and the men of the fyrd there"—he pointed to a place on the right. "Get camp set up quickly and we'll drill the fyrd with spears until suppertime."

The thegns bowed in their saddles and rode back down the hill. Cynewise considered telling her father that she would give the orders, that he made her look weak by preempting her, that nearly half of the men in their army were her men, not his, the thegns hers to command. But she kept her mouth shut. She would appear pathetic if she protested in that way, and her father would just ignore her in any event.

"You'll sup with me, Father, once you're done with your drills?" she asked instead.

"Yes, yes, of course," Ceorle said, his eyes still on the distant church tower. "You go have your servants set up your tent and whatever fancy things you've brought with you in the field, and I'll be by once I've seen that the men get their supper."

Dining with her father was as pleasant as Cynewise might have hoped. When Ceorle spoke she bit her tongue and held her temper like a mad dog on a leash, and nodded and smiled, and that kept things calm and civil. They discussed what they might do next, and to

Cynewise's astonishment, they agreed on how they would proceed, genuinely agreed.

"We'll send Oswin with a guard to the priory, to speak with the heathens," Cynewise said. "We'll send the silver with him and he can pay them off and we'll get our captive men back. Once we have them, we'll have an army large enough to crush the heathens and Nothwulf as well." She waited for her father to raise some objection, make some argument, but he did not, so she continued.

"Not that we wish to bother ourselves with the Northmen. They're not our chief worry. They may plunder a few more churches, but they'll do no worse than that," Cynewise said. She waited for Ceorle to comment on that, and when he did not she continued. "Nothwulf is our greatest concern, as long as he pretends to a claim on the ealdormanship. If he's in the neighborhood then I suppose we should speak with him. Assure him we're here to fight the Northmen, not him. See what sort of army he has, and if it is not so great as ours, which I would think it is not, then we turn on him once the Northmen are gone. Father, are you well?"

Ceorle was looking a bit glassy-eyed. He shook his head and for a moment said nothing, then muttered, "I'm fine, fine, just worn out from the travel, I should think."

Cynewise turned to Aelfwyn, who was standing off to the side, ready to do her lady's bidding. "Aelfwyn, don't just stand there like some gaping fool! Go get my father's manservant, his Lordship obviously needs to take to his bed."

It was a few moments, no more, before Ceorle's manservant arrived and escorted Ceorle from Cynewise's tent, supporting his master under one arm while one of the guards supported him under the other. Cynewise made a great show of fussing over her father, and once they were gone she called for Oswin. The shire reeve had been waiting for a summons, and so he stepped into Cynewise's tent before she could even begin to grow impatient.

"You must go to the heathens again and bring them the danegeld. My father has generously agreed to aide us in paying this, so you will have the full one hundred and fifty pounds of silver."

Oswin nodded and Cynewise signaled for two of her servants to fetch the chest of silver that was stashed in a corner of the tent. Ceorle had indeed come around, after considerable prodding, and added one hundred pounds of silver to the danegeld, which meant that Cynewise could secret away fifty of it, which she already had, and Oswin could deliver the one hundred and fifty pounds the Northmen demanded.

"You go speak to the Northmen, this Thorgrim, if that's his name...I hardly recall such things...and you deliver this," Cynewise continued. "And you return with two hundred of my father's men-at-arms. Men, swords, shields, mail, all of it. These bastards demand a high price, but for that we'll get what's rightfully ours. Do you understand?"

"Yes, lady," Oswin said with a short bow.

"We have scouts searching out Nothwulf and Leofric, that traitorous bastard," Cynewise continued, but before she could say more a servant—she recognized him as one of her father's men—came tentatively into the tent, hat in hand.

"Beg pardon. Lady, but Aelfgar...your father's manservant, lady..."

"I know who he is," Cynewise snapped.

"Yes, lady. He commanded me tell you your father's illness grows worse, and he...."

"Yes, yes, tell Aelfgar my prayers are with my father and I'll need no more news in that regard," Cynewise said, gesturing toward the door of the tent. The servant nodded, bowed, and backed away, a puzzled look on his thin face.

"You father, ma'am, is ill?" Oswin asked.

"He'll be fine," Cynewise said. "A stomach ailment that troubles him from time to time."

"I see," Oswin said.

"As I was saying," Cynewise continued. "We have men looking for Nothwulf, and when he's found, and when we have the men back who were taken at Christchurch, and the damned Northmen are gone, then we'll see to him and be done with all of this."

"Yes, ma'am," Oswin said. "Nothwulf's army must be near. The heathens themselves expect him to attack."

"I pray he'll fling his men at the heathens," Cynewise said. "It could rid us of two nuisances and save me one hundred and fifty pounds of silver. But my guess is that Nothwulf is too great a coward to fight, so we'll have no choice but to pay them off. So, go now."

"Yes, m'lady," Oswin said, bowed, and then signaled to the guards outside the tent to enter. They grabbed the handles of the iron-bound chest and lifted it with more difficulty than seemed appropriate for a relatively small box, then carried it out.

"Aelfwyn," Cynewise called, still staring at the door through which Oswin had gone, and in a heartbeat Aelfwyn was standing beside her.

"Ma'am?"

Cynewise remained silent for a moment, her mind still working. Then she said, "In Sherborne, you played the little whore for Nothwulf, and you did it well."

Aelfwyn said nothing to that, and after a moment's silence Cynewise looked up at her. "Well?"

"Yes, ma'am," Aelfwyn said at last, apparently not appreciating the compliment.

"Do you think you could get in his good graces again? Use your...charms?"

"Oh, ma'am, I wouldn't think so," Aelfwyn said. "Nothwulf found me out, took me as his prisoner. I was treated terribly, ma'am."

"Hmm," Cynewise said. "Well, we'll see. There may still be some opportunity there. But for now, pray see my bed is made ready. It's been a trying day and I'm quite ready to retire."

The bed, an oak frame cleverly made to come apart for ease of transport, supporting a fine, down-filled mattress, was made ready. Aelfwyn helped Cynewise into her sleeping clothes and soon Ealdorman Cynewise was sleeping the good sleep of the innocent.

The gray light of dawn was illuminating the tent, but just barely, when she woke to Aelfwyn, who was gently shaking her shoulder.

"What?" Cynewise snapped, but the word came out more like a croak and she cleared her throat irritably.

"It's Oswin, ma'am, the shire reeve..."

"I know who Oswin is, you idiot," Cynewise said, her voice now its proper tone and pitch.

"Oswin's outside, ma'am, and he would speak to you."

Cynewise scowled. The damned shire reeve had something so important to say that he had to wake her at such an hour? She could not imagine. She was about to send him away when the fog of sleep cleared a bit more and she realized he might indeed have something important enough for such a transgression.

"Very well," Cynewise said, tossing her silk blanket aside. "Get me my cape and then send him in."

By the time Oswin stepped into the tent, a scowl on his face, Cynewise was seated on her throne-like chair, her embroidered cape around her shoulders, half-covering her sleeping gown, her shoes and stockings on her feet.

"Oswin? What news? " Cynewise asked.

"I rode to Christchurch Priory, ma'am," Oswin said. "Off to pay the danegeld, see that the heathens bugger off, and I come on Nothwulf's army."

"Indeed?" Cynewise said. "Where?"

"Christchurch Priory," Oswin said and Cynewise felt her stomach sink. If Nothwulf had defeated the heathens in battle he would come off as the savior of Dorsetshire, and she could not allow that. It was why she was willing to pay the Northmen to make them go away. But now it seemed she was too late, that Nothwulf had already won his victory.

"Have they…" she began, but Oswin cut her off.

"Seems the heathens abandoned the priory and set up some sort of defense on the beach," he said. "And Nothwulf has them surrounded. Which means there's four hundred or more of Nothwulf's damned men-at-arms between us and the damned Northmen."

Cynewise nodded. She was not entirely surprised. She knew that Nothwulf and his army were somewhere in the area, and it made sense that he would be where the enemy was. As much as she despised Nothwulf, considered him weak-minded and feckless, and was happy to refer to him as a coward, still she did not actually doubt his dedication and his courage. She had to keep that in mind, because nothing could lead to ruin quicker than underestimating one's enemy.

"Four hundred men-at-arms between us and the heathens," she said softly. It was not a question and Oswin knew better than to make reply. She was thinking now, and it helped to voice those thoughts. Four hundred men-at-arms. That was very bad. Or very good. It would be up to her to see which it was.

"Well, we can't pay the Northmen to leave, not now," Cynewise said, addressing Oswin this time. "We'll look like cowards doing that, with Nothwulf there and ready to fight. Hell, we can't even get to the heathens, with Nothwulf surrounding them. We'll have to join him in fighting those whore's sons. But we must be leading the thing, or seeming to."

"Yes, ma'am," Oswin said. "But if we drive the Northmen off, our men and Nothwulf's drive them off, then we find ourselves just where we are now. Stalemate."

"Perhaps," Cynewise said. "It will depend on how the battle plays out. There's danger here, but opportunity as well." She fell silent, staring vaguely at the ground on which Oswin stood. Oswin, she knew, would wait patiently. They had had dealings enough that the reeve knew when to shut up and let her consider the next move. Finally she looked up.

"Horsa!" she snapped and the servant named Horsa who had been standing at Cynewise's side, half asleep on his feet, snapped awake.

"Ma'am?"

"How does my father?" Cynewise had instructed Horsa to visit her father's tent on and off through the night and get the news as to his health.

"Not well, ma'am, but his servants are hopeful. He's a strong man, even at his age, and he seems to be past the worst of it."

"Good to hear. Pray send them word that I would have my father attend me here." To Cynewise's further irritation she heard Horsa shuffle his feet a bit and she turned in her chair to glare at him.

"Well, ma'am, I can bring word, but his men, I think they'll object, begging your pardon. They'll say his lordship ain't strong enough to move."

Cynewise glared at the servant for a moment longer, then let out a long sigh of exasperation, a tone that suggested all the burdens of the world invariably fell on her shoulders.

"Very well," she said, "I'll go to him, if I must." But it was worth it, she knew. In that moment, staring at Oswin's boots, she had seen how this all might play out if handled right. It was worth the trouble of talking to a sick old man.

Chapter Ten

I sing to thee the second,
as thou hast to wander
joyless on thy ways.

The Poetic Edda

Nearly four hundred Northmen were crammed into a half-moon fortification two hundred feet long and a hundred feet wide at its widest part and pressed against the bank of the river. Six of their seven ships were floating in the shallow water, tethered to the shore by lines run over their bows and made fast to anchors set in the soft dirt. The seventh ship rode at anchor one hundred feet out in the river with two hundred English prisoners crammed miserably aboard.

The Northmen had no shelter to speak of, no means of provisioning, save for the food and drink they had with them on the shore and aboard the ships. They were surrounded by a powerful army lurking just out of range of their arrows and spears. How large an army they did not know, but large enough to completely envelope the makeshift log walls of the longphort. They had no reason to doubt that an attack would come at any moment, and if it did, it could well end in bloody defeat.

And yet the Northmen were jubilant, celebrating with the sort of abandon for which their kind was famous.

They were well-on drunk. Barrels of ale and mead and even wine were stacked on the ground, and as quickly as one was drained the head of another was stove in. The priory at Christchurch, stripped bare now, had been well-stocked when Thorgrim's fleet arrived. Thorgrim had been generous in doling out the food to the townsfolk who had lent a hand in building the walls—there was far more in the storehouses than he and his men could carry away—but he was more

84

parsimonious with the drink. He did not want the townsfolk to gain the courage found in ale and mead. That would only lead to trouble. And he did not want to deny his men the thing that they most desired, far more than the salt meat and fish and bread that they also took with them.

The ale and mead and wine had been flowing since just after *hádegi*, midday. A big fire was built on the dirt and the men sat around it and they sang and they laughed and they dipped their cups in the stove-in barrels and drank some more.

They drank in recognition of the feat they had pulled off, one which the skalds would sing about for generations. How, under the command of Thorgrim Night Wolf, a man whose fame was spreading like the light at dawn, they had built a longphort in a single night and confounded their enemy once again. They drank to the plunder that was stored down under the deck boards of their ships, and to the two hundred prisoners who would bring them even greater riches, either ransomed for silver or sold as slaves.

They drank because they had ale and mead to drink and they drank because they liked to drink.

Thorgrim made no protest. The men had earned this. He was proud of them and happy to let them indulge. He did not think the enemy would come that night, or perhaps ever. The walls of the longphort were not high, and they were no marvels of construction, but they were built of heavy logs and timber, and the ground before them was strewn with debris that would be a nightmare to cross in the dark. And if any managed to make it through those haphazard obstructions they would have to scale the walls in the face of wild, drunk Northmen wielding swords, axes and spears.

He had lookouts posted, sober men standing on the walls, but he did not think the enemy would come. So he sat with his men by the fire and celebrated along with them.

Failend was not celebrating. She was off toward the western end of the longphort, hidden by shadow, sitting on a short length of log, staring out into the dark. She was about as far from the fire as she could get in that place, which was not very far, a hundred feet or so. Her thoughts, however, had stayed so far afield she might as well have been in Frankia, or back in her native Ireland.

For three days now she had shunned Thorgrim's bed, gone off to sleep by herself in some corner of the priory. And he had said nothing about it. She was not even sure he noticed.

Damn him, damn him... she thought. And her next thought was, *Well, what in the name of God did you expect?*

Thorgrim Night Wolf had never pledged his love to her. Had never made any promises, had, in truth, never pursued her at all. She had gone to him, crawled into his bed, lain with him. Nearly a year before. Did she really think he or any man would object to her giving herself to him, would decline her advances? She was very attractive to men and she knew it. Did she think that fornicating with a heathen would lead to his loving her?

"Yes," she said out loud. Yes, she had thought that. Or hoped it, anyway. A half-formed, unexamined thought, one that would not bear up to scrutiny. But yes, she had thought that Thorgrim would love her.

Because she loved him. It was never her intention, or even a thought in her head at first. Her life had been turned upside down at Glendalough. No, not just turned upside down. It had been shredded like a banner flying in a gale, torn to ribbons and remade into something she did not recognize. She had gone from her numbing existence as wife to an old, wealthy man, a woman who tried to satisfy her undefined yearning by bedding various men, to what she was now.

Which is what?

A killer. She had killed her husband, killed men in battle. Put arrows through them, which was easy. Driven the point of her seax into their guts, which was not quite so easy, either for her arm or her conscience. She had killed Christians. In the service of heathens she had put Christians in their graves.

Sharing Thorgrim's bed had been a part of all the madness. Thorgrim Night Wolf was a mystery, a danger, a thrill. That was how it had started for her. Thorgrim was just part of the wild abandon, the insane recklessness into which she had voluntarily leapt. She told herself that she would not fall in love with him. And she believed it. Thorgrim was a heathen, and if he was attractive in an animal sort of way he was also vicious and brutal, thoughtless in his cruelty.

But actually he was not. She had assumed that all Northmen were like that, and she found that some were, but Thorgrim was not. He was not a mindless predator; he was more complicated than that. He was intriguing to her. And he was desirable. Very desirable. Of course love would grow in that soil.

And now, through the smoke of love and madness, the truth was starting to appear. She had become a heathen and a killer, and she loved a man who did not care if she slept with him or not.

How would he feel if I bedded another? she wondered. She had no intention of doing so, she just wondered if Thorgrim cared enough to be angry or jealous.

She did not hear the steps on the soft ground, and the voice was soft, but it surprised her nonetheless.

"Pensive tonight." It was not a question, but a statement.

Failend looked up. The figure was only a dark outline, backlit by the fire, but she recognized the shape of the man. And even if she had not, there was no mistaking the voice. There was no one among all of them who had so odd an accent as Louis de Roumois.

"Mmm," Failend said. No words came to mind. Her thoughts were twisting like eddies of wind. She wanted to be left alone, and she welcomed Louis's company, all at the same time.

For a moment they remained silent, and Failend guessed that Louis was looking at her as she was looking at him, but she still could not see his face.

"You may as well sit," she said, nodding toward the unoccupied section of log.

"Thank you, I will," he said, stepping past her. Failend realized they were speaking in Irish, Failend's native tongue and the one Louis had used for the past year or more, a language they shared. It sounded odd to her now.

She had been speaking only the Northmen's language for some time. Even when they had been in Ireland, she had little call to speak Irish after she had joined with Thorgrim's band. Instead, she had stumbled along in Norse until she grew more adept with that tongue.

The same was true for Louis, but he, like Failend, was still more comfortable in Irish. He sat and they did not speak and Failend remembered that that was something she liked about Louis. Talkative as he could be, he could also be silent, and be comfortable in the silence. Silence was not something Failend enjoyed very often in the midst of several hundred Northmen.

"You've not been with Thorgrim of late," Louis observed at last.

"You've been watching me?"

"I see things. A leader of men must be aware of all things around him. Of course, I don't lead so much as a flock of sheep anymore. But it's an old habit."

Failend did not reply. She had no intention of discussing with Louis her relationship with Thorgrim. She was not even sure she could discuss it with herself. But there were other things.

"We're Christians," she said. "We *were* Christians. I suppose we still are. Does it bother you, Louis, to help these heathens?"

She could not see him in the dark, but, knowing Louis, she was quite certain that he had shrugged his shoulders. "These heathen Northmen have tried to kill me, the Irish Christians have tried to kill me. The English have tried to kill me. I don't feel much love for any of them. Now, I think of myself just as a Frank."

"Didn't the Franks try to kill you?" Failend asked, and she heard a short chuckle in reply.

"No," Louis said. "My brother wished to kill me, but he didn't dare. Instead he sent me to the monastery in Glendalough where he hoped I might die of boredom. And I almost did."

"I was dying of boredom in Glendalough, too," Failend said. "That's why we took to entertaining each other."

"I recall," Louis said. "You're not bored now, are you?"

"No," Failend said. "Not bored. Confused."

"You love Thorgrim," Louis said. "You don't know if he loves you."

"No," Failend said, the word more emphatic than she had intended. "Yes. I don't know. You're lucky, you know. You know what you want to do. Get back to Frankia, avenge yourself against your brother. You have a purpose, for what it's worth. Me, I'm drifting, like a boat that's been pushed out into the water."

"I don't feel terribly lucky," Louis said.

They sat in silence a while longer. There was a bond between them, Failend could feel it. They had been lovers. They had been soldiers together, and outlaws and prisoners of the Northmen. They had been strangers in the heathens' camp and they had become part of Thorgrim's army, each in their own way. And yet they were still strangers there, the two odd ones, the ones who did not hear the song of Odin and Thor.

"You could speak to Thorgrim, you know," Louis said at last. "He's not an unreasonable man."

"He tried to kill you," Failend said. "Several times."

"That's how I know he's not unreasonable."

Failend smiled. "He does not want to hear from me and my petty worries. He has worries enough. I'd look like a complete fool, talking to him about the things that are troubling me. Silly girlish things."

They could hear voices, men coming closer. They sat in silence and Failend hoped they would not be noticed. She did not expect trouble of any kind; she just did not wish to speak to anyone. Anyone besides Louis. It felt good to talk to Louis.

The men staggered past, five of them framed against the firelight. They were laughing and talking loud and walking on none too steady legs. They lined up against the longphort wall, invisible in the dark, and Failend could hear the sound of them urinating against the logs.

She and Louis sat still for what seemed a long time, but Failend imagined that the Northmen were quite full of ale and had a lot to expel. At last the liquid sounds came to an end and the men came stumbling back toward the fire.

And then they stopped. "Who's there?" one of them called and he seemed to be looking in their direction, though it was not entirely clear. "Are you folk who won't come drink with us?"

"Are they buggering each other?" another voice called out, the words smeared together. "Let them be!"

"No, we'll see who's buggering who," the first voice called and Failend saw the men stumbling toward them.

They appeared out of the dark, and in the light of the fire falling on their faces Failend saw that they were men she did not know. Not well, anyway. They had been part of Jorund's crew, joined with Thorgrim's army back at Loch Garman. They had all come together as one army, and Jorund had pledged his loyalty to Thorgrim, but still Jorund's men remained Jorund's, and Thorgrim's men Thorgrim's.

Failend recognized these men. She had spoken with a few of them on occasion. She might have known their names once, but she could not recall any of them. She felt herself tense.

"Oh, see here, it's the pretty little one," one said.

"And the pretty Frankish one!" another cried.

Louis stood and Failend did as well, though at just around five feet in height her standing had no great dramatic effect. In truth she guessed it made her seem more vulnerable.

"Which of you will have the girl," the first asked, "and which the Frank?"

When Failend had first been taken prisoner by Thorgrim and his men she had all but assumed they would rape her. But they did not, and soon she realized that they would not, and after that she never felt afraid in the company of any of Thorgrim's men.

Until that moment. There was something ugly and brutish about these men, drunk with mead and triumph, feeling invulnerable and ready to take what they wanted. It was something she had not encountered before, at least not directed at herself.

But she would not let that fear show. "Even sober you would not be man enough, Gaut," Failend said, the man's name suddenly flashing in her mind. "You certainly are not man enough now."

That brought howls from the others, but Gaut looked less amused. He took a step toward her and she rested her hand on the hilt of her seax, hanging like a sword at her side.

"Thorgrim might not be enough for you, but I can show you what it's like to lay with a real man," he said.

Louis stepped up, not between them, but close. "No need of this," he said, and though his Norse speech was rough his voice was smooth. "Like you said, she's with Thorgrim Night Wolf, and you do not want to cross him."

For all Louis's good intentions, Failend still felt herself flush with anger. If this pig Gaut did not rape her it would be because she herself stuck a blade in him, not because he feared Thorgrim Night Wolf. She drew her seax and lifted her chin, and said, "A real man, you say? I'll make a real gelding of you."

The others laughed even harder, but still Gaut did not laugh at all. His expression was a mix of anger and lust and humiliation, an ugly brew. Louis took another step, imposing himself between them. Failend swung her seax and struck Louis in the stomach with the flat of the blade, hard enough to stop him and make him bend at the waist, and as he did she stepped forward, past him.

The fury was really bubbling now, steaming and roiling. The whoreson Gaut was only a part of it, and not even the biggest part, but he would be the one to pay.

Gaut stepped back, surprised to have Failend advancing on him. He drew his sword, which was half again as long as Failend's seax, and held it loosely at his side. "I can hump you or I can kill you, your choice, you little whore," Gaut said.

He might have expected a verbal retort, but he did not get one. Failend darted forward and before Gaut could even lift his sword to the horizontal she drove the point of the seax into his gut. He was wearing only his tunic and leggings and the blade passed though the linen cloth without hesitation. She felt the point drive into flesh and then hit the thicker muscle and she pulled her arm back. She was happy to deliver a painful wound, but even in her fury she could not drive her blade clean into so pathetic a creature as this.

Gaut howled and leapt back and showed none of the restraint that Failend had. He swung his sword in a great sideways arc and would have taken Failend's head clean off if she had not ducked down and let the blade pass with a humming sound over her head.

She pushed herself back to her feet, stumbling as she did. Gaut was holding his sword high, over his left shoulder, ready to swing again. Failend stabbed him once more, delivering another shallow but painful cut, this time to his shoulder. She expected him to stagger back, drop his sword, but he did not. The drink in his gut and the fury in his brain blinded him to the pain.

Gaut swung his sword again, a backhand stroke with terrific force behind it, and in that instant Failend knew that she could not get her seax up in time to block it, and even if she could it would do nothing to counter Gaut's blow. She had time enough to think she was about to die, not time enough to think about what that meant, and then there was a flash on her right hand side and Louis's blade was up in front of her.

Gaut's blade hit Louis's with a loud ringing sound, but Louis's parry was not enough to overcome the momentum behind Gaut's sword. His blade continued on in its path and hit Failend's shoulder, but it had slowed enough by then that it just knocked her sideways and made her stagger.

Failend heard the sound of swords scraping from scabbards, a sound she now knew well, and she knew the fight was far from over.

This is ridiculous, she thought, she and Louis in a desperate fight with their ostensible friends. But her mind and her body were separate spirits now, and her body knew only to eliminate the nearest threat, then go for the next.

She recovered from the stumble, which had put her between Gaut and Louis. She felt Louis's hand on her shoulder, trying to push her aside, but she twisted free of it as she turned and thrust her seax at Gaut. Gaut was just raising his sword again when the point caught him once more in the gut—it was hard for Failend to reach much higher—and this time she did not pull back. The point pierced flesh and slowed as it hit muscle and then continued on, sinking deep. Gaut shrieked as if the seax had released some demon buried inside him.

Failend jerked the point free and thought, *You're done, bastard.*

And indeed he was, at least as far as that fight was concerned. But the four men with him were not, and they had weapons in hand. One had a sword and he and Louis were locked into it now, trading blow for blow. Another had an ax and he pushed the staggering Gaut aside and came at Failend and it seemed any thoughts of rape he might have had had turned to thoughts of murder.

"Come on, you worthless pile of shit!" she shouted, crouching low, seax held just in front of her.

The one with the ax was as drunk as the rest, and probably not very graceful even when sober. He took an ungainly swing at Failend, roaring as he did. But Failend had recovered from her blind rage and her mind was working again. She leaned back and let the ax whip by her face, close enough that she could feel the breeze.

The man was still shouting as the ax sailed past and he stumbled, having put everything behind that stroke. He was open to her— throat, heart, stomach, balls—she could have driven her seax into any one of them. But instead she took half a step forward and drove her foot into his crotch.

The man's scream changed abruptly, rising in pitch, and the ax fell from his hand. Failend knew he was done, too, and she turned fast to see where the next man was. Behind her. He had circled around in hope of snatching her from behind, and he seemed surprised to suddenly be confronting her face to face. Failend lunged and he jumped back and took an awkward swing with his own seax.

And then Failend saw something else. Movement beyond this man, this Northman she was fighting. It barely registered out in the dark, at the very edges of the light from the bonfire, just shadows and flickers as the light caught it. But somehow she knew what it was. Instantly, from just the merest hints, she knew what she was seeing.

"The English!" she shouted at the top of her none too impressive voice. "The English! They're coming over the wall!"

Chapter Eleven

Evil is his eye's
as the raging snake;
his teeth he shows,
when the sword he sees.

The Poetic Edda

The distance from Odd's farm to Halfdan the Black's hall in Grømstad was usually a day's ride, but it took Odd and his neighbors two days to make the journey. There were sixty-six riders all told, as Odd and each of the ten others had brought five of their men with them. The men were ostensibly there as added protection on the road, though such a force was hardly necessary. There was little danger to be found in Fevik or Vik. In truth they were there for show, there to make the small party seem more formidable and substantial. Because they were going to meet with the king.

And they did indeed look formidable. Neither Odd nor any of the others brought their shepherds or blacksmiths with them. They brought grown sons and men-at-arms and prosperous tenants, many of whom had gone a'viking and knew the use of their weapons. They wore mail and helmets and swords, and carried bright-colored shields on their saddles. Their horses were tall and powerful and well fitted out.

It was not the numbers that slowed them down. Even that many men could have covered the distance in a single day, riding on the good, summer-dry road. It was the cart that held them back. Odd knew better than to arrive at Halfdan's hall expecting hospitality with nothing in the way of tribute to offer. Halfdan or any other king might call on one of his subjects, offering nothing but the honor of the royal presence, and expect to be well fed and well housed, he and his entire retinue. But it did not work like that in the reciprocal.

The cart was heavy loaded. It carried casks of honey from Odd's own hives and mead made from that honey, cured hams and bacon, baskets of carrots and rutabagas and radishes and legs of lamb. A cargo worthy of a king's hall. The cart groaned and creaked and rattled along and Odd spent most of the trip worrying that he had piled more on it than the axels could endure.

But endure they did, and the entire parade—men, horses, oxen and cart—arrived at Halfdan's homestead in Grømstad with a showy presence that did them credit, and gifts of which no one would be ashamed.

Odd had been to Halfdan's hall several times, but it had been many years now, not since well before Ornolf and Thorgrim had sailed for Ireland. The royal compound never failed to impress, but now it seemed more impressive still. Because it was.

When last Odd had been there, the great hall and other buildings were surrounded by an earthen wall topped with a palisade fence. The wall had been nearly circular and perhaps two hundred feet in diameter, the roofs and upper part of the building's walls clearly visible over the top, but it was not like that any longer.

There was an earthen wall still, but Odd knew it was higher than it had been since now he could see only the top of the great hall's roof. The wall was no longer round but rather oval in shape, and the long side ran a good three hundred feet before curving away on the rounded ends. The palisade that topped the wall stood ten feet high and was made of new-cut trees, straight and sturdy looking, with ends shaped to uniform points.

The road they were on ran right up to the two tall oak doors set in the earthen wall. Odd reined his horse to a stop fifty feet from the doors and waited for some acknowledgement from within, and he heard the rest come to a stop behind him. Amundi Thorsteinsson walked his horse up beside Odd's.

Odd nodded his head in the direction of the wall. "Impressive," he said.

"It's meant to be," Amundi said. "Every time Halfdan takes control of a new part of the country he adds another building or another foot of height to the wall."

Odd smiled. "I guess he does it because he can."

"And because he must," Amundi said. "Each new conquest brings new enemies as well."

There had apparently been some discussion among the guards on the wall, perhaps someone of higher rank summoned, because it took some time before a man called out, "Who's there?"

"Odd Thorgrimson," Odd replied, "And Amundi Thorsteinsson. And others. We've come to speak with Lord Halfdan."

There was more discussion on the wall, but not much, and then the big oak doors creaked open and Odd led his little parade through. The improvements to the wall had impressed him, but they paled in comparison to what was being done on the grounds within. The great hall bore little resemblance to the building Odd remembered. It was a third again as long as it had been. The formerly straight roofline was now a long, gentle arch lengthwise, and the walls bowed out near the center of the building, so the entire thing resembled a massive ship turned keel-up. Smoke came trickling out of several smoke holes under the roof, which was shingled, not sod or thatch-covered, and the walls were built of vertical wooden planks carefully smoothed.

There were more buildings on the grounds than he recalled from earlier visits. Some were clearly new, the wood not much weathered at all. A barn and larger blacksmith shop and another building Odd took for a storehouse. Off to the left yet another building stood half-built, the carpenters actively setting up the posts that would support the roof.

Odd and Amundi looked at one another as they rode. Amundi raised an eyebrow at the show of wealth. Odd nodded his understanding. They rode on, heading for the hall at the center of the grounds, where stable boys waited to take their mounts.

But not just stable boys. Odd could see several guards, Halfdan's *hirdmen*, warriors who had sworn an oath of allegiance to the king. And standing at their head was a man whom Odd was fairly certain was Einar Sigurdsson, the king's *sœlumadr*, enforcer of Halfdan's will.

Odd and the rest stopped when they reached that knot of men and boys and he and Amundi and the rest slid down from their horses. Odd was just beginning to stretch his sore muscles—he was rarely in the saddle for so long a time—when Einar approached. He looked neither pleased nor displeased to see Odd and his band, but he did not offer a hand in greeting.

"Odd Thorgrimson, so good to see you again so soon after our last meeting," he said, and his voice was as neutral as his face. "And Amundi Thorsteinsson, and the rest of you distinguished gentlemen. What brings you to this place?"

"We would speak with King Halfdan," Odd said. "We've brought gifts for his table." He nodded toward the wagon rolling up. Einar gave the wagon a casual glance and showed no more reaction to that than he had to their arrival.

"On what subject would you speak to the king?" Einar asked.

"On business of mine," Odd said. "And the other hauldar who ride with me."

Einar nodded. "The king, as you no doubt know, is a very busy man. Better that you should have sent word first. I'm not certain he's even in residence, but I'll see, and see if he has time for an audience with you." He gave a hint of a bow, then turned and headed for the hall as the stable boys led the horses away.

"Not certain that the king's in residence," Amundi said in a disgusted tone. The other men, the nine other landowners who had ridden with them, gathered around, having stretched their own weary muscles.

"What does Einar say?" Ulfkel Ospaksson asked.

"He's going to see if the king's in residence," Odd said.

Ulfkel spit on the ground. "Whore's son, of course the king is in residence. Does that little puke have no better way to show off his authority?"

"Probably not," Amundi said. "But if the king tells him to say he's away, then we'll know where we stand in his royal eyes."

They waited a few moments more until Einar returned through the big doors. He stopped a few feet from the waiting men and his eyes flickered down to Odd's waist. He looked Odd in the eyes.

"The sword you wear, is it Blood-letter, the sword of Ulf of the Battle Song?" he asked.

"It is," Odd said, and he felt a slow rise of anger. "My grandfather's sword."

Einar nodded and gave Odd a knowing look. "A beautiful blade, I know it well," Einar said. There was nothing in his words at which Odd might take offense, and that made the whole thing even more humiliating. Because Odd knew what Einar had left unsaid. *Too beautiful for a farmer like you.*

"Well?" Ulfkel said in a voice that was loud and unpleasant. "Is Halfdan *in residence?*"

"Gentlemen," Einar said, finally addressing them all. "You are in luck."

And for the next few hours it did appear that they were in luck. The cart was led away and the servants were sent to escort the warriors who had accompanied the eleven hauldar off to a barracks where they would be housed, where they would find food and drink. Odd and his fellows were led into the great hall and there shown where they might find places to sleep. House servants offered them food and drink, better quality no doubt than that offered to their men.

Odd and his fellows spent the bulk of the afternoon in final discussion of what they would say to Halfdan when they were given an audience. Politeness, humility were in order, on that they agreed. But a humble man was not necessarily a lick-spittle, and a lick-spittle was not a man who would get what he wanted from a king. They would make it clear that Thorgrim's farm was not to be simply taken at Halfdan's whim. If taxes were owed then the farm would pay for them. But the farm would remain in Odd's care.

That was what they would say out loud. The implications ran deeper than that. They were there to remind Halfdan that the hauldar were important men, powerful men. They would not be trifled with. Neither Halfdan nor any other would trample on their rights. And an attack on one would be considered an attack on all.

They knew better than to say these things explicitly, as they might be construed as a threat, but they wanted the message to be clear as a winter sky

As the discussion went on, Halfdan's servants and slaves began setting up massive trestle tables on either side of the long hearth that ran down the center of the hall. At the head of those tables and perpendicular to them they set another, the head table.

"Looks like a royal feast is to be had," Ragi Oleifsson observed.

"And we better be invited," Ulfkel Ospaksson said. "I've spent silver enough, and used up enough of my food and drink entertaining the king and his men when they pass through. About time some of that comes back my way."

"I'm sure you'll get your fill," Odd said. "I'm sure we're invited. Truth be told, this feast might be in our honor."

Odd believed his own words, but not entirely. Halfdan had not snubbed them yet, had not refused to see them or pretended he was away. But if he staged a feast and did not invite the hauldar who were guests in his house, that would be the ultimate humiliation. If a neighbor were to do such a thing to a neighbor it might start a war between the families. But what if a king did it to his subjects?

But once again Halfdan did not choose to humiliate his unannounced guests. Even as the long hall was being set up for the banquet, one of the servants, one of higher rank, judging by his clothing, approached and gave a shallow bow. "King Halfdan begs you gentlemen will sit at the head table by his side," the man said. "And begs all your men be invited to the feasting as well."

"Please tell the good king that we're grateful for his invitation," Odd said and the others nodded their agreement. When the servant had left them, Odd turned to the others. "This should give us the chance to speak our mind. Maybe when Halfdan gets some drink in him, he'll be more agreeable still."

But Odd was wrong about their chance to speak with Halfdan, and was never able to discover if the king was more talkative with drink in him. The feast was well on, the guests eating and drinking, the volume increasing with each cup or horn of ale and mead that went down their throats. But Halfdan was not there.

Odd looked off down the length of the hall, the far reaches lost in shadow. There were doors to rooms built off the hall and he guessed that one of those was Halfdan's bed chamber, and Halfdan might well be there. Two days ride, a wagon of expensive gifts, the king not fifty feet away, and they could not speak with him.

"Odd?"

Odd turned the other way. Einar was standing there, his face expressionless as usual.

"Yes?" Odd had to speak loud to be heard over the noise of the feast.

"King Halfdan sends his regrets," Einar said. "He's not well tonight and has decided to retire. He begs me ask you if you will be available to speak with him in the morning?"

The first reply that jumped into Odd's mind was neither polite nor helpful so with some effort he kept it to himself.

"Very well," Odd said. "We would not wish to put the king out. In the morning, then."

With no chance of an audience that night Odd would have been happy to just retire as well. But that was not going to happen as long as the feasting raged on around him, the raucous sound filling the hall. It was some time later that the noise had tapered off enough, and Odd was exhausted enough, that he was able to crawl off to his makeshift bed. He was asleep before he managed to pull the shoes from his feet.

Odd woke before dawn, as he always did, but in his semi-aware state, as he pulled himself from the world of sleep, he was not sure where he was. In a barn, that much he knew, with hundreds of animals all around, more animals than he had ever seen. Strange.

Then he was fully awake and he understood that the dream of animals had been prompted by the rumble of dozens of men snoring at impressive volume—the feast-goers of the night before, sleeping in their beds or facedown on the table or on the floor where they had fallen. Odd smiled and worked his way out from under the blankets.

A servant brought him a bowl of water and he washed himself and combed his hair.

"Is King Halfdan up?" he asked the servant when he came to fetch the bowl away.

"I wouldn't know, master," the servant said. "I've not seen him, that's all I know."

Odd nodded. As far as he could tell, he was the only one besides the servants who was awake. It was early, too early for an audience with the king. But he could wait.

And he did wait. He stepped out of the hall into the morning air as the sun was edging above the palisades on the earthen wall and the servants were hurrying about on their morning routines. He waited for Halfdan as the morning meal was served out and the remnants cleared away. He waited through an uncertain discussion with the other men who had come with him.

Finally Einar made his appearance. Odd, who had been sitting on a bench at the table, stood, as did Amundi and the others. Einar stopped a few feet away where he could address them all.

"Gentleman, the king decided this very morning that today would be a fine day for hunting. He and his party are gone already, but he begs me tell you he would welcome it if you could join him in the field."

Odd felt his face flush and burn. *Like a cat playing with a mouse,* he thought. *Bastard.* But there was nothing he could do.

The horses were brought around and Odd and the others mounted up. One of Halfdan's men joined them so that he might lead them to where the hunting party had set up.

They rode through the big gates and out into the open country. It was a beautiful day, the full flower of summer, skies blue, the grass green, the breeze warm. Birds whipped past and bees worked busily around the bright flowers.

It is a perfect day for a hunt, Odd admitted to himself.

They continued on for some time, up, over and down a series of hills that marched away from the walls of Halfdan's compound. At last they crested a hill and saw the hunting party below them. Two great trestle tables were laid out with food and drink. Servants attended the tables and attended the dozen men who were clustered on a small rise a hundred feet away. In the middle of them, unmistakable, stood Halfdan the Black. Odd had not seen him in years, but he recognized him right away, even from a distance.

They rode down the hill and the servants waiting there took their horses. They dismounted and Odd wondered what the protocol was, whether he should approach the king. Then Halfdan called out from his place on the hillock.

"Is that Odd Thorgrimson? And Ulfkel Ospaksson? Amundi Thorsteinsson? All of you, come over here, come over here!"

Odd led the way as the little band followed the king's command, walking through the stiff, knee-high grass. The crowd around Halfdan parted and Odd could see the king was waiting for them, a smile on his face. Halfdan wore a leather gauntlet, and perched on the gauntlet was a white bird, a massive, proud-looking gyrfalcon.

The falcon was magnificent, the bird of kings, nearly two feet tall with a snowy breast and black and white striations on its wings. Jesses dangled from its legs and a leather hood with a boar's bristle crest covered its head.

Halfdan looked more impressive still. He was nearly five decades old, older than Thorgrim by a few years, but he did not have the worn, broken appearance of many men his age. Why should he? His had not been a life of brutal labor and scarce food or the hardships of seafaring.

He was no stranger to battle; he was well known for his courage and skill on the field, but even a lifetime of fighting had left him unmarked. He was smiling now, and his teeth were straight and white and they were all still there. He wore a tunic of red silk, with cuff and hems intricately embroidered, and tall black leather boots that flashed in the sun.

"Welcome, my friends, welcome!" Halfdan said. "Forgive me for being so elusive!"

"It's good to see you, lord," Odd said. He began to raise his hand as he approached, meaning to offer it to Halfdan, but he saw that the king had his bird in one hand, and a lure in the other, so Odd lowered his hand again. "I thank you for your hospitality."

Halfdan waved dismissively. "My pleasure entirely," he said.

Your pleasure, indeed, Odd thought. The mead and the ham served at the feast the night before had been excellent, which was no surprise, since Odd knew for certain it was part of the cartload of gifts he had brought for the king's table. *Easy for you to entertain when the guests bring their own food and drink, and enough for all.*

"For the son of Thorgrim Night Wolf? Grandson of Ornolf the Restless?" Halfdan continued. "It's my honor. By the gods how I miss old Ornolf! Killed so far from home."

Odd nodded. "He's missed." He wanted to add that unlike Ornolf, Thorgrim had not been killed far from home, as far as he knew, but he did not think such a statement would go over well.

"Lord, I...we...we had hoped to have a word with you," Odd said, gesturing toward Amundi at his side and the others who were standing in a loose group behind them.

"Of course, of course!" Halfdan said. "But hold a second. I'm about to let this beauty fly!" He tossed the lure aside and eased the hood off the falcon's head. The bird's eyes were dark and alert. It jerked its head side to side as it scanned its surroundings.

Halfdan lowered his arm and then raised it quickly and the falcon took off in a great flutter of beating wings. Odd watched it soar high above, fast and effortless.

"See here," Halfdan said. "I have a handful of slaves out there flushing rabbit. I make them wear black caps on their heads. The bird is trained to look for the caps, and it knows when they're about to flush a rabbit or a quail!"

"Excellent, lord," Odd said. "A beautiful bird. But if you'll give me leave…"

"Wait! Wait! They have a rabbit!" Halfdan said, pointing up at the soaring bird of prey. "Just watch this!"

Odd watched, as did everyone else. They heard the rustle and the call of the slaves out in the grass, and occasionally they could see one of them thrashing around.

But the bird was seeing things they could not. It banked hard to the right and then went into a sharp dive, plummeting to earth, wings tucked back, speed building, until it flared and hit the ground, talons first. The men watching could see a glimpse of brown and white, the unfortunate rabbit that thought it was escaping from the flushers and never knew where the real danger was.

The knot of men around the king gave a soft cheer and clapped their approval. Halfdan beamed.

"What say you, Odd?" Halfdan asked.

"Excellently well done," Odd said. "Magnificent bird."

"He is," Halfdan said. "Do you hunt?"

"No, lord," Odd said. He frowned. This was not how he had envisioned this happening. He had hoped to have a private meeting with Halfdan, just him and the others and the king, alone, but it seemed that was not how it would be.

"But…I'd hoped we could speak," Odd tried again. "You, me, these gentlemen. It's about my father's farm, lord," Odd said. "Thorgrim's farm."

"Yes, a fine farm, I've been there often." Halfdan said. "What of it?"

"Well, lord, I understand you wish to take it. For taxes."

"I wish to what?" Halfdan looked puzzled.

"To take it, lord. To pay taxes that are supposed to be owed you."

"Who owes me taxes? You?"

"No, lord. It's said you feel taxes are owed on Thorgrim's land. And you wish to take it."

Halfdan shook his head. "Who told you this?"

"Einar Sigurdsson, lord. He was there with some of your hirdmen, and he said you wish to claim the farm as your own."

Halfdan waved his hand. "Einar gets ahead of himself!" he said. "I don't know if I have any claim to your father's farm. I'll have to speak with Einar, see what he's thinking."

"Thank you, lord," Odd said, but he did not want to leave it at that. There were bigger issues, other principles at stake, things that needed clarifying.

"We...the hauldar...your subjects, we would not care to see the rights we have enjoyed for generations..."

What? What could he say? Trampled? Ignored? Pissed upon? Odd wished he had thought of the right word beforehand, one that imparted his meaning but would not be seen as a demand or a threat or an insult.

Then he looked at Halfdan and he saw a shadow pass over the man's face and he knew he need say nothing more. His meaning had been clear enough and the king was not at all pleased with that meaning.

I've made a mistake now, Odd thought and his mind reached for the words to set it to rights. He felt as if he had been knocked on the side of the head, his thoughts scrambled. But even as he faced the horrible blankness of his own thoughts the shadow passed from Halfdan's face and he smiled and slapped Odd on the shoulder.

"Come now, this is such a fine day. No time for weighty matters of state!"

Odd nodded without enthusiasm. He had spent a week organizing this visit, and two days travel and a cartload of his finest just so he and Halfdan could have this discussion, and he was not ready to abandon it now.

But clearly Halfdan was. He turned from Odd and looked out at the field. One of the slaves was heading toward him, the broken, bloody rabbit in his hand. Overhead the gyrfalcon soared in long, lazy circles.

"Forgive me, Odd, Amundi, gentlemen," Halfdan said. "I must get my bird back and see to him." He gestured toward the tables at the bottom of the hillock. "There's food and drink, please help yourself, and we'll continue this discussion when we can." Then he turned and looked up at the bird, the conversation over.

Odd and the others made their way down the hill toward the tables and their bounty, but Odd's mind was not on food or drink. He was thinking of his conversation with Halfdan, a talk that was now clearly at an end.

That did not go well, Odd thought, and he felt the humiliation smoldering in him. Halfdan had treated him like a fool. An impotent fool.

That did not go well at all.

Chapter Twelve

Wake, maid of maids!
Wake, my friend!
Now there is dark of darks;
we will both to
Valhall ride,
and to the holy fane.

The Poetic Edda

"The English! The English! There!" Failend shouted her warning again. If it was a full-on attack or a small party she could not tell, but she knew she had to stop them, no matter. *They* had to stop them.

The man with the seax, the one who had hoped to grab her while she fought with the other, seemed not to have heard her warning, or if he did he took it for a ruse. Recovered from the surprise of Failend's attack, he widened his stance, held his weapon out to one side, his empty hand out to the other, ready to grab her wrist if she lunged again. Failend could see his eyes shining in the light, and the dull mass of a red beard.

And behind him, where he could not see them, men-at-arms, the enemy, coming silently over the wall.

How many, she could not tell, she could see no details, just the movement in the dark. Her eyes shifted from them to the man in front of her and back again. She heard Louis's blade clash with that of the Northman he was fighting, and she thought that the Northman must be a good swordsman to have stood so long against Louis de Roumois.

"The English! They're coming over the wall!" Failend shouted again. The red-bearded man did not alter his stance, did not look any

106

less ready to attack, but she thought she saw a shade of doubt, or at least confusion, come over his face.

Failend, too, was in a half crouch, blade held ready, but now she stood straight, exposed and vulnerable, and pointed out over the man's shoulder with her seax and yelled, "There! They're coming over!"

Now the uncertainty was clear on the man's face and he looked quickly over his shoulder, then back, in case this was some sort of trick, but Failend's mind was no longer on him. She turned, turned her back on the man, and hit Louis on the shoulder with the flat of her seax.

Louis jerked his head in her direction. He was still fighting the one with the sword, and the fifth man was circling around to the side. That one had a seax, not a sword, and seemed to be looking for an opening in which to use the shorter blade.

"Louis, the English!" Failend shouted. "They're coming over the wall!"

"What?" Louis yelled back. He parried a thrust from the sword man, then lunged at the other to keep him at bay.

"The English..." Failend began again, but the red-bearded man she had been fighting came pushing past her, waving his seax toward the wall behind them.

"The bastard English are coming over the wall!" he shouted, still gesturing, and everyone stopped and turned, as if they had all suddenly forgotten about their own fight. And then they started to run.

Not back to the fire and the crowd of armed Northmen, as any reasonable person might do, but at the invaders. There was no thought, much less discussion. They just reacted. Failend, Louis, and the three men left standing, who paused long enough to grab up the more substantial weapons their shipmates had dropped.

"At them, at them!" Failend's erstwhile attacker yelled, and the rest joined in, shouting as loud as they could, hoping to surprise and frighten the invaders and attract the attention of those back by the fire. Failend let out a banshee yell, a scream that harkened back to the druids of her native land, and then the five of them flung themselves into the fight.

The English had been trying for stealth, that was clear, but they had time enough to prepare as Failend and the rest charged at them.

Louis was on them first, slashing left and right with his sword, an attack that might have seemed wild and disjointed if not for Louis's grace and control. The first man in his way went down fast, and the two behind were having a hard time keeping clear of his quick blade.

How many, how many? Failend wondered. She could see a dozen or so men in the dark, though so far from the light of the fire they were shadowy at best. The English had, for obvious reasons, come over the wall at the darkest place and that made it impossible to see how many they were, and nearly impossible to fight them.

The red-bearded Northman had snatched up the ax from his companion who, last seen, was still lying on the ground clutching his balls. Now he barreled into the line of English, swinging the ax in front of him. His attack was as frenzied as Louis's was controlled, but it was just as effective. An English sword reached out for him, and Failend saw the ax come down on the blade and snap it in two. The Northman screamed again and raised the ax high and brought it down on the Englishman's helmeted head.

The helmet did the Englishman little good. The ax split it like cordwood and drove on down into the man's skull. His knees buckled and he slumped to the ground, the ax still embedded in his skull. Failend could see the Northman struggling to free the blade, could see the Englishman just behind bring his sword back to deliver a backhand stroke. She shouted, leapt forward, drove her seax into the Englishman, right into his chest under his upraised arm.

The man screamed, the sword fell, the Northman yanked his ax free. He and Failend turned and faced the next two stumbling into the fight.

The other two Northmen had also driven themselves into the melee. One was thrusting and slashing with his sword, but the other had taken a vicious cut across the neck. He was staggering back when an English spear shot out from the dark, impaled his chest and doubled him over, eyes wide, mouth open. The spear was jerked back and he fell to his knees.

Failend watched this for a heartbeat, no more. No time for distractions. The spear that had killed the man thrust out again, looking for her this time, but she batted it aside with the seax in her right hand, grabbed the shaft in her left and jerked. The spearman, not ready for that, stumbled forward, near enough for Failend to get her short seax into him.

She was still screaming, the Northmen and Louis were screaming, the English were screaming. Someone was shouting something that sounded like orders. Weapons were clashing on weapons and Failend knew that this could not go on much longer. She knew they should not have attacked the enemy, they should have raced back to the fire, alerted the others, but they had not been thinking when they charged, and now there was no extricating themselves.

The English were pushing them back, step by step, and circling around the outside. It was their surprise attack that had kept them alive so far. The shock of their unexpected and wild charge had knocked the invaders off balance and allowed Failend and the others a moment of opportunity. But that moment was over. The English had figured out it was only five people, and one was already dead. It was a small defense and they could end it soon.

And in that frenzied attack, that fight for their lives, that desperate moment when the entire world shuts down to just those things within reach of a weapon, Failend forgot that there were others on the beach. She remembered Louis and the two others fighting with her, but she forgot the four hundred back by the fire. Until they arrived.

Damn, damn... she thought as she became aware of the running feet and the shouting men behind her. She thought the English had circled around behind, that any second now she would feel a spear or a sword or an ax in her back. In that second of distraction the man in front of her thrust out with his spear, thrust the point straight for her belly, and she knew she was too late to stop the weapon from striking home.

She was frozen, watching death come, when a sword came flailing down in front of her like a sword from Heaven, and Thorgrim Night Wolf was at her side. It was his sword, Iron-tooth, a blade she knew well, and it struck just as the tip of the English spear was touching Failend's tunic. It struck the Englishman's wrist and kept on going, taking his hand clean off. The spear, with the hand still gripping the shaft, dropped to the ground and the spear warrior screamed and grabbed the bleeding stump with his left hand and Thorgrim drove Iron-tooth through his chest.

"Thank you," Failend said in a conversational way, but Thorgrim had already driven past her, thrusting and slashing, and on her left side Godi came smashing into the line, hacking with his ax. Then, through the cacophony of shouting men, came the war cry of Starri Deathless, like a razor-sharp knife through soft flesh.

It was a sound that was familiar to Failend by now, from all the scrapes she and Starri had been in together, but she still found it frightening. Not nearly as frightening as it was to those whom Starri was attacking, however, and once again Failend saw the war cry work its magic. She could see the pause, the uncertainty in the line of men before her, the step back and then another as the English heard the Angel of Death coming for them.

Run, you bastards, run, she thought, and, as if she were directing them with her mind, the English broke and ran. Back ranks first, those not locked in the fighting. There was just light enough from the distant fire for Failend to see them throw their weapons away and turn and flee, presumably back over the wall, the way they had come.

Those in the front could not turn and see what their comrades were doing, but they seemed to feel the absence of the men behind. One by one they, too, turned and ran, some getting clean away, some dying under a sword or ax or spear before they had taken two steps back. Others flung their weapons away and fell to their knees with arms raised. And some of those were struck down anyway in the battle frenzy, and others were pushed down flat on the ground by Northmen who had retained enough presence of mind to not kill everything before them.

Then, in that odd way of battle, it was over. The Englishmen who were caught halfway up the wall were pulled down and shoved to the ground. The rest who had not escaped were already down, surrendered or dead. The sound of struggling men, the clash of weapons, was gone, and in its place were the groans of the wounded and the thrashing and cursing of Starri Deathless as his shipmates held him down to stop him from further slaughter.

Failend was breathing hard. She held her seax loose at her side and the blood ran down the blade and dripped from the point. She felt an ache in her thigh which she had not noticed and looked down to find the cloth of her breeches cut through and hanging open, revealing a wide and bleeding laceration beneath. She felt the pain redouble now that she was aware of it, and her leg buckled a little. Not enough to put her down, but enough that she was standing at an odd angle.

She felt a hand on her shoulder and looked up. The light of the bonfire illuminated one half of Thorgrim's face and she could see concern there, along with streaks of blood and sweat.

"You're hurt," he said. "You should sit."

"I'm all right," Failend said, though they both knew that was not true.

"You were here before us," Thorgrim said. "You and Louis the Frank."

Failend nodded. She tried to hear something in Thorgrim's voice. Suspicion? Jealousy? Worry? Concern? There was something there, but she did not know what.

"Louis and those others from Jorund's crew," Failend said. "I don't know their names. We were just talking."

Thorgrim nodded. "Good thing you were here," he said. "But it was a foolish thing, running into the fight like that."

"Not the first foolish thing I've done," Failend said.

They were silent for a moment, not an easy silence, then Failend asked, "The English…what were they about, do you think? Was this supposed to be a full-on attack?"

"I don't think so," Thorgrim said. "They killed the man who was on lookout. I guess he wasn't looking out so well. But if they meant this to be a real battle they would have tried to come over the wall in a few places. I think these men were sent to discover what they could. There was only a couple dozen of them, no more."

Failend nodded and the silence fell on them again.

"I haven't seen much of you," Thorgrim said next, as hesitant and unsure as Failend had ever heard him.

"I've been around," she said, but she could not manage to put much reconciliation in her tone. "Did you miss me?"

Thorgrim frowned a little. He nodded his head.

"Did you miss me? Or just miss humping me?" Failend asked. She saw the surprise on Thorgrim's face. She could see he did not know what to say to that.

This is stupid, she thought. Dead men lying at their feet, her thigh pulsing blood, an enemy gathered on the other side of the makeshift wall, and she was worried about whether Thorgrim loved her or just loved to fornicate.

"Go," she said. "I'll be fine. I can bind this wound. It's nothing, and you have more important things by far to concern you." She wiped the blade of her seax on her tunic, slid it into the scabbard, turned and hobbled back toward the stump of log where she had sought some quiet before this had all begun.

Chapter Thirteen

Then I, too, left—a lonely, lordless refugee,
full of unaccountable desires!
But the man's kinsmen schemed to estrange us,
divide us, keep us apart.

The Wife's Lament
10th Century English Poem

It was still dark outside, but there was light in Nothwulf's tent, thrown off by the several candles burning in their stands. Light enough to see the rent in the sleeve of Captain Ailmar's mail shirt, the dried blood that covered his hand where it had run down his arm, the dirt and presumably more blood streaking his face, the weariness in his eyes.

Ailmar was Leofric's most trusted captain, commander of his hearth guard. It was why he had been chosen to lead the nighttime raid over the Northmen's walls. But in the end it seemed they did not need a trusted man so much as a lucky man, and Ailmar was not that, apparently.

"The heathens was to the west end of their works, lord," he was explaining to Nothwulf. Leofric sat off to Nothwulf's side. He may have been Ailmar's master, but Nothwulf was his ealdorman, and so the report went to him.

"We knew they'd be to the west. Their fire was to the west. We moved to the east side, sent one of the men up on the wall and he done for the lookout. Very quiet, no one heard anything. Not that anyone could, over the heathens singing and carrying on like the devils they are. So we went up and over the wall and everything was good, but then we realized there were some of the bastards on the ground right where we were coming over, hidden in the dark."

"How many?" Nothwulf asked. "Did they seem to be waiting for you?"

"No, lord. I think we took them by surprise. But there were a lot of them, two dozen I would reckon. And they attacked screaming like lunatics. We might have beat them anyway, but the screaming brought the rest and that was an end to it."

Nothwulf nodded. He had seen the men on their return. Cuts from swords and axes, ripped chainmail. But none of them were too badly hurt, because the ones who were too badly hurt did not make it back over the wall.

God knows what the heathens did to those poor bastards, Nothwulf thought.

"So the Northmen are numerous, and they're not drinking themselves into insensibility, is that what we've learned?" Leofric asked.

"Yes, lord, that seems to be it," Ailmar said.

"How many men did we lose?" Nothwulf asked.

"Ah…not sure, lord. I've not had the chance to determine that," Ailmar said.

You mean you don't want to tell me, Nothwulf thought. Which was ironic. Ailmar considered the losses to be a poor reflection on his own leadership. But Nothwulf did not blame Ailmar, he blamed himself alone. Nothwulf was more anxious about the number of casualties than Ailmar was.

"Very well," Nothwulf said. "You and your men did good work tonight. You couldn't have known there'd be some of the Northmen skulking about in the dark. Now, go get some rest."

Ailmar stood and bowed and left the tent as fast as he could. Nothwulf turned to Leofric. "You were right. It was a stupid, pointless endeavor."

"I did not say that. I just worried that it couldn't be carried out with success," Leofric said.

Leofric was a gentleman of the highest order. That was why he did not remind Nothwulf that he had questioned Nothwulf's plan to send men over the wall, and the purpose for doing so. In the end it had been the disaster that Leofric had predicted, and now, in his present state of mind, Nothwulf could not even recall why he had ever thought it was a good idea.

"So, what now?" Nothwulf asked. He was quite done with making decisions.

"As you said to Ailmar," Leofric said. "Rest. We'll figure the next step in the morning."

But there was no need for figuring, because the next step came to them. It rode right into camp in the form of Oswin the shire reeve, followed by a dozen of the finest men-at-arms in Cynewise's army.

Where the hell did they come from? Nothwulf wondered as he watched them approach down the wide path between the rows of tents. Cynewise's army, he realized, must be closer than he thought.

Nothwulf was standing outside his tent, a wash bowl in front of him, his face lathered with soap, when Oswin reined to a stop fifteen feet away. In his surprise Nothwulf had forgotten about the soap, but in that moment remembered. He grabbed a towel and wiped his face and tried to hide any consternation that might have crept into his expression.

Oswin slipped down from his horse and approached. Nothwulf's guards took a step forward, but Nothwulf waved them off. Oswin stopped a few feet from Nothwulf and bowed.

"My lord, it's my pleasure to see you again." He was well practiced in subservience and his words truly sounded sincere.

"Oswin," Nothwulf said, nodding his head in acknowledgement. "You'll forgive my surprise at seeing you here."

"Of course, lord," Oswin said. "I come at the behest of my lady Cynewise. She asks if you would be so gracious as to meet with her at your convenience."

"It's hardly convenient for me to ride to Sherborne, what with the heathens trapped here under our noses." Nothwulf nodded toward the makeshift log walls, which were two hundred feet away across the open ground between the river's edge and the first of the houses that made up the village of Christchurch.

Oswin looked over at the walls as if they were of only minor interest. "I see the masts of their ships," he said. "If their ships are there, and they're able to sail away, I wonder how trapped they could be. In any event, my lady is not at Sherborne. She rides at the head of her army, not three miles from here."

"Indeed?" Nothwulf said, showing no more interest than Oswin had in the Northmen's defenses. He had not really thought that

Cynewise was in Sherborne. He did not know where she was, but he was desperately anxious to find out.

"Yes, lord, about three miles away," Oswin said. "And she begs you'll meet with her."

"She's welcome in my camp any time," Nothwulf said. "She is my sister-in-law, after all."

"An honor she feels deeply," Oswin said. "But she begs me give her apologies, but she is too occupied to leave her army at the moment."

And I'm not? Nothwulf thought. But he understood that there was a time to stand on a point of honor and a time to compromise. At the moment it was more important that he speak with Cynewise and get an idea of what she was up to than to sit petulantly in camp and insist she come to him.

Actually, it was to his advantage to go to her, to see for himself the size and makeup of her army.

"Very well, if Cynewise is too out of sorts to come here, then I will go to her," Nothwulf said. "Pray wait while I dress."

Nothwulf dressed, he breakfasted, he spoke with Leofric, he ordered Bryning, captain of his hearth-guard, to assemble an armed escort, he gave instructions to his servant, all the while leaving Oswin to wait outside the tent. Finally, when all was in readiness, he mounted, and he and Oswin and their respective contingents of men-at-arms rode from the camp.

Nothwulf would have preferred to lead the procession, which was his proper place, but of course he did not know where Cynewise was to be found. So he opted for the next best thing, which was to ride side by side with Oswin. And they did not ride for long: Cynewise's camp was indeed just three miles away.

As they approached, Nothwulf undertook the difficult task of looking uninterested in what was in front of him while simultaneously taking in every bit of it that he could. There were a lot of men. Some he could see were part of the fyrd, but many were proper men-at-arms. There were quite a few horses, a sign of professional warriors, men of means, or those employed by men of means. There had to be five hundred men all told, pretty much the same as he commanded. All that he was able to see while trying not to look around. And he saw a few other things that caught his attention in a serious way.

They came at last to the big tent that housed Cynewise in a level of comfort not generally enjoyed by soldiers in the field. Oswin stopped and Nothwulf stopped and they both swung out of their saddles and dropped to the ground. They approached the tent and the guard to the right of the door called, "Lord Nothwulf and Shire Reeve Oswin!"

That's "Ealdorman," not "Lord," Nothwulf thought, but the thought was cut short by a voice, Cynewise's voice, from within, calling, "Come!"

Oswin ducked through the canvas flap of a door and Nothwulf followed. The interior of the tent was nearly as grand as a bed chamber in a royal house: a wide bed with a feather mattress, a wardrobe, a table with wash basin, mirror and combs, another with wine and glasses and cheese and bread.

Cynewise was seated in a large chair opposite the bed, nearly facing the door. The chair resembled a throne somewhat, which was not by chance. There were a few other chairs of lesser stature around it. One was occupied by Bishop Ealhstan, which surprised Nothwulf so much he was not quite able to keep it from his face.

Oswin bowed and Nothwulf gave a halfhearted nod of the head. He turned to the bishop. "Your Grace, I'm surprised to see you here. Delighted, but surprised."

"My Lord Nothwulf," Ealhstan said. "The heathens have invaded one of my priories, one of the holy places of God. Of course I must be here."

"Of course," Nothwulf said. He turned to Cynewise. She, too, was something of a surprise. When he had seen her in Sherborne, sitting on the dais, she had looked like a little girl, frightened and overwhelmed, seated in a grown-up's chair. But she looked that way no longer. She sat erect, confident, wearing a silk gown which was both elegant and austere, feminine but not soft or compromising. Her face was composed and Nothwulf could read nothing in it. She wore a cape around her shoulders which gave her a vaguely martial look.

"Thank you, Lord Nothwulf, for responding to my summons," Cynewise said.

Summons? Nothwulf thought, but he did not react to that. Instead he replied, "Of course, sister. How could I not come to your assistance when your need is so great?"

Cynewise took on a thoughtful look. "So great? I'm not so sure…"

"I believe I saw the banner of Devonshire at the north end of the camp," Nothwulf said before Cynewise could finish the thought. "Has your father come to your aide?"

"My father has come with a few of his men," Cynewise said. "You know how he loathes the Northmen and will do anything to see them driven off."

"Indeed," Nothwulf said. "I'm sure you welcome his experience, having none of your own in such things." He made a show of looking around. "I would have thought he'd be here, to join us in this conference."

"He's not well," Cynewise said. "He's taken to his bed."

"I'm sorry to hear that," Nothwulf said, though he was anything but. "Nothing too serious, I hope?"

"Something he ate," Cynewise said, waving her hand to dismiss the subject.

"But to more important matters," the bishop chimed in. "It seems you're both here, each with an army, and the same thought in mind, which is to drive the Northmen into the sea. Which would be most pleasing to God. Now, surely that would be best done with the two of you fighting side by side?"

Nothwulf looked at the bishop, looked at Cynewise and then back at the bishop. He wondered if Ealhstan was sincere in this, or working with Cynewise on some nefarious trick, but he concluded in that instant that the bishop was not playing tricks. Ealhstan was a clever man, and a manipulative one, but he was not the sort who would put himself in the middle of such a thing as this and play one side against the other. There was too much risk of picking the wrong side, and losing all he had gained.

"Of course, your Grace," Nothwulf said. He turned to Cynewise who was most certainly playing tricks. "You agree with his Grace?"

Cynewise nodded. "I do," she said, and Nothwulf could not help but think of the first time he had heard her say that, at her wedding to his brother, seconds before the thegn Werheard had stepped up and killed his brother right at the altar. She had been a frail, weak thing, notably unattractive, and Nothwulf had wondered if she would have substance enough to give birth to Merewald's heirs. But now she looked very different indeed. Attractive, actually. Quite attractive.

"We have twice the heathens' numbers, between us," she said, and Nothwulf pulled his attention back to the moment. "I propose that I march my men to Christchurch and there we'll join up and launch our attack on the Northmen. We can't help but grind them into the dirt."

Nothwulf nodded. "Yes, I believe you're right," he said even as he tried to untangle the knot of Cynewise's real intentions. She couldn't let him fight the Northmen alone. If he won and she was not there then it would greatly bolster his status among the thegns. Cynewise would find it impossible to carry on as the pretender to the ealdormanship. So she would join him in the fight, and she would look for some way to make him seem the fool. Or die in battle. Either one would suit her needs.

But he was not the only one who could be made to look a fool. Or die. He pulled a chair closer and sat down, unbidden. "Let's discuss when we might make our attack, and how we might do it," he said. "But perhaps you should call the thegns who march with you. And your father, if he's well enough. These are military matters, you know, and not really the sort of things a young woman would understand."

It was late in the afternoon by the time Nothwulf and his hearthguard rode back into their camp on the edge of the village of Christchurch. His first thought was not for his own men, but rather the heathens, and his eyes were fixed on their fortifications across the open ground. He could still see their masts rising above the rough wooden walls, and he felt a sense of relief. All of his plans rested on his beating the Northmen in a way that made him look like a proper leader and Cynewise the incompetent slut that she was. But if the Northmen were gone, then all was for naught.

He called Leofric and the other thegns together and told them of his plans. Explained how Cynewise was there with an army about the size of their own, that she would march to Christchurch to join them and together they would crush the heathens under foot.

"Who will lead this fight?" Leofric asked. He was the only one of them who would dare ask such a question, and expect a genuine answer.

"I will, obviously," Nothwulf said. "The thegns who follow Cynewise, they do so because they think she'll manage to hold on to the ealdormanship. Not because they see her as a great leader. They certainly would not care to allow a child such as her to lead them in a fight."

Heads nodded. If any were skeptical they kept it to themselves.

Night came at last and Nothwulf listened to the camp settling down. The dark seemed to smother the sounds made by the hundreds of men and animals, and sleep pushed its way through the tents. Off in the distance, soft, like small waves on the beach, he could hear the Northmen carrying out their nightly pagan ritual of drinking and singing around the fire.

The bastards had much to celebrate, having sacked Christchurch Priory, tricked the English by shifting to their new fortification and, most recently, beating off Nothwulf's ill-advised attack. They probably felt he was unlikely to try such a thing again. And they were right.

Sleep did not visit Nothwulf. His mind reeled and staggered like a drunken fool, careening off this and that. Cynewise's army would be there by late the next day. Where would they camp? How would he assert his dominance from the outset? Would her father, Ceorle, be well enough to take part? If so, that was a problem. Nothwulf might be a more experienced leader than Cynewise, but he was not more experienced than Ceorle, and not nearly as powerful or influential with the king.

At last he undressed and slipped into his camp bed, but still sleep stayed clear. His mind turned to Cynewise, moving on its own, like a horse that knows which way it wants to go, regardless of what the rider wishes. He saw her sitting on that ersatz throne, her head slightly tipped back, revealing that long, smooth neck. He thought of how her slim body would feel wrapped in his arms. He thought about how her long legs would feel wrapped around his waist.

Then he thought of something else, an idea that had not occurred to him before, and his eyes flew open, thoughts of Cynewise gone. He toyed with this new thought a bit, explored it from different angles, and the more he looked at it, the more intrigued he became.

And then he was back with Cynewise, and she was on top of him, young and strong and energetic, her long blond hair half covering her face, her eyes closed, her mouth open.

And then he was asleep. And in his dreams he was with Cynewise once again. He could feel her touching him and he saw her in a vast hall that was half filled with down pillows, warm and luxurious.

And then he opened his eyes with a start and he saw that there was in fact a woman touching him, touching his face with gentle fingers. He first thought it was Cynewise, then the fog began to clear from his mind, and the light of the single candle still burning fell on her face and he saw it was not Cynewise—it was Aelfwyn.

Nothwulf gasped in surprise and scooted back in the bed, pushing himself up to a sitting position as he did. He saw Aelfwyn smile.

"You were never so shy with me in bed before," she said. Her voice had a quality that was utterly familiar to him, though it seemed like it was from an earlier age. Quite a bit had happened since last he heard it.

"How did you get in here?" he demanded. It was the least important of the many questions he needed to ask, but it was all he could think to say.

"Your guards searched me for weapons," Aelfwyn said. "They were very thorough, the lecherous bastards. But once they saw I was unarmed they figured you would not be disappointed to see me. Are you?"

Nothwulf ignored the question. His mind was clearing. "You're here at Cynewise's command. Like last time. What mischief do you have in mind now?"

"I'm here on my own," Aelfwyn said. "I learned from your hearth-guard where your camp was. I walked here. Cynewise does not know."

Nothwulf smiled at that. "I should have you flogged right now for thinking me such a fool as to believe you."

"You may flog me if you wish," Aelfwyn said. "You could hardly use me worse than Cynewise has. Making me play the whore for you was the least of it. Actually, I didn't mind that so much. But she'll whore me out to another, one less desirable than you, if she needs to. The beatings and the yelling, that I could do without. I *will* do without."

Nothwulf was silent as he regarded her. *Beautiful*, he thought. He had forgotten how beautiful she was. Cynewise's beauty could show through on occasion, but Aelfwyn radiated it.

No wonder Cynewise hates the little vixen.

"So, what do you want of me?" Nothwulf asked. "I have no doubt you miss rutting with me, but I doubt you would walk miles in the dark just for that."

"I might," Aelfwyn said. "But in truth I want nothing from you. I want only to get free of that bitch Cynewise, and I had nowhere to go but to you. So here I am. And I'm willing to be of use to you."

"I imagine you are," Nothwulf said. "Just as you've been of use to many men, I would suspect."

"No, not that. By warning you. Cynewise means to betray you. I know it."

Again Nothwulf was silent, considering this. "How will she betray me?" he asked.

"She's agreed to join you in fighting the Northmen," Aelfwyn said. "I know that. She told you that each of you, you and her, will take a fair share of the fighting. But she's gone to her father and begged him to take her place. Told him she's just a woman and not able to lead warriors like a man."

"That's true enough," Nothwulf said. "I'm only surprised she's willing to admit it."

"She's admitting nothing," Aelfwyn said. "She doesn't believe that. The way she figures it, her father leads an attack on the Northmen, you lead an attack on the Northmen, Cynewise hangs back and lets the two of you and your men get slaughtered. It solves two problems for her."

Nothwulf frowned. He could see how that might work out well for Cynewise. He knew Ceorle and he knew that if there were armies to be led, the old man would insist on leading them.

"But what if Ceorle and I beat the Northmen?" Nothwulf argued. "What if we're not killed in the fighting?"

"Cynewise would be happy to see you beat the Northmen, rid her of that problem," Aelfwyn said. "And she has ways to make certain you two are killed."

Then another thought came to Nothwulf.

"But Ceorle's sick. He won't be able to lead men in battle."

Aelfwyn waved a hand as if she were shooing a fly. "Whatever Cynewise gave the old man, I'm sure it wasn't enough to kill him. He'll be up in a day or so."

Nothwulf sat up a little straighter. "You're saying Cynewise poisoned her father?"

"Of course she did," Aelfwyn replied, and her tone suggested that she thought it a stupid question. "She was sick to death of the old goat, wanted to shut him up for a few days. Let her think and plan in peace."

Nothwulf shook his head. Not because he didn't believe Aelfwyn, but because he realized that he did not appreciate the lengths to which Cynewise was willing to go. Such as arranging for the death of her husband of two minutes. And her father.

They were silent again for a moment, then Aelfwyn continued.

"Cynewise doesn't care a bit about the Northmen. She was going to pay them danegeld to leave. The only thing she cares about is making sure you don't come off looking like the proper leader. Or, better still, that you're dead. Like your brother. I don't think she believed you would be this much trouble for her."

"If she was going to pay the Northmen to leave, why didn't she?"

"Because you're here, you fool! Oswin had one hundred and fifty pounds of silver that he was to deliver to them, but he couldn't because your army is between him and the heathens."

"How do you know all this?" Nothwulf asked.

"I'm Cynewise's lady's maid! I am always attending her. I hear everything, even though she reckons me just another bit of her furniture, always there but unable to listen or speak. She beats me and she yells at me and she whores me out and she expects me to be loyal as a dog to her."

Nothwulf frowned again. Aelfwyn sounded sincere enough, but then, she had also sounded sincere back when she was helping implicate him in his brother's murder.

"Are you not loyal as a dog?" Nothwulf asked. "What cause do I have to believe you?"

Aelfwyn shook her head. "I don't care if you believe me or not," she said. "I truly don't. I've said what I want to say, and if you won't offer me protection I'll find someone who will. But if you think I'm here by Cynewise's command, then tell me how Cynewise could benefit by my telling you to be on your guard."

Nothwulf thought about that. She was right. He could envision no benefit to Cynewise in what Aelfwyn had to say, no reason she might have sent Aelfwyn with that message. Now he felt foolish for having trusted Cynewise even the tiny bit he had.

Then he thought of that other idea, the one that had come to him just as sleep approached and snapped him awake. He felt a sense of relief, like warmth from a fire. Surely God Himself had put that idea in his head, to save him from the snares of Cynewise. He reached out and placed a hand on Aelfwyn's thigh.

"You've done me a great good turn, coming here, warning me thus," he said. "And you must be cold and worn down from your dangerous trip. Pray, lie beside me and let me warm you up again, and ease your fears."

Chapter Fourteen

From the saddle we will talk:
let us sit,
and of princely
families discourse,
of those chieftains
who from the gods descend.

The Poetic Edda

The three of them: Odd, Vermund Jurundsson, the overseer of Odd's farm, and the old shipwright Ari, were leaning on the wagon watching the six men approach from the south. They were on horseback, riding slow. They would be tired, but there was nothing for it. They were Odd's men and they had been sent to do a job, and now they were coming back and they would be put to a bigger job still.

"So, Halfdan was not so keen on listening to your concerns?" Ari asked. It had been two days since the king's hunting party, but Ari had been gone searching for suitable timber when Odd returned and they had not spoken until that moment.

"No," Odd said. "But he's a clever bastard. I forgot how clever, to my peril. Never refused to see us, even made us feel welcome, but he would not be pinned down for any real talk. I had no satisfaction from him."

Recounting his meeting with the king made the humiliation rise again like bile in Odd's throat. "We didn't speak again while he was hunting. We returned to his hall and the next day Einar informed us Halfdan had gone off south and would not be back for some time."

"Did he?"

"I don't know," Odd said. "Not that it matters. He was done talking about it. And I was done being played with."

"And the others?" Ari asked.

"No happier than I was," Odd said. "But Halfdan was careful to give no real offense. Amundi and the rest, they figured we could do naught but hope Halfdan heard us and will take care about snatching up property that isn't his."

Ari gave a snorting laugh. "You know how a dog is, once it's killed a chicken and got that taste of blood in its mouth?" he said. "It won't stop killing. Well, I fear your father's farm will be Halfdan's first chicken."

"Not his first," Vermund said. "He's taken land to the south. He's tasted it. Thorgrim's farm will just be his first taste in Vik."

The riders came up the hill toward Odd's hall, toward the wagon the men were leaning on and the five other wagons behind it, all the wagons Odd owned or could borrow. The one riding at the head of the band was a man named Gnup, strong and reliable, if not the sharpest arrow in the quiver, who assisted Vermund in running the farm. He had a shovel strapped across his saddle, as did the others. He stopped his horse by the wagon and climbed, weary, down from the saddle, and the rest did the same.

"All's well, Gnup?" Odd asked, and Gnup nodded his large head.

"Done, and it looks well."

"You look tired. You and your men."

Gnup nodded again. "It's the riding, not the digging."

"I'd think so," Odd said. Gnup and the others were competent riders, but not much used to it. In truth they would rather have walked, but there was no time for that. They were, however, farmers and good hands with pick and shovel.

"Well, you men eat and rest," Odd said. "Tomorrow we're off again. And then the real digging will begin."

Another man might have had a clever retort to that, but Gnup just said, "Yes, Master Odd," and snatched up his horse's reins and led the animal off toward the barn, the rest still following behind.

"Will any of those others, your neighbors, the hauldar, will they join you in this business?" Ari asked.

"No," Odd said. "They seemed to think it was best if we let things be, let Halfdan make the next move. Wait and see how he reacts to our visit."

126

"If they think Halfdan will just let this go, they're fools," Vermund said.

"Yes," Odd said. "But honestly, I don't think any of them really believe Halfdan is done with us. Because they're not fools. In any case, I didn't tell them my plans. This isn't their fight. At least not yet. And I don't want to drag them into it."

Odd suddenly felt a weariness come over him. He had done no digging that day, but he had done quite a bit else. He and Ari and Vermund retreated to the long hall where *náttmál*, the evening meal, was waiting. They ate with Signy and the children, along with a few of the more prosperous freemen who rented land from Odd.

The freemen were, for the most part, a few years older than Odd, and unlike Odd all had gone a'viking in their younger days. For that reason Odd always felt a little out of sorts in their company. He liked them, and they liked him, as best he could tell. Odd was certainly the highest born and the wealthiest of all of them. But they had endured the privations of voyaging at sea and the horror of genuine battle, and Odd had not, and he could not forget it.

They ate well—thick cuts of beef and fresh greens and root vegetables and fish, and to drink, ale and mead—and they discussed what would definitely happen the next day, and what might happen, and what they would do.

The men went to bed earlier and more sober than was their wont, because they would be up early and would need their rest. Odd, too, went to his bed closet and lay down beside Signy, who had her back turned toward him. She had said little during *náttmál*, and she said nothing now, and Odd tried to gauge just how angry she was. But after a moment she shuffled toward him and pressed her back and legs against him. He reached his arm around her and she made a soft sound in her throat and he guessed she was not as angry as he feared.

It was still dark when they all rose, and the sun was just breaking the horizon out where the sea and sky met when the parade of men and wagons moved out, rolling south from Odd's farm. Odd led the way with Ari and some of the freemen, all on horseback. Behind them came the six wagons, empty and moving easily. Each carried a driver and a couple of the farm hands. The rest of the freemen followed behind. They were in total nine mounted warriors and sixteen laborers. Not a terribly impressive war band, but then they were not a war band, necessarily. That would be determined later.

The wagons were empty and rolling over dry roads in generally good repair, but they still could not move terribly fast. It was not until midday when they finally came rumbling down the long hill that led to Thorgrim's farm, the hall at the center of the numerous outbuildings. Odd could see folk moving around, but there seemed to be no purpose or hurry to their actions, as if the entire place was simply bracing for what might happen next.

They were nearing the buildings when Skafti Hrappsson came hurrying up at a pace somewhere between a fast walk and a run.

"Master Odd!" he said as he reached Odd's horse, turned and walked back alongside.

"Skafti, good man," Odd said. "Are any of Halfdan's men here?"

"No, no," Skafti said. "They've come a few times since last you was here. I think just to look things over. And then they're gone. Usually don't even bother saying a word to me, or any of the others. I...we...don't interfere, as you never made your wishes known on that score."

"Quite right," Odd said. They reached the beaten ground outside the hall and the mounted men dismounted and Skafti called for the stable boys, cursing them for being a bunch of slow and lazy curs.

"We went to Grømstad to speak with Halfdan, me and some of the neighbors," Odd said. "Amundi Thorsteinsson was there."

Skafti nodded. Amundi was the neighbor whose land abutted Thorgrim's property, and Skafti understood the man's high status. If there was any man in Vik to whom Halfdan might listen, it was Amundi.

"And the king? Did he heed what you had to say?" Skafti asked.

"That was not actually clear," Odd said. "Halfdan made sure it wasn't clear. He would give us no real answer, didn't ever hear us out, really. We don't know what he intends. So I think it's time to remove anything of value from here."

"Master?"

"I've brought wagons," Odd said, gesturing behind him as if Skafti had not noticed them. "We're going to take all the food in the storerooms and the smokehouse. All the grain. Barrels of salt fish. The ale and mead. The honey. And the bee hives. I want you to personally fetch the bee hives and bring them over here."

"Master Odd?"

"I'm kidding," Odd said. "We'll leave the bees for later." Now that they were there and taking action rather than just talking about it, Odd felt his mood rise.

"Very well, Master Odd," Skafti said, visibly relieved.

"Not just the food," Odd continued. "All the blacksmith tools, the shipwright tools, the farm tools, any weapons, clothes, blankets, furs, anything of value. The cattle up in the hills can stay there for now. We'll drive them to my land later."

"You'll keep Halfdan from getting whatever you can, is that it?" Skafti asked.

"Exactly," Odd said. "If I could take the buildings as well, I would. You and the rest had better come to my farm, too. It might not be safe."

"Indeed it might not," Skafti said, looking around as if Halfdan's men might be sneaking up at that very moment. "But see here, young master. This won't go unnoticed. I have a feeling Halfdan has men watching all the time. I haven't seen them, but I have a feeling they're there."

"I'm sure you're right," Odd said. Of course Halfdan had men watching Thorgrim's farm. Halfdan had men watching everything he possessed, or wished to possess.

There was an awkward pause as the obvious but unasked question hung between them. *If you know they're watching, and you know it will provoke Halfdan, why do this?*

Odd could not have answered the question if it had been asked. He could not answer it when Signy asked it. He might have told her that he felt in his gut it was the right thing to do, and that his pride would not allow him to just submit to Halfdan's capricious land grab. That would have been true, but it would not have swayed Signy, so he had said nothing.

"Well, we had better get on with it," Odd said. He slapped Skafti on the shoulder. "Go gather up your people and I'll set mine to work as well."

Skafti hurried off, Odd turned to Vermund, and soon the wagons were brought around to the various buildings and gangs of men and women set to the job of emptying the buildings out, stacking their contents on the wagon beds. The wagons that belonged to Thorgrim's farm were rounded up as well, oxen hitched up, and those, too, were loaded with the contents of the farm.

It was a considerable amount of work, but they had many hands, and it was not long before the wagon beds were full, the axels threatening to snap under the load. Skafti and Vermund came to Odd as the last of the wagons came groaning round the back of the hall to join its brethren, each with its patient teams of oxen waiting in the traces.

"That's it," Skafti said. "Half of the back storehouse is still full, but there's not an inch of space left on any of the wagons. If so much as a mouse were to climb aboard they'd collapse, so I guess we'll have to leave it."

"For now," Odd said. "We can return." He looked past the men to the country to the south, where the road disappeared over a hill. Nothing. No movement.

"Let's get the people something to eat, and then we'll be off," he said.

Skafti cocked his head and gave Odd an uncertain look. "Master Odd," he said, "is it wise, really, to waste time with eating now? The wagons are full up and we should be on our way. It'll be dark in a few hours and we won't be making much speed with this load."

"Exactly," Odd said. "There'll be no chance to eat on the road, and the people are very hungry after such a hard day's work. Just a quick meal and we'll be off."

Skafti nodded slowly, clearly dubious but in no position to argue. It was not the dark that concerned him, Odd was sure, but the possibility of Halfdan's men returning. And it was not the people's hunger that was on Odd's mind, but the fear that he would miss the chance to show Halfdan he was no slave to the king.

The meal was as quick as it might be. Bread and butter and dried fish were served out and each person took their share and found a place to sit and eat, with Skafti hurrying them along.

They were just swallowing the last bites when the riders appeared. Off to the south, coming up the dry road, pushing their horses as hard as they could. Odd had posted a man to keep watch in that direction and now he called out his warning.

Odd was sitting on the back of one of the wagons, his legs dangling down, and at the lookout's cry he hopped off and walked over to where he too could see.

"There, Odd," the lookout said unnecessarily, and pointed, which was just as unneeded. The riders were clearly visible, half a mile away.

Odd counted them as best he could. Twelve, it seemed. He thought he could count twelve.

"Those will be Halfdan's men," Odd said. He turned and walked back to where the others were getting to their feet. Some were crossing the ground to where they could also see down the road.

"Those will be Halfdan's men," Odd said again, louder now, so that everyone could hear. He looked over at the freemen who were standing by themselves. They had removed swords and helmets and the other weapons they carried so that they could help load the wagons, but now they had armed themselves once again.

"You men," Odd said, nodding toward them. "Let's mount and be ready to meet our guests properly." The freemen, farmers turned warriors, mounted their horses, and Ari and Vermund, who were similarly armed, did as well.

"Skafti, get the rest of the people back, well away from here," Odd said. "I'm not expecting any trouble, but let's keep them clear, to be safe."

Skafti nodded and began herding the people back beyond the line of wagons. The sound of the riders' horses was audible now in the still air of the afternoon. Odd adjusted the way his sword hung on his belt, put his foot in his stirrup and swung himself up into his saddle.

There were fifteen of them, it turned out. Odd had miscounted. He could see that as the riders came down the sloping road and covered the last hundred yards into the farmyard. And he could see that Einar Sigurdsson was on the lead mount, his green and red cape flogging behind him.

Einar and the rest reined their horses in and walked them toward Odd and the other mounted men. The horses' flanks were covered in sweat and Odd could see Einar was breathing hard and he approached slowly so he could catch his breath. Ten feet away he stopped and when he spoke it was with admirable calm.

"Odd, whatever are you doing here?" he asked. "I thought King Halfdan made it clear that he intended to take this property for taxes."

"King Halfdan made nothing clear," Odd said. "In any event, it appears he has not taken it. The property is still here."

"Don't try to be clever," Einar said. He gestured toward the wagons. "This is all a part of the property. Halfdan's property."

"We haven't really determined that, have we?" Odd said. "Maybe Halfdan should have given me the courtesy of a real interview." His eyes moved from Einar to the men behind. They were part of Halfdan's hirdmen, professional warriors, not the one-time raiders turned farmers who had Odd's back. They wore mail and helmets and carried fine swords. Their horses, though panting for breath, were good-looking animals that had surely never known a plow or a wagon.

"It's not for you to determine what's proper for the king to do," Einar said. "Now, I order you and your men to leave, and leave now. The people who belong to this farm will put these stores and tools and such back where they should be. Until the king determines who shall have it."

"No," Odd said.

The single word seemed to take Einar by surprise. "No?"

"No. It's you who must leave, and leave now. All of you. Go."

Einar's eyebrows came together and he frowned, which made his moustache twitch. His horse shifted under him. For a moment he said nothing. And then the words returned, even as his calm deserted him.

"I've had enough of your arrogance, you trumped up little farmer. You wear a sword when you should be pushing a plow. Now leave us before you get hurt."

Odd felt his face flush. There was nothing feigned in the fury he felt as he pulled Blood-letter free of the scabbard. "Bastard!" he shouted as he kicked his horse in the flanks. The animal bolted forward and Odd slashed at Einar, but in those few seconds Einar had managed to pull his own blade, and he held it up to stop Odd's in mid-stroke.

"You dare..." Einar shouted. Odd twisted his horse around in a tight circle and slashed at him again, and again Einar met Blood-letter with his own blade. Behind him the fifteen mounted warriors drew their swords, but Odd did not hear any of his freemen do likewise. Fifteen against one. That was not a fight he wished to have.

"Run! Run! Go!" Odd shouted, turning his horse once again, sliding his sword back into the scabbard as he did. He kicked the horse's flanks harder this time and whipped the reins as he goaded the animal to a run. He could see glimpses of the faces of his own men, the surprised looks, looks bordering on panic. They, too, whirled their horses around and urged them forward, fast as they could move.

"Go! Go!" Odd shouted again as his horse flew past his own men, pounding off for the road down which they had come, the road that led back to his own farm and relative safety. He heard Einar shouting behind him, calling for his men to follow. He heard the confused sound of men trying to sheath their weapons and force their tired mounts to run once more.

Then Odd was past them all, his horse's speed building as he fled. He looked back over his shoulder. The freemen had responded quickly, charging after him, driving their mounts forward. And behind them, Einar and the hirdmen sorting themselves out, recovering from the surprise. There was already fifty feet between Odd and his men and Halfdan's, and the distance was widening as the men from Fevik raced away.

Odd looked straight ahead. His horse was charging for the road, already heading up the slope that led up from his father's farm. He whipped the reins back and forth once more. *Run, run, you whoreson,* he thought. Einar and the hirdmen were coming now, and Odd had only his short head start and the horse's speed to keep him from being cut down like a dog.

Chapter Fifteen

I sing to thee the fourth.
If foes assail thee ready
on the dangerous road,
their hearts shall fail them

The Poetic Edda

Odd was just cresting the hill that ran up from Thorgrim's farm when he heard hoofbeats close behind and he thought, *May the gods grant those are my men and not Einar's.*

He was standing in the stirrups, leaning forward, and he turned his head half around to see behind. Vermund was there, right on his heels, and he caught a glimpse of the other freemen behind.

Odd straightened a bit and turned his head further until he could see back down the road, until he could see Einar and Halfdan's men. They were coming hard after them, but there was a good hundred and fifty or two hundred feet between the two groups of horsemen, such was the lead that Odd's surprise retreat had opened up.

Good, good... Odd thought, as his horse and the others came up over the high part of the hill. The road stretched off in front, tending off to the left, as familiar to Odd as anything on his own farm.

He had lived there, on his father's farm, until he was a man and married. While his brother, Harald, only seventeen years old, had already seen a good part of the Western world, Odd, in his first nineteen years, had rarely left the farm. And when he did leave, he had only gone as far as his own land in Fevik. It was something he thought about. Often.

The road dipped a bit, then leveled out and ran straight for half a mile before bending around a steep hill where it was lost from sight.

He looked behind once more. Three hundred feet between the last of his men and Einar's. That would do.

Einar's horses were fast, certainly faster than those of Odd and his men. But after the long, hard ride from Halfdan's hall Einar's mounts were nearly blown, whereas Odd's had done little but walk that day. That was what Odd had counted on.

They were closing fast with the hill on the side of the road and Odd pictured what he would see on the other side. He had taken careful note on the trip down, even dismounting to see that part of the road from various angles, and he felt he knew it well.

"Follow me, now!" Odd shouted, as loud as he could, though he had no idea if the others could hear him over the hoofbeats and the wind rushing past. He could barely hear himself. But he leaned a bit and nudged the charging horse off to the right side of the road, where the worn path met the summer grass. He could see the hill off to his left, and the road that had been hidden by the short, steep ridge began to open up. He could see the place in the road where Gnup and the others had been at work, and the beaten grass where the wagons had left the road to avoid it just that morning. He shifted a bit more to the right. His horse left the road and continued running over the short grass, racing along the long, narrow grooves left in the wake of the wagons' wheels.

Odd gritted his teeth and listened for the sound of disaster behind, but he heard nothing above the cacophony of the running horses. Thirty feet, forty, fifty, sixty, and he began to ease his horse back from its flat-out run, bringing the speed down slowly so the animal would not hurt itself. He heard the sound of the wind in his ears die off and the sound of the other horses slowing as well. And beyond them, now out of sight around the steep hill, the sound of Einar and the others racing after them.

"Wait for it," Odd said, "Follow my lead..."

They waited, heaving for breath, horses heaving for breath, but they did not wait long. They had barely stopped when Einar and the others came charging into sight, pounding down the center of the road, coming into view as they rounded the hill. They were close enough that Odd could see the surprise on Einar's face as Einar realized that the men they were pursuing had stopped and turned and were waiting for them. Einar was just starting to rein his horse in when the animal's feet broke through the thin cover that hid the ditch from sight.

It was not deep—only a foot or so, which was as deep as it needed to be—and six feet across, so there was no chance of a running horse simply leaping over it. Gnup and his men had done it just as Odd instructed, and they had done it well.

The ditch ran from one side of the road to the other. Once dug, it had been covered with a screen of wattle fencing set over it like a lid, straw over that, and last, a layer of dirt deep enough to hide everything beneath. It was visible enough on close examination, but Odd did not think that Einar, chasing after them, would see it at all. And he was right.

Einar's horse stumbled as its front feet dropped under it. Odd saw Einar's eyes go wide as he pitched forward, saw his cape come swirling around as the momentum tossed Einar over his horse's head. The rider just behind Einar had no time to react before his horse hit the ditch and Einar's flailing mount at the same moment, and they, too, went down.

In an instant the orderly column of riders was turned into a frantic jumble. The first rank of riders could do no more than shout in surprise as their horses hit both the ditch and the other horses and fell into a trashing pile.

The last of the riders had time to react, as much time as it took their running mounts to cover the thirty feet between them and the ditch, but that was not much time at all. They jerked reins left and right, trying to twist the horses out of the way. Two hit the ditch and went down, and three managed to stop in time, the horses whinnying loud, bucking and twisting and prancing at the sudden stop and the terrifying sight in front of them.

Those men still mounted leapt to the ground and swung the shields off their backs and drew swords. Einar and the men in the ditch fought their way free of the tangle of screaming, kicking horses and as they climbed out they also took up swords and shields. They were fighting men, trained warriors, and they knew what would come next.

"With me! With me!" Odd shouted and he swung his leg over his saddle and dropped to the ground. He pulled the leather strap of his shield over his head, thrust his arm through the loop fastened to the back and gripped the handle of the boss with his left hand. With his right he drew Blood-letter, and for the first time he felt the sword dance in his hand the way that his grandfather had described it to him and Harald, when they were very young boys sitting by the hearth.

"Let them live! Let them live!" Odd shouted next as he hurried over the fifty feet from where their horses stood on the road to where Einar and the others were just pulling themselves from the ditch. He had told his men all this before. They were sending a message to Halfdan, not starting a war.

Odd was at the head of his men and Einar was at the head of his, at least those who had extracted themselves from the trap, and both had sword and shield in hand. Their eyes met and Odd could see the fury and hate in Einar's face and he guessed it matched his own. He lifted Blood-letter as he ran.

Then from behind Einar another of Halfdan's men pulled himself from the ditch. He was taller and broader than Einar, his face streaked with blood, his mouth open. He might have been shouting, but Odd could not tell over the great noise made by the downed horses and riders. The man had a crazed look in his eyes, and he must have been crazed indeed, because he shoved Einar out of his way, took shield and sword in hand and took a step toward Odd. As much as Odd wished to cross swords with Einar, he knew he had to forget him for the moment and deal with this one first.

The big man brought his sword back, backhand over his left shoulder. He was shouting, a meaningless animal roar, as he swung the sword in a circle that nearly slashed Einar's arm on its way around. It was a powerful stroke but an awkward one and Odd let the blow glance off his shield as he lunged straight in with Blood-letter. He saw the sword pierce mail and taste blood once more.

It was not a fatal wound. It might have gone straight through the big man's gut, but he had the presence of mind to twist as the point came at him and he took it in the side: painful but not enough to end the fight.

Odd glanced to his right. Vermund had charged past him and now he was engaged with Einar, sword to sword, but Odd could spare them no more than a glance. Not even that. He turned back in time to see his opponent's sword stabbing at him like a heron hunting minnows.

Odd jerked his shield up just as the sword point bit into his left shoulder. The rim of Odd's shield caught the sword blade and knocked it aside, but the point was still in his flesh and it tore its way free. Odd could feel the spread of blood and he had a barely formed thought that the wound should hurt more than it did, but that thought was washed away by the wave of blind fury that swept over him.

The big man drove forward with his shield, hoping to push Odd off balance, but Odd leapt back and the man's push met only air. He stumbled, having expected resistance and meeting none, and Odd stepped forward as he drew Blood-letter back.

Flat of the blade! Flat of the blade!

A voice in his head told him to hit the man, not slash him, as he had instructed his own warriors to do. But it was only a voice in his head, which he could ignore, so he thrust Blood-letter right through the man's neck.

It was like stabbing a wineskin. The blood came out in a great burst, the man's eyes went wide, his knees buckled and Odd pulled Blood-letter free. In the corner of his eye he had seen another of Einar's men coming up on his left side. He raised his shield and was surprised to find he was barely able to do so. The man's sword came down and Odd felt the jarring impact of the sword slamming down on the flat wood, and a heartbeat later the agonizing pain radiating out from the wound in his shoulder.

"Bastard!" Odd shouted. He twisted as he pushed the sword aside and thrust and felt Blood-letter stab into the other man's shield. He twisted and pulled the blade back and the man stepped forward and hit Odd hard with his shield.

The blow made Odd stagger back and the pain in his shoulder redoubled, but he was moving without thinking now. His muscles remembered the many hours of training in private and sparring with whomever he could find to spar, practicing with sword and shield, ax and spear and bare hands. Odd Pig-binder he might be, but he was still the son of Thorgrim Night Wolf, grandson of Ornolf the Restless and Ulf of the Battle Song. He might spend the bulk of his days at farming, but he would not be found wanting in a fight.

He glanced to his left and down. One of his freemen was on the ground, grimacing as he clutched his bleeding thigh, and others were fighting Einar's men in a line along the edge of the ditch. He saw Ari, who was old but still strong and quick, dodge a sword's thrust, step up and hit his adversary hard on the side of the head, knocking him back into the ditch where the hurt and frantic horses were still thrashing around.

Odd took all that in as if he were looking at some elaborate tapestry, interesting but of no concern to him, because all he could feel was the rage that was driving him now.

The one who had shoved him with his shield thrust his sword at Odd's chest. Odd brought Blood-letter straight up and he felt the blade scrape along the other man's blade. Odd caught the man's sword with Blood-letter's cross guard and pushed the thrust out of line.

The man was off balance, vulnerable, but too close for Odd to drive Blood-letter into him. Instead he cocked his arm and drove the pommel of the sword down on the man's forehead and sent him staggering back. A hard shove would have sent him flying back into the trench, but that thought did not even cross Odd's mind, because no thoughts were forming there at all. He brought Blood-letter back and drove the point right through the man's mail shirt, right through his chest. He jerked it free and turned to take the next man on and did not even bother to watch that one fall.

The fight was nearly over, he could see that. Some of Einar's men had been flung back into the ditch, some were lying on the ground with the freemen standing over them, holding them down at sword-point. Some were lying still. But not Einar. Einar was still fighting.

Vermund had gone after him first, but now Vermund was ten feet back, sword and shield at his feet, right hand clamped over a bleeding gash on his left forearm. Another of the freemen lay at Einar's feet. And yet another, a man named Aslak, was engaged with Einar, blow for blow.

"Einar, you whore's son!" Odd shouted as he advanced. Einar slashed at Aslak and made him jump away and Odd stepped in between them. He had a notion to slam Einar with his shield, but his shoulder was burning and he was not certain he could lift it, let alone drive it forward, so instead he lashed out with his foot and kicked Einar hard in the leg.

It was apparently not what Einar expected. By the time he moved to block the kick it was too late. Odd connected with his Einar's thigh, just above the knee, a solid, powerful blow. Einar staggered and his leg nearly folded. Odd brought his sword up over his head and cut down with the considerable strength of his still-intact right arm.

But Einar was quick, and he managed to get his shield up and take the blow, though it threw him further off balance. He took an uneven step back. Odd stepped forward and swung at him with his shield and the two shields struck and Odd shouted with the agony in his shoulder.

Einar took a feeble stab at Odd and Odd knocked his sword away with his own blade. He drew Blood-letter back. He was looking at the wide gap between Einar's sword and shield, the clear path from Blood-letter's tip to Einar's heart. And he was just starting the thrust when he felt hands on his sword arm, hands on his shoulders, pulling him back.

He looked right. Aslak had his sword arm gripped in two hands. Ari, on his left, had him by the shoulders and someone else did too, but he could not turn far enough to see who it was.

"Sons of bitches!" Odd cried and tried to twist free, but the others held him tight.

"We weren't to kill them!" Ari said, loud, so his voice could pierce the madness. "Your orders, Odd! Let them live!"

Odd gave one last shake of his shoulders and then stopped as Ari's words began to register. It was indeed what he had said. It was his plan. He was certain Halfdan would send men to stop the goods from Thorgrim's farm from being removed. His intention was to fight those men, subdue them, humiliate them. He knew they would be more powerful than his own band of ad hoc warriors, so he devised the trap.

Fight them, subdue them, make they walk back to Halfdan's compound with a message to deliver. But somehow, once the blood was up and the sword was in his hand, Odd had ignored his own directions.

He lowered his sword and shield and his body relaxed and the men holding him let him go. Two of the freemen were flanking Einar. They had taken his sword and shield and now Einar stood straight, trying to project as much fearless dignity as he could.

Odd said nothing as he looked around and let his breathing settle. A few of his men, a few of Einar's lay sprawled out on the ground. Some were still moving, some were not, but most of them seemed to be intact, with Einar's defeated warriors stripped of weapons and held at bay by the freemen. They, at least, had heeded Odd's words not to kill, even if Odd himself had not.

Einar was the first to speak. "This was a very, very stupid thing to do, Odd Thorgrimson," he said. "I don't know what you hoped to get out of this. Maybe the wrath of Halfdan the Black. If so, you'll have it."

Odd dropped his shield to the ground and found he could move his left arm better than he had hoped. He stepped toward Einar, and Einar, to his credit, did not react in any way. Odd grabbed a corner of Einar's cloak and used it to wipe Blood-letter clean before sliding the blade back into the scabbard.

"I went to Halfdan, humbly, to speak with him, but he would not hear me. So I did this to make certain he would listen," Odd said. "I am a loyal subject of my king. I pay him his due. I'll fight for him if he asks. But I am not a slave, and I am not a fool. None of us are. You tell Halfdan that we expect to be treated like the freemen we are, and then we'll treat him like the king he is."

Odd turned and walked away before Einar could reply, and Vermund and Ari began to issue orders. Einar's men were made to coax the horses that could still walk from the ditch and kill those that could not. They bound their fellow warriors' wounds and used the fit horses to drag the dead ones well clear of the road. They were given shovels and made to fill the ditch back up.

When all that was done they were set free. Three of Einar's men had been killed, two by Odd's hand, and they were loaded onto horses. Four were too wounded to walk and they, too, were given mounts. Einar took one of the remaining horses for himself.

They had been stripped of weapons and mail, and now a pile of swords and shields and helmets and mail shirts lay by the side of the road. Odd had been considering the pile, and now he came to a decision.

"Give them their swords back," he said. The others looked at him, uncomprehending for a moment, then they retrieved the weapons and handed them back to their owners. Halfdan's men would suffer enough recrimination and humiliation without having to return without their swords.

Einar took his sword and held it across the saddle. He looked down at Odd. "This will not help you," he said. "This will not calm Halfdan's wrath in the least."

"It was not meant to," Odd said. "You just tell Halfdan the things I said to you."

Einar held Odd's eyes for a moment more, and then without a word he nudged his horse to a walk, heading back the way he had come, and the others followed behind. Odd and his men remained silent as well as they watched them go.

It had played out just as Odd had envisioned, save for his own rage, which he had not seen coming. The message was sent. But still Odd heard Einar's words, over and over in his head.

This was a very, very stupid thing to do. He was starting to fear that Einar was right.

Chapter Sixteen

Long he sat, until he slept;
and he awoke of joy bereft:
on his hands he felt heavy constraints,
and round his feet fetters clasped.

The Poetic Edda

Thorgrim Night Wolf walked along the top of the longphort's wall, staring out into the dark. He stopped and listened. He walked some more. He spoke softly with the sentries he encountered along the way. He walked on, stepping carefully over the uneven surface of the makeshift barricade.

There was an army out there. For days now, five or six days, they had remained camped in a semicircle around the longphort. They had come, as Thorgrim guessed they would, hoping to attack him and his men while they took their ease at the poorly defended monastery. It might have been an easy victory for them. Instead, it was the Northmen who had a good laugh when the English launched their attack only to find there was no one there.

How they must curse us fin gall, Thorgrim thought, and then he corrected himself. *No, not fin gall. The Irish call us that, not the English.* He wondered what the English called them.

I can well imagine, he thought.

He moved on further west along the wall. Five days, and save for that one minor raid, the enemy had shown no inclination to do anything. Of course, that raid might well have turned to something bigger if it had not been found out by Failend and the others.

Failend...

She, more than the enemy out in the dark or any other matter really, had been chiefly on his mind.

Did you miss me? Or just miss humping me?

The question had taken him aback. It was like an arrow shooting out of the dark. He had no notion it was coming, no sense of the potential danger, until it struck.

Did you miss me? Did he? He had never given her much thought, in truth. They had taken her prisoner...how long ago? Three lifetimes? She and Louis. And she had gone from prisoner to warrior to lover and Thorgrim had just gone along with each change because each was certainly to his benefit and came at no cost at all.

He had been a widower for five years now. He had been with other women since, but only in a carnal way. He had not loved any of them. Since the loss of his wife he had given little thought to his feelings about any woman, and likewise had given little thought for any woman's feelings toward him. He had men and ships to command and keep whole, he had raiding and fighting to consider, he had his son Harald always on his mind. He was trying to return to his home in East Agder and had been for three years now. Women and their concerns were not generally a part of going a'viking, and they had not been thus far.

But Failend, apparently, did not feel the same.

Thorgrim came to one of the ladders that stood at various intervals along the wall. He took one last look out toward the enemy's camp. If the sun had been up he would have been able to see their tents in a line and the wagons and horses further back. He would have seen smoke from cook fires and men moving about. But it was dark, well past midnight, and all he could see were a few points of light that indicated where torches or small fires burned. Every once in a while he could hear the clatter of something dropped or the sharp note of someone calling out, but those minor punctuations of sound only served to emphasize how very quiet it was.

He climbed down the ladder. He had not yet been to bed. Or, more correctly, he had gone to his bed and once again found it empty, but this time he did not feel like climbing under the covers alone. He realized that he missed Failend's presence, and that realization had come as a surprise, because he had never thought of it before, one way or another.

Now he walked slowly around the camp, checking that weapons were placed in such a way that they could be easily taken up, that the men were not insensible with drink, that there was no chance of fire reaching the ships pulled up on the beach.

He looked out over the water toward where *Blood Hawk* and her cargo of future slaves lay at anchor. He had hoped to ransom them, not sell them, but the English had sent an army rather than the one hundred pounds of silver promised, and so slaves they would be. Thorgrim had put off leaving in hopes that the ransom might still come through, but he had abandoned that hope. On the morrow they would begin loading the ships for sea.

He walked on and he pretended to himself that his path was aimless, a random night inspection of the longphort and its defenses, but he knew it was not true. And soon he found himself walking past heaps of sleeping men, great lumps of wool and fur, hair and weapons just visible in the low light of the dying bonfire and the sliver of moon overhead. The crew of *Sea Hammer*, his own men.

Louis de Roumois was sleeping a little ways from the rest, under a light-colored wool blanket, which made it stand out in the dull light. Thorgrim wondered if the Northmen insisted that Louis sleep set apart, or if Louis, a haughty Frank and a Christian to boot, wished to keep his distance from the savage Northmen. The latter, Thorgrim suspected.

He paused for a moment and looked down at Louis's prone form hidden by the blanket. He looked away and took a step and he heard Louis's whispered voice say, "She's not here."

"What?" Thorgrim asked, also speaking soft, not wishing to disturb the others, not wishing them to know he was there. He saw Louis toss the blanket aside and sit up.

"If you look for Failend, she's not here."

Thorgrim felt his face flush and it made him angry. "I'm not looking for anyone. I'm seeing to the defenses. It's what I do."

"Mmm," Louis said, noncommittally. He kicked the blankets off the rest of the way and stood, stretching his arms. "I can't sleep either," he said. "Damned English. I wish they'd do something. Leave, attack, I don't care. Just stop sitting on their fat asses looking at us."

"Yes," Thorgrim said. It occurred to him that Louis had become very fluent in the Norse language. His accent was odd, but the words came to him nearly as well as they did to one raised to that tongue.

The result of living and sailing and fighting beside heathens for as long as he had.

"I'm done waiting," Thorgrim said.

"Will we attack them?" Louis asked. It was just a question, with no hint of whether Louis would approve of such a thing or be frightened by it. But Thorgrim had fought side by side with Louis often enough now that he did not think the man would fear battle. His feelings for the Frank were fluid, more so than his feelings for almost any other man he had known. Thorgrim tended to see men as black or white, good or bad. But with Louis, Thorgrim wanted sometimes to embrace him and sometimes to run a sword through his gut.

"No reason to attack," Thorgrim said. "We've taken everything to be had in this place. We'd just be killing and dying to no end. No, we'll load the ships and be off to sea. Sell the prisoners in Frisia. Where you can find a ship to Frankia and we'll be free of you."

"And I of you, and I'll thank the Lord for it," Louis said, but there was no malice in his voice. They stood for a moment, looking out into the dark, then Louis said, "You came looking for Failend?"

Thorgrim opened his mouth to deny it, then closed his mouth, thought about what he would say. There was no point in lying, just as there was no point in attacking the English.

"Yes. She's not been in my bed for many nights now."

"Nor mine," Louis said. "Not since we joined with you fine fellows."

"I didn't think she was in your bed," Thorgrim said. "But you're quick to deny it. Are you afraid you'll make me angry?"

Louis made a grunt of a laugh. "No, I'm not afraid," he said. "I just won't have my honor questioned. Or hers."

Thorgrim was not sure how to take that. "You think I'm questioning Failend's honor?"

"No," Louis said. "As far as I can see you've treated her honorably. If there were mistakes made, it was Failend who made them. It's her responsibility."

"What mistakes has she made?" Thorgrim asked. This was not the sort of conversation he was accustomed to having, and he wondered if he would speak this way to one of his fellow Northmen. He did not think so. But somehow with the foreigner, Louis, it was different.

As to Failend's mistakes, Thorgrim figured he knew the answer, or at least what Louis would say. Failend had embraced the ways of the Northmen, from their language to their dress to their desire for battle. A Frank, and Christian, like Louis would certainly see that as a grave mistake indeed.

"Her mistake was falling in love with you," Louis said.

That was not what Thorgrim had expected. He frowned and stared out toward the water. "You think she's in love with me?"

"Of course she is!" Louis said. "By God, you're a blockhead. You don't see it?"

Thorgrim was caught between his surprise and his desire to reprimand Louis for calling him a blockhead, reprimand him in a very physical way, but the surprise won out.

"No, I guess I didn't see it..." Thorgrim said and even as the words came out he could hear how stupid they were. He had been so long out of the company of women that he could hardly recall how they thought and felt. And even before that he had been nearly twenty years married to Hallbera and he had never had to wonder about her love or loyalty. With Failend he had just floated along, never giving a thought to her feelings about him. But now she seemed to him foreign and odd, a mysterious being with whom he could not communicate, just as she had when she had first been taken prisoner.

"So what is she thinking now?" Thorgrim asked, and he could see Louis shrug.

"It's not for me to say."

"Say it anyway," Thorgrim growled.

"Well, I think at first she could tolerate loving you, even if you did not love her in return. Now? I think she's afraid she's wasting her time. That nothing will come of this. It hasn't been easy for her, you know, leaving Ireland. It's all she knew. She tries to believe she's taken on a new life with you heathens, but she hasn't, not as much as she thinks."

"She's told you all this?" Thorgrim asked. He was not comfortable with the thought of Failend sharing such intimacies with Louis and not with him, and that discomfort surprised him.

"She's told me some," Louis said. "Mostly I can just see it in her. What she does, what she says. How she reacts. You can hear these things if you listen. And you're not a blockhead of a heathen."

Again Thorgrim was caught between his surprise and the notion that he should not let Louis's words go by without a response, and this time he opted for a response. But even as his hand was lifting to grab Louis's throat he heard footsteps running, a soft, padding sound on the trampled ground.

"Father! Father, there you are!" Harald appeared in the dull light of the dying flames.

Thorgrim lowered his hand. "Harald?"

Harald stopped a few feet away and Thorgrim could see he was sweating and breathing hard. "I've been all over looking for you," he said. "You weren't asleep and you weren't by the fire..."

"Yes, " Thorgrim said, "I know where I wasn't. Why are you looking for me?"

"The sentries, on the wall," Harald said. "They tell me they heard something, something going on out there." He pointed vaguely toward the wall, in the direction of the village beyond.

"Come," Thorgrim said. He knew it was pointless to try to get anything more from Harald, so he hurried toward the nearest ladder with Harald and Louis following.

He scrambled up the ladder and back on top of the wall. The sentry there took a step toward them and Thorgrim saw that it was Hall, who was crew on his own ship, *Sea Hammer*.

"There," Hall said, pointing out into the dark, and he had sense enough to say nothing more. Thorgrim cocked his head and strained to hear. At first there was nothing, and then, as his ears grew used to the quiet, he began to hear it. There was a soft, muffled undercurrent of noise, like the combination of men moving about and speaking softly and every once in a while the quiet clink of two hard things hitting one another. It was not much, but certainly more noise than they were accustomed to hearing from the enemy's camp so late at night.

Thorgrim turned to Hall. "How long has this been going on?"

"Not long," Hall said. "I first heard something halfway through this watch. I listened for a bit before I thought it was worth calling you."

Thorgrim nodded. He turned to Harald and Louis. "Well?"

"Sounds like a lot of men, doing something," Harald offered.

Thorgrim hesitated, just a beat, and then said, "Well, Louis, what do you think?"

"I agree with Harald," he said. "That's not the sound of a camp asleep. Whatever they're doing they're trying to be quiet about it. But an army can only be so quiet."

Thorgrim turned to Hall. "Go find Starri and have him join me here. Harald, go spread the word for the men to wake and get under arms. Find Jorund and Godi. Have them help. Tell them to be quiet, no noise, no talking. If those bastards over there are going to attack, it's better they think we're not prepared."

The two men nodded and raced off as fast as they could along the precarious wall. Louis and Thorgrim stood side by side looking off into the dark.

"There are no fires," Louis said.

"What?"

"Every night we look out, we see some fires in the English camp. Cook fires or lanterns or something. Some light. Now, nothing."

"Hmm," Thorgrim said. Louis was right. No fires at all. There had been earlier, he recalled, and generally they would see a few fires burning all night. But now the fires were gone. Which you would expect from an army trying to hide its movements, because even low fires cast light.

Then they heard the thud of something heavy hitting the ground followed by a horse's whinny.

"I better go get my own weapons," Louis said and he disappeared down the ladder. Thorgrim continued to look into the darkness that hid the open ground and the enemy on the other side. He heard the creak of the ladder behind him. He turned, expecting to see Starri, but instead he saw Failend stepping awkwardly onto the wall, her arms full of something.

"I brought you this," Failend said, and Thorgrim, now listening to her words with care, thought he heard a touch of uncertainty, a touch of contrition. But perhaps it was something else.

He looked down at her arms. She held his mail shirt, as well as Iron-tooth and his belt and seax. "I can go fetch your shield, if you like," she said. "I couldn't carry it with the rest."

"No, thank you," Thorgrim said. He took the mail shirt and slipped it over his head. Failend was already wearing her mail. She had her seax, the weapon he had given her more than a year before, hanging from her belt, and her bow and arrows over her shoulder.

Next Thorgrim took up his sword belt and buckled it around his waist. "I'll get my shield if I think I need it," he said. He settled Irontooth in place and then there was a silence between them, and not one that was particularly comfortable.

"Thank you, Failend, for bringing my sword and such. I'm not sure what's going on out there..." Thorgrim began because he could think of no other place to begin. He was searching for the next thing to say when the scene was happily interrupted by Starri Deathless flying up the ladder and out onto the wall, his two battle axes thrust into his belt.

"Are they attacking, Night Wolf?" he asked in a loud whisper. His hand reached for the arrowhead that he wore on a cord around his neck and he rubbed it between thumb and forefinger as if that charm might bring the enemy forward.

"No, not attacking," Thorgrim said. "Not yet. I need your ears." He pointed out into the dark. "Listen, tell me what you hear."

Starri cocked his head and leaned forward a bit. It was harder to hear now, with several hundred Northmen rousting themselves from sleep and making ready for battle, and no matter how hard they tried they could not be terribly quiet. But Starri seemed completely absorbed in listening and seemed to not even notice the muted din behind him.

At last he nodded and said, "There's a lot of men moving around. They're talking low. I can hear horses and mail jingling. And footsteps."

"What are they doing?" Failend asked.

"Moving around," Starri said. "Other than that, I can't tell."

Thorgrim nodded. For Starri that was a surprisingly rational conclusion. "Keep listening," Thorgrim said. "Failend, come with me." He climbed down the ladder and Failend followed and Thorgrim wondered why he had told Failend to come. He had no task in mind for her. But somehow it did not seem right to abandon her on the wall. He felt like he had abandoned her enough already.

By the remains of the fire, Thorgrim saw Jorund gathering the men who had formerly sailed under his command and who still looked to him as their leader. He could see Godi a little ways off, looming over the others. He turned to Failend.

"Would you go find Harald and Asmund, Halldor, all the captains and tell them to come join us here?"

Failend nodded, turned and raced off. Thorgrim pushed his way through the men to Jorund's side.

"Thorgrim! What's going on?" Jorund asked, his voice in a whisper.

"Not sure," Thorgrim said. "Some activity with the English army. An attack, maybe. We had better be ready."

Jorund nodded, and in a moment Failend returned with the other men in tow. Thorgrim waved them over and they formed a circle.

"I was just telling Jorund," Thorgrim said. "The English are... doing something. We can't tell what. But they might be making ready to attack. They're being quiet about it, to be certain. So here's what we'll do. Each of you take command of your ship's crews. Keep a few men on top of the wall but most hidden behind. There we'll have a man with an unlit torch every ten feet or so, and a flame, hidden from sight, ready to light the torches. If we see them coming, we wait until they're nearly on the wall, then on my command the torches get lit and thrown over the wall. That'll light them up and we'll kill them as they come over. Understand?"

Heads nodded all around the circle.

"Any questions?" There were none, so Thorgrim sent the men off to get the crews of their ships arrayed behind the wall. He and Failend and Harald climbed back up on top of the wall where Starri was still listening. He looked as if he had not moved even the tiniest bit.

"If those drunken buffoons behind me would make less of a racket I could hear more," Starri said without being asked. "But things have changed over there, I can hear that much. The noise has picked up. Whatever they're up to, they're busier at it now."

"Good," Thorgrim said. He hoped they would not take too long, whatever they were doing. He knew that the waiting was always the worst. It was the thing that wore men's spirits down.

He turned and looked anxiously behind him. Much as he wanted the English to attack soon, he did not want them to attack too soon. If they came out of the night just then, with the Northmen still sorting themselves out, they could be up and over the wall before any defense was in place.

For some time they remained like that, on top of the wall, Thorgrim swiveling between facing the English and looking behind to mark the progress of his own men. It was not long before he could see his people gathered behind the wall below him, and he guessed that the others were in place as well, standing ready with torches and with weapons and a rising blood-lust.

Very well, Thorgrim thought, *Very well, you English bastards, you can come any time now...*

But the English did not come. Still Thorgrim and the others listened, still they looked out into the dark, and still they could detect no sign of an attack. The stars wheeled overhead, the moon sunk toward the horizon, and no battle was joined. Behind him, and along the wall, Thorgrim could sense the sharp edge of the men's readiness start to dull as the night rolled by, quiet and uneventful.

His legs grew weary and he wanted very much to sit, but he knew he could not, though some of the men on the ground behind him were now planted on their hind-ends. He found his eyes starting to shut and he paced back and forth a bit.

In the east, the sky began to grow pale.

"Oh, come on, you bastards, come on!" Starri shouted out toward the English camp. In his frustration he did not even bother to speak softly. Thorgrim looked behind him and down. Half the men waiting behind the wall were asleep.

The sky grew lighter, and more and more of the village revealed itself. And then, finally, there was gray light enough for them to see clear to the village, and what they saw was not what they had expected.

The evening before there had been tents and sentries, banners and horses and hundreds of men moving about the camp, and wagons further back in the town, but now there was nothing. Just a village, nothing more, with no sign that an army had ever been there at all.

Thorgrim smiled. "You remember, Harald, how we laughed to see the English attack the monastery? After we had abandoned it for this longphort?"

"Yes, Father," Harald said.

"Well, it seems they have played a trick of their own."

Chapter Seventeen

[I]t was determined that tribute should be paid to the Danish men because of the great terror they were causing along the coast.

Anglo-Saxon Chronicle

Oswin, shire reeve of Dorset, spent some long moments wondering if there was some crucial point he had forgotten. The most obvious question: was he in the right place? He thought back to his last time there, when he had brought Cynewise's request to Nothwulf that he attend her.

He shook his head in disgust. It was ridiculous to even think such a thing. Of course he was in the right place. He was not that addled in the brain, not yet.

That being the case, was there some arrangement he had failed to remember, or one of which he had not been told? Was Nothwulf to move his army to some other strategic location, some other place from where he was to launch his assault on the Northmen? Some plan that Cynewise had not told him of?

"Of course not," Oswin said out loud, but soft enough that the men behind him—a guard of half a dozen riders, one bearing Cynewise's banner—could not hear. Cynewise would not have told Nothwulf to move his army. She wanted him here. That was the idea. She would give him the honor of leading the attack, Nothwulf and her father. And hopefully she would have the honor of seeing their armies decimated by the Northmen while hers remained intact.

No, she would not have told Nothwulf to move.

And therein lay the mystery, because Nothwulf and his army were most certainly not there. Oswin had come to meet with Nothwulf, to organize the movements of his men and Cynewise's, but now there was no one there to meet.

Oswin nudged his horse forward, riding at a slow walk. The signs of the army that had once encamped there were all over the ground. There were blackened fire pits and beaten paths between where the tents had once stood. There were beef bones strewn around and a trampled place, dotted with piles of horse manure, where the horses had been tethered. He could even see the wide footprint of the pavilion that had been Nothwulf's home in the field.

Oswin slid down from his horse and walked over to the nearest fire pit, crouched down and held his hand over the charred wood in the center. He felt nothing. He lowered his palm until it was no more than an inch above the wood, and then he could feel the heat emanating from the spent fuel. The fire had been dead for a while, but not too great a while. That morning, perhaps. The tracks in the soft ground were sharp and clearly defined. Recently made.

He stood and looked across the open ground toward the Northmen's makeshift fort. The heathens were still there, he was sure. It was the first thing he had looked for, even before reaching Nothwulf's camp. The Northmen were the keystone here, the excuse on which everything relied, the ostensible purpose for the presence of the armies, which were really there to wipe one another off the map. If the Northmen escaped, new excuses would have to be found.

Worse still, if the Northmen left they would take the two hundred prime men-at-arms they held as prisoners and sell them as slaves. Which would be too bad for the men-at-arms, but worse for Cynewise, who would lose their service.

But they had not left. Oswin could see their masts jutting up beyond the fortifications. He could see flagstaffs set into the walls with banners waving in the breeze. He could see smoke rising from the other side of the barricades. They were still there, which meant they still needed to be driven off in some way, so that Cynewise could appear to be the savior of Dorset and then get on with the real business of eliminating Nothwulf.

Oswin heard the sound of a rider approaching, coming at a gallop, and he looked in the direction of the sound. It was Eadwold, one of Cynewise's hearth-guard, one of the men who had come with Oswin so they might make a proper show riding into camp, mail gleaming, banners flying.

He reined his horse to a stop five feet from Oswin.

"Well?" Oswin said.

"They marched off to the east, to a ford on the River Avon," Eadwold said, getting the words out between labored breaths. "I saw their tracks go over the ford, but I didn't follow farther."

Oswin nodded. Christchurch Priory sat on a point of land at the juncture of the Rivers Avon and Stour, both of which ran inland and vaguely north. Anyone going east or west would have to cross one of those rivers. So Nothwulf had marched his men off to the east, a direction pretty much opposite of the way to his hall in Blandford or his house in Sherborne.

Where the hell are you going, you bastard? Oswin wondered. Eadwold had made the right decision, not going after Nothwulf's column. It would have taken too long to catch up with them, left Oswin waiting for word longer than he could afford to wait. But still it left unanswered the one, crucial question. Where was Nothwulf going? What was he up to?

Which meant he would not be able to give Cynewise answers to those questions. And that would not go well.

Oswin sighed. None of this was going well, and it was not likely to get better. He climbed back on his horse and turned to the guards milling around behind him. "Doesn't seem as there's anything here to amuse us," he said. "Let's head back to camp."

It was near noon when they arrived. Oswin found Cynewise outside her tent, waiting as her groom saddled her horse. She was dressed in her mail shirt, her cape over her shoulders, her helmet in her hand and her sword hanging from her belt. Oswin noticed that the sword was shorter than a typical such weapon. A man's sword would have made her look ridiculous, but the one she wore was well proportioned to her size. He wondered if she had ordered the blade made specifically for her.

He pushed that thought aside. He knew he was just trying to not think of the unpleasantness soon to come. He slid down from his horse and bowed to Cynewise.

"Lady Cynewise, we've come from Nothwulf's camp, and...ah...in truth, he's not there. Him or his army."

Cynewise's lips went down and her eyebrows came together, but she said nothing. She would have so many questions that demanded answers that Oswin guessed they were fighting to get out of her mouth, like a panicked crowd trying to flee a burning building through a single door.

"Not there..." she said at last. "Where are they?"

"I don't know, ma'am. They marched off to the east, but they were gone when I got there, and I didn't think I had time to pursue them. Rather I chose to come back and report this news. To you."

Cynewise nodded slowly. "The Northmen?"

"Still there, ma'am. Haven't moved, apparently." Oswin could actually see the moment in Cynewise's face when her surprise gave way to the rage he had anticipated. Her frown deepened and with a sudden movement she whirled around and flung her helmet on the ground with an impressive display of force.

"Son of a bitch! Son of a bitch!" she shouted. "You incompetent bastard, how could you have let this happen?"

I didn't let it happen, you stupid tart, Oswin thought, but he kept his mouth shut, his expression neutral.

"That whore's son is up to something, and you had better find out what it is!" Cynewise spit. She reminded him of an angry cat, a small bundle of fury, more dangerous than one might expect.

"I've already sent..." Oswin began, but before he could go further he was distracted by the sight of Cynewise's father, Ceorle, approaching. He, too, was wearing mail and a fine silk cape, sword on his belt. He was flanked by two of his warriors who had their arms around his waist, while Ceorle's arms were around their shoulders. They seemed to be pretty much carrying the old man.

"What is it now?" Ceorle barked, his voice hoarse, though there was still strength in it. "What God-almighty mess have you made now, daughter?"

Cynewise pressed her lips tight together and turned toward her father. "Father, surely you're not well enough to be up and dressed for battle."

"Bah!" Ceorle said. "If I stay abed the Northmen will overrun this shire. Kill us all!" He looked Cynewise up and down. "What, dressed in your men-at-arms costume again?" he asked. "You look like you're part of some damned troupe of players."

Cynewise turned to Oswin. Oswin could see that her father's words, his simple presence, had doubled her fury, which she was about to unleash on someone, and that someone was not Ceorle.

"We're done with the damned Northmen," she said. "May they all be damned to Hell, we'll give them the danegeld and be done with them. It's Nothwulf we need to finish, not them. You get back on your horse and return to the priory and get rid of them as you should have done days ago."

Oswin bowed. "Ma'am," he said, eager to take his leave, but Ceorle stopped him.

"Northmen? Danegeld?" he sputtered. "Are we not done with that? Why are we still concerned about the Northmen? I thought you were buying them off. What have you done with the silver I loaned you?"

"You loaned me nothing, Father," Cynewise said. "You gave me one hundred pounds of silver to buy the freedom of your men-at-arms."

"Made prisoner by your incompetence! And I want those men back, do you hear? By God, I see I must step in here, to make certain you don't make a hash of things." Ceorle's words were strong, but his voice was growing noticeably weaker with the strain that his anger was putting on his constitution.

Cynewise looked past her father, snapped her fingers and shouted, "Horsa!" and her servant hurried over.

"My father is ill. Fetch a chair for him to sit," she snapped and Horsa nodded and hurried off. A moment later he returned with a chair in his hands and Bishop Ealhstan hurrying behind, a worried look on his face. Horsa set the chair down and Ceorle was eased down into it. Ealhstan, chins jiggling, opened his mouth to speak, but before he did he looked from Ceorle to Cynewise and back. He shut his mouth again.

Cynewise watched this all play out, and when Ceorle was seated she led Oswin out of earshot.

"What of Aelfwyn?" she asked. "Did you find that little whore?"

"No, ma'am. I had my men search the camp and the roads in all directions, and we saw no sign of her."

Cynewise held Oswin's eyes with her own, which were pale blue and reminded Oswin of pure, untainted ice. Again he marveled that so tiny a creature could in turn become so very menacing. He had taken her for a weak vessel when she first arrived at Sherborne. But the two of them had come to an understanding after her husband's murder, before actually, and it had been Cynewise who had initiated it. They had worked together. She had listened to him, agreed with much that he had to offer. She had been reasonable, to the extent that a person in her situation could be.

But no more. She had changed since then. Considerably. And Oswin found himself less and less sanguine about that change.

"This is the second time you've managed to fail in a single morning, Oswin," Cynewise said at last. "You've been a help to me until now, but now I find myself paying the price of your failures, and I won't pay it long. Get the danegeld to the Northmen, get my father's men-at-arms back, with their weapons and armor, do you understand? If we're to crush Nothwulf we need those men. So you get them back, you find Nothwulf, and then I'll see to destroying him. Clear?"

"Yes, ma'am," Oswin said. How any of this had been the result of failure on his part he did not know, but he did not think it wise to argue. He bowed again, turned, and hurried off toward Cynewise's tent where the chest of silver, the danegeld, was stored. As he stepped past the seated Ceorle, Bishop Ealhstan hovering around him, he heard Cynewise call out, "Horsa! My father is weak and needs refreshment. Fetch some of the broth, and be quick about it."

Chapter Eighteen

At the gates of death I wake thee!
if thou rememberest,
that thou thy son badest
to thy grave-mound to come.

The Poetic Edda

It was tiring, standing watch through the night, keyed up for battle, and so by dawn Thorgrim's men were very tired. All save Starri Deathless, who sat sullenly against the longphort's makeshift wall, hacking thoughtlessly at a stray chunk of wood with one of his battle axes and muttering about what cowards the English were.

Cowards or not, the English were gone. That much was clear. If it was some sort of trick, Thorgrim could not imagine what it might be. Nor did he care. He was more than ready to abandon that place, and he and his men would leave much wealthier than they were when they arrived.

He set a watch and ordered the rest of his men to sleep. He would give them until noon when the tide was high, and then they would be off, rowing their longships through the channels between sandbanks and out the narrow entrance through which they had come.

Thorgrim felt that he himself should remain awake, but he also felt that he would fall face-first to the ground if he tried. On weary legs he ambled off to his own bed, a pile of furs on the afterdeck of his ship which was pulled up on the beach, the place he felt most comfortable and at home. He took off his sword and mail and lay down, letting the luxury of reclining sweep over him. He was starting to drift off when he heard the soft sound of someone stepping aboard. He opened one eye and in early morning light he saw Failend as she came aft. He opened the other eye and turned his head as she stood next to the pile of furs on which he lay.

"Do you mind if I lie down, too?" she asked. Thorgrim shook his head. Failend nodded. She took off her sword belt and mail shirt and deposited them on the deck. Thorgrim wondered if she would take off any more—not because he felt like having a romp under the furs, which he did not—but because he genuinely did not know what was going on in her mind. She remained fully clothed, however, and lay down beside him, tunic and leggings intact. Not touching him, just next to him. She was facing him but her eyes were closed and she looked relaxed, like she was already near sleep.

I should say something, Thorgrim thought. But he had no idea of what to say. What's more, Failend looked to be asleep already, and he did not wish to disturb her. Nor did he wish to have the conversation that he knew they would have if he said anything at all. So he closed his eyes again and soon he, too, was asleep.

He woke when he hoped to wake, when the sun was near its high point above. He stood and stretched and Failend opened her eyes and looked up at him.

"Not much of a rest," she said.

"No," Thorgrim agreed. "But it's all we get. Too much to do. The tide's high and it's time we were gone from here."

Failend nodded. For a moment they looked at one another and Thorgrim again had the unhappy thought that he really should say something. But then Failend jumped to her feet and said, "Very well. Let's be at it."

Men were already stirring by the time Thorgrim made his way to the great black pile of charred wood where the bonfire had once burned. He called in a loud voice, loud enough to wake those still sleeping, for Harald and Godi and the other captains.

"It's time to get underway," Thorgrim said when all were assembled. "We've been in this accursed place long enough, and I'm done with it and with the English here. Your ships are fit to sail, right?"

The ships had been made ready to leave days before, and so everything was pretty much loaded aboard and stashed where it needed to be stashed. They had only to load the weapons and the last of the food and they were ready to get underway.

"*Blood Hawk* still needs loading and fitting out," Godi said. *Blood Hawk* had been used as a floating prison and Godi, to whom Thorgrim had given command of the ship, was not pleased. He let his tone reflect that displeasure, to the extent he thought he could do so without provoking Thorgrim. "Other than that she's ready for sea. As far as I know."

"Very well," Thorgrim said. "Let us haul your ship back to the beach. It looks like we're taking those miserable English with us. We'll distribute them around the ships. If they don't know how to row, I'm sure they can learn quick enough."

The others nodded. But as it turned out, it would not be that simple.

Thorgrim had never thought about his prisoners jumping off *Blood Hawk* and swimming to freedom because he guessed no more than a handful of them would be able to do so. He was more concerned that they would cut or cast off the cable that held them anchored to the bottom and drift away to the far shore. To avoid that possibility the cable had been affixed to the ship in such a way that it was nearly impossible to reach, and even if it was reached the prisoners had no blades with which they might cut the thick walrus hide rope. And apparently they had not even tried.

But they had been at work sabotaging the ship. When it was hauled up to the beach Thorgrim and the others found a foot or more of water in the bilge, deep enough that some of the deck boards were floating free. *Blood Hawk* was sinking.

"Look here," Harald called from a place on the starboard side near the mast. He was on hands and knees peering down into the bilge. "It looks like they found some means to half pry up one of the planks. Managed to crack it, they pried so hard. Started it leaking bad."

Godi was standing at Thorgrim's side up by the bow and he voiced the very thought that was on Thorgrim's mind. "What by all the gods did they think they would achieve doing that?"

"No idea," said Gudrid, standing beside him. "It wouldn't have done them much good for the ship to sink under them. If they wanted to drown themselves, it'd be easier to just jump overboard."

Thorgrim frowned. He could not imagine what the English were thinking and he did not care at all. His only thought was to get the ship repaired and then get to sea.

They tilted the *Blood Hawk* over on her port side so they could get at the damaged plank from underneath and the men most skilled at the shipwright's trade were set to work. Others were set to gathering the food, ale, sea chests, oars and other gear that would be loaded aboard *Blood Hawk* once she was made seaworthy. Still others were put to the task of dividing up the English prisoners and driving them off to the ships that would take them to the slave markets in Frisia.

Thorgrim looked at the water's edge. There was a line of dark earth where the retreating tide had left its mark. If the repairs to *Blood Hawk* were not done fast then the tide would be out by the time they were ready to leave. He remembered the tricky channels and the sandbars hidden just below the surface that he had seen when they first came to that place. The Englishman, Sweartling, who had piloted them in was long gone. Thorgrim did not want to leave when the tide was out.

He walked over to where Godi and the others were working on the sprung plank. He peered over the shoulders of the crouching men. He said nothing. They were doing just what he would have done, and doing it as quickly as he would have done, but he did not know if it would be quick enough.

"Lord Thorgrim?"

Thorgrim turned. One of Jorund's men was there, a man named Bjorn.

"Lord, Harald sent me to say there's a man outside the wall. An Englishman, lord, with a dozen men-at-arms with him. Harald says it's the same who come to see us at the monastery, when we first took that place."

Thorgrim nodded and frowned. *English?* he thought. *I thought those whore's sons marched off.*

"Very well, tell Harald I'll be there directly," Thorgrim said.

A few minutes later Thorgrim climbed the ladder on that section of wall where he saw Harald standing. He stepped up beside his son and looked down at the ground below. There were thirteen horses and riders at the edge of the line of branches and debris and other obstacles that the Northmen had thrown out in front of the walls. The riders were well armed and wearing mail. One held a staff and banner which Thorgrim recognized, just as he recognized the man at the head of the small contingent.

"This is the one who came to see us before," Thorgrim said. "Isn't it? The one who offered us danegeld?"

"I think so," Harald said. "I wonder what he wants now."

"I guess we had better ask him. You're able to translate his words?"

"Yes, I think so," Harald said, sounding more confident than the words would suggest, then he called out in English to the man below.

The man on the horse swung himself down to the ground and began to pick his way through the obstacles toward to the wall. "I told him to come closer," Harald said and Thorgrim nodded.

The man stopped at the base of the wall and spoke. Harald turned to Thorgrim. "He says he has brought the danegeld," Harald said.

"Danegeld?" Thorgrim said. "Why would they bring danegeld? I thought they all marched away this morning." He did not actually intend for Harald to relay this to the Englishman, but in his enthusiasm Harald did anyway. The man below replied.

"He says the other army was not his men, not friends of his. He says the prisoners we have, they are his men and he wants them back. That's why he brought the danegeld. That, and so we would leave."

"I see," Thorgrim said. "It seems we've wandered into some sort of civil war. Don't say that to this bastard," he added and Harald nodded.

"Anyway, we want no part of this," Thorgrim continued. "But we do want their silver. Tell him to fetch it and we'll put a ladder down for him. Tell him he won't be harmed."

Thorgrim expected to see fear, or at least reluctance on the part of the Englishman, being asked into the wolf's den, but he showed no sign of either, and Thorgrim was impressed. Instead, the Englishman returned to the others and gave an order and four of his men climbed down from their horses and retrieved sacks that had been tied to their saddles. Then the five of them walked back toward the wall as two of Thorgrim's men lowered a ladder down.

The one in charge climbed halfway up the ladder, moving awkwardly as he carried with him the sack, which was apparently quite heavy. Thorgrim was pleased to see that. He expected there was at least twenty-five pounds of silver in the sack, and in the other three as well.

The gods are doing us a great kindness, Thorgrim thought. *Or at least the English are.* If *Blood Hawk* had not been damaged then they would have sailed away before the danegeld arrived. The English would have lost the prisoners but would have rid themselves of the Northmen for free.

Harald reached down and took the bag from the man, and the other three were passed up as well. As the fourth bag came up, the man on the ladder did so too, bringing the bag with him. He pulled the top open so that Thorgrim could see the dull gleam of the silver inside, then set the bag down with the others. He stood and looked Thorgrim in the eye.

Yes, I remember you... Thorgrim thought. And he did. He remembered the calm and expressionless face, the assuredness, bordering on arrogance. The Englishman spoke, and even though he knew by now that Harald was the one who understood, he held Thorgrim's eyes.

"He says the silver is there. One hundred pounds, as agreed," Harald said. "He says he would like his men-at-arms back."

"And the priests?" Thorgrim asked. "I thought he was paying for the priests as well."

Harald translated. "Yes, he says the priests as well," Harald said, though it was clear that the men of God were an afterthought.

"Tell him he'll get his men when we sail, which should be soon," Thorgrim said. He waited as the words passed back and forth.

"He says he'll expect the men to be healthy and assembled with their armor and weapons," Harald said and Thorgrim laughed. He could not help himself.

"Ask him, does he really expect me to give the men back fully armed and set them right here where they can join in an attack against us?"

Harald translated the words and Thorgrim saw the flicker of doubt cross the Englishman's face. "He says you made a promise to return the men," Harald said.

"Yes, I did," said Thorgrim. "The men. Not the armor or weapons. Nor did I say where I would leave them. Tell him we'll sail..." He glanced out at the tide line. Already lower than he would like, and the men were still working on *Blood Hawk*.

"Tell him we'll sail tomorrow. We'll take his men and we'll leave them on the south side of the big harbor east of here. We'll leave them with the clothes they wear, nothing more. And if this fellow continues to annoy me we won't leave them with even that much."

Harald translated and once again Thorgrim saw the concern on the man's face. He hid it well, it was just a shadow of worry, but Thorgrim could see it. And he knew that if the Englishman showed that much concern on his face, then he was holding quite a bit more in his heart.

Thorgrim folded his arms. He waited for a reply, for a counter-offer. But he guessed the Englishman was no fool and would understand that he had nothing with which to bargain. There was no argument that he could make, so his reply consisted of just two words.

"He says, 'tomorrow, then,'" Harald translated.

Chapter Nineteen

That which I will ask thee,
and I desire to know:
who here holds sway,
and has power over these lands
and costly halls?

The Poetic Edda

The meeting was much like the previous one, and much different. The same ten men seated in the same hall, Odd's long hall, and seated at the same table. Even seated at the same places. The food and ale were the same, the same servants scurrying back and forth.

But it was not the same mood. Before, it had been serious, but friendly as well. Neighborly. Now the anger was palpable. It hung like the smoke from the hearth fire. It hung in the silence, the stunned silence, as the men tried to understand what Odd had said, and all it implied.

"You had this all thought out beforehand?" Ulfkel Ospaksson said, the first to speak. "You knew Halfdan would send men, and you had your men dig this...hidden ditch? A trap?"

"Yes, I did," Odd said. He could hear in his voice a mixture of guilt and defiance, anger and contrition. Those were the same emotions that had been roiling his thoughts since he had pulled off that ambush, and since he had realized that this meeting could not be avoided. He had no choice but to inform the hauldar of what he had done. He could not let them find out in some other way and think that he was trying to hide from his actions. He could not let them think he was avoiding their wrath.

"This was in no way a good idea," Amundi Thorsteinsson began, and the others fell silent. As the oldest and wealthiest among them,

166

Amundi commanded their respect. "I understand why you did it, Odd. And maybe it would have had the effect you hoped for. Sent a message to Halfdan. If you had not shed blood. That was your mistake. That's something Halfdan cannot ignore."

Odd pressed his lips together and he looked at Amundi and considered his reply. He had anticipated this point, struggled to form an answer long before his actions would be questioned. But he had come up with nothing. Nothing but the truth, which he did not particularly wish to speak.

"It was a fight," Odd said at last. "A hard fight. Halfdan's men were in no mood to yield, and they did not. Sometimes blood is spilled in battle."

He looked from man to man. They all knew it was the truth, but not one of them was mollified by that explanation.

Ulfkel Ospaksson took a drink, shook his head, took another drink. "This won't go well, I reckon. Halfdan won't just let this go. He can't."

Vifil spoke next. "He ignored us once. When we went to speak to him. What a great show of friendship he made, but it was just his way of putting us off so he might continue to do as he wished. But he won't ignore this."

"He's a clever one. He'll try to divide us," Amundi said.

"Divide us?" Ulfkel said with sudden vehemence. "Divide us? He has no need to divide us. Odd did that himself, dividing us. Did a fine job of it, killing Halfdan's men without a thought of telling us that he planned to do it."

"Maybe Odd was wrong in that," Vifil broke in, "but still we cannot..."

Odd held up his hands. "Please!" he said, loudly, and the others stopped talking.

"Please, my friends, let's not have this argument, at least not until I've said what I need to say. And then I hope there'll be no more call for argument."

No one objected. They sat quiet, regarding him with looks of frustration, anger, curiosity, any of the many things they were feeling at the moment.

"When I asked you all to come here the first time, I only wanted to tell you what Halfdan was trying to do. Trying to grab up my father's farm. Honestly, that was all I wished, just to tell you that, and to hear what you had to say about it. The idea of us going to Halfdan, voicing our concerns, that just came into my head. That was not my intention."

"But it was not a bad thought," Amundi said. "Something had to be done, and even Halfdan couldn't find fault in talking."

"Yes, talking's fine," Ulfkel said. "But now Odd is talking with his sword, and Halfdan can certainly can find fault with that."

"I don't regret the talking," Odd said. "I agree it had to be done. Words must always be tried first, before blood is shed. But I'm sorry now I made you all part of this. It was my fight."

"You said that Halfdan wouldn't stop at taking Thorgrim's farm," said Ragi Oleifsson. "That he was greedier than that. I thought that was true when you said it, and I think it's doubly true now." As the least influential of the lot, Ragi's lands were the most vulnerable to Halfdan's efforts to expand his holdings.

"We don't know…" Ulfkel started, but again Odd held up his hands.

"Please!" He waited until it was quiet once more. "Come morning, I will ride to Grømstad. I'll give myself up to Halfdan, explain how the ambush and the bloodletting were my responsibility alone—not any of yours—and I'll take what punishment he sees fit to give."

Once again there was silence at the long table, brought on by yet another surprise from Odd. No one had any illusions as to where Odd's actions would lead. At best Odd could hope to lose Thorgrim's farm and his own as well. Somewhat worse, he would lose his life. Worst of all, he would die an ignoble death after seeing his family taken and sold as slaves.

If there was something even more terrible than that, Odd did not care to think about it.

He waited to hear if there were any objections. In some dark corner of his mind he hoped there might be. He hoped the others might talk him out of it. And he chastised himself for a coward for even thinking such a thing, no matter how half-formed the thought might be.

The irony, of course, was that even if one of the others tried to talk him out of this decision, Odd would never allow himself to be swayed. It was pointless to hope that any of them might try. And indeed, no one did. They all knew it was the right thing to do. The only thing.

"Very well, then it's decided," Odd said in a brighter tone. "And I'm glad we don't have to think on that anymore, because I intend to get very drunk tonight."

He clapped his hands and more ale and mead and wine appeared. There was food on the table already, but soon that was replaced by what would more rightly be called a feast, with servants carrying out platters piled with meat and vegetables and bread and butter and cheese. Business done, Odd's family joined them, as did Vermund Jurundsson and Ari and the captains of the guards that some of the other landholders had brought with them.

Despite his words, Odd did not get drunk. That was not what a good host did, and Odd knew well the advice given by the gods:

> Less good than they say for the sons of men
> is the drinking oft of ale:
> for the more they drink, the less can they think
> and keep a watch o'er their wits.

Odd's guests, however, did not adhere so closely to that advice and they downed ale and mead in varying quantities and grew more boisterous and loud. But that was expected of guests in a hall and no one, least of all Odd, took any offense.

The evening turned into night and the singing and laughing and storytelling went on, cresting like a wave and then losing force, until one by one the guests began to drift off, to collapse where they had staked out a place to sleep on the long platforms that lined either side of the hall.

Odd remained awake, sitting on one of the few chairs the hall boasted, feet thrust out near the hearth fire. He was as sober as he could be, and, indeed, he doubted that any amount of drink could quell the turmoil in his mind.

Of the guests, Amundi Thorsteinsson was the only one still awake. He sat near Odd, facing the fire as well, while the servants cleared away the last of the extraordinary mess spread over the table, benches and floor. Amundi seemed as sober as Odd, and Odd guessed he was. Amundi was not a young man and he was not the sort to give himself over to drink.

"It's a brave thing you're doing, going to Halfdan, admitting what you did," Amundi said, breaking the long silence.

"Hmm," Odd said. "It's not so brave when you have no choice."

"You have a choice. You could choose to save your life."

"I could save my life and lose my honor. As I said, it's not really a choice."

They were silent again for some time, and then Amundi said, "When you thought of this idea, of setting a trap for Einar and his men, you did not intend to wound anyone, or kill them, did you?"

"No," Odd said. "Even I could see that it would be foolish to start the killing. That sort of thing does not end well."

"And I'll wager that your men did as you said. They did not draw blood."

Odd looked up from the fire, over at Amundi. "I don't think they did. No. I know they didn't. They obeyed my command."

Amundi nodded. "So it was you, wasn't it? In the heat of it, you drew blood. Cut Einar's men down. You weren't even thinking. You just let the madness take you."

Odd did not reply. He tried to see what Amundi meant by saying such a thing. Was there accusation in his voice? Criticism? Odd could not hear it.

"That's right," Odd said at last. "It was me. I'm ashamed to admit it. And ashamed I didn't admit it to the others, earlier. But it was me. I went mad."

Amundi looked up and met Odd's eyes. "I thought so. You are so very much like your father," he said.

Those words came as a great surprise to Odd. It was not something that he had ever considered, not once. "My brother, Harald, he's the one who's like our father," Odd said. "Not me."

Amundi shook his head.

"Harald is the one who went a'viking," Odd continued his argument. "Like our father did. And you. I stayed home and tended my farm."

"Did you want to stay home?" Amundi asked. "Or did your father talk you into it? Talk you into staying with your family?"

Odd said nothing. Amundi knew the truth. Odd thought of the harsh words he and his father had exchanged, the anger and disappointment and resentment he had felt. Resentment toward Thorgrim and Harald and Signy. To be left behind in such a way. It was like a bitter taste in his mouth. A taste he had forgotten, but now was tasting again.

170

"I've known Thorgrim and Hallbera since we were all young," Amundi continued. "And I've known you children all your lives. Your brother, Harald, he is very much the mix of your parents. He has a lot of Hallbera in him. And Ornolf the Restless. But you, you are very much the image of Thorgrim Ulfsson."

Odd frowned, but he did not know how to reply, so he looked back into the flames.

"That's how I knew what happened when you fought with Einar," Amundi said. "As you said, your father and I went a'viking when we were about your age. I've seen how battle could bring the madness on him. Sweep him away."

"I...I don't have...the wolf dreams," Odd said.

"Good," Amundi said. "I don't think your father looked on them as a gift. But Thorgrim is much more than just the wolf dreams. As are you."

They were quiet again for a long time. Then Odd said, "I wish I was like my father, but I'm not. My father built great wealth. Fame. A place of honor. And now I'm going to lose it all, everything he built and I built, because of my own stupidity."

"And yet...I don't think there's anything you've done that your father would not have done."

"No...save for ruining everything, and bringing harm to the people he was sworn to protect."

"Your father risked everything, many times," Amundi said. "But the gods favored him, because he was worthy of their favor. Now you, too, have chosen to take the bold path, to shun the coward's way. And I think the gods will look with favor on you as well."

Odd hoped very much that the gods would look on him with favor, because he knew that his wife, Signy, most certainly would not. It was one of the reasons that he had spent so long sitting by the fire: he dreaded the thought of going to his sleeping closet and confronting her.

She had only learned of his decision to go to Halfdan when he had told the others. She had raised no objections in front of their important company, but in private she would voice her concerns, and most vehemently.

It was the duty of any man to face his enemies without hesitation. This was a truth that Odd had been taught from the time he was old enough to learn. And he would never do anything less. But facing one's wife was a different matter. That was something he was very hesitant to do. Nor was he afraid to admit as much, and he doubted that any man would be.

Still, he could not put it off forever. So when Amundi retired at last, Odd did the same. He stripped down, crawled in bed with Signy, hoping that she was asleep. But even before he was settled she rolled over and faced him, and he could see her eyes gleaming in the dark.

Their discussion went much as he thought it would—sharp words spoken in hushed tones. Signy, incredulous that Odd would trade away his life and his family and his farm for his honor. That he would not plead with Halfdan for mercy, and offer anything short of his life and his children's lives to be forgiven his transgression. That he could be so utterly selfish.

And Odd, trying to make her see that doing such a thing would leave him unmanned, a pathetic and pitiable creature. A man not worthy of being called a man, and certainly not worthy of being her husband. Stripped of everything that made him who he was: master, husband, father. Warrior. He would be none of those things and so he would be nothing.

He assured her he would not risk her life or the lives of his children. He would send them someplace safe until this was over, one way or another. She was not mollified. By the time they were done talking, with dawn in the offing, nothing was resolved, but there was nothing left to say.

Odd was up not long after that, having not really slept much at all. He pulled on his clothes and washed his face, then stepped out into the cool of the early morning. Some of the servants and farmhands were already moving about, preparing for the day. Signy, too, would normally have been up at that hour, but she was not, and Odd guessed that she was shunning him and his company.

Though Odd was not eager to make the ride to Halfdan the Black's hall in Grømstad, and suffer whatever would come next, he was eager to get it over with. Still, he could not leave without seeing his guests off, and his guests seemed none too eager to rise, being each in varying states of pain from the debauchery of the night before. The morning was well along when they finally began to stumble from their beds and call for water and ale and for their horses and their men to be made ready. They each had long rides ahead of them as they returned to their respective farms, and most were not much looking forward to it.

The boys from the stable brought Odd's horse around, saddled, bit and bridle in place. Odd stepped out of the long hall, adjusting the hang of Blood-letter, working his shoulders to settle the mail shirt. Behind him, silent, came Signy and the children.

Amundi, sober and clear-headed, was already up and getting his men mounted for the ride back. He greeted Odd with a quick hug and pat on the back. He glanced over Odd's shoulder and then looked back at him.

"Signy is not so happy about this," he said in a soft voice.

"No," Odd said.

Amundi nodded. "A woman's chief concern is very different than a man's," he said. "A woman thinks of her children, her family. A man thinks of his honor. Even if he says he's thinking of his family, he's really thinking of his honor."

Odd smiled. "You're right," he said. "And now I must say goodbye to Signy and my children and they'll be mad at me, and if I never see them again that will be the last image I have of them." Those words had been meant mostly as a joke, but as he spoke them, Odd felt a sense of despair sweep over him.

He took a breath, turned toward Signy. Their eyes met and Odd heard someone yell from somewhere beyond the hall and he and Signy both looked off in that direction. There were three riders coming from the north, and even from a few hundred yards away Odd could see their mounts were tired. They were riding three abreast, and the man on the middle horse seemed barely able to hold himself upright. As they drew closer Odd could see his head was bound with a bandage and the light-colored fabric of his tunic was stained dark in great patches of what Odd took to be blood.

All eyes were on the riders now. They drew up to the long hall and Odd saw that the one in the middle was a man named Frodi who lived in the shielding, the small house in the hills, with the others who tended the herds there in the summer months. His clothes were torn, his face battered, the bandage on his head was soaked with blood on either side of his head. His ears had been cut off, Odd was sure of it. The men on either side were also herdsmen in Odd's employ, but they seemed unharmed.

"Frodi!" Odd shouted. "What...who did this?" Even as he spoke Odd could see Frodi was in no condition to give an answer.

The man to Frodi's left, whose name was Valgerd, answered instead. "He doesn't know. We don't know. We were out looking for a stray, and when we came back, they were dead. All dead, or carried off. Except Frodi. And he...well, you can see for yourself."

Frodi gasped and shook his head, sucked in air and spoke. "Don't know who. They drove off the herds. Men on horseback. Don't know who."

But Odd did know, or he had a very good idea. He felt the fury building in him. And he felt relief as well. Because he would not be riding to Halfdan's fortress after all.

Chapter Twenty

[S]pear spilled
rivers of blood,
and it ran from
wound red on sword.

The Poetic Edda

Whatever evil had happened at the shielding, it would have to be met with warriors under arms, but Odd had no men under arms.

Odd had meant to ride alone into the storm of Halfdan's fury. He would not make any of his people join him in that. It was entirely possible that Halfdan would punish not just Odd but anyone in his company for the crime of loyalty to the king's enemy.

As a result, all of the men who would normally take up arms, such as Ari and Vermund, were scattered around at their various tasks. They were certainly not ready to ride into a fight, but when the alarm was raised and the call to turn out with weapons and shields came echoing around the yard and the fields, turn out they did, and quickly.

Odd watched with forced patience as the stable boys brought the horses out into the yard and his men mounted. Amundi stepped up beside him. "I have some of my men with me, of course, and we'll ride with you," he said. "The others, they'll all come as well."

Odd nodded. He had hoped the others would choose to ride with him, but he would not put them on the spot by asking. Still, he knew that no man would want to be seen riding off in one direction when there was a fight to be had in the other.

The sun had not reached its noontime height by the time they rode out, a formidable line of warriors, the wealthy landowners leading their own columns of armed men. They would be more than enough to deal with the raiders, if the raiders could be found, unless

Halfdan had sent a genuine army. And no one would send an army to kill unarmed herdsmen and drive off cattle.

Odd led the way, riding at a fast trot while the others fell in just behind him, until there was nothing to be heard save for the pounding of the hooves and the breathing of the mounts. He had made this trip to the shieling many, many times. The distance was about fifteen miles and he knew just how hard he could push his horse along the uphill path to arrive as quickly as possible without exhausting the animal. Even then the afternoon would be well on by the time they arrived.

They were a few miles away when they saw the smoke, a weak column rising up from the last of an unseen fire somewhere up ahead. But Odd did not need to see the fire to know what was burning. He felt his stomach twist up.

He held up his hand and slowed his horse to a walk and heard the other horses behind him slow as well. Amundi came up on his left side and Ulfkel Ospaksson on his right and they rode in silence, side by side. At that pace they would have been able to hear anything there was to hear, such as the raiding party still at work, but there was nothing.

"This fire," Ulfkel said, nodding ahead. "This is your shieling?"

"Yes," Odd said. "And the sheep, they're usually kept in the fields here." There were no sheep to be seen now.

"Bastard," Ulfkel said.

Odd looked over at the man and he was surprised by what he saw. Aging and corpulent, but there was an alertness, even eagerness, in Ulfkel's manner now. He sat more upright in the saddle, eyes fixed ahead, the reins held with purpose. It was as if the raider in him, long asleep, was waking up.

They rode on, and finally they could see the blackened heap of charred wood where the small house had once stood, the last gasps of smoke roiling up from it like the remnants of a funeral pyre. Odd felt his stomach turn further. It was not because of the house, the house meant nothing. But strewn around he could see bodies, motionless on the summer grass.

The riders approached, slow and hesitant. The first of the dead men was splayed out on the grass, his bearded face pale and yellow, eyes open. There was a gash in the back of his tunic, torn flesh visible through the rent, gleaming in a wash of fresh blood. A foot from his hand was the splitting ax he had been using as a weapon. Odd was glad to see he had died fighting. The gods would look with favor on that. It was the smallest of consolations, but it was something.

They continued along the wide path toward the burned-out wreckage of the shielding, passing more dead men scattered about. They all had weapons of some sort: axes or clubs or staffs. Spears. One man even had a sword. But no shields, no helmets, nothing to indicate they had had warning enough to do any more than grab what was on hand.

Odd stopped his horse and climbed down from the saddle. He looked around. He said nothing. He did not know what to say. The others climbed down as well and stretched sore limbs. It was very quiet. Odd was accustomed to the sounds of the sheep, and the cattle if they were nearby, the shouts of the herdsmen, but now there was nothing.

"Livestock's gone?" Amundi asked.

Odd nodded. "The sheep were kept nearby here. They're gone. Cattle were usually in a field about a mile up from here, but I have no doubt they're gone as well." But Odd was no more worried about the livestock than he was the house. It was not the livestock that was making his stomach churn to the point where he feared he might vomit.

For a long moment they all stood in silence and Odd studied the scene around him with growing anger and disgust. When at last he trusted himself to speak he said, "There's no women."

"Women?" Amundi said.

"Most of these men," Odd said, making a sweeping gesture to indicate the dead lying scattered around the grounds, "had their wives with them. There were half a dozen women. More."

Amundi said nothing, and neither did anyone else. They all understood the implications. Halfdan's men had carried the women off. Halfdan might keep them as slaves or sell them as slaves or give them to his men.

Ulfkel spoke next. "We had better bury these ones," he said. "Then we'll figure what we'll do about this. It was a brave thing you intended, Odd, going to Halfdan. But I don't know if it will answer now. Not after this."

Odd nodded, a noncommittal gesture. None of the others seconded Ulfkel's words. Enthusiasm for joining in Odd's feud with the king was by no means universal.

"Ulfkel's right, we'd best bury these men," Odd said. He wanted to change the subject before each man was forced to declare where he stood. Odd felt sick enough at having dragged these men as far into his fight as he had already. At having done things that had resulted in the slaughter of his shepherds, the enslavement of their women. He did not intend to allow anyone to involve himself further.

Vermund and Ari, well familiar with the shieling, headed off to the small outbuilding where the picks and shovels would be found. Odd's other men, and his neighbors' men as well, spread out and began to carry the dead to a place near the burned-out building where they might be interred. Odd watched them work, but his mind was far afield.

Ragi Oleifsson broke the silence. "This was a cowardly thing," he said. "Kill shepherds. Steal cattle and women. This sort of thing is not worthy of a king, that's for certain."

"We're all assuming Halfdan did this," Vifil said. "But we don't know that. Like Ragi said, this isn't the kind of war you'd expect from a king."

Odd frowned. He had been thinking along those same lines. It was no surprise that Halfdan would have his revenge for what Odd had done, that he would strike out, hurt Odd as badly as he could. But this was hardly it. Stealing cattle? Killing hired men and thralls? It was a terrible thing, but far from the worst that Halfdan might do.

"I think Halfdan's sending a warning here," Ulfkel said. "He doesn't want a war. Doesn't want to do something so bad that we'll all turn on him. So he did this."

Heads were nodding, but not Odd's. That did not seem right to him either. Halfdan was many things, but measured was not one of them. He might not want a war, but he certainly would not stand for any threat to his rule.

"I think Ulfkel's right," Ragi said. "That's why the men who did this, they left the one alive, just cut his ears off. They wanted word to get to Odd."

There was nodding again, but still this did not ring true to Odd. There was no need to leave Frodi alive to bring word of the raid. The slaughter. Odd would have found out about it soon enough. There were always men going between the farm and the shielding, and that was true of any shielding in that country. Halfdan would have known that. But still he made certain that Odd knew of the attack immediately after it had happened. Why?

Because Halfdan knew that Odd would lead his men up to the shielding in hope of catching the raiders. That he would leave his farm unprotected.

He looked up, the motion so fast and sharp that everyone turned to him. "This is a distraction," he said and he could not keep the urgency, the mounting panic, from his voice. "Halfdan wanted us gone from my farm."

That was met with silence. They all understood why that might be.

"If Halfdan wants his revenge on you," Ragi said, "why would he want you gone from the farm? Wouldn't he want to catch you there? Isn't it you he wants?"

Amundi spoke before Odd could answer. "Halfdan knew we were all gathered at Odd's. Of course he has men watching. And Ulfkel is right about him not wanting a war. He does not want to attack Odd's farm when we all are there."

"But that doesn't answer why he would trick us to leave," Ragi replied. "Why not wait until Odd's alone?"

Ulfkel spoke next. "Because Halfdan does not want Odd dead. If he attacks when Odd's there, then Odd dies fighting. A hero's death, sword in hand. Too easy. Halfdan wants Odd to suffer more than that."

There was no denying the logic in that, and no other explanation that seemed more probable. They had been led away. And that meant that something was happening at Odd's farm that was far worse than the destruction that had been visited on the shielding. And in that instant of realization, the solemn and necessary work of burying the dead was forgotten in a rush of anxiety and panic.

"Everyone! Mount up! Mount up!" Odd shouted, again trying and failing to keep the fear from his voice. "Leave off what you're doing, just leave it! We have to get back to the farm."

Everyone stopped, motionless, like that moment when something thrown up in the air pauses before falling back to earth. Then they all broke at once, dropping the corpses they were carrying, tossing shovels and picks aside. None of them had any idea what this new emergency was about, but they were disciplined enough to not ask, just act.

Odd was back on his horse, had put the spurs to its flanks and was pounding off, back the way they had come, before most of the other men were even mounted. The animal under him was running hard, but it had just completed a fast run, fifteen miles uphill, and it was worn. Odd considered kicking it with the spurs again but he held off.

The others were right behind him now, galloping on, downhill at least, but still their mounts were tired and quickly growing more tired still. Odd grit his teeth, breathed deep, trying to keep the terror down. They covered a mile, then two, then in the corner of his eye Odd saw Amundi pulling up beside him.

"We have to slow down!" Amundi shouted. "We'll blow the horses, and then they'll be of no use at all!"

Odd wanted to argue. He wanted to refuse. But he knew Amundi was right. He did not reply because he did not trust his voice, but he eased the reins and brought his horse to a walk. He heard the others do the same. He heard sighs of relief.

It was the longest and most agonizing ride of Odd's life. They alternated between trotting and galloping and walking, and when they were walking it was everything Odd could do to keep himself from dropping to the ground and running, flat out.

Odd came up over the last hill between him and the farm and he could see it all below him: men and horses swirling around the grounds, one of the storehouses on fire, his people on foot running in all directions. He heard little pinpricks of sound, shouting and screaming and metal clashing on metal.

He kicked his horse to a full-on gallop, pushing the beast as hard as it could go. He did not care now if the horse dropped dead under him. Now he was close enough to run the rest of the way.

Not too late... Odd thought, and with that came a huge wave of relief. No matter what had happened, or what would happen, he would be in the middle of it, blooded sword in hand, and not standing around miles away, dumb, unaware and impotent.

The horse was heaving for breath, its flanks a sheen of sweat, but Odd had no thought for the animal.

Why are they still here and fighting? he wondered. He would have thought that Halfdan's men would strike fast and be gone, long before he and the others could return from the shielding. And yet they were still there.

And then he understood what had happened. These men attacking the farm were the same men who had sacked the shielding. They had doubled back, hoping Odd and the others would not guess at the deception. Halfdan could not risk sending enough warriors to attack both farm and shielding. It would have left his own homestead too ill-defended.

At least they are as tired as we are, Odd thought. He was close enough now to see the mail shirts and helmets worn by the men on horseback. He could see swords raised and men on foot with spears—his men—fighting back as best they could. He could see women huddled by the blacksmith's hut, guards with spears standing over them. Men putting the torch to the outbuildings and others trying to stop them and men crawling wounded on the ground and men lying still.

"At them! At them!" Odd shouted, loud enough for the men behind him to hear, and loud enough to be heard by Halfdan's raiders as well. Odd saw heads snap up, look over. He saw men waving their arms and shouting. Giving orders, he had to imagine. He saw all of them, all the warriors below, break off with what they were doing and rush to form some sort of defense as this new threat swept down on them.

Odd looked over his shoulder. His horsemen were riding abreast, a very impressive line of mounted warriors charging into the fight. He looked forward again. Halfdan's men must have thought it was impressive as well. They were scrambling to form a shield wall, running with panicked urgency. Fifty yards ahead the wall started to coalesce, bright colored shields overlapping, spears reaching out from behind.

"Right at them! Right at them! Behind me!" Odd shouted. He had Blood-letter in his hand now, holding it up over his head as he charged the shield wall. The horse was heaving for breath and its footing was becoming unsure. Odd thought of reining to a stop, sliding down to the ground, grabbing his shield and racing for the line.

No...sons of whores... he thought. He would slam right into the shield wall with his horse, barrel right through the line, make a hole through which the men behind him could ride.

Twenty yards away and Odd could see faces behind the shields, bearded faces and clean-shaved faces and helmets of iron and leather. He thought he could see Einar, but he was not certain.

Then the horse under him stumbled. Odd pulled his eyes from the shield wall and looked down. The horse's eyes were wide, its mouth open, and it was starting to stagger as it ran. Odd looked up. Fifteen yards. The horse took a wild step and Odd felt it going down.

"Aaaahh!" Odd shouted in surprise as he felt the horse fold up under him, front feet first. He saw the ground coming up at him and he felt himself pitching forward. He grabbed at the edge of the saddle as the horse's chest hit the dirt, its hind legs still driving. The horse was screaming and twisting as it went down and Odd had an image of its body coming down on his leg and crushing it.

Man and beast were still traveling with the speed and momentum of twelve hundred pounds of horse running at full gallop as Odd kicked his foot free of the stirrup. The horse was nearly all the way over on its side when he pushed himself off and jumped clear.

Odd had just enough time to grab onto two half-formed thoughts. The first was to hit the ground with his shoulder. The second was to not let go of Blood-letter. He had no sense for where he would come to a stop, or what shape he would be in when he did, but he knew that if he was still alive he would need his sword.

He hit the ground with his shoulder, mostly. He came down on his left side, shoulder and back. He felt himself tumbling, turning end over end. He had images of men and shields and legs flashing by. He saw the horse just a few feet behind him, sliding and thrashing. He felt his hand tighten on Blood-letter's grip until he could not distinguish between hand and sword.

Then he came to a stop. He lay still, but only for an instant. Every part of him was shouting with deadly urgency for him to stand. He pushed himself to his knees and felt the pain rip through his arm and leg, but they seemed to still work so he ignored it. He felt blood, warm and liquid, on his left shoulder and he knew the wound from the last fight, halfway healed, had opened up again. He turned and held his sword up and he got to his feet.

The shield wall was no more. What had a moment before been a semi-organized defense was now chaos. The horse was still on its side, screaming and thrashing, its hooves lashing out. Men were piled on men where they had fallen, and now were clawing at one another to get clear, to regain their feet. Those further from the horse were colliding with the men racing to get away.

Einar was shouting, waving his sword, trying to regain control. His green cape was half torn from his neck and he jerked it free and flung it aside. He grabbed one of his men as he ran past, turned him around and shoved him toward the fight.

A discarded shield was lying at Odd's feet and he snatched it up and thrust his arm through the leather strap, surprised to find the agony in his shoulder gone. Through the gap made by the flailing horse he could see Amundi and Ulfkel and the others. They had stopped their charge and were climbing down from their horses and advancing, shields on arms, weapons held high. Odd had stood up ready to fight, but in the confusion no one had even noticed he was there.

All eyes were turned toward Amundi and the advancing line, but Odd did not let that situation last for very long. With a shout he shoved the man in front of him with his shield, made him stagger into the next man in line, and when the man turned in surprise Odd hacked down on him with Blood-letter.

The man, eyes wide, lifted his shield in time to stop Odd's blade with the iron rim. He pushed the shield up farther and Odd knew what would come next: the slash of a blade from under. Odd stepped back, dropped his own shield, felt it connect with the seax the man was thrusting at him low. He lifted the borrowed shield and pushed the man and he staggered back. He was off balance, just for an instant, but that instant was long enough for Blood-letter's tip to find his throat.

The man spun away, choking, blood whipping around. Odd could see Einar fifteen feet away, still shouting and waving his arms and trying to get his men in some kind of order. Odd took a half dozen steps towards him—his desire to run a sword through the man had not diminished—but another fighting man came between them, wild-eyed, bearded, ax-wielding.

Odd raised his shield up and the ax came down. The blade hit the wooden face of the shield and shattered the thin boards. Odd could see the bulk of the ax head where it had broken through, but now the weapon was lodged in the shield and the man could not pull it free. Odd jerked the shield to the left and yanked the handle of the ax from the man's hand, stabbing out with Blood-letter as he did. But the man could see what was coming and he twisted and jumped back and Blood-letter sailed right past.

Before Odd could even draw the blade back, Amundi and Ulfkel, Ragi and Vifil and the rest, and all their men, collided with Einar's line. Odd didn't see it, focused as he was on the fight in front of him, but he felt it, felt the weight of the attack as the two small armies crashed into one another. There was no cohesion, no plan or thought, just two bands of angry, brutal men coming together like beasts disputing territory, shields up, weapons flailing, voices shouting.

Einar was still very much on Odd's mind. Einar, Halfdan's man, the one who made manifest Halfdan's wishes. Who had led the slaughter against the shielding, and come back to do worse to Halfdan's home and family.

The ax warrior, whose ax was still buried in Odd's shield, was drawing a seax now, the fight not out of him yet. Odd thrust again and the man raised a mail-clad arm to push the blade aside, but Odd twisted his hand, just a bit, and the sword's sharp edge ran over the man's exposed wrist, drawing blood and a shriek of agony as it did.

Odd hit him with his shield, pushing him out of the way, and gained another step toward Einar, who still had not seen him coming. The fight was wild and chaotic, but Odd had the sense that it was not going well for Einar's men. No surprise. The men on Odd's side were more numerous, and they were driven by fury at this wonton attack. Einar's men had been taken by surprise in the middle of doing a job in which they had no real stake. In such circumstances, fury usually won out, and it seemed to be doing so again.

The space was open between Odd and Einar, five steps and Odd would be there and he could run Blood-letter through the man, when another of Einar's men stepped into the gap. He had shield and spear and there was blood on both, and blood on his face, and for some reason the sight of the blood sparked Odd's anger. It was like blowing on a hot coal, seeing it ignite where before it had only smoldered.

Odd shouted as the fury came over him. The man thrust his spear tip at Odd's chest. Odd caught the tip with the remnants of his shield and pushed it aside, but the man at the far end of the shaft was too far for Odd's sword to reach. He hacked down with his sword and the blade caught the wooden spear shaft and split it like kindling, leaving the man with a broken butt end in hand and a surprised look on his face.

Two quick steps and Odd was within striking distance, but the spearman seemed to have lost interest in the fight. He threw the broken end at Odd and stepped quickly back. Odd saw his eyes and mouth open wide with surprise and the tip of a sword rip through him, back to front, as the men who had come with Odd pressed against the other side of Einar's line.

But he did not care about any of that. He wanted only to get to Einar. He turned again and hacked at the next man who stood between them. Einar looked up and their eyes met and Odd saw the fury sweep across Einar's face to match his own. And then the whole thing collapsed.

Einar's men were done. Taken by surprise, outnumbered, exhausted, there was not much fight left in them in any event. It did not take long for Odd and the others to make them break and run.

Run they did. They raced off in every direction, some grabbing nearby horses, some racing for the road that led back toward Grømstad, some just running. Einar shouted and grabbed men as they ran by and tried to shove them back into the fight, but it was pointless, and he realized it was pointless even before Odd could push his way through to get at him.

Einar turned and raced a dozen paces to where his horse stood. The animal was shifting nervously, but it was well enough trained to stay where it was, even in the middle of the fighting.

"Einar, you bastard!" Odd shouted, but Einar seemed to have forgotten all about him, and that made Odd more furious still. One of Einar's men was struggling to get his foot in a stirrup and Odd cut him down where he stood. The man dropped and the horse ran off, dragging the man, wounded or dead, behind.

"Kill them all! Before they escape!" Odd shouted, and behind him another voice called out, just as loud and emphatic.

"No! No!" It was Amundi. "No! Let them go, let them go!" He was running in front of his own men, and Odd's men, arms up, shouting. "Let them go!"

You son of a whore, I'll kill you too! Odd thought, and even as the thought formed in his head he felt a flush of shame and his fury collapsed like a wooden house burned through. What was he thinking? He was insane. He let the tip of Blood-letter rest on the ground and he tilted his head back and gulped air and let his mind settle.

Signy... He thought of his wife for the first time since riding into the fight. Signy. And the children. They were the singular reason he had been so frantic to return, and in the madness he had forgotten them entirely.

He looked around, turning a complete circle as he scanned the yard. Einar's men were racing off and it was only the men with Odd, and the wounded and dead, remaining. He remembered seeing the women under guard, over by the blacksmith's shop.

Odd wiped Blood-letter on the tunic of a dead man at his feet and slid it back into the sheath. He jogged off toward the blacksmith shop where the women and the children were on their feet now. He could see Signy, their children huddled around her and clutching at her dress. She held a spear in her hand. Odd could see the blood gleaming on the head and shaft.

"Signy!" he shouted and she looked over and he could see the relief on her face. He grabbed her, hugged her, and she hugged him back with the arm not holding the spear. He felt the arms of his children wrapping around his legs.

Odd straightened his arms, holding his wife so that he could see her. He looked her up and down but could see no visible injuries. He looked at the spear. He looked down at the man who had been guarding them. He was lying face down on the ground, his helmet a few feet away, blood soaking his torn tunic. He looked back at Signy.

"He wasn't paying attention," Signy said by way of explanation.

Odd nodded.

"You're letting them get away?" Signy asked. "Halfdan's men, who did this?"

Odd nodded again. "If we slaughter them it will only make things worse." He was sure that was why Amundi had let them go, and now, as the anger subsided, he could see it was the most sensible thing to do.

"You think Halfdan will be satisfied now?" Signy asked. "What he did here, and at the shielding, for what you did to his men?"

"We can hope," Odd said.

"We can hope," Signy repeated.

"And we can make ready, in case he is not."

Twenty-One

Has the sea him deluded,
or the sword wounded?
On that man
I will harm inflict.

The Poetic Edda

Thorgrim's ships were ready, with time to spare. The tide line was still creeping up the beach when Godi declared *Blood Hawk* seaworthy. Hundreds of willing hands heaved her up onto an even keel and guided her down the rollers, back into the shallow water of the river against which the *ad hoc* longphort was backed.

Godi and Harald and a few others were aboard as the ship eased into the water and then floated free. Their eyes were fixed on the repairs that had been made to the damaged plank. They were quiet for a moment, and then Godi called, "Good! It's good! Once the wood takes up it'll be tight as can be."

Thorgrim nodded. That was indeed good, good for many reasons. He was ready to get out of that place. They had the spoils from the monastery. They had the danegeld, one hundred pounds of silver, even though they had intended to leave without it. They had won all those riches with just a little hard fighting, nothing more. Thorgrim did not know how long such good luck would last, and he did not wish to push it.

"We are not so far from Frankia now, you know," Louis de Roumois said. He was standing beside Thorgrim, one of the last of the men remaining on the shore. "A week or two's sailing would get us there."

Thorgrim watched Harald vault over the *Blood Hawk*'s side into water up to his knees, then come wading ashore. He turned to Louis.

187

"You're a navigator now?" he asked. "If you can turn yourself into a sailor, maybe you can turn yourself into a bird and fly home."

Louis shrugged. "We're both guessing as to where in Engla-land we are. If our guesses are right, then it is a week or two to Frankia."

Thorgrim looked out over his fleet, the bows of the ships pointing roughly east into the flooding tide. They were all manned up, the men using their sea chests for rowing benches, oars held straight up, waiting for the order to ship them and row. The English prisoners had been distributed around the fleet. Gudrid and Harald had told them of their fate, explained that they would be set ashore on the far side of the harbor, but it was pretty clear from their faces they were skeptical at best.

"My family is very wealthy," Louis continued. "Once I have regained my place you would be paid well, you know. A lot more than a pathetic hundred pounds of silver."

Thorgrim smiled. He did not consider a hundred pounds of silver to be an impressive haul, riches beyond his imagining. He wondered if Louis thought he did.

"You've told me this before," Thorgrim said. "More than once."

"And I'll probably tell it to you many times more," Louis said. "Because we seem to grow closer to Frankia all the time."

"If you go to Frankia, and become king or whatever you say you are, would you bring Failend with you?"

The question seemed to startle Louis, and his reaction was visible. "Failend is with you, not with me," he said. "Do you question her loyalty? Or my designs on her? Because you should not."

"I don't worry about you," Thorgrim said. "You yearn for Frankia more than you yearn for any woman. Failend? She's given me her loyalty, I believe that, though I never asked her for it. But I wonder if she's growing worried about being with one such as me. One who doesn't follow your Christ god."

"You could be a follower, you know. You could be…" Louis said a word that sounded like *baptized* but Thorgrim did not understand. He guessed the word was Frankish, that there was no such word in his language, or if there was, Louis did not know it.

"What is that, that word you said?" Thorgrim asked.

"It is how you become a Christian. There are priests here, they could do it."

Harald approached. "The repairs to *Blood Hawk* are holding," he said, "and everything seems ready for us to leave."

"Good," Thorgrim said. He turned to Louis. "No time for me to become a Christian now," he said. "But if we are where we think we are in Engla-land, and we are on our way to Norway, which we are, then Frankia does indeed lie in between. So take cheer."

Louis nodded, a smile playing over his face. Thorgrim stepped closer and spoke in a lower voice. "I would not hurt Failend, but I fear she'll be hurt by me, because I've grown too weary of this world to care much for anything. And if she were to love you, I would not stand in the way, or challenge you."

He was not certain why he had said that, any more than he was certain about much that had to do with him and Failend, a complication he had not foreseen. His feelings for Failend were not the feelings she had for him, that was true, but still he did care. Nor was he so obtuse that he could not understand the tangle of emotions with which the girl was wrestling. He would spare her that, if he could, even if it meant forgoing the comfort she brought him.

He left Louis standing there, and he and Harald walked off toward the place where *Sea Hammer* floated in the stream. Thorgrim looked around the longphort which had been their home for so brief a time. The makeshift wall, a number of broken barrels, a few heaps of half-buried offal from slaughtered animals, blackened fire pits and the trampled earth were all that was left to mark their stay.

They reached the water's edge and waded out as far as they could toward the low midships where they might more easily climb aboard. Thorgrim set his hands on the sheer strake, ready to heave himself up over the side. He knew it would not be so easy as it had been in his younger days, or even a few years ago, after the battering he had endured since leaving his home. He thought of a wolf pack, how the leader of the pack would face a challenge to his position as soon as he showed any sign of weakness.

With a soft grunt he pushed himself up and swung one leg over the sheer strake, then the other, then hopped easily down to the deck, as smoothly as one might wish, and the effort that it took had not shown on his face.

I guess I am lead wolf still, he thought as he walked aft to the tiller, stepping with care down the crowded deck.

Most of his men were at the oars, each one double-manned, or at work on various tasks. But forty or so of the English prisoners were packed into the open area down the ship's centerline, sitting on the deck. Some looked with blank curiosity at him as he passed, some averted their eyes, some glared with undisguised anger. The priests wore their simple brown robes; the rest wore only tunics and leggings. They looked more like farmers than men-at-arms and Thorgrim was sure that only made them angrier still.

He stepped up onto the small raised deck aft. He looked aloft. *Sea Hammer*'s yard had been lowered and swung fore-and-aft, resting on the gallows, as had the yards of the other ships. There would be no need for sails in the tricky harbor, not until they were well free of the land.

Starri Deathless was already on his perch at the top of the mast. He looked down at the river. The water was running visibly down the ship's side. The tide was still flooding and would be for a while more, and that was good. In those confined waters, with shallows and sandbars and mudflats just below the surface, it was better to be pushing against the current than to be swept along by it. Better to go aground on a rising tide than a falling one.

"Ship oars!" Thorgrim called and the long oars came down to larboard and starboard, the blades were thrust through the oarports and the long shafts of the looms run out.

"Take the anchor up!" Thorgrim called next and a dozen hands in the bow heaved on the seal hide rope and pulled the heavy anchor from the bottom. *Sea Hammer*'s bow began to swing as the ship came untethered and Thorgrim ordered to rowers to pull. The blades of the oars dug in, the ship began to make headway, and Thorgrim felt the rush of excitement and relief he always felt when his last connection to the land was broken and he was once more fully afloat. The sea might bring its own troubles and dangers, but Thorgrim would take those over the intrigues of men ashore any day.

They pulled past *Blood Hawk* and, as soon as they were clear, Godi ordered his anchor heaved aboard, and then *Long Serpent*, *Dragon*, *Oak Heart* and the rest, one after another, freeing themselves from the bottom and falling into line astern of *Sea Hammer*, a waterborne parade, silent and dangerous as a wolf pack on the hunt.

"Water looks deep enough here, Night Wolf!" Starri cried down from aloft.

"Thank you, Starri!" Thorgrim called back, but he knew that already. Thorgrim Night Wolf did not care for surprises, or to leave anything unknown that could be known. Over the past few weeks he had taken several opportunities to row down the river and across the wide bay, sounding the bottom as he did, getting a sense for where the safe water ran. But things changed, sandbars shifted, and he had not been able to explore it all, so he was happy to have Starri's sharp eyes aloft.

The river narrowed as they pulled against the current, the scrubby banks only fifty feet away on either side. Thorgrim ran his eyes carefully along the shore, and he saw the others doing so as well. On the water they were safe from any substantial attack unless the English suddenly appeared in ships of their own, which Thorgrim was all but certain would not happen. Archers on shore, however, could do plenty of hurt over so short a distance. But other than a few herdsmen and their flocks there was nothing but vegetation to see.

Soon the river began to widen again as *Sea Hammer* moved out into the delta, or what might well be called a bay. Thorgrim moved his eyes from the near shore and ran them along the more distant banks north and south. A flat, marshy, scruffy land, not much good for anything. Even if he had planned on staying in Engla-land, he would not have chosen that place for a home.

"Sandbar to starboard!" Starri sang out. "You'll miss it on this heading!"

Thorgrim thanked him, though he had already seen the sandbar, and knew it was there even before they had seen it. He smiled to himself. Starri knew little about seafaring and cared even less, but he delighted in sitting at the masthead and shouting down directions.

Harald, who had just finished overseeing the retrieval of the anchor, stepped up beside him. Harald had assumed a leadership role aboard *Sea Hammer*, and now it was time that he had his own ship, Thorgrim knew. He was certainly a competent enough seaman and comfortable and experienced enough with command for that.

If one of those other captains dies or such, or if we get another ship, then it will be Harald's, Thorgrim thought.

It was not the first time he had thought that. There had been several opportunities to give Harald his own command, but Thorgrim had let them slip by, making this or that excuse. But he knew the truth of it: he did not want to lose Harald's company, and he did not want to let his son wander too far from his sight.

It was not how a father should treat his son, not a son who had reached manhood and proven himself the way Harald had, but Thorgrim could not help it. The loss of Hallbera had changed something inside him.

"We still have to rid ourselves of these English prisoners," Harald said. "Do you know where you'll put them?"

"I do," Thorgrim said. "Last time I rowed down this way I saw a beach, just to the south there, and it looks to have water enough with the high tide for us to drop these sorry bastards off."

Thorgrim nodded toward the starboard bow. The long stretch of light brown sand that marked the beach was just coming into view around a low spit of land. In his explorations Thorgrim had poked around in the water off the beach and found nothing to impede their landing.

Sea Hammer crawled past the spit of land and Thorgrim pushed the tiller gently away and the bow swung south, angling toward the beach. He looked over his shoulder. *Blood Hawk* was following in their wake, and behind, the rest were maintaining their neat line until it was their time to turn. The oarsmen were in a steady rhythm now, pulling easy, and the ship was moving nimbly in the calm water, the current not as strong in the wider harbor as it had been in the river.

They closed quickly with the beach, and through a few low places in the dunes Thorgrim could get tantalizing glimpses of the ocean beyond, flashing in the sun. But they could not reach the open water that way. They would have to run the narrow, tricky channel through the dunes to the east before they could enjoy such freedom as that.

"Take a pull, then rest on your oars!" Thorgrim called, and the rowers pulled once more, then straightened and pushed down on the handles of the oars. The blades came up dripping from the water, but *Sea Hammer* had enough way on that she kept moving, silent and steady, toward the beach. Ten feet from where water met shore, the bow ran itself into the soft sand and with a barely perceptible lurch the ship came to a stop.

For the rowers it was a moment to rest, but for the prisoners it was a moment of confusion and growing fear. Thorgrim could see them looking around again, heads up, more alert now that there had been some change in their condition. He turned to Harald.

"Should be shallow enough here for them to go over the side, at least forward of the beam," he said. "Tell them to get off."

Harald nodded and headed forward. In their tunics, sitting in a cluster on the deck, it was impossible to tell who among the prisoners might have authority over the others, so Harald pushed past them and chose the man closest to the bow. Thorgrim saw his son gesturing over the side and to the shoreline beyond. He could hear the sound of his words but could not make them out and would not have understood them even if he could. He saw the prisoner look at Harald, look at the shore beyond, look back at Harald. He did not move.

Harald's gestures became more animated, his words a bit more emphatic. The Englishman looked over his shoulder at the man behind, as if to get his opinion on the matter or to ask what trick was being played.

Before Thorgrim could speak, Harald did the very thing Thorgrim was about to tell him to do. He leaned down and grabbed the Englishman by the collar of his tunic. The prisoner was not a small man, but Harald, despite his age, was enormously strong, and he jerked the Englishman to his feet without the slightest difficulty. The Englishman started to make some sort of defensive gesture with his arms, but before he could do more than that Harald spun him around and threw him clean over the sheer strake and into the water below, dropping him neatly between two extended oars.

There was a loud splash, a moment of thrashing around, then the man found his feet and stood and pushed his way through the water to the shore. Harald leaned down to grab the next man, but there was no need. Like a flock of birds lifting from a field, the prisoners leapt to their feet and raced for the side of the ship, starboard and larboard. They stumbled over the rowers' legs and shoved one another out of the way as they vaulted over the sheer strakes, some bouncing off the looms of the oars on their way to the water.

Thorgrim looked off to either side. *Blood Hawk* and *Long Serpent* were also aground, and the prisoners there seemed to have taken their cue for those aboard *Sea Hammer*. They were leaping into the water all along the side of the ship, some jumping into water that was too deep to comfortably stand, but they all managed to thrash their way ashore.

The rest of the fleet came up behind, each ship running its bow aground, disgorging its panicked cargo. Soon there were more than two hundred drenched yet relieved men-at-arms and priests standing in a disordered line on the shore. They seemed to still be unsure of what had just happened, or what they should do next.

"It'll be some time before those ones are a threat," Gudrid said. He had been standing near the afterdeck, spear in hand, in case the prisoners had decided on some heroic course of action.

Thorgrim grunted. "Should take them the rest of the day just to get to the other side of the river," he said.

"We could sell them back their weapons," suggested Armod, "if they had anything to pay with."

The prisoners disembarked, Thorgrim ordered the rowers to pull astern. *Sea Hammer*'s bow eased off the sand and the ship began to draw stern-first away from the beach. Once clear, he ordered starboard oars to pull ahead, larboard astern, and the longship spun like a dancer. Then they pulled together and *Sea Hammer* gathered headway, threading her way carefully between the tricky mud banks, Starri happily calling out directions from on high.

They were going north now. Thorgrim looked out past the bow. Ahead was a strip of light-colored sand just a bit higher than the water surrounding it, a place where the bottom rose up above the surface and created a long, thin island of sand. He knew from his explorations that he wanted to head more or less straight for it, then turn to the east when he had closed to within a few hundred feet.

"Night Wolf!" Starri called. "There's a sandbar right ahead, and you're heading right for it like a blind fool!"

"Thank you, Starri," Thorgrim called. "I'd be lost without you."

"You'd be aground, anyway," Starri called back. Thorgrim pushed the tiller away and *Sea Hammer* made her turn to the east and once again the ships astern followed in her wake. Thorgrim could see, or at least he thought he could see, the spit of land forming the west entrance of the channel that connected the harbor to the sea.

He had been through it only once, when the fisherman Sweartling had guided them, but then they were coming in from the sea, east to west. At the time Thorgrim had made as close a study as he could of the entrance, knowing that barring a complete disaster he would have to go back out again. But that was it. In his recent poking around he had not made it that far east. This water was largely unknown to him.

"I see mud to the north!" Starri called out. "Best go a little south here!"

Thorgrim pushed the tiller over. Starri's words were in line with his memory, that there was a mudflat at the mouth of the channel and he would have to skirt around it to be safe. They rowed on, and now Thorgrim could see for certain the mouth of the channel, the gap in the long, sand beach through which they would row to gain the sea. Like open, welcoming arms. He turned *Sea Hammer* toward them.

The channel itself was long as Thorgrim recalled, a mile at least, but he could not yet see beyond the mouth of it. He knew once he came around the bulge of land on the eastern shore that he would be able to see it open up before him, a long, straight, watery road to the sea. But it, like the harbor, was deceptive, with more sand and mud waiting to snag the ships' bottoms.

He looked at the shoreline as it grew closer. The tideline was all but gone, which meant that the tide was nearly at its highest point, and that in turn meant it would soon turn and start sweeping them out the channel. And that was not good. It meant less control in that tricky waterway.

"Stroke oar, step it up!" Thorgrim called. Hall, who had been setting the stroke, increased his speed, and the others followed suit, and *Sea Hammer* began to move more quickly toward the channel's mouth.

Here we go, Thorgrim thought as the land came up on either side of his ship and they moved from the harbor into the narrower confines of the channel. Astern of *Sea Hammer* the other ships had also increased their pace, keeping their spacing even, one to the other.

The change was abrupt, from the wide open harbor to the narrow strip of water that cut through the shore, the banks no more than sixty or seventy feet away on either side, close enough to cause some real problems.

Thorgrim's eyes were glancing from shore to shore, but focusing mostly on the water just ahead, his chief concern. He was tense, ready to react if some eddy or other quirk of the current began to twist *Sea Hammer* off her course. His arms and hands were sensitive to the feel of the tiller as he judged how much steerage he had, if the ship was still being driven by the oars or if the tide had turned and was sweeping them along. But the rudder still seemed to have a solid bite in the water, allowing him to maintain control.

Then he heard Starri Deathless shout from the masthead, not his usual imperious command but a yell of genuine surprise, with a note of pleasure in it. At the same time he heard others calling out with at least the same degree of surprise.

He looked up quickly, eyes moving from south to north. On either bank he saw the one thing he had not expected to see at all: makeshift fortifications, much like those at the longphort he and his men had built. And standing on them and in front of them were men-at-arms. Hundreds of men-at-arms. Waiting, apparently, for the Northmen to come.

Twenty-Two

False are thou, Freya!
Who temptest me:
by thy eyes thou showest it,
so fixed upon us;
while thou thy man
hast on the dead-road
the young Ottar...

The Poetic Edda

Ealdorman Nothwulf stood on top of the uninspiring but functional wall that his men had so recently built, watching the longships coming on, and he felt a deep, warm sense of satisfaction. Pleasure, even. It was ironic, and he knew it. One did not generally feel pleasure at the sight of half a dozen ships, each crammed with bloodthirsty heathens, approaching fast. But this was different.

He pulled his eyes from the lead ship and looked across the few hundred feet of water to the other side of the channel. There was another wall, another slapped-together fortification, much like the one on which he stood. Leofric stood on that one, looking at the ships just as he was. He saw Leofric raise his arm and wave and Nothwulf waved back.

And you doubted me, didn't you, old man? Nothwulf thought. He, Nothwulf, had seen the brilliance of this idea from the beginning. Leofric had not been so sure.

The first suggestion of an idea had come to him in his tent, while camped with his army beyond the walls of the Northmen's fortification. A nebulous, half-formed thing, this plan, but it had solidified with Aelfwyn's appearance and the information she brought about Cynewise's desire to be rid of the Northmen so that she could concentrate on killing him.

Cynewise would pay the Northmen to leave. And to leave they would have to row through the narrow confines of the channel. There they would be vulnerable to archers and spearmen and other hazards. He could stop them, kill them, make himself the hero of Dorsetshire. There was nothing King Æthelwulf admired more than men who killed heathens. He might be growing more addled, but he would not ignore that.

The worst possibility was that the Northmen would escape Nothwulf's trap, but in doing so they would certainly lose many men, and that made the worst possibility not so bad. Best case, Nothwulf and Leofric managed to get one or more of the ships to run ashore and they captured them, slaughtering the crew. Then Nothwulf would have the glory, and he would have the danegeld Cynewise had paid, and he would have the plunder that the Northmen had taken. That last might be a bit tricky, given that the priory they had robbed was on Leofric's land, but Nothwulf figured he could find some way around that.

"Stand ready!" Nothwulf cried out, loud enough to be heard all along his littoral defenses, but of course the men had been ready for some time. They had been ready for days.

Once Nothwulf had hit on this plan, and half convinced, half bullied Leofric into going along, they had marched quickly to this place and set to work. Trees cut down, driftwood logs collected, houses pulled apart, they fetched timber from every source they could to erect their walls, Nothwulf on the northwest bank, Leofric to the southeast. They had rounded up archers and bows and arrows. They had made ready and then they had waited. For this moment.

Nothwulf looked behind him. A series of small fire rings had been built behind the wall where they were hidden from the water. They made a line parallel to the wall and running its whole length. Each ring had kindling and wood arranged so that it would light up as soon as a glowing coal was put to it. But they were not yet lit. A line of smoke columns might alert the Northmen while they were still some ways away, put them on guard, or even make them turn around. But now it was time, because now it was too late for the Northmen to react.

"Go ahead, stoke the fires!" Nothwulf called, and the men who had been standing by, blowing gently on the embers, now set the embers to the kindling, and in no time at all each of the fires was burning well, the smoke rising up in a line. He looked across the water and could see the first columns of smoke rising up from the fires on Leofric's side.

He looked back at the channel and the lead ship pulling toward them. It was a big one, maybe the biggest he had ever seen. It had the tall, elegantly curved prow that the Northmen preferred, with some sort of carving at the end, though Nothwulf could not make out what it was. Some pagan god or such. A row of bright-colored shields painted in various patterns lined the ship's side, and the long oars were thrust out below them, moving with an impressive synchronization. The deck was crowded with men.

The ship had slowed, Nothwulf could see that as well. They had been pulling hard when they first came into view, coming around the south entrance to the channel, but they had slowed at the no doubt surprising sight of the fortification and the men standing there and waiting.

Nothwulf nodded his head. "Good, good," he said. "Come on, you can do it...you can run past these miserable defenses...go ahead and try, you heathen bastards."

There was another ship a short distance behind the first and nearly as big, and behind that, another. Nothwulf knew that there were seven ships in all, but the last three in line were not yet visible, which was also good. They would come blundering into whatever mess the first in line were tangled up in.

Nothwulf did not know a lot about ships, but he did know some things. He knew that they had more control going into the current rather than being pushed along by it. He knew they needed a certain amount of room to maneuver and turn, and wide as the channel looked, it was deceptive, with mud banks here and there below the surface. He knew they needed a certain depth of water in which to float.

"Good, good," he said again. He turned back once more and looked down behind the wall. The archers were standing near, ready to climb up to the top of the wall, where they would get the most advantageous shot. The fires were all burning well. Next to each fire stood a half dozen men. Some held arrows with oil-soaked rags bound tight around the ends of the shafts. The others stood ready to touch the rags off in the fires and hand them up quick to the archers on the wall.

"Now!" Nothwulf shouted. "Now! Light them up!"

The defenses on shore, the handful of men standing on the walls, seemed to pose no real danger to *Sea Hammer* or the rest of the fleet, as long as their crews did not go ashore. And Thorgrim did not intend to go ashore. Not at all. He wanted to get clear of the channel as quickly as he could and leave the shore behind.

And even if they did go ashore, Thorgrim was certain that they could just brush the Englishmen aside. No, there did not seem to be any danger there. And that fact sounded a warning, loud and clear, in Thorgrim's mind.

So why build the walls at all?

"Hall, slow your stroke," Thorgrim called. Hall nodded and with the next stroke he pulled back on the oar with half the force he had been using, and the rest did the same. *Sea Hammer*'s speed through the water slowed noticeably and the momentum came off her. No sense in rushing into this unexpected situation.

"Starri, what do you see?" Thorgrim called aloft.

"Just the walls," Starri called out. "Some of those miserable bastards standing on them, more shirking behind. Some cook fires."

Thorgrim was about to tell Starri to stay put, that he needed him as lookout, but even before he could speak Starri grabbed onto the shroud and came down, half sliding, half hand-over-hand, until his feet hit the sheer strake and he hopped to the deck. There would be no keeping him at the masthead now. Starri would remain aloft as long as navigating was the greatest fun to be had, but now there were men-at-arms near, and the possibility of a fight, and there was no chance Starri would be willing to watch from on high.

Indeed, Starri had hardly recovered his footing before he pulled his tunic up over his head, preferring to go bare-chested into battle. His arms were starting to do that strange jerky thing they did when a fight was near.

Thorgrim looked behind. *Blood Hawk* was in his wake, about a hundred feet astern. He looked from bank to bank. The men-at-arms were lining the top of the walls and more were climbing up to join them.

What do you think you'll do from way over there? Thorgrim thought. Then, as if in answer to his question, he saw an archer raise his bow, an arrow on the bowstring. He was more than a hundred feet away, not an unreasonable distance for a good bowman. Thorgrim could not make out the details, but the motion was unmistakable. Still, there was something odd about the whole thing, something that did not look right, but Thorgrim could not tell what.

The archer drew, he released, and the arrow made a dark streak through the air as it sailed over the water and embedded itself in one of the shields mounted on *Sea Hammer*'s side. It quivered there for a moment, dark smoke whirling up from its head, and then the painted canvas face of the shield burst into flames.

"Oh, Thor's arse!" Gudrid shouted. Thorgrim was thinking much the same thing. *Flaming arrows.* And immediately the next thought came to mind: *The sails!*

It would be a hard thing to set a ship on fire with flaming arrows. Even covered in tar and pitch as they were, the timbers were too big to easily catch. But the sails were something else. Oiled wool, they would ignite easily. The burning sail might take the whole ship with it, and even if it did not, they could not afford to lose the sails. They had fought and died at Loch Garman to make these sails, and they could not be replaced now.

"Hall! Double time! Go!" Thorgrim shouted. Hall was not surprised by the order. He leaned forward quick, dipped his oar and pulled back hard. The muscles in his arms and the sinews in his neck stood out with the effort. Behind him, on either side, more than a hundred men on the double-manned oars did the same. *Sea Hammer* lurched ahead, her speed building with each stroke.

The arrows were coming fast now, flying in from either side. The shield that had ignited had been thrown overboard, leaving a gap in the line like a missing tooth. More arrows struck shields and the mast and lodged in the prow. As fast as they came in, men grabbed them and jerked them free and tossed them aside. Or, nearly as fast. Here and there an arrow remained lodged in the wood, smoking and sputtering. One, stuck in the mast, was dropping flaming bits of its oil-soaked cloth on the sail lashed to the yard below.

Harald was there, a bucket in hand. The arrow was too high to reach so he flung the water in the bucket up at it, a well-aimed shot that extinguished the flame, much to Thorgrim's relief. Now Harald was shouting orders to those not manning an oar and they grabbed up buckets, hauled water up from the channel and doused the sail with it, soaking the cloth, making it more difficult to light.

Sea Hammer was almost even with the *ad hoc* walls on the beaches on either side, the shoreline sliding quickly past as the rowers leaned in hard. The arrows were like a swarm of bees, flying in from either side, making a steady drumbeat of thumps in the wood where they struck. Up on the foredeck Failend stood with her own bow, a quiver of arrows leaning against the ship's side. She was nocking and shooting as fast as she could, which was very fast. Thorgrim had no doubt that her arrows were finding their marks, that she was taking down their tormentors as fast as she could, but she alone was not enough to do much harm to them.

The walls were abeam of them now, *Sea Hammer* halfway past. Astern of them *Blood Hawk* was also enduring the rain of arrows. Thorgrim could see men grabbing for the flaming shafts and tossing them into the water. But *Sea Hammer* had nearly run the gauntlet, with *Blood Hawk* right astern, and then they would have the safety of sea room. The other ships were smaller targets and they would be moving even faster. These defenses, the flaming arrows, it all seemed a lot of effort for naught, and Thorgrim was surprised the English would not have realized how easily the fast ships could slip through it all.

Maybe they don't know how fast our ships are, when pulled with a will, Thorgrim thought, and at that moment *Sea Hammer* struck something, something hidden by the muddy water, and lurched to a stop. Thorgrim was flung forward and he grunted as the tiller drove into his gut. To larboard and starboard rowers were tossed to the deck. The oars, which an instant before were moving in beautiful symmetry, now pointed off in every direction.

"Bastard!" Thorgrim shouted, straightening and looking around. *Sea Hammer*'s bow was lodged on some obstruction hidden below the surface and the ship was pivoting on that point, turning broadside to the channel as the now-ebbing tide pushed her along.

"What by all the gods..." Thorgrim began. He saw Harald jump to his feet and bound forward, leaping onto the foredeck where Failend was just pulling herself up. Harald looked over the side, down into the water.

"It's a ship!" he shouted aft. "A ship, sunk in the channel! More than one, I think!"

Bastards, Thorgrim thought. But angry as he was with the English, he was angrier with himself. He had wondered how the English could be such fools as to think their arrows would stop the longships. But they were not the fools, not at all. It was him, Thorgrim, who was a blind idiot thinking that his fleet could just run past the fortifications with never a problem. He had underestimated his enemy, a common, often fatal mistake, and they had hooked him and hauled him right in like a fat cod flopping on the deck.

He turned quick and looked astern. *Blood Hawk* was only a hundred feet away, maybe less, and coming down on them. Godi was seaman enough to know not to try to turn his ship: with the current running with him, *Blood Hawk* would get swept down on *Sea Hammer* as she turned broadside to the channel. Instead he had the oarsmen rowing astern for all they were worth, trying to back away, but it was not at all clear that it would be enough. Beyond *Blood Hawk* Thorgrim could see *Long Serpent* coming on, rowing ahead, but slowly, apparently unsure of what was happening. Farther back, *Oak Heart* was just rounding the point and coming into view.

Forward, *Sea Hammer*'s rowers were sorting themselves out, those who had been flung to the deck pulling themselves up, those who had managed to stay seated on the sea chests getting control of the long oars. The current had *Sea Hammer* now, turning her crosswise to the channel. Thorgrim looked over the starboard side. He could see the indistinct shape of a ship just below the surface, like a vessel of drowned sailors, ghostly and frightening. The English must have weighted it with rocks, moved it in place, knocked a hole in the bottom. They knew the Northmen would wait for high tide to get through the channel. High tide, when the sunken ship would be hidden by the deep water.

The rain of arrows had built to gale force, sweeping in from both sides, the thump of arrowheads in wood as steady as the beat of hail on a canvas tent. Thorgrim heard a scream forward, short, loud, and sharp. The arrows, fired from the top of the walls ashore, were coming in over the shields on the rail, and one had found a living target up near the bow.

It was a man named Vandrad, long beard, shaved head, wearing a brown tunic that was now all but engulfed in flames. An arrow was sticking out of his chest, but somehow the man was still alive, screaming and flailing and still on his feet. Then Gudrid leapt over one of the sea chests and came down nearly on top of him, knocking him to the deck and beating at the flames with a blanket. Gudrid's intent, Thorgrim knew, was to save the ship. Gaut was done for. Even if he could live with those burns, he would not want to.

The arrows were coming in faster than the men could pull them free and toss them overboard, and fire was spreading fore and aft. A number of the shields were fully involved, forming a wall of flame and smoke along parts of the ship's side, keeping the rowers from their benches. Something up by the foredeck was in flames and Harald and two others were throwing buckets of water on it. An arrow took one of the men in the back and he arched and tumbled forward, knocking into Harald as he fell. A little farther aft another man took an arrow in the thigh, and he screamed in pain even as he beat at the flames.

"Rowers, take up your oars!" Thorgrim shouted. The men on the sea chests, those far enough from the flames, grabbed onto the grips of the oars, brought the looms up so they rode parallel to the water.

This won't be easy, Thorgrim thought. The current was pressing *Sea Hammer*'s starboard side against the wreck, and the oars on that side would foul with the sunken ship as the men tried to pull. But without the drive from the starboard bank of oars, there would be no getting free.

Amidships, larboard side, Gudrid and four others drove the butt end of spear shafts into the burning shields. They thrust again and again and finally the shields gave way, breaking apart and falling down into the water. They might have made a sizzling sound, but Thorgrim could not hear it over the shouting and the crackling of flames and the screams of wounded men.

"Starboard oars!" he shouted, but before he could say the next thing he heard a voice cry out from behind him, surprising since he was the farthest aft. He looked to his left, back up the channel. *Blood Hawk*'s bow was twenty feet away, but rather than driving down on *Sea Hammer* and tangling with her, the other ship seemed to be completely stopped, hanging motionless in the water. Standing on the sheer strake, one hand on the prow to steady himself, a rope clenched in the other, was the massive form of Godi.

"Thorgrim!" he shouted. "I have an anchor out! I'll throw you a line!" He held the rope up to make his meaning more clear.

Thorgrim waved his hand in acknowledgement, then stepped up to the ship's side, his arms outstretched to catch the rope. *I'll give you a dozen silver arm bands for this, Godi, if we live through it,* he thought.

Godi brought his arm back, then swung it in a wide, sideways arc. The rope flew away from him, unwinding neatly in the air and dropping on Thorgrim's outstretched arm. Thorgrim did not even have to grab for it. Line in hand, he dropped down to the deck and took three steps forward, ready to make the rope fast to the heavy cleat mounted to the ship's side.

Then he stopped. *Not by the stern, by the bow,* he thought. If they were going to be towed off, they should be towed off bow-first, so that the men at the oars could pull with force, not push the oars to make sternway. He turned back to Godi.

"Is there enough rope for me to take this to the bow?" he shouted. He got a lung-full of smoke and he coughed hard. He saw Godi look down at the rest of the rope coiled out of sight on the deck. He looked up and nodded.

"Yes!" he shouted, and then, in a less certain tone, "I think so!"

That was all Thorgrim needed to hear. He grabbed the bitter end of the tow rope and began to race forward, stepping up on the sea chest farthest aft, larboard side. Vali was there, oar in hand, and before Thorgrim could tell him to get clear he shifted inboard and pushed the grip of his oar down to make it easier for Thorgrim to step over. Vali could see what was going on and knew what he had to do.

The same was true of the next man forward. All along the larboard side the rowers slid inboard, making a path for Thorgrim to race forward. But the men were not the only obstacle. There were still shields on fire all down the ship's side, and arrows whipping in from the nearby shore.

Thorgrim leapt from sea chest to sea chest, pulling the rope along as Godi, across the water, payed out more and more of its length. Just forward of the beam, three shields were blazing, forming a wall of flame and smoke, but there was nothing to do but race past, dragging the rope, and with any luck moving quick enough to keep the flames from catching on it, or him. He plunged past, feeling the searing heat on his left side, on his face and hands and through the cloth of his tunic.

The rope caught on something. It pulled him up short and the end of the rope was nearly jerked out of his hands. Through the flames Thorgrim could not see what the rope was caught on, but he held tight and flicked the end, shouting at the intensity of the heat. The rope leapt free and Thorgrim continued his race forward. An arrow ripped past him, close enough to brush the front of his tunic, but he did not pause.

He reached the forward-most sea chest at last, jumped down to the deck and whipped the bitter end around the big cleat near the bow. He straightened and looked along the length of the line where it stretched from *Sea Hammer*'s bow to *Blood Hawk*'s. He feared he would see the rope engulfed in flame, but the tough strands of walrus hide were intact, with only a few inconsequential embers clinging to it. He lifted his arm and waved to Godi.

Godi waved back, then dropped down to *Blood Hawk*'s deck and disappeared behind the bow. Thorgrim turned and faced aft.

"Stand ready on the oars!" Thorgrim shouted. "*Blood Hawk* will pull us off, but once we're clear you bastards row like your asses are on fire!" Which they would be soon, if they tarried a moment longer.

Through the noise of the fires and the shouting, and the whir and thud of arrows, Thorgrim heard Godi's voice calling out an order. *Blood Hawk*'s oars bit into the water and the walrus hide rope lifted and drew straight. Somewhere at *Blood Hawk*'s stern Thorgrim imagined every man not on an oar was hauling on the dripping anchor line, helping the rowers to move two ships at once.

Then *Sea Hammer* began to move. Her bow, pressed by the current against the sunken ship, began to swing free. Thorgrim moved aft, pushing his way down the centerline of the ship, running his eyes over the sail bound to the yard as he did. Nothing, no flames, no charred holes. Harald's wetting and the vigilance of the others standing ready with buckets had kept the precious cloth safe. He hoped the same was true on *Blood Hawk*, and on *Long Serpent*, which had also become a target of the archers ashore.

Thorgrim reached the afterdeck, stepped up and pulled the rudder amidships. The bow was still swinging, the north shore of the channel sweeping past. Thorgrim could see the rough walls of the English defenses, the archers standing on top, the banners snapping in the breeze. Arrows were still flying in at an astounding rate and he was looking right into the storm.

"Starboard side, stroke!" Thorgrim shouted and the rowers all along the starboard side leaned forward, lifted the grips of their oars, and then leaned back, putting their considerable strength of arm, leg and back into the effort. *Sea Hammer* reacted to the force of the drive, turning faster to larboard, making things a bit easier for the men aboard *Blood Hawk*.

"Larboard and starboard, pull together!" Thorgrim shouted next and now both sides leaned aft and pulled forward, ignoring the fires burning around the ship, the chaos of men trying to put them out, the smoke that carried on it the smell of burning flesh, dead men with clothes still in flames.

"Pull!"

Again the men heaved on the oars. Thorgrim tried to see through the confusion on deck, see how the tow rope was fairing. Hanging slack he guessed, but he could not be sure. Still, with *Sea Hammer* rowing ahead, the proper way, she would have considerably more drive than *Blood Hawk,* rowing astern. It would not take them long to pass *Blood Hawk* by, and then they would switch around, with *Sea Hammer* taking Godi's ship in tow.

Fewer arrows seemed to find their mark. Thorgrim glanced over the starboard side, then the larboard. They were already drawing clear of the fortifications and the line of archers who stood on top of the walls. He heard a thudding sound nearby, felt a tremor in the tiller under his hands. He looked to starboard. A flaming arrow had embedded itself in the head of the rudder, just above the point where the tiller met it at a right angle.

I'll see that you pay for this, Thorgrim thought as he held the tiller with his left hand and reached out with his right, though he wasn't sure who exactly he was threatening. Not that whore's son Oswin. No reason for Oswin to have set this trap. So who was it? The other army that Oswin had mentioned? He cursed the sunken ship that was keeping him from getting free of the land. He longed to get to sea and be done with all the horse manure in which men ashore loved to wallow.

He could feel the flames on his hand as he grabbed the shaft of the arrow stuck in the rudder. The fire lapped onto his sleeve as he wiggled the arrow and pulled it free. He tossed it overboard and beat his flaming cuff against his chest. Small bits of burning cloth rained down on the deck by his feet, but they were not enough to set *Sea Hammer* on fire.

He looked forward. The flames burning *Sea Hammer*'s deck and the shields and the dead were nearly under control, men beating at them with blankets and furs. Others hauled water up over the side in buckets and dowsed the flames and kept the sail well soaked. *Blood Hawk* was considerably closer now, *Sea Hammer* quickly overhauling her. He looked past *Blood Hawk*, up the channel toward the harbor from which they had just come. His stomach lurched and a curse came unbidden from his throat.

Long Serpent, Jorund's command, was sideways in the channel, just a few hundred feet from *Blood Hawk*'s stern, and the current was sweeping her down on *Blood Hawk*. Jorund must have seen what was happening and tried to turn his ship around. Something had gone wrong—*Long Serpent* might have run up on a mud flat, might have gotten caught in an eddy or found the current too fast to turn in— but whatever it was, she seemed unable to swing her bow up into the ebbing tide.

It was not for want of trying. *Long Serpent*'s oars, at least those that Thorgrim could see, were moving fast, the men clearly pulling hard, trying to bring the ship's head around. But they were failing.

Set your anchor, Thorgrim thought. An anchor over the bow would turn the ship into the current. *Or stream something astern.* Anything, a board, a couple of buckets, tied to a rope and run over the stern would likely do the same. But it did no good for Thorgrim to think it, and *Long Serpent* was too far for him to shout the words across the water. He did not know if Jorund was a good seaman or not. He had kept his ship alive during the horrendous gale that had blown them to Engla-land, and that was something, but it could have been luck.

"We'll see," Thorgrim said grimly.

Others on *Sea Hammer*'s crew saw what was happening, and met it with considerable shouting, waving and pointing. The rowers twisted at their places, trying to see what the excitement was about. They were working harder now as the ebb tide grew in force, and that same tide was driving *Long Serpent* quickly down onto *Blood Hawk*'s stern.

Thorgrim pulled the tiller toward him. If he could skirt around *Blood Hawk*, avoid being caught up in the collision, he might be able to get both ships on a tow line, pull both free. *Sea Hammer*'s bow began to swing and Thorgrim called forward for Harald to cast off the tow line that connected *Sea Hammer* to *Blood Hawk*.

And then *Long Serpent* and *Blood Hawk* hit. *Long Serpent* had managed to get halfway through her turn when she slammed into *Blood Hawk*'s stern, her starboard quarter coming hard against *Blood Hawk*'s sternpost. Thorgrim could hear men shouting on the two ships, and his own men shouting as well.

"Pull, you bastards! Double man the oars!" Thorgrim shouted. *Sea Hammer*'s men tossed buckets aside and scrambled to find seats at the oars. There was little danger from fire now; it was the disaster up ahead that was the greatest threat.

Thorgrim looked out past the bow. *Blood Hawk* and *Long Serpent* were entangled and the current was sweeping them down onto *Sea Hammer*. Thorgrim pulled the tiller a bit more, turned his ship's bow another degree, but he did not dare turn too far or the current would grab the bow and turn *Sea Hammer* broadside as it did *Long Serpent*.

Then, to Thorgrim's surprise, both *Blood Hawk* and *Long Serpent* stopped where they were, motionless in the middle of the channel. Had they run aground? Hit another submerged obstacle? Thorgrim could make no sense of it.

Then he remembered. *The anchor! Blood Hawk* had set an anchor. Thorgrim thought they had hauled it up by then, but apparently not, and now both ships were hanging on that single, tenuous wood and stone hook.

Hold on, hold on... Thorgrim thought. If *Blood Hawk* and *Long Serpent* could both hang on the anchor long enough for *Sea Hammer* to get clear and up-current of them, then there might be a chance to tow them both off. He wanted to tell his men to row harder still, but he could see in a glance that they could not. They were rowing as hard as they conceivably could. *Sea Hammer* could go no faster than she was.

He looked at the open water ahead. He looked over at the ships just in time to see *Blood Hawk*'s anchor line part. One moment the ships were motionless and then suddenly they were moving again, turning in the current and sweeping down on *Sea Hammer*. They were going to hit him; there was no way to avoid it now, and Thorgrim's only choice was where they would strike his ship—on the bow or amidships or somewhere in between.

"Get your oars in! Get them in!" Thorgrim shouted, and surprising as that order was the men obeyed, and quickly, sliding the long shafts inboard through the row ports.

He pushed the tiller away and turned *Sea Hammer*'s bow toward the drifting vessels. If they hit bow-on it would likely do less damage. He grit his teeth and braced for the collision.

Blood Hawk was spinning from the force of *Long Serpent*'s impact, turning broadside to *Sea Hammer*. *Sea Hammer*'s bow hit her just about amidships with a shudder that ran through the ship's fabric and the terrible sound of grinding and cracking wood. And they continued to spin, the three ships locked together, turning as the current pushed them down the channel.

Not done yet, Thorgrim thought. There was one more collision yet to come, and it came at almost the same instant that Thorgrim thought those words. *Sea Hammer* once again ran up on the dead ship sunk in the channel. She leaned a bit to starboard as her momentum came to a sudden stop, and she groaned, pinned between the wreck below and *Blood Hawk* and *Long Serpent* up-current of her.

From either bank the arrows continued to come, their ends burning, their numbers swelling. And with the arrows came something worse, something that made Thorgrim even more furious still: a cheer of victory, English victory, loud and long.

Chapter Twenty-Three

Hear a great wonder,
hear of peace broken,
hear of a great matter,
hear of a death
— one man's or more.

Gisli Sursson's Saga

The room at the western end of Halfdan the Black's great hall served as a throne room of sorts. It was the domain of Halfdan alone, separated from the rest of the hall by a doorway, and entered only at the king's bidding. It was small compared to the rest of the hall, but still bigger than the houses in which most of Halfdan's subjects lived.

There were benches built against the walls on either side of the room, and a raised platform at the far end on which sat a large and elaborately carved oak chair. The roof, fifteen feet overhead, was partially supported by a half dozen posts which also bore intricate carvings, serpents and vines winding their way around bas relief images of Halfdan's heroic deeds. There was a hearth in the middle of the floor, and a fire was burning with the intensity of Halfdan's anger.

"Say again who was there," he said, his voice a low growl. He had been staring into the flames for some time now without speaking at all. It made the others in attendance—Einar and his captains and other men of import in Halfdan's court—shift and squirm with trepidation. They all knew him well enough to know that the quieter he became, the angrier he was. And that day he was very quiet indeed.

"Odd, of course, was there," Einar said. "His family, the people on his farm…"

"I know that, you idiot," Halfdan said.

"Amundi Thorsteinsson, Ragi Oleifsson, Ulfkel Ospaksson, all of them who came with Odd to see you," Einar continued on quickly. "They each of them had their *hirdsmen*, or whoever they took as guards. They must have. Odd could not have that many men, at least not that many he could put under arms."

Halfdan wanted to call Einar an idiot once again. Odd might well have that many men under arms. How could Einar know? Halfdan had thought Odd to be no more than a farmer, a man who would not push back against the ambitions of his king, who could not find it in himself to push back. A man not worthy of being called Thorgrimson. But so far Odd had proved Halfdan wrong every time. He had challenged Halfdan. And the only thing Halfdan hated more than to be proved wrong was to be challenged.

"And they all stood with Odd? They came with him to fight you?" Halfdan said.

"Yes, Lord," Einar said. They had covered all this, but Einar knew better than to let any note of exasperation creep into his voice. "We waited until they were in the hills, and then we attacked the farm. Those who were left, they fought. More than I would have guessed. Odd's wife, whatever she's called, she rallied what few there were there and they put up a good fight. But not that good. We had captured the lot of them and we were ready to return here when Odd and the rest came back from the hills. They must have guessed what we were up to. Or we were betrayed, somehow."

"Hmm," Halfdan said. He was silent. More squirming, more trepidation. "I guess your trick of luring them up to the shielding was not so much of a trick after all," he said, finally.

"Lord, we would have had the whole household if..." Einar stopped talking.

"If what?"

"Ah...nothing, Lord," Einar said. "I forget what I was thinking."

You were thinking that if I had let you take more men you could have attacked the shielding and the farm at once, isn't that what you were going to say? Halfdan thought. Einar nearly slipped up by speaking his mind, a mistake men did not make twice in Halfdan's company. But Halfdan let it go, because Einar was right. He had made a mistake not giving Einar and the raiders enough warriors, though he was not about to admit to that.

Halfdan looked around at the faces of the other men. The platform on which Halfdan's throne sat was at the same height as the benches, but the throne itself put Halfdan about three feet higher than the rest, which forced them to look up at him. Not an accident.

"Anyone else?" Halfdan said. So far Einar was the only one who had spoken. He had been in charge of the raid, it had been his failure, and the rest were happy to let him do the talking. But in Halfdan's mind they had all failed, and he would not let the others off so easily.

"The raid on the shielding, that went just as we wanted," said Onund Jonsson. Onund was the captain of Halfdan's *hird*, a fearless and skilled warrior, but for all that he was obsequious, eager to please his king. Those were both qualities that Halfdan liked. He kept Onund close because he knew that a king such as himself had many enemies, but Onund was not one of them. It was why he had not, until that last raid, sent Onund and the hird to accompany Einar. He preferred to keep his trusted guard close.

"We killed all but one of Odd's people there," Onund continued. "Took a dozen women, near a hundred head of cattle, sheep... It's all yours now, Lord."

Halfdan looked back into the fire. He did not reply. He was in no mood to admit being pleased about any of this. And the women and the cattle were nothing compared to what he really wanted. He wanted Odd's wife. He wanted Odd's children. He wanted to make Odd suffer as payment for his audacity. And even more than that, he wanted everyone to see the price that a man would pay for standing between Halfdan the Black and that which Halfdan desired.

"Cattle, yes," Halfdan said. "Women." He said the words dismissively because he felt they warranted dismissal. He turned his attention back to Einar. "Why, pray tell, were all of the hauldar gathered at Odd's farm? Were they meeting? Plotting?"

"All I know is what one of Odd's slaves told me, lord, one we carried off. She works as a servant in the long hall, so she would be in the place to overhear. She told me that the hauldar were angry with Odd, furious that he should set the trap he did, and give them no warning that he meant to do so. They were angry that Odd had incurred your wrath, lord."

Really? Halfdan thought. That was interesting, if true. He had thought—feared—that the hauldar were united in this. They had come to see him as one, had fought Einar as one. But maybe they were not so united. Maybe Odd was more on his own than he had thought.

And that would be a good thing, because for all of the warriors that Halfdan had under his command, the haulder, collectively, had more. They represented a lot of potential power in that country.

For a long time Halfdan was silent. Quite a long time. But his mind was not quiet at all. His thoughts were getting away from him, free-ranging through the past.

That family, that bastard family he thought.

They had never made trouble for him, but he knew they would, one day. They were poised to do it, like a boulder teetering on a cliff edge, ready to roll down with the barest nudge and crush everything in its path. He, Halfdan, had been young, and years away from being king, when Ulf of the Battle Song had died. But Ulf was legend enough to carve the family's good name in stone. His deeds were still praised by the skalds.

And Ornolf the Restless. He and Ulf had been friends, had gone raiding together. Ornolf was no warrior like Ulf was, but he had outlived Ulf by half a lifetime, and he had a quality that was probably more dangerous than any that Ulf possessed. He was liked.

Fat, loud, drunken, still Ornolf the Restless had a touch that made men enjoy his company. He was generous, welcoming, and could even be wise and quick-witted at times. He had seemed pleased when Halfdan became king, and he had never done anything to undermine his rule. He had hosted Halfdan and his company at his great hall many times.

But he had never been obsequious, either. He had treated Halfdan more as an equal than as a sovereign. He had never done anything to explicitly give offence, but still Halfdan had his suspicions. If Ornolf had wanted to start trouble, had wanted to turn the king's subjects against him, then he would have been in a good position to do so. Buffoon though he was, men listened to Ornolf, and followed him.

And from them, Ulf and Ornolf, came Thorgrim Night Wolf, son of one, son-in-law of the other. Thorgrim, too, was liked, but not in the way Ornolf was. Thorgrim was also generous and welcoming, but there was nothing jovial or open about him. There was instead a menacing quality, a sense that you did not want to be an enemy to that man. And of course there were the rumors of what he was. A shape-shifter. Kveldulf. There was more to be feared from Thorgrim than from Ornolf.

Thorgrim and Halfdan were near the same age. Halfdan had known Thorgrim, though not well, for as long as he could recall, and he saw how that feeling of menace Thorgrim exuded only grew more pronounced as he won fame and wealth raiding with Ornolf the Restless. Then, when he married into Ornolf's family, when those two lines joined, he became more of a threat still.

Halfdan the Black had kept his eyes on Thorgrim all through the years, watched for any sign of betrayal, any indication that Thorgrim was plotting against him, but his suspicions were never confirmed. Thorgrim grew prosperous, and had children, and expanded his holdings, and Halfdan never had any reason to think the man's ambitions went beyond that.

Still, he was pleased when word came a few years back that Thorgrim and Ornolf had gone off raiding once more. Halfdan was happy to have the two of them out of the country, and Thorgrim's son Harald as well. Harald was just a boy, but then every wolf started out as a playful cub.

It was a good thing, having them gone. Even better if they never returned, but Halfdan dared not hope that. Yet, it seemed that that was exactly what had happened.

The other son, the older one, remained. Odd was married and settled peacefully on his farm. He seemed more like Ornolf than Thorgrim, less threatening, but without Ornolf's loud, raucous and undisciplined ways. Odd was well liked, but men were not drawn to him. He did not seem like a man to be worried about.

Halfdan looked up. "Thorgrim Night Wolf is dead," he said out loud and the men seated around him nodded, though neither they nor Halfdan knew if that was actually true. "And taxes are owed. Thorgrim owes us taxes, and if he is not here to pay them, then they must come out of his estate."

The others nodded again, though, in this too, none of them knew for certain that Halfdan's words were true. No one but Einar, who knew for certain that they were not. But that did not matter in the least.

"We've underestimated Odd Thorgrimson, I'll be the first to say so," Halfdan continued. "But we can do so no longer. Decisive action, that's what we need." Around him heads nodded more vigorously still.

"We'll assemble the hird, and all the warriors here, and we'll..." Halfdan began and then he stopped. The image of a ship popped into his mind. A ship hauled up on rollers and him poking around where the strakes met the keelson.

Sometimes you found a bit of rot in the wood there. Usually it did not look like much, and sometimes it wasn't. Easily cut out and replaced. But sometimes when you started to poke at it you found that the rot ran much deeper than you thought. Keep poking, and soon you find that the whole thing is rotten, through and through, and there is nothing to do but burn it all down to the keel.

"Hold..." Halfdan said. "First fetch riders. I would send word out, around the countryside. Arrangements must be made before we move on Odd Thorgrimson."

First, he thought, *we see how deep the rot runs in this.*

Chapter Twenty-Four

Bloody he was
on his breast before,
at the father of magic
he howled from afar...

The Poetic Edda

From the top of the makeshift wall, Leofric watched the disaster, the beautiful, beautiful disaster, play out on the water just a few hundred feet away.

"The boy was right," he said out loud. Ailmar, the captain of his guard, was standing next to him, but he did not hear, and Leofric wasn't really talking to him in any case.

"Damn my eyes, but the boy was right."

Leofric had not been so sure. Not sure that Nothwulf's idea would work, not sure it was even a good idea in the first place, trapping the Northmen there rather than just letting them sail away. They had discussed it, Leofric taking care to not let the discussion devolve into an argument. And of course, Nothwulf did not need to argue. He was the ealdorman, even if only half of Dorset agreed that he was. He could do as he wished.

On the other hand, Nothwulf needed all the friends he could muster, and Leofric was an important and powerful one, and they both knew it. For that reason, Nothwulf too kept things civil. And in the end he prevailed.

Because Cynewise was winning. It could not be denied. The majority of the thegns were with her, and she had the backing of her father, who secured the backing of the bishop, which could well mean the backing of King Æthelwulf. If she received the credit for driving the Northmen off, then it would further secure her position.

Even if paying danegeld was not the most admirable way of ridding the shire of the heathens, still it did the trick. They would be gone, and it would be her doing.

But stopping them, slaughtering them, reclaiming the stolen riches, that would make Nothwulf a hero indeed. It would be hard for Cynewise to claim the title of ealdorman after that.

Leofric smiled and shook his head as he watched the chaos unfold. They had sunk three old wrecks in the channel, and the first of the Northmen's ships had hit them and they stopped the Northmen dead. Now the flaming arrows had set the heathens' ship on fire in a dozen places. The crew looked like lunatics running back and forth, dousing the flames.

Those ships... Leofric thought. The sunken wrecks had come from Lymington to the east, the only ships in that port town, at least the only ones with which the owners would part. And little wonder: they were pretty much rotten even before his men had sunk them in the channel. It seemed a miracle to Leofric that they had survived the voyage to Christchurch, which was all of ten miles over calm seas.

The ships had served one last purpose above water before being sent to their final rest. They had been used to convey Leofric's men across the channel, so that they could fortify the southern shore just as Nothwulf had fortified the northern.

Leofric had pointed out as forcefully as he dared that the army was thus divided, and the only means of reuniting them was about to be scuttled and lost. Nothwulf had acknowledged the problem but did not consider it worth the worry. Leofric's men could march around and join Nothwulf's again before Cynewise even knew what had happened.

Dubious as he was, Leofric had to admit that judging by what he was seeing just then, playing out on the water, Nothwulf had been right about all of it. Thus far.

In the channel below, the next ship in line had come to the aid of the first, pulling it free from the wrecks. But now the third was coming down the channel and it seemed to be out of control, turning sideways and drifting. Even a landsman like Leofric could see something was terribly wrong.

He turned to Ailmar and spoke louder. "What say you, captain? What's happening there?" He nodded toward the channel below them, the three ships.

"Looks to me like the one in the middle, they anchored and they're pulling the other off. The one sideways in the channel? I think they're in some sort of trouble."

Leofric nodded. It did look that way. He had seen many things in his years, but he had never seen anything like that: three ships struggling in the narrow water, great flights of arrows whipping in from either shore, fires burning on board the vessels, his men cheering, the Northmen shouting and screaming.

The third ship, the one sideways in the channel, struck the second. For a moment they remained motionless, hanging on the one anchor. Then the anchor line broke, apparently, and the two ships drifted down onto the first, and the lot of them were swept along, stuck together, until the first fetched up on the sunken wrecks once again.

"Oh, that's done for them," Ailmar said and Leofric could hear the mirth in his tone. And he was probably right. Leofric looked to the west. The fourth of the heathens' ships was just coming into the mouth of the channel, but he could not imagine they would be stupid enough to follow the first three into that killing field.

As to those first three, Leofric did not see how they could get themselves out of this trap. The arrows were coming in faster than the men could put out the flames. They were almost beyond the range of Nothwulf's archers on the far shore, but they were an easy target for Leofric's, and his bowmen were taking full advantage. Soon, surely, the ships would be overwhelmed, the fires too numerous to be extinguished.

"See here, lord!" Ailmar said, pointing. The first ship was hard up against the submerged wreck, but the other two were still being driven by the current, pivoting around the first ship like a huge gate on hinges, swinging toward the south bank where Leofric's fortifications were built. His men were enjoying every moment, watching their target come closer, as if God were laying the heathens in front of them like a sacrifice.

Leofric watched in silent fascination. *Amazing...* he thought. The ships were massive, and they moved in utter silence. Even with all the shouting and the twang of bow strings and crackling of fires it seemed as if there was a noise missing, the sound that should have come with something so huge as those ships moving so swiftly.

The middle ship was caught partway on the first ship and partway on the wrecks and it stopped there. The third kept swinging but stopped before it came against the wrecks. Its stern was hung on the second ship, its bow seemingly fixed in place.

"Run aground!" Ailmar shouted.

"What?"

"That last ship! The bow's run up on the mud. See, there's a mud bank there, coming off the shore. That ship's hung up on the mud!"

"Ah," Leofric said. That explained why it had stopped where it was. And it also presented an opportunity.

The downside of Nothwulf's plan had always been twofold. The first problem was that half of the army was stranded on the south shore with only the few fishing boats they had to move them. Leofric was mortally certain that Cynewise's men were watching the goings-on, and would attack Nothwulf's weakened forces once the Northmen were dealt with, leaving Leofric to march as quickly as he could around the harbor, which would not be quick enough.

The other concern was that if Nothwulf's plan worked out right the heathens' ships would burn and sink in the channel. Bad for the Northmen, but not ideal for Nothwulf or Leofric either, who would lose most if not all of the plunder. Sure, some of it might be retrieved when the tide went out, but only some, and likely not much.

But now the Northmen's ships were stuck on the mud and within reach. Now Leofric could lead his men forward, capture them intact so they could be used to move the army back across the channel. Capture them without Nothwulf there, which was better still, since Leofric was quite certain Nothwulf would try to find some way of keeping the plunder for himself. That was not a harsh reflection on Nothwulf; it was just how men were.

"Ailmar, I have a thought that we might..." Leofric began when his words were cut short by a cry from the ships below. There had been plenty of noise from that quarter already, the shouts of panicked men, the shrieks of the wounded. But this was not that. This was something new. A man shouting, or screaming, or some mix of both, with a sharp keening thrown in. A frightening sound.

Leofric's and Ailmar's heads snapped up, their attention drawn to the strange cry. The swirl of frantic activity aboard the ships had not diminished: men running here and there, fighting the fires, throwing burning material overboard, dragging the wounded clear, trying to lever the ships apart. Chaotic and disorganized. And one man doing something that none of the others was doing.

One man. His movements stood out because they were so in contrast with the rest: this one Northman seemed oblivious to all that was going on around him. He raced down the center of the first ship, running in a near straight line, stern to bow. He seemed to be the one who was screaming that weird, beastly sound. He reached the front end of the first ship and clambered onto the middle ship, dropped to the deck and raced down the length of that one as well. He moved with astounding agility, dodging and weaving through the crowd of struggling men.

Leofric and Ailmar and the men near them, indeed most of the men on the wall, were watching him run, their bows forgotten. He reached the bow of the middle ship and flung himself over onto the last, the one closest to Leofric's defenses, the one run up on the mud. Once again he made his mad run down the length of the ship, and when he reached the bow he stepped up onto the side of the ship and hurled himself off, coming down in water up to his waist, but never breaking stride.

"What is this lunatic doing?" Ailmar said, but if he hoped for an answer he was disappointed because no one had any idea.

By the look of him he was a Northman like most Northmen: long hair, beard, though not so impressive a beard. Savage looking. Most Northmen, however, went into battle with shield and spear, or ax or sword. Many wore helmets, the fortunate ones wore mail. But this one had none of those things. Not even a tunic. He was bare-chested, wearing only leggings, and he carried two of those fearsome battle axes the Northmen used, one in each hand.

He ran though the water, lifting his legs high in an almost comical way. He reached the shore and ran up the sand beach halfway to the wall on which Leofric stood. There he stopped, maybe seventy feet away, and raised his axes over his head. The screaming changed from the demonic shriek to something else, and it took Leofric a moment to realize they were words. This thing was speaking. Leofric had heard Northmen speak before, and their language did not sound too different from English, but this man's words sounded very savage indeed.

"Something's not right with this one," Leofric heard one of his men say.

Leofric shook his head. He seemed to be transfixed by this odd sight, but there was no time for that. If they were going to attack the Northmen, board their ships, then it had to be done soon.

"Shoot him!" Leofric shouted. "Someone shoot that lunatic bastard."

This was sport the archers would truly enjoy, and he knew it. Two dozen bows came up almost at once, as the crazy Northman began to twist and turn in some sort of manic dance. Two dozen arrows flew free of their bowstrings. The Northman hopped side to side and spun in circles, axes held at arm's length, and two dozen arrows flew right past him. Not one found its mark.

"You stupid, blind bastards!" Ailmar shouted. "Shoot him, he's right bloody there!" But the archers did not need Ailmar's encouragement. Furious now, they nocked arrows, fired as fast as they could as the madman with the axes raced side to side, leapt up and down, even turned a summersault, screaming and shouting all the while. Taunting. The arrows whipped past, embedding themselves in the sand. The Northman seemed untouchable.

"Very well, damn this madman!" Leofric shouted. The man seemed imperviousness to the arrows and it was unnerving him. Time to move.

"Take up your shields and your weapons! We're going to capture those ships! We'll kill them all!" Leofric shouted and the rest shouted with him and he guessed they were as eager to be done with the specter in front of them as he was. All along the wall the archers climbed down to the ground behind them where their shields and armor and other weapons sat ready for them to grab up. The other men-at-arms, a hundred or more, those who were not archers as well, were already set and ready, equipped and awaiting their orders. They were all eager to be at it. The frustration of not being able to kill the madman was driving them.

"Go! Go!" Leofric shouted from the top of the wall. They had worked this out well before the longships had come into the channel, prepared for the possibility of actual combat on the shore. Half the men would charge around the east end of the defenses, half around the west, then they would meet in two columns and advance on the ships. They had thought it unlikely they would get the chance— neither Leofric nor Nothwulf imagined the vessels would be within reach—but here it was working out better than they had hoped.

From his vantage point, Leofric watched the columns of men sweeping around either end of the wall. "Very well, Ailmar, let's get on with it," he said. He crouched and reached down with his toe and found a foothold in the front of the wall, then scrambled down the fifteen feet to the sandy ground. He turned and swung the shield off his back and drew his sword just as the men from either end of the wall were meeting in the middle, falling in behind him, where he could lead them into the fight. Leofric might have been twenty years older than the next man there, but he would be second to no one when going into battle.

Ailmar was at his side now, and the rest of the men-at-arms arrayed behind. The lunatic Northman was still there, still doing his odd dance on the sand.

"We'll see how long this one keeps dancing his jig with two hundred armed men ready to drive spears up his arse," Ailmar said.

Leofric smiled and stepped off, leading the men forward. The madman saw them coming and he stopped and stood motionless on the sand, watching, seemingly transfixed.

That's right, you mad bastard, Leofric thought. *Here we come. Time for you to run.*

And the madman did run. He went from standing motionless to a full-on sprint in just a heartbeat's time. But he did not run back to the ships, as Leofric had expected. Rather, he charged, screaming, axes raised, straight at the English line.

Starri Deathless had reached the bow of *Sea Hammer* before Thorgrim even knew he was in motion. He heard Starri's scream through all the noise aboard his ship and the other two ships, but he was so caught up in the unfolding disaster in front of him that it hardly registered.

And then it did. "Oh, by the gods..." Thorgrim said, looking up, his eyes following the sound of Starri's war cry. Starri had just reached the bow and Thorgrim watched him swing around the stem and leap over to *Blood Hawk*'s stern and then race the length of that ship as well.

Thorgrim was not in the least bit surprised by this. He had been waiting for it. He knew Starri would not be able to remain in the presence of an enemy such as this without fighting them, hand to hand, even if he had to do it alone. But despite knowing it, Thorgrim had not considered trying to stop him, because he knew that would be impossible, and he had not considered what he would do when it happened.

He looked back at *Sea Hammer*'s deck. The flaming arrows were still coming in, but not so many now. He turned and looked to the north and the other defensive wall, but the archers there were too far away to have much hope of reaching the stranded ships. That was half the problem solved. The men on board his ship had the fires in hand, and the sail seemed safe for now. Harald had knocked the gallows out of the way and lowered the yard nearly down to the deck, where it was more protected and easier to dowse with water.

"I guess we had better go get Starri," Thorgrim said out loud, though he was talking to himself. He grabbed up his shield and slung it over his back and made his way forward. "Louis!" he shouted to the Frank who, alone among the men, was not doing much of anything. He was not lazy, Thorgrim knew, or a shirker. He simply had no idea what to do in virtually any situation on shipboard.

But he did know what to do in a fight.

"Get your shield and helmet and come with me. Harald! Gudrid!" Thorgrim called to men as he walked forward and the men grabbed up weapons and shields. Even those men whose names he did not call armed themselves and followed. Starri was not the only one who wished to come to grips with this vexing enemy.

Thorgrim reached the bow. He looked past *Blood Hawk* to the beach, where Starri was now dancing around, yelling and waving his axes. Along the wall the archers raised bows and let loose a flight of arrows. Thorgrim grit his teeth and braced for the sight of Starri pierced through and through, but the arrows flew past and Starri continued with his taunting dance unscathed.

And you think the gods favor me? Thorgrim thought. He climbed up onto *Sea Hammer*'s sheer strake and reached over to grab *Blood Hawk*'s sternpost. He stepped across, a bit awkwardly compared to the ease with which Starri had made that leap, as if he were walking on a beaten path.

Godi was there on the afterdeck, his face smudged black from fighting the fires and one hand covered with someone's half-dry blood.

"Going to fetch Starri?" Godi asked.

"We are," Thorgrim said, stepping clear so the men behind him could climb from *Sea Hammer* to *Blood Hawk*. Thorgrim looked down

Blood Hawk's deck. There were fires here and there, and half a dozen dead, most with clothing burned. There were black holes in the sail where the arrows had struck, but the damage did not seem irreparable.

Thorgrim looked past the ship to Starri on the beach. No more arrows that Thorgrim could see; most of the archers were gone from the wall. *Now what are they about?* Thorgrim wondered, but he thought he knew.

"They're going to attack us," he said. Just as Starri had been able to use the bridge of ships to get ashore, the English were going to use the same path to launch an attack. Obviously they would prefer to capture the ships and the plunder rather than burn and sink it all, and now they saw their chance.

And that changed everything. The Northmen were not just dragging the berserker Starri back aboard, they were going to defend their ships, the loss of which would undoubtedly mean the loss of their lives as well.

"To arms! To arms!" Thorgrim shouted in a voice to be heard across the decks of three ships. "To arms and follow me! The English whores' sons will be attacking us directly!"

Others took up the cry as Thorgrim raced forward. He reached *Blood Hawk*'s bow and made the step onto *Long Serpent*, an easier crossing, he was glad to see. Forward, the men of *Long Serpent* were gathering up weapons. The ship itself was in good shape, little sign of damage from arrows or fire, because she had not been long in the archers' range.

Once again Thorgrim hurried forward. He looked up in time to see the English men-at-arms swarming around either end of the defenses. They must have been ready for this very thing. They would want to catch the Northmen as they were coming ashore, when they were most vulnerable, and not after they had had time to form up. There was one hundred, two hundred of the men-at-arms, and only Starri Deathless standing against them.

But as far as Starri was concerned, he was all that was needed. He renewed his battle cry and broke into a run, charging straight at the English columns. Thorgrim could see the surprise in the English lines as the men-at-arms hesitated in their advance, clearly thrown off by this ridiculous attack.

Starri was on them in an instant. The man leading the lines of English soldiers stepped forward to meet him, shield in one hand, sword raised and ready in the other. Starri came to a stop a foot from the man and dropped low as he swung his shield. Starri dodged sideways, the shield passed him without striking, and the Englishman followed with a thrust of his sword. But Starri, quick as a snake, was hard to hit and the man missed with both.

Then Starri was up again. He hooked the edge of the man's shield with the curved blade of one ax and swung the other ax hard at the man's head. He connected and the man was down and Starri leapt over him and flung himself at the next in line.

Thorgrim smiled. Starri had just bought them the few moments they needed to get ashore and get in some sort of order. He reached *Long Serpent*'s bow and vaulted over the sheer strake. The water was nearly waist deep where he landed and he felt his shoes sink into the soft mud on which the ship's bow was grounded. He pushed his way toward the shore, taking exaggerated steps through the water, and heard the splashes and grunts of the men dropping into the water behind him.

Up the beach, near the wall, he could see a knot of thrashing, wild men, weapons hacking here and there, confusion, like a fox bringing panic to a chicken coop. This was what Starri Deathless could do to even a well-disciplined column of men. Thorgrim had seen it before, many times.

"Form up! Form up! Make a swine array!" Thorgrim shouted, waving and pointing where he wanted his men to go. They would arrange themselves in a wedge shape, with himself and Godi and Harald as the point, and drive into the English line.

Thorgrim raced a ways up the beach, gesturing to Godi and Harald to join him, shouting for the others to make their wedge formation, which they did, quickly. Thorgrim drew Iron-tooth and held the weapon high. He adjusted his grip on his shield and shouted as he ran forward, his eyes fixed on the line of Englishmen ahead.

He was aiming for the spot where Starri was doling out a single-handed beating, where the line was a tangled mess of men trying to sort themselves out. Where the confusion was the greatest. The sand was soft underfoot, the running hard, but the distance was not great, and suddenly he was there, plunging into the fight.

The Englishmen on the flanks, those not fighting with Starri, had seen them coming, and they closed in as the wings of Thorgrim's wedge came charging up. But the men-at-arms occupied with Starri had not seen this new threat, did not know the Northmen were there until Thorgrim and Harald and Godi slammed into the line with the weight of the rest of Thorgrim's men behind.

The first men-at-arms died with looks of shock on their faces, shields hardly raised in defense, but once those men were down the real fighting began. Thorgrim worked his shield left and right, knocking aside any weapons coming for him, thrusting with Iron-tooth, sometimes hitting shields, sometimes hitting flesh, sometimes hitting air.

There was little strength in the English line; the defense was not solid. Thorgrim could feel it, as he had before, on many battlefields. The two armies might be evenly matched in numbers and weapons and training, but one had the fighting spirit in them, and one did not, and he could feel that the English did not. He wondered if maybe Starri's madness had unnerved them.

Shield up, Thorgrim took the blow of an ax on its face, saw the blade break through the wood, then jerked it aside and thrust straight out, past the edge of his opponent's shield, right into his belly. He pulled the blade free as the scream was just building on the man's lips.

Thorgrim thought about the first man whom Starri had taken down, the man in front who had stepped up to fight. Was that man the leader of the Englishmen here? Were they now leaderless? Did the sight of that man falling so quickly demoralize the rest? It was possible, certainly. It could explain why the fight was draining out of them so fast.

Someone slammed against Thorgrim's left side and he half turned to see if it was friend or foe, but it was neither. It was Louis the Frank, eyes wide, sweat running down his face and making streaks in the blood splattered on his face. He was fighting with an Englishman right in front of him, while behind that man another was trying to get at Louis with the point of a spear.

The English sword came down and Louis caught it with his blade, inches before it would likely have cut his arm off. He lashed out with his foot and drove it into the man's knee. The man crumpled and Louis's sword found his neck as he went down and Thorgrim stepped up and drove Iron-tooth in the spearman's shoulder as he lunged forward.

Louis turned to Thorgrim and shouted, in Frankish, Thorgrim guessed, since he did not understand the words, but he did understand the look in Louis's eyes and the frantic gesture toward the beach. Thorgrim looked back over his shoulder as long as he dared, which was not long, but long enough to see what Louis meant. *Long Serpent* was on fire.

Perhaps one of the small fires had caught and spread, perhaps the archers were still shooting into her, but either way the ship was on fire and the flames were spreading fast. The fire was concentrated amidships mostly, running over the few shields still on the shield rack and crawling up the heavily tarred shrouds. It surrounded the base of the mast, which looked like a tree in a burning forest. It would catch the sail soon; there was no stopping it now.

"Oh, you bastards!" Thorgrim shouted as he turned back to the fight. He did not want to lose *Long Serpent*. She was a good ship, Jorund's command, and he wondered why Jorund was not leading the fight against the fire.

But more importantly, *Long Serpent* was their bridge to the other ships. If she burned to the waterline she might take *Blood Hawk* and *Sea Hammer* with her. Thorgrim and his men would be trapped on shore where they would eventually be killed. They could not hold the English off forever.

Louis was not the only one who had noticed this change of circumstance. The English men-at-arms began a cheer which spread like the fire on *Long Serpent*, jumping from man to man until the entire line of fighting men was yelling. And that in turn, put renewed vigor into them. Whereas a moment before Thorgrim could feel they were ready to break and run, now they surged forward, pushing back against the Northmen's line.

"Hold them! Hold them!" Thorgrim shouted, loud as he could, trying to be heard over the cacophony of the fight, and, he knew, likely failing. "Back away! Step by step, back to the ship!"

He batted a spear point away and took a step back and Harald and Godi and Louis did the same. Thorgrim stole a glance to the left and right. The others along the line were also backing away, yielding the ground foot by foot. This was an extraordinary danger, backing away, trying to reach their only avenue of escape before it burned and sank into the water. It was an invitation to panic, to his own men turning and running in fright.

Another step, and another. Another glance left and right. The men were looking behind them as they backed away, looking back at the ships which were their only means of escape and Thorgrim did not like the expressions he saw. He slashed at the Englishman in front of him, then looked quickly over his shoulder while the man was flinching from the blow.

Long Serpent was all but engulfed now, her sail and yard a bold line of flames running fore and aft, her mast burning. There would be no getting through that, and even if they could, it would do no good. The few men left aboard *Blood Hawk* had pushed *Long Serpent*'s stern free to keep the flames from spreading. Fifteen feet of water separated the stern of the one ship from the bow of the other.

That's that, Thorgrim thought. His arms wielded sword and shield while his mind scrambled for a way out of this. *Oak Heart, Fox...the other ships*, he thought. *Get to the other ships...*

How? His men were on the verge of breaking, and once they did they would be killed piecemeal. The Northmen were bold and skilled warriors in battle, more so than nearly any other men, but they were still just men. They could still be set to route. And Thorgrim did not even know where the other ships were.

"Hold! Hold!" Thorgrim shouted again. He could feel the hesitancy, and he thought he saw in the corner of his eye one of his men turning and running for the shore. He thought of stepping back, putting himself in a position to kill any man who tried to flee. Make them remember that he, Thorgrim Night Wolf, was more dangerous than the English would ever be.

Thorgrim took another swipe at the Englishman in front of him, an obstinate man with a sword who refused to be run through. He saw another of his men, far off on the left end of the line, break off from the fight and race for the beach.

Time to push forward, he thought. Backing away was pointless. It was time to surge ahead.

Then he heard the yelling.

It was not from the front, not from the English line, but from the right, and some ways away from the fighting. He frowned and looked in that direction, but he could not see through the lines of warriors, English and Northmen.

He took another step back, slashed again at the man in his front. They had been trading blows for what seemed like a half a day. Thorgrim's arm was tiring and he could tell his opponent's was as well. It would all have to end soon.

The yelling was closer. Thorgrim still could not see it but suddenly he felt it: some blow to the line of men in front of him, something that staggered the English and seemed to throw them into confusion. Thorgrim looked right again. The line of men-at-arms was crumbling, breaking apart, men running wildly as if a furious bear had been dropped in their midst. They ran for the walls and they ran toward the water and they ran east, straight away from the fight.

The wall of men thinned and Thorgrim was able to finally see. He could see the men who had come, and they were Northmen who had apparently run right up the English flank, hit them unawares and rolled on through. He looked west along the bank of the channel. *Oak Heart* was pulled up on the shore, and just beyond her, *Fox* sat with her bow in the sand. Further out on the water, *Dragon* and *Black Wing* were backing down on *Sea Hammer* and *Blood Hawk*, ready to tow them off.

Asmund, captain of *Oak Heart* pushed through the men, over toward Thorgrim, with Hardbein of *Fox* at his side. Thorgrim took their hands, shook them, slapped them on the shoulders.

"Well done," he said. "Well done."

They stood in awkward silence for a moment, looking around, then Asmund said, "Looks like you need taking out to your ship."

Thorgrim looked back at *Sea Hammer*. She and *Blood Hawk* were well clear of the flames, thanks to the gods and the men left on board. *Long Serpent* was burning end to end and starting to settle in the water.

"We do," Thorgrim said, then he called out to the other men on the beach, "Let's get aboard *Oak Heart*! Let's leave this place. Get the wounded and the dead! Some of you drag Starri along if he won't come." Starri was still wailing and struggling, trying to get at the fleeing enemy, while six men held him back, a harder task than fighting the English men-at-arms.

Thorgrim's eye caught a glint of metal on the beach and he looked down. Fifteen feet away a man lay motionless on the sand, one of many. But the helmet that he wore was polished bright—that's had caught Thorgrim's eye—and his mail was as well. Thorgrim stepped closer. The man was no common soldier. He had a thin white beard and moustache, and the clothes he wore under the armor were made of fine linen and embroidered around the edges. This was the man who had first stepped up to fight Starri, Thorgrim was certain.

He knelt down and pressed his fingers into the man's neck. Most did not live through an encounter with Starri Deathless on the field of battle, but this one did not look dead. And indeed Thorgrim could feel a pulse, a strong pulse, beating under his fingertips.

He stood. "Take this one," he said to a handful of his men standing nearby. He pointed to the man on the ground. He was not sure why he had given that order. Better to just kill him there and be done with it. But something told Thorgrim to do otherwise.

"Grab him up and bring him along and let's get off this stinking beach."

Chapter Twenty-Five

He who makes blades bound,
the warrior wont to rule supposes
our fate's in his two strong fists...

The Saga of Ref the Sly

Amundi Thorsteinsson was riding back from an inspection of his fields when he saw the riders coming. Three of them, and one held a shaft with a banner flying at the end. He was still too far off for Amundi to see what banner it was, but in truth he didn't have to.

He sighed. "Here we go," he said to Thord, his overseer, who rode next to him.

"Lord?"

"Things have been peaceful here for...what? A week now? But I think that blessed interlude is over."

This would be the perfect cap to the past few days, Amundi thought. His thoughts had been in a whirl ever since returning from Odd's farm, where they had done battle with Halfdan's men. Battle. It was not something he had experienced in a long time.

He had fought often in his younger days, raiding on foreign soil or in feuds with neighbors or hunting down cattle thieves. He had been a decent warrior. Nothing like Odd's grandfather Ulf, or even Thorgrim Night Wolf, but decent enough. He had liked it. It made him feel alive.

He'd tasted that again, fighting at Odd's farm, and it made him more acutely aware of something he had long understood: they, he and his neighbors, all of Vik, had been very lucky with the peace they had enjoyed for many years now. Twenty at least, he imagined, since the last time there had been any real trouble in that country. They had become used to it. They had become like weapons whose edges were left to grow dull.

"Is this trouble, lord, do you think?" Thord asked. "Should I get our men under arms?"

"Trouble, probably," Amundi said. "But I don't think we'll be fighting today. I think these men bring trouble, but they will not give it. No, ride ahead and see the boys are ready to care for these fellows' horses, and see my wife sets a good meal for them."

"Yes, lord," Thord said and put the spurs to his horse, riding on ahead of Amundi toward the stables and the hall.

Amundi followed after him, riding more slowly, walking his horse toward the stables. He was not eager to plunge into whatever was about to happen.

His spirit had been low for some time now. On his way back from Odd's farm he had ridden through the property owned by his neighbor, Thorgrim Night Wolf, whom he had not seen in several years. It was a melancholy experience.

Thorgrim's farm had always been a bustling place, well-tended and prosperous. There were workers and servants and thralls and they were all well cared for and content in their lot. Thorgrim had always been welcoming to Amundi, unless Amundi arrived in the evening on a day when Thorgrim was taken by the black mood. But at those times Thorgrim was generally absent, and in his place Hallbera was a kind and thoughtful hostess.

Even after Thorgrim and Ornolf had sailed away, little had changed. Odd kept a close watch on the farm. Skafti Hrappsson, the overseer, was honest and competent, and if he was not as exacting as Thorgrim had been, still he made sure all was in good order. Thorgrim's farm, Amundi's neighbor's farm, was run with care and consideration, and was as prosperous as one might expect of such a place.

No more. Amundi had ridden through the fields, which were quickly being overgrown with weeds and tall grass. He had ridden though the farmyard, past the outbuildings, the smith and the stables and the storehouses. Past the empty great hall.

There was no one there now. Some had gone to live at Odd's farm, some had simply left. Odd had removed pretty much anything of value, and Halfdan and thieves unknown had removed the rest. There were no chickens, no ducks, no cats or dogs. The buildings were already starting to show signs of neglect. There was a lifeless quality to the place. A hall of the dead.

It had given Amundi an uneasy feeling that he still had not shaken off, because he knew that the change that had come to Thorgrim's farm was just a harbinger of the change that was coming to Vik, and to all of the country around. They had enjoyed twenty years of peace and abundance, but that could not go on forever.

He reined to a stop in the middle of his yard. There were still chickens and ducks at his farm, and they scattered as he rode past them and the stable boys came out to take his horse. Servants bustled around, and the blacksmith's hammer rang with its semi-musical note. His farm was every bit as well-run and successful as Thorgrim's. In truth, Amundi had always been aware of an unspoken and generally amiable sense of competition between him and Thorgrim. Amiable, perhaps, because there was no clear winner, neither of them obviously outstripping the other.

Alfdis, Amundi's wife of twenty-five years, came hurrying out of the hall, wiping her hands on her apron. "Who are these visitors, husband?" she asked.

"Halfdan's men," Amundi said. The two of them looked off to the south. The riders were close now, minutes from arriving. "You've set out food and drink for them?"

"Yes," Alfdis said, making no effort to disguise her concern. "What do they want?"

"I don't know," Amundi said, which was true, but he had a pretty good idea, at least of the general nature of their business.

They were still standing there, husband and wife, when the riders came trotting into the yard. Amundi could see now that he had been right about the banner: a long, red, pointed silk flag with the black head of an ax at the widest part. The banner of Halfdan the Black.

"Amundi!" the lead rider said as he slipped down from his horse and one of the stable boys took the reins.

"Thorstein, welcome," Amundi said. Thorstein was one of Halfdan's hirdsmen, part of the elite house guard, whom Amundi had known for many years. Amundi had expected Einar to be leading this contingent, but on second thought he was not surprised that Einar was not there. He guessed that Einar was not much in favor with Halfdan just then.

"Welcome, Thorstein, it's been too long," Alfdis said, stepping up and giving the man a perfunctory hug.

"Thank you, Alfdis," Thorstein said. "It has been too long." There was an odd note in Thorstein's voice, as if he was trying and failing to be more formal than he would naturally be in that company. It seemed Thorstein did not relish the task he was on.

"Please come in, you and your men," Alfdis said.

"We've not come for a visit," Thorstein said. "There's business we must..."

"Of course," Alfdis said. "But you've ridden hard, I can see that, and I'm sure you're hungry and thirsty. Come, come." Alfdis was not a woman who would stand to be found wanting in hospitality, whether that hospitality was desired or not.

Soon they were seated at the hall's center table, meat and cheese and bread and ale spread out before them, and they ate and drank. They spoke about many things, but Halfdan and the recent events were not among the topics. Thorstein had not been at the fight at Odd's farm, Amundi was all but certain. Halfdan would not have risked his precious hird for a task he must have thought would be easily accomplished.

"Very well," Amundi said at last. Thorstein clearly had something to say, and with every bite of Amundi's food, every sip of his ale, he was growing more reluctant to say it. "Please, Thorstein, tell us why you've come."

"Of course," Thorstein said. "I bring word from King Halfdan. He sends his regards and asks that you and as many of your warriors as you can spare ride to his hall in Grømstad. He reckons you should be able to bring a dozen men, at least."

"Does he?" Amundi said. "Well, he should know."

Thorstein shifted on his bench. "I need not remind you of your obligation to the king. Your obligation to serve under arms, you and your men," he said.

"No, you need not. And when does he want us there?"

"As soon as you possibly can. Tomorrow. Can you get there by midday?"

Alfdis spoke next. "This is a very busy time on the farm, Thorstein, you know that. This is not the time for the men to be gone. My husband especially. Being ready for the winter could well depend on this week."

"Of course..." Thorstein began, but Amundi cut him off. Thorstein certainly knew all this. He might even have been sympathetic. Further discussion was pointless: there was no chance of Thorstein changing his decision because the decision was not his to change. Amundi could either comply or he could drive Thorstein off, and he was not about to drive the man off. Amundi did indeed have an obligation to his king. He had not forgotten that.

"I understand, Thorstein," he said. "I can assemble the men, and we can try to make it by midday. Will that do?"

"Yes, that will do," Thorstein said. He did not offer to tell Amundi the reason for the summons, and Amundi did not ask. He did not need to.

Thorstein accepted Amundi's invitation to spend the night, it being too late to make it back to Grømstad until well after dark. But he and his men were up early the next day and gone before Amundi had even called for his men and told them of this unexpected summons.

It was not midday, but late afternoon, when Amundi finally arrived at Halfdan's hall. He could have pushed harder and arrived earlier if he had been eager to get there, but he was not, so he timed his arrival to be as late as it could be without sparking Halfdan's anger.

He rode at the head of a column that numbered a dozen men. They were the free men who worked his farm and some who rented land from him. The armor they wore, the weapons they carried, had been handed down from father to son, or acquired in one way or another, or given by Amundi as gifts for good and faithful work.

Amundi led the men through the big gate, well-guarded but open, and into the open area by the great hall. He saw there what he expected to see: a crowd of men, all ready for battle. And beyond them, staked out, the horses on which they would get there.

Ulfkel Ospaksson was the first to greet him, hurrying over in his quick though ponderous way. "Amundi! Thor's arse, I supposed you'd be here first. You're not the sort to dawdle, I know that. Then I wondered if you'd decided not to come to the party."

Amundi slipped down from his horse and signaled for his men to do likewise. "Wouldn't miss this, Ulfkel, even if I could. Which I can't."

"None of us can," Ulfkel said, then lowered his voice in what he reckoned was a conspiratorial tone. "That whore's whelp Halfdan's got some plan, and I don't think we'll like it."

"I think you're right. As usual, Ulfkel," Amundi said, also speaking in a near whisper. He looked around. He saw Vifil at the far end of the ground and Ragi Oleifsson with his own men, and a few of the other farmers in the area, men with holdings of various sizes. All of the men of status except for Odd, and that was as he guessed it would be.

"I think we should get us all together: you, me, Ragi, all the leading men here. Talk this out," Ulfkel said.

"We should," Amundi said. "But I doubt we'll have the chance."

And he was right. By the time he and his men had staked out the horses, Einar had come from the long hall and called for the attention of the men gathered there. Amundi looked close at Einar, tried to see if he had sustained any injury from the fight at Odd's farm, or, more likely, injury from Halfdan on his reporting what had happened. But Amundi could see nothing of the sort.

"Gentlemen, listen here," Einar said, then paused a moment as the buzzing of talk settled down. "King Halfdan is most pleased that you've come to his summons, and in a willing and timely way. You do, as you know, owe military service to your king, and King Halfdan is satisfied that you take that obligation seriously."

Einar paused, apparently waiting for some to argue or object, but no one did, so he continued. "It's not often that King Halfdan calls on you, but when there's a genuine threat to this kingdom then it's necessary that he do so. And such a threat has arrived now."

Again Einar paused. Amundi figured he was waiting for someone to ask what that threat might be, a question to which Einar doubtlessly had an answer ready to go. Amundi wondered if anyone would in fact ask. He glanced over at Ulfkel. If anyone was willing to speak up it would be him. But Ulfkel was standing with arms folded and mouth in a frown and he did not look poised to speak.

I wonder if there's any here so foolish that they can't guess at the reason we've been called, Amundi thought.

"Good," Einar said with a tone that suggested the talk was over. "It's late in the day, now. King Halfdan will not ask you to ride through the night. He asks you feel welcome in his hall, where you will all sleep, and then in the morning, we ride."

The men were ushered into Halfdan's hall, and though they were near two hundred warriors, the hall was enormous and accommodated them all with ease. They ate and drank and Halfdan did not join them. But Einar was there, and Amundi and the others who had brought fighting men with them were very aware of his presence, as well as that of Onund Jonsson, captain of Halfdan's hird, his personal army, the paid warriors of his house guard, as well as other members of Halfdan's retinue. They were being watched, and much as Amundi would have liked to gather with the others and talk this out, he knew that such seemingly conspiratorial activity would get back to Halfdan, and Halfdan would not look charitably upon it.

So they slept, and they woke, and they had their morning meal, and then Einar said, "Pray, get your mounts and make ready to ride out. This business will not keep you long from your farms, we don't think."

The men put on what armor they had, belted on weapons and stumbled out of the hall to where their horses waited. They mounted up and formed themselves into a ragged column. At the end of the column stood two heavy wagons loaded with food and ale, enough to feed the entire army for a few days, at least.

I guess maybe we'll be gone longer from our farms than you would have us believe, Amundi thought.

They were all on horseback and waiting when Halfdan made his first appearance, stepping through the big door. On his head was a bright shining helmet and over his shoulders a cloak made of red silk, like his banner, trimmed in ermine and clasped with a massive jeweled broach. His mail glinted like sunlight on the breeze-rustled surface of clear water.

Stable boys held Halfdan's horse as he mounted, and behind him half a dozen of his hirdsmen mounted as well. Thorstein was among them, as was the flag bearer who had come with Thorstein to summon Amundi. The hirdsmen were armed and outfitted nearly as well as Halfdan himself.

They rode out, heading north along the road Amundi had followed the day before to get to Halfdan's hall. They rode mostly in silence, with just a word here and there and the occasional sound of a horse's whinny or a cough or curse from one of the men. They stopped for their midday meal and then resumed their travels. Their pace was not leisurely, but two hundred or more men could not move as swiftly as a dozen could, and they were still riding as the sun began to drop in the west.

Amundi had only a vague idea of where they were heading when they left Halfdan's compound, but as they traveled he felt more certain, and his stomach tightened as it became increasingly clear to him that he was right. Then at last Halfdan, riding at the head of the long column, turned off the main road and led the men down another, smaller road that Amundi knew well—the road to Thorgrim Night Wolf's farm.

The place looked just as forlorn as it had when Amundi had ridden though some days before, more so even, with the daylight fading away. They rode down the long hill to the yard around which the buildings were built, the empty and deserted buildings, and when they were all there, Halfdan told the men they could dismount, though he himself remained on horseback.

"We'll spend the night here," Halfdan said, and his voice sounded odd in the unnatural quiet of the place. "This farm is mine now, forfeited by the family of Thorgrim Ulfsson for failing to pay his taxes. So you may sleep in the hall, or wherever you wish. It's all here for you to use. In the morning we get on with our business."

Ulfkel Ospaksson, who among them was the least given to restraint, could bear no more. "What business is that, Lord Halfdan?" he called. "We've ridden until our arses are numb, and with no idea why."

Halfdan wheeled his horse so he was looking directly at Ulfkel. He must have been anticipating that question all day, Amundi imagined, and there was a practiced quality to his words.

"Your king requires it, that's all you need to know," Halfdan replied. "All you need to know for now. In the morning you'll all be told what we're about, what our work is. In any event, Ulfkel, if I tell you now you'll just forget by morning anyway, and you know it."

That dig at Ulfkel brought a chuckle and broke the mounting tension. A fire was built in the long hearth in Thorgrim's hall and barrels of food and ale unloaded from the wagons, and once that began to flow the mood grew lighter still. For most.

The noise of eating and drinking and talking faded as the night progressed, and finally there was just snoring, copious and loud. But sleep did not come for Amundi. He was used to the snoring, that would not have disturbed his rest, but the turmoil in his mind was something new, and he fought with that beast all through the night.

He drifted off at last, and woke to the bustle of Halfdan's men cooking a great caldron of porridge over the revived flames in the hearth. They ate, the more important among them at the table, the others on the raised platforms on either side of the hall. Halfdan sat in the high seat, the seat of honor, which Thorgrim Night Wolf had once occupied.

"You've shown yourselves to be good and loyal men," Halfdan said when the meal was finished. He spoke loud and his words carried throughout the long, high-ceilinged hall. "You came when I summoned, and did not show discontent. But that's not true of all the men who live in the country of Vik, no, not at all."

No one spoke now, no one moved. They looked at Halfdan and they listened. "Odd Thorgrimson, whose father once owned this farm, has chosen to defy me. To put himself outside the law. And worse, he has used violence against his king's men. He has unsheathed his sword. And that cannot be forgiven. No man can defy his king, not when good men like you come and do your duty when summoned. So today we ride to the farm of Odd Thorgrimson and we capture the villain and his family and we see that justice is done. And when it is, you all will be rewarded."

Silence followed Halfdan's words, and Amundi thought, *And there it is…and I can put off choosing no longer.* But he had already made his choice, lying awake in the dark hall.

He stood. Halfdan looked at him and all the others did as well.

"Lord Halfdan," he said. "I have always been loyal to my king. To you and to your father, and I am just as loyal today. I'm ready to take up arms when you give the word. But we're free men here." He made a sweeping gesture, indicating all the men in the hall. "We're not slaves. What we own—land, houses, thralls, cattle—we'll let no man, king or thief, take from us. And that's how Odd Thorgrimson feels, too. What he did is not right, setting a trap for your men, but neither is taking his land with no cause."

He stopped. It seemed as if the quiet had redoubled. No one moved or spoke as Amundi met Halfdan's stare and held it. The others might have expected Halfdan to explode in anger, but Amundi knew better. Halfdan the Black had far too much control for that.

"Odd is an outlaw," Halfdan said at last, his voice calm and smooth, just as Amundi knew it would be. "His land was not taken without cause. It wasn't his land to begin with. It was his father's land, and his father owed taxes he did not pay."

Neither man, Halfdan not Amundi, moved, nor did anyone else in the hall. "Thorgrim Night Wolf is my neighbor and my friend," Amundi said. "Whether he owed taxes or not, it's not mine to say. But you tried to simply take his land for yourself, without giving Odd a chance to speak, or to make it right. That's not how a free man should be treated. There are laws about this, about how a man's property is to be confiscated. I don't deny it, what Odd did was wrong, but it's what a free man, a free man of honor, would be expected to do."

Silence again. Then Halfdan said, "Then what do you propose to do?"

"I would implore you to speak to Odd. To let him make this right. If Thorgrim's farm is to be confiscated, then do it according to the law. As for me, I won't be part of any attack on Odd Thorgrimson and his family. I'll go back to my farm, me and my men. You have warriors enough, you won't feel our loss."

Amundi nodded toward Thord and the others who had ridden with him and they stood and filed over to stand by him. Then Ulfkel Ospaksson stood as well.

"I'm in agreement with my friend Amundi," he said. "We're free men. We have our rights. Our land is not to just be taken, not Odd's, not any of ours." He nodded toward his men and they stood and came over to him as Amundi's had done.

And then the others. Vifil, Ragi Oleifsson, Thorgeir Herjolfsson, the rest of the landowners there, each stood and summoned his men and in a long file they left the hall and found their horses. They were silent, save for Ulfkel, who muttered and cursed under his breath. It was a profound choice they had made.

"Amundi," said Vifil as he settled on his horse. "Are you returning to your farm?"

"Yes," Amundi said. "I've stuck my nose too far deep into this already. It's no business of mine."

And then he thought, *Odd will know soon enough what a world of hurt I've just unleashed.*

Halfdan the Black was still standing by the high seat as the men shuffled out of the hall. He watched them go and his face wore no discernable expression. Then, when the door closed behind the last man, he sat. Einar was on his right side, Onund Jonsson on his left. Scattered around the table seven other men, part of his hird, all the men he had left for his attack on Odd's farm.

No one spoke. No one would dare speak before he did. He knew that. These men were loyal. They would sit here until they died of thirst before they would speak their minds unbidden. And Halfdan was not ready to speak, not just then. He had to let his rage settle, let his thoughts order themselves.

After some time, when he trusted that his voice would sound as calm as if he were exchanging pleasantries, he said, "Well, Einar, I suppose now we see how deep the rot is running."

"Yes, lord," Einar said.

"Did you think it ran so deep?" Halfdan asked. It was a terribly cruel thing to ask, because any answer that Einar could give might be expected to meet Halfdan's wrath. Halfdan watched the man fidget a bit. He knew the question was cruel and he did not care in the least. Einar had made a hash of a number of things recently. It was his fault, really, that Halfdan was in the position he was in. But he did not intend to overtly punish Einar. That would be over too quickly. Instead he would subject him to subtle torture, drawn out over weeks and months.

"No, lord, I didn't," Einar said. "Amundi, certainly. No surprise there. But not the others."

Halfdan nodded. In truth, he had not expected so much rot either. He knew Amundi would be disloyal, the bastard. And he had expected one or two of the others as well. But not all of them.

"Amundi is a problem," Halfdan said, mostly to himself. Amundi was growing too rich and too powerful. But Amundi was not as much of a problem as Odd was. The people would follow Odd because, like Amundi, he was rich and well-liked and admired. And unlike Amundi, he was the son of Thorgrim Night Wolf, grandson of Ornolf the Restless and Ulf of the Battle Song. The irony, Halfdan had come to realize, was that he understood the power that Odd could wield even more than Odd himself did.

So Odd needed to be crushed, before he came to fully understand his place in Vik and the potential it offered.

Halfdan knew that some men in his place might listen to the landowners' grievances, consider that they might have a valid point, maybe come to some accommodation. But only weak and uncertain men would do that, and Halfdan was neither of those things. He had no doubt that he was right, and the others were wrong. And disloyal. And because he was certain of his righteousness and more clever than the others, he had anticipated this very thing, this near rebellion, and made ready for it.

"This is good," Halfdan said. "This is good. We're getting at the rot now; we'll cut it out. If they're all disloyal, then they'll all forfeit their land. We'll see that it goes to men who know how to serve their king." He spoke loud to make certain that everyone in the hall heard him. This was a rumor he wanted to spread, the notion that the king would be handing out the best farms to the men who served him most loyally.

"Where are the others?" Halfdan asked Einar.

"Just a few miles from here," Einar said quickly. "Two hundred warriors. They made camp last evening. I sent Thorstein to speak with them. To make certain they were there and ready to move."

Halfdan nodded. Einar was being very careful not to make any further blunders.

Knowing that at least some of the landowners would desert him, Halfdan had ordered two hundred of his best men, including the remainder of the hird, to follow behind and wait for his word. Two hundred men he could lead in an attack against Odd, and crush him and anyone else who proved disloyal.

And now he knew the truth, the depth of the rot. They were all disloyal. He and his men would have more work on their hands than he had originally thought, cutting the rot away.

Chapter Twenty-Six

I guess that before he gets me,
the ring-giver, craver of sword-crashing
will meet with tricks — there'll be
a victory ode for me.

The Saga of Ref the Sly

There was quite a lot to do and little time in which to do it. Thorgrim Night Wolf could hear the shouts of the English men-at-arms and he guessed they were getting their warriors back in order and would renew the fight soon. He made his way through the crowd of men, the crews of four longships, shouting orders, pointing here and there, pushing men in various directions. The dead and wounded had to be found and carried off to the waiting ships. Any discarded English weapons worth keeping had to be collected up. Armor and shoes and purses had to be removed from the English casualties left on the beach.

Oak Heart was the larger of the two vessels run up on the beach. Most of the wounded and dead were loaded aboard her, and when they were secure, the men who could still walk climbed aboard, and aboard *Fox* as well. Thorgrim, Asmund, Godi and Hardbein were the last to go, as was befitting their place as captains. Harald, too, waited until the others were safe aboard because that was the way Harald was. Thorgrim took one last look around.

"Good," he said. All of his men had been carried off. There were only English on the beach now, some moving feebly about, most lying motionless.

How by all the gods are we going to get out of this miserable harbor? Thorgrim wondered, but that question he kept to himself. He turned and gave the others a nod and they climbed aboard the ships,

Thorgrim, Harald and Asmund aboard *Oak Heart*, Hardbein aboard his command, *Fox*. Asmund, Thorgrim noted, had brains enough to not run the bow of his ship too hard up on the beach, and to drop an anchor behind him as he headed for shore. Between rowing astern with the oars, double-manned, and hauling on the anchor rope it was little problem to back her off. The same with *Fox*.

Asmund said nothing other than to call a few orders forward as he saw to getting his ship underway. Thorgrim looked aft, out toward the channel. *Dragon* had *Sea Hammer* under tow and had already pulled her clear of the sunken ships and the burning *Long Serpent*. Likewise, *Black Wing* was towing *Blood Hawk* clear. The tide was against them now, but with the men pulling hard at the oars the shallow-bottomed vessels were able to make decent way against it.

"We'll get you over to *Sea Hammer* directly," Asmund said.

"No," Thorgrim said. "I'll stay here for now." It was a hard choice—every man naturally wanted to be with his ship, particularly when there was danger—but *Sea Hammer* and *Blood Hawk* seemed safe now, more or less, and trying to come alongside and get aboard them would just put them in greater jeopardy. So Thorgrim swallowed his anxiety and remained where he was and watched his fleet crawl free of the killing trap into which they had blundered.

A few desultory arrows flew their way, some striking the ships, but the enthusiasm had gone out of the English and there was little effort made to stop the Northmen's retreat. *And why should there be,* Thorgrim wondered. The English had done almost all they had hoped to do: they stopped their enemy's escape, burned one of their ships, killed any number of them in a fight on the beach. They had trapped them like wolves in a pit.

"Let me tend to that."

Thorgrim pulled his eyes from the beach and the makeshift walls they were leaving astern. Failend was standing in front of him. Small as she was, she looked smaller still with him standing on the raised after deck and her on the deck below.

"What?"

Failend pointed to Thorgrim's leg. He looked down. The leggings on his left thigh were neatly sliced and through the rent in the fabric he could see dried blood and the red gleam of blood still flowing. He had not even been aware of the wound.

He looked up at Failend. Her hair was a tangle and there were streaks of blood on her face. She wore no expression that he could see. In her hand were some strips of cloth.

"Yes, thank you," Thorgrim said. Failend nodded and knelt on the after deck. Thorgrim watched her hands as she peeled the cloth back and dabbed at the wound, then began to carefully wrap the cloth around it. He was aware of the laceration now, and the pain came rushing in like a storm-driven wave, as if all the pain he had not felt came on all at once. He sucked in his breath.

"It must hurt," Failend said, but there was still little expression in her voice. "We might have to sew it later."

"It's mostly your sewing that's holding me together these days," Thorgrim said. Failend tied the bandage off and stood.

"Mine and others," she said.

Thorgrim looked her up and down. "You're unhurt?"

She shrugged. "The English didn't hurt me," she said.

"Good," Thorgrim said. "Thank you, for your help on the beach."

"Well, I'm a heathen now," she said. "And I guess this is what heathens do. Can you stand?"

"Yes, I think so," Thorgrim said. "I seem to be standing now, mostly." He was favoring his intact leg and trying not to think about how much his wounded leg hurt.

"I'll sit here," Failend said, gesturing toward a place near the break of the after deck. "Let me know if you need help."

Failend sat and what seemed a look of exhaustion washed over her, but Thorgrim had other things to think about.

"Mud bank, off to starboard!" Starri's voice called out. Thorgrim looked up. Starri was in his place at the head of the mast.

"What's he doing up there?" Asmund asked. He was standing at the tiller behind Thorgrim and his voice was like a growl. Asmund was not much of a talker.

"Serving as lookout," Thorgrim said. "He likes it up there, and he does no harm." He paused, and then said, "Actually, he can be pretty helpful at times, doing that. Not just fighting."

Asmund made a grunting noise and Thorgrim directed him to turn *Oak Heart* a bit to larboard to avoid the wide mud bank north of them. He looked astern. The rest of the ships were falling in behind. *Dragon* and *Black Wing* still had the other, short-handed vessels in tow, but the work of pulling them became easier as the ships left the confines of the channel where the water ran fast and hard, squeezed in by the banks.

Now what? Thorgrim wondered. The route to the sea was blocked. There were English armies scattered all over the countryside, and he had no way of knowing where they were or how large. Going ashore anywhere, even to their makeshift longphort, could be a fatal proposition.

He looked off the starboard bow. A sandbar rose up from the harbor, a long, light brown, sandy stretch of dry land. There was nothing else there besides sand—no trees, no water, no food, nothing to form a defense. But more importantly, there was no army of Englishmen.

"There," he said, turning toward Asmund. "See that sandbar? That's where we're going."

The ebbing tide grew less swift as the bay opened up around them, and soon *Oak Heart*'s sharp bow drove into the edge of the sandbar. The ship came to a stop, so easily that it could not be felt. One moment she was moving and the next moment she was not. The oars came in and men jumped over the side and waded ashore. Anchors were lowered down, carried up the beach and driven into the soft, warm sand. On either side of the ship the rest of the fleet did likewise until they were all there, all run up ashore.

Thorgrim hobbled forward, toward the bow. Harald was there, a worried look on his face, which irritated Thorgrim mightily.

"Father, can I help you?" he asked. "Let me get a line, we can set you down on the beach. Or at least rig a gangplank."

"No, Harald. Thank you. It's fine, my leg. Just a small thing." He continued forward, Harald half a pace behind. He swung one leg over the ship's side and then the other. He pushed off, knowing how much it would hurt when he landed, how foolish he was to not take Harald's offer just for the sake of pride. He knew how much worse his dignity would fare if he screamed in pain like a little girl.

All that he thought in the heartbeat it took him to drop from the sheer strake down into the water. He took care to take the weight on his right leg, but that nearly buckled under him, so he put his left leg down and felt the pain shoot up his side. He clenched his teeth. He did not scream. He chastised himself for an aging fool.

Just behind him Harald dropped effortlessly into the water. Thorgrim was certain the boy wanted to take his arm and offer support as they made their way ashore, and he was equally certain that Harald knew better than to try.

"Come on," Thorgrim said.

They walked ashore through the knee-high water and onto the soft sand and Thorgrim found himself breathing deep from the exertion. He stopped, hands on hips, and looked around. A handful of men were already there, seeing to anchors and mooring lines, but the rest were still aboard the ships. They sat on their sea chests, resting from the terrible exertion of that day: rowing, fighting fires, fighting their enemy, rowing harder still, all with their brethren dying around them.

Let them rest, Thorgrim thought.

But there was no rest for him, at least no respite from making decisions. Because now they were stuck on a sandbar, trapped in that miserable harbor, and ringed in by enemies on every shore.

He was about to tell Harald to summon the other captains when he saw they were coming already. Asmund from *Oak Heart* and Hardbein from *Fox* were heading toward him, and further along the beach Godi Unundarson, Halldor, commander of *Black Wing* and Fostolf from *Dragon* were approaching.

Jorund, Thorgrim thought. Jorund was the one he wanted to talk to. Much of the debacle in the channel had been the result of his ill-advised attempt to turn his ship in midstream. Now *Long Serpent* was burned to the waterline and more men were dead than needed to die. Thorgrim wanted very much to talk to Jorund.

But Jorund did not arrive. Rather, one of Jorund's men, a man named Ofeig, stepped up to the gathering. "Jorund's dead," Ofeig said. "Just as we were coming down the channel. He saw what was happening, that your ships had struck something and were stuck. He was getting the rowers to back oars, ordered an anchor over the stern, so we could come down slow and pass a tow line. Then one of those arrows got him, right in the chest. We had to put him out...the fire...on his clothes and his beard." Thorgrim could hear the pain in the man's voice. Jorund was well-liked by his men. That was why few seemed to mourn when their old chief, Ketil Hrolfsson, was killed and Jorund took his place.

"And then...?" Halldor prompted.

"It was just madness. Jorund on fire. Dead. Fires breaking out all over. Next thing we knew we were sideways in the channel and that was the end of it."

Heads nodded all around. Thorgrim felt a touch of relief. He did not like to think that Jorund had made such a hash of things.

"His body?" Thorgrim asked.

"Burned with *Long Serpent*," Ofeig said. He gave half a smile. "I guess he had a proper send-off to the corpse hall. A funeral fit for such a man. Or nearly."

The others nodded. The funeral pyre of a man like Jorund should have included horses and tack, tools and food and ale and a slave girl to serve him on his journey. But at least his death was as good as any man could hope for.

Ofeig turned and walked away. The others were silent for a moment, thinking about Jorund and his death at the end of a flaming arrow. And where he might be now. Surely he had been lifted up to Valhalla by the Choosers of the Slain.

"Very well," Thorgrim said at last. "We don't all get as lucky as Jorund."

He looked past the gathering at the sandbar and the shores of the harbor beyond. The land was not very far away, a quarter mile at most. But Thorgrim had never seen any vessel bigger than a fishing boat in that harbor, and even if the English rounded up everything that would float they would not be able to get enough men onto the sandbar at once to launch a credible attack. They would be butchered if they tried, and so Thorgrim doubted that they would.

"We have wounded men," he said to the others. "And repairs that the ships will need. It seems we're safe enough here. For now. We can stay a few days, anyway. So let's get the wounded ashore and get some sort of shelter rigged and a fire going. Each of you, let me know the conditions of your ships, once you've worked that out."

The others nodded. There was not much to add to that. When they had prepared the fleet to sail they took aboard food and ale and water and firewood since they could never count on finding those things when they beached the ships for the night. Thus provisioned, they could live on the sandbar for a while. But using up their stores would mean having to replace them before they sailed too far off.

The captains returned to their ships and Thorgrim hobbled along after them. Orders were shouted, and soon each ship was swarming with activity as the men made ready to set up camp, unloading the food and ale and firewood they would need, at least for one night. A cask was set down in the sand near where the wood for the fire was being laid out, and Thorgrim took advantage of that, sitting down on the barrel, relishing the relief he felt as the weight came off his leg and the throbbing pain eased a bit.

For some time he remained there, watching the activity on the beach. He tried to keep his mind on the one question that mattered to him and to the rest of them on the sandbar—how would they get out of the hole in which they were stuck? He tried to concentrate, but again and again his mind drifted off and he tried to pull it back. He was more exhausted than he could recall every being and he could not make his mind work the way he wished. So he stopped trying.

We're safe for the night, at least, and we're not going anywhere until daybreak, he thought. *Time for food and sleep.* With that thought, Thorgrim felt a great sense of relief. No reason to make any decisions just then, because there was nothing to be done immediately in any event.

They spent the night on the sand, with only a perfunctory watch set, relying on the water surrounding them to keep the English at bay. Thorgrim slept well, and he woke feeling more ready to make a decision, but he still had no notion of what that might be.

He was on his barrel seat once again, staring off in the direction of the channel entrance, considering his choices while the men stoked fires and got breakfast together. Hall approached and spoke, hesitantly, not wanting to break Thorgrim's concentration, apparently.

"Lord Thorgrim?"

"Yes?"

"That prisoner you took, after the fighting back there? Well, he's still alive. Surprised me. Didn't think he'd live the night. He's an old man and he took a hard hit to the head. Starri hit him, and Starri doesn't usually leave them alive, as you know. Anyway, he's awake now. I don't know what he's saying, talking his foreign talk, but he seems like he's saying something that's supposed to make sense."

The prisoner... Thorgrim had forgotten all about him. "Good. Bring him to me. And fetch Harald. He seems to know their tongue pretty well now."

Hall nodded and trotted off. Thorgrim thrust his wounded leg straight out, adjusting the angle, finding the position in which it hurt the least. By the time he had found that position the prisoner was coming down the gangplank they had rigged over *Oak Heart*'s bow. Hall was leading him and Harald was coming behind. The prisoner was moving slowly and with care, as one might expect of a man whose head had been nearly knocked in, but beyond that he did not seem reluctant to come.

Thorgrim watched them approach. The man's helmet, mail and sword were gone, of course, and he wore a black tunic and leggings. As he drew closer Thorgrim could see that the tunic was linen, very fine linen, and highlighted with gold thread.

The man himself had longish hair and a neat-trimmed moustache and goatee, all of which were mostly white and shot through with strands of black, somewhat the opposite of Thorgrim's own hair and beard. Thorgrim guessed he was older than himself by at least ten years, but he looked hale and fit, not ravaged by the struggle to survive. Not a man who had seen hard labor all his life, but still one who was willing to stand in the center of a shield wall.

A jarl of some sort, or whatever these English call it, Thorgrim thought. The man carried himself with dignity and not a trace of fear, despite having no idea of his pending fate, and having every reason to fear the worst.

Thorgrim gestured toward another barrel a few feet away and the man sat. He folded his hands on his leg, met Thorgrim's stare and held it.

"Father, this man is named Leofric," Harald said, pronouncing the odd name with surprising ease. "He was the leader of the men who set the trap. The men on the east side of the channel."

Thorgrim nodded. He turned to a knot of men nearby who were staving in the head of an ale cask. "Fetch this man some drink," he said, gesturing toward Leofric, "and me as well."

A moment later he and Leofric held horns full of ale, and they lifted them and each took a long, deep drink. Leofric did not pause to let Thorgrim drink first. He did not seem worried that the Northmen would poison him. Good.

"Ask him, is he the king hereabouts?" Thorgrim said to Harald. "Tell him to speak the truth."

Harald translated, and Thorgrim could hear the boy put a threatening tone in his words, warning this man not to lie. But the man's expression did not change, and still he showed no sign of fear or even vague concern when he replied.

"He says he's the lord of the lands around here," Harald said. "But he serves an...overlord, I guess. The overlord rules a bigger part. Not all of it, just a part they call...I couldn't understand the word."

Thorgrim nodded. Before he could speak, the man was talking again.

"He says they all serve a king, who is king of all this country. This country is called Wessex."

"Hmm..." Thorgrim said. It was very complicated, but then again he knew that his own country would seem that way to a stranger. Nor did the hierarchy of this country—Engla-land, Wessex, whatever they called it—matter in the least to him.

"Just to be clear," Thorgrim said, "this fellow, and his overlord, they are not the ones who paid us the danegeld?"

Harald translated. "No, Father, that was not Leofric's overlord. It was another who wishes for that title."

Thorgrim sighed. This was doing nothing for his temper, or the throbbing in his leg. "Ask him why they tried to stop us. This other lord paid us to leave. They could have been rid of us for free."

When Leofric had answered, Harald said, "He says they did not want the other one to get credit for driving us off. If they could have stopped us, it would have done them honor. That, and they would have taken the danegeld and our plunder for themselves."

"The dog is honest, I'll give him that," Thorgrim said. He and Leofric held each other's eyes. The Englishman did look honest, a man of honor, though Thorgrim had lived long enough to know that the way a man looked was hardly proof of anything.

Leofric spoke next. "He says we seem to be trapped here, in this harbor. He says we can't get through the channel unless they remove the sunken ships."

Thorgrim had already realized as much. It would take considerable effort to clear the channel, and he and his men could not do it if they were being fired on from either shore by the deadly English archers. They could try to drive the men-at-arms off, but he doubted they could hold them at bay long enough to get the wrecks clear. And the English armies could be reinforced. His could not.

He wondered just how important this Leofric was, if by holding him hostage he could get the English to remove the wrecks. He doubted it. This whole business seemed to rise above the life of any one man, save perhaps the king whom Leofric had mentioned.

The Englishman spoke again, and again his calm self-assurance was quite clear, even if his words were not.

"Leofric says if we return the plunder then they'll allow us to leave," Harald said. "He says we may keep the danegeld."

Thorgrim smiled at that. "Tell him he's very amusing."

Harald translated. Thorgrim had no way of knowing how accurately Harald rendered the words, but Leofric gave a slight nod of the head and Thorgrim thought he saw the hint of a smile on the man's lips and he imagined that Harald got it about right.

They were quiet for a moment. "Tell him we seem to have trapped one another," Thorgrim said to Harald. "Tell him if we must, we'll fight our way out, and that will not go well for him, or for his overlord."

Harald relayed the words. Leofric's expression did not change as he considered them. He seemed ready to speak and then he stopped, as if a thought had brought him up short. He turned and looked back toward the east, toward the channel that led to the sea. He turned the other way and seemed to be looking at the Northmen's still impressive fleet, run up on the beach. He spoke.

"Leofric says he may have thought of something that would be of great benefit to us both," Harald said.

Chapter Twenty-Seven

*"There is no reason to hesitate in killing all of them.
It will also," said Helgi, "deter others from attacking us."*

Bolli Bollason's Tale

There were few secrets in Fevik. Word flew so quickly from place to place it seemed to be carried by the larks and the sparrows. For that reason Odd knew, for some days before, that his neighbors had been summoned to the king's hall in Grømstad. Those same neighbors who had gone with him to speak with Halfdan. Those same neighbors who had been standing with him, more or less, until then.

He and Signy were together when they heard the news. They were lending a hand with the butchering and smoking—hard work, unpleasant, but vital to seeing the farmstead through the long winter that seemed always to be fast approaching. Vermund Jurundsson came riding with purpose down the trail from the lower fields, and brought word of the meeting to them.

"The king has called our neighbors?" Signy asked, as if she did not hear Vermund's words clearly. "With their men? Under arms?"

"Yes, ma'am," Vermund said. "What I heard. And I don't doubt but it's true."

She turned to Odd. "Will you go if Halfdan calls you?" she asked. "Will you bring armed men to serve the king?"

Odd studied his wife for a moment. He tried to divine whether this was a genuine question, or if she had misheard Vermund, or if she really did not understand. That last seemed unlikely—Signy was usually more perceptive than he was.

She doesn't understand because she does not want to understand, Odd concluded.

"I would go if I was called," Odd said. "I'm loyal to my king, I always have been. But I won't be called, because Halfdan is gathering the men to come against me. Against us." He gestured to indicate the hall, the farm, all of the buildings and land and people that Halfdan was coming for.

Signy's eyebrows came together, her mouth slightly open. She turned to Vermund for confirmation.

"It's true, ma'am," he said. "At least, I think it is. No one knows what Halfdan will do, save for Halfdan. But I'd wager all that he's coming here."

The three of them were quiet for a moment, then Signy said in a much more subdued tone, "What will we do?"

It was, of course, the very question Odd had been considering in the few moments since Vermund had given them the news. Actually, he had been considering it for more than a week, because he had guessed it would come to this, him and Halfdan. There was no one, simple answer. What he, Odd, would do was different from what he would ask his people to do, and that was very different from what he would tell his family to do.

"*Sea Hawk* is all but ready to get underway," Odd said. *Sea Hawk* was the ship that Ari had been building since the early spring. She had been launched just a few weeks before, a little ahead of schedule, Odd sensing that the time to have a ship handy might be near. He had named her *Sea Hawk*, rather than something more war-like, to convince both Signy and himself that he had not built her to go a'viking.

"If Halfdan comes here with an army, you and the children and the other women will go in her," Odd continued. "I'll send men enough with you to work the ship. We'll get you safe, then the rest of us will see to some sort of defense."

"You mistake it, husband," Signy said. "The children and the other women will go in the ship. And the men to work it. But I will not."

Odd looked at his wife. She wore an expression which he had seen before, often enough to understand the futility of arguing the point.

"Yes, just the other women and children," he said. "You and me, we'll see to things here. But remember, all we know is that our neighbors have been summoned by Halfdan, and even that's just a rumor. We don't know if it's true. We'll say nothing to the others. There's no need to cause a panic yet."

"Odd..." Signy said, and there was a strange note in her voice. Worry. It was not something Odd had often heard from his wife. "Odd, will we have to fight Halfdan...by ourselves? Just us, here on the farm?"

"I don't know," Odd said. It was as truthful an answer as he could give. "I hope not. But I don't know. All we can do is wait and see."

But rumors continued to wing their way to Odd's farm. They grew in detail and frequency until finally they became something more than rumors. Until the people knew with certainty that Halfdan had summoned armed men, and Odd was not one of them.

All that time Odd and Signy continued to work with the butchers, turning the slaughtered hogs into smoked hams for the winter. The rhythms of the farm work did not change, but the sense of impending danger did, building like summer storm clouds. And finally Odd could ignore it no longer.

There were preparations to be made. Odd had been putting them off because he did not want to believe his king would do such a thing as lead his neighbors against him. Which was ridiculous. He knew what Halfdan was willing to do. He called Vermund over even as the final decision was forming in his mind.

"We have to get ready for a visit from Halfdan and the others," he said. "Let's get anything of value out of the hall: stores, cookware, clothes, blankets, anything. Secure them in one of the outbuildings. But no panic. I don't want to frighten the people. I don't want them to know what's going on."

"I reckon they know already," Vermund said. "They probably knew before you and me."

If they know what's going on, they know more than I do, Odd thought. He said to Vermund, "Signy and me, we'll carry on here a while more. Then we'll come lend you a hand."

They worked through the rest of the morning, Odd and Signy and the butchers, cleaning out carcasses and cutting up what remained and hanging it in the smokehouse. Sharpening tools and shoveling entrails. And off in the hall a steady line of servants and slaves moved whatever there was of value from the big building to a smaller storehouse a hundred yards away. They moved with urgency but not panic, and Odd was happy to see that.

It was getting near midday when Odd and Signy finished turning their live hogs into preserved meat, scrubbing the blood from their hands and arms, which was no easy thing. Odd's thoughts were turning toward eating when one of his people called across the open ground.

"Master Odd! Riders!" The man pointed toward the south. Odd could see them as well, a dozen or so mounted men. They were riding slow, their horses at a walk. They did not look like a column of warriors riding to the attack, bent on savaging the farm.

"Who is this?" Signy asked. "Do you know?"

"No, I don't," Odd said. "But I have an idea."

He and Signy walked toward the path along which the riders were coming, a worn brown trail cutting across the open fields on which the milch cows grazed. They stopped there and waited for the horsemen to approach, and soon Odd could see that his guess had been right.

"Amundi Thorsteinsson!" Odd called as the riders drew into earshot. He lifted his arm in greeting and Amundi lifted his arm as well. Odd tried not to show how relieved he was to see the man, tried and largely failed. Because he was very relieved. Because even if Amundi was not there to fight with him, at least he was not joining Halfdan to fight against him.

Signy turned and waved for one of the servant girls and the girl rushed over. "Get some of the others and fetch food and ale for these men," she said.

"Ma'am, we're taking the food and the ale from the hall now, ma'am," the girl said. This all seemed too confusing for her to follow.

"Then bring some back, enough for these men, the best we have," Signy snapped. Her usual patience and charity were deserting her.

Amundi climbed down from his horse. The others behind him did as well. They were Amundi's men. Dressed for battle. Odd recognized many of them.

He stepped over and took Amundi's proffered hand and shook and the men slapped one another on the shoulder.

"Amundi! Welcome!" Odd said. "I don't know what brings you here, but I can guess. Though I'm sure there's much more to the tale I don't know."

Odd was right on both counts. Soon after, he and Amundi, Signy and Amundi's man Thord were seated on benches outside the hall with ale and platters of meat and bread. The rest of Amundi's men were seated at various places around, similarly outfitted. For five minutes Amundi had been speaking without interruption.

"This morning Halfdan told us why we had been called together. Not that any of us hadn't guessed. We were to ride against you, take you and your family prisoner. Claim your farm."

"You wouldn't have taken me prisoner," Odd said.

"I'm sure Halfdan knew that," Amundi said. "And that would have been fine, too."

"But you didn't join Halfdan?" Signy asked.

"No," Amundi said. "I told him that we have laws, that free men should not be treated that way, but he wouldn't hear it. I left, me and my men. Not to come warn you, I'll admit that. I was on my way home. Pretending to myself I could just stand aside and watch. But of course I couldn't, I knew that, so I turned about and came here."

Odd nodded. That was pretty much how he guessed it had played out.

"But the others?" Signy asked. "The other men, they stayed with Halfdan?"

"No," Amundi said. "Ulfkel was the first to join me. And then the others. We all walked out of Thorgrim's hall and rode away. As angry as the other landowners are with you, Odd—and they are very angry, don't doubt it—they wouldn't stand for Halfdan treating a fellow free man in that way. Setting such a precedent."

"They're taking a brave stand," Signy said. "Boldly returning to their farms and their beds."

Amundi raised his eyebrows. "Don't judge too harshly, Signy," he said. "It's what I meant to do."

"Yes, but you changed your mind," Signy said, and there was bitterness in her voice.

But as it happened, Amundi was not the only one to change his mind. Soon after Signy spoke those words, Ragi Oleifsson came riding down the path with his own men behind him. Then came Ulfkel Ospaksson with a dozen warriors, and his neighbor Vigdis with ten, and then Vifil behind him. Last came a man named Bolli Thorleiksson. Like the others, he led the armed warriors he had brought to Halfdan.

Odd greeted them as they came, and Signy greeted them as well and called for more food and ale, and each of them expressed surprise to see the others there. Each apparently thought they alone had the mettle to join Odd in his stand for a free man's rights.

Soon they were all settled on benches and stools, their men and horses in the care of Odd's servants, and they told their tales of standing with Amundi and joining him in leaving Halfdan's company.

"I'm not keen to defy Halfdan," Ragi Oleifsson said. "He's king, after all, and that has to mean something. But it doesn't mean he has the right to take whatever man's farm he pleases. He must respect the free men under his rule. If we let him get away with this once, well, who knows where he'll stop?"

There was muttered agreement with that notion. Ulfkel spoke next.

"What we're doing here, we're making it so Halfdan has to talk with us, right? I mean, he might crush Odd like a bug, or any one of us, but he can't crush us all. Who would be left for him to rule?"

There was muttered agreement to that as well, but it was growing less certain.

"Fevik is not the only place Halfdan rules," Amundi said, injecting some largely unwelcome truth into the discussion. "He holds sway over quite a bit of the country to the south of Grømstad. You all know that well. His kingdom grows bigger and he grows richer. And as he grows richer he grows more powerful."

There was silence for a moment, then Ragi said, "All the more reason to stand up to the man now. Let him see how it is. If you're going to train a dog, you don't wait until the cur is too big to mind you."

"Halfdan meant to lead you men against me," Odd said. "He wants to divide us. But you refused to help, and you left him without an army. That gives us time to try to talk with him one more time."

"How do you figure that?" Thorgeir asked.

"He has no warriors now," Odd said. "So there's no danger of him raiding my farm any time soon. Even if he's still set on doing it, he'll have to ride back to Grømstad and raise more men, then ride back here. We can go to him."

"Really?" Amundi said. "Talk? You still think we should talk with him?"

"Yes," Odd said, but in truth the words cut across every instinct he had. He wanted to fight. He wanted to drive Blood-letter through

Einar's heart and Halfdan's heart. The thought of letting the blade sing in his hand excited him.

He thought of the trap in the road, or the fight when they had returned from the shieling. Those things had thrilled him in a way he had never been thrilled before. And that realization worried him. And that worry made him want to choose diplomacy once again.

"I was ready to talk with Halfdan before," Odd said. "Before his cowardly attack on those poor bastards at the shieling. I'm ready still." He glanced around to see if Signy was near, but she was off instructing the servants regarding the banquet they would have later. "I was ready to go alone and I'm still ready to go alone. I wouldn't ask any of you to ride back into the wolf's lair."

"You're a very reasonable man, Odd Thorgrimson," Amundi said. "Too reasonable, maybe. Or maybe I should say too hopeful that Halfdan will see reason."

Odd nodded. He did not think himself particularly reasonable. But this newfound bloodlust had put him off balance, and an excess of reason seemed the only way to set himself right again.

"Reasonable or foolish," Odd said. "We'll know which pretty soon, I think."

The day was getting on and the danger seemed to have passed, at least for the time being. Halfdan could not pose much of a threat when nearly all the warriors he had called to his side had left him and were gathered at the home of the man he intended to attack. Signy called for their guests to join her and Odd and their men in the hall. A feast would be laid out, and places for sleeping provided. It was not an offer that was easy to decline, and no one did.

They saw to their horses and sent riders off to their farms to tell wives and overseers what was going on. They filed into the long hall, the fires already blazing in the hearth that ran down the center of the building. They shed mail and set helmets and shields aside, unbelted swords and set them aside as well, until none of the guests were armed with more than their knives and a few with seaxes hung horizontally from their belts—practically naked by the standards of the Northmen.

Odd was glad to see it. It was a sign that he was trusted, and that was a good thing. Son of Thorgrim Night Wolf, grandson of Ornolf the Restless and Ulf of the Battle Song. The man who wielded Blood-letter. He thought of what Signy had said: *Halfdan knows who you are, and what you come from, and what you are capable of. You frighten him.* He had dismissed those words then, and he still dismissed them. But he had not stopped turning them over in his mind.

Lambs and pigs turned on spits over the hearth fire. The smoke lifted up toward the high roofline and the noise in the hall rose as the contents of the barrels of ale and mead were drained away. Servants moved deftly through the men, the boisterous men, under the command of Signy who kept them at it like a captain on a field of battle. Odd had no musicians in a formal sense, but a few of the men who worked the farm had talent in that way, and he set them to playing in a space beyond the long tables.

It was a good banquet, better than the last few gatherings there, weighed down as they had been by consideration of the ugly goings-on. Now there seemed a sense of optimism, as if heavy covers had been lifted off and they could breathe fresh air again.

None of them thought the trouble with Halfdan was done—they were not so foolish as that—but they knew the trouble had been set aside for the time being, and that and the ale and mead and companionship made for a buoyant mood.

As the effects of the drink reached their high water mark and began to ebb Odd called for his skald, who, like the musicians, was not really a skald. He was one of the butchers with whom Odd had been working at the smokehouse, but he was also a poet of some ability. The hall settled, the men sprawled on the benches, and the skald began.

He told ancient stories of the gods, familiar stories but comforting in their familiarity. He told stories of men long gone, ancestors of Odd Thorgrimson and of many of the other men who sat in the hall, men whose families had tended the soil around there for generations, and who had put off from those shores to go raiding in far off countries or fought wars on their home soil. Who brought wealth back to Fevik, and with it fame for themselves and their families.

Odd's mind drifted back to the great hall in which he had grown up. His father, Thorgrim, was also a talented skald who wrote and told stories of gods and men. It was not always easy to get him to recite his tales, but when he could be prevailed upon he could hold his listeners in a spell. It was not a talent one would expect from a man like his father, and it surprised people when they first heard Thorgrim perform.

Father…Father… Odd thought. *Where are you? Do you live still, or are you in Odin's corpse hall?* The thought of his father, the thought of the great hall on Thorgrim's farm, his home for far longer than his own farm had been, gave rise to a strange feeling surging up in him. He spoke out loud, but softly so only he could hear.

"You'll not have my father's farm. Bastard. You won't have it."

It was quiet: only the crackle of the fire in the hearth and the slow, melodic voice of the skald, telling his tales. It was so soothing that some of the men had already fallen asleep, heads down on the table, and they were thumped soundly when their snoring threatened to drown out the poet.

Odd looked into the flames and let the skald's words flow through his head like water through a net. His thoughts were a jumble and he didn't even try to bring them into any sort of alignment, just let them toss around, heaping one upon the other.

Then he looked up quickly, staring off into the dark, not even sure why he did that. The farm, the hall, often felt like part of him, like part of his own body. And just as he could sense when something was wrong with his person, now he could sense there was something wrong with the hall.

He frowned and knitted his brow. His eyes moved along the roof above. He could smell smoke. The hall of course was full of smoke, with only a bit able to escape from the smoke holes at either end of the peak of the roof. He had been smelling smoke all night. But this was different. It was something burning that had not been burning before.

His eyes continued to sweep the thatch above, though it was only just visible in the fading light of the dying hearth fire. He shifted a bit and then he stopped. A bright point of light, off at the far end of the hall. The big room was lost in darkness there, but Odd knew that the light was a flame and it was just at the point where the thatch roof met the heavy timber walls. And he knew that the roof of the hall was on fire.

Chapter Twenty-Eight

*And so for each man
the praise of the living,
of those who mention him after life ends,
remains the best epitaph*

The Seafarer
Ninth Century English Poem

There was good news. And there was bad news. And there was bad news that was, in truth, good news. And it was all so amorphous and confusing that it made Cynewise profoundly annoyed.

Confusion was not a thing she wrestled with much. She had always been a person of clarity, clarity, as unadulterated as her pure blue eyes. She had always been one to fix on what she wanted and to pursue it with singular focus until it was hers. She had done that all the way to ealdormanship of Dorset. But now things were clouding up.

It was people, that was the problem. As long as she had only herself to rely on then there were no concerns, because she was always utterly reliable. It was only when she had to call on others—her father, Oswin, the thegns—that things became confused, because there were few who were as competent as she was. None, in truth.

She was seated in her not coincidentally throne-like chair in the relative luxury of her spacious tent. Oswin, who had just returned to camp, was standing in front of her now. His news was the good news, which was lucky for him after all the ill news he had brought her as of late. Nothwulf's marching away to parts unknown was one thing, but worse, much worse, was the Northmen, despite the payment of danegeld, sailing off with her father's men-at-arms and

263

leaving only a promise to drop them on the far side of the bay. Oswin had managed to lose the danegeld, the men-at-arms and the Northmen, all in one stroke. Quite a feat.

"Yes, Lady Cynewise, we found Nothwulf and his army," he was saying. "They're on the west bank of the channel that runs from the harbor to the sea. They've built fortifications there."

Cynewise squinted. "Fortifications? Why?"

"Well, ma'am, it seems they mean to stop the Northmen from leaving," Oswin said. "In truth, they've already fought them. Yesterday. The Northmen tried to leave and Nothwulf and Leofric and the thegns who stand with them prevented it. I hear they sunk ships in the channel. Blocked it."

Cynewise was quiet for a moment. "Why, for the love of God?"

"I don't know for certain, ma'am. But I think they didn't want you to get credit for ridding the shire of the heathens. They wanted to defeat them in battle. To boost Nothwulf's claim to the ealdorman's seat, and to get their hands on the danegeld and the plunder."

"And did they defeat them in battle?"

"Not entirely. They kept them from getting to sea, but they did not beat them. The Northmen returned to the harbor. They're encamped on a sandbar now, where no one can get to them. What they'll do next is anyone's guess."

Cynewise shook her head. *Nothwulf, you are a blundering idiot,* she thought. *You've got these wolves caught in a trap and you have no way to get them out. Right there is proof enough I should be ealdorman.*

"But here's the good thing, ma'am," Oswin continued. "Nothwulf and his men are still there, waiting for the Northmen to try again to leave. But only half of his army is on the west side. Leofric and his men and some of the other thegns are on the east side. That was their plan, to catch the Northmen between both armies and burn their ships with flaming arrows. It nearly worked, so they're ready to try it again."

Cynewise considered the situation that Oswin had just described. Nothwulf was encamped with his back to the water and only half his army with him. And not even with his back to the water. Facing the water, his back exposed to an attack from the land.

"Surely they have boats to move from one side to the other?" she asked.

"Not that I know of. We took some prisoners, questioned them. They all said the same. They used the ships to move Leofric's men before they sunk them. Now they have only a handful of boats, and small ones at that. If Leofric wants to join his men up with Nothwulf's they'd have to march clear around through Christchurch. It would take them a day at least."

Now Cynewise was growing excited. She could see the possibilities here. They could strike at Nothwulf at first light—he was no more than a day's march away—and wipe his army out. Leofric would have to join with her then, and the Northmen could do whatever they pleased as long as it involved getting their filthy selves out of Dorsetshire.

She was about to call for Eadwold, captain of her hearth-guard, and tell him to get the men ready to march within the hour. Before she could, Horsa, her servant, appeared through the door, bowing, nodding, and clearly not wanting to say what he had to say.

"Lady Cynewise, it's Bishop Ealhstan," he said. "He's been wishing to speak with you, like I said before, and I don't think I can put him off much longer."

Cynewise sighed. This might have all been easily handled, Nothwulf cut down while he had so stupidly exposed himself, but that was not to be. Here were complications on complications.

She looked at Oswin who was making no effort to hide his curiosity. "The bishop will want to speak to me about my father," she said. "Why this is so urgent I don't know. He's dead and there's not much to be done about it."

"Dead...ma'am?"

"Yes, he died this morning," Cynewise said. She knew that grief was in order, some display of mourning for the old man's passing, but she was having a hard time summoning it. In front of Oswin it didn't really matter, but she'd have to put on a better show for Bishop Ealhstan. She'd have to appear as if her father's death meant more to her than just another problem with which to deal.

People, she thought. *It's people who make it so damned difficult to make a thing happen. Even when they're dead, it seems, they're still a great nuisance.*

She turned to Horsa. "Very well, see the bishop in."

Horsa disappeared and Cynewise forced the irritation out of her expression and replaced it with a look of resolve mixed with grief. Horsa reappeared with Bishop Ealhstan following behind, and behind him a man named Sigeric who was captain of her father's men-at-arms.

"Oh, Bishop Ealhstan, thank God above you've come!" Cynewise said, happy to hear the genuine-sounding note of sorrow in her voice. "We must arrange for mass to be said for my beloved father, who even now rests in the arms of our Lord."

"Yes, ma'am, of course. Arrangements are being made," Ealhstan said. Cynewise tried to gauge how real the bishop thought her grief to be, but Ealhstan was a hard one to read. He came off as a fat, doddering fool, but Cynewise knew it was a mistake to think him so.

"We'll do what we can, here in the field, in our rude camp," Cynewise went on. "And when his earthly remains are returned to his beloved Devon, then we'll see to a proper funeral. But now I fear there are military matters that must take precedence."

"Of course, Lady Cynewise, of course," the bishop said. "But see here, Sigeric would speak with you, ma'am. We've been in talks all morning, and he would speak with you now."

'Been in talks all morning,' Cynewise thought. *That does not sound good.*

"Of course," Cynewise said. She turned to Sigeric. "I had meant to send for you this morning, Sigeric," she said. "But the shock of my father's passing has much affected me. Still, we must be strong. It's what Ceorle would have wished."

"Yes, ma'am," Sigeric said, and before he could say more she launched in again.

"Oswin brings news that Nothwulf is nearby and he's vulnerable. If we move quickly we can catch him with but half his army, and his back to the water. We can finish him off, be done with all this." She knew she was talking now just to keep anyone else from talking for fear they might say something she did not want to hear. But she also knew that she couldn't keep doing that.

Sigeric cleared his throat. "Yes, ma'am," he said, "but I must tell you...we cannot join you in this."

"We...?"

"The men under my command, ma'am. Your father's men. We're Devon men, and what goes on in Dorset isn't our business."

"You're here in Dorsetshire under orders from my father," Cynewise reminded him. "Your business is what he says is your business." Then, seeing immediately the flaw in this argument, she added, "And now that he's gone your business is what I say it is."

"No, Lady Cynewise, I'm afraid it's not," Sigeric said and there was no subservience in his voice, no suggestion that he was at all intimidated by her. "You are ealdorman of Dorsetshire, but not Devonshire."

"I am the eldest of my father's house!" Cynewise reminded him. "It has yet to be seen if I am not ealdorman of Devonshire as well."

"Ah, Lady Cynewise," Bishop Ealhstan piped up. "Such a heavy burden to carry! Too much to ask of a young, frail woman such as yourself. Certainly it would be best, and proper, for your brother to assume the ealdormanship of Devon."

"My brother is fourteen years old," Cynewise said and stopped. She stopped because she understood at last what was happening here. Ealhstan would see to it that her brother was ealdorman while he, Ealhstan, was there to guide him in matters spiritual and political. And financial, no doubt, the treasury of Devonshire an irresistible temptation. And Sigeric and his men-at-arms there to see the bishop's will be done.

You greedy, lying bastards, Cynewise thought. But there was nothing she could do to stop them. She would be lucky just to hang on to what she had gained in Dorset.

"Very well, go. Do as you will. I dare say my father would not be pleased…is not pleased, I should say, in his heavenly home, but you do as you think is right. And God have mercy on you."

"Yes, ma'am," Bishop Ealhstan said, and with tolerably respectful bows he and Sigeric took their leave.

"Bastards," Cynewise said once they were gone. "But it doesn't matter, we have men enough still to see to Nothwulf, if half his army is stuck on the far side of the channel. Oswin, summon the thegns so that I might enlighten them as to our plans."

Oswin nodded and ducked out of the tent, and soon he was back with the half-dozen thegns who had come in support of Cynewise. They were not there because they liked her or championed her cause, she knew that, but because she had made it clear from the onset that it would be to their advantage in many ways to see her as ealdorman of the shire. For the thegns this had never been about whether she or Nothwulf had proper claim to the title. It was about which of the two could do the most good for those who supported them.

But she did not care why they supported her, or were willing to fight for her, as long as they did.

As each of the men entered, they stepped up in front of Cynewise and expressed their condolences at the death of her father, which she acknowledged with grace. When that weary exercise was done, the men sat in the various chairs arranged around the tent and were handed cups of ale while Cynewise looked from one to the other, studying them.

She felt secure enough with their loyalty, but how much of Dorset did they represent? How many thegns were standing with Nothwulf? Leofric, the traitor, but how many others? How many thegns were there in Dorset? She should know that, but she didn't and she chastised herself for her ignorance.

Oswin would know, but she did not care to ask Oswin anything. She did not want to display ignorance of any kind.

"Gentlemen," Cynewise said. "Oswin brings us good news. Nothwulf had divided his army, and he has managed to put himself in a place where he can be easily trapped. If we move swiftly then we will be able to crush him on the morrow."

A man named Aegenwulf, who had great holdings to the west, spoke up. "Lady Cynewise, there's word in the camp that Sigeric is marching your father's men back to Devon. Is that true?"

Cynewise shifted a bit. "Yes, that's true. Sigeric sees fit to ignore my father's final wishes, but that's no matter. We do not need those men."

The thegns glanced at one another and said nothing until Aegenwulf spoke again. "We're sorry to hear that, Lady Cynewise," he said. "We'd looked on your father's men as a great help to us."

Cynewise felt a creeping sense of panic. Had these men supported her only because they thought she had the support of her powerful father? Was Bishop Ealhstan turning on her and taking these men along, the way he had Sigeric? If so, this was not the time to show weakness of any sort.

"See here, Aegenwulf, all of you," she said. She stood now, and though her height was not impressive it was helped by the fact that the chairs the men sat on were purposely short. "By law and by King Æthelwulf and by God Himself I am made ealdorman of this shire. I rule here, in the place of my late husband, and I will stand for no pretenders like Nothwulf. He is vulnerable now, and we will crush him now, on my command. Is that clear to all?"

Her voice was low and she looked each of the men in turn right in the eye. Cynewise, daughter of Ceorle, ealdorman of Dorsetshire, knew how to take command. No one protested. No one moved.

"Good. Your loyalty will be well rewarded. As it has been so far. Now go and get your men ready to march to battle."

One by one they stood, bowed to Cynewise, and shuffled out of the tent. Their enthusiasm was underwhelming. But they were doing as they were told, and once they had crushed Nothwulf, and Cynewise had doled out a good portion of Nothwulf's wealth to them, then they would be more animated in their support of her.

Still, she was not happy. In fact, she was furious, her anger like a red-hot coal burning in her chest. The pain was as great as that, and the only way to rid herself of the coal was to give her fury full vent.

And the only one there worth unleashing it on, the only one who truly deserved it, was Oswin, the shire reeve.

She turned to him and held him in her merciless gaze until he began to fidget. "Do you see that?" she said, nodding toward the door through which the thegns had left.

"Ma'am?"

"The thegns," she hissed. "Do you see how they treat me? How they make just enough show of loyalty to avoid my wrath? How utterly unable I am to depend on them? This is your doing, you incompetent fool."

Oswin's eyebrows came together and he frowned. He clearly had not expected this. "My doing?" he said.

"Yes, your doing. Losing Nothwulf. Losing the danegeld. Losing the fine men-at-arms my father sent, who might have made the difference in this battle." Her momentum was building now, and she could feel the rage spilling out of her, and it was good.

"You have made one stupid blunder after another, ever since I became ealdorman. I kept you on because I thought you might be of some use, but now I wonder. I can tell you one thing—the loss of the danegeld will be made up from your purse, even if I must take your property and sell it. I will not stand for your idiocy a moment longer!"

She paused, aware that her breathing was labored from the effort. Oswin's mouth formed a tight line between his beard and moustache. She waited for him to reply, but he did not and she guessed he did not trust himself to speak. He would not risk further enraging her. He had nowhere else to go.

"Be gone from here before I take your position of reeve from you and give it to a man actually worthy of the title. Go back and keep an eye on Nothwulf and if his army moves a rod either direction, or if that bastard Leofric crosses the channel and joins him, you let me know. Is that clear?"

A pause, long enough for Oswin to register his anger, not so long as to require another outburst from Cynewise, and he said, "Yes, Lady Cynewise." He gave a quick bow and then he was gone.

Chapter Twenty-Nine

From their saddles they alighted, at the house's gable,
thence went in through the hall.
See they bow's on bass rope drawn,
seven hundred, which the warrior owned.

The Poetic Edda

Odd shifted again on his bench. He met the skald's eye and held up a hand for the man to stop and he did, mid-sentence. The guests who were still awake waited for him to continue, but instead Odd stood, slowly, his hand still held up, palm out. He wanted their attention, and he wanted quiet and he did not want roaring panic.

"The south end of the hall, low down on the roof," he said. "If you look you'll see there are flames. I can just see them. The roof is on fire." There was silence in the wake of those words, tired and drunk men trying to grasp the meaning and the importance of what he had said. Heads slowly turned to the south end of the hall, and Odd turned his head as well. The flames were already spreading. What had just been a point of light a moment before was now a small but visible fire. In the quiet they could hear the sharp crackle of dried thatch as it burned.

"Well, by the gods!" Ulfkel shouted. He stood quickly and knocked his bench over as he did. "Let's get some buckets, some water! Looks like it's early on, we'll put that whore's son fire out! Everyone, out of the hall!"

"Wait!" Odd shouted, loud enough to be heard over the noise of dozens of men reacting at last, loud enough to get their attention and make them stop what they were doing.

"Wait!" Odd said again. "I don't think the fire's an accident. I think it was set. And I think the hall is surrounded by Halfdan's men, waiting for us to come running through that door."

Again there was quiet as the men absorbed this surprising news, but the quiet did not last long. Near the door to the store room one of the servant girls saw the fire, which until then had been unnoticed by anyone but the men at the table, and her scream cut though the silence.

Heads jerked around at the surprising sound. The girl had her hand over her mouth and she was pointing and backing away, as if the fire, one hundred feet from where she stood, might be an immediate threat. From the storeroom more of the servants came racing out, and thralls and servants from other quarters, and the sound of fear, the worst sort of fear, fear thrust at them suddenly, rose up from them.

"Don't panic, don't panic!" Odd shouted, desperate to stop the people from doing something stupid in their terror, but his words were ineffective, shouted over that distance. It was an ugly irony: the more the servants let fear drive them, the greater their danger became.

Odd took a step in their direction, but before he could move beyond that he saw Signy burst out of the store room, her face equal parts fury and confusion. She looked at the far end of the hall, where the fire was starting to mount. She looked at the servant girl, still screaming uncontrollably. She took two quick steps toward the servant, knocked the girl's arm aside and cuffed her hard on the side of the head.

The girl went down in a heap and the screaming stopped. In the absence of that panic-inducing noise, Signy began issuing orders to the servants and the thralls. Odd could not hear the words, but he knew Signy was perfectly able to give commands that could not be ignored, and instantly the people were racing off in every direction.

"Why do you think it's Halfdan has done this?" Vifil asked. "Why don't you think the fire's an accident?"

"I don't know," Odd said. He could see the others were eager to take action, to get out of the hall and fight the flames, which was no surprise. But some voice—his father's voice?—was telling him to be more thoughtful.

"I don't know," Odd said again. "But I feel certain I'm right."

James L. Nelson

"If it is Halfdan who's done this, how by all the gods could he have the hall surrounded?" Ragi asked. His voice was calm, as if he were not standing in a burning building. "We are all the army he had with him."

"We might not be," Amundi said. "Halfdan's no fool. He might have seen this coming and had more warriors waiting nearby. He might have called us all up as a test of our loyalty. If that's the case, then we failed, as far as he's concerned."

"So he'll be happy to be rid of us all," Vifil said, a statement met with nodded heads.

"We don't know if that's true or not!" Ulfkel said. "And yet we stand here and make guesses while the hall burns around us! If we want to know if Halfdan's outside then we only have to open the whore's son door and see!"

"You're right," Odd said. "I'll do just that. None of you move."

He jogged across the floor, through the semi-dark of the hall, lit only with the hearth fire and a few lanterns and, increasingly, the fire burning at the far end. He reached the big oak door, which had been barred from the inside. He paused there, turned his ear to the door and listened. He could hear nothing through the thick oak planks or the timber walls, but that was not surprising. If there was a full-fledged battle raging outside he doubted he would have heard it.

Moving with care, Odd lifted the bar from the door and set it aside, then he pushed gently on the door itself, which swung easily on greased iron hinges. He eased it open just an inch or so, the opening so narrow that it was unlikely to be seen in the dark. Then he peered through the crack.

His view was considerably limited, but it was expansive enough for him to see what he needed to see. A loose line of armed men, shields on arms, spears, axes, swords ready. He could only see a dozen or so from where he stood, but that was enough. He was quite certain that the line extended the length of the hall, with clusters of men at each of the doors ready to strike down anyone who fled the burning building. This was not some new and clever tactic, burning down a hall with your enemies inside. It was tried and true.

Odd eased the door closed and replaced the bar. He jogged back toward the big table in the center, the remnants of the banquet still spread over its surface. His guests and their men were slipping mail shirts or leather armor over their heads, strapping on swords or

273

thrusting battle axes through belts. Whether there was a fight in the offing or not they knew they would not be staying there and they would not leave their weapons behind.

One of the servants stood holding Odd's mail shirt, his helmet and his belt on which hung Blood-letter. Odd nodded his thanks and gestured for the man to set them on the table.

"Well?" Ulfkel demanded.

"As I feared," Odd said. "Halfdan's men are out there, lined up and ready for us. I only saw a few, but I don't doubt there are more." He lifted his mail shirt and slipped it over his head.

"Then out we go!" Ulfkel shouted. "Halfdan can bite my arse. I'll go down fighting before I burn up in here. I'm first out the door. You sorry bastards can follow me and kill any I leave behind!"

There was no doubt in Odd's mind that Ulfkel would happily charge out the door and right into the bulk of Halfdan's warriors. And he would likely take a few of them with him to the corpse hall. But not many. Because the men in the burning hall had to come out through the door one at a time, and in that manner Halfdan's men could cut them down as they came.

The alternative was to remain in the hall and burn to death. Neither choice was terribly attractive.

"There are two doors," Amundi said. "We'll divide our men, come out each at the same time. That will at least give us…"

Odd buckled Blood-letter around his waist, then raised his hand to cut him off. "This," he said, gesturing to the hall, the men, the fire spreading through the thatch, "is no great surprise to me. Anyone in my situation would be a fool to not see it coming. And make ready for it."

He turned to Vermund Jurundsson and Gnup and Ari the shipwright who were standing nearby, waiting, and he nodded his head. The three men stepped up onto the platform that lined the back wall of the hall, right next to Odd and Signy's sleeping closet. They grabbed the furs and blankets that lay strewn around and tossed them aside, then dropped to their knees. Odd's guests watched, silent, bewildered, and overhead the fire spread along the thatch, illuminating the hall in a wild, undulating light.

Vermund nodded to the others and together they lifted a section of the platform, five feet square and heavy built. They stood together, then moved the section to one side before setting it down again. Odd plucked a torch from a holder mounted on one of the carved posts that supported the roof beams overhead, then climbed up onto the platform. He held the torch over the open space where the section had been removed. The top of the ladder and a half dozen rungs were visible until it was all lost in the dark below.

"Vermund, you lead the women and the servants out first, then the rest of us will follow," Odd said, handing the torch to Vermund. "Signy," Odd continued, speaking louder, "get the women and the servants and you'll all follow Vermund out." The children were already hidden aboard *Sea Hawk*, which was ready to put to sea if necessary.

The guests could no longer swallow their questions. Amundi was the first to speak. "All right, Odd, by all the gods, what have you done?" He climbed up on the platform beside Odd, and Vifil and Ragi and the rest did as well. They looked down at the open place where the section of platform had been removed.

"A hiding place?" Ragi said. "A place to wait out Halfdan and the fire?" He did not sound terribly enthusiastic at the prospect.

"No," Odd said. "A tunnel. From here to the storehouse two hundred feet to the north."

"A tunnel..." Vifil said. There was no attempt to hide his surprise.

"A tunnel?" said Ulfkel. "What bastard digs a tunnel from their hall?"

Amundi answered. "A bastard who has wit enough to see what might happen. And make ready for when it does."

They stepped aside as Vermund came through holding the torch aloft. He stepped onto the ladder and climbed down into the pit, and behind him came the women, the servants and thralls, each moving with various levels of uncertainty. One after another they climbed down and moved off, Signy last of all, until all that the men on top could see was the glow of Vermund's torch growing dimmer as he led the refugees on.

Odd stepped down off the platform and grabbed another torch from a column, then climbed up again. "Come," he said. "Gather your men. I'll lead the way. Some of you others, take up torches as well." He waited for a minute as they sorted themselves out, then he turned and stepped down onto the top rung of the ladder, then onto the next one and the next, down into the secret hole that Gnup and the others had laboriously dug over the past weeks.

He reached the bottom of the ladder, the earth soft under the leather soles of his shoes. He turned and moved slowly off, deeper into the shaft, quick enough so the others would not get bunched up around him, slow enough that he didn't outpace them with the light. Far ahead he could see just a bit of a glow from Vermund's torch and he guessed that he and his people were just emerging from the far end of the passage and into the storehouse.

Odd moved on, crouching a bit though he didn't have to. The tunnel was deep enough for him to stand upright. It really wasn't a tunnel at all, in truth. Gnup and the others had dug a long trench, six feet deep and four feet wide, in a straight line from the hall to the storehouse. Once that was done the trench had been roofed over with heavy planks, pine boards thick enough to bear the weight of a wagon, and set a couple inches into the ground. Then the entire thing had been covered over with the dirt that had come from the digging. In a day or so it was impossible to tell that anything had been disturbed.

It was made just like the trap he had set in the road near Thorgrim's farm, writ large, except that the top of this trench was built to stand up to the weight of a horse, not collapse under it.

This was only the third time Odd had been through that underground passage. The first two times were for inspecting, making certain the work was done to his satisfaction, which it was. It was very well done. Gnup would get a silver arm ring for that, if he and Odd lived through the night.

Behind him, Odd could hear muttered comments, speculation, soft exclamations of surprise.

The tunnel seemed to go on forever, though Odd knew exactly how long it was, which was not very, and soon he saw the ladder at the far end appear in the light of his torch. He paused and thrust the base of the torch into a small hole dug in the side of the tunnel and left it there, then scrambled up the ladder and into the storehouse above.

The night air was cool and fresh and it made Odd realize how foul the air in the tunnel was. Of course he had never envisioned so many men moving through it. He had built it for his family and the servants to escape the hall, not an army of near two hundred warriors. He hoped the men at the far end of the line would not faint, but there was nothing he could do about it now. It would be up to their fellows to rescue them.

Vermund had left his burning torch inside the storehouse, set in a bracket, and in the light Odd could see that the storehouse was empty of people. Vermund and Signy had led them out the door, which was hanging open, and if they were still following his orders, had sent them running for safety, as far from the burning hall and Halfdan's men as they could get.

Odd stood aside. As the others began to emerge from the shaft, he gestured for them to head out the open door. The storehouse would stand between them and the hall and Halfdan's men would not see them there. Odd doubted they would even think to look in that direction for an army of warriors coming up out of the ground.

Finally Amundi came up from the hole in the floor. "I'm the last," he said. He had a hint of a smile on his face. He looked as if he was about to say something, but instead he just shook his head in a gesture of disbelief and headed out the door.

Odd came last out of the storehouse. The air carried the powerful, sharp smell of burning thatch and the crackling sound of the fire was loud. There was light enough from the fire consuming the roof of the hall, and the stars and moon overhead, for him to see the men waiting for him: his neighbors in a small cluster, and behind them the warriors they had brought along with them. Warriors summoned by Halfdan to help kill Odd and his people.

"Well, it seems Halfdan won't burn us alive in the hall, or cut us down like dogs," Odd said, speaking just a little softer than normal. "You and your men can make your escape now, you should be safe. You'll lose your horses, and I'm sorry for that, but there's nothing for it. But if you head out into the night Halfdan will never hunt you down."

"Doesn't have to," Ulfkel said. "He knows well enough where our farms are."

"But he doesn't know you were here," Odd said.

"You're saying we should leave? Leave you behind?" Vifil asked. "What are you going to do?"

"I'll go speak with Halfdan," Odd said. "Give myself up to him in exchange for my family's safety. Like I meant to do before."

Amundi made a snorting sound. "Too late for that. You'll be cut down before you speak one word, and it will be the worse for your family."

"What else can I do?" Odd said. "Do you expect me to flee?"

Odd could sense something uncomfortable passing through the men, a shuffling sort of indecision. Then Ulfkel said, "You can fight, by Thor's arse. *We* can fight. We can all fight this bastard."

Odd shook his head. "I wouldn't ask that of any of you. I couldn't ask." But even as he spoke the words he chastised himself for a hypocrite. It was true that he would not ask, but it was also true that he wanted very much for those men to offer. He was willing to give up his own life, ready to give it up, but he did not want to sell it cheap.

"You don't have to ask," Amundi said. "I don't think Halfdan sees much difference between you and us anymore. He might not know we were in the hall, but it won't matter. This started with you, and with your father's farm, but we're part of it now. By our choice. He'll certainly come after us, so we might as well make our stand here."

Heads nodded among the assembled free men. Behind them, Odd could see the warriors who were close enough to hear the discussion nodding as well. Nearly two hundred men, and he doubted that Halfdan had many more than that with him. And Halfdan's men were staring into the flames of the burning hall, waiting, unaware that their enemy was behind them, out in the dark.

There were worse ways to go into a fight.

"Very well," Odd said. He tried to keep the relief out of his voice, and that effort made him feel like even more of a hypocrite and a fraud. "Fighting it is."

Chapter Thirty

Long is the journey,
long are the ways,
long are men's desires.

The Poetic Edda

Halfdan did not know they were there. That advantage, the chance to launch a surprise attack, was worth another two dozen warriors. For that reason Odd and the others wanted to be certain that Halfdan continued to not know, right up until the moment the first of the king's men fell to their swords.

Amundi and the others hustled to arrange their men in columns, two long lines of one hundred men each. The plan was simple, as most good plans were. Nearly all of Halfdan's men were on the far side of the hall because that was where the doors were. But Odd did not think Halfdan would be foolish enough to leave the near side of the building completely unwatched. And if that was the case, then those men had to go before they could raise an alarm.

He and the other free men stood at the head of the columns and led the way carefully toward the edge of the storehouse, the only thing that stood between them and the burning hall. Odd raised his hand and the men behind came to a stop, some, not getting the message, cursing as they ran into the men in front of them. Odd and the other leaders edged to the corner of the building and stepped out into the open where they could see.

The hall was blazing now, the whole north end a great pyre reaching up high into the night sky. It was hard to look at, and Odd felt a sadness flood over him. In all the worry of getting his family and the servants and the others to safety, of wondering what Halfdan might do next, he had not thought of what this meant.

His hall, his home, the place where his children had been born and raised, and now it was being consumed by flames and soon it would be nothing but a charred heap, a mound of smoldering wreckage. He felt his sorrow slowly shift into something else: a rage deeper and more profound than he had thought possible.

Odd pulled his eyes from the blaze and looked along the length of the hall. Halfdan had indeed set guards on that side. He could see them, half a dozen or so, moving back and forth, silhouettes against the burning building. He turned to Amundi and the others.

"I'll kill those men," he said, nodding toward the hall. "And then we'll bring our men forward and attack around each end." He turned and slipped off before anyone could object.

And well they might object. Odd was the youngest of them, the least experienced in the use of arms. The others had all gone a'viking in their younger days, and even if it was many years before, still they had done this sort of thing and lived to tell of it. They had stood in shield walls and fought desperate battles hand to hand. They had killed men with swords and spears and knives and seaxes. They had likely killed men with their bare hands. And Odd had done none of that. Odd Pig-Binder.

Odd had killed before, certainly. Not just pigs but men, killed them in the usual course of things: feuds and robberies and repulsing minor raids by outlaws. He had probably killed more men since the start of his fight with Halfdan than he had in his whole life leading up to it. But in the eyes of the others he was a farmer, not a warrior. And even if he was a very fine, very well-respected farmer, he was a farmer nonetheless.

It was this understanding, and a sense that this was his fight, work that he alone must do, and the rage in his soul that was pushing him like a gale of wind toward the burning hall.

He moved quickly through the dark, his shield slung over his back, Blood-letter still in its scabbard. He could see the guards looking in every direction, but mostly they were staring at the burning hall, a rare sight, which meant they would be nearly blind when looking the other way, out into the dark. A wagon stood almost halfway between the storehouse and the hall. Odd reached it undetected and ducked down in its shadow. He swung the shield off his back and laid it aside.

The nearest guard was no more than thirty feet away. He had a shield on his arm and a spear in his hand. The fire glinted off a polished helmet on his head.

Odd made a moaning sound, like a man, or maybe an animal, in great pain. He did it again, louder this time. His eyes were on the guard and he could see him react as the strange noise reached his ears and registered as something that should concern him. He paused, looked up, cocked his head, then looked side to side. Odd moaned again and this time the man could tell the direction from which the sound came.

He was not fool enough to come rushing over. Rather, he took careful steps in the direction of the wagon, shield on his arm, spear horizontal and poised. Odd remained motionless, watching him come, waiting to see which end of the wagon he would investigate first. The world seemed to close down on him until it was just Odd and the wagon and the advancing guard and the rage like a sharp knife in his temple.

The guard stepped to his left and headed toward the front of the wagon where the shafts rested on the ground and Odd moved in the other direction. This was something entirely new to him. He had hunted, certainly, had become quite adept at stalking prey, but he had never played this sort of game with another human. But strangely, it did not feel foreign. Not at all. Odd felt as if the spirits of his grandfathers were leading him on.

He came around the far side and drew the long knife from the sheath on his belt, stepping with care, making no noise. The guard had reached the wagon now and was peering cautiously down into the shadows, shield still at chest level, spear point reaching out into what Odd knew was only darkness.

Odd straightened and took three steps. The guard sensed he was there just as Odd's left arm came up and around the man's head and his hand clamped over his mouth. It was all so very strange: the warm bulk of the man pressed against him, the smell of his flesh, the strength of his body as he suddenly realized he was in mortal danger and began to fight back. Odd could feel the man's teeth pressed into his palm and he could feel his warm breath through calloused skin as Halfdan's warrior screamed into Odd's hand.

The muscles in Odd's left arm tightened and the man's head was pulled back, his neck elongated and he began fighting harder still as he understood what was coming. He swung the edge of his shield up over his left shoulder, trying to hit Odd in the face, but Odd flinched right and the edge of the shield just grazed his cheek. Then Odd whipped the knife around and brought it up to the man's throat.

Odd had cut the throats of hundreds of animals of all sizes and he knew the sensation well: the press of the steel against resilient flesh, then the feel of the flesh parting under the sharp blade, the slight tug as the blade was drawn through muscle and sinew, the fine vibration as it ran over the bones of the neck. The blast of hot blood over the knife hand.

And here it was again, in every way, but this time it was a man, and Odd was very much aware that it was a man, a man who could think and speak and love and hate. Who might have a wife, who might have children. Odd felt the great profundity of that, and he felt a numb detachment as well.

All this Odd thought and felt in the three heartbeats' time it took him to grab the warrior and cut his throat. He felt the man thrash a bit more and he held him tight, like a grieving lover he was trying to console, and then the man went limp and Odd eased him down onto the ground.

Odd dropped to one knee beside the motionless body. He stabbed his knife into the ground and wiped his blood-soaked hand on the tail of the man's tunic, and once most of the blood was gone he grabbed the knife and wiped that as well. He did those things without thought, his eyes on the remainder of the men on that side of the hall. They, too, would have to be removed.

He looked down at the body sprawled out in front of him. The man's arm was flung out and his shield had come halfway off his arm, and without really thinking about it or making a decision Odd knew what he would do next. He slid the knife back into his sheath, then plucked the helmet from the man's head and set it on his own. He picked up the shield and slid it over his arm, then grabbed the man's discarded spear and stood.

The next closest of Halfdan's men was a couple hundred feet away. His shield was on his back, his spear resting easy on his shoulder. He wore a tunic and no mail. He seemed to not be very concerned about much. Odd began jogging toward him, a pace calculated to allow him to remain unconcerned.

By the time the man paused in his casual pacing and turned to face him, Odd had halved the distance between them. The man took the spear off his shoulder and rested the butt on the ground but took no other precautions beyond that. In the light of the burning hall he would see the familiar face of the shield Odd held, the glint of his helmet, the spear in Odd's hand. Just what he would expect to see.

"What is it?" the man shouted as Odd drew closer. There was curiosity in his tone, perhaps a touch of concern. The next word out of his mouth, and the last word, was, "What?" as Odd, still jogging, lowered the spear he was holding and with his right hand alone drove it straight into the man's gut.

The man's eyes and mouth opened wide. He doubled over the spear and Odd was certain a scream was coming so he swung his shield in a wide arc and slammed it against the man's head. The man's helmet made a dull ringing sound as the wooden shield struck. The man twisted sideways and sprawled out on the ground, the spear jerking free from his body as he fell. Odd paused to see if he needed to hit the man again, but he seemed to be out cold, a mercy as he bled out through the vicious stomach wound.

Odd straightened. That little performance had not gone unnoticed. Two more of the men patrolling that side of the hall were running toward him now, the first about fifty feet ahead of the second.

"This bastard tried to kill me!" Odd shouted, pointing with his spear toward the man at his feet. He didn't think the warrior running at him would believe that, or care, but if it created even a hint of doubt in the man's mind that could be an advantage.

"He tried to kill me!" Odd shouted again. The man coming at him was thirty feet away and as he ran he slung his shield around off his back and onto his arm. Odd was sorry to see that. It would make this all the more difficult. He held his spear at his side, waited until Halfdan's man was twenty feet away, too close to miss, and then he whipped the spear up and flung it straight and true.

The shield was a problem, as Odd guessed it would be. The man never broke stride as he lifted the shield and let the iron spear point embed itself in the wood. But that instant when the shield was over the man's face was all that Odd needed. He leapt forward and drew Blood-letter as he ran. The man lowered the shield, the spear still hanging from the face, only to run straight into the point of Odd's sword.

He was still running as the blade slid into his chest. He started to scream, then the scream turned to a choking sound as the blood erupted from his mouth. Odd held up his shield and the man hit it hard, coming to a jarring halt, and Odd pushed him away, pulling Blood-letter clean out as he did.

The next man was almost on him, a great brute with a shield and an ax and crazed look on his face, wild eyes peering out from a mass of wild facial hair. He raised the ax and screamed as he hacked down with a strength of arm that would easily cleave a helmet in two and still have force enough to cleave the skull beneath it.

Odd did not raise his shield. Instead he raised Blood-letter, held sideways, and the man's bare wrists came down on the blade's wicked edge. The force of the blow pushed the sword down and all but separated the man's hands from his arms. The ax flew clear and Odd had to dodge to one side and the man shrieked and held his arms up to his face, his hands flopping sideways at unnatural angles. He started to scream again but Blood-letter cut it short.

Odd was breathing hard, but the rage was up and the urge to keep on killing was overwhelming. There were no more guards that he could see on that side of the hall; any others were lost in the darkness further down. It was his duty to go back and get Amundi and the others so they might launch their planned attack, but even the notion of moving away from the fight was more than Odd could endure.

He looked back at the storehouse, trying to organize his thoughts well enough to make a decision, when he saw that no decision was needed.

The others must have seen what was happening, maybe guessed that Odd would just keep going on his own, so they broke from their hiding place and advanced, two lines of warriors surging toward him. Odd could see Amundi leading the line of men closest to him, Ulfkel, leading the other. They split up as they approached the hall, Ulfkel heading for the north side, the side fully engulfed, Amundi going for the south end, leading his men seemingly straight at Odd.

"Come along! Now we kill the lot of them!" Amundi shouted as he ran closer. He had his shield on his arm and his sword raised and he seemed more alive than Odd had ever seen him.

Odd took a step toward him, ready to join the charge, ready to run at Amundi's side around the far end of the hall and plunge into the fight, hitting Halfdan's men on one side while Ulfkel hit them on the other. But he didn't.

Instead he stood and watched. Amundi, with Ragi and Vigdis in company, raced by, and after them the hundred warriors they commanded.

Go with them, go with them! Odd commanded himself, but he remained fixed where he was, watching the warriors race past. He did not know why. It wasn't cowardice, that he understood. He was more than willing to plunge into the thick of it. It wasn't any misgiving, as if he might think this was a bad idea. He knew it wasn't. He knew they had every hope of success.

Why don't I go with them?

He could see the battle playing out in his mind, Halfdan's men pressed in on either side, Halfdan's hird standing circle around him, fighting off anyone who might break through the shield walls at either end of the hall while the fire spread and the heat began to singe their flesh.

Then he understood. This was his fight. Him and Halfdan. He could not be just another warrior going into battle, one small part of a company of men, an anonymous sword and shield. No. He was too much a part of this to be simply one of many.

It was too personal for that. He did not wish to fight Halfdan's men. He needed to fight Halfdan himself.

And with that realization he was ready to move. He jogged down the length of the hall, into the dark where flames from the burning roof could not yet reach, over the ground where Amundi had just led his line of warriors. There were dead men strewn around, the last of Halfdan's men who had been sent to that side of the hall. The side which had no doors, and so did not need men positioned there in great numbers.

Except it did have a door. At the back of the storeroom just past the platform on which Odd and Signy's sleeping closet sat there was a door that led out to the grounds. It was there for the servants to go in and out, for food and such to be brought into the hall without going through one of the two big doors on the other side. It was very difficult to see in the dark, hard to find if you were not intimately familiar with the hall. Which Odd was.

He found the door easily. He lifted the latch and pushed, but the door, barred from inside, did not move, which was what he had expected. Odd took a step back, lifted his right leg and drove his heel into the door, right at the level of the latch. He felt the pain in his foot, the shudder of the impact up his leg, but he also saw the door flex inward and he heard the splintering sound of the bar giving way. He cocked his leg again, drove his heel in again, and this time the door swung open with the crushing noise of shattering wood.

Odd stepped quickly through the door and into the storeroom. The room itself was lost in dark, but beyond the room Odd could see the brilliant light of the fire that was consuming his hall. He stepped across the room, caught his foot on something, stumbled and recovered. He continued on, a bit more cautiously, until the firelight fell on the floor where he was walking.

He took a tentative step out of the storeroom and into the hall itself. It was a step he feared to take. Not because he thought there would be anyone there—he knew no one would be so foolish as to enter that inferno—but for the heartbreaking sight that would greet him.

And in that he was not disappointed. The entire north end of the hall was lost in a mass of fire that was devouring the walls and roof and tables. Black smoke roiled up, and if the roof had not been so high the entire space would have been nothing but choking blackness, backlit by flames.

Odd stood motionless and watched the destruction and he felt a strange sickness in his stomach. He knew every little bit of that hall, every beam, every post, every rafter that supported the dense thatch. Much of it he had built himself. The familiar walls and roof were illuminated now more brightly than he had ever seen. He could trace their length from overhead right to the point where they were lost in the terrific blaze.

As he stared, one of the great beams broke free and dropped twenty feet to the floor and burst into a spray of sparks and flames and smoke. Above, the roof sagged and the fire redoubled.

"Odin, give me strength to avenge this!" Odd shouted the words, as loud as he was able, but he could still barely hear himself over the sound of the fire that was consuming his home. He stepped out from the shelter of the storeroom door and raced across the floor, vaulting over the long hearth that ran down the center of the room. There were still coals smoldering there and they seemed ridiculous in the light of the massive blaze.

The southern door was off to Odd's right and he changed direction and ran straight for it. He stopped just inside and leaned against the wooden planks and pressed his ear to them. He could make out the sounds of fighting, the shouting and clash of weapons. It sounded far off through the door and the roar of the fire. But it was fighting, there was no doubt. His neighbors had done as they said, had swept around either end of the hall and charged straight into Halfdan's men.

Odd lifted the bar and pushed the door open, just a few inches. At first he could see nothing but dark shapes moving against a darker night, but his eyes adjusted and he could make out men fighting just beyond the door, and further away. Dozens of men. There were no shield walls, no organized attack, just dozens of individuals in combat.

He pushed the door wider and half-stepped from the hall. He could not see Halfdan or his hird. He looked north along the wall and saw them at last: Halfdan mounted, high above the fray, his hird surrounding him as the fight swirled around. The fire from the burning hall made his fine mail and helmet glitter and undulate with red and orange light. Odd could see the look of calm on his face, the look of a man who did not expect to see defeat that day.

Beside him, also mounted, sat Einar, his green cape looking black in that light, his face as calm and sure as his master's.

Odd clenched his teeth. He looked around again. There was no getting through that mass of fighting men. To get at Halfdan he would have to hack his way through the thick of the battle, and even if he lived to do that he would be facing the best of the hird protecting their king.

But there was another way.

Odd stepped back into the hall and closed the door and barred it. His presence had not been noticed—the men outside the hall were too distracted by far to see him. He turned and ran along the wall toward the burning end of the building. He jumped up onto the platform that ran the length of the wall and continued on. Small fires were burning here and there, ignited by flaming debris dropped from the roof, and Odd leapt over them as he ran.

The heat from the flames was all but intolerable. Odd felt his skin grow hot and he felt the searing pain, head to toe, as if he, like the roof overhead, had burst into flames. With every foot he ran, the pain grew worse and he heard himself shout with the agony of it.

The walls seemed to tremble, and a cracking and roaring noise rose up from the flames. Then another of the massive roof beams broke free and came thundering down to the floor just twenty feet away. It was a timber thirty feet long, hewn from a great oak that had once stood on the far hills and was now a flaming shaft, a lance of the gods, flung from on high. It hit the floor and made the platform under Odd's feet shudder. Burning thatch came down in a rain of fire. A scrap the size of a shield fell on the arm of Odd's mail and ignited the cuff of his tunic. Odd beat the flames out as he ran, still screaming with the agony of being cooked alive.

At last he leapt down off the far end of the platform right in front of the north door of the hall. On the other side of the door and fifteen feet away were Halfdan, Einar and the hird. Odd knew it, he had seen it from the south door. No need to fight his way to the enemy king: he was there already.

He grit his teeth and lifted the bar from the door, tossed it aside, then paused. He had a vision floating in his imagination of a madman bursting out of the burning building, and he realized the advantage he would gain from so shocking an appearance. He half turned. A pile of burning thatch lay on the floor a few feet away, the flames rising as high as his head. He stepped toward it and held his shield over the fire. The flames licked around the edge and he could smell the paint on its face burning. And then the entire shield ignited.

Odd spun around and took three quick steps to the door. He reached down and lifted the latch and kicked the oak door open, drawing Blood-letter as he did. He stepped out into the night, the shield on his left arm a ball of flame. He could feel the heat through the metal boss and knew he would not be able to hold it much longer, and he knew he had to get the maximum effect while he still could. So he took a step forward and he screamed.

The scream came from deep down, deeper than he thought was in him. It was a scream made up of many parts: the rage of seeing his hall burned, his wife and children threatened, of seeing his father's farm stolen from him, of being treated like a piece of something that could just be kicked around at will. Of remaining behind on a farm while his father and his brother went a'viking, of knowing that as respected as he might be he would never be respected the way a warrior was respected. Of knowing that his wife loved him but not knowing if he had earned even a part of that love, or was worthy of it.

It was a scream that cut right through the clash of weapons and the shouts of men and the cries of the gravely wounded. It was a scream that made eyes turn quick in his direction and when they did they saw an image of a man, or something like a man, coming out of a burning building in which no man could hope to live and bearing a shield of living flame. It was the image of a demon from the fire, born of the fire, son of the fire.

Odd saw eyes go wide, the men of the hird who surrounded Halfdan, just ten feet away, turning toward him and taking a step back, mouths open. Odd felt the flames from the shield burning his face. His left hand, holding the grip of the shield, was in unbearable pain. He was still screaming as he took two steps in Halfdan's direction and flung the shield at the cowering men. It spun through the air like a massive fireball and slammed into the warriors who surrounded Halfdan's horse, and they flinched and ducked and cowered from the assault.

"It's Odd, you fools!" Halfdan's voice roared out as the scream died in Odd's throat. "It's Odd! Kill him!"

The shock lasted only an instant, but that instant was long enough. The men of the hird were still regaining their senses when Odd was on them, Blood-letter lashing out like lightning striking here and there. A man's throat was rent, another felt the bite of the sword in his shoulder. Odd still had sense enough to know he did not have to kill these men, only get them out of the way, out of the fight.

The man to his right was down, his shield on the ground and Odd snatched it up even as he held Blood-letter aloft to deflect a blow coming for his head. He slipped his arm through the strap and wrapped his aching fingers around the grip as he stood. He pushed the shield into the man in front of him, half turned and thrust at the man to his left, missing, leaping clear of the counter thrust.

Now he sensed movement in front of him and he turned, shield held up, just in time to catch the point of a sword aimed at his chest. A lucky move on his part, an accidental move, but it saved his life, at least for the moment. He pulled the shield back, felt the point of the sword pull free. He looked over the top edge of the shield, into the eyes of the man who had nearly killed him. Einar.

"Come on, you sorry swineherd!" Einar taunted. His moustache made a black line across his face and down his cheeks and his helmet and teeth reflected the light from the fire. "I'll have that sword from you! It needs a warrior to carry it, not you!"

Einar's words were as sharp and quick as his sword and Odd felt the rage swell again. He glanced side to side to see who else was there, if he would be fighting Einar alone or the rest of the hird as well. But the warriors ringing Halfdan seemed to be busy now with fighting of their own.

"There's no help for you, you bastard!" Einar shouted, misinterpreting the look, or choosing to. "In the name of King Halfdan I'll cut you down myself!"

He was still speaking the last of those words when Odd lunged, driving straight at him with the point of Blood-letter's blade, right past the edge of Einar's shield. Einar twisted at the waist, twisting out of the path of the blade. The point caught Einar's mail shirt on the side and went right on through. Odd saw it come out through the mail on the far side and he braced for Einar's shriek of agony, but it did not come.

Instead, Einar twisted back, the sword still caught in his mail, and Odd realized the blade had slid between mail and tunic and not through Einar's body at all. He realized this at the same instant that Einar turned and Blood-letter's hilt was jerked from Odd's hand.

For a second both men stopped, unsure of what had happened. Einar looked down and saw Odd's sword still thrust through his mail shirt. Odd saw that this was the perfect instance to lash out at Einar and kill him, but he had no weapon. Then the instant passed and Einar was at him again.

He pushed Odd with his shield, pushed him away to get room to fight. Odd stumbled back and saw the point of Einar's sword coming at him so he stumbled back again and Einar's thrust fell short by inches. Odd knocked the extended blade aside with his shield, leapt forward, drawing his knife from its sheath as he did.

His shield hit Einar's and the two of them went down, Odd on top of Einar, shield against shield. Einar swung his arm around and his fist, gripping the hilt of his sword, slammed into the side of Odd's head. Odd felt the stunning blow and for an instant seemed to lose sense of where he was, what he was trying to do. But it was an instant, no more, and then he drove the point of his long knife down at Einar's face.

Einar's eyes went wide and he twisted his head to the side. Odd's knife sliced through Einar's ear and stabbed deep into the ground. But Einar seemed not to notice the wound. He pushed hard with his shield, trying to push Odd off of him. Odd pulled the knife free and brought his arm back, eyes fixed on Einar's face, intent on driving the blade through Einar's head. His arm was just starting the down stroke when he felt a sudden agony in his right shoulder, as if he had been touched with a red-hot metal bar.

He shouted and jerked back with some half-formed notion that Einar had managed to stab him. But as he straightened he saw the great bulk of a horse looming over him, not three feet away. He looked up at Halfdan and understood Halfdan had just driven a sword into his shoulder. Now Halfdan was bringing his sword up once more, ready to strike again, a backhand stroke that would take Odd's head clean off.

"Bastard!" Odd shouted and leapt to his feet. He still had the shield in his left hand so he raised it high and stepped on Einar's chest and launched himself at Halfdan. The shield hit Halfdan's side and Odd hit the shield and the impact sent waves of pain radiating out from his fresh wound. He felt Halfdan's sword come down, but Odd was so close that Halfdan's arm, not his blade, struck his shoulder and bounced uselessly off.

Odd had only the knife, but it was enough. He shifted the shield on his left arm and swung the knife around with his right, sure the weapon's wicked point would pierce Halfdan's mail. But even as the knife was in mid-swing Halfdan jerked his horse's reins and the animal pivoted around, slamming its neck into Odd's shoulder.

The blow from the horse knocked Odd sideways and he screamed with the agony of it. He stumbled and his foot caught on Einar, still on the ground, and he stumbled further.

Odd was sure he was going down, and all he could think was how much it was going to hurt when his wounded shoulder hit the ground. But he caught himself, regained his footing. He straightened and saw the horse rearing up, saw its hoof lash out like a whip. It struck him in the shoulder and sent him staggering again.

Odd dropped the knife and yelled. He tried to clamp his left hand over the wound, but with the shield on his arm he couldn't reach it. He saw the horse leap toward him, teeth bared, ready to tear at any flesh not covered with iron—his hands, his face.

The shield was all Odd had now, so he swung it at the horse and felt it connect. The horse reared back again and Odd braced for the flailing hooves, but they did not come. He lowered the shield. The fighting, which had been manic just a moment before, seemed to have all but stopped, as if some signal had been given. Odd found himself looking at Halfdan's horse, lit up red in the blaze of the burning hall, Halfdan's mail still glinting in the light as he rode off. The pounding of the horse's hooves on the soft ground seemed unnaturally loud, and then faded as Halfdan raced away.

Odd looked to his left. Men were standing, men were lying on the ground. Men were breathing hard and holding hands over wounds and staring straight up, mouths open gulping air. Some of Halfdan's men were on their knees, hands held up in what looked like supplication.

And then he saw Amundi coming through the press. His mail was rent and there was blood on his face and he seemed to be limping. But he was smiling. A weary smile, a wounded smile, a tempered smile. But a smile of victory.

Chapter Thirty-One

Then he must consider that the wise Lord
often moves through the earth
granting some men honor, glory and fame,
but others only shame and hardship.

Deor's Lament
Early Anglo-Saxon Poem

It amazed Nothwulf how often it happened. One could wait days for
some change in circumstance, some indication of which direction to
move. And then, suddenly, everything seemed to happen all at once.
That was certainly the case now.

In truth it had been just one day, but in the wake of the battle and
all that hung in the balance it certainly felt as if he had been stewing
much longer than that. And now, at last, the momentum seemed to
be building again.

The signs of the fighting were still visible: the humps of fresh-
turned earth where the dead had been buried, thankfully not too
many, the tent set up to shelter the wounded, the series of dark
patches on the ground where the fires had burned to light the arrows
shot at the Northmen. The tide had gone out and the burned hulk of
the Northman's ship was mostly exposed, run up hard against the
ships Nothwulf had sunk in mid-channel to prevent their escape.

It had worked just as he had envisioned. Except for the bit where
the heathens had escaped by rowing back into the bay and
ensconcing themselves on a sandbar where they could not be
reached.

Other than that it had worked well. The one ship burned, the
others damaged. Heathens killed. When it was over Nothwulf had
sent a boat out to poke around the hulk of the burned-out ship. They

had managed to retrieve a few things of value: some swords, a small chest full of silver, some arm rings. Not all that Nothwulf had hoped for, but something.

And there was the other thing. Leofric had been captured. Ailmar, Leofric's second in command, had come over himself in one of the boats to give Nothwulf the news. Leofric had been leading the counterattack against the Northmen, he had been wounded, and when the Northmen ran off they took Leofric with them. What they wanted with Leofric Nothwulf did not know. Ransom, likely. Leofric looked like a man of means and some importance. But no word had come.

So Nothwulf waited to see what might happen next. He knew he should act, take the initiative, rather than simply wait for something to happen, but he was not entirely certain what he should do. He wished Leofric were there to advise him. That was not something he cared admit to himself, and certainly not to anyone else, but he knew that it was true.

"Leofric..." Nothwulf muttered. He assumed the demand for ransom would be coming soon and then he would have to decide what to do. He wanted the old man back, certainly. But it was also true that Leofric was growing timid in his advice, like an old woman. Nothwulf found him irritating at times. Leofric was a royal thegn, his lands given to his father by the king himself, and he was close to King Æthelwulf, so there was no way for Nothwulf to lay claim to his holdings even if Leofric was gone. Still, he had to wonder if he was better off with or without the man.

I guess we'll just have to see how much ransom is demanded, Nothwulf concluded. He would need a price before he could determine whether or not it was worth buying Leofric's freedom.

But Nothwulf did not hear from the Northmen, at least not at first. His first sign of pending change came in the form of two horsemen, riding in from the west.

Nothwulf understood how exposed he was to an overland attack, and he knew Cynewise was out there somewhere, so he had put sentries far out behind his makeshift fortifications. One of the two riders approaching was one of those sentries, he was pretty sure. Who the other was he had no idea.

He waited on top of the rough log wall as he watched them approach. They stopped a hundred feet from his position and dismounted and Nothwulf could see now who the second rider was: Oswin, the shire reeve. Cynewise's man.

Now what? Nothwulf wondered.

Oswin climbed up one of the ladders leaning against the wall and made his way over to Nothwulf, moving in the unhurried, self-assured way that Nothwulf associated with the man. He stopped when he reached Nothwulf's place and gave a nod of the head that might have been construed as a bow. The sort of bow a man might give if he wished to show no real sign of subservience.

"Oswin, what brings you now?" Nothwulf said, careful to sound not at all curious, even slightly bored by all this.

"I came to tell you Cynewise and her army will attack you at first light," he said, looking Nothwulf in the eye, his expression calm and unwavering.

That took Nothwulf by surprise, and despite himself he let the surprise show.

"She...sent you here to tell me this?" Nothwulf asked. His mouth was speaking those half-considered words while his mind was scrambling to figure out what sort of game they were playing, Oswin and Cynewise.

"No," Oswin said. "She sent me to watch you. I decided to bring you the warning myself."

Nothwulf squinted and stared at Oswin, unspeaking, for a long moment. "Do you honestly expect me to believe anything you say? You're a lying dog and you always have been. And now you lie in service of Cynewise."

Oswin nodded. "I'll own up to that," he said. "Except I'm not lying for Cynewise anymore. I'm done with her. Her father's dead and his men-at-arms are going back to Devonshire. The thegns who were with her, well, they're with her still, but their loyalty is shaky at best."

Again Oswin was quiet for a moment. "You own up to being a liar," he said at last. "Why should I believe you now?"

"You don't have to. I won't pretend that I do anything but what's in my own self-interest. So...I think it's in my interest to come to your aid. Because I think Cynewise is done for. And when she's finished I would hope to keep my office, if possible. If not that, then at least my head."

"Your loyalty is commendable," Nothwulf said.

"I am utterly loyal," Oswin said. "To myself and to whoever I think can do me the most good. And more and more that seems to be you."

"Your words make perfect sense," Oswin said. "And yet...I have a hard time seeing past your lying, sniveling, boot-lick past."

"Of course," Oswin said. "So let me say this. Cynewise knows that you're caught here on this point of land with your back to the channel and half your army, Leofric's half, stuck on the other side. She still has more than enough men to crush you and they're on the move as of now. You can believe me or not. But when this is over, and if you're still alive and ealdorman of Dorsetshire, I would beg you remember I gave you valuable information, and I gave it truthfully and willingly."

Nothwulf was not certain what to say to that. Oswin would not be the first to turn on that little bitch Cynewise. Aelfwyn, too, had been driven to abandon her and had also provided him with valuable information.

He was about to reply with something noncommittal when the sentry, fifty feet away, shouted, "Lord Nothwulf!"

"Yes?"

"There's a boat coming, Lord," the sentry called, pointing out over the water. "Coming from the heathens, I think!"

Nothwulf and Oswin looked off to where the man was pointing. A single boat, about a quarter of a mile away, was pulling toward them. It did indeed seem to be coming from the direction of the sandbar on which the heathens were encamped. There seemed to be two men at the oars and one in the stern, though it was hard to tell from that distance. In any event, they did not seem to pose any significant threat.

"Ah, yes, the heathens," Oswin said. "As if this all wasn't complicated enough."

"Coming to seek terms, I should think," Nothwulf said. "We did them great hurt yesterday, have them fairly well trapped in that sandbar."

"Hmm," Oswin said. The sound dripped with disbelief.

"You may wait there," Nothwulf said to Oswin, indicating the ground on the landward side of the wall. He did not want Oswin to know that Leofric had been taken hostage, or anything else for that matter. Oswin gave a quick bow and climbed down the ladder to wait, and Nothwulf sent two guards to help him with the waiting. Then he turned back to watch the boat's approach.

Here comes the demand for ransom, Nothwulf thought. He moved to the far end of the wall, eyes on the Northmen, his mind racing around like a rabbit trying to get away from a dog. Oswin's words had unsettled him because he believed them. He knew that he was vulnerable where he was, with half his army on the other side of the channel. They were only about two hundred feet away, he could see them perfectly well, but they might as well have been in Frankia for all they could join with him.

It was not as if he hadn't seen this coming from the start. But he always had a vague idea that they would be able to capture at least one of the Northmen's ships, and that would allow them to move men back and forth with relative ease. But it hadn't worked out that way, and now all they had to move the men were a couple of little boats.

To fight Cynewise he needed his army all together. To fight the Northmen he needed them on both sides of the channel. He had no quick or easy means to get men from one side to the other. And now here came the Northmen, and God alone knew what demands they would make, how much worse they might make the entire situation. Nothwulf wanted to scream in frustration at times, but he kept it to himself.

Nothwulf climbed down the ladder that led to the beach and walked over to where the boat had run up on the sand. The three heathens climbed out in the face of ten of Nothwulf's men, standing in a half circle with spears lowered.

The guards stepped aside as Nothwulf approached, making an opening in their circle but never lowering their spears or their vigilance. Nothwulf stepped through the gap and stopped ten feet from where the Northmen stood waiting, calm and unmoved by the weapons pointed at them.

So how do we talk with these whores' sons? Nothwulf thought when one of them took a step forward. He was not terribly tall, but very broad and powerful-looking. A young man with long blond hair tied in a braid down his back and the wispy attempts at a beard on his jaw.

"Good day," the heathen said in passable English, passable enough that Nothwulf could understand him. "My name is Harald. I come from the camp of the...fin gall." He said that last word as if he knew it was not right but he did not know what else to say. And he was correct insofar as Nothwulf had no idea what it meant, but he guessed it meant the Northmen.

"I am Lord Nothwulf. I am ruler of these lands around."

The young man Harald nodded. "I am looking for you," he said.

Who told you to look for me? Ah, Leofric! Nothwulf thought, and he said, "Well, here I am."

"My father is chief of the people there," Harald said, indicating with his thumb the sandbar a half a mile away. "You blocked the channel. We're stuck. But we have Leofric. Hostage."

Nothwulf wondered if this Harald was going to suggest he let the Northmen leave in exchange for Leofric, which he was not about to do. It would cost them a lot more than one man's life to get through the channel.

"Yes, go on," Nothwulf said.

"You're in danger, too," Harald continued. "Leofric's men are there." Harald pointed to the eastern bank. "Can't cross the channel. And your enemy is ready to attack."

How did he bloody know that? Nothwulf wondered. *Did they torture Leofric?*

"Leofric and my father have talked," Harald continued. "Found a way out of all this. Good for you and for us."

Nothwulf was listening now.

"Leofric sent me to tell you this," Harald continued. "Leofric and my father, Thorgrim Ulfsson. We have ships and we have men. We don't care about your fight. We only want to leave. You clear the wrecks from the channel, we bring the ships there." He pointed to the eastern shore. "When your enemy attacks, we get Leofric's men, bring them to join you. And then we'll go."

Nothwulf nodded, but every word Harald spoke made him think, *This is a trap.* He folded his arms and stared at Harald, looking for some sign of a trick. Finally he said, "Why should I believe that Leofric is helping you?"

Harald dug into a purse that hung from his belt. "Leofric sends this, as a sign to you." He held out his hand, a ring resting on the palm. Nothwulf picked up the ring and looked at it closely. A gold ring with Leofric's device worked into it. It was certainly Leofric's, he had been wearing it for years.

"For all I know you cut that off Leofric's finger," Nothwulf said.

"Maybe," Harald agreed.

Nothwulf was silent as he considered all this. If the Northman was telling the truth then here was an answer to his biggest problem—how to bring his army together in the face of Cynewise's attack.

"You Northmen won't come ashore?" Nothwulf asked. "You won't fight?"

"No," Harald said. "Your fight, not ours. We'll bring your men across. Or if you don't agree, we'll watch your army be killed by this woman, Sinwhy…" Harald stumbled over Cynewise's name, but added, "It will be fun. Entertainment."

Nothwulf pressed his lips together. He needed to think on this, give it a few hours, even better, sleep on it before making a decision. But he did not have that luxury. A decision was needed and it was needed immediately. So he made one, made it with his gut because he could not get his mind to work fast enough.

"Very well," he said to Harald. "I agree. I think Cynewise—my enemy—will attack first thing tomorrow. Have your ships ready to go. Land them out of sight around that point of land." He pointed to the shore across the channel, just south of the entrance where a ship would not be seen from the side Nothwulf was on. "Once you hear the fighting start, bring the men-at-arms across and land them here. Leofric included." Nothwulf was starting to think he might get away with not paying any ransom at all.

Harald looked at the point to the south where Nothwulf indicated, then back at Nothwulf. "And you'll have the channel clear for us?"

"Yes, we'll do that tonight. Once the men are landed you can be on your way."

Harald nodded. "Good. I'll tell Leofric. And my father. You see that the men on the other side know of our bargain." He turned and climbed into the boat, then the other two heathens shoved the boat into the water, hopped aboard and took up the oars. Soon they were underway, back to their sandbar encampment.

Nothwulf watched them go. It seemed to him things were working out, moving in his favor at last. And then he remembered that his entire plan was based on what he had been told by Oswin and by one heathen who barely spoke English and he felt the panic rising again.

Chapter Thirty-Two

*Three things
threaten a man's existence
before his final hour:
either illness, old age
or sword's-edge-malice.*

The Seafarer

Well, at least Nothwulf didn't do anything stupid, Leofric thought as he watched the boat pulling back to the sandbar, Harald's yellow hair clearly visible. *At least, not yet.*

This had all been Leofric's idea, the plan that was unfolding. The heathen named Thorgrim did not know the players in this drama, nor did he understand the complex machinations going on in the shire of Dorset. And why should he? Sometimes Leofric didn't think that he himself could follow it. But for all that, their needs, his and Thorgrim's, were simple. Thorgrim needed to get out of the harbor. Leofric needed to get his men across the channel to help Nothwulf in the coming fight. Each was in a position to help the other.

As long as Nothwulf played along. Leofric had his concerns. He was afraid Nothwulf might not believe Harald and get it in his mind to hold the boy and the others in the boat as hostages. Leofric figured that sending his ring would help, but it would be no guarantee, because Nothwulf might well not believe that Leofric himself had actually sent it.

But so far things looked good.

He and Thorgrim were standing side by side watching the boat approach. For Leofric, the hours spent among the Northmen, the heathens, had been the most fascinating he had ever had. He felt like

Daniel of old: half a day in the lion's den and God had thus far preserved him.

Waking up that morning on the deck of a Northman's ship, head wracked with pain from the blow to his skull, weapons gone, Leofric had figured it was about over, and it was only a question of how torturous the final hours would be. But far from doling out an agonizing death, Thorgrim had proved himself a good host. He fed Leofric and gave him a cup of ale kept constantly filled. They had negotiated like civilized men, carrying on a most enlightening conversation, with Harald there as translator. And after they reached an agreement Thorgrim even restored Leofric's sword and mail to him.

Still, these Northmen were the enemies of Wessex, and Leofric recognized this as an opportunity to learn more about them, with an eye toward beating them on future fields of battle. When Thorgrim left him to attend to other business, Leofric spent his time making a careful study of the goings on. He wanted to see how this heathen army functioned.

He noticed one thing right off: it wasn't really an army at all. Thorgrim aside, Leofric had a hard time telling who were the leaders, the captains or whatever the heathens called them, and who were the regular men-at-arms.

Some of the men wore silver arm rings and carried swords and appeared to be of greater importance, and Leofric guessed they were in command, but no one seemed to be telling anyone what to do or where to go. They all seemed to know, and they did what needed doing with no orders given. That would not be the case in an English army. A hearth-guard, perhaps, could function on their own, and maybe the more elite of the warriors, but the fyrd certainly needed to be supervised as if they were children.

The Northmen seemed to be organized by ship, the crews of each keeping together, making their own fires and seeing to their own provisions, which made sense. But Leofric did not see any jealousy or ill-will from one crew to the other. They were more like a band of brothers than any army he had ever led.

They fight for themselves, they fight for their fellows. They don't fight simply because they are commanded to fight, Leofric thought. *They fight for plunder that they'll all share.*

Was it any wonder they were so damned hard to beat?

Leofric's observations were interrupted by the sight of Harald's boat returning. Once the boy was ashore his news led to another discussion with Thorgrim. This time the meeting also included the captains of the other ships, and Leofric saw he had for the most part guessed right about who they were.

Harald explained, in Norse and English, that Nothwulf had agreed to their plan. He would be ready, and he would expect the Northmen to be ready as well. Leofric could not understand the discussion that took place between the heathens, and Harald did not translate it for him, but it did seem that no one objected.

They have no cause to object, Leofric thought. *They only need to play the part of ferrymen once and then they're on their way. Don't even have to draw their swords.*

Discussion done, Leofric was free to continue his observations. Evening came and the Northmen cooked and ate their supper, and then everything that had been unloaded from the ships was loaded back aboard. They bedded down for the night on the sand, which Leofric guessed was preferable to the decks of the ships, and soon the dark was filled with the rough snoring of four hundred or so half-drunk, half-wild men.

Leofric was not accustomed to such rude accommodations, but he slept well nonetheless, with the sand soft beneath him and himself wearier than he could recall. He woke to the sound of movement, a muted but purposeful sound. He opened his eyes to find that it was still dark. He pushed himself to his feet and looked around.

The stars were brilliant overhead and they gave off enough light that he could make out the bands of men moving toward their ships, and the last of anything important still on the beach being carried off. He was just wondering where he should go or if they meant to leave him behind when Harald appeared beside him.

"My father says please join him on his ship," Harald said and without waiting for an answer he headed off toward the water's edge, leaving Leofric to follow behind. They waded out into the water, knee-deep. Harald put his hands on the edge of the ship and hoisted himself up, swinging easily over the rail and down to the deck.

He turned and looked back. "I can send you a line, or put down a plank," he said.

"No, I can manage," Leofric said, wondering if that was true. He set his hands on the rail, pressed his lips together, jumped as high as he could and pushed down with his arms. As he came up he felt a shot of pride at still being capable of such a thing, and then a shot of panic as he realized he was not going to make it. But then Harald grabbed a fistful of his mail shirt and pulled him the rest of the way aboard.

It was the mail, Leofric thought as Harald helped him to his feet. *I could have made that easily if I hadn't been wearing the mail.*

The two men made their way toward the center of the ship where they could walk aft without stepping over the sea chests that served as benches. Leofric stumbled once on something in the dark, but he caught himself before he fell. At the very stern of the vessel he could just make out a raised platform, and standing there was Thorgrim, a fur wrapped around him against the morning chill. He was looking forward, looking up at the mast and the stars, turning and looking out over the blackness of the water. He seemed to miss nothing.

Thorgrim looked down and said a single word and Harald said, "My father says 'Good morning.'"

"Good morning to him," Leofric said, and he noticed for the first time a hint of light off to the east.

Thorgrim spoke again. "My father says we'll wait for a bit more light, and then we'll go," Harald said.

Leofric nodded, figured that would not need translation. He turned and looked forward. He could see the dark outlines of the men as they took the long oars down from the rack that ran along the center of the ship and slid them out through holes in the ship's side. They settled on the sea chests and held the oars up the way seabirds will hold their wings to dry. They waited and Leofric waited.

They did not wait long. Soon the shadows began to soften and the men became more discernable and Thorgrim shouted out an order, loud enough in the still air to be heard all over the sandbar. Leofric felt the ship lurch a bit and he realized there were still men ashore and they were pushing the vessel back into the water. He felt a change in the ship's motion, a sensation of floating. Thorgrim called another order and the oars came down and the men bent as they rowed and the huge vessel began to slowly back away from the sand.

Leofric watched it all, all that he could see, with fascination. He had a naturally curious mind, and this was something well beyond any previous experience. He had been in boats and ships before, certainly, but nothing like this, the powerful war machine of a powerful enemy. If he felt like Daniel in the lions' den on the beach, now he felt as if he were in the jaws of the beast.

The light continued to spread and he could see the men down either side of the ship, moving with an easy rhythm, the ship moving fast and silent in the still water. He could make out the dark shapes of the other ships slipping off the beach and following behind, a wolf pack falling in behind its leader.

With a few words Thorgrim made the ship stop and turn in its own length, as if he had uttered some sort of magic incantation. But to Thorgrim or Harald or the others there seemed to be nothing magical about it. They just watched it happen and said nothing.

Leofric could see only the vaguest outlines of the shore, but Thorgrim seemed to know where he was and where he wished to go. With a few gruff orders the ship began to gather way while Thorgrim shifted the tiller slightly forward and back.

Harald was standing at Leofric's side, so Leofric asked him in a soft vice, "How does Thorgrim know where to go?"

"He looks at the stars," Harald said. "He looked last night, saw how the stars should be for the direction he wants to go. And he knows the harbor well. He made sure of that."

"It sounds like he is a good mariner," Leofric said.

"He is a great mariner," Harald said and the pride was obvious in his voice.

They pulled on through the growing light of dawn, slowly, like men feeling their way through a dark room. But the light continued to spread and soon Leofric could see where they were and where they were headed and it was exactly where he had meant for Thorgrim to land his ships, south of the channel entrance. They were less than a quarter mile away.

Soon after, Thorgrim's ship bumped up on shore and one after another the others did as well. There was light enough that Leofric could see the full length of the ship now. He could see men going over the bow with ropes in hand, no doubt to secure the ship in place. One of the Northmen came back and spoke a few words to Thorgrim.

Harald turned to Leofric. "That man says there's an Englishman waiting to talk to us," he said. Thorgrim hopped down from the afterdeck and waved for Leofric and Harald to follow, and the three of them made their way forward, walking down the centerline of the ship.

At the bow Thorgrim leaned over the side and looked toward the beach and Leofric did likewise. Thirty feet away, looking not at all comfortable, stood Ailmar, captain of Leofric's hearth-guard, commander of the men there in Leofric's absence. Leofric could see the relief wash over the man's face when he saw his thegn looking down toward him.

"Lord Leofric! You're unhurt?" Ailmar called.

"Yes," Leofric called back. "And if you need to say anything to the Northmen, Harald here can translate. Speaks our language." Leofric wanted Ailmar to know that, before he said anything the Northmen should not hear.

"Very good, lord," Ailmar replied. "We got word from Nothwulf. The men are under arms and ready."

Leofric heard Harald translate the words to Thorgrim and Thorgrim replied. "My father says have your men come to this place and wait on the beach. When we hear the sounds of the fight, then we go."

Leofric nodded. *Sensible*, he thought. *Keep English and heathens apart until there's need for them to mix.*

Ailmar hurried off and it was not long after that he was back, walking at the head of his column, two hundred men or so strong. A good-looking, capable-looking army. More disciplined, less loose than the Northmen, not as savage-looking. Leofric wondered, if it came down to it, on level ground, who would win in an all-out fight, his men or Thorgrim's.

Dear God, I pray we don't have to find out, Leofric thought.

He and Thorgrim headed aft again and Leofric could see Thorgrim's limp had become more pronounced. They reached the stern and Thorgrim sat on the edge of the small raised deck and extended his leg with a stifled groan.

One of his men, a mere boy by the looks of him, came over and spoke a few words. Thorgrim looked reluctant about whatever the boy had said, but he seemed to give in. The boy knelt down in front of him and peeled back a tear in Thorgrim's leggings to reveal bloody bandages beneath.

They spoke again, and with continued reluctance Thorgrim stood and pulled his leggings down. His tunic hung to his knees and pale legs extended down from there. His left thigh was wrapped tight with bandages, soaked through with blood.

Leofric, sure that Thorgrim's tunic covered the things he had no desire to see, watched with interest. The boy carefully peeled the bandages away, pulling them free of Thorgrim's leg, eliciting a grunt of pain as the cloth pulled on the wound. The boy's hands were delicate and sure. Leofric looked at his face, which was set in concentration.

That's a woman! he realized. He was not entirely sure at first, but as he studied the face he became certain. She was dressed in a tunic and leggings, like the rest of the men, and wore a mail shirt and a seax on her belt. But she was without a doubt a woman.

Leofric shook his head. The more he learned about the Northmen the more mysterious and strange they seemed.

With the bandage gone, the woman took a wet cloth and washed the wound as well as she could, then began to dress it again. She had two wraps around Thorgrim's thigh when another of the Northmen came running aft. This one looked more manic than Thorgrim, or any of the others. He was wearing only leggings, and his arms and body were lean and muscular and crisscrossed with scars, with one particularly vicious one at his shoulder, the result of a spear thrust or a sword, Leofric guessed. His hair was unkempt and fell in a great heap over his shoulders. There was a wild look on his wild face.

This is the one who hit me! Leofric realized. He remembered the man now, how he had launched himself at Leofric's men-at-arms, had seemed impervious to the swords and spears and axes that had tried to do him in. Instinctively Leofric laid his hand on the pommel of his sword.

But the wild man did not attack him this time. Rather he stopped in front of Thorgrim and pointed off to the north and said something in a tone that conveyed his excitement. Thorgrim nodded and cocked his head as if to listen.

"What is it?" Leofric asked Harald.

"This is Starri," Harald said, nodding toward the crazed man in front of him. "He has the best hearing of anyone aboard. He says there's fighting, on the western bank of the channel.

Leofric felt a surge of excitement at those words, a sense of movement, things happening now. All the Northmen within earshot of Starri were also cocking their heads to listen, and Leofric did as well. He strained to hear, tried to filter out the other sounds, the lapping of the water, the grinding of the ship's bow in the sand, the shuffling and murmuring of the men aboard. He thought he heard it—the clash of weapons, the shouts of men, the familiar sound of fighting. But Leofric was not a young man, his hearing was not what it had been, and he was not certain.

He looked at Thorgrim and saw the same look of uncertainty. He looked at Harald and Harald seemed more intent, more determined than his father did.

Harald said a few words to Thorgrim. Then he turned to Leofric. "I told my father I hear it, too. I'm pretty certain I hear it, anyway. Fighting. I can hear the clanging of weapons and I can hear men shouting."

Leofric shook his head. "I don't hear it," he admitted. "But if younger ears...or this Starri fellow says it's so, I'll believe it. And if it's so, then it's time for us to move."

This was the moment Leofric had been waiting for, the moment Cynewise committed her men to battle. She would never have launched an attack if she saw that Nothwulf's army was complete, and certainly not if she saw the Northmen's ships heading into the fight. Leofric wanted the battle fully joined before he sprung his surprise on her.

Harald translated his words to Thorgrim and Thorgrim nodded. The young woman bandaging his leg finished and Thorgrim pulled up his leggings even as he began calling orders forward. Then he turned to Leofric and said something else.

"My father says get your men on board," Harald said.

Leofric nodded and turned and jogged down the length of the ship, as well as his old legs and the obstacle-strewn deck would allow. It would not take long to get his men aboard. During the waiting time Ailmar had divided the men up into six divisions, one for each ship, and positioned them on the beach near their assigned vessels.

He reached the bow and looked down. Ailmar was standing there, waiting for word.

"Do you hear that?" Leofric asked, pointing to the north. "Fighting?"

Ailmar listened for a moment. "I think so," he said, but he sounded unsure. No matter.

"The Northmen say they hear the fighting, so time to go. Get the men aboard."

Ailmar nodded and raced off. Leofric reached the back of the ship just as the first of his men came climbing over the side and stepping aboard, hesitant and uncertain. Like him, the men-at-arms must have that into-the-lions'-den feeling. But the Northmen simply indicated with gestures and minor shoves where they should stand, and they found places clear of the rowers.

Leofric looked over the starboard side. His men were climbing aboard the other ships as well, the embarkation quick, smooth and efficient. He was glad of that, and felt both pride and relief. He wanted Thorgrim to see that English men-at-arms were no less able than the Northmen.

The last of Leofric's men had just pulled himself aboard when Thorgrim called for the rowers to lower oars. Men ashore pushed the bow off, then came scrambling over the side as the men sitting on the sea chests heaved their oars.

Once again Leofric watched and marveled at the way Thorgrim brought the ship out into the deeper water, then made it spin in place and head off to the north. It seemed even more impressive now, with the sun up and Leofric able to see the smooth coordination of the rowers as they reacted to the perfunctory orders that Thorgrim called out.

These men have been bred to this, Leofric thought. *Born and bred.* Skill such as this could only be the result of a lifetime of experience at such things.

The fleet did not have far to go. Off the starboard side the low sandy beach slipped past, and very soon the mouth of the channel opened up off the starboard bow and Leofric could see part of the wall that Nothwulf had built. And there was no longer any doubt that the battle had begun. Even Leofric could hear it clearly now: shouts and screams and the clashing of weapons carried on the still morning air.

It was all working out as planned, so perfectly it made Leofric uneasy.

Thorgrim reached over and prodded him, and when Leofric looked, Thorgrim pointed to his ear and to the distant shore, asking in sign language if Leofric heard the sound of the fighting. Leofric nodded and Thorgrim nodded as well. Thorgrim spoke to Harald, Harald spoke to Leofric.

"My father asks where do you want the men landed?"

Leofric looked off toward where the fighting was taking place. He could see most of Nothwulf's wall, but he could see none of the men-at-arms or any of the battle. That did not surprise him. Nothwulf would not have kept his men behind the wall for fear of Cynewise's army coming around the ends and encircling them.

"Tell Thorgrim to land us in front of the wall," Leofric said, pointing to the spot he meant. It was perfect. Cynewise would not see the ships coming. The first indication she would get of Leofric's joining the fight would be the sight of his two hundred men-at-arms surging out from behind the barricade.

Harald relayed that request. Thorgrim nodded and adjusted the tiller a bit and the ship's bow turned until it was pointed like a spear at the place Leofric had indicated.

He felt his pulse quickening, his excitement building. This trap, this battle, could put an end to all of the nonsense, all the confusion and struggle for power and duplicity that had started with the murder of ealdorman Merewald, Cynewise's husband of two minutes. Before the sun reached its zenith that day, the pretender might be crushed, Nothwulf in his rightful place, peace in Dorsetshire once again.

Thorgrim called another order. The rowers pulled one more time, then lifted their oars and once again the ship's bow ground up on the shore. The tide, Leofric could see, was high and the ship made it nearly to the wall before going aground. Even better.

He looked at Thorgrim and Thorgrim nodded. Leofric extended a hand, offering his thanks to this heathen, well aware of how odd this was. Thorgrim looked at the hand and gave a hint of a smile, suggesting he, too, saw the irony in the gesture. Then he grasped Leofric's hand in his and shook.

Leofric let go of Thorgrim's hand and hurried forward. "Over you go! Over you go! Get ashore now!" he shouted as he ran and the men-at-arms began to race for the sides of the ship, up by the bow, and swing themselves over.

Leofric was last, and he went over as gently as he could, landing in water up to his thighs. He waded ashore behind the rest. On either side of Thorgrim's ship the other vessels were also running up onto the sand, the Englishmen leaping over the sides and thrashing their way up onto dry ground. It took blessedly little time to get them ashore, and then Thorgrim's ship and the others began to draw off again, turning to head down the cleared channel and out to the open sea.

The men were shifted into their divisions, one under Leofric's command to go around the south end of the wall, one led by Ailmar to go around the north. Once they came in sight of the battle each man would lead his soldiers into the attack wherever they judged best. They had planned it all out.

Leofric stepped up to the head of his column. His helmet and shield were long gone, but he was too fired up now to care about those things. He drew his sword and with a shout led the men forward.

They came around the end of the wall and right into the fighting. It was chaotic and Leofric could not tell at first what was going on. A ragged line of men were pushed back nearly to the wall and they were fighting off a half-circle of attackers, so many that the attackers were two or three deep. Nothwulf's men, pushed back by Cynewise's greater numbers, Leofric realized. And with that, the point of attack became obvious.

"There! There! Right at them!" Leofric shouted, pointing with his sword to the left flank of the attacking line. The men behind him raised a cheer as they surged forward and Leofric could see looks of surprise on the men laying into Nothwulf's army. They looked up, looked over, mouths opened in shock. As well they might. They were moments from a bloody and final victory, and now this, like the hand of God come to smite them.

Leofric let his men race past him. He would join them in the fight, but first he had to find Nothwulf, if Nothwulf was still alive. He had to talk to the man, make certain their intentions were coordinated.

He moved off to his right, toward the makeshift wall, his eyes on the fight in front of him. His men were racing into battle in no real order, but they had complete surprise on their side, and Cynewise's men had no time to prepare to meet them. The best they could do was turn and face the on-rush, weapons raised.

Who commands you? Leofric wondered. Certainly not Cynewise. Clever and wily as she was, he doubted she had the mettle to lead men in battle. Indeed, she was probably too clever to even try, to risk her life in that way.

So one of the thegns who followed her. Aegenwulf, maybe. He was the most powerful of those who took Cynewise's side. Or Eadwold, captain of her hearth-guard, perhaps. Whoever it was, Leofric figured he'd learn soon enough, once the fighting was done and they found his body, broken and bleeding on the field of battle.

He might already be dead. There were bodies enough even now. Leofric stepped carefully over and around them, backing toward the wall, figuring he would find Nothwulf somewhere near the center of the line.

And he was right. Nothwulf was in the middle of the fighting. His face was red and sweating from exertion and his shield was half shattered, but beyond that he looked whole. He also looked confused and relieved.

"Nothwulf!" Leofric shouted. He hurried on, eyes moving between Nothwulf and the battle in front of them. "Nothwulf!" Nothwulf looked his way. A smile spread over his face and he opened his mouth and shouted in exhilaration.

"Leofric! Dear Leofric!" he called and held his arms out, sword in one hand, shield in the other. Leofric met him and they embraced, then pushed apart again.

"Leofric, you're just in time, I must say!" Nothwulf shouted. "Cynewise's men didn't hesitate in their attack. Aegenwulf was leading them, I'm quite sure. They came on like a pack of wolves. I thought we were done for!"

"We came as fast as we could," Leofric said. "Thorgrim... he's the leader of the Northmen... he did just as promised."

"Seems to have played out how you thought!" Nothwulf said and pointed with his sword toward the battle. Leofric's men, along with Nothwulf's who had found new life in the sudden assistance, were pushing Cynewise's men back, encircling them. It was clear to Leofric that their enemy, seeing the trap close around them, would break and run at any moment.

"Excellent!" Leofric said. "And you were able to get the channel free of the wrecks? I suspect Thorgrim and his lot are out to sea already."

"No," Nothwulf said. "The wrecks remain."

"What? Were you not able to move them?"

"We didn't try," Nothwulf said. "The Northmen still have the plunder and the danegeld and I want it back. We have our army together now, and soon there'll be no threat from Cynewise. Nothing to stop us beating the Northmen as well!"

"But...I gave my word to Thorgrim that the channel would be clear," Leofric said.

Nothwulf shook his head. "Giving word to a Northman means nothing. There's no honor among those lying animals. I didn't think you really meant it. No call for us to keep our word."

Leofric's mouth hung open, but he said nothing. He did not know what to say. And the only thought that came into his head was, *Oh, you stupid little bastard...*

Chapter Thirty-Three

How the injustice assails me—my lord's absence!
Elsewhere on earth lovers share the same bed
while I pass through life, half dead...

The Wife's Lament
10th Century English Poem

Thorgrim watched the last of the Englishmen climb over the sheer strake of his ship and of the other ships as well, and he thought, *Glad to be shed of those bastards.* Leofric seemed a decent one, a warrior, a man of honor. He liked Leofric, or at least felt that he could have come to like him. The same might be true of other men in England. But he did not intend to remain long enough in that country to find out.

"Rowers! Backwater!" he shouted and the rowers leaned back, then dropped their oars and pushed them away as they leaned forward. *Sea Hammer* slid back off of the sand, though not far enough to dislodge the bow. They went through the motion once more and Thorgrim felt the bow come free.

Another pull and *Sea Hammer* was turned bow first in the channel. Beyond that, Thorgrim was looking at a stretch of water half a mile long, hemmed in on either side by low shores of sand and scrubby brush. And beyond that, the sea, the glorious open sea.

"Pull!" he shouted and *Sea Hammer* shot forward, driven by the combined force of the oars and the ebbing tide. He pulled the tiller toward him and swung the ship toward mid-channel to give the other longships room to make their own way off the bank.

The sound of the fighting was loud and distinct, but Thorgrim could not see the actual battle, which was taking place on the other side of the makeshift wall, the wall from which the English had showered them with flaming arrows. He shook his head at the strangeness of it all. His life, he thought, was like a ship at sea, with so many forces working on it in so many ways, pushing in divergent directions, and him struggling to keep it on course. Trying to keep it afloat.

He looked astern. The other ships were underway now. *Blood Hawk* was in his wake, and *Oak Heart* and *Black Wing* were astern of *Blood Hawk*, rowing abreast, and the rest falling in behind. Six ships, each fighting the current to position themselves in the channel.

Thorgrim looked ahead again and gave the tiller a small pull. *Sea Hammer*'s speed was still building as the ebbing tide drove her along. Ahead and to starboard he could see the charred remains of *Long Serpent*'s stem and sternpost, like two black claws reaching up from below, markers for Jorund's final resting place. He pulled the tiller a bit more, directing *Sea Hammer* ship to give the wreck a wide berth. He pulled his eyes from that eerie sight and looked out over the open water ahead.

He was thinking of the brutal fight that had taken place there just a few days before, and how placid the water looked now, when *Sea Hammer* slammed into the sunken ship still there, still hidden just below the surface. She hit with far more force than she had the first time and Thorgrim was launched forward, knocking the tiller aside as he tumbled off the afterdeck and down onto the deck below. He felt the wound in his leg tear open as he came to rest on his side and he howled in pain.

"Bastards! You bastards!" he shouted in rage and in agony. He put his hands down on the deck and began to push himself up when the ship shuddered again. The air was filled with the sound of shattering wood and shouting men and he knew that *Blood Hawk*, unable to check her forward way in time, had slammed into them. The impact tossed him to the deck once more. He felt the warm blood running down his leg.

His men were running and shouting. He heard Harald yelling, "Fend off, there! Fend them off!" Thorgrim grit his teeth and began to push himself up once again. He braced for the next ship to hit and to toss him down again, but this time he managed to regain his feet.

He had one hand on the sheer strake when *Oak Heart* hit *Blood Hawk* and drove her into *Sea Hammer*'s stern with renewed force. The three ships began to pivot sideways, pushed by the tide. They swung through ninety degrees until *Sea Hammer* was broadside in the channel, hung up on the wrecks below. *Blood Hawk* hit the charred sternpost of *Long Serpent,* snapped it off and continued to swing into the wrecks. Beyond that, *Oak Heart* also hung up on the ships hidden under the water.

The three ships came to rest, but the disaster was not over, not at all. *Black Wing,* which had been abreast of *Oak Heart,* struck *Blood Hawk* bow-on, driving into her larboard side like a spear hefted by a powerful man. Thorgrim could hear the crushing sound as she struck. He saw a section of her side cave in and he hoped the damage would not go clear to the waterline, or below.

Fox and *Dragon* were still underway, but would not be for long. Their oars were flailing as they tried to backwater, to keep themselves off the tangle of ships and gain enough room that they could turn and get their bows into the current. If they could, they might be able to tow the others free. Thorgrim watched the effort. The ships' captains, Hardbein and Fostolf, were doing exactly the right thing. But it would not work.

"Good try," Thorgrim said to himself as he saw *Fox* pushed sideways in the stream and begin drifting down on *Sea Hammer.* Fostolf, in command of *Dragon,* put his tiller over in hope that he had room enough to turn. But he didn't—Thorgrim could see that—and he guessed Fostolf could see it too, but it was worth the effort, just in case. The ship turned sideways in the channel and before they could turn any further they came hard up against *Black Wing.*

And there they were. Six longships, piled up against the shipwrecks below, like so much sea wrack on a beach, held there by the powerful current of the ebbing tide. A great tangle of oars, half of them sheared off, the shattered remains of shields still mounted on the shield racks, and hulls broken like eggshells. Men were shouting and wood was grinding and cracking, and beneath it all, the sounds of a battle that was raging, unseen behind the wall on shore.

Thorgrim stepped up onto the afterdeck where he could get a slightly better view of the scene. He stepped up with his right leg, dragging his left behind him, and this time, having been able to brace for the pain, he was able to resist shouting in agony.

Sea Hammer lay starboard side to the wall of sunken ships, her bow pointing toward the shore where they had left Leofric and the others. *Blood Hawk* was astern and the rest in a jumble beyond her. Men were shouting and using oar shafts as levers to try and force the ships apart. It was chaos and it was pointless and it had to stop.

"Hold up! Hold up!" Thorgrim shouted, reaching down deep to put all the force and volume he could into his voice. "Hold up!"

His words pierced the noise of ships and men. The various crews fell silent, and those who could see him turned and looked in his direction.

"Are any of you sinking?" he called next. There was silence. Only the sound of water piling up against the sides of the ships was audible, that and the noise of battle, which seemed to be dropping away. Then Godi, commander of *Blood Hawk*, called back in a voice that even Thorgrim could not hope to match.

"We're stove in pretty bad," he called. *Black Wing*'s bow was still jammed into his ship's side. "But we won't sink. At least not unless the seas get up."

"Get *Black Wing* free and lash her alongside!" Thorgrim shouted.

From behind Thorgrim heard Failend say, "You're bleeding a river." He turned back. She was at the edge of the after deck, strips of cloth in her hand. She nodded at Thorgrim's feet. He looked down. His left shoe was planting in the middle of a pool of blood.

"Just bind it up," he said, voice like a growl. He was too furious now to care about his leg or to feel any gratitude for Failend's concern. Nor did Failend sound as if she was offering him help from any sense of love or compassion, but rather for some unspoken obligation she seemed to feel.

She hopped up on the afterdeck, kneeled and began wrapping the cloth around his leg. "Tight, tight," he said. He wanted the blood held inside long enough for him to kill anyone he needed to kill, and he numbered those in the dozens. Failend pulled the bandages tight. He could see the strain in her neck as she pulled, as if she was trying to hurt him. As if when she looked at his leg she saw his neck.

"Father..." Harald was standing beside him now. Thorgrim could see on Harald's face that the boy was reading his mood correctly, and was approaching him now with great reluctance.

"Father, there's no one on the shore over there." He pointed astern, toward the eastern side of the channel where Leofric's men had been. "We can shift the ships closer there, so they can't reach us with their arrows. Then when the tide is out..."

"No." Thorgrim cut him off. "We'll shift *Sea Hammer* that way, get her bow ashore." He pointed to the other side of the channel, the side from which the sounds of fighting could still be heard. "Then we'll get the other ships astern, each overlapping. We'll make a bridge so we can all get ashore there. Then we'll kill every one of those lying, miserable whore-son English dogs."

Cynewise sat on her horse several hundred feet behind the battlefield and watched the fighting as it unfolded. She was wearing her mail shirt and her sword, her helmet on her head. The armor her father had mocked. She smiled, just a bit.

Not so funny now, is it, you old bastard? she thought.

But for all that, she did feel a bit self-conscious wearing it. She was smarter than Nothwulf, of that she was certain, and more dangerous by far. More able to bend men to her will. Certainly more able to lead Dorset and see it rise to its proper place in the kingdom of Wessex. But she was not a warrior. And meaningless as that was, she knew it meant something to the thegns. So, to the extent that she could, she knew she had to at least appear as such.

Whatever good was happening on the battlefield was none of her doing. It was Aegenwulf's. Aegenwulf was the most powerful of the thegns, at least those who sided with her, and he was a campaigner of old, veteran of many battles. He had fought Englishmen and Welshmen and Northmen. She had consulted with him in private, and when he had told her how best to approach the fight she had explained those plans to the rest. As far as she could tell, the fight was going as it was supposed to go.

Standing around her in a loose circle were six others, men on horseback. Five were members of her hearth-guard, there for her protection, under the command of Eadwold, who was at her right-hand side. The other was Oswin, the shire reeve, to her left. Her servant, Horsa, stood on the ground by her horse's head.

"Eadwold, what do you make of the fight thus far?" she asked. She tried to sound as if she had her own opinion of what was going on, but in truth she didn't. All she could see was a great swirl of men and weapons. The clash and the shouting drifted back from the battle. She could not tell who was winning, or even who was who.

"It goes well, m'lady," Eadwold said. "It seems, as Oswin said, that but half of Nothwulf's men were on this side of the channel. See how Aegenwulf outnumbers them and presses in on three sides."

Cynewise did not see that, and the mention of Oswin irritated her. She was trying to put him out of her mind, even though he was sitting his horse just a few feet away. She blamed a good part of her recent troubles on his incompetence. Worse, she was having doubts about his loyalty. It would be a problem if any man under her command was disloyal, but Oswin in particular knew a great deal. He certainly could not be allowed to just run amuck.

She pulled herself back to the issue before her. "Certainly, yes, I see how Aegenwulf is attacking just as I instructed him to do." Oswin made a short sound, like a stifled cough, infuriating but not blatantly insubordinate enough for Cynewise to turn on him.

"You think this will end soon?" she asked.

"I think, ma'am..." Oswin said but she cut him off.

"I was speaking with Eadwold," she said. "Eadwold?"

"I would think so," Eadwold said. "Nothwulf, he was a fool, he got the men's backs against that wall there and now Aegenwulf's pressing in on him and there's nowhere to..."

Now it was Oswin who cut them off. "Dear God," he said with genuine astonishment.

Eadwold and Cynewise had been looking at each other, but with Oswin's exclamation they both turned back to the fight. As far as Cynewise could see, nothing had changed. Hundreds of men running about, wielding weapons, some lying on the ground, dead or wounded, she supposed.

But whatever Oswin had seen, Eadwold saw it too. "What...?" he said, his tone shocked and incredulous.

"What?" Cynewise asked. "What is it?"

"More men-at-arms, Lady Cynewise," Oswin said. "Coming around the wall, do you see? They are on Aegenwulf's flanks. This is not a good thing."

Cynewise turned to Eadwold and glared at him.

"I don't know where they came from, m'lady," he stammered as if this were his fault, which was indeed the impression Cynewise was giving him. "Hiding on the other side of the wall? Held in reserve for this moment?"

Cynewise turned the other way and glared at Oswin, but Oswin did not meet her eye. "I thought you said Leofric's men, half of Nothwulf's army, were stuck on the far side of the channel. Where did these men come from?"

Oswin shrugged. "I can't imagine," he said. "Maybe Leofric found some way to get them across. He didn't have boats enough that I knew of. Maybe the Northmen are helping him."

Cynewise felt suddenly ill. With Leofric's men on the other side of the channel, her army had been twice the size of Nothwulf's. Even with Leofric's men there, and with her father's men gone, she still had as many men-at-arms as Nothwulf. But if the heathens had thrown in with Nothwulf...

"Still, we were beating Nothwulf and we are beating him still," Cynewise announced. Eadwold made a sound in his throat that might have been construed as a reply, though not an answer of any sort. Oswin, however, made a genuine reply.

"Oh, I think not, Lady Cynewise," he said. "These new men are fresh, and they've taken Aegenwulf quite by surprise. See, now they're pressing in on him. I fear the worst, ma'am."

"You sound pretty damned smug for someone who fears the worst," Cynewise snapped.

Oswin finally took his eyes from the fight and turned to her. "Forgive me, ma'am," he said. "I'm only telling you the truth. If my tone doesn't suggest the terror I feel for you, I apologize."

Cynewise turned back to the battle, teeth clenched, and she knew her face was red and that made her angrier still. The fighting seemed to be getting closer. Before, Aegenwulf had been pushing Nothwulf's men back, but now it seemed to be the other way around. Her anger at Oswin filled her mind, but she reminded herself that if Aegenwulf was defeated on the field of battle then she had bigger problems by far than his impudence.

The mounted band was silent after that, watching the battle unfold. From the few things that Oswin and Eadwold had said Cynewise had a better idea of what was happening, and she thought she was making sense of it.

She hoped she was wrong. She wanted to ask but she didn't dare. Because what she was seeing suggested things were now going very badly for her indeed.

*　　　　　*　　　　　*

The two things that Leofric thought would happen did happen, and at almost the same moment. The first was the Northmen's ships hitting the wrecks sunk in the channel. The other was Cynewise's men breaking and running.

Leofric was just finding his voice again. "What have you done?" he demanded of Nothwulf. "You left the wrecks in the channel?"

"Of course!" Nothwulf shouted over the noise of the battle. "I guessed that was what you wanted! I couldn't imagine you really meant to let the heathens sail off with all the plunder of Christchurch! And Cynewise's danegeld!"

Leofric was about to reply to this when he heard the sudden burst of shouting, panicked cries, cries of rage and at least once voice apparently yelling out in pain. Not from the battle, but from behind him, from the other side of the wall, and he knew that Thorgrim had just found out that he had been betrayed. Leofric recalled the savage, cunning, lethal undercurrent that seemed to float just below Thorgrim's stoic surface. A good ally, a frightening enemy, he had thought. They had experienced him as the first, now they would meet him as the second.

"Think of how fine a thing it will be to have the danegeld Cynewise paid the Northmen," Nothwulf said.

"Yes, but first you must take it," Leofric said. "And the taking will not be so easy."

Nothwulf reached over and clapped Leofric on the shoulder as if to reassure him. "Fear not, old friend," he said with a smile. "We beat them once, we'll do it again!"

Leofric was about to remove Nothwulf's hand from his shoulder, he was about to tear Nothwulf's arm off and beat him on the head with it, when a cheer rose up from the fighting men at their front and drew their attention. It was not clear what was happening, hard to see through the press of warriors standing shoulder to shoulder. But something had changed. Whereas a moment before Leofric and Nothwulf's men had been holding their ground, going blow for blow with Cynewise's men, now some of them seemed to be running. Not in flight but in pursuit. Which meant Cynewise's line had broken and now they were fleeing for their lives.

"Huzzah! See here, we've won!" Nothwulf yelled in triumph, but celebration was not foremost in Leofric's mind. He pushed Nothwulf aside and hurried after his men.

"Stop running! Stop running!" he shouted. "Stand your ground! Ailmar, stop those men, keep them in place!"

Most of the men were beyond earshot and they continued to run, but many were not, and they obeyed. Ailmar, younger than Leofric, was more energetic in pushing his way through the men and forcing them to listen. Those who heard him stopped and lowered their weapons. Leofric could see them gasping for air, happy and thankful no doubt to stop running.

The rest continued on, but as they ran they seemed to realize that many of their number were not with them. One by one they slowed and looked back, and seeing the pursuit was not universal they, too, came to a stop. And finally it was only Leofric and Nothwulf's men standing and sucking air and Cynewise's men running off, fast as they could, and the many dead and wounded scattered about.

"Leofric! What are you doing!" Nothwulf yelled. He ran up beside Leofric, pointing with his sword across the field. "Now's our moment!" he said. "They're on the run, we can go after them and cut them down like wheat! We can kill ever man who was stupid enough to stand with Cynewise!"

Leofric looked at the young man and did not like what he saw. Nothwulf had been growing bolder by the day. He had managed to pen the Northmen in at Christchurch and outwitted Cynewise by marching his men off before she could betray him. He had come up with the notion of trapping the Northmen in the channel and convinced the others that it was a good idea. And it had worked out almost as well as Nothwulf had hoped, even if he had not completely considered the outcome—that the Northmen would be trapped in the bay where they could still cause trouble.

Nothwulf was pleased with himself, very pleased, that was clear, and it was giving him more confidence than was warranted, by far. What's more, the thought of the riches to be had in killing the Northmen was in the young man's head, and the ealdormanship in his sight. Greed and hubris. Leofric had seen their effects before, on other men. It did not generally end well.

"Cynewise and her army are no threat," Leofric said. "They've run off, and they'll be in no position to attack again, not for some time. But now, thanks to you, there are four hundred or more angry Northmen just on the other side of this wall. I think that is a more immediate concern."

Nothwulf made a dismissive gesture. "Their ships are hung up on the wrecks in the middle of the channel. We have time enough to collect our archers and light fires and finish them off as we did the first time. When the tide goes out and the crabs and the gulls are feasting on their corpses we'll retrieve all the riches they stole from us."

"Honestly, Nothwulf, you arrogant little bastard—yes, I called you a little bastard and I don't give a damn if you are to be ealdorman—you should learn you must kill a man before you declare that the crabs and gulls will eat him."

With that Leofric turned and headed off toward one of the ladders still leaning up against the wall. "Where are you going?" Nothwulf called. He tried to make his voice sound as if he demanded obedience, but Leofric could hear the worry in it.

"I'm going to see just how stuck the Northmen actually are," Leofric called over his shoulder. He grabbed the rough rungs of the ladder and climbed, twenty feet up, then stepped off onto the wall itself. He looked out across the water and saw pretty much what he expected to see.

Near mid-channel all six of the Northmen's longships were piled up against the underwater obstructions. The tide was running out, the current moving fast and pinning the ships in place. The lower the water became, the more stuck they would be.

The ladder shook a bit and then Nothwulf stepped out into the wall beside him. For a moment the two men were silent, watching the Northmen on their ships, a couple hundred yards away. The ships were motionless but the heathens were not. They swarmed over the vessels, doing something, but what it was Leofric could not tell.

"There, what did I tell you?" Nothwulf said. "They're stuck, just as I knew they would be, and now they'll be as easy to kill as a hart cornered by hounds." His voice did not sound as confident as his words suggested.

"Indeed?" Leofric said. He was furious with Nothwulf and what he had done. It was stupid for many reasons. Worse, it was dishonorable. Worse still, it was he, Leofric, who would seem to Thorgrim to be the treacherous one.

"Yes, indeed," Nothwulf said. "Where can they go? They're within arrow shot and they're stuck fast."

"See here," Leofric said, pointing toward the tangle of ships. The one closest to them was Thorgrim's ship, of that Leofric was nearly sure. And far from being stuck fast, it was beginning to move. Slowly, torturously, it was inching its way along the wall of submerged wrecks. How they were doing it, Leofric could not tell. Using the oars to push off and move themselves ahead, he guessed. But whatever they were doing, it was working. Slowly, but it was working.

"Now what are those heathen bastards doing?" Nothwulf asked.

"I don't know," Leofric said. "But if I were to guess, I'd say they're moving that ship up to the bank of the channel. So they can get ashore, there at our feet. Thorgrim strikes me as the sort who'll want vengeance before he wants escape."

"One ship? What do they hope to do with the men from one ship?" Nothwulf asked. "We'll kill them as they come."

"Look," Leofric said. The ship just behind Thorgrim had a smaller vessel lashed alongside, and the two of them were inching along behind Thorgrim's ship. He could see movement in the ship behind those two as well.

"You think they mean to come ashore? To fight?" Nothwulf asked.

"Fight, yes," Leofric said. "Or plunder, if there's no one to fight."

"Oh, there will certainly be someone to fight," Nothwulf said. "We just beat Cynewise's army, and now we'll stand ready to beat them. Slaughter them. Moving their ships to the shore? That will just make getting at their plunder easier than I thought."

"We'll slaughter them?" Leofric said. "No. Not 'we'. You, perhaps, but I won't be part of this. I won't sacrifice my men for your folly."

"What?"

"I won't fight with you. This is your doing."

"But..." Nothwulf stammered, the words struggling to find a way out. "I am ealdorman. I just defeated Cynewise and I am ealdorman now. You know right well you have an obligation to me for military service. I demand you honor it."

"Demand? Please," Leofric said. "I've stood with you all through this debacle, through every stupid thing you've done, even when you had no idea what was going on. But now you've sullied my honor. Be glad I don't demand satisfaction for that." Then Leofric turned and went back down the ladder to rejoin his men—half of Nothwulf's army—waiting there.

Chapter Thirty-Four

Bravery in the world
against the enmity of fiends,
daring deeds against devils,
thus the sons of men
will praise him afterwards,
and his fame will eternally
live with the angels.

The Seafarer
Ninth Century English Poem

At first it was not clear to Cynewise what was going on. Both Eadwold and Oswin said that more of Nothwulf's men had arrived on the field, from where, no one knew, and suddenly what had looked like an easy victory was now in doubt. She studied the fighting in the distance and she thought she understood what they were talking about, but it was very hard to make any sense of the confusion.

And then her men turned and ran in panicked flight, and that she understood immediately as she found the stench of defeat reaching her nose.

"Are they running? My men-at-arms, are they running?" Cynewise asked, unwilling to believe what she was seeing with her own eyes.

"Yes, Lady Cynewise," Eadwold said. "Yes, they are." Eadwold sounded nervous as he spoke. As well he might. His chief duty was protecting her, and now he was watching her own army stampeding toward them, the enemy right on their heels.

"Now, lady, we really must fly from here," he said next. "Nothwulf's men are coming after ours and they'll be on us directly."

"No," Cynewise said. She was her father's daughter, not a timid sort, and now her rage smothered any spark of fear she might have felt. She kicked her spurs into her horse's flanks, but rather than turn and flee as Eadwold wished, she rode right at the men coming toward her.

In no time she was among them, sword drawn, pointing toward Nothwulf's army and shouting, "Turn and fight! You damned cowards! Turn and fight!" She slashed at the men close at hand as they streamed around her prancing mount. They did not turn and fight. They did not even acknowledge her.

Behind them all came Aegenwulf, mounted on his white horse. He was not racing away from the field of battle, frightened and beaten. Rather, he was riding slowly, just keeping up with the running soldiers, like a man simply resigned to what had happened.

"Aegenwulf, what the devil is going on?" Cynewise demanded as she reined up beside him. Aegenwulf stopped his horse and turned it in a half-circle so that he could look back over the battlefield. Then he turned back to Cynewise.

"Seems Nothwulf is not giving chase," Aegenwulf said. "I wonder why? Well, whatever the reason I guess it's our good fortune. First we've had today."

"This is intolerable!" Cynewise said, struggling to avoid shouting. "How did this happen?"

"Nothwulf had men in reserve, it seems. I don't know where they came from. Leofric's men were still on the other side of the channel as of last night. We checked, you'll recall. Either they got over somehow, or there were more on this side than we thought. In any event, they sprung their trap and sent our men to flight."

"Well, collect the men up and get back and continue fighting!" Cynewise demanded.

Aegenwulf shook his head. "No, Lady Cynewise, it's over, I fear. No fight left in those men."

"It's not over, damn you…"

"No, truly, it is," Aegenwulf said. "When your father's men abandoned us it took a lot of the spirit out of the others. The fyrd, the men-at-arms. Even the thegns. They did not like the odds against them. But they were willing to fight anyway. But now they've been beat, and they won't be willing to fight again."

For a long moment they just held one another's eyes while Cynewise flailed around for the right words. She considered reminding him that she was ealdorman, and as such she could insist on him fulfilling his military obligation to her. But in truth her being ealdorman was now in question. She had no leverage over Aegenwulf. Actually, as the most powerful thegn to side with her, and the commander of the largest faction of men-at-arms, and a dear friend of the king, Aegenwulf was the one with the leverage here.

So, commanding him was not in order. But neither could she look weak. "We must be careful, Aegenwulf," she said. "These are dangerous times. If Nothwulf becomes ealdorman he won't look with favor on those who opposed him. I think we must see this business through, or it will be the ruin of us all. You and me, and the other thegns as well."

Aegenwulf looked unmoved. Then he sighed. "If Nothwulf becomes ealdorman he'll know that half of Dorsetshire opposed him, and he'll know that his hold on the seat is very precarious indeed. He'll be too in need of friends to start looking for enemies."

And he was right. Cynewise knew it. "So what would you have me do?" she asked.

"You still have soldiers in the field," Aegenwulf said. "Nothwulf does not yet know how few are left." He turned in his saddle and nodded toward Nothwulf's men, most of whom had now returned to the wall and were standing about, not doing anything in particular.

"I suggest," Aegenwulf continued, "that you take your hearth guard and ride over there. Seek out Nothwulf and see if you two can't come to some sort of accommodation, while you still have something with which to bargain."

He turned back, gave his reins a shake, and walked away in the direction that his men had run off, leaving Cynewise alone on the field.

Damn the old man. I didn't need him before and I don't need him now, Nothwulf thought. He climbed a few rungs up the ladder so that he could address the men from there. His men and the thegns who supported him were gathered around in loose ranks near him. Leofric's men and the thegns in his camp were also standing in a loose group, fifty feet away and quite purposefully separate from Nothwulf's.

"You men did fine, damned fine!" Nothwulf shouted. "Butchered Cynewise's men and sent them running. Showed them how real men fight!"

Nothwulf had expected a cheer, but it didn't come and that unnerved him a bit. There were smiles and murmurs of appreciation at those remarks, certainly, but the men were too exhausted and too uncertain to yell with any gusto.

"So now that we've vanquished one enemy we'll vanquish another! The Northmen we drove off the other day, they're back now, and once again the fools have run up on the wrecks we sunk in the channel."

The pleased look on the men's faces faded to confusion with those words. The murmuring spread and redoubled. Even Bryning, captain of Nothwulf's hearth guard, was taken by surprise, and he alone of the men dared to speak up.

"Lord Nothwulf, the heathens are caught on the wrecks? Now?"

"Yes, Bryning, now," Nothwulf said, but Bryning still did not look as if he understood.

"You mean, lord, just the other side of this wall are the heathens and their ships? I thought they meant to sail away, lord, after setting Leofric's men ashore."

"Yes, Bryning, they meant to, but we would be fools to let them, wouldn't we?" Nothwulf said. He could see how stunning this news was to them, and no wonder. Here they had been thinking they won a great and final victory, only to find there was another enemy just on the far side of the makeshift wall.

"Will we do for them with arrows, lord, like last time?" one of the others chimed in.

"No, no time," Nothwulf said. "They'll be coming ashore directly. We'll wait behind the wall, and once they begin to land, while most are still aboard their ships, then we'll fall on them and cut them down. We'll attack when we still outnumber them three to one!"

Nothwulf tried to infuse the words with confidence, as if this had been the plan all along and not something he was concocting as he spoke, which it was. He hoped the notion of greatly outnumbering the heathens would give the men heart, because they seemed to very much need it.

"And Leofric and his men?" another asked "They're with us?"

"No, not initially," Nothwulf said. "When the moment is right, then they'll join in. As they did with the fight against Cynewise's army."

He hoped that was true. Leofric had in fact made it clear that he would not join Nothwulf in this. But if things were going against him, Nothwulf figured that the old man could not help but come to his aid.

He couldn't just watch as we all get butchered, could he? Nothwulf wondered. He didn't think so, but then, he didn't think Leofric would have been so angry about his leaving the channel blocked.

"Let's divide up, divide up with your captains, half to the north end of the wall, half to the south," Nothwulf called. "We'll keep out of sight, and once I give the word both divisions will attack at once, come at 'em from both sides. Do you follow?"

Heads nodded. The minor thegns and their captains began to gather their men and lead them north or south to the ends of the wall. Nothwulf climbed up the ladder just high enough that he could see over it and stopped there.

The nearest of the longships had moved quite a bit since he and Leofric had first observed them. In fact, even as Nothwulf watched, the ship's bow seemed to strike the sand under the water and the ship came to a stop, as close to shore as she could get. He watched as the men moved toward the bow. They had shields on their backs and some wore mail and some helmets. They were too far off for Nothwulf to see what sort of weapons they carried, but he knew from experience what they would be: swords, seaxes, axes, spears.

Surely the water's too deep right there for them to get off the ship, Nothwulf thought. If the heathens had to wait for the tide to go out before they could get ashore then it would buy him and his men some time. For what, he did not know. Setting up with flaming arrows, perhaps. But any delay would be welcome, because the thought of going right into another fight, particularly against Northmen, was not appealing.

One of the Northmen vaulted over the side of the ship, but rather than sinking out of sight he stood with the water just below his waist. He pushed his way to the shore, and more and more of his fellows came over the rail and followed behind.

Damn it... Nothwulf thought.

The bow of the second ship was butted up against the stern of the first, the men climbing over and using the first ship as a bridge to the land. Nothwulf watched the activity and tried to work out how many he should let get ashore before he launched the attack. Not so many that they posed a real threat to his men. He did, however, want to kill as many as he could, so he needed to let a goodly number get off the ships.

How many that was he did not know. He watched as more and more of them came ashore. And then he knew it was time. Something inside told him so, and also suggested that he might have waited too long.

Nothwulf scrambled down the ladder and onto the ground. He would lead the men at the northern end of the wall, since they were closer to where the heathens were coming ashore. He ran to the southern end, told Bryning to wait for his advance before launching his own attack, and then raced off to the north, taking his place at the head of the men waiting there.

"Very well," Nothwulf said. He peeked around the corner of the wall, then adjusted his helmet, took the shield off his back and drew his sword. "Let us go!"

He came around the barricade, his men following behind. He had no plan of battle, really. He just meant to surprise the heathens and attack while they were unprepared. As he moved down the slight slope to the water's edge he called for his men to spread out, form a line like a loose shield wall. That should be enough to drive the Northmen back. He looked to the south to make certain Bryning was with him, and he was, getting his men in a line just as Nothwulf was doing.

He turned back, getting his first good look at the heathens from ground level. Those on shore were considerably outnumbered by his own men, which was good. They were in no sort of order as they gathered on the beach. They watched in silence as the English men-at-arms came around the ends of the wall. Nothwulf looked for signs of panic, but he saw none.

Nothwulf was leading at a quick walk. He wanted to hit the enemy before they could organize, but he did not want his men running, their order and discipline breaking down. The heathens were just a couple hundred feet away and Nothwulf figured even at that pace they would reach the enemy while they were still in disarray.

But he figured wrong. He heard the man near the center shout a few words, point left and right with his sword and the Northmen fell into two loose lines. Then the Northmen began to advance, one line toward Nothwulf and the other toward Bryning, as more and more of them poured over the bow of the grounded ship.

Nothwulf slowed his advance with some vague thought that he should not be too quick to engage these men. The one in the center, the one who had given the orders, was making right for him. He walked with a painful limp, but that did not seem to dampen his apparent desire to get into the fight. Beside him walked the young, yellow-haired Northman who had come to negotiate. Harald.

The two lines continued to close with one another and Nothwulf began to feel less certain about his decision to attack. He was no coward, and this was far from the first time he had fought Northmen, but it was the first time that he alone had led men into a fight. The first time it had been his decision. His pace slowed a bit more.

One of the Northmen banged his ax on his shield and the sharp noise made Nothwulf jump. Then another did so, and another, axes and swords and spears banging on the faces of shields. Then the Northmen began chanting a rhythmic chant, yelling in time to the beat of the weapons, and all the while moving toward Nothwulf's men.

Harald leaned over and spoke to the man in the center of the line, then pointed with his sword directly at Nothwulf, and the man in the center gave a quick nod. Nothwulf remembered Harald had said his father was the leader of this band. Was that him? He would not be happy about the trick played on him.

Then another scream cut through the sound, a single cry, like something that might come from the mouth of Satan himself. One of the Northmen, shirtless, no helmet, no armor of any sort, and carrying two axes, burst from the crowd and went running at Bryning's line. Nothwulf glanced over in time to see him crash into Bryning's men with the axes whirling like threshing flails, knocking the soldiers aside.

Nothwulf looked back at the line advancing toward his own men. They were still chanting and beating their weapons, save for the man who had given the orders, the man with the limp. He was close enough now that Nothwulf could see his face. His beard, like his hair, was dark but shot through with gray. He wore no helmet, and the parts of his face that were not covered by hair seemed streaked with blood. He held his sword with an ease that spoke of long use.

But it was his eyes that stopped Nothwulf in his tracks. Dark eyes peering out from the weathered face. Strange, animal eyes that radiated threat like heat coming off of red hot coals. Nothwulf had looked into the faces of many enemies on the field of battle, English, heathen, but he had never seen anything like this. Nothing as unearthly as those predator eyes that were staring right into his.

Now, rather than advance, Nothwulf took a step back. The Northman's eyes did not waver, they did not blink. Nothwulf took another step back. The heathens continued to come at them, their pace unwavering, the banging of weapons on shields rhythmic and unceasing. The limping man's eyes did not let go of his.

Nothwulf's mouth was suddenly very dry and he felt his hands and legs trembling, just a little. Then, suddenly, mindless panic rolled over him like a freak wave. He whirled around, plunged through the press of his own men, and ran.

Standing on *Sea Hammer*'s deck, looking toward the shore, Thorgrim Night Wolf had never felt anything like the rage he felt burning in his gut and spreading out from there, crackling like lightning through his arms and legs and driving him along. He pushed his way through the men until he reached the forward end of the ship, then vaulted over the side. He felt the water, cold and briny, envelope him up to the waist. He felt the wound in his thigh pulse and radiate pain, but the agony was delicious, and he welcomed it.

He found his footing and made his way ashore, stopped a dozen yards from the water's edge. The men already there parted before him. No one tried to speak to him, and he spoke to no one.

Right in front of him was the wall, the wall from which the English had assailed them with their flaming arrows. Burned *Long Serpent* to the waterline, killing Jorund in the process. Nearly burned *Sea Hammer* as well. The wall. He would burn it to ashes once he was done with the killing.

The English were hiding behind the wall. Thorgrim could not see them, but he knew they were there. In the still-reasonable place in his mind he wondered if he was lapsing into a wolf dream. It had never happened that way before, a wolf dream coming on him while wide awake and heading into battle, but that didn't mean it could not. Any number of changes seemed to happen as the years spilled by. He wondered what it might be this time.

He could feel the press of men around him as more and more came wading ashore. He took his shield off his back and slung it over his arm. He was not wearing his helmet, but that didn't matter because he felt certain that he could not be hurt, could not even be touched.

Harald stepped up beside him just as the English came around the end of the wall. A hundred men-at-arms at least, Thorgrim guessed. He looked to the south and saw another hundred coming from that direction.

"Make a line!" he called. He pointed with Iron-tooth to his right and left and his men fell quickly into order. "Another to meet the bastards to the south." He waited for a moment as the men sorted themselves out, then stepped off, the pain in his thigh blinding, but rather than hinder him it seemed to drive him on. Harald was at his side, his men a pace behind.

He lifted Iron-tooth above his head, and off to his right someone started banging a weapon against a shield. The gesture was taken up by the others until soon a world of sound seemed to precede them up the beach. And then the men started to chant.

The English would not understand the words, Thorgrim knew, but he could see that the sound alone was having the right effect. The man at the front hesitated and those behind him did as well. The chanting grew louder.

"That one, Father," Harald said, pointing to the Englishman who was leading the slow charge. "That's the one I spoke with, the one who agreed to remove the wrecks."

Thorgrim nodded, but his eyes did not leave the man whom Harald had pointed out. *You die first*, Thorgrim thought. He tried to quicken his pace, but his thigh would not allow it.

From somewhere behind him Starri Deathless screamed. Thorgrim had heard the sound too often to be moved by it, but he understood how terrifying it was to an enemy on the field. Starri would be flinging himself at the other line, the one to the south, because even in his madness Starri knew better than to get in Thorgrim's way.

Thorgrim's eyes remained on the Englishman in the front, locked on him as if a cable were binding them to the man's face. He could see the man take a step back, then another, the panic building.

Don't run, Thorgrim thought, but he knew it was useless, and just as the thought came to him the man turned and fled.

That was the end of the English attack. As the one commanding the men-at-arms clawed his way through the line and raced off, the line itself fell apart, and the others followed as fast as they could, shields and weapons flying in the air as they were cast aside. Thorgrim looked to his left. Starri was on the ground, a confused look on his face, head turning side to side, looking for an enemy to fight, but they, too, were running as fast as they could.

Thorgrim wanted to run after them, but he could barely walk, let alone run. But he did not want the others to go on without him, so he continued on, his pace unchanging, and the men followed behind.

Get around the wall... Thorgrim thought. *Get around the wall, see what the bastards are doing.*

Four more painful steps and then a man stepped out from behind the wall, the very spot where Thorgrim was heading. Thorgrim squinted, thinking this might be a renewed attack, but it was only one man. He waited for more to come behind him, warriors bolder than those who fled, but there were no more. One man, walking toward him. No shield, no weapons, his hands held out at his sides.

They closed for a few more steps and then Thorgrim saw who it was. Leofric. The man he had mistaken for a man of honor. The man he wished to kill more than any other. He felt the rage surging up again and he lifted Iron-tooth a little higher. But Leofric did not flinch. He did not slow as he walked toward Thorgrim, his hands still out by his side.

He stopped four feet in front of Thorgrim, a perfect distance for Iron-tooth to split his skull. He met Thorgrim's eyes with his own unwavering stare. There was no fear on his face, no emotion at all. For a moment the whole world hung suspended as the two men stared at one another. Then Leofric spoke.

"He says you may kill him if you wish," Harald said. "But he says he did not know the channel was still blocked. He swears it on his honor. He says if you choose to not kill him, then on the low tide his men will help remove the ships so we may get to sea."

Thorgrim stared at him for a moment more. Then he sighed and lowered Iron-tooth until the sword's tip rested on the dirt.

Epilogue

Victory to his sons he gives,
but to some riches;
eloquence to the great,
and to men, wit.

Poetic Edda

The fight outside Odd's burning hall ended much more abruptly than it began. The better part of Halfdan's men had run off into the dark. Some gave up the fight on seeing their king flee the field of battle. Others had taken their leave once it became clear just how the battle was turning out. The rest were prisoners, or they were dead.

Those who ran off were allowed to go. None of Odd's men had the strength or desire to go after them.

Amundi wiped the blade of his sword on the hem of his tunic, slipped it into its scabbard and embraced Odd in a hug. They held each other for a moment, then Odd let Amundi go and said, "Hold a moment." He stepped over to where he and Einar had been fighting and scanned the trampled ground. The hall was still burning, even more so now as the fire worked its way down the long building, and the light cast moving shadows like spirits of the dead over the ground. And in that light Odd saw Blood-letter, trampled and half sunk in the mud.

He felt a mixture of relief and dread as he bent down and snatched it up. He held it up to the firelight, turning it side to side. It was well coated with blood and dirt, but it seemed unharmed, the blade still straight and true. Odd bent down and wiped it on a dead man's tunic and slid it back into his scabbard.

He looked up at his hall. The flames were well past the north door now, the one he had barely been able to get to. It was likely the fire

336

had reached his and Signy's sleeping closet. His first impulse had been to rally the men and set about fighting the flames, maybe preserve part of his home so that when it was time to rebuild he would not have to start with nothing. One look now told him that the effort would be pointless.

He turned away from the burning building and walked back to where Amundi stood.

"We wondered, or I wondered, where you had gone off to," Amundi said. "I thought you were right by my side." There was no censure in his words, but Odd could well imagine the accusations of cowardice that must have run though Amundi's mind, if not out of his mouth, when he realized Odd had left them.

"The fight was not going well," Amundi continued. "These men that Halfdan had with him, they're good warriors. His best, I would imagine. Better trained than our men, more accustomed to this work. I had my doubts that we could beat them. And then suddenly this fire demon comes screaming out of the burning hall."

Odd gave a weak smile and shrugged. He looked around him, his thoughts settling. "I wanted to get at Halfdan. And I failed. I might have hurt some of his men, or killed some, I don't know. But whatever I did, it didn't do much good."

"Oh, that's not so," Amundi said. Ragi and Vifil appeared through the crowd of half-stunned men, their right sides lit up orange from the flames, their left nearly lost in shadow. They, too, were carrying sundry wounds and tears it their armor. They, too, were smiling.

"Here's that fire-spirit!" Ragi said. "I'll swear on my sword I nearly pissed myself when you came out of that door, flaming shield in hand!"

"That's it," Amundi said. "You coming out of that door. It shook everyone. Distracted them. And then Halfdan's hird had to fight you, and they were not even sure you were of this world, I imagine. At least not immediately. Everyone was in such confusion, then Halfdan's men just folded up in front of us. I've never seen the like."

I've never seen the like, Odd thought. Amundi had seen many such battles and he, Odd Pig-binder, had not. That was all Odd heard in those words of praise.

"What will we call you now?" Vifil said as if Odd had spoken his thoughts aloud. "Odd of the Burning Shield? Odd Shit-fire?"

Odd gave a weak smile.

"Maybe Odd Fire Eater would be better," Amundi said. Odd continued to smile but said nothing. He had no idea if such a name would stick. He had no idea if he would welcome it if it did.

But there was no time for such trivial things as nicknames. Odd and the others spoke of what needed doing next, then called out orders to those who served them, instructing them first to see to the wounded, both their fellows and Halfdan's men as well. Odd could see that the men were already attending to Halfdan's dead and wounded: purses cut away, arm rings, bracelets, seaxes and swords liberated.

"Where's Ulfkel?" Amundi asked. The fight had been over for some time, but they were only just noticing his absence. Had their heads not been swimming from the noise and strain and shock of the fight they would certainly have noticed earlier. Ulfkel was not an easy one to miss.

They walked north, the direction from which Ulfkel had led his men, and it did not take long to find him, though they walked right past him at first. Two of Halfdan's men, or the corpses of two of his men, lay on top of Ulfkel's body, mostly obscuring it. Ragi and Odd grabbed the first corpse and rolled it aside. A seax was jutting from the man's chest, and Ulfkel's hand, which presumably had still been gripping the weapon, fell free. They did not have to guess how the second man died. The blade of Ulfkel's sword was run clean through him and it stood up through his back like a flagpole.

The four men looked down at Ulfkel and for a moment they were silent. A knife was sticking out of Ulfkel's chest, right at his heart. His mail was slashed and they could see the pale skin and the blood around the vicious wound in his flesh. His helmet was gone and a part of his scalp had been cut away and now hung off the side of his head. The ear on that side was gone as well. There was another gaping wound in his thigh that looked as if it had been made by the tip of a spear.

"There's no doubt that he went down fighting," Amundi said. "The Choosers of the Slain will look well on our friend." Odd reached down and closed Ulfkel's eyes, which seemed to be looking up in surprise. Once the needs of the living had been attended to, Ulfkel would get the send-off to Valhalla that a man such as he deserved.

The wounded were moved off to a place where they could be cared for and a messenger was sent to fetch the women and the thralls that they might return and lend a hand. The dead were moved to another place and laid out in a row. The prisoners were stripped of weapons and armor, hands bound, and set in a third place under guard. Sentries were posted. The rest of the exhausted men were allowed to sleep.

But sleep would not come for Odd. He knew it would not and he did not even try. Instead he sat with his back to an old barrel, close enough to his burning hall to feel the heat from the flames, far enough that they did not scorch him. Signy found him there and admonished him, as he knew she would, for ignoring the wound that Halfdan's sword had made in his shoulder. She tended to it, starting the blood flowing again as she peeled the stiff, rent cloth of his tunic away and then applying bandages wrapped tight around him.

When she was done she sat down on his left side and leaned against him. She did not speak, and Odd was grateful for that, because he did not know what he would say to her. Soon he could hear her breathing soft and steady and he let her sleep propped up against him while he stared out into the dark.

Morning came and there was much to do. Signy and the servants sifted through the great, scorched pile of ash and charred wood that had once been the long hall. The fires had burned themselves out, though many spots were still too hot to approach. In any event there was nothing much of value left there. Odd had ordered most of it removed days before, and the flames had taken the rest.

Because the food had been moved to one of the storehouses and thus saved, there was enough on hand to feed the warriors and the prisoners alike. Odd and Amundi and Ragi and Vifil and Vigdis ate together and discussed what they would do next.

"We can kill them," Ragi said. The talk was now of the prisoners. "Or we can sell them or put them to work for us."

"First they'll work for us," Odd said. "They'll do what we need them to do. And then we'll see what their fate will be." He was giving orders, not asking, but no one seemed to question his right to do so. Even he, the most critical of all of them where his own status was concerned, did not question himself.

The prisoners were set to work digging graves. They were set to work clearing away the rubble of the hall once it was cool enough to touch. They were put to the task of building a funeral pyre worthy of Ulfkel Ospaksson, which was touched off at day's end, sending Ulfkel to Odin's hall of the slain in a manner befitting the man.

For three days the prisoners from Halfdan's army were made to work, and then on the morning of the fourth day they were summoned before Odd and the other free men. Einar, who had survived the fight, stood at the head of the band, but Odd did not feel the need to address him as if he was any sort of leader.

"You men fought well, and you did good work for us," he said, speaking loud enough to be heard by the forty or so men standing before him. "You've been in the service of Halfdan the Black. If you would serve me instead, I would welcome you."

He waited as the men looked at one another and a low muttering spread over the crowd. Finally one man pushed his way through and stepped up behind Odd. Then another and another until twelve in all had left Halfdan's service and joined with Odd. Which was, Odd was willing to admit, twelve more than he had expected.

"Good," Odd said. "The rest of you are free to go."

This was met with more silence and looks of raw suspicion.

"Go?" Einar asked.

"Go," Odd said. "All of you. Go. Back to Halfdan, off to Niflheim, wherever you please. Just get off my land and stay off."

There was more silence, more confusion. No one moved. Then one man, toward the back, turned and walked off down the beaten track that ran south. The others watched, as if to see what terrible fate would befall him, what trick was being played. And when they saw he was just walking away, unmolested, they turned and followed him.

Einar remained where he was, his eyes fixed on Odd's. He scowled and his moustache twitched. His eyes narrowed. Odd could see on Einar's face all of the things boiling inside him: rage, humiliation, suspicion, relief. It was not a healthful mix. Einar half opened his mouth as if to speak, held it that way for a moment, then closed it again. He turned and walked away and Odd could see he was trying to do so with as much dignity as he could. Which was not much.

Amundi was standing at Odd's side. "Mercy?" he asked. "You think those men deserved your mercy?"

"No mercy," Odd said. "Killing them would have been a mercy. Now they're wanderers. They've seen Halfdan's cowardly flight. They won't be welcomed by him, not with the tales they could tell. They might sell their service elsewhere, I don't care. But Einar, he's the one who'll suffer. He wouldn't dare return to Halfdan, not after the hash he's made of things. Everyone in this whole country knows him and hates him. He has nothing now, and nowhere to go."

Amundi nodded. "I see," he said. "You have no authority to make him an outlaw, but you did it anyway."

The others were there and they stood in a circle and for a long moment no one spoke. "Well," said Vifil at last, "we've beaten Halfdan the Black!" The words came out flat. Vifil and all the rest knew how untrue that was.

"We beat him in battle," Odd said. "But I fear there's a war now."

Heads nodded. "What will Halfdan do, do you suppose?" Ragi said. "What should we do?"

There was silence again and Odd hoped someone would give an answer, but he realized that they were all waiting for him to give an answer. So he did, the only answer he could truthfully offer.

"I don't know," he said. "I don't know what Halfdan will do, or what we will do. Before this all started I knew many things, but now I know nothing. But I'll learn. We'll all learn, soon enough."

Even through the heavy red carpet Nothwulf could feel the granite against his knees. It was becoming uncomfortable, soon to be painful, and he wondered how much longer he would have to kneel like this. It was like penance. It was all like penance. Though if he was going to be honest with himself—and he had made a vow to be honest with himself—penance was no more than he deserved.

Bishop Ealhstan was speaking, and had been for a while, but Nothwulf had stopped listening some time ago. He knew what the old man was saying, in any event. He had heard it all many times. It was, incredibly, just a few months since he had last heard those words spoken. It seemed much longer than that. A lifetime. More.

He shifted his knees a bit. Along with Ealhstan's voice he could hear the soft, cumulative sound of dozens of onlookers attempting to be quiet. He heard the occasional muted cough, the rustle of fabric, the shuffle of feet. Occasionally a sharp noise from outside made its way through the thick walls and made Nothwulf start, just a bit.

He was not comfortable with this, and his increasingly aching knees were the least of it. It was a fool thing to do and he knew it. Foolish and dangerous. Physically, morally, spiritually dangerous. But he could think of no other way out of this situation

There were no weapons in the cathedral, he was certain. Fairly certain. Explicit instructions had been given—no swords, no knives, not even the fancy, decorative sort, worn to show off their bejeweled hilts and not intended to ever cut anything. Bryning had made certain that those instructions were carried out, to the extent he was able, carefully observing each person as they entered. That was the best he could do. The people gathered in the spacious knave were the most important men and women in Dorsetshire, and Bryning was not about to inspect their persons more closely.

Nothwulf shifted a little, turned his head just a bit, trying to look over his shoulder without appearing to do so. He could not see what he wished to see, so he craned his neck a bit more.

"Will you stop that, for the love of God?" Cynewise whispered, her tone more disgust and exasperation than anger. She was kneeling beside him, their heads not two feet apart.

"What?" Nothwulf whispered back.

"No one is going to stab you, you bloody fool."

Nothwulf turned his head and looked straight forward. *You should know, you little tart,* he thought. *Murdering men at their weddings seems to be your business.*

"Dearly beloved, we are gathered here in the sight of God..." Ealhstan continued.

Yes, sight of God. You hear that, Cynewise? He's watching you, you viper, Nothwulf thought. He knew the moment of danger was coming. Not now, but once the vows were said. That had been the end for his brother. But for all his concern Nothwulf did not really think Cynewise would have him murdered, right there, every man of note in the shire looking on. You could get away with that sort of thing once, but the second time was bound to raise suspicions.

So, if there was a moment of danger, it would likely come later.

He glanced over at Cynewise who had her head lowered and was doing a very good imitation of a pious and obedient woman. She was not unattractive. Quite the opposite. When Nothwulf was able to view her with disinterested eyes he had to admit she stirred something in him. He intended to explore that further when the wedding feast was done, when they had headed off to their bed chamber. Regardless of what she might want, she would be his wife, and that office came with certain obligations. The thought excited Nothwulf and it frightened him as well.

A wave of doubt came over him, just as it had many times since this whole thing started. Their courtship had really been a negotiation, about as romantic as haggling over the boundaries of a piece of land or the price of a cow. It had begun just as Nothwulf stopped his ignominious flight from the Northmen on the bank of the channel, when he had stopped running and the men behind him had stopped running. He was gasping for breath, wondering how he would ever recover from such a shameful thing, when he had seen her, alone, approaching on horseback.

She rode up, unhurried, as Nothwulf's breathing was returning to normal.

"Nothwulf, we must talk," she said. "As Christians, it's only right that we talk." She looked around at the men behind him. "Have you just been routed by some foe?"

Nothwulf looked behind him. He had thoroughly anticipated seeing the heathens racing around the wall, howling and waving their weapons, but he saw nothing. Leofric's men had moved off, half a mile to the south. Now, other than the wall, there was nothing to see.

"We fought the Northmen," Nothwulf said. "The Northmen you so shamefully paid to go away. We drove them back to their ships. We would not let such enemies go so easy."

"Hmm," Cynewise said. "Well, it was bravely done, I'm sure. Which makes one wonder why you felt the need to run." She looked off to where Leofric's men were clustered. "I see you have only half the men you did before. Those over there, have they left you?"

"Left? No. They're standing ready to fight again. You, the heathens, we've beaten you all today, and we'll do so again."

"Hmm," Cynewise said again. "I'm not so sure about that. My father has sent more men. We're greatly reinforced. But, as a Christian, I thought it my duty to speak with you before more blood is shed."

And so they spoke. Argued. Nothwulf began to suspect that Cynewise was much weaker than she let on, all but deserted by the men who had supported her. But then, the same was true of

Nothwulf. Two claimants to the seat of ealdorman and neither with any force to back up their claims.

And so, marriage. Joining their houses. It had been Cynewise's idea, in truth. Nothwulf pointed out the obvious—if they were married, he would be ealdorman. There could be no debate about that. Not between the two of them, not among the thegns of Dorsetshire, or the bishop or the king.

Cynewise agreed, but Nothwulf did not take much comfort from her easy cooperation.

"I now pronounce you man and wife," Bishop Ealhstan said. Nothwulf and Cynewise stood and the bishop made a discreet gesture to indicate they should kiss. Nothwulf turned to his bride, lifted the veil from her face. She was indeed beautiful, though the look she was giving him was not particularly inviting.

Shun me if you will, I can manage, Nothwulf thought. He had brought Cynewise's former lady's maid, Aelfwyn, into his household, to serve in some capacity. What her official duties would be he was not certain. Her unofficial duties included keeping Nothwulf company in his bed when Cynewise would not, and driving Cynewise mad by her mere presence.

He leaned forward and touched Cynewise's lips with his own and received a flicker of a response in return. He felt himself tense, felt every muscle in his body crying to straighten and spin around and defend against the dagger that must surely be coming for his back.

He pulled his lips away and straightened, slowly and in a dignified way. He sensed a general easing of tension in the cathedral, as if all the guests had been holding their breath and were now letting it go, and he realized he was not the only one braced for the possibility of bloody murder. Again.

Leofric, standing in the front rank, began to clap and the others joined in until the space was filled with the sound of their clapping, a loud and enthusiastic sound, happiness mixed with relief: relief that no one had been killed, that this marriage had gone off as had been planned, that the wounds that had so injured Dorsetshire might finally be let to heal.

Nothwulf smiled. The deed was done. Now, if he could find a way to rid himself of his wife before she found a way to murder him then their marriage would be a happy one indeed.

*   *   *

Of the eight ships in Thorgrim's fleet which had been blown clear of the Irish coast, six remained, and they were not in terribly good shape. Battered and repaired, battered and repaired, neither ships nor men could take such treatment for long. The throbbing in Thorgrim's left thigh reminded him of that.

Leofric's words, his willingness to let Thorgrim cleave him in two on the shore, had drained the rage out of him like the tide pouring out of the harbor. He just nodded his head—he felt as if he did not have the energy to do more—then turned and led his men back to the ships, leaving Harald to explain to them what happened.

The tide fell and rose again during the dark hours, and it was on its way out once more when Thorgrim and the others awoke. In the early light Thorgrim could see Leofric's men, a few hundred at least, gathered on the beach. They huddled around small cooking fires and the smell of wood smoke and food filled the air. A man came splashing out to *Sea Hammer*'s side and said, through Harald's translation, that Leofric asked that they join his men in breakfast.

The Northmen piled ashore, dropping into water that was just ankle deep now and still falling. They walked ashore, both hungry and wary. But soon they were given porridge and meat and ale and the wariness faded like the darkness of night.

The tide ran out and Thorgrim finally had a clear look at the ships that had stymied his attempts to get to sea. Three of them, sorry wrecks of old trading vessels. He guessed it had been no great task to sink them since they must have been in a sinking condition to begin with. He could see there was a single spot where they might have broken through the wrecks if they had hit it just right, but they could not have known that when they were hidden by the water.

Tearing three ships apart, even just down to the waterline, was no easy task, but having four hundred determined men to do it removed much of the burden. Once breakfast was over they went at the sodden wrecks with axes and hammers and whatever else they could use to mete out destruction.

They started on the ship nearest the shore and as the tide continued to fall they waded farther and farther into the channel. They climbed aboard the ship sunk midstream and standing on the half submerged deck continued to reduce it to its individual timbers, letting the broken wood drift off with the ebbing tide.

By late morning the tide turned and the sea water began to pour back into the harbor, but before it rose too high the last of the obstructions were broken up. Thorgrim, exhausted, weak, wracked with pain, pulled himself aboard *Sea Hammer* which, like the other ships, had been anchored once it floated free from the bottom. He ordered the men to ship oars, and the captains of the other ships followed suit.

He turned and looked toward the shore to the west, the crude wall, the black spots where the cook fires had burned, the English men-at-arms standing there in a scraggly line. Leofric was near the center of the line, a few yards closer to the water than the rest. He and Thorgrim looked at one another. Thorgrim gave a nod of his head and Leofric did the same.

Turned out to be a man of honor after all, Thorgrim thought, then he called for the rowers to make way.

They were fighting the current this time, making for the open water against the flood tide, but they did not have far to go. They worked their way through the curving channel and soon Thorgrim could see that the water was getting deeper below them, the ocean spreading out on the starboard side.

"A little farther, Night Wolf, and then deep water all around!" Starri called from his perch on the masthead. "Well, all around to starboard. That's how you should turn. To starboard."

Thorgrim smiled a thin smile. The shoreline lay to larboard, not a hundred yards away. He was not likely to turn in that direction.

He looked to the west, the low, scrubby hills, the long white beach, and on the other side the wide harbor in which they had been trapped. *No, no chance I'll be turning that way,* Thorgrim thought again.

The sun was out, the breeze was light and from the northwest, and that was all good. Crucial, in fact, because all of the ships had suffered some sort of damage. The least hurt was *Dragon*, which only had a few of her oars broken. The most hurt was *Blood Hawk*, her larboard side stove in by *Black Wing*, which had also suffered mightily in that encounter. Now *Blood Hawk* had a piece of heavily tarred canvas stretched over the gaping hole in her side, which would keep the water out, mostly, unless the seas got up too high.

They continued out into the open water. To the north Thorgrim could see nothing but a long half-moon of sandy beach arching around for ten miles or so until it ended at a point of land to the east, just barely visible in the distance. Thorgrim shifted his tiller until *Sea Hammer*'s bow was on a heading to pass just south of that point.

They set an easy pace, and all through the afternoon they pulled for the point of land and watched as it seemed to rise up out of the sea. The day was getting on when Thorgrim saw a broken gap in the shoreline, a mile wide or so, in what he had thought was an unbroken stretch of land. It might be an entrance to a bay, or the mouth of a great river. It might be open water right through, the land to the south of it an island, and not part of the mainland at all. He could not tell. He didn't much care.

The sun was at their back and low down, casting long shadows over the deck, when the little fleet rounded the point at the far end of the bay. This time the shore was not made up of long, sandy beaches, but rather high, jagged cliffs, an inhospitable coast. It was not a place for ships to land, certainly not damaged ships. Thorgrim was about to turn his fleet around when he saw an indent in the shore, like a section scooped out of the rock wall, and inside that section, a place to come ashore. White sand. Shelter.

In the last bits of red evening light the ships drove their bows into the sand, anchors run up the beach, scouts sent out to make certain there was no one who might launch some surprise on them. When they returned and declared the country empty as far as they could make out, fires were lit, food and ale and mead brought ashore.

Gudrid found a log and half a dozen men rolled it up by the fire. He knew better than to suggest Thorgrim have a seat on it, but Thorgrim knew that was why he brought it there. Everyone else knew as well, and no one sat and it remained unoccupied until Thorgrim relented and with a grunt eased himself down in silent gratitude. He sat for some time, looking into the flames, his mind in a swirl of exhaustion and pain. Ships to repair, men to repair, they would start it all again in the morning.

"Louis," he called, looking up from the flames. Louis the Frank, standing off to his right, turned and walked toward him.

"Where are we?" Thorgrim asked.

Louis shrugged. "Why do you ask me such things?" he said. "Engla-land. I think. I should ask you, where we are going."

That was easy enough for Thorgrim to answer. "East," he said. "East."

East. To Louis's home in Frankia. East to his own home. He was ready to go home. His home in Norway, his home in Valhalla, either one would be fine with him.

Would you like a heads-up about new titles in The Norsemen Saga, as well as preview sample chapters and other good stuff cheap (actually free)?

Visit our web site to sign up for our (occasional) e-mail newsletter:

www.jameslnelson.com

Other Fiction by
James L. Nelson:

The Brethren of the Coast:
Piracy in Colonial America
The Guardship
The Blackbirder
The Pirate Round

The Samuel Bowater Novels:
Naval action of the American Civil War
Glory in the Name
Thieves of Mercy

The Only Life that Mattered:
The Story of Ann Bonny, Mary Read and Calico Jack Rackham

Glossary

adze – a tool much like an ax but with the blade set at a right angle to the handle.

Ægir – Norse god of the sea. In Norse mythology he was also the host of great feasts for the gods.

Angel-cynn - (pronounced Angle-kin). Term used in the writing of Alfred the Great and the Old English Chronical to denote both the English people of Teutonic descent, namely the Angles, Saxons and Jutes, and the land they occupied. This seems to be the only term used to denote the country of England until the Danish conquest, after which the island was referred to as Engla land.

Asgard - the dwelling place of the Norse gods and goddesses, essentially the Norse heaven.

athwartships – at a right angle to the centerline of a vessel.

beitass - a wooden pole, or spar, secured to the side of a ship on the after end and leading forward to which the corner, or clew, of a sail could be secured.

berserkir - a Viking warrior able to work himself up into a frenzy of blood-lust before a battle. The berserkirs, near psychopathic killers in battle, were the fiercest of the Viking soldiers. The word berserkir comes from the Norse for "bear shirt" and is the origin of the modern English "berserk".

block – nautical term for a pulley.

boss - the round, iron centerpiece of a wooden shield. The boss formed an iron cup protruding from the front of the shield, providing a hollow in the back across which ran the hand grip.

bothach – Gaelic term for poor tenant farmers, serfs.

brace - line used for hauling a **yard** side to side on a horizontal plane. Used to adjust the angle of the sail to the wind.

brat – a rectangular cloth worn in various configurations as an outer garment over a *leine*.

bride-price - money paid by the family of the groom to the family of the bride.

byrdingr - a smaller ocean-going cargo vessel used by the Norsemen for trade and transportation. Generally about 40 feet in length, the byrdingr was a smaller version of the more well-known *knarr*.

cable – a measure of approximately 600 feet.

clench nail – a type of nail that, after being driven through a board, has a type of washer called a rove placed over the end and is then bent over to secure it in place.

clew – one of the lower corners of a square sail, to which the **sheet** is attached.

ceorl – a commoner in early Medieval England, a peasant, but also a small-time landowner with rights. Members of the ceorl class served in the **fyrd**.

curach - a boat, unique to Ireland, made of a wood frame covered in hide. They ranged in size, the largest propelled by sail and capable of carrying several tons. The most common sea-going craft of mediaeval Ireland. **Curach** was the Gaelic word for boat which later became the word curragh.

dagmál – breakfast time

danegeld - tribute paid by the English to the Vikings to secure peace.

derbfine – In Irish law, a family of four generations, including a man, his sons, grandsons and great grandsons.

dragon ship - the largest of the Viking warships, upwards of 160 feet long and able to carry as many as 300 men. Dragon ships were the flagships of the fleet, the ships of kings.

dubh gall - Gaelic term for Vikings of Danish descent. It means Black Strangers, a reference to the mail armor they wore, made dark by the oil used to preserve it. *See* **fin gall**.

ell – a unit of length, a little more than a yard.

eyrir – Scandinavian unit of measurement, approximately an ounce.

félag – a fellowship of men who owed each other a mutual obligation, such as multiple owners of a ship, or a band or warriors who had sworn allegiance to one another.

figurehead – ornamental carving on the bow of a ship.

fin gall - Gaelic term for Vikings of Norwegian descent. It means White Strangers. *See* **dubh gall**.

forestay – a rope running from the top of a ship's mast to the bow used to support the mast.

Frisia – a region in the northern part of the modern-day Netherlands.

Freya - Norse goddess of beauty and love, she was also associated with warriors, as many of the Norse deity were. Freya often led the **Valkyrie** to the battlefield.

fyrd – in Medieval England, a levy of commoners called up for military service when needed.

gallows – tall, T-shaped posts on the ship's centerline, forward of the mast, on which the oars and yard were stored when not in use.

hack silver – pieces of silver from larger units cut up for distribution.

hall – the central building on a Viking-age farm. It served as dining hall, sleeping quarters and storage. Also known as a **longhouse**.

halyard - a line by which a sail or a yard is raised.

Haustmánudur – early autumn. Literally, harvest-month.

Hel - in Norse mythology, the daughter of Loki and the ruler of the underworld where those who are not raised up to Valhalla are sent to suffer. The same name, Hel, is given to the realm over which she rules, the Norse hell.

hersir – in medieval Norway, a magistrate who served to oversee a region under the rule of a king.

hide – a unit of land considered sufficient to support a single family.

hird - an elite corps of Viking warriors hired and maintained by a king or powerful **jarl**. Unlike most Viking warrior groups, which would assemble and disperse at will, the hird was retained as a semi-permanent force which formed the core of a Viking army.

hirdsman - a warrior who is a member of the **hird**.

hólmganga – a formal, organized duel fought in a marked off area between two men.

jarl - title given to a man of high rank. A jarl might be an independent ruler or subordinate to a king. Jarl is the origin of the English word *earl*.

Jörmungandr – in Norse mythology, a vast sea serpent that surrounds the earth, grasping its own tail.

knarr - a Norse merchant vessel. Smaller, wider and sturdier than the longship, knarrs were the workhorse of Norse trade, carrying cargo and settlers wherever the Norsemen traveled.

Laigin – Medieval name for the modern-day county of Leinster in the southeast corner of Ireland.

league – a distance of three miles.

lee shore – land that is downwind of a ship, on which a ship is in danger of being driven.

leeward – down wind.

leech – either one of the two vertical edges of a square sail.

leine – a long, loose-fitting smock worn by men and women under other clothing. Similar to the shift of a later period.

levies - conscripted soldiers of ninth century warfare.

Loki - Norse god of fire and free spirits. Loki was mischievous and his tricks caused great trouble for the gods, for which he was punished.

longphort - literally, a ship fortress. A small, fortified port to protect shipping and serve as a center of commerce and a launching off point for raiding.

luchrupán – Middle Irish word that became the modern-day Leprechaun.

luff – the shivering of a sail when its edge is pointed into the wind and the wind strikes it on both sides.

Midgard – one of nine worlds in Norse mythology, it is the earth, the world known and visible to humans.

Niflheim – the World of Fog. One of the nine worlds in Norse mythology, somewhat analogous to Hell, the afterlife for people who do not die honorable deaths.

Njord – Norse god of the sea and seafaring.

norns – in Norse mythology, women who sit at the center of the world and hold the fate of each person by spinning the thread of each person's life.

Odin - foremost of the Norse gods. Odin was the god of wisdom and war, protector of both chieftains and poets.

oénach –a major fair, often held on a feast day in an area bordered by two territories.

perch - a unit of measure equal to 16½ feet. The same as a rod.

Ragnarok - the mythical final battle when most humans and gods would be killed by the forces of evil and the earth destroyed, only to rise again, purified.

rath – Gaelic word for a **ringfort**. Many Irish place names still contain the word Rath.

rod – a unit of measure equal to 16½ feet. The same as a perch

rove – a square washer used to fasten the planks of a longship. A nail is driven through the plank and the hole in the washer and then bent over.

ringfort - common Irish homestead, consisting of houses protected by circular earthwork and palisade walls.

rí túaithe – Gaelic term for a minor king, who would owe allegiance to nobles higher in rank.

rí tuath – a minor king who is lord over several **rí túaithe**.

rí ruirech –a supreme or provincial king, to whom the **rí tuath** owe allegiance.

sceattas – small, thick silver coins minted in England and Frisia in the early Middle Ages.

seax – any of a variety of edged weapons longer than a knife but shorter and lighter than a typical sword.

sheer strake – the uppermost plank, or strake, of a boat or ship's hull. On a Viking ship the sheer strake would form the upper edge of the ship's hull.

sheet – a rope that controls a sail. In the case of a square sail the sheets pull the **clews** down to hold the sail so the wind can fill it.

shieldwall - a defensive wall formed by soldiers standing in line with shields overlapping.

shire reeve – a magistrate who served a king or ealdorman and carried out various official functions within his district. One of the highest ranking officials, under whom other, more minor reeves served. The term shire reeve is the basis of the modern-day *sheriff*.

shroud – a heavy rope stretching from the top of the mast to the ship's side that prevents the mast from falling sideways.

skald - a Viking-era poet, generally one attached to a royal court. The skalds wrote a very stylized type of verse particular to the medieval Scandinavians. Poetry was an important part of Viking culture and the ability to write it a highly regarded skill.

sling - the center portion of the **yard**.

sœslumadr – official appointed by the king to administer royal holdings. Similar to the English **shire reeve**.

spar – generic term used for any of the masts or yards that are part of a ship's rig.

stem – the curved timber that forms the bow of the ship. On Viking ships the stem extended well above the upper edge of the ship and the figurehead was mounted there.

strake – one of the wooden planks that make up the hull of a ship. The construction technique, used by the Norsemen, in which one strake overlaps the one below it is called *lapstrake construction*.

swine array - a Viking battle formation consisting of a wedge-shaped arrangement of men used to attack a shield wall or other defensive position.

tánaise ríg – Gaelic term for heir apparent, the man assumed to be next in line for a kingship.

thegn – a minor noble or a land-holder above the peasant class who also served the king in a military capacity.

thing - a communal assembly.

Thor - Norse god of storms and wind, but also the protector of humans and the other gods. Thor's chosen weapon was a hammer. Hammer amulets were popular with Norsemen in the same way that crosses are popular with Christians.

thrall - Norse term for a slave. Origin of the English word "enthrall".

thwart - a rower's seat in a boat. From the old Norse term meaning "across".

tuath – a minor kingdom in medieval Ireland that consisted of several **túaithe**.

túaithe – a further subdivision of a kingdom, ruled by a **rí túaithe**

Ulfberht – a particular make of sword crafted in the Germanic countries and inscribed with the name Ulfberht or some variant. Though it is not clear who Ulfberht was, the swords that bore his name were of the highest quality and much prized.

unstep – to take a mast down. To put a mast in place is to step the mast.

Valhalla - a great hall in **Asgard** where slain warriors would go to feast, drink and fight until the coming of **Ragnarok**.

Valkyrie - female spirits of Norse mythology who gathered the spirits of the dead from the battle field and escorted them to **Valhalla**. They were the Choosers of the Slain, and though later romantically portrayed as Odin's warrior handmaidens, they were originally viewed more demonically, as spirits who devoured the corpses of the dead.

vantnale – a wooden lever attached to the lower end of a shroud and used to make the shroud fast and to tension it.

varonn – springtime. Literally "spring work" in Old Norse.

Vik - An area of Norway south of modern-day Oslo. The name is possibly the origin of the term *Viking*.

wattle and daub - common medieval technique for building walls. Small sticks were woven through larger uprights to form the wattle, and the structure was plastered with mud or plaster, the daub.

weather – closest to the direction from which the wind is blowing, when used to indicate the position of something relative to the wind.

wergild - the fine imposed for taking a man's life. The amount of the wergild was dependent on the victim's social standing.

witan - a council of the greater nobles and bishops of a region, generally assembled to advise the king.

yard - a long, tapered timber from which a sail was suspended. When a Viking ship was not under sail, the yard was turned lengthwise and lowered to near the deck with the sail lashed to it.

Acknowledgements

Once again I find myself indebted to the usual suspects: Steve Cromwell for the covers which have really helped make this series, and Alistair Corbett for his photography. Alicia Street at iProofread and More for her careful and thorough editing. The maps by Chris Boyle have brought a dimension to the books that they were sorely lacking, and I am very grateful to him. Nat Sobel, Judith Weber and all the folks at Sobel Weber Associates, Inc. have helped bring the series to an international audience, which now includes translations in German, Spanish, Italian and Russian.

I am indebted to Caroline Connolly for her expertise regarding horses. This includes not just help with the book but also giving my kids their first taste of horseback riding. My thanks to Nathaniel Nelson for his IT work, his suggestions of how I can pull myself into the twenty-first century and, most important of all, his support and enthusiasm. Thanks to Stephanie Nelson for her help with...well, everything.

And of course, my shipmate for three decades, my beloved wife, Lisa.

42269948R00224

Trilogía de la ciudad

LOS ESPEJOS
DE LA NOCHE
(AMIGOS)

Jordi Sierra i Fabra

SiF
EDITORIAL

Prólogo

LOS SENTIMIENTOS

Paz

En realidad éramos tres parejas tan distintas, tan... Es difícil explicarlo, especialmente ahora. Puede que antes fuéramos como tantas, iguales a otras, pero de pronto fue como si los años no se hubieran movido lo mismo para todos.

Una no ve el abismo hasta que está sobre él.

Y nuestros abismos ni siquiera estaban bajo nosotros, sino entre nosotros.

Rafael

Todos tenemos un mal día, pero en ocasiones la suma de muchas pequeñas cosas convierte ese mal día en un cataclismo total. Así que creo que eso fue lo que sucedió. Cuando las circunstancias se encadenan es imposible detenerlas, pierdes el control sobre el entorno, y lo que es peor, sobre ti mismo.

Fue eso, solo eso: un mal día, y una asquerosa noche.

Nadie tuvo la culpa, ¿verdad? Nadie.

¿O sí?

Sixto

Me gusta la cerveza sin espuma. Cuando se echa el contenido de la botella o la lata de golpe en un vaso, pasa lo que pasa: que la espuma se derrama. Yo lo odio. Por esa razón comparo esa noche con ello. Derramamos la cerveza de golpe, y la espuma se desbordó. Demasiada presión. Demasiadas carambolas no previstas. Es como cuando quieres encajar las piezas de un puzzle y no encuentras una, o incluso resulta que hay una pieza que no encaja en ninguna parte. Bueno... no sé si me explico. Hay cosas que no tienen una lógica.

Simplemente, suceden.

Y lo de esa noche sucedió, sin más.

Como la jodida espuma imparable rezumando por el borde del vaso.

Salvador

Ser médico no es un trabajo, es una religión, por eso mismo ahora me siento más vulnerable, incapaz de entender no ya lo que sucedió, sino qué estaba haciendo yo allí, ¿por qué...?

No era la mejor noche para examinar una vida, el pasado, el presente, el futuro, Paz, Octavio, Vanessa, yo mismo, todo. Tampoco era la mejor noche para ir de un lado a otro con Rafael y con Sixto. Se notaba en el ambiente.

Soy médico, tenía que haberlo comprendido. Un simple diagnóstico previo suele ayudar a detener una enfermedad. Bastaba con ver los indicios. Pero no los ví, no supe valorar la situación, y cuando en un quirófano se te va un paciente sin que puedas evitarlo...

Todas las guerras tienen un resumen para el que las pierde, y es muy simple, se define con dos palabras: demasiado tarde.

Natalia

Éramos seis personas, no tres parejas, sino seis personas. Eso implica seis emociones distintas, seis formas de ver las cosas, y cuando cada una de las seis tiene algo que ocultar y se expone a verlo todo claro, o a estallar, en mitad de la noche, lo que puede llegar a suceder es imprevisible.

Nadie pone seis elementos químicos juntos en una probeta para ver qué pasa, que tipo de reacción se desata.

Nosotros lo hicimos, inconscientemente.

Ya sé que es tarde para lamentar nada, pero... ¿hace falta que diga que no lo podíamos prever, que fue un accidente, que...?

No éramos más que tres hombres y tres mujeres, como tantos y tantas, saliendo a cenar y a pasar el rato en una noche de viernes cualquiera.

Encarna

Fue cosa de mala suerte, nada más, no hay que darle más vueltas. No creo en destinos ni en tonterías así. Unas veces estás en el lugar adecuado en el momento preciso, y te sale bien. Otras es al revés.

¡Por Dios! ¿Hace falta explicarlo?

¡Yo lo siento, como la que más, y punto!

Eso es todo, ¿no? Quiero decir que...

¿Qué otra cosa puede hacerse?

Primera Parte

LAS PIEZAS

1

Paz arrojó el tercero de los vestidos seleccionados sobre la cama, con cuidado pero sin dejar de exteriorizar su malestar. Cogió el cuarto, que colgaba de una percha al lado del quinto y último, y se embutió en él sin más convencimiento que con los anteriores. El resultado, después de mirarse de arriba abajo, de frente y por ambos lados, fue el mismo. Se lo quitó y antes de proceder a ponerse el que le quedaba, observó su imagen en el espejo con todas las dudas impresas en sus ojos. Después de todo, no se trataba de los vestidos, sino de ella misma, y eso resultaba evidente.

Lo que vio, una vez más, aunque ahora le hizo más daño por alguna extraña razón, acabó de demoler su frágil estado de ánimo. El pecho caído, el abdomen demasiado pronunciado, las caderas ensanchadas, el cambio progresivo y natural que distanciaba cada vez con mayor rigor el pasado y la proyectaba hacia la vejez a través de una madurez que sobrevolaba como un avión a reacción.

Odió sus sentimientos, porque no le gustaba tenerlos y menos que la afectaran, y como solía hacer, los barrió a base de aplastarlos en el fondo de su ser. Cogió el quinto vestido y cuando se lo estaba poniendo por la cabeza entró en la habitación Vanessa, con su natural sonrisa colgándole de los labios.

—¿Te ayudo? —quiso saber la niña.

—No... bueno, sí —se resignó su madre—. No sé qué ponerme.

—¿Adónde vais?

—A cenar, con los Martí y los Planas.

—¿Los Planas? ¿Ha vuelto ella con su marido?

—Ah, no, perdona. Me refiero a él y la nueva.

—¡Oh, vaya! —pareció comprender Vanessa—. ¿Qué tal es?

—Joven.

—Capto la indirecta.

—Hija, que él tiene cuarenta y dos y ella veintinueve.

—Pues no es tanto. La mayoría de los separados se las buscan de veintidós. Es la edad ideal.

—Supieras tanto de matemáticas como de eso.

—Mamá, te digo lo que hay. Espera... —la ayudó a subir la cremallera y, tras separarse un paso y mirarla a través del espejo, aseguró—: Estás muy bien.

—¿En serio? No sé, no sé —vaciló Paz—. Natalia es tan elegante, y esa chica tan...

—Joven, ya lo has dicho. Pruébate este —señaló el segundo que se había puesto—. Lo que no entiendo, es cómo Natalia acepta salir con ella.

—¿Y yo? La verdad es que estamos en una posición embarazosa, porque seguimos siendo amigas de Sole, y este cambio... No sé porque Sixto se empeña en que todo sea como antes, porque no lo es. Esa mujer no pega ni con cola. Pero eso tu padre y Rafael no lo entienden, o será que Sixto es un liante, ya sabes. Ni siquiera sé cómo quedamos en salir esta noche.

—¿Sole aún lo está pasando mal?

—¿Tú que crees? Son tres hijos, y Sixto se portó fatal.

—Mira, mamá, cuando dos rompen la culpa es mitad y mitad. Y de eso sí que puedo hablar. Acuérdate de que en mi clase los hijos de los separados son mayoría.

Acabó de ponerse el vestido elegido por su hija y, una vez más, se enfrentó al espejo. Vanessa fue el árbitro decisivo, después de que examinara los otros cuatro y fuera eliminándolos uno a uno.

—Este, sin duda —asintió la niña—. Iréis a cenar y luego a tomar una copa o un batido de frutas o algo así, ¿no? —y sin esperar respuesta insistió—: Sí, sí, este. Hazme caso. Estás elegante sin cantar, y se te ve bien.

—¿Estás segura, hija? —tuvo su último atisbo de duda ella.

—Completamente.

Eso zanjó el tema y Paz volvió a quitárselo para plancharlo y buscar los complementos adecuados.

Todavía era temprano.

Paz

Mi nombre es Paz Antich, tengo cuarenta y cuatro años y dos hijos, Octavio, de dieciocho, y Vanessa, de catorce. Mi marido es Salvador Marcos, médico de profesión. Pediatra, para más detalle. Mi vida hasta hoy ha sido un cruce de estabilidades, satisfacciones, normalidades y sencillez. Probablemente ha sido la vida que siempre he buscado y he necesitado, sin otra cosa que no fuera la sensación de tenerlo todo en orden y al alcance de la mano, todo controlado, aunque sin excesos. Mi hija estudia y es una gran chica. Mi hijo está en la edad difícil, y es el que más miedo me da, pero tengo confianza en él. Siempre he tenido confianza en los demás, mucho más que en mí misma. Por ejemplo, los problemas que tienen Salvador y Octavio, yo los entiendo, puedo hacerme cargo de ellos, pero en modo alguno pienso que sean tan trágicos como mi marido interpreta. Salvador ha olvidado ya sus años juveniles, aunque él se acoja al tópico y cuando se lo recuerdo me dice eso de que "eran otros tiempos". Los tiempos cambian, pero las personas tienen los mismos problemas aunque los vistan con otros sentimientos. Y un problema es siempre un problema, algo que nos absorbe al completo.

Yo no trabajo. He sido "esposa y madre". No sé si eso es bueno o malo, pero está hecho y no sirve de mucho pensar en ello. Al comienzo, en los días difíciles y duros, trabajé en la consulta de Salvador, como enfermera, recepcionista y todo lo que hiciera falta. Luego, entre la necesidad de cuidar de mis hijos y el hecho de que las cosas empezaran a ir bien... ya se sabe. Me quedé en casa y punto. Lo malo es que ahora estoy en esa edad en la que empiezan las preguntas, las dudas, y mi cuerpo ya ni siquiera me acompaña. Hace cinco meses que no me viene el período, y no es un nuevo embarazo, que más quisiera yo. Es el azote de cualquier mujer, la menopausia.

Me siento deprimida, más de lo que nunca hubiera imaginado llegar a estar. Y ni siquiera se lo he dicho a Salvador. Todavía no. Es curioso, porque es la primera vez que le oculto algo. No sé de que tengo miedo, pero lo tengo.

Amo a mi marido. Para algunas puede que sea rutina, hábito, tiempo, constancia, no haber conocido a otro... Pero para mi es amor. La fidelidad es amor, y el día a día, y los años que tal vez te endurecen el alma pero no los sentimientos, y la compañía, y el mutuo apoyo y tantas otras cosas. Le amo porque ha sido un buen hombre, trabajador, dedicado, respetuoso, familiar, estable. No sé si me explico. No quisiera hacer el retrato de un hombre aburrido, o dar a entender que lo sea yo. Para mi no es aburrimiento, sino edad y madurez, y estabilidad, sí, especialmente estabilidad. Creo que todo funciona, pero el mismo miedo del que hablaba hace un instante me hace experimentar una cierta angustia, no por él, sino por mi. Es como si tuviera miedo de fallar, de no estar a la altura, de envejecer sin más. Conozco a Salvador, y sé lo que necesita, por esa razón temo no poder dárselo en un momento dado.

Pueden ser manías, recelos e inseguridades, pero lo tenía todo muy presente en las horas previas a la salida.

2

Rafael colgó el teléfono de forma airada. Más que un final de conversación fue el inicio de una explosión densa, soterrada, cargada de iras y furias. Apretó los puños y de sus labios solo fluyó una palabra, una expresión que resumía en ese instante todas sus frustraciones:

—¡Mierda!

Como si hubiera llamado a alguien, o ese alguien lo hubiera interpretado así a tenor del tono de su voz, la puerta del despacho se abrió un par de segundos después y por ella apareció la figura de un hombre especialmente bajo, con escaso cabello en la cabeza y gafas de miope. Tanto el recién aparecido como él, se quedaron mirando en silencio otro par de segundos, hasta que el primero preguntó:

—¿Y bien?

Fue el detonante para el nuevo estallido de Rafael.

—¡Que no puede pagar, y que lo siente! ¡Coño, me dice a mi que lo siente! Me ha venido con el cuento de que aunque le ponga una pistola en el pecho, no tiene salida. ¡Maldita sea! ¡Pues no haber hecho el pedido, no te digo!

Se levantó de golpe, descargando su rabia sobre la mesa en forma de puñetazo, y dando un par de pasos sin rumbo por el despacho, como un león enjaulado. El hombre de la puerta permaneció en el mismo lugar, poniendo cara de circunstancias, hasta que Rafael se detuvo frente a él y tuvo que levantar un poco los ojos para mirarle a la cara.

—¿Tenemos alguna solución, Gonzalo?

—Hablar con el banco el lunes.

—Nos van a coser a intereses. Todavía más —lamentó Rafael—. ¿Y si llamáramos a los de Capdevila y Gimpera? Tenemos esa partida de camisas que trajimos de Bali.

—Al precio de mercado no van a quererlas a estas alturas, y si bajamos más perdemos dinero. Además, son de manga larga y no da tiempo a colocarlas ahora, por eso decidimos guardarlas hasta septiembre.

—¿Me lo dices o me lo cuentas? ¡Coño, Gonzalo, que todo esto ya lo sé! ¿Y si les cortamos las mangas? Tenemos todo el fin de semana. Un par de mujeres podría hacerlo, ¿no?

No parecía muy conforme, pero miró al dueño del negocio con el respeto del empleado sumiso y consecuente con las circunstancias, que no eran las mejores. Él mismo estaba asustado ante la más que seria posibilidad de que en dos meses estuviera en el paro.

—Podría hacerse —concedió sin vencer sus reticencias—. Lo malo es que se notará demasiado, y querrán atornillarnos con el precio. Encima, las perspectivas de esas camisas para septiembre eran muy buenas y es una lástima...

—¡Pero para septiembre faltan tres meses, joder, y el dinero lo necesitamos ahora, o el maldito banco nos pondrá el pie en el cuello!

Su empleado parpadeó asustado ante el nuevo brote de violencia verbal y emocional. Bajó la cabeza, o más bien se le cayó sobre el pecho, y no dijo nada más.

Rafael comprobó la hora en su reloj de muñeca y regresó a su sillón dando largas zancadas.

Rafael

Añoro los 80. Dijeran lo que dijeran, y se piense lo que se piense, fueron buenos años, el dinero se movía rápido, existían otras agallas, y nadie dejaba de mojarse el culo porque el mismo riesgo era tan mínimo en el fondo como embriagador en esencia. Todo el mundo tenía su oportunidad y era más fácil ganar, porque se sabía a lo que se iba. En cambio ahora... que si la crisis, el paro, el miedo y todo lo demás, y a joderse. Nadie mueve un dedo, todo Dios está a la expectativa. Ni reactivación ni leches. Y así nos va.

No todo consiste en tener energía, visión del negocio, del que sea, o conocer el mercado y sus posibilidades. Te sale un cabrón, solo uno, y te jode lo mismo que si te abriera en canal. Por eso las cosas van tan mal, porque un solo imbécil es capaz de...

Maldito viernes.

Me llamo Rafael Martí, tengo cuarenta y tres años, estoy casado con Natalia y nuestra hija Gloria ha cumplido hace poco los siete de edad. Un cuadro perfecto si no fuera porque todo cuanto creé hace diez años, a base de paciencia, empuje, créditos y muchas horas abrasadas más que quemadas, puede irse al garete en menos de lo que cuesta decirlo. Y lo peor de algo así es que para el éxito te salen muchas manos, pero para el fracaso... No recuerdo haberme sentido más solo en la vida, porque esto es algo que no puedo decirle a Natalia.

Ni a Mercedes.

Encima está lo de Mercedes, ¡joder!

Sixto rompe con su santa, la deja con tres hijos, y no pasa nada. Ya tiene a Encarna, que está realmente bien, más que bien, ¡y a follar que son dos días! Pero yo...

Cuando conocí a Mercedes no pensé que las cosas pudieran llegar tan lejos. Una cana al aire y nada más. Pero no, a mi la vida se me ha de complicar, siempre, hasta las últimas consecuencias. Así ando ahora, encoñado, entre dos aguas, sin tener nada claro, y con ella presionándome hasta el punto de que...

No creo que sea justo.

Si le hubiera dicho a Natalia que me iba a alguna parte, a por género, o a cerrar una operación importante, nada habría sucedido, Mercedes hubiera estado feliz y contenta, y yo... ¿Pero cómo irme con el lío que tenía montado? El lío y la dichosa cena con el muermo de Salvador y el cabrón de Sixto, luciendo nena.

A veces todo te viene a la contra, y lo ves, pero no puedes hacer nada, y menos apartarte. La mierda acaba cogiéndote de lleno.

3

Sixto Planas pulsó el interruptor de apagado del ordenador y la pantalla se quedó oscura al instante. La misma oscuridad que trató de hacer llegar a su cerebro cuando cerró los ojos y se dejó caer hacia atrás, para relajarse unos segundos antes de ponerse en pié y dar por concluida la jornada laboral. Aunque solo fuera por un día, se largaría temprano.

Tenía que hacer.

La oscuridad duró muy poco. Escuchó unos golpecitos en la puerta de su despacho, y sin darle tiempo a decir nada, en un sentido o en otro, alguien la abrió. Él también abrió de nuevo los ojos y se encontró con la figura de Jacinto, con una expresión de cara que no le gustó nada.

No en viernes por la tarde, justo a la hora de irse.

—¿Qué pasa? —fue el primero en hablar.

Su visitante no se anduvo por las ramas. No era necesario.

—Van a darle la campaña de los preservativos a Estrada —le informó.

—¿Qué?

—El lunes. He pensado que querrías saberlo.

—Pero, ¿qué estás diciendo?

Su expresión no dejaba lugar a dudas. Simplemente no podía creerlo. La de Jacinto García tampoco dejaba lugar a dudas. Esperó, apoyado con ambas manos en la mesa, y finalmente, ante el silencio del dueño del despacho, volvió a hablar.

—Se lo he oído decir hace una hora a Peláez, en el lavabo, y me ha parecido demasiado fuerte, así que he tirado de la manta hace un minuto, con Enrich, y me lo ha cantado. Van a apostar por él.

—¡Esa campaña era mía! —gritó—. ¿Puede saberse...? ¿Y tú por qué no me lo decías hace una hora, a la primera? —se puso en pié de golpe—. A esta hora y en viernes el jefe es capaz de haberse largado.

—Ya se ha largado —le informó Jacinto—, y desde luego lo que te he dicho es confidencial, no jodas. A ver si ahora...

—¿Y de qué me sirve que sea confidencial? —protestó Sixto airado—. ¿Es que no ves de qué va esto? ¡Si le dan la campaña a ese niñato de mierda se acabó! ¡Adiós al puesto de Ruiz! ¡Mierda, mierda... mierda!

—¿Y si la fastidia? —tanteó sin seguridad Jacinto.

Sixto dejó de moverse como un perro rabioso.

—¿Fastidiarla? —rezongó—. Esa campaña es una pera en dulce, un bombón. ¿De veras crees que ese hijo de puta de Roberto Estrada va a meter la pata cuando ha estado buscando algo así desde que llegó?

—Tal vez le estén poniendo a prueba.

Era justamente lo que estaban haciendo, pero no en el sentido negativo que trataba de buscar su compañero, sino justo en el opuesto, el positivo. Y era tanto una victoria del otro como una derrota suya. El pulso se decantaba por primera vez y no le gustaba nada.

No en un momento como aquel.

Y en viernes.

Toda la rabia que sentía se condensó en su cerebro hasta producirle un peso insostenible que le obligó a sentarse de nuevo.

—Hijos de puta... —suspiró finalmente haciendo llegar su amargura al mundo en general.

Sixto

Me llamo Sixto Planas, tengo cuarenta y dos años de edad y mi vida pasa por la encrucijada por la que atraviesan muchos hombres de mediana edad en el momento en que todo, absolutamente todo, cambia de manera radical alrededor suyo.

Personal y profesionalmente estoy en mi mejor momento, o creía estarlo. A veces basta un giro, por pequeño que sea, de los acontecimientos, para que todo lo que antes estaba arriba ahora esté abajo y viceversa. Vivo una segunda juventud con Encarna, pero no puedo dejar atrás tantos años de matrimonio con Sole, y no por ella específicamente, porque sin amor... Lo digo por nuestros hijos. Esa es una carga pesada y dura. Tengo al alcance de la mano el puesto que siempre ambicioné en la empresa de publicidad donde trabajo, pero justo cuando creo estar al final del camino, y me dispongo a disfrutar del premio, aparece otro gallo en el corral. Y es un gallo de pelea. Lo sé bien porque me recuerda a mí mismo hace doce años, cuando entré en la firma y me pasé por el rodillo a aquel hombre, Estanis Gaspar, arrebatándole sus últimos sueños, antes de que se fuera por dignidad.

Me pregunto si tendré que hacer yo lo mismo.

Por dignidad.

Hace doce años no había tres millones de parados. Se podía tener dignidad, y orgullo, y amor propio, y otras cosas parecidas.

Cosas capaces de hacer que uno se sienta bien consigo mismo.

Me casé con Sole demasiado joven. La historia de siempre. Yo tenía veintiún años y ella era preciosa. Preciosa y romántica. A los dos meses de casados me anunció que estaba embarazada y ese fue el detonante. El Titanic se hundió en cuestión de horas. Nuestra vía de escape fue mucho más lenta. Un hijo de veinte años, Domingo, una hija de diecisiete, Marta, y otro hijo más, Guillermo, a contrapié, a modo de guinda, con cinco años de edad. En medio, demasiados esfuerzos, demasiadas penalidades hasta lograr la estabilidad, el éxito, el buen dinero. No me considero uno de aquellos ejecutivos agresivos de que tanto se hablaba en los 80, pero hay que ser de una pasta especial para trabajar en publicidad, hacer lo que yo hago, y estar al día, moviéndome siempre por el filo de la navaja. En mi trabajo no importa lo que hayas hecho, sino cómo funciona la última campaña, y cómo será la próxima. Cuenta tu último spot, tu nueva idea, el sí o el no de ese cliente por el que te has pasado días y noches sin pegar ojo y por el que has sacrificado tus vacaciones o lo que sea.

Sole no podía entenderlo.

Encarna sí, porque es joven, ambiciosa, actual. Ella es perfecta para mí y para mi futuro. Formamos una buena pareja.

Perfecta salvo en el caso de que suceda algo y no pueda darle lo que espera de mí, aquello que forma mi equilibrio, mi propia vida: mi trabajo y mi éxito.

Mal día un viernes para enterarte de que el nuevo gallo del corral está pisando fuerte, tanto que ya le ves la suela del zapato a punto de aplastarte, cuando no hace ni seis meses era él quien se apartaba temeroso para dejarte tomar primero el café.

El lunes iban a darle a Roberto Estrada la campaña de los preservativos Aura, una campaña agresiva, de impacto, que podía dar mucho que hablar, y con la que yo esperaba alcanzar el puesto de Nacho Ruíz cuando se retirara en unos meses.

El lunes podía ser el primer día del declive de mi vida si antes no hablaba con Marcelino Escobar, el jefe, y lo impedía. Lo que menos necesitaba ese fin de semana eran problemas, y lo que más, divertirme, no hacerme mala sangre, pasarlo bien.

Aunque fuera con Salvador, Rafael y sus mujeres.

Lo hacía por Encarna, en serio. Para que se integrara.

No sé, quizás estaba equivocado después de todo.

4

Natalia abandonó la sala de aparatos completamente empapáda, aunque no tan agotada por el trabajo como otras veces. No quería empezar la noche cansada después de haberse dado una paliza de gimnasio por la tarde. Por esa razón imaginó que ese medio kilo que le sobraba no debía de haberse esfumado. Cinco días sin ir por allí pasaban factura. Claro que no hubiera podido dejar sola a Gloria teniendo fiebre, aunque estuviese su madre, o la chica. Gloria siempre la necesitaba a ella.

Su niña.

Llegó al vestuario, abrió la taquilla, sacó la bolsa del interior y tras depositarla en el banco extrajo de ella la toalla y el jabón en gel, luego se metió en las duchas sin esperar un segundo, dejando que el agua tibia devolviera a su cuerpo el buen tono a través de la reacción inmediata. Cuando salió del baño, cinco minutos más tarde, otras dos mujeres estaban culminando su puesta en forma para el fin de semana. Las dos parecían tener prisa. Las dos hablaban en voz alta y reían.

Las dos mostraban el desparpajo de quienes se sienten jóvenes y fuertes, seguras, hasta el límite de la insolencia.

No estaban solas, pero eso les importaba poco.

—Te aseguro que va a comprarme ese anillo, como me llamo Ana.

—Dale tiempo, mujer. Ya sabías que tenía fama de difícil.

—Difícil no sé, pero es todo un caballo, y cuando ha corrido una buena carrera y ha llegado... es capaz de lo que sea. Así que este fin de semana le voy a hacer correr el Grand National.

Se echaron a reír al unísono. La morena estaba desnuda, sin ocultar la perfección de su cuerpo, sin un átomo de grasa, pechos generosos y altos, sexo rasurado, piernas delgadas y muy largas. La de cabello castaño llevaba puesto el sujetador y las bragas, pero podía equipararse en todo a su amiga, salvo por el pecho, que parecía menos abundante, a tenor de su mayor delgadez. Las dos eran exquisitamente atractivas y sensuales, de rostros exuberantes, labios armónicos, ojos grandes, piel bronceada en pleno mes de junio, manos coronadas por largas uñas.

Natalia estaba segura de que la morena era la amante de Juan de Blas, el de la Catalana.

Se vistió antes de que las dos bellezas, típicas del Iradier tanto como lo eran las esposas maduras de un buen número de ejecutivos y gerifaltes de Barcelona, terminaran de arreglarse, y se marchó del vestuario sin prestar atención a sus nuevos comentarios y bromas. Le dolían. Por más que tratara de ignorarlo, le dolían.

Siempre habría una como ellas, dispuesta a conseguir por la vía fácil lo que para una mujer normal y decente costaba toda una vida.

Siempre.

Trató de apartar el sabor amargo, próximo a la derrota, que le apareció inmediatamente en la boca, pero no lo consiguió, al llegar a la calle éste ya se había apoderado por completo de ella.

Natalia

Tenía treinta y tres años cuando di a luz a Gloria. En aquellos días, para mí, se trataba casi de mi última oportunidad para ser madre. Por ello no vacilé en engañar a Rafael, mi marido. No fue un accidente. Simplemente dejé de tomar la píldora para quedarme en estado. Si no, de qué. Rafael nunca habría dicho que sí. Además, se lo revelé cuando ya estaba de dos meses, y lo preparé a conciencia, con la cena, sus padres y los míos, una puesta en escena ejemplar. No pudo decir nada. Puso cara de póker y sonrió. Besitos y resignación. Después, aquella misma noche, las preguntas, mis lágrimas, el tanteo para ver si quería tenerlo, mi decisión final —él sabía que yo le tengo pánico a los quirófanos—, y punto.

Si no fuera por mi hija, ahora me estaría volviendo loca.

De eso hace siete años, y para cuando sucedió, ya llevaba otros siete de casada. Tengo cuarenta años y siento que todo cuanto hay a mi alrededor se está desmoronando.

Siempre habrá leonas como las de Iradier, dispuestas a todo.

El relevo de todas las santas del mundo, en el momento en que las santas naufragan y sus maridos buscan otra tabla de salvación con la que volver a sentirse jóvenes.

Recuerdo que mi madre me dijo una vez, siendo yo adolescente, que lo peor que puede tener una persona es orgullo. No la entendí. Para mi, el orgullo era un signo de identidad, una señal de casta. Años después, se lo recordé, y me insistió en ello. Me dijo que solo los flexibles llegan al fin de sus días colmados, habiendo ganado más que perdido, mientras que los orgullosos, ¡ay de ellos!, lo perdían todo en el camino. Desde luego la filosofía de mi madre era característica de las mujeres de antes, esposas solicitas, con la pierna rota y en casa. Amén. Sin embargo ahora me toca a mi decidir que es más importante, si mi orgullo o mi matrimonio.

Aun así, Rafael puede escoger por sí mismo, y hacer como Sixto.

¿Qué les pasa a los hombres en determinados momentos de su vida?

Ni siquiera sé cómo es ella, por qué ha sucedido. Yo he hecho todo lo que he podido.

Estaba tranquila, relajada, pero las dos mujeres del gimnasio me habían puesto a mil, me hicieron enfrentarme a un problema que, por el hecho de ser viernes y tener que salir a cenar, había decidido aparcar. Entonces recordé que Sixto volvería a meternos a su Encarna por las narices y eso me acabó de conmocionar.

Orgullo o matrimonio.

Todavía me molestaba que mi madre tuviera razón en algo.

Fue ella la que me dijo que no me casara con Rafael, aunque yo ya tuviese veintiséis años y me sintiera prisionera de mi soltería caduca.

5

Salvador puso el estetoscopio sobre el pecho del niño, y este se estremeció ligeramente al notar el frío contacto del metal. Le envió una mirada acusadora que él ignoró. A través del estetoscopio escuchó los sanos, sanísimos latidos de aquel joven corazón. Pese a ello, debió de poner algún tipo de cara insólita, porque escuchó la voz de la madre del pequeño, preguntando ansiosa:

—¿Qué tal, doctor?

—Fuerte como una roca, señora Elías —aseguró.

—Bueno, es que estos días, con la primavera... ya sabe. Ha estornudado varias veces y temía...

Madres con un solo hijo. Eran las peores. Las temía. Y si además eran hipocondríacas, como la señora Elías... Cuando ella tenía frío, tapaba a su hijo, y cuando ella tenía calor le quitaba la ropa. Sus hijos nunca tenían voz, más bien eran prolongaciones de sí misma. Una vez, una madre preocupada, le preguntó qué podía hacer para que su hijo no se constipara siempre y no andara tan delicado de salud, y él le contestó que lo mejor que podía hacer era darle un hermano, o dos, y por supuesto dejar que la naturaleza siguiera su curso.

Terminó la revisión, pura rutina. Hubiera podido estar más rato, montar más el número, hacerle ver a ella que se lo tomaba muy en serio, pero era viernes, tenía aún gente en la consulta y no estaba para perder el tiempo. Las revisiones trimestrales de Pablito Elías no ofrecían secreto alguno. Se preguntó quién diablos podía ser el médico de ella.

Y le compadeció.

Se estaba despidiendo de la señora Elías y de su hijo, que aún le miraba sospechosamente y sin hablar, pese al caramelo que siempre le daba, cuando sonó el teléfono. Le dio la mano a ella y regresó a su mesa, sentándose en el instante de levantar el auricular de su soporte.

—¿Sí, Gemma?

—Es su señora, doctor.

—Gracias —pulsó una tecla del aparato y cambió el tono de su voz al preguntar—: ¿Paz? ¿Qué hay?

—Solo quería recordarte que esta noche hemos quedado, y que no llegues tarde, o con el tiempo justo —escuchó la voz de su mujer.

—Tranquila, que ya me acordaba. Aún no estoy menopáusico —bromeó él.

Le pareció que ella tardaba algo en volver a hablar, pero no supo entender el motivo. Quizás Vanessa estuviera por allí, o tal vez Octavio. Paz se olvidaba de todo cuando tenía cerca a sus hijos.

—No sé cómo la gente tiene ganas de ir al médico en viernes —suspiró su esposa.

—No todos se van de fin de semana, ni tienen una segunda residencia.

—Claro —se despidió ella—. Bueno, no tardes. Hasta luego.

Se cortó la comunicación por parte de quien había llamado, pero Salvador no depositó el auricular en el teléfono. Pulsó el botón rojo señalizado con el número 1 e inmediatamente la voz de su enfermera llegó hasta él.

—¿Sí?

—¿Cuántas visitas me quedan, Gemma?

—Tres, doctor, pero uno es Vicente García. Está aquí con sus padres.

—Ah, vaya —mencionó él haciendo una mueca de resignación y pesar antes de decirle a su enfermera—: Puede hacer pasar al siguiente.

Colgó y llenó sus pulmones de aire mientras esperaba que se abriera de nuevo la puerta de su despacho. El niño de la señora Elías y los niños de todas las señoras Elías del mundo eran fuertes y sanos. Otra cosa es que, además, fueran felices.

Vicente García tenía ocho años, y era seropositivo.

El virus del sida empezaba ya a manifestársele de forma imparable.

Salvador

Hay momentos en la vida en los que, sin saber el motivo, empiezas a hacerte preguntas, a cuestionarte las cosas, a mirar hacia atrás y a tu alrededor, dudas sobre si pudo haber sido distinto, si en algún lugar del camino, habiendo tomado otra dirección, todo habría sido diferente. No creo que sea cosa de una determinada edad. No creo que los hombres, por el simple hecho de cumplir los cuarenta, entren en crisis. He conocido a hombres que la han pasado a los treinta y hombres que la han pasado a los cincuenta. Y he conocido a hombres que nunca han estado en crisis. Ni siquiera creo que sea una crisis.

Simplemente te paras y te examinas.

Yo lo estaba haciendo desde hacía unos meses, a mis cuarenta y seis años de edad, con veintitrés de casado, es decir, con la mitad de mi vida unido a Paz. Y la consecuencia más directa de ello es que en las últimas semanas empezaba a ver a mis pequeños pacientes como monstruos, vampiros devoradores de sangre y energía. Ellos y ellas siempre eran niños y niñas, siempre tenían la misma edad. Solo cambiaban las caras, pero en el fondo eran los mismos, mientras que yo, tenía diez años más, veinte años más.

—Hazte pediatra —me dijo mi viejo profesor—. Siempre hay niños.

Tenía razón.

Pero sigo sin saber por qué me hice pediatra, cuando lo que yo quería era ser cirujano, operar, salvar vidas, ser un héroe.

O quizá si lo sepa, o me engañe con ello, no sé.

Paz

Esa es la razón de mis preguntas y de mis dudas, de mis incertidumbres, y el motivo de que sea ahora es porque ahora las cosas están cambiando muy deprisa, en mi y a mi alrededor, aunque no sea un cambio vertiginoso, sino más bien situacional. El cambio de los sentidos y los sentimientos, las fuerzas y las debilidades. El cambio silencioso que llega con el terremoto de la edad. Puedo percibirlo. Me siento rutinario y recuerdo cuando, de joven, la palabra rutina me daba todos los miedos del mundo.

Examinando a Vicente García, sabiendo que su mal ya era imparable, me sentí peor de lo que jamás me había sentido en la vida, mezquino, inútil, vacío. Y fue entonces cuando pensé en Paz, en su pérdida de ilusión, y en Octavio, el hijo del que me separaba un abismo y al que no entendía, y en Vanessa, mi pequeño latido, casi lo mejor de mí mismo en estas circunstancias.

Asomándome al interior enfermo de aquel niño, fue como si me asomara a mi propio interior, lleno del cáncer de la desesperación.

No me gustó verlo, y mucho menos lo que sentí.

6

Encarna observó cómo su jefe atravesaba la oficina a buen paso, con la misma cara de vinagre de siempre, sin siquiera despedirse de ella o de las restantes secretarias de dirección repartidas por la antesala del Gran Cerebro, como llamaban ellas al núcleo en el que reinaban los dirigentes de la empresa. Nada más tragarse la puerta del departamento al hombre, se relajó y echó un vistazo a su reloj de pulsera. Faltaban menos de veinte minutos para la hora.

—Tengo unas ganas de perder de vista todo esto para siempre —suspiró.

—Y cuando lleves casada un par de años lo echarás de menos, ya verás —manifestó la mujer sentada frente a ella.

—Lo dudo.

—Bueno —su compañera se encogió de hombros—, ya me dirás —cambió el tono de su voz y la expresión de su cara, invadiéndola de misterios, para preguntar—: ¿Qué haces este fin de semana?

—No gran cosa —la respuesta de Encarna fue más bien seca—. Sixto tiene no se qué de una campaña que ha de preparar, y esta noche vamos a cenar con sus amigos y sus mujeres.

—¡Qué fuerte! —mencionó la otra—. Eso de entrar en un grupo de gente más o menos establecido y tratar de integrarte... Supongo que debían ser amigos de la ex de tu novio, ¿no?

—Ellos pasan bastante, ya te lo dije. El médico va a lo suyo y parece vivir en su mundo. Es un hombre distante. En cuanto a Rafael... ese es de los que te mira de arriba abajo y te desnuda, pero poco más. Se nota que le gustaría estar en el sitio de Sixto, ya me entiendes. Lo peor son ellas. Les cuesta digerirlo, no me tragan.

—Hija, pues vaya plan.

—¿Quieres que te diga la verdad, Amparo? No sé qué hago en medio de ellos. Pero son sus amigos, y deberé acostumbrarme, al menos por ahora. No voy a cometer el error de pedirle que corte con todo su pasado. Cuando nos casemos será otra cosa. Entonces él mismo verá que es mejor empezar de cero y formar nuestro propio entorno.

—¿Y cuándo será eso, porque al ritmo que vais...?

—¿Te crees tú que un divorcio es cosa de coser y cantar? La ex le está presionando mucho.

—Mujer, con tres hijos tú harías lo mismo.

—Yo no me casé recién destetada y me puse a parir críos a la primera, qué quieres que te diga.

Dejaron de hablar al entrar en la oficina un hombre joven, de poco más de treinta años, pero las dos siguieron su paso de reojo, hasta que él miró abiertamente en dirección a Encarna y se le aproximó. Cuando se detuvo frente a las dos mesas encaradas, actuaron con naturalidad levantando la cabeza para atenderle. El recién llegado se dirigió a ella, como si estuvieran solos.

—¿Se ha ido ya el señor Peralta, Encarna?

Sonaba a excusa, y era una excusa. El despacho de Mario daba al pasillo por el cual acababa de pasar su jefe, y él tenía que haberle visto.

—Sí, hace un minuto —respondió la mujer entrando en el juego con una sonrisa cálida—. ¿Querías algo especial?

—Puede esperar hasta el lunes, tranquila —aseguró él.

No se movió. Amparo fingió estar concentrada en su trabajo. Encarna por contra sostuvo la mirada del ejecutivo, alto, elegante, con buena imagen.

—¿Todavía vas a esquiar? —preguntó suavemente.

—No, ya no hay nieve —sonrió displicente Mario—. Mañana subiré al apartamento de Tossa. ¿Quieres venir?

Encarna hizo un mohín mitad pesaroso mitad juguetón.

—No, no puedo —dijo.

—Vamos, mujer. Sol y mar, ¿qué más quieres?

—¿Qué pasa, te ha fallado el ligue ésta semana? —le pinchó ella.

—¿Ligue? Cualquiera diría —Mario hizo un gesto de discreta seguridad—. Ya sabes que soy un buen tipo, o al menos deberías saberlo. En fin, si aceptaras una cita...

—Tengo un compromiso, lo siento —se excusó Encarna.

Mario alzó sus dos manos, plegó los labios y enmarcó las cejas. Después inició la retirada, rápida, sin llegar a insistir, sin mostrar signos de derrota, elegante. Amparo le dirigió una mirada envolvente, como tratando de decir que ella estaba libre y dispuesta. El ejecutivo pasó por encima de ese fuego apagado y levantó una mano neutra en dirección a Encarna.

—Algún día, ¿de acuerdo? —se despidió chasqueando un dedo.

—Algún día, claro —dijo ella revestida de educada cortesía.

Caminó con paso firme y decidido en dirección a la puerta, y en el instante en que salió por ella, Amparo casi se abalanzó sobre la mesa.

—¡Eres una coqueta! —estalló sonriendo y fingiendo estar escandalizada—. Ya sé que no puedes evitarlo, pero... ¡Es que no paras, hija!

—No soy coqueta —le reprochó Encarna—: soy educada.

—¡Ya, y yo una monja de clausura! ¡Si en cuanto ha entrado le has echado la red, aunque venía a por ti, claro, que no me chupo el dedo!

—Bueno, ¿y qué? —Encarna irradiaba cierto orgullo y seguridad—. Me encanta jugar un poco, y ver lo que veo en sus ojos. Cuando me case se habrá acabado todo, ¿no? Pues para lo que me queda...

—Un día tendrás un disgusto —manifestó Amparo.

—No seas tonta —rezongó su compañera—. Todo el mundo va a lo que va, que es lo mismo. Y nunca pasa nada. ¿Qué quieres que pase? ¡Tú, que eres una dramática y te van los melodramas y todo ese rollo! ¿Por qué no te diviertes un poco, sin problemas, sin manías?

Amparo, con los ojos abiertos como platos, iba a responder con airada quietud, para hurtar sus palabras a las demás secretarias, pero en ese momento sonó el teléfono en su mesa y ya no pudo hacerlo.

Encarna se levantó para ir al lavabo.

Encarna

No soy coqueta, nunca lo he sido, pero me gusta gustar, me encanta ser mirada y admirada, disfruto sintiendo lo que siento cuando entro en un lugar y una docena de rostros se mueve en mi dirección. Y cuando digo rostros, hablo igual de hombres que de mujeres, aunque preferentemente sean ellos los que se agiten a mi paso.

Soy consciente de mis limitaciones. No soy una belleza, pero me cuido, trato de vestir bien, de ir a la moda y de resultar sexy sin parecer agresiva, sin pasarme. Mi única concesión en este sentido es el rubio de mi cabello, que no es natural, pero me encanta.

¿Qué más puedo decir?

Sí, tal vez que suelo ser una persona animada, feliz, despreocupada, a la que gusta pasárselo bien y que suele arrastrar a los demás a hacer lo mismo. Pero eso no es malo. Simplemente creo que se trata de estar viva o estar muerta, y yo me siento viva, muy viva.

La vida pasa muy rápido, y va dejando huellas, aunque finjas ignorarlas.

Cuando conocí a Sixto todo fue uno de tantos juegos, pero de la misma forma que hay partidas que se hacen muy largas, la nuestra fue tan breve como intensa. Después de lo de Quique no me creía capaz de volver a enamorarme, y me equivoqué. En parte porque Sixto era parecido a Quique, la misma fuerza, la misma convicción, el mismo desparpajo ante la vida. Con Quique viví cuatro años sin esperanzas, y lo sabía. Con Sixto es distinto, porque fue él quien me habló de otra vida, de casarnos, de empezar partiendo de cero, que es lo que más necesito. Lo mismo que él.

Es cuestión de paciencia. Vivimos juntos, ha roto con su mujer a pesar de los hijos, y todavía navega entre las dos aguas de su pasado y su futuro. Trato de no presionarle, no empujarle en ninguna dirección. Necesita encontrarse a sí mismo. Por esa razón aceptaba salidas como la de esa noche, con sus amigos y sus mujeres, porque para él era importante la sensación de naturalidad, como si no pasara nada. Necesitaba tiempo.

El tiempo dicen que todo lo cura, aunque no estoy del todo segura. A veces aún pienso en Quique y en lo que pudo ser.

A veces...

Me llamo Encarna Cuxart y tengo veintinueve años.

A veces es necesario aferrarse a todo para sentir la vida.

7

Iba a colgar, al comprobar que nadie descolgaba el teléfono al otro lado, cuando una voz irrumpió en la línea en tono desabrido.

—¿Sí? —escuchó el asomo de grito.

—¿Paco? Creía que ya no había nadie. Soy Rafael, ¿está Roque?

—¿A estas horas? Es viernes, hombre. Me pillas a mi porque tengo un lío de mil pares de demonios, como siempre, y a este paso, con plastas como tú llamando a cada momento, me dan las doce. ¿Qué quieres?

—Hablar con Roque, ¿qué va a ser? ¿Donde puedo encontrarle?

—¿Estás de broma? Roque se ha largado a media mañana.

—¿Adónde?

—¿Y yo que sé? —el tono aumentó en hastío—. Llámale el lunes.

—Oye, que es urgente —trató de insistir Rafael.

—¿Para él o para ti?

—¡Joder, es urgente para los dos! Hay una...

—Rafa, tío —le interrumpió Paco—, no me lo cuentes. No puedo hacer nada, y Roque no está, ¿vale? ¿Qué quieres que te diga?

Podía decirle que tenía aquel puesto gracias a él, pero prefirió callarse. Podía decirle la verdad, pero optó por lo mismo. En lugar de eso escogió la calma. No hay nada peor en el negocio, en cualquier negocio, que dar señas de pánico. Todo el mundo detecta el pánico, y este, además, se extiende como una mancha de aceite.

—Está bien, de acuerdo —le restó importancia al tema aunque sin lograrlo del todo—, pero si te llama dile que le estoy buscando, que me localice en mi casa a la hora que sea.

—Bien, hombre, bien.

—Gracias, Paco.

No supo si el otro le había oído, porque la línea se interrumpió casi al unísono. Entre volver a colgar el auricular dejándose llevar por la ira y hacerlo con suavidad, esta vez se inclinó por lo segundo. Como siguiera dándole golpes lo rompería y sería peor. ¿Cuántos llevaba en la última media hora?

Se echó hacia atrás, y el silencio de su entorno le hizo aún más daño que el fracaso de sus más recientes gestiones. Todos se habían ido, solo quedaba él. Recordó el símil del capitán que se hunde con el barco y lo encontró adecuado.

Aunque no quiso ceder al desánimo. Él no.

Entonces se acodó de nuevo sobre la mesa, descolgó el auricular una vez más, y empezó a marcar un número.

No llegó a pulsar los siete dígitos. Se detuvo en el quinto.

Fue justo al pasear su acorralada mirada por encima de la mesa y encontrarse con la fotografía de Natalia y de su hija Gloria, abierta como una ventana sobre el ángulo opuesto de su mesa.

Mercedes desapareció de su mente barrida por un silencioso viento, de forma tan súbita como se le había aparecido al desear estar lejos de allí y de la tormenta que tenía en la cabeza.

Se quedó sin fuerzas y tras depositar el auricular sobre los huecos del aparato volvió a echarse hacia atrás y esta vez cerró los ojos.

8

Dejó la plancha caliente en el receptáculo metálico de la tabla para darle la vuelta al vestido cuando su hijo Octavio apareció ante ella, surgiendo de la nada, porque salvo cuando oía música, siempre era tan silencioso como una puesta de sol en mitad de un océano quieto. Ya no retomó la plancha.

—Mamá, ¿me das el dinero del fin de semana?

El gesto de Paz fue de contenido cansancio. Primero, los hombros descendieron unos milímetros por debajo de su posición natural; segundo, su rostro se llenó de cenizas indisimuladas; tercero, sus ojos se apagaron levemente, por espacio de unos breves instantes, hasta volver a centrarlos en él, revestidos de agotada determinación.

—Octavio, por favor...

—¿Qué pasa? —se extrañó el muchacho.

—Sabes muy bien lo que pasa —manifestó su madre dolorida—. Y luego me las cargo yo. Así que vas a esperar a tu padre, ¿de acuerdo?

—¿Esperar a papá? ¿Y si llega a las tantas? ¡Mamá, que me están esperando!

—Tu padre vendrá temprano, tenemos una cena.

—Es que... —trató de insistir Octavio.

—No voy a darte el dinero, hijo —le detuvo ella—, y si llegas tarde, llegas tarde. Llama que para eso está el teléfono. No quiero volver a disgustarme con tu padre, ¿entiendes? Y además, esta vez tiene razón —le miró como si lamentara tener que decirle esto—. No te ve en todo el fin de semana, porque de día duermes y pasas toda la noche fuera, así que no vas a irte ahora. Te esperas, hablas con él, te da la paga y en paz.

—¡Jo, mamá, no me vengas con rollos!

—Jo, Octavio, lo mismo te digo, ¿vale?

Se quedaron mirando frente a frente, ella con su vestido a medio planchar entre las manos, él con su vieja cazadora por encima de una camiseta en otro tiempo probablemente nueva, unos vaqueros ajustados y sucios y unas botas ennegrecidas por su uso continuado y sin descanso desde que salieron de la zapatería. Con el cabello largo, por encima de los hombros y hasta media espalda por detrás, la incipiente pelusa de la barba sin afeitar, el rostro enteco y su más de metro setenta de extrema delgadez, el aspecto de Octavio era más bien indefinible. En la calle tal vez pareciera un "colega" más. Allí en cambio daba la impresión de haber sido atropellado por un camión hacía menos de diez segundos.

No hubo más intercambio de palabras inútiles.

Su hijo dio media vuelta, en silencio, como siempre, y aún antes de que ella volviera a tomar la plancha para continuar su labor, de su habitación emergió el torrente sonoro de las primeras notas de un agresivo tema tan cargado de adrenalina como solían ser todos los suyos.

Rock duro lo llamaban.

9

En el momento de entrar Natalia por la puerta de su casa, un torbellino en forma de niña salió de alguna parte y, trotando a lo largo del pasillo, se le echó encima de un salto.

—¡Mamá!

Abrazó a Gloria, con intensidad, antes de preguntarle inmediatamente:

—¿Cómo te encuentras, cariño?

—¿Otra vez? —la niña puso cara de fastidio supremo—. Ya te lo he dicho, ¡bien! Tan bien como a mediodía, y como ésta mañana.

—Bueno, parece que ya pasó, ¿verdad? De todas formas el lunes te llevaré al médico. No te irán mal unas vitaminas.

—¡Ecs! —Gloria reflejó todo su asco haciendo una mueca dramática—. ¿Más vitaminas? ¡Pero si no las necesito!

—Estás muy desganada últimamente, y claro, te pones enferma. Eso es debilidad.

Habían llegado a la sala-comedor, grande y espaciosa, profusamente ornamentada, sin que la recién llegada hubiera podido dejar la bolsa del gimnasio. En el momento de depositarla en el suelo apareció una mujer relativamente joven, apenas la treintena, surgiendo de la puerta más próxima a su derecha. Ya iba vestida para salir a la calle, con un liviano jersey por encima de los hombros y un bolso negro, barato, colgado del brazo doblado sobre el pecho.

—¿Ya se va, Margarita?

—Señora, ¿podría...?

Gloria tiraba de su madre, arrastrándola hacia su habitación. Tuvo que detener el empuje de su hija de forma terminante.

—¡Gloria, por favor, un momento!

—¡Vale! —protestó de nuevo la pequeña haciendo un gesto de resignación y soltándose de su mano.

—¿Qué quiere, Margarita? —se interesó Natalia.

—Verá, señora... —vaciló inicialmente, como si tuviera miedo de seguir hablando, aunque al momento arrancó de forma decidida—. Sabe que vengo aquí tres días a la semana, y que tengo otra casa para los otros dos, pero ahora... en fin, que en esa otra casa quieren que cambie, que vaya allí tres días, y con el cambio gano más dinero, ¿entiende? Yo aquí estoy bien, ya lo sabe, pero necesito ese dinero porque en casa... bueno, usted ya sabe. Solo que usted me iguale lo que me dan, yo me quedo y les digo que no puede ser, pero si no es así...

Era algo inesperado, y en aquel momento demasiado incómodo para ella, con tantas cosas más urgentes en la cabeza. Buscó la forma de mantener la calma, de congelar la situación.

—No puedo decirle nada, Margarita, al menos ahora. Hablaré con mi marido, por supuesto. ¿Cuándo necesita una respuesta?

—Cuanto antes. Como va a llegar el verano y las vacaciones y todo eso... La semana próxima si fuera posible...

Gloria se había ido a su habitación. Estaban solas. Natalia no tuvo más que asentir con la cabeza, en silencio, casi con resignación, para que su asistenta no insistiera más acerca del tema. Eso fue suficiente. Ni siquiera hablaron de dinero. Margarita farfulló unas palabras de despedida, bastante cortada por lo que tal vez sintiera como un chantaje o una excesiva intromisión, y acabó retirándose en dirección al recibidor. Lo último que las dos mujeres intercambiaron fue un sucinto "hasta el lunes" que sonó como un eco doble. Apenas diez segundos después la puerta del piso se cerró tras Margarita.

Natalia aún tardó otros diez antes de fruncir el ceño con preocupación.

Llegaba el verano, sí, y con él su intención tal vez no tuviera sentido, o la tuviera del todo. No era una decisión fácil. Ni cómoda. Lo cómodo sería esperar, callar, tener atada a Margarita y muchas otras cosas, y en septiembre...

Se sorprendió de su aparente frialdad.

¿Acaso no le importaba?

No pudo plantearse el tema a fondo, buceando en el interior de su alma. Gloria reapareció en ese instante y la paz quedó borrada por la siempre temible vitalidad de su hija.

—¡Oh, mamá! ¿Qué haces? —gritó enfadada la niña—. ¡Te estaba esperando en mi habitación! ¡Vamos, ven!

Y se llevó a su madre tirando de ella con todas sus fuerzas.

10

Sixto insistió más por rebeldía que por la convicción de un posible éxito, y marcó por enésima vez el número de teléfono de Marcelino Escobar, su jefe. El hecho de que no hubiera dejado puesto el automático le daba ciertas esperanzas de que todavía pasara por casa antes de salir. En esta ocasión cruzó los dedos y se animó a si mismo murmurando un alentador:

—Vamos, ¡vamos!, cógelo maldito cabrón.

No tuvo fortuna. Dejó que el zumbido sonara una docena de veces al otro lado y acabó colgando con fría contención. Tras hacerlo comprobó la hora en su Rolex.

No tenía sentido que siguiera allí, perdiendo el tiempo. Cuanto antes se marchara, antes podría intentarlo por última vez desde casa. Y estaba lo de la cena. No quería llegar tarde, por Encarna. Lo que más necesitaban era naturalidad, normalidad. Aunque de poder cancelar la cena, o al menos su presencia y la de Encarna en ella, lo habría hecho. No estaba de humor.

Bien, tal vez se tratara de eso, de recuperarlo cenando con los amigos, hablando, pasando un poco del imbécil de su jefe, la campaña y Roberto Estrada.

Se levantó de su butaca, decidido, y recogió la chaqueta, que se había quitado al quedarse solo en el despacho y en la empresa. Se la puso, cuidando los detalles de su apariencia física a través del reflejo de la imagen que le daba el cuadro de una de sus campañas colgado de la pared, y finalmente salió de allí caminando a buen paso. El vigilante de la oficina, en recepción, fue la única alma viva que halló a su paso.

—Adiós, Fermín —le deseó.

—Buen fin de semana, señor Planas —le correspondió el hombre.

Buen tipo, Fermín. Leal, considerado, silencioso. Cuando Encarna iba a verle al despacho fuera de horas, al comienzo de sus relaciones, siempre actuaba como un verdadero amigo, y no era por la propina que a veces le caía o el regalo de Navidad. Hay buenas y malas personas, y Fermín pertenecía a la primera categoría.

El ascensor le llevó directamente al parking, vacío en el sector destinado a su empresa salvo por su automóvil. Sacó las llaves y accionó el dispositivo de apertura a distancia desde unos diez metros. Los cuatro pilotos del vehículo se iluminaron un par de veces, saludándole al acercarse. Tuvo tiempo de mirar la forma agresiva y mágica del BMW, otra de sus señas de identidad preferidas, aunque daría lo que fuera por tener algo más, el coche de sus sueños, un Porsche.

La campaña de Aura quizá se lo hubiera proporcionado.

Cuando se introdujo en él no lo puso en marcha de inmediato.

Toda su rabia emergió, sorda, densa, agarrotándole los movimientos y produciéndole la misma sensación que la de estar en un trampolín gigante de saltos de esquí, a punto de echar a rodar hacia abajo.

Y sin esquíes.

11

Despidió a la última madre, con su niña de cara pecosa, en la puerta de la consulta, mientras Gemma permanecía discretamente a dos pasos de ellos, manos unidas, sonrisa de ternura, rostro envuelto en colores, como parte inmóvil de la escena. Cuando la puerta se cerró y quedaron solos, ella no perdió ni un ápice de su actitud. Él sí. Dejó de parecer feliz y su cara se trastocó por completo, exteriorizando el cansancio que sentía, el peso de un malestar inexplicable pero que avanzaba desde dentro hacia afuera por todos los conductos de su ser.

—Se acabó —dijo Salvador.

—Parece cansado, doctor.

—Lo estoy, Gemma, para que voy a engañarla. Yo también tendría que ir al médico para que me recetara vitaminas, como hacen todas las madres de hoy. ¡Dios! —se burló—. Nunca he visto niños y niñas más sanos, por lo menos en su mayoría, y todas las madres empeñadas en que necesitan vitaminas. Es una epidemia.

—Pero son tan ricos, ¿verdad doctor? —manifestó la enfermera refiriéndose a los pacientes de la consulta.

Se la quedó mirando, y entonces pensó algo tan evidente, que la simple realidad del descubrimiento le dio de lleno en el centro de su ánimo.

Pasaba mucho más tiempo con Gemma en la consulta que con Paz en casa, y aunque llevara veintitrés años casado, los quince en los que su enfermera había estado allí, codo con codo con él, probablemente sumaban más horas de compañía y contacto que los primeros.

Y lo ignoraba todo de ella, salvo que era soltera, eficiente, discreta, callada, tierna con los niños y las niñas, y una amiga para todas las madres.

Un mundo aparte que compartía sin saber nada de él.

—¿Qué va a hacer este fin de semana, Gemma? —se oyó preguntar inesperadamente.

La mujer también acusó la sorpresa, aunque de forma apenas imperceptible. Solo fue un destello en sus ojos. Los dos sabían que era la primera vez que el médico le formulaba una pregunta así, por asombroso que pareciera. La primera vez en quince años.

—Oh, nada especial —se encogió de hombros—. Me quedaré en casa, me pondré unas zapatillas, y me dedicaré a limpiar, ver la tele, leer... Un fin de semana tranquilo.

Como el suyo, salvo por la cena de esa noche. Tranquilo. Con Paz a su lado, Octavio durmiendo y Vanessa estudiando. Un mundo de silencios en el que siempre había creído vivir a gusto.

¿Cuánto hacía que Paz y él...?

¿Tendría novio Gemma? ¿Lo habría tenido alguna vez?

¿Era soltera por vocación? ¿Qué clase de aventuras podía haber tenido a lo largo de su vida? ¿Y su edad? ¿Qué edad tenía Gemma, treinta y cinco, treinta y siete? Sí, la empleó con veintidós, cuando era una tímida muchacha recién salida del aprobado final. Paz le había dicho que sería buena, tal vez porque ya entonces Gemma era un modelo de discreciones y silencios.

¿Haría el amor Gemma con sus amigos?

¿Y si aún era virgen?

Se le antojó absurdo, pero curioso. Ni siquiera sabía por qué todo aquello aparecía en un momento como aquel, y en una simple fracción de segundo, ¿o era más? Los dos seguían mirándose como si cada cual esperara algo del otro.

—Váyase, doctor Marcos —dijo la enfermera—. Yo cerraré la consulta.

Doctor Marcos.

Quince años después aún le llamaba doctor Marcos. Y no era culpa de ella, sino de él.

12

El timbre del teléfono, que escuchó al abrir la puerta del pequeño apartamento, la hizo correr hacia el aparato y descolgarlo con urgencia. Aún antes de que pudiera preguntar quien llamaba, escuchó la voz de su madre, tan habitual como siempre.

—¿Encarna? Hija, ¿eres tú? ¿Encarna?

—Sí, mamá, soy yo —jadeó ella recuperándose de la breve carrera—. Es que acabo de llegar a casa, déjame respirar.

—Vaya horas —protestó la mujer—. ¿No tenías una cena?

—Mamá, trabajo, ¿sabes?

—Ya, y no tienes tiempo para nada. Si estuvieras aquí, ahora lo tendrías todo listo, y tú, como una rosa.

Nunca perdía la oportunidad. Ni en los cuatro años que vivió con Quique, ni ahora, a pesar de que la idea de que iba a casarse, parecía tranquilizarla un poco más. Claro que su madre todavía lo dudaba. Siempre había estado llena de dudas, aún en vida de su padre.

¿Por qué no habrían tenido más hijos? Ahora no dependería tanto de ella, aunque lo que más la aterraba era el futuro, cuando su madre se hiciera realmente mayor y mucho más insoportable.

—¿Qué quieres, mamá? —quiso saber Encarna.

—Nada, saber si vendrás a comer el domingo.

—¿He dejado de venir algún domingo sin avisarte antes?

—¿Te hago algo especial? —preguntó la mujer dando la impresión, como siempre, de estar manteniendo su propia conversación al margen de las respuestas de la otra parte.

—No, lo que quieras.

Nunca preguntaba por Sixto. Jamás le pedía que le llevase a comer. Ella tampoco trataba de imponer nada. Todo a su tiempo. Y hablando de tiempo, si no la detenía antes de que cogiera carrerilla, después sería mucho peor. Le hablaría de sus hermanas, y de las hijas de sus hermanas, todas casualmente casadas, y con hijos maravillosos.

—¿Qué vas a ponerte esta noche? —y sin esperar respuesta continuó—: Yo que tú, me pondría el vestido azul. Es elegante y discreto. Piensa que para esas dos señoras, tu eres la otra, así que...

Cualquiera menos el azul. Le echaba años encima, era aburrido, insípido. Y al diablo con ellas. Quería lucir sus encantos, que los tenía. Fuera como fuera, ellas siempre la verían como a "la otra", como decía su madre.

—Vale, mamá. Ya te contaré el domingo, ¿eh?

—Sí, el domingo. ¡Uy la de cosas que me cuentas tú! —rezongó su madre tan hiriente como de costumbre—. Matildita sí que le cuenta todo a su madre, porque dice que es su mejor amiga, pero tú... Si no fuera por...

—Mamá —la detuvo—, he de colgar.

—Pero hija, si no...

—Ha llegado Sixto —mintió—, y tenemos el tiempo justo.

Fue suficiente. A su madre solo le faltaba hacer el signo de la cruz cada vez que lo mentaba, lo mismo que hizo con Quique durante cuatro años. Otra cosa sería cuando fueran marido y mujer, legales. Otra cosa.

La despedida fue rápida. Tanto como tensa.

13

Gloria jugaba en su habitación, tras la breve sesión de relaciones materno filiales impuesta por la ansiedad de la pequeña cada vez que ella regresaba a casa de dónde fuera. Natalia empezó a desnudarse en la suya, para quitarse la ropa con la que había ido al gimnasio. Se quedó completamente desnuda y entonces se miró a sí misma en el espejo del armario, poniéndose tanto de frente como de perfil. Trabajo le costaba mantenerse en forma, pero aun así... el decaimiento de los senos empezaba a ser evidente, y la formación de las bolsas en las caderas, y la flacidez de muslos y antebrazos, mientras que el abdomen... En un par de años necesitaría una liposucción, y ya, de paso, un lifting en la cara.

Si tomaba aquella decisión ¿lo haría antes o después de verano? quería ser una mujer nueva, aunque no pensara en...

¿O sí? Mónica se había separado de su marido con cuarenta y siete años y los dos se habían vuelto a casar.

Claro que Mónica era mucha Mónica.

Apartó los ojos del cuerpo reflejado en el espejo y fingió no darle importancia a nada. Cogió la bata de la cama y se cubrió con ella. Sin embargo le dio la espalda a la idea de empezar a maquillarse para que luego no le viniera con sus habituales prisas Rafael. Sentía una extraña lasitud. Salió de la habitación y deambuló por la casa hasta detenerse en la sala. Paseó una distraída mirada por ella que se detuvo en las dos docenas de fotografías repartidas por encima del piano. Nadie tocaba el piano, aunque mantenía su ilusión de que Gloria, un día, se decidiera. Pero era un hermoso objeto decorativo. Quedaba muy bien en aquel rincón, y aportaba solemnidad y dignidad al conjunto. Los portarretratos de todos los tamaños y de todas las clases, formaban una alfombra de imágenes sobre la regia madera.

Se paró frente a ellos, y paseó sus ojos por aquellas dos docenas de segundos capturados a las vidas de cuantos allí estaban, preferentemente Rafael y ella, y más aún Gloria pese a su corta edad, y luego su madre y su padre, y la madre y el padre de Rafael, y su hermana, su prima, su...

Rafael y ella el día de la boda, y durante aquel fin de semana en Andorra, y en las vacaciones de dos años atrás, en Cancún, y con Gloria, más y más con Gloria, en cada uno de sus siete cumpleaños, y en la piscina, y en el día de Reyes, y con sus abuelos. Si no fuera por ella.

Cogió la fotografía del día de la boda, cuando tanto ella como él parecían dispuestos a comerse el mundo. Bastaba con ver su sonrisa, y los ojos desafiantes de Rafael. No se sentía especialmente nostálgica, ni sentimental, pero sí indiferente, como si la de la foto fuera otra persona. Y era esa indiferencia la que más la asustaba ahora. Algunas mujeres cogían al marido y le ponían firmes, algunas más callaban y esperaban, dejando que la naturaleza siguiera su curso, sabiendo que tenían ganada la batalla de los hijos y la honorabilidad, y otras optaban por lo más directo, sintiéndose heridas y rebelándose como un gato panza arriba. En su caso parecía vivir un paréntesis.

¿Por qué no podía sentir, llorar?

Se esforzó en hacerlo, buscó un dolor interior capaz de arrastrarla, pero lo único que consiguió fue agitar su respiración y sentirse ridícula.

Eso la decidió a dar la espalda a los recuerdos y regresar a su habitación para empezar a pensar en la dichosa cena y en qué ponerse.

Natalia

Hay cosas que no pueden explicarse, por más que se intente. A veces miraba a Salvador y a Paz, y sentía envidia. Sabía que ellos llegarían a viejos juntos, estables, en equilibrio permanente. Por la misma razón siempre había sabido que Sixto y Sole acabarían separándose. Ella es emotiva, sentimental, con ese sentido dramático de la vida que la hace vulnerable, y él... demasiado depredador, demasiado pagado de sí mismo, demasiado ambicioso a medida que el éxito profesional le había ido afianzando en la vida. Al comienzo no era así, pero luego... Sole me decía a veces que el mundo de la publicidad era una selva, cuando aún le defendía. Yo le contestaba que no conocía el de Rafael.

Creo que ni yo misma conozco el mundo de mi marido.

Mirando aquellas fotografías, me daba cuenta de que lo peor de la vida es ver el pasado desde la perspectiva del presente, sin entender por qué ha sido así, y preguntándote si pudo haber sido de otra forma. Algunos lo llaman dudas, otros análisis. Yo pienso que es inseguridad.

Y si es así, el mundo está lleno de inseguros e inseguras.

Cuando Sole me contó que se separaba de Sixto, y tuve que consolarla y todo eso, reconozco que no sentí pena ni rabia, solo asombro, tanto como incertidumbre, porque inmediatamente pensé en mí misma, en lo que haría si eso me sucedía a mí. Supongo que fue una reacción natural. Es igual que cuando una amiga te dice que tiene cáncer de mamá y tú recuerdas que has encontrado un bulto en tu pecho. Lo de la amiga te duele, pero tras el dolor aparece el miedo e inevitablemente acabas pensando en ti. Encima, lo ves claro, y te dices que, en el fondo, ya lo veías venir.

Sole era mi amiga, es mi amiga, y nunca se me ocurrió decirle que lo veía venir.

¿Cuántas de mis amigas pensarán que ya lo veían venir en mi caso?

¿Tendrá alguna la certeza que confirme mis sospechas?

Trataba de ser fuerte, de mostrarme entera, y especialmente de ser digna, pero pensar en la tal Encarna durante la cena, y en Sixto, radiante y feliz, como si no pasara nada, y en Rafael, exactamente lo mismo cuando a lo peor habría querido estar con su amante, o lío, o lo que sea...

Tenía ganas de estar muy guapa. Así que empecé a aplicarme a ello.

14

—Paz, ¿puedo decirte algo en confianza?

—Por supuesto, Sole, ¿qué sucede?

—He encontrado un preservativo en el bolso de Marta.

Lo dijo como si hubiera anunciado el comienzo de la Tercera Guerra Mundial, soltándolo igual que una bomba silenciosa. La espera que siguió a sus palabras dotó de mayor dramatismo a su tono de voz.

—Bueno, ¿y qué? —dijo finalmente Paz—. Tiene diecisiete años.

—Pero, ¿qué dices? —no era escándalo, solo horror—. ¡Si lleva un trasto de esos significa que lo hace, y ni siquiera sé con quién sale! ¡Nunca cuentan nada!

—¿Te preocupa que lo haga o que no sepas con quién?

—¡Hay, hija, a veces eres tan frívola!

—¿Yo? —Paz tuvo ganas de reír. Si no lo hizo fue en consideración a lo mal que lo estaba pasando su amiga, magnificando todos los detalles que sentía como negativos en su vida—. Prefiero que mi hijo, si lo hace, que seguro que sí con dieciocho años, tome precauciones, a que pueda pillar el sida.

—Desde luego —suspiró Sole—. Antes solo teníamos miedo de quedar embarazadas, y ahora... ¡Pero de todas formas me he sentido fatal!

En otras circunstancias le hubiera dicho que se sentía vieja, como ella misma, porque los hijos ya andaban en cosas mayores. Pero no en estas, así que calló. Tampoco le preguntó qué estaba haciendo con el bolso de su hija. Estaba segura de que Sole era de las que registraba las habitaciones de sus hijos. La conocía bien.

—Habla con ella, mujer —le insinuó Paz.

—¡Ya, que no sabes tú, casi tan bien como yo, cómo es Marta, y más ahora! Es la que lo lleva fatal. Ya sabes lo unida que estaba a su padre. Se siente muy herida. Traicionada, ¿entiendes?

Salía el tema de la separación, una vez más, como siempre a pesar de las semanas transcurridas. De todas formas era inevitable.

—Sole, escucha, yo precisamente te había telefoneado para decirte algo importante.

—¿Que es?

—Esta noche cenamos con Sixto y con ella.

Hubiera podido ser más comedida y delicada, pero de cualquier manera era absurdo. Y quería decírselo, para sentirse más tranquila. El silencio al otro lado del hilo telefónico la hizo volver a hablar.

—Lo siento, Sole, fue algo que me pilló de improviso, y lo mismo a Natalia —dijo sabiendo que no era más que una excusa.

—Claro, claro —la respuesta fue un murmullo.

—No quiero que pienses que todo será como antes, solo que con ella en tu lugar. Por parte de Sixto estoy segura que trata de que sea así, pero por parte nuestra... Que no, vamos, que no. Seguro que será una velada difícil. Yo ni siquiera sé de qué hablar con esa chica o qué decirle.

El nuevo silencio fue más ominoso que el anterior.

—Sole, ¿estás bien? —preguntó Paz.

—A veces me siento tan sola, tan desesperada, que sé que si volviera... le perdonaría.

—¿Estás loca? ¿Después de lo que te ha hecho? ¡Ya no se trata de esto, sino de todo lo de antes! ¡Sole, por Dios!

Demasiado tarde.

Precedida por una soterrada carga de dolor, que pudo percibir a través del auricular, supo que su amiga estaba llorando.

Paz

No sé que hubiera hecho en lugar de Sole. No sé como habría reaccionado, pensando tanto en mí misma como en mis hijos, máxime cuando ella tenía uno de cinco años de edad, pero su sumisión... me hacía rebelarme, sentirme feminista y encima radical. ¿Perdonarle? Sixto había ido a lo fácil, así de simple. Y en cuanto a ella, a "la nueva", seguía preguntándome cómo podía una mujer joven enamorarse de un hombre mayor, casado y con tres hijos. Y si eso ya no era ninguna maravilla, menos cabía considerarle una maravilla a él, aunque Sixto siempre hubiera ido por la vida de guapo y seductor, de hombre seguro avalado por el éxito de sus últimos años como publicista.

El éxito, tal vez la clave fuera esa.

En momentos así, mi idea de que mi existencia fuera aburrida y monótona, se me presentaba como todo lo contrario, una bendición, algo capaz de desterrar mi miedo, convertir la menopausia en un hecho natural y hacerme ver que esa estabilidad de la que me siento orgullosa es el pasaporte de la felicidad matrimonial, si se entiende como felicidad matrimonial poder alcanzar el tiempo y la edad en que solo importa mirar hacia adelante con esperanza y hacia atrás con el orgullo de haber hecho las cosas bien, o lo mejor posible en cualquier caso. Salvador y yo teníamos algo. Pero, ¿cómo se le dice eso a la amiga que ha visto hundir todas sus secretas esperanzas? Una cosa así ni siquiera podía decírsela a Natalia.

Ella también era distinta, y últimamente, hasta luchaba, de una forma tal vez patética, quizás ridícula, contra el tiempo, contra sí misma, contra la inevitable progresión del tiempo.

En el fondo, éramos tan distintos... Creo que me di cuenta en ese momento, cuando Salvador aún no había llegado y yo ya estaba preparada para salir, nada más acabar de hablar con Sole. Tan distintos que no me entraba en la cabeza qué podía unirnos ya. En otro tiempo ellos habían sido amigos, pero ahora... ¿qué clase de nexo mantenía a mi marido con Rafael o con Sixto? ¿O a mi o a Natalia con ellos? Natalia y yo sí éramos amigas, no íntimas, pero sí amigas, como con Sole. Salvo eso, ya no había nada.

Y cuando Sixto se casara con Encarna, si era verdad que lo hacía, desde luego sería el fin. Si ellos no se daban cuenta, Natalia y yo sí lo haríamos.

Probablemente ni tan solo hiciera falta esperar a que se casaran.

Después de la cena de esa noche...

Puede que, después de todo, lo que pasó fuese una consecuencia de esas crispaciones.

No creo en las casualidades.

15

Rafael había hecho la última llamada casi diez minutos antes, también infructuosa, pero seguía en su despacho, buscando una salida, o intentando imaginar una estrategia para salir del atolladero el lunes por la mañana, a primera hora, antes de que tuviera que ir al banco con las manos vacías y la cola entre las piernas. Menudos eran los banqueros. Todas las sonrisas, palmadas en la espalda y reverencias del comienzo, se tornarían caras largas, muestras de pesar y palabras de sentido abatimiento, mientras le preparaban el ataúd. Para los bancos no existían "mañanas" ni tan siquiera "en unas horas". El dinero era su sangre. Sin dinero se les ponía el corazón negro, aunque se tratase de una minúscula gota en su incesante fluir.

Y no había salidas, lo sabía, salvo que hiciera una operación fulminante, con dinero fácil pero a la baja, o sucediera un milagro. El lunes en una hora debía dar con la clave, o probablemente sería como echar la primera palada de tierra en la tumba de sus sueños.

Odió el fin de semana.

Y esta vez se sorprendió de que, al pensar en Mercedes, ella se materializara allí delante, como por arte de magia.

—¿Qué estás...?

—La puerta estaba abierta. Ni siquiera sabía si te encontraría.

—¿Por qué no has llamado?

—¿Quién lleva más de una hora comunicando?

El tono no era pacífico, ni su rostro agradable pese a su belleza natural, inmaculada. Tenía los brazos cruzados sobre el pecho, el desafío tintando de rojos la mirada y la nube de tormenta diseminando sombras por todo su cuerpo envarado. Vestía informalmente, pero aun así estaba atractiva, con el cabello revuelto y la sensación de haber salido de un anuncio de la tele.

—Lo siento, cariño —él se levantó, pero cuando trató de abrazarla y besarla ella se le escabulló de entre las manos.

—¿Lo has arreglado? —quiso saber.

—¿Cómo querías que lo hiciera? —lamentó Rafael con cansancio—. Es una de esas estúpidas salidas de matrimonios.

—Y en viernes, claro.

—¡Todos trabajan, coño! ¡La gente suele salir a cenar los viernes!

—Desde luego, tienes razón —repuso ella—, y es lo que pienso hacer yo, porque no pensarás que voy a quedarme en casa como una imbécil, ¿verdad, cariño?

—¿Vas a irte sola a cenar por ahí?

—¿Quién te ha dicho que voy a ir sola?

Bufó lleno de súbito cansancio, pero sin dejarse arrastrar por la ira. La conocía, y era capaz de todo. Esa firme voluntad, su fuerza interior, su carácter agresivo, era lo que más le había gustado y le gustaba de Mercedes, aunque en ocasiones como aquella, su sola proximidad echara chispas.

—No lo dirás en serio —tanteó.

—¿Que no lo digo en serio? —la carcajada no fue natural pero sí firme—. Ya lo verás. Tú sales con tu mujer y tu panda, y yo con mi gente. ¿Pasa algo? Que yo sepa no estamos casados.

—Vamos, por favor, no quiero peleas —Rafael se rindió, agotado—. Si supieras el lío que tengo aquí, y lo que me espera este fin de semana, y el lunes. Los problemas que...

—¡Ah, ya, TÚ tienes problemas, YO no! —gritó Mercedes—. ¡Esto es fantástico! ¡El gran hombre!

La vio dar un par de pasos nerviosos por el despacho, agitando los brazos, hablándole a las cuatro paredes que les envolvían, y acabó perdiendo la calma. Quiso evitarlo, pero no pudo. No en aquellas circunstancias.

—¡Coño, Mercedes, no jodas!

Ella se detuvo en seco, atravesándole con sus ojos acerados.

—¿Joder? —dijo despacio—. No, hijo, no, tranquilo. De joder nada, a no ser que te lo hagas esta noche con tu mujer, que es lo que quieres en el fondo. Yo me voy y en paz, y si quieres algo, me llamas, ¿vale? Pues eso. ¿Ves? Ningún problema.

Y dio media vuelta, saliendo del despacho, sin darle tiempo a reaccionar.

Hubiera podido detenerla, pero no lo hizo.

Tampoco habría podido cambiar las cosas aunque hubiera querido.

Rafael

Había perdido el culo por esa niña. ¿La verdad? Pues sí. Desde que la conocí nada fue lo mismo, y desde que la tuve... Dios, Dios, Dios... ¿Puede tenerse un átomo de energía? ¿Cuánto hacía que no echaba tres polvos seguidos en una noche? ¿Y cuánto que no repetía cada día durante una semana seguida? Lo malo es que Sixto ha sabido superar los problemas por la vía rápida y directa, mientras que a mi, se me han caído encima, todos, como un alud.

Y le gusto, eso es lo más alucinante. Si hubiera sido una aventura... aquí paz y después gloria. Pero le gusto, y no es una broma. Mercedes se había enamorado de mí tan a la primera como yo de ella. A lo peor le recuerdo a su padre, o a lo mejor es sincera, o tal vez se trate de una fantasía, ¿cómo saberlo? Siento que estoy caminando por el filo de la navaja, con un abismo a cada lado. No puedo dejarla, pero tampoco puedo dejar a Natalia. ¿O sí? Empezar de nuevo con Mercedes sería...

Ella es adulta para su edad, lo sé, y no está jugando. Me presiona porque me ama, porque es de sangre caliente, porque no quiere esperar ni ser la segunda de los martes y jueves de ocho a nueve o la cita en el avión para ir a pasar el fin de semana a Mallorca mientras yo finjo estar comprando una partida de camisetas Made in Taiwan.

El fin de semana de Mallorca, justo. Eso había sido...

Cuando se marchó del despacho, dejándome plantado como un idiota, con toda su mala hostia por bandera, hubiera asesinado a alguien, comenzando por Natalia y por Sixto, y el orden daba lo mismo. Lo de la cena era cosa de él, para restregarnos a su nena por las narices. Lo raro era que Natalia, y la misma Paz, hubieran aceptado. ¿Quién había sido el primero en proponer lo de ir a cenar, como antes?

No quería perder a Mercedes, era en lo único que pensaba además de la crisis de mi negocio.

Cuando reaccioné y salí corriendo, para detenerla, para decirle... qué sé yo que le hubiera dicho, ya no le encontré.

Se había dado buena prisa en esfumarse.

Eso acabó de ponerme a tope.

16

Sixto detuvo el coche en doble fila, conectó los pilotos de los cuatro lados y tras parar el motor bajó de forma apresurada para comprobar si el vehículo obstruía el paso. No valía la pena que perdiera el tiempo aparcando y disponía de menos de diez minutos para...

Levantó la cabeza. Juraría que en el balcón de su ex-casa alguien se acababa de retirar precipitadamente. No pudo asegurarlo. Llegó hasta el portal y pulsó el timbre del piso. La espera fue mínima.

—¿Sí? —reconoció la voz de su hija Marta.

—Soy papá, bajad.

—Está bien.

Ignoró la asepsia. Marta era la más difícil, la que peor lo estaba llevando, además de Sole. Estaban tan unidos que ella ahora lo tomaba como una traición, un golpe bajo. Incluso era posible que estuviese celosa. Celosa de compartirle con otra mujer.

A sus diecisiete años, Marta también lo era, y muy sensible además.

Solo por su hija, más que por su mujer, habría continuado con la mentira de su matrimonio sin amor.

Paseó arriba y abajo de la acera, vigilando el coche, y por dos veces examinó la hora en menos de un minuto. ¿Cuánto se tardaba en bajar, en ascensor o a pié, desde el tercer piso? Llegaba muy tarde, por supuesto, y ya debían saber que la visita sería una mera cortesía, pero aún así podían comprender que a veces las cosas...

No, no comprendían, ya no. Les habría importado un pito lo de Roberto Estrada y la campaña de los preservativos Aura, aunque dependieran de su sueldo como dependían.

Una exhalación en forma de niño de cinco años salió finalmente por el portal y se le echó encima. Él se agachó para cogerle en brazos. Marta apareció casi a continuación, pero no Domingo. Le buscó inquieto y la niña se dio cuenta de ello. No hizo falta que preguntara.

—Se ha ido —reveló—. Ha estado esperado pero ya no podía más. Había quedado —y agregó cortante—: Y yo también.

—Lo siento, cariño. Ha sido un día horrible —intentó besarla, pero su hija se apartó sin disimulo, mirando hacia otro lado como si buscara algo. Tuvo que cambiar de actitud, dedicando sus sentimientos a quién sí los estaba necesitando y pidiendo a gritos—. ¿Y tú qué, bicho? ¿Qué has hecho hoy?

—Me he peleado con Nati —anunció orgulloso el niño.

—¿Con Nati? ¿Y quien es Nati?

—Una niña tonta —manifestó Guillermo.

—¿Y por qué es tonta?

Se sentía ridículo. Antes, en casa, esa era la clase de conversación que concluía sin más, fingiendo una atención que no prestaba. Ahora, en la calle, con visos de ser lo más importante del mundo, se le antojaba a falsedad y castigo, con Marta rehuyéndole y con Domingo ya lejos, en otra galaxia, aunque él, a sus veinte años, fuera el más imparcial.

—Escucha —detuvo el torrente oral de Guillermo—, la próxima semana estaremos juntos, ¿de acuerdo? Tienes ya pensado a dónde quieres ir.

—¡Al Tibidabo! —gritó el pequeño.

Pronto le harían socio de honor. Había ido más veces al Tibidabo en las últimas semanas que en toda su vida. No sabía ni por qué preguntaba.

—Yo tengo planes —le advirtió Marta.

—Claro, claro —asintió su padre sin fuerzas para imponer nada—. Aunque...

Se encontró con los ojos de su hija y se calló de nuevo.

Sixto

Los hijos son duros, implacables, y casi siempre crueles, porque en su natural egoísmo basan el epicentro de su universo. Mientras tú eres el sol de ese universo, estás en casa, cuentan contigo, les das dinero, luchan contra ti por ser la autoridad y se cobijan bajo el invisible paraguas de la seguridad que aportas, aunque ellos ni siquiera sepan si tú te sientes seguro, feliz o convencido de algo, puedes llegar a sentir o creer que son tuyos o que forman tanta parte de ti como tú de ellos. Cuando todo esto termina, parcial o totalmente, y se sienten solos, desprotegidos, engañados o frustrados... su venganza es terrible. Y para un padre, basta una mirada, un gesto, una palabra. Hay muchas formas de morir, pero solo un hijo o una hija sabe cómo matarte con un simple desprecio.

¿Y qué podía decirles, que su madre y yo ya no nos queríamos? Lo había intentado al comienzo, pero eso no funciona. Para los hijos el concepto del amor es una abstracción. Los padres son padres y ya está. Incluso creen que una pareja de más de treinta años y con hijos ya no hace el amor. El sexo es para los jóvenes. Yo había intentado mantenerme entero, estable. Para dramas ya estaba ella, su madre, y ahora lo que debía contarles de mí... No quería ni imaginarlo.

¿Cómo se le dice a una hija de diecisiete años que quieres vivir, amar y ser amado, tener algo más que una rutina? Marta me habría dicho que me lo hubiera pensado mejor antes de casarme con Sole, o incluso antes de engendrarla a ella.

Estaba tan orgulloso de mi hija y de su fortaleza de carácter.

Nunca pensé que eso se pudiera volver contra mí.

Lo malo es que descubres que les necesitas cuando ya es demasiado tarde, y también que en el fondo muchas familias pueden llegar a estar formadas por extraños y extrañas debido a la falta de tiempo de los padres para con los hijos, falta de comunicación, falta de otros vínculos salvo los impuestos por ley, vida y naturaleza.

¿Me estoy justificando?

Cuando dejé a Guillermo y a Marta tenía la peor de las sensaciones, entre lo laboral y personal, en la boca del estómago.

17

No había dejado de pensar en las sensaciones experimentadas en la consulta minutos antes. Para él, eran tan desconocidas como lo que pudiera haber en la mente de su hijo, y tan desconcertante como desconcertante era Octavio. Descubrir como había descubierto que Gemma estaba allí, y que eso formaba parte de su vida de una forma mucho más intensa que otros hechos u otras personas, se le antojaba una revelación. Y si de algo estaba seguro era de que Gemma le quería, le adoraba, con esa clase de adoración respetuosa y callada, amable, constante, capaz de labrar día a día durante años un vínculo especial, basado tan solo en la compañía, el contacto, la síntesis de lo humano y lo profesional, tal vez lo divino.

Recordó que una vez, tal vez un año o dos antes, Paz se lo había dicho:

—Tu enfermera besa el suelo que pisas.

Era una clase de amor, una clase de pasión, una clase de ternura, tal vez más fría, quizá más platónica de lo normal, y seguramente más eterna. Y lo que más miedo le daba era haberlo descubierto ahora, en este momento, cuando se estaba planteando una serie de dudas. Era como estar abriendo los ojos al mundo después de haber estado de espaldas a él.

Demasiado tiempo.

Miró a una mujer que caminaba en dirección opuesta a la suya por la calle. Llevaba un maletín negro en la mano, vestía traje chaqueta de color gris, con pantalones, con el cabello recogido y gafas oscuras, sus rasgos no eran desde luego femeninos, sino más bien masculinos. Daba la impresión de ser feroz, o de andar metida en muchos problemas. Pisaba fuerte, con convicción. Cuando pasó por su lado, arremolinó el aire de forma feroz.

Por detrás vio a otra, más joven, falda corta, piernas largas, blusa blanca y sin sujetadores, lo cual permitía el cadencioso movimiento de los pechos en el vaivén de cada paso, cabello suelto, perfectamente maquillada, femenina, con expresión abierta. Incluso giró la cabeza cuando le superó.

Dos mujeres, dos mundos

¿Cuando dejó Paz de ser simplemente eso, femenina?

Se sintió machista ante ese pensamiento, pero ya no le abandonó hasta que llegó a su casa, abrió la puerta y se encontró con el torbellino de su hija Vanessa entre los brazos, anunciando con su voz imitación actriz gangosa a todo pulmón:

—¡Atención al personal, el eminente doctor llegó a casa, estén dispuestos para la revisión!

Y se echó a reír, porque era imposible no hacerlo con ella tan vital y alegre como solía estarlo siempre, aún en tiempo de exámenes.

Salvador

Le estaba dando vueltas a esa y otras preguntas.

¿Cuándo dejó Paz de ser simplemente eso, femenina?

¿Y yo? ¿Qué era yo? ¿Un simple proveedor de las seguridades familiares, sin derechos, solo con deberes? Si no se podía vivir sin aire, ¿podía vivir el ser humano sin ternura, sin cariño, sin intensidad? La pasión es necesaria para existir, y en este caso... bueno, no sabía lo que Paz podía exigir de mí, nunca me lo había dicho, pero yo sí sabía lo que hubiera exigido de ella de haber podido: feminidad, seducción, fantasía, que se cuidara un poco más y tratara de no envejecer, no física, sino mentalmente. Incluso Natalia iba a un gimnasio, para no perder el ritmo de la vida. Rafael no habría consentido que su mujer engordara y se pusiera horrible. Rafael necesitaba mantenerse joven consigo mismo y con todo su entorno. Un caso claro, aunque al fin y a la postre, Sixto era el que lo había hecho más radical todo, rompiendo con Sole y buscándose un cuerpo joven, en el que la pasión, la feminidad, la seducción, la fantasía y el cariño fueran aún posibles. Un cuerpo joven con sentimientos jóvenes.

Como él decía: "a follar, que son dos días".

Ahora no sé si incluso puedo culpar a Paz por lo que pudo ser y no fue.

¿Me hice pediatra por ella, para darle la seguridad que pedía y necesitaba, o por mi mismo, porque no supe si llegaría a ser el famoso cirujano que pretendía? Estaba tan enamorado... Y aún lo estoy, ¡lo estoy! Para mi no puede haber otra mujer salvo Paz, la quiero, deseo envejecer a su lado, pero... ¿cómo insuflar entusiasmo a quien lo ha perdido? Pasión, seducción, fantasía... eso son términos de los que siempre careció, ahora lo sé, pero con los que me habitué a no vivir. Sin embargo, siempre hay un momento en el que te haces preguntas, te planteas cosas, intentas agarrar con desesperación el tren de la existencia antes de que pase por la última estación y luego ya no se detenga hasta el fin.

Dios... nunca he vuelto a sentir lo que sentí aquel 17 de enero de 1969, nunca. Y un día, en el Juicio Final, quizás solo tenga eso como exponente de lo que ha sido mi vida. Fue mi momento de gloria, de borrachera personal, y pensé que tras eso, ya nada se me resistiría, que sería capaz de todo. Si solo pudiera volver a sentir una vez aquella adrenalina, mientras gritaba las consignas con mis compañeros, mientras subíamos la escalera de la universidad como una turba enloquecida pero fuerte, mientras echábamos el maldito busto de Franco por la ventana, mientras quitábamos la bandera nacional y poníamos la roja con la hoz y el martillo...

Aquel día yo era el Che, y Fidel, y Kubala, y Kennedy, y Dylan, y Lennon y todos los dioses de mi juventud.

Aquel día yo supe que estaba vivo, y que había nacido para algo.

Pero soy pediatra, tengo una mujer a la que amo pero con la que he dejado de sentir la verdadera intensidad del amor, un hijo al que no entiendo, una hija a la que adoro y he convertido en la luz de mi futuro, y una enfermera solterona que a lo peor incluso está enamorada de mi aunque nunca, nunca, pueda llegar a pasar nada entre los dos, porque para eso son las adoraciones platónicas.

Si pudiera volver a aquel 17 de enero de 1969.

Si pudiera hacer que mi vida entera hubiese sido un 17 de enero de 1969.

18

Encarna abrió la puerta completamente convencida de que el que llamaba era Sixto, que no encontraba las llaves o llevaba las manos ocupadas con sus carpetas y papeles. Por esa razón no se preocupó de ponerse antes unos pantalones o una simple falda. Incluso en la blusa que llevaba por encima y le llegaba hasta la mitad de los muslos, estaban desabrochados la mayoría de los botones. Con el cabello suelto y descalza, era una visión demasiado turbadora para cualquiera, y más lo fue para Carlos, su vecino del piso de arriba, cuando la vio.

—Oh, eres tú —dijo ella desconcertada llevándose una mano a la parte superior de la blusa.

—Hola... Vaya, siento molestarte. Es que... Venía a devolverte el compact que me dejaste ayer.

No sabía dónde mirar, pero tampoco hacía muchos esfuerzos para no hacerlo. Casi parecía que su mayor duda consistía en saber qué parte de su anatomía le gustaba más o merecía más su contemplación. La mano sujetando las dos partes abiertas de la blusa impedía ver el nacimiento de los senos, como un segundo antes, pero las piernas desnudas, los pies con las uñas pintadas, el rostro franco y abierto con su sonrisa...

—¿Te ha gustado? —quiso saber Encarna.

—Mucho, es muy fuerte.

—Ya te buscaré los demás. Aún no he abierto algunas cajas desde que llegué, y eso que han pasado... Bueno, como esto es provisional, aunque a lo mejor...

No estaba cortada por la escena. Carlos tenía veinticuatro años, y era muy agradable, muy guapo. De haber estado sola habría salido con él, lo tenía claro. Durante los primeros días, cuando él no sabía que ella y Sixto vivían juntos, se le había insinuado un par de veces.

Ahora ya no lo hacía directamente, pero le pedía discos, siempre se cruzaba con ella, y desde luego no era una casualidad. ¿Por qué iba a estar cortada?

Ni tan solo enfadada por su constancia. Encarna nunca se enfadaba. Y procuraba reír siempre. En alguna parte había leído que la gente que ríe tiene más arrugas que los demás, pero a cambio vivían más años. Sus mayores esfuerzos estaban encaminados desde hacía tiempo a reír sin forzar los pliegues de la piel.

Carlos no se movía, y ella parecía una estatua, con la imagen recortada al contraluz debido a la iluminación del recibidor y la oscuridad de la escalera. Probablemente él hubiera seguido hablando, de cualquier tema, como solía hacer, y a ella no le hubiese importado en absoluto que lo hiciera, de no haber sido porque en ese instante sí sonó el timbre de la puerta de la calle y supo que era Sixto.

No tuvo que decirle a Carlos que se fuera.

—La próxima semana te bajaré la cinta de ese grupo que conozco —se despidió él iniciando una rápida retirada.

—¡Oh, bien! —le envolvió ella con su sonrisa de adiós.

Encarna

Carlos me recordaba a Quique, no solo por su aspecto, varonil, fuerte, atractivo, de talante abierto y predisposición a la libertad, sino por otros detalles, desde la forma de mirarme a la manera de buscar la forma de seducirme. Se puede saber mucho de un hombre por la manera en que te aborda, te dice las primeras palabras, te envuelve y se define en su táctica. Y tanto da que haya unos que lo único que pretenden sea acostarse contigo a la primera, o que haya otros dispuestos y capaces a esperar y hacer las cosas bien, sabiendo que lo bueno merece la pena y que esperar refuerza el placer final. Eso es otra cosa. El primer contacto es lo mismo que esa fuerza magnética que te atrae hacia una persona sin más, desde el momento en que la ves por primera vez.

Quiero a Sixto, y quiero casarme con él, tener hijos con él, sentar la cabeza y tratar de ser "madura" aunque sin renunciar a ser mujer, es decir, seguir siendo yo misma, que es como le gusto, porque nunca, nunca, querría llegar a convertirme en una esposa modelo, aburrida y carente de vida como Paz, o una pija de Iradier tan vacía como Natalia, aunque al menos ella trata de estar al día y disfruta de lo que tiene, que tampoco está mal. Quiero hacerlo y estaba en camino de conseguirlo, porque desde que Sixto y yo vivíamos juntos, existía un verdadero vínculo. Pero a veces, de noche, me despertaba y en la oscuridad aún me preguntaba si todo aquello no era un sueño, y si al extender mi mano, en lugar de tropezar con Sixto encontraría a Quique.

Para algunas personas, cuatro años son una vida.

Y mis cuatro años con Quique lo habían sido, plena, intensa, fuerte, densa y extraordinaria. Cuatro años vividos a tope, a mil por hora.

Por esa razón lo habíamos quemado y gastado todo en ese tiempo, sin dejar nada para un mañana que ya no iba a llegar.

Quique era dibujante, un buen dibujante. Hacía ilustraciones para varias revistas y maquetas para otras, como estilista gráfico. No tenía horarios, trabajaba en casa, podía hacer el amor a cualquier hora, entraba y salía, íbamos a cenar fuera cada noche, y al cine y al teatro. Se gastaba todo lo que ganaba al día, sin preocuparse de otra cosa. Solo presente. El mañana era una ilusión estúpida. Nunca tuvimos mucho, pero a mi no me importó. Ahora es diferente. Ahora sé que tener garantiza un poco el futuro, porque el mañana, cuando pasan las locuras de juventud, sí acaba existiendo. De no haber sido por mi sueldo, muchos meses habríamos estado con el agua al cuello. En cambio, cuando a él le pagaban algo importante o hacía un trabajo que nos dejaba un buen dinero, podíamos reventarlo en un fin de semana en Londres, yendo a los teatros del West End y a comprar discos, o en una escapada al Caribe.

Todos mis recuerdos con Quique están tan vivos, y son tan fuertes...

Carlos me lo recordaba, por esa razón a veces hablaba con él sin importarme nada el hecho de que las cosas ya no fueran distintas. A fin de cuentas Quique nunca quiso comprometerse, y lo que Carlos buscaba era lo mismo, un revolcón, tirarse a la vecina de abajo. Todavía un sueño juvenil. Eso me parecía encantador.

Sobre todo porque con Sixto había momentos en que me sentía "una señora casada", y no precisamente por los beneficios de las "señoras casadas", sino por las desventajas.

En cuanto llegó él supe que tenía el día, o la noche.

19

Dejó de sujetarse la blusa y ésta se entreabrió mostrando parte de sus encantos. Encarna sabía que a Sixto le gustaba llegar a casa y encontrársela así. No habría sido la primera vez que nada más llegar acababan en la cama, si es que llegaban. A Sixto también le gustaba tenerla en cualquier parte, en el suelo del pequeño apartamento o entre los cojines de la diminuta sala repleta de cosas. Por lo visto su ex era cómoda. Solo quería hacerlo en la cama, sin fantasías.

A su ex, probablemente, la seducción de Jessica Lange por parte de Jack Nicholson en la cocina del remake de El cartero siempre llama dos veces le habría parecido una estupidez, cuando era la auténtica sal del amor y del sexo.

Pero en esta ocasión, Sixto entró en el piso sin verla, atrapado por una tormenta interior tan evidente como las sombras de su cara. Le dio un beso de marido, fugaz, lejos de la avidez de otras ocasiones en las que semejaba un náufrago encontrando una tabla de salvación en mitad del mar, y entró dejando el maletín y una caja sobre la mesita de la sala.

Fue directamente al mueble bar y cogió la botella de whisky.

—¿Me he perdido el fin de semana, cariño? —preguntó ella.

—¿Qué? —Sixto pareció salir de una abstracción.

—Es que como llevas puesta la cara de los lunes, no sé yo sí...

—¿Estás sarcástica o qué?

—Mejor o qué. ¿Pasa algo?

Llevó ambas manos a su cintura, con lo cual la blusa se abrió casi por completo en la parte superior, y subió en la inferior descubriendo la oscura presencia de su sexo muy cerca de los extremos de la tela. También abrió las piernas, apoyándose en la izquierda al culminar su gesto de desafío.

Por raro que pareciera, estuvo segura de que, por una vez, Sixto no sentía nada.

—Vengo de mi casa, bueno... —intentó rectificar, pero ya era tarde—. No ha sido lo que se dice agradable.

—¿Lo es alguna vez? —dijo Encarna—. ¿La has visto a ella?

—No, a mi hija y a Guillermo.

—Y te ha puesto mala cara, claro.

No le contestó. No era necesario. Sabía lo que Marta significaba para él. Escanció tres dedos de whisky en un vaso y se lo llevó a los labios. Le bastaron dos tragos.

—No empieces a beber, ¿quieres? —protestó Encarna.

—¿Qué pasa, vas a darme el coñazo ahora tú?

—No, hijo, no —levantó sus dos manos a la altura del pecho, con las palmas vueltas hacia él, y acto seguido le dio la espalda, encaminándose al cuarto de baño.

Encarna nunca discutía. Tal vez fuera una de sus ventajas. Siempre optaba por largarse en cuanto se torcían las cosas. Al revés de Sole.

Sixto se escanció otros dos dedos de whisky.

Lo necesitaba.

20

Salvador abrió la puerta de la habitación de su hijo, y al verla tan revuelta como siempre, pero vacía, hizo un gesto de desagrado. Lo peor fue la oleada de mal olor que le atufó la pituitaria, mezcla de sudor y tabaco. Cerró la puerta y se encaminó a su propia habitación, donde había creído escuchar los últimos movimientos de Paz. No se equivocó.

—¿Y Octavio? —preguntó en un tono que no dejaba lugar a dudas sobre su estado de ánimo—. ¿Ya se ha marchado?

—No, hombre, no —le tranquilizó su esposa—. Ha ido a por tabaco.

—¿Pero cuántos paquetes fuma al día este hijo tuyo?

—Uno, que yo sepa, aunque a veces, como todo el mundo le pide...

—Pues que le pidan menos, y que controle más. ¿No emplea siempre esta palabra? —rezongó hastiado—. De todas formas este no va a pasar de los cuarenta, y a los que hará polvo será a nosotros, porque lo que es él... ¡Jesús!

—¿Has tenido un mal día?

—¿Yo? No, ¿por qué?

—Es que has llegado hace cinco minutos y no has

parado de protestar y refunfuñar por todo. Por eso.

Iba a decirle que no era verdad, y a mentirla hablándole del pequeño Vicente García y su sida infantil pero tan mortal como cualquier otro, y a comentarle incluso la sensación producida por Gemma antes de salir de la consulta. Pero en lugar de todo ello aceptó su culpa, la responsabilidad, y no quiso pasar a hablar de su mal humor ni de las causas que le motivaban, por otra parte tan profundas que ni con un sacacorchos las habría logrado sacar a flote.

Paz se estaba arreglando, llevaba puestas únicamente las bragas y los sujetadores. Unas bragas enormes, desde el vientre hasta la mitad de los muslos, para presionar sobre la carne. Los sujetadores también eran muy grandes. Nada que ver con las braguitas livianas de las chicas de los anuncios, ni tampoco con los modelos de sujetador para pechos minis. Se sintió aún más extraño cuando apartó la mirada y no quiso verla de aquella forma. A veces prefería recordarla como...

—¿Quieres arreglarte de una vez en lugar de dar vueltas por ahí buscando con quién meterte? —le reprochó Paz.

—Pero si luego hemos de esperarles igualmente —protestó él—. No sé porque no va cada pareja en su coche.

—¡Ay, para ya, querido!, ¿quieres? Y ponte el traje azul, que te hace más jovial y con tus dos amigos arrasando...

¿Arrasando?

Salvador tampoco quiso hacer preguntas en torno a ello. Sixto iba de nuevo joven, tanto a nivel de aspecto como de talante, pero Rafael... Optó por dirigirse al cuarto de baño para afeitarse y refrescarse un poco. No quería descubrir lo que ya sabía: que Paz estaba un poco harta de ellos, y más aún de salidas como aquella, en la que había una nota de discordia.

Bueno, Encarna estaba loca, pero era simpática.

21

No era el momento adecuado, ni la oportunidad más idónea, pero se escuchó a sí misma diciendo aquello que le había estado rondando por la cabeza en los últimos días. Ni siquiera sabía si era una prueba de fuego, para ver cómo reaccionaba él, o si realmente estaba dispuesta a hacer lo que pensaba.

—Rafa, creo que voy a volver a trabajar.

Su marido dejó de atarse el zapato derecho y levantó la cabeza. El tono de sus ojos y la expresión de su cara no dejaron lugar a dudas acerca de sus sentimientos.

—¿Qué? —preguntó como si no hubiera oído bien.

—He dicho que estoy pensando en volver a trabajar.

—¿Por qué?

—Hoy en día todas las mujeres lo hacen.

—Querrás decir que hoy en día todas las mujeres jóvenes lo hacen.

—¿Qué quieres decir con eso, que soy mayor?

—Yo no me refería a que tú seas mayor, sino a que ya no es lo mismo que antes, ¿me explico? Hoy en día las chicas salen de la universidad dispuestas a todo, y quieren ser abogadas, economistas, licenciadas, competir con los hombres y todo ese rollo. Vale, de acuerdo, no digo nada. Pero para las que lo dejasteis al casaros o poco después de casaros, no digo que no sea imposible, pero sí muy difícil. Hay tres millones de parados —cambió de pronto el talante, y casi con miedo preguntó—: ¿O quieres que te meta en la empresa?

—No, nada de trabajar contigo, sería insoportable. Hablaba de otro trabajo, no sé.

Rafael pareció aliviado. Volvió a su primera actitud, defensiva y reticente tanto como de velada oposición.

—Sigue estando complicado, Natalia. Llevas muchos años fuera del mercado laboral, y sinceramente, para que hagas una tontería por cuatro cuartos...

—No es por el dinero, y lo sabes.

—No, no lo sé. ¿Por qué es?

No le gustaba aquel tono agresivo, de acorralamiento, de acoso y derribo, pero no quería discutir. No esa noche. Le bastaba con verle la cara.

—Olvídalo —dijo ella—. después del verano ya veré.

—¿Después del verano? —el hombre hizo un gesto de pasmo—. Desde luego... es fantástico. ¿Crees que encima puedes elegir el momento? ¿Sabes cómo está el país, y el tinglado, y todo? ¡Natalia, por Dios, no seas infantil! —estuvo tentado de hablarle del negocio, y de los problemas, y de que todo se estaba yendo al garete, y que a lo peor sí tendrían que buscar trabajo, los dos, y parar el tren de vida, y recortar gastos, y... , pero no lo hizo. Logró contenerse. Lo peor que podía pasarle ahora era tener una esposa aburrida incordiando. No era un juego. Y optó por acudir a lo más fácil pero efectivo—: Tienes una hija de siete años que te necesita. ¿Has pensado en ella?

Natalia sostuvo su mirada unos segundos, hasta que plegó velas, mitad cansada mitad rendida. Desde luego no era el momento, aunque nunca lo era ni lo sería. Y fuere como fuere, todo dependía de su actitud, de su decisión, de lo que finalmente hiciera con su vida y la de Gloria.

Hacía mucho que veía a Rafa como un extraño, pero nunca como hasta ese instante.

22

En ésta oportunidad, y por ello casi no lo pudo creer, el teléfono fue descolgado al otro lado de la línea.

—¿Sí? ¿Quién es? —escuchó la voz de Marcelino Escobar, y no precisamente alegre o cordial.

—Soy Sixto.

—Coño, ¿qué pasa? —se extrañó su jefe.

Se sintió ridículo, de golpe. Allí estaba él, por importante que fuese en la empresa, y creía serlo, llamando a su superior, al hombre que tenía la llave del destino de todos los que estaban a sus órdenes, en viernes por la noche, para cuestionarle una decisión que ni siquiera era oficial, y que podía cambiar el mismo lunes por la mañana.

¿Se había vuelto loco?

Sintió una oleada de calor y un estremecimiento recorrió su piel.

—Es que este fin de semana voy a trabajar en la campaña de Aura, ¿sabes? —consiguió decir con más naturalidad de la que sentía—. Y quería consultarte unos detalles importantes. Cosa de un minuto.

Una buena salida. Reflejos. Si él le atendía, le escuchaba, aunque no tenía ni idea de lo que podía decirle, significaba que le mantenía en liza.

No lo hizo.

—Escucha, Sixto —le detuvo el director de la agencia—, imagino que debía haber hablado contigo antes de irme pero... chico, es viernes, tengo un compromiso y...

—¿De qué querías hablarme, de la campaña?

Su corazón latía muy rápido. Si de algo tenía fama Marcelino Escobar era de implacable, de no casarse con nadie, de ir al grano, directo, sin perder un instante en rodeos u otras disquisiciones.

—Es mejor que no hagas nada, Sixto —le soltó su jefe—. Voy darle una oportunidad a Estrada, para ponerle a prueba. Como tenemos tiempo ya que para este verano va a estar la cosa muy justa y el cliente así lo ha entendido, quiero ver como se sale.

—¿Vas a darle la campaña de Aura a Roberto Estrada?

—¿Algún problema?

No era una pregunta, era una advertencia, pero Sixto sentía demasiada ofuscación para entenderlo así, y aunque lo entendiera no pudo detenerse.

—¡Esta campaña es una pera en dulce, y era mía!

—Sixto —el tono de voz fue paciente pero tenso—, sabes muy bien la filosofía de la empresa.

La sabía. "Nada es de nadie, sino del que mejor lo hace". La había diseñado él mismo, cuando se cargó a sus dos socios y se hizo con el timón de la nave.

—Pero...

—Sixto, si lo prefieres hablamos el lunes, o si quieres trabajar igual, y me vienes con algo sensacional, lo haces. No voy a impedirlo. Pero es tarde, tengo prisa, y no quiero discutir esto por teléfono. ¿Crees que soy idiota? He hablado con Estrada, y lo que me ha dicho me gusta, es bueno, así que punto. Yo que tú me lo tomaría con calma. Y además, coño, no vas a hacerlo todo tú, ¡deja algo para los demás! —se rio de su gracia, pero no la tenía—. Confía en mi instinto, ¿quieres? Creo que ese Estrada traerá sangre e ideas nuevas, y en publicidad esto es como un seguro de vida, ¿no?

No se lo decía con palabras, pero sí con cada inflexión de voz, y con el trasfondo del tema, y con la experiencia que ambos tenían y les sobraba. ¿Sangre e ideas nuevas? La publicidad era un mundo de depredadores, y la única sangre era la que se derramaba entre los perdedores. A

Roberto Estrada le estaba poniendo la directa. De ahí a que fuera "uno de ellos" solo había un paso. Y de este a ocupar el puesto de Ruiz...

Su puesto.

—Claro, Marcelino. Perdona —intentó retroceder a tiempo de salvar su dignidad, al menos de no quemarse en una batalla inútil y perdida.

—Hasta el lunes, Sixto. Y tómate el fin de semana para disfrutar con tu nena, que no todo es trabajo, creéme —volvió a reírse levemente antes de despedirse y colgar tras un lacónico—: ¡Salud!

Era un hijo de puta. El mayor hijo de puta del mundillo de la publicidad. Por esta razón era además el mejor de todos los hijos de puta.

23

No tuvo que llamar a Octavio cuando este regresó, porque su hijo entró directamente en el cuarto de baño, buscándole. Salvador le vio por el espejo, mientras apuraba el rasurado de su barba, crecida desde que se había afeitado a primera hora de la mañana. El cabello largo y la cara de despiste solían incomodarle tanto o más que su aspecto, por lo general astrado. En alguna parte había leído que eso era una moda. *Dirty look* lo llamaban, y también *grunge*. No tenía ni idea de lo que quería decir salvo que en esencia la cosa estaba en ir pringados de piés a cabeza. En los 50 hubo *beatnicks* y en los 60 *hippies*. De ahí no pasó. Y en España, ni eso. En España en los 70 aún se iba con traje y corbata y cara de gilipollas. Franco no se largó hasta el 75.

—¿Me das la pasta?

No podía ser más directo. Si un día le decía: "Papá, estoy harto de pedirte dinero cada semana. Por dignidad y por orgullo, me voy. Trabajaré y me buscaré la vida por mí mismo", en el fondo se sentiría radiante. Ojalá hubiera podido hacerlo él, que tuvo que quedarse en casa, como estaba mandado, hasta que se casó. Pero eso formaba parte de un pasado asombrosamente lejano. Era mejor parar la mano y olvidar tonterías decimonónicas como lo de la dignidad y el orgullo. Era una generación práctica.

Y demasiado desconocida.

—¿Ya te vas?

—He quedado con los colegas hace rato.

—Podrías...

—¿Vais a cenar en casa? ¿No, verdad? Pues me abro, ¿qué pasa?

—¿Qué has hecho hoy?

—He mirado unas cosas para este verano.

—¿Qué clase de "cosas"?

—Pues cosas —se encogió de hombros Octavio—. Ya te lo diré cuando salgan.

—Y si no salen, como el verano pasado, a tocarte las... narices tres meses, sin dar golpe, como el resto del año.

—Hombre, que no es eso.

—¿Entonces qué es?

—Pues que va a ser si la cosa está chunga.

Él, u otros como él, ¿subirían alguna escalera gritando por unos derechos, defenestrando un busto odiado y plantando la bandera de su revolución, tuviera los colores que tuviera y significara lo que significara?

Su hijo no esperó su nueva andanada.

—Bueno, dame la pasta, va, que se van a cansar de esperarme.

—¡Pues que esperen! —gritó—. ¡Total, vas a pasarte la noche con ellos, y luego regresarás al amanecer, como el otro día, borracho como una cuba y vomitando antes de llegar a tu habitación! ¡Para eso no hace falta correr!

Lo aguantó impertérrito. Solía hacerlo siempre cuando él subía de tono. Lo único que deseaba era "trincar la pasta", como lo llamaban, y "abrirse" cuanto antes.

Paz apareció en el pasillo, por detrás de su hijo.

—¿Ya estáis discutiendo? —protestó.

—Yo no digo nada —se defendió Octavio.

Salvador tampoco quiso decir nada más. No con Paz delante. No servía de mucho si ella desplegaba su manto protector por encima del chico, y luego le acusaba de intransigente, de no entender nada, de haberse quedado atrás y de otras cosas parecidas.

Nunca creyó que después de haber vivido la revolución de los años 60, pudiera tener un "conflicto generacional" con sus hijos. Bueno, con su hijo. Vanessa era distinta.

—Tengo la cartera en mi chaqueta —dijo con fastidio, dando por concluído el conato de pelea.

—¿Cuánto cojo? —preguntó Octavio.

—Cinco mil, ¿por qué?

Puso cara de fastidio, como si cinco mil, a los dieciocho años y para un fin de semana, fuera una bagatela, pero esta vez su madre se lo llevó, empujándole para que no rebrotara la tensión. Todavía la oyó murmurar y cuchichear algo, tal vez que ella iba a darle mil más, por ejemplo.

Estuvo a punto de salir, para controlarlo y evitarlo.

Pero no lo hizo, se detuvo. Fuera como fuera no podía luchar contra Paz. Nunca había ni habría podido.

Salvador

Siempre deseé un hijo para ser su amigo, para ir al fútbol con él, hablar con él, discutir con él, vivir con él, crecer con él. Y cuando nació Octavio, me sentí colmado. Ahora me pregunto en qué parte del camino nos separamos y nos hicimos extremos de una cuerda tan corta pero también tan distante y llena de nudos.

Aunque desde pequeño, incluso ya con dos y tres años, Octavio fue así, diferente, cerrado, con un mundo propio y un universo especial, fuera de lo que en otros niños era normal. Odió el fútbol, jamás fue violento como cualquier niño a su edad, no hablaba apenas, costaba arrancarle un simple "sí" o un "no", se pasaba el día leyendo, ¡al menos! No quiso estudiar pero leía y leía sin parar, lo cual hacía pensar a su madre que era inteligente, capaz. Yo también lo hubiera creído así, de no ser porque ahora sé que en la vida se necesita mucho más.

Ojalá esté equivocado.

A veces Octavio dice que a él le bastará con una casa, en una montaña, para vivir y ser feliz. Carece de ambiciones. Extraño en un mundo tan ambicioso y competitivo, pero tal vez saludable para enfrentarse a los cambios del siglo XXI. La utopía de los años 60 sirvió para que un montón de ilusos pudiéramos crecer creyendo en algo, y creo que en el siglo XXI se necesitarán otras utopías para vencer la implacable ley del progreso, el deterioro de la vida y la naturaleza, la caída de los valores...

¡Dios! Si alguien me oyera hablando de "valores".

Cuando defenestramos el busto de Franco cambiamos los valores de arriba abajo, y sabíamos por qué lo hacíamos, creíamos en ello. Pero hoy, ¿de qué valores estamos hablando? Los mataron todos en los 80, en los años del gran acaparamiento, los años del dinero fácil y la continua huida hacia adelante de los nuevos dioses.

Octavio fuma hierba, "porros". Él lo niega, e insiste en que de drogas, nada, que no está "pirado", que pasa de esos "malos rollos", y hasta cuenta que un gramo de cocaína —jaco, o farlopa, me parece que lo llamó— vale doce mil pesetas, y una pastilla para subir el tono en la noche cinco mil. No podría pagarlo, claro, y ese es el miedo de todo padre, que después de todo caiga y para tener acceso a esas mierdas acabe negociando y traficando. Un miedo atroz. Pero según Paz, Octavio y sus amigos solo beben. ¡Solo beben, como si eso fuera un mal menor! Hemos llegado a considerar que lo menos malo es mejor que lo muy malo.

Me siento tan y tan lejos de él.

De aquel niño con el que quería ir al fútbol, crecer, vivir...

Toda la noche estuve pensando en Octavio. Puede que esa fuera la clave de... Al menos mi clave.

A cada momento me preguntaba dónde estaría, con quién, haciendo qué, y hasta imaginándome que podía encontrármelo en mitad de la calle, en el instante menos esperado, yendo con Rafael, Sixto y las mujeres.

Me decía a mí mismo que si eso sucedía, no lo soportaría.

Sentía vergüenza de mi propio hijo, y piedad por mi.

¿Hay algo peor para un padre?

24

Rafael se quedó mirando a la canguro mientras la chica caminaba de espaldas a él, en dirección a la sala. No cerró la puerta hasta que ella hubo desaparecido de su vista, y lo hizo en el momento en que la voz de Natalia le llegaba desde el dormitorio preguntando:

—¿Es Cristina?

—Sí, ya está aquí —anunció él.

Solo tenía que coger la chaqueta, pero prescindió del detalle. Caminó por el pasillo hasta la sala, y al no ver allí a Cristina se dirigió a la habitación de Gloria. Antes de llegar la oyó hacer planes con la recién llegada.

—...así que primero veremos el vídeo de Dirty dancing, y después...

—¡Eh, eh! ¿Conspirando para montaros la juerga por vuestra cuenta? —dijo entrando de pronto en la habitación de su hija.

—¡Oh, vaya! —Gloria hizo un gesto teatral, llevándose una mano a los ojos, mientras se dejaba caer de espaldas sobre la cama, en la que estaba subida—. ¡Nos ha pillado in fraganti!

La canguro le hizo cosquillas y la niña se retorció entre sus manos, pero Rafael no miraba a su hija, aunque sonriera de forma mecánica, sino a la muchacha, diecisiete años, alta y esbelta, con un cuerpo de mujer lleno de excitación y promesas, un pecho generoso, una cintura breve, unos ojos expresivos, unos labios tan carnosos como fresas maduras, el cabello revuelto...

Crecían rápido, y desde luego entendía que actores como Robert de Niro tuvieran amores con chicas como Cristina, de diecisiete años. ¿Infanticidas? ¡Y una leche! Todas las que hacían anuncios en televisión eran niñas, y las mejores modelos, las top más iniciáticas, comenzaban con quince y dieciséis años. Eran el puro deseo, y ningún hombre normal podía resistirlo, fingir y pensar en "niñas". Cristina no era una niña. Y si lo era, su cuerpo la traicionaba, y engañaba a cualquiera, como él. Por si eso fuera poco, la naturaleza hacía lo demás: desde los 80 las chicas dejaban de ser vírgenes a los catorce. Lo decían las malditas estadísticas.

Dejaron de jugar sobre la cama, y Gloria se zafó de las manos de la canguro, levantándose y echando a correr sin dejar de reír más allá del amparo de su habitación. Cristina no la siguió. Se incorporó y se arregló el cabello, luego el jersey, liviano y muy ceñido, lo mismo que los vaqueros. Lo hizo despreocupadamente, pasando de que él estuviera delante. Incluso se ajustó el sujetador por encima de la ropa.

Rafael no reaccionó hasta que lo hizo ella, mirándole revestida de inocencias al pasar por su lado, tan libre como natural.

La turbación no desapareció hasta que Natalia apareció junto a él.

—¡Venga, vamos! ¿Se puede saber a qué estás esperando?

25

Sixto examinó los papeles de la campaña de los preservativos Aura. Ni siquiera la mejor de sus ideas, y las había tenido de geniales en los últimos diez o doce años, derrotaría la cerrazón de Marcelino, ahora lo sabía. El simple hecho de que él presentara una idea, cuando le había dado la campaña a otro, equivaldría a retratarle. Así que estaba acorralado. No perdido pero sí acorralado. Roberto Estrada subía. Él bajaba. Era la ley de la bolsa en publicidad. Vales lo que vale tu última campaña, y la de aquella condenada pelotita "viva", que no paraba de dar botes, no había sido precisamente lúcida. En tres meses el último en llegar podía ocupar el puesto de Ruiz, a la derecha de Dios Padre. Y si eso sucedía, su declive estaba anunciado, y la primera paletada de tierra sobre su tumba dada.

No era agorero, ni se dejaba llevar por el dramatismo. Era realista.

Conocía el terreno que pisaba.

Si hubiera matado a Roberto Estrada el primer día, si le hubiera borrado su estúpida sonrisa —aún más de lo que lo hizo con aquel corte, que desde luego le puso en su contra inmediatamente—, si le hubiera dicho a Marcelino que no servía... ¿Por qué tuvo que ser tan perdonavidas, y decirle que "no estaba mal" y que "podía aprender"? ¿Por qué había tenido que ser tan bocazas y sentirse tan seguro de sí mismo?

Desde que trataba de iniciar una nueva vida, normal y feliz, con Encarna, todo le salía mal. Era como si hubiera pisado mierda.

Demasiada turbulencia.

—Sixto, ¿has visto mi pulsera de...?

Demasiada tensión.

—¡Coño y a mi qué me cuentas! ¿He estado aquí todo el día? !Acabo de llegar hace diez minutos!, ¿no? ¡Si pusieras un poco de orden en este caos de casa! ¡aquí es imposible encontrar nada, y encima tú, que lo vas dejando todo donde te sale de...!

Encarna ya no estaba allí para oírle.

26

Entreabrió la puerta de la habitación de Vanessa, y metió la cabeza por el hueco buscando la figura de su hija al no verla sentada de espaldas a él frente a su mesa de trabajo. Le llegó su voz aún antes de que la descubriera, en la cama, que quedaba detrás de la hoja de madera.

—Pasa, papá.

—¿Te encuentras mal? —se inquietó Salvador.

—No, es que hacía un break.

—Ah.

—Llevo todo el día, y no quiero que se me caigan las pestañas. Aún no se hacen trasplantes de pestañas, ¿sabes?

Solía tener ocurrencias de las más diversas, y hablaba con un lenguaje propio y una entonación que le divertía tanto como le fascinaba. Vanessa estaba llena de vitalidad, y estaba seguro de que tenía ante sí un futuro mágico, esplendido, sobre todo por su actitud ante la vida, su forma de ver y entender el mundo, su talante positivo. No era brillante en los estudios, pero su voluntad lo resistía todo, y su caparazón daba la impresión de estar hecho a prueba de bombas. A veces Paz le decía justamente lo contrario, que ella se sentía débil, y que trataba de superar su complejo de inferioridad con la determinación de lograr cuanto se había propuesto. Para una adolescente de catorce años, eso ya era suficiente.

Aunque fuera curioso. Paz estaba preocupada por Vanessa y no por Octavio, mientras que él, era todo lo contrario. Uno de los dos estaba equivocado.

Aunque, ¿por qué no era posible que los dos acertaran en lo bueno?

Se sentó en la cama, junto a la niña, y le pasó una mano por la mejilla. Vanessa sonrió con ternura. Precisamente por eso le sorprendió lo que dijo.

—Has de confiar más en Octavio, papá.

—¿Qué quieres decir?

—Es muy buen tío, y muy legal. Lo que pasa es que va a su aire. Si supieras la buena fama que tiene.

—¿Entre sus "colegas"? —se burló sin ganas.

—Entre sus "colegas", sí —asintió Vanessa—. Es la persona más desinteresada y honesta que conozco, de las que se puede confiar.

Si algo le gustaba, por lo menos, era aquello, que sus hijos estuvieran unidos pese a ser tan distintos de carácter, pertenecer a sexos opuestos y llevarse cuatro años de diferencia. Siempre les había dicho que confiaran el uno en el otro, y que en los temas que no quisieran hablar con él o con Paz, que por lo menos los hablaran entre sí, que no se engañaran ni se mintieran. Se sentía orgulloso de ello.

Y también de que Vanessa defendiera de aquella manera a Octavio.

—Sé que es especial —concedió—, pero fuma, bebe...

—Papá, eso lo hacen todos, pero él controla.

—Oh, ya salió la palabra mágica: control.

—¿Qué te crees que voy a hacer yo en cuanto me dejes salir de noche?

—Perfecto —bromeó de nuevo sin ganas—: otro problema.

—Venga, hombre, no seas carca. ¿Y tus batallitas de cuando eras joven? Antes mucho contarlas, y ahora, hace años que nasti de plasti, por si tomamos nota. Eres un tramposo.

Y a lo peor tenía razón: otro problema. Octavio era un chico, Vanessa una chica. Con quince años la mayoría ya salía de noche, con amigas o con amigos. Cines, discotecas, los arañazos al reloj y a la libertad... Y con diecisiete o dieciocho, también ella pasaría toda la noche "de marcha", hasta el amanecer, porque se trataba de eso. Lo de llegar "antes de las diez" pertenecía al tiempo de los dinosaurios. Su tiempo.

—¿Te quedarás estudiando todo el fin de semana? —quiso saber.

—¡Que remedio! —bufó la chica—. ¡El lunes tengo las malditas mates, y quiero nota!

—Tómatelo con calma —le dio un beso y se levantó de la cama.

—¿Consejo de médico?

—Sí.

—¡A la orden, doc! —cantó imitando a Bugs Bunny.

Siempre le hacía reír, aunque no quisiera, o pensara que no estaba de humor, o sintiera los nubarrones del malestar. Siempre lo lograba.

Era como una bocanada renovada y constante de aire fresco.

—Bien mirado —dijo—, si no me traes nota será mejor que no aparezcas por casa.

—¡Oh, cielos, repudiada por mi propio padre, no puedo creerlo! —volvió a cantar Vanessa empleando su más eficaz y divertido tono gangoso de voz al tiempo que hundía su cabeza debajo de la almohada.

Encarna

No aguanto los malos rollos. No aguanto las malas caras, los gritos y toda esa parafernalia que agria las relaciones entre las personas, y más entre las parejas. Tengo mis propias teorías, lo de que si uno no quiere pelea el otro ya puede darse de cabeza contra la pared.

Mi relación con Quique estuvo formada por tres años y medio intensos, de vida y magia en común, y otro medio año de declive y deterioro, que coincidió con su engaño y mi choque con la realidad, aunque de ese medio año solo los tres meses finales resultaran realmente duros, y la amargura de la separación fuese algo de un abrir y cerrar de ojos.

Pero no hubo peleas. Recriminaciones sí, peleas no.

Sixto solía trabajar en casa, estaba volcado en su trabajo, y yo sabía que era su vida, pero por lo general se dejaba los problemas en la puerta, si es que los tenía. En el momento de gritarme, sin más, me metí en nuestra habitación y pasé de él. Si había tenido un mal encuentro con sus hijos... Lo único malo es que su futuro iba a estar lleno de malos encuentros con ellos, con su ex y consigo mismo. Y en eso poco podía hacer yo, salvo tener paciencia si le quería.

Y le quiero.

Me da igual lo que piensen las mujeres de sus amigas. Le quiero. No estaría aquí si no le quisiera.

Iba a vestirme, porque ya se hacía tarde y no quería que luego me echara la bronca por no estar lista y a punto cuando él decidiera irse. Ni siquiera sabía la hora en que había quedado con ellos. Me desnudé, por completo, y fue en ese momento cuando él entró en la habitación.

27

Quería pedirle perdón, o cuanto menos excusarse. Encarna no tenía la culpa de nada, y la idea de pasar la noche con ella disgustada en presencia de Salvador y de Rafael, con sus respectivas... Aunque nunca se enfadara, aunque siempre estuviese contenta y pareciera feliz, todavía estaban empezando, y si no quería perderla tenía que ir con cuidado. Encarna era la fuerte. En una relación como la suya, la fuerte siempre es la parte más joven, aunque él creyera tener el poder, económico y ambiental. Si encima de como estaban las cosas hundía lo mejor de si mismo en un momento como aquel, sería tanto como fastidiar por completo su vida. Empezaba a darse cuenta de que ahora dependía más y más de su nuevo amor.

Era una droga.

Cuando al entrar en la habitación la vio desnuda, con los brazos en alto sujetándose el cabello, los pechos aún más altos gracias a ello, los muslos brillando a través de su reluciente contorno y la masa oscura y frondosa del vello púbico destacando como un poderoso reclamo en su cuerpo vibrante, supo que además de amarla la deseaba.

Las otras siempre fueron simples destellos, sensaciones fugaces, amores de una noche, o de una semana. Incluso las dos o tres relaciones más largas no le aportaron nada salvo placer y las luces de lo prohibido en el limitado horizonte de una vida volcada en el trabajo. De no haber encontrado a Encarna habría seguido igual, dando tumbos entre la agencia y la vulgaridad de su vida con Sole. Ahora la necesitaba.

Se detuvo detrás de ella, y le puso ambas manos en la cintura. Encarna dejó de sujetarse el cabello y este cayó por encima de los hombros, desparramándose hasta ellos y la nuca con sus rubios acentos. Sixto elevó su mano derecha para apartarle los de la parte derecha y le besó el cuello sin que su compañera opusiera ninguna resistencia o dijera nada. El beso fue largo, dejó un rastro húmedo hasta la oreja y una vez en ella le mordisqueó el lóbulo antes de introducirle la lengua en su interior.

Encarna ya no pudo permanecer quieta.

—Va, que sabes que me gusta, estáte quieto.

No se estuvo quieto, la hizo girar despacio entre sus brazos, hasta quedar de cara, y entonces buscó sus labios. Al encontrarlos, ya entreabiertos y con aquella especial vibración que tanto le gustaba , acabó de perder el frágil equilibrio de su consciencia. Cerró los ojos y se dejó llevar y arrastrar por todas las sensaciones que buscaba y necesitaba en un momento como aquel. Su mano derecha descendió primero hasta el pecho, orlando el pezón, endureciéndolo con su caricia, y después hasta la cúpula pélvica, arremolinando los dedos entre el vello antes de buscar, un poco más abajo, la dulce textura de las vulvas.

Solo entonces ella trató de retirarse un poco.

—¿Qué haces? —susurró—. Es tarde. Vamos a...

—Que se jodan —murmuró él.

—Pero...

Fue un último y fallido intento de detenerle. Sixto ocupó la vagina, y su humedad le volvió definitivamente loco, como solía sucederle cada vez que juntos asaltaban el palacio de sus sueños. Encarna gimió, disparándose de manera inmediata. Abrió más la boca para mantener el beso y también abrió las piernas para que él la acariciara.

Cuando cayeron sobre la cama, un minuto después, sus movimientos ya no eran acompasados ni cadenciosos, sino la resultante de la guerra de sus sentidos.

28

Paz sacó la cabeza por la puerta de la habitación al oir el timbre exterior con el zumbido mucho más agudo que el del piso.

—¡Llaman! —gritó—. ¿Puedes ir tú? Yo aún no estoy lista.

Primero no oyó ninguna respuesta. Iba a salir igualmente, para abrir la puerta de la calle desde arriba, y recabar ayuda inmediata para que Salvador o Vanessa hicieran lo propio con la del piso, pero no fue necesario. Olvidaba a veces que su marido hablaba poco, pero eso no significara que estuviese sordo. Pasó por su lado, obediente y ya correctamente trajeado y a punto, y ella volvió a meterse en la habitación para terminar de arreglarse. Solo le faltaba subirse la cremallera del vestido, ponerse los pendientes, escoger que collar o que pulseras llevar. Odiaba las ornamentaciones, pero Natalia solía ir muy enjoyada y tampoco quería parecer una pobretona a su lado.

Cuando finalmente se decidió por un collar muy sencillo, de plata, y dos pulseras igualmente de plata, se encogió de hombros y decidió que de todas formas ya estaba bien. Como complemento final se puso un broche en la parte superior izquierda del vestido. También era de plata, puro diseño, regalo de Vanessa y Octavio por su último cumpleaños.

Hasta ella llegaron las voces de Rafael y Natalia, junto a la de su marido.

—¡Hombre, Salvador! ¿Ya has dejado de comer niños por hoy?

—Hola, ¿cómo estas, querida?

—¿Y Paz?

—Acabando de arreglarse. ¿Cómo va todo, Rafa?

—Si todos los críos que visitas compraran la ropa que vendo, me iría mucho mejor. ¿Por qué no regalas unos vaqueros o una *T-Shirt* por cada tres visitas?

—¿Qué es una *T-Shirt*?

—Una camiseta, hombre, una camiseta de esas con cosas escritas.

Las voces y las risas se aproximaron por el pasillo. Paz salió en ese momento, justo a tiempo de encontrarse a Natalia, que parecía buscarla caminando un par de pasos por delante de los dos hombres.

—Hola, Natalia —la saludó ella, y a continuación ponderó—: Caramba, qué vestido más bonito llevas, y qué bien te sienta.

—Lo vi ayer y no pude resistir la tentación, ¿a que es divino?

También Vanessa apareció por el pasillo, apartada de sus estudios por la irrupción de las visitas.

—¡Eh, familia! ¿Qué hay? —gritó anunciando su presencia.

Hubo nuevo reparto de besos, abrazos, palabras agradables dirigidas a la adolescente, mientras avanzaban ahora más despacio hacia la sala. Natalia preguntó por Octavio. Paz por Gloria. Salvador y Rafael volvían a reír a causa del modismo anglosajón recién empleado por el segundo. Vanessa observaba a Natalia de arriba abajo, con atención, para poder cotillear después con su madre. Al llegar los cinco a la sala se desparramaron por ella de forma relajada, y solo Rafael se dejó caer en una butaca, como si estuviese agotado antes de empezar la noche.

Salvador aprovechó el primer instante de silencio global, tras el estallido habitual de todas las llegadas o despedidas, para preguntar como correspondía a un perfecto anfitrión:

—¿Queréis beber algo? Ya sabéis que la puntualidad no es cosa de Sixto, y más ahora.

29

Regresó del baño, aún desnuda, y pese a que acababa de poseerla sintió de nuevo la punzada del deseo, de acariciarla y besarla, tenerla a su lado en la cama.

—Vamos —le azuzó Encarna—. ¿Has visto la hora que es?

—Vale, vale, ya me visto —dijo él sin hacer la menor intención de moverse.

—Oye, que si quieres no vamos, ¿eh? —le miró como si esperase una reacción positiva por parte de Sixto—. Llamamos dando una excusa y...

—No, mujer, no. Ya me levanto.

Lo hizo, de un salto, recuperando la flexibilidad y elasticidad de las piernas después de la tensión pasada y la descarga erótica. Encarna se había puesto encima, así que estaba más agotado por haberse tenido que mover con el agravante de su peso, aunque no era nada comparado con el de Sole. Claro que Sole nunca se ponía encima. Era clásica.

—Oye, ¿qué te pasaba, o qué te pasa esta noche?

—¿Por qué? —mencionó él abriendo el armario para escoger la ropa que iba a ponerse.

—Más que hacer el amor parecías estarte tirando al mundo entero.

—Tenía ganas, mujer.

—Tienes ganas cada día, y a cada momento, y no lo haces como acabas de hacerlo ahora. Y además... está tu cabreo de antes. ¿Qué sucede?

—Nada —escogió un traje deportivo, elegante, una camisa azul, ¿corbata? Seguro que los otros dos iban con corbata—. ¿Qué quieres que...?

—Oye, te pasa algo y no me vengas con chorradas. Si no quieres confiar en mi, o si tienes miedo de que me asuste o que se yo que se te ocurre, es otra cosa, pero no me digas que no te pasa nada cuando me has dado un... bueno, que me has puesto a mil, y estabas disparado.

—¿En serio? —se acercó a ella para atraparla una vez más.

—¡Ahora ya no estoy a mil, quieto! —se apartó Encarna decidida a no volver a caer en la trampa.

—Si quieres vengo cabreado cada noche.

—No me lo cuentes, no. Tú a lo tuyo —protestó ella plegando los labios.

Se resignó. La verdad es que había sido una estupidez gritar como lo había hecho. Encarna no era una de sus niñas de veinte años. Era una mujer adulta y madura, aunque a veces por su aspecto y su carácter, pudiera parecer más joven. Si quería mantenerla apartada de sus problemas laborales no tenía porque haber demostrado que los tenía, aunque también estaba lo de Marta, el divorcio y todo lo demás, incluida Sole. Siempre Sole.

Una separación no mata los recuerdos, ni ahoga las voces, el dolor.

—Mi hija me ha puesto mala cara —justificó sin mucha convicción.

—Tu hija te pone mala cara desde que te fuiste, y a no ser que hoy haya sido muy, pero que muy mala cara, sueles resignarte, no cabrearte.

—Le van a dar la campaña de los preservativos al gilipollas de Estrada.

Logró decirlo, sin más, aunque con cansancio y sabor a derrota. Lo hizo apartando sus ojos de ella, paseándolos por la habitación a la búsqueda de una salida que no encontró. La reacción de Encarna fue directa.

—No sé de qué te extrañas. Llevas un mes hablándome de ese tío, o sea que ya le veías venir y te temías algo así. Tenías que haberle parado los piés antes, aunque no quiero decirte que te hayas equivocado —le tranquilizó ella—. Solo te digo que esto te servirá para la próxima. Tampoco es tan grave. ¿O sí?

¿Le recordaba que la campaña era un plato de primera? ¿Le recordaba lo de Ruiz? ¿Le recordaba de qué iba el lío de la publicidad?

—Ven.

No fue a por ella. Se lo pidió.

Y ella no le recordó la hora que era, ni protestó, ni dijo nada. Le bastó con verle la cara, dejó los sujetadores que iba a ponerse y cubrió la breve distancia que les separaba.

Sixto la abrazó, con ternura, pero fue Encarna la que ésta vez le besó a él.

Todavía estaban desnudos.

Y no era necesario hablar inmediatamente, aunque uno estaba dispuesto a hacerlo y otra dispuesta a escuchar.

30

—He hablado con Sole, hace un rato.

—¿Ah, sí? —se interesó enseguida Natalia—. Yo es que no me atrevo, mira. Me da un no sé qué... Y como acaba siempre llorando. ¿Cómo está?

—¿Cómo quieres que esté? Fatal. Y a mi también se me pone a llorar, tú dirás, pero hija, hay que estar a las duras y las maduras.

—Sí, claro, pero... ¿Ha llamado ella?

—No, yo.

—¡Qué valor tienes! —ponderó Natalia.

—Quería decirle lo de esta noche, que salíamos a cenar con ella.

—¡Por Dios! ¿Qué necesidad había de contárselo?

—¿Y si alguien nos ve y se lo dice, qué? Mira, he preferido ser clara, no andarme con tapujos. Lo otro hubiera sido peor, porque entonces, y en su estado, igual le hubiera dado por pensar que la estábamos olvidando y engañando y qué se yo cuántas cosas más.

—No, si visto así... —dudó Natalia—. ¿Y cómo se lo ha tomado?

—Bueno, no sabría explicarlo. De entrada le he dicho que tanto tú como yo nos habíamos metido en esto sin saber cómo, pero que la cosa ya era inevitable.

—Menos mal que le has dicho que yo...

—Claro, mujer —justificó Paz—. Y también le he dicho que lo íbamos a pasar mal, porque no sabía ni qué decirle o de qué hablar.

—¡Si es que es la pura verdad! No tenemos nada en común, y a estas alturas de nuestra vida, eso de tener que ser amiga de alguien solo porque está con una persona... vaya, que no.

—¿Sabes qué me ha dicho? —se acercó a su amiga y menguó el tono de su voz, como si cerca hubiera alguien capaz de oirlas o interesado en el tema—. Que si él volviera, le perdonaría.

—¡No!

—Lo que oyes.

—Pero si ha sido una... —no encontró la palabra adecuada y acabó moviendo la cabeza negativamente ante lo que consideraba una atrocidad.

—Supongo que son muchos años, y están los hijos.

—Y ella, que es muy boba.

Se arrepintió de haber hablado así de su amiga. A modo de ramalazo, se preguntó qué haría ella misma acerca de su propio drama. A veces creía estar viendo una película, como en el caso de Sole y Sixto, en la que los protagonistas eran otros, no ella y Rafael.

—Solo espero que la cena sea pacifica y tranquila, y que no haya ninguna tensión —suspiró Paz—. Mañana le diré a Salvador que las cosas ya no son como eran antes, y que si Sixto tiene una nueva pareja me parece muy bien, pero que a nosotros no nos complique la vida.

—Yo le diré lo mismo a Rafael.

—¿Qué pasaría si Sole rehiciera su vida y también nos trajera a su nuevo compañero, marido o lo que sea?

—Claro, claro. Esto no es América, de momento.

—Ya, y seguro que nuestros maridos no lo verían tan normal.

—Eso por descontado, Paz.

Estaban de acuerdo, y se solidarizaron una con otra a través de sus miradas, aunque Natalia apartó la suya de forma inmediata.

Fue entonces cuando Paz se dio cuenta de la forma en que unía y desunía sus manos, y del aire nervioso que la envolvía, y también de la extraña tensión que parecía destilar. Y por puro instinto, tuvo la sensación que más que de Sole, a lo peor al final no habían estado hablando de su amiga separada, sino de alguien mucho más próximo.

Y desde luego no era ella.

31

—¿Y tu hijo? Hace mucho que no le veo.

Salvador dejó el vaso sobre la mesita. No había mucho que decir, pero menos aún por donde escapar. Fingió indiferencia, pero su voz atrapó toda la carga emocional que sentía ante el tema que más le preocupaba de su vida familiar, además de lo que atañía a la propia Paz y a la amarga rutina de su matrimonio.

—Estará por ahí —suspiró—. ¡Es viernes!

—Lo dices como si fuera el Nombre de la Bestia —bromeó Rafael.

—¿Te acuerdas de cuando el fin de semana empezaba el sábado a mediodía?

—¿Que si me acuerdo? ¡Como que yo trabajaba en sábado!

—Hoy en cambio empiezan el viernes y acaban el mismo lunes por la mañana.

—Sí, ya, pero ojalá lo hubiéramos pillado nosotros, tú, que en nuestra época... ¡Ya nos jodieron bien, ya! Yo cada vez que lo pienso...

—Nos putearon, pero eso nos enseñó a valernos por nosotros mismos, y nos hizo madurar antes, saber lo que queríamos y cómo conseguirlo —dijo Salvador—. Esto de ahora no sé yo qué sentido tiene.

—Coño, pues pasarlo bien, ¿qué sentido va a tener? Son jóvenes, y hay menos chorradas que cuando lo éramos nosotros.

—Tú tienes una hija, y es aún pequeña —le recordó Salvador.

—¿Qué pasa, que tu hijo lleva los pelos largos y se va de marcha? ¡No va a quedarse en casa!

—Muy liberal y progre eres tú con los hijos de los demás.

—Y muy carca te estás volviendo tú, revolucionario de pacotilla —se burló Rafael—. A la edad de Octavio ya te habían corrido a palos los grises un par de veces, y te habían detenido en otra ¿no?

—Sí, hombre, compara la lucha de entonces con el pasotismo de ahora.

—¡Coño, que han pasado la tira de años, Salva!

—Así que hicimos "la revolución" para esto, para que hoy nuestros hijos salgan el viernes por la noche, se emporren, se pongan ciegos de cerveza, y puedan decir libremente que todo es una mierda y que no hay futuro y que, total, para lo que viene, no hace falta hacer nada.

—¡Uy, cómo estás tú esta noche! —cantó Rafael apurando el último sorbo de su vaso—. A este paso acabarás votando al PP, como está mandado.

—Sabes perfectamente a quien voto. Aquí el facha es Sixto.

—¡Anda ya!

—¿Que no? Preguntárselo. Aquí todo Dios era del PSOE en los 80, cuando había dinero que ganar, como tú. ¡La gente guapa! Pero estamos en los 90, y ahora es cuando todos se están quitando la careta. Yo siempre me he mantenido fiel a mis ideas.

—¿No te habrás pasado a lo del Colom?

—Tampoco es eso. Hay que defender un nacionalismo serio y real, posibilista.

—No me hagas campaña, va. Total, para decirme que estás preocupado por Octavio, tampoco vamos a discutir de política.

—Sé muy bien que en este país no puede hablarse de política ni de fútbol a no ser que todo el mundo sea del mismo partido y del mismo equipo, no me lo recuerdes —aclaró Salvador—. Y no estoy preocupado por mi hijo, es solo que...

—Que lo tienen mal, Salva, que sí —le detuvo Rafael—. Que tú estás en tu consulta, y te vienen las mamás con sus nenes y sus nenas, y te dan esos papelitos de la médica y te ganas la pasta tan tranquilo, pero los que tenemos negocios lo vemos, y lo notamos, ¡y joder cómo está el patio! Y eso la gente joven lo ve y lo sabe. ¿Qué te crees, que si pudiera no me iría yo de marcha el fin de semana entero, pasando de todo? ¡Si lo único malo de ahora es que haya tanto maricón suelto!

Salvador iba a responder cuando pensó en algo, inesperado.

Ni siquiera sabía si su hijo salía con chicas.

Tuvo que levantarse, para servirse otro poco de bebida, ante la súbita ira que le dominó.

32

—¿Qué te sucede? —preguntó Paz.

—¿A mí? Nada, ¿por qué?

—Te noto algo nerviosa, tensa. Ya sabes.

—Pues no, vaya... no sé —Natalia hizo un gesto vago, demasiado artificial—. Será que estos días he estado intranquila por Gloria.

—¿Ha estado enferma?

—Sí, un poco resfriada.

—Pero no llamaste a Salvador.

—No, mujer, ya veía que no era nada.

—Pues es toda una sorpresa —consideró Paz burlona—. Por lo general a la que tu hija estornuda ya estás llamando a urgencias.

—¡Cómo eres! Es que a veces me asusto.

—A veces..., muchas veces.

—Cómo se nota que los tienes ya mayores y te despreocupas.

—Oh, sí, me despreocupo mucho, como que ahora es cuando de verdad hay que empezar a preocuparse —anunció Paz—. ¿Sabes que la hija de Sole llevaba un preservativo en el bolso?

—Tiene diecisiete años.

—Es lo que le he dicho a ella.

—¿Y Sole, como lo ha encontrado, registrándoselo, claro?

—¿Tú qué crees?

—Eso es algo que nunca haré con Gloria, de verdad.

Paz iba a decirle que lo dudaba, que si alguien era capaz de registrarle las cosas a su única hija, era ella, pero no quiso pincharla más. De hecho, y gracias al giro de la conversación, hablando de hijos, Natalia había eludido la pregunta inicial.

Pero ella seguía inquieta, sus ojos se revestían de un halo ceniciento, perdiéndose más allá de sí mismas y sus voces. Era una suma de detalles. Pequeños detalles.

Como el hecho de que ahora ella mirase de aquella forma tan densa la fotografía de su boda.

—Pensaba llevar a Gloria el lunes a ver a Salvador, para que le recete unas vitaminas —dijo en voz baja, aunque la dicotomía abierta entre su voz y el color de sus pensamientos fuese evidente.

—Tienes la hija más sana del mundo, mujer.

Era su tema favorito, Gloria, pero esta vez ni la rebatió ni se sintió ofendida ni buscó uno de sus característicos cuerpo a cuerpo maternales. Cogió el marco de plata con la fotografía y lo observó más de cerca.

—Estabais muy bien los dos aquí, ¿verdad?

—Salvador era muy guapo de joven.

—Y tú también.

—No, era del montón, aunque para él...

—Siempre ha estado muy enamorado —susurró Natalia—. Y pronto haréis los veinticinco años juntos, ¡Jesús!

—Juntos ya los llevamos. Recuerda que estuvimos dos de relaciones.

Dejó el portarretratos en su sitio, y la luz que titilaba en los ojos de Natalia se hizo más evidente para Paz.

Sin embargo, la nueva pregunta que iba a formularle acerca de su estado, murió antes de alcanzar los labios.

—Oye, qué raro que aún no estén aquí, ¿verdad? —dijo Natalia cambiando de pronto su tono de voz y su aspecto—. Sixto es un poco viva la virgen, pero yendo con ella, por lo menos podrían ser más puntuales, ¿no? ¿Qué hora es?

Rafael

No sé como se me ocurrió la idea, fue algo parecido a un flash mental, una de esas cosas que de pronto aparecen en tu cabeza, y que se disparan, y que en ese momento, además, te parecen plausibles, casi geniales, porque cuando estás desesperado, cualquier solución, por insólita que sea, te resulta genial.

Allí estaba yo, con la mente puesta en otra parte, en mi negocio, hablando de hijos y demás tonterías de matrimonios con Salvador, mi amigo Salvador, médico para más señas.

Siempre había imaginado que él estaba forrado, pero forrado de verdad, es decir, con pasta, buena pasta en el banco. ¿Y si no, de qué trabajar tantas horas tomándoles la temperatura a los críos, en la consulta, visitando casas, y antes en todas las entidades médicas por las que había pasado? ¿Era por amor a su profesión? Desde luego sí, eso entraba de lleno dentro de lo posible, pero los médicos van sumando, y sumando, y sumando, y la mayoría escaquean a Hacienda porque es lo más sencillo. ¿Quién controla si en un día se han hecho veinte o treinta consultas? Si a mi me pagaran en metálico y sin necesidad de hacer facturas o recibos, como él, otro gallo cantaría. Pero a mi me tienen cogido por las pelotas. A él no.

Y Salvador no gastaba apenas nada, llevaba el mismo coche de hacía diez o doce años, vestía a lo clásico, su mujer no era de las de llevar joyas o cambiar el vestuario cada temporada, ni gimnasios ni polladas de esas. Nunca se tomaban unas vacaciones decentes, ni viajaban. Encima su hijo no había estudiado nada y la niña aún no había empezado en serio su futura carrera.

Salvador tenía dinero, seguro, y tal vez...

Solo tal vez...

33

Respiró a fondo, inundó sus pulmones de aire, atemperó la excitación que sentía ante la relevancia de su idea, y buscando la forma de parecer normal, sin que su voz sonara ansiosa o su ánimo le delatara, le pasó de pronto un brazo por encima de los hombros de Salvador y le dijo:

—Oye, ¿tú qué haces con el dinero?

—¿Cómo que qué hago? —Salvador intentó mirarle girando la cabeza hacia él—. ¡Vaya preguntas haces!

—Quiero decir que si lo dejas en el banco o inviertes o compras cosas y todo eso, hombre.

—¿Comprar? ¿Qué quieres que compre?

—Bueno —se dio cuenta de que parecía reacio a soltar prenda—, hay gente que va comprando algún piso, para los hijos, para alquilar, o locales comerciales. Conozco a uno que tiene una docena de locales comerciales. Los bancos dan cada día menos intereses, y tú no jugarás en bolsa, por supuesto.

—Por supuesto —le aclaró Salvador—. Prefiero los fondos de inversión.

—¿Fondos de inversión? Bueno, sí, son rentables y seguros, pero...

—En quince años, si no tocas nada, ni pagas a Hacienda.

—Ya, pero hay cosas más rentables, más inmediatas. Eso de los quince años... ¡joder, tú!, suena a jubilación.

—Es que se trata de eso, de tener dinero para cuando seas mayor. La pensión que pueda quedarme del Colegio de Médicos estará bien, pero por si acaso.

—O sea que eres una hormiguita.

—Llámalo así.

—¿No te interesaría invertir en un negocio?

Se lo soltó de golpe, cansado de darle vueltas y de buscar la forma de interesarle en el tema. Le conocía lo bastante bien como para saber que su amigo era conservador en eso, defensor del ahorro, contrario a la especulación, de los que busca, ante todo, la seguridad. Los tiempos del "lanzarse a la piscina sin mirar si hay agua" habían pasado para él, si es que un día los hubo, a pesar de que en su juventud fuera todo un rebelde.

En los días en que se podía ser rebelde.

—¿Un negocio? —dudó Salvador—. ¿Qué clase de negocio?

—El mío. Estoy buscando un socio para hacer una ampliación de capital, pero para ya mismo, porque tengo una oportunidad única de comprar una enorme partida de género de Indonesia y es cosa de un par de días. Beneficio seguro, ya sabes, aunque en los negocios siempre es mejor mantener el capital y buscar más...

—Creía que el momento era bastante malo —le detuvo Salvador.

Rafael congeló su sonrisa para mantener su tono distendido y eficaz, seguro y empresarial. Era un buen vendedor, siempre lo había sido, aunque era la primera vez que trataba de venderle una pompa de jabón a un amigo.

Lo que necesitaba era salvarse, no un socio, aunque si para ello debía vender su alma al diablo...

—Al contrario —aseguró—. El momento es bueno para los que saben invertir bien, jugar sus cartas. Mira, los orientales venden barato porque nadie compra, y el que se arriesgue ahora es el que se llevará el gato al agua. Es evidente, ¿no?

—No sé, chico. Ya sabes que yo de negocios ni entiendo ni he querido entender nunca. Eso lo dejo para los que tenéis visión de la jugada, como tú. Cada cual, a lo suyo.

—Pero te interesaría, ¿no?

—¿A mí? —se extrañó Salvador—. No, por Dios. Ya me va bien como estoy.

—Con el dinero en el banco y esos fondos de inversión, mínimo pero seguro.

—Exacto.

—¿Te das cuenta de que puede que estés tirando la posibilidad de...?

Volvió a detenerle, y ahora con un gesto que fue decisivo, hasta para alguien tan vehemente y tozudo como Rafael.

—No, no, no, gracias por pensar en mi pero... no. Nunca lo he hecho, y nunca lo haré. Es como si te pidiera que fueras mi socio en una nueva consulta que fuera a abrir.

—Si es una buena oportunidad, la estudiaría y a lo mejor, si pudiera, invertiría, ¿por qué no? Además, somos amigos.

No tenía que haberle dicho esto último. Se dio cuenta de ello. Ahora ya no le ofrecía dinero fácil en una inversión de negocios. Ahora se lo acababa de pedir.

Acababa de decirle que estaba mal y con el agua al cuello.

—Los amigos son malos para los negocios —dijo Salvador—. Siempre es mejor alguien con quien puedas hablar sin más lazos que los económicos. Y en tu caso, si lo que me has dicho es bueno, encontrarás a alguien, seguro, o le pides dinero al banco y te lo montas solo.

—Bueno, yo lo hacía por ti, ya sabes —manifestó Rafael—. Lo otro ya lo tengo seguro, pero prefería que... En fin, olvídalo.

Y le dio la espalda, fingiendo buscar el aparador con las botellas, para que el médico no viera sus mandíbulas apretadas, ni el rictus de rabia que difícilmente logró atemperar al sentirse inundado por ella durante dos o tres breves pero intensos segundos.

Salvador

No me enfadé con él. Conozco a Rafael. Pero me supo mal que me propusiera algo como aquello, primero, conociéndome, y segundo, sabiendo como sabíamos los dos que me estaba engañando, y que sí existían dificultades para todos, y más para los que, como él, habían montado pequeñas empresas en la vorágine económica de los 80, buscando un crecimiento rápido, a veces unos beneficios inmediatos a caballo de sus muchos riesgos y que en los 90 naufragaban o vivían al límite de lo irreal, azuzadas por la crisis, la recesión, los impuestos y los cambios políticos y económicos del mundo entero.

Rafael era listo. Es listo. Siempre lo fue. Pero es de esa clase de personas que te asustan, porque no caminan por la vida, corren, y más que correr, a veces da la impresión de que siempre están huyendo hacia adelante con su vertiginosa forma de hacerlo todo. Compran, venden, especulan, ganan, pierden, se juegan el infarto a los cuarenta y pico y con toda seguridad la muerte antes de los sesenta. Gente que dice que vive la vida a tope, pero que para mi lo único que hacen es quemarla. Vivir a tope es marcharse a la India a curar leprosos, o al Africa a ejercer en un hospital sin medios en un campo de refugiados de cualquier guerra tribal y barbárica, o escalar el Everest si eso es lo que te gusta. Pero vivir a tope con la única bandera del dinero y el placer de tenerlo para volver a tratar de ganar más, no creo que sea lo mejor que pueda hacerse, aunque desde luego yo, ahorrando como una hormiguita, como decía Rafael...

Puede que siempre fuera viejo de antemano, pensando en el futuro, guardando, temiendo. Viejo o prudente. Siempre he sido viejo desde que conocí a Paz, acabé la carrera, me hice pediatra...

Si no quise vivir el riesgo de ser lo que quise ser cuando pude hacerlo, ¿cómo pensar ahora que iba a darle mi dinero, aunque solo fuera una parte, por pequeña que fuese, al loco de Rafael?

Sé que se enfadó, se lo noté. Fue una descarga eléctrica tan inmediata como reveladora. Y me dio pena. Yo también podía haberme enfadado, porque quería liarme, pero no lo hice. Pensé que tenía que estar muy desesperado para llegar a algo como eso. Si me hubiese pedido dinero directamente... Aunque no, tampoco se lo hubiese dejado. No creo en los negocios, ni en las inversiones, ni en las especulaciones, si no eres negociante, inversionista, especulador. Y yo solo soy médico.

Pediatra.

No sé que habría sido de la escena, de nosotros, si en ese momento no hubiera sonado el teléfono.

34

Alguien descolgó el aparato al término del primer zumbido. Casi coincidiendo con la voz de Salvador, Encarna salió de la habitación luciendo un vestido de una sóla pieza, relativamente breve, aunque no era el más ínfimo de los que tenía. El escote, en V, llegaba hasta más abajo del punto de contacto de ambos senos, apretándoselos hacia el centro de su pecho. La falda, mini, alcanzaba la mitad de los muslos, permitiendo ver la perfecta linea de las piernas, rematadas por unos zapatos de tacón alto que aún las hacían más largas. El cabello rubio, suelto, contrastaba con el negro austero del vestido.

—¿Sí? ¿Quién es? —creyó oir por segunda vez a Salvador antes de llegar a reaccionar.

—Soy yo, Sixto.

—¡Eh! ¿Qué pasa? Habíamos quedado a esta hora, ¿no?

—Mira, que he tenido una complicación y como a fin de cuentas hemos de ir en dos coches, mejor nos encontramos directamente en el restaurante, ¿vale?

—Ah, muy bien —al otro lado de la linea Salvador pareció informar del cambio de planes a los demás, probablemente a Paz, Natalia y Rafael—. Es Sixto, que dice que se le ha hecho tarde y que nos vemos en el restaurante directamente —volvió a ponerse al aparato y agregó dirigiéndose a él—: La Venta, ¿eh?

—La Venta, sí —confirmó Sixto.

—Hasta ahora.

Colgó y se quedó mirando a Encarna, casi ajeno a la conversación que acababa de sostener. La encontró preciosa, deseable. Demasiado preciosa y deseable. Se maravilló de lo bien que sabía arreglarse, lo bien que sabía gustar, y también de su suerte al tenerla.

Pero aquella era una salida de matrimonios, no una escapada solitaria de ella y de él.

—Oye, ¿no tienes nada más discreto? —preguntó tratando de parecer normal.

—¿Más discreto cómo? —dijo Encarna sin detenerse, buscando algo por la mesa y el mueble de la sala.

—No sé, más... bueno, menos llamativo.

—La llamativa soy yo, no el vestido, ¿recuerdas? —le dirigió una sonrisa punzante y le guiñó un ojo.

—Llámalo como quieras, pero con este vestido...

No acabó la frase, y esta vez Encarna se detuvo frente a él, brazos en jarras, desafiante.

—Siempre he vestido como yo quiero, no al gusto de los demás, pasando de a dónde fuera o con quién —le dijo sin acritud pero con firmeza.

—Si es que solo vamos a cenar —insistió sin mucha fuerza Sixto, con miedo de hacerla enfadar teniendo en cuenta lo mucho que disfrutaba con la ropa su compañera.

—¿Y qué? Si las mujeres de tus amigos son mayores, yo no. Que se vayan acostumbrando. ¿O es por otra cosa?

—¿Otra cosa?

—A lo peor no quieres que sean ellos los que me vean así.

—Vamos, no digas tonterias.

—Entonces dejémoslo, y ayúdame a encontrar mi pulsera o no nos vamos.

—Ponte otra, mujer —se rindió él.

—¡Si, hombre, otra! ¿Y tú estás en publicidad? Las personas no se ponen esto con aquello y lo de más allá con esto otro. Y menos las mujeres. Hay que ir a tono, ¿no lo sabes? Además —volvió a mirarle fijamente y con decisión—, eso de que solo vamos a cenar, olvídalo. Después tomaremos algo y nos iremos a bailar.

—No creo yo que ellos...

—Hablo de ti y de mi. Si se apuntan, bien, pero si no, pasando, ¿vale?

Había descubierto un nuevo horizonte con ella, aunque a veces acabara demasiado agotado. Esta vez no quiso decirle que no tenía ganas. Lo del vestido la había puesto combativa, aunque no guerrera. Solo combativa. La conocía ya muy bien, o estaba en camino de hacerlo.

Era viernes por la noche.

¿Y cuando había hecho el amor, de aquella forma intensa y alucinante, en un viernes por la noche al llegar a casa, o por la mañana al despertar, o en lugares y momentos de lo más insospechado, antes de conocer a Encarna?

Aquello no tenía precio.

35

—El precio que ha pagado es muy alto —dijo Paz.

—Estoy de acuerdo contigo —confirmó Natalia lanzando una rápida mirada en dirección a Rafael—. Perder a la familia solo por tirarse a una chica joven es...

—Bueno, será algo más que "tirársela" cuando vive con ella y van a casarse al acabar el papelamen del divorcio —repuso Rafael haciendo un gesto de reflexión.

—Es lo mismo —le increpó su mujer—. Para mi, se case con ella o no, resulta igual de patético. Sixto ha ido a lo fácil, y como hay un montón de niñas, y no tan niñas, dispuestas a saltarse las normas y conseguir lo que se proponen por la vía rápida... Así va todo.

—Entonces no estás de acuerdo con que todo el mundo pueda tener una segunda oportunidad —manifestó Salvador, callado hasta ese momento y al margen de la conversación suscitada tras colgar el auricular telefónico.

—Una segunda oportunidad sí, si te quedas viuda o viudo, o si tu matrimonio va mal. Pero eso de cambiar solo porque te entra la neura de la juventud perdida y lo de que el tiempo se acaba y hay que apurar la copa... Qué quieres que te diga.

—Tú no sabes si su matrimonio iba mal —dijo Rafael.

—Conozco a Sole, y tu también. Sabes que fue Sixto el que conoció a Encarna y se olvidó de todo. Hasta ese momento eran una pareja normal.

—¿A que llamas tu normal? —quiso saber Salvador.

Paz miró a su marido.

—Pues normal, estable, con mucho de bueno forjado a lo largo de los años y los pequeños problemas habituales en todas las parejas —exclamó Natalia subiendo el tono de voz y el énfasis de sus palabras.

—Sabes perfectamente que la mayoría de matrimonios que se casan excesivamente jóvenes, sin haber vivido la vida, y que encima amontonan hijos rápidamente, acaban mal —puntualizó Salvador.

—Será ahora, con la moda del cambio, porque antes no era así.

—No, antes había que aguantar, y por eso había tanto asesinato —bromeó Rafael con más cinismo que ganas de hacer una gracia.

—Como se nota que sois hombres —espetó Natalia—. Y como Sixto es vuestro amigo.

—Eso no tiene nada que ver —dijo Salvador—. ¿Sabes? Ni siquiera sé si fue él quien le echó el lazo a Encarna, o si fue Encarna la que se lo echó a él.

—¡Sixto siempre ha sido un calavera, con la bragueta fácil, por Dios! —gritó Natalia—. Y ésta vez ha encontrado a una que no se ha contentado con pasar el rato. Una listilla.

—Creo que Encarna también tuvo una relación fallida antes.

—¿Quien te lo ha dicho, Sixto? —Natalia volvió a fulminar a su marido—. ¿Y eso que significa? ¡Todo el mundo ha tenido un amor frustrado o un desengaño! ¿Y qué? Si yo soy soltera y sé que un hombre está casado... vamos, es que ni me ve el pelo, faltaría más.

—Terreno vedado, propiedad privada —volvió a bromear Rafael—. ¿Y el amor qué?

—¿El amor? ¿Pero de qué amor estás hablando, por favor? Lo de Sixto es sexo y nada más que sexo, una locura presenil, y lo de ella... A ver, ¿que puede haber encontrado en él, con cuarenta y pico de años y dejando mujer y tres hijos, uno de ellos de cinco años, ¡por Dios!

—Mujer, no te alteres —intentó calmarla Paz.

—¡Si es que esas cosas me ponen...! —Natalia miraba todavía fijamente a su marido, tanto que tuvo que hacer un esfuerzo para dejar de hacerlo, y con él apretó los puños hasta hundir las uñas en su carne. Acabó rezongando con evidente desprecio—: Lo que no sé es que estamos haciendo nosotros saliendo con ella. ¿Darle carta de normalidad? Porque no la tiene, ¿sabéis? No la tiene.

—Podíais haberlo dicho antes —desgranó en tono cansino Salvador.

—¿Quién quedó para cenar todos juntos esta noche? —preguntó Paz.

Se miraron los cuatro, sin que ninguna tuviera una respuesta segura. Había sido como otras veces, por inercia, o al menos eso hubieran jurado. O tal vez hubiera sido el mismo Sixto, que dijo...

—Bueno, eso ya no importa —se encogió de hombros Salvador—. ¿Nos vamos o qué? A este paso aún llegarán antes Sixto y ella, y la mesa estaba reservada para hace diez minutos.

Paz

Fue como si de pronto... empezaran a llover cuchillos de punta. Les conozco bien, a todos. Son muchos años. De entrada, Salvador, y de salida, Natalia.

Algo le sucedía a ella.

Y algo, más indefinible, más remoto y oscuro, le sucedía a él.

Intenté mirar a mi marido, penetrar en el interior de su conciencia, pero no lo conseguí. Fue el primero en moverse, el primero en salir de la sala, el primero en meterse en el cuarto de baño con la excusa de orinar, y cuando salió ya nada era igual, la dinámica del grupo, pese a la tensión, era otra, y hablabamos de no sé qué más. En el caso de Natalia, la evidencia aún era más fuerte. Estaba nerviosa, crispada, y no era por salir con Encarna y sentirse culpable de abandonar a Sole con ello. Era por algo más. Su forma de hablarle a Rafael, de mirarle, de interpelarle... Muchas parejas aprovechan la presencia de los amigos para pelearse "bajo vigilancia", decirse lo que no se atreven a decirse en privado, temerosos de desencadenar la guerra o de no saber luego cómo apagar un fuego provocado por su falta de control. Pero Natalia no se había peleado con Rafael, solo había dado rienda suelta a sus nervios, como el niño que mucho antes de llegar al puesto de refrescos ya insinúa que tiene sed. Y Rafael estaba irónico, mordaz.

Salvador llevaba unos días, tal vez más, serio, perdido.

Pensé que hablaría con él después, al regresar, o al día siguiente.

Antes solíamos hablar más.

En cuanto a Natalia, sabía que ella misma estallaría y me lo contaría a lo largo de la noche. A ella también la conocía bien.

Natalia

No sé qué me molestó más, si la postura cínica y despreocupada de Rafael, hablando de Sixto y de su fulana, o el hecho de que fingiera tanta indiferencia en un tema en el que ahora estaba tan hundido casi como el propio Sixto, porque para mi, el simple hecho de la traición, ya era tan grave como lo otro. Ni siquiera sabía si estaba preparando el terreno para darme la patada, o si es que se sentía furioso por no estar dispuesto a hacer lo que había hecho su amigo.

Esa era una de las claves de todo aquello.

Porque si él iba a dejar a su querida, o lo que fuera, y yo metía la pata antes de hora... lo único que haría sería clavarme un cuchillo en la espalda yo misma. Pero si por el contrario su devaneo progresaba, y yo callaba, las consecuencias podían ser peor, tal vez dejarme sin nada. Las amantes son avariciosas. Ya que no se llevan a tu hombre en el mejor momento, se llevan lo que han ganado para que su momento sea mejor.

Paz no paraba de mirarme, así que imaginé que ella sospechaba algo. Había querido contárselo varias veces, a lo largo del rato anterior, estando sola, pero una y otra vez, por orgullo o por miedo, lo evitaba. De pronto comprendí que era una tontería, que hay cosas que no pueden llevarse solas, porque son indigeribles. Yo estaba ofuscada, y por contra, Paz era tan equilibrada, tan consecuente.

No acabábamos de irnos nunca. Primero fue Salvador el que se metió en el cuarto de baño, después Rafael. No me extrañó que tuviera acidez y dolor de estómago, con lo que ya había bebido. Y luego alguien llamó por teléfono, una madre preocupada porque a su hija la fiebre no se le iba. Pensé que Salvador tendría que ir a visitarla, y que no habría cena.

Ojalá hubiera sido así, aunque en este momento yo quería salir. No sé la razón, puesto que sabía que no iba a sentirme cómoda con Encarna, pero quería salir, hacer lo que fuera menos regresar a casa y meterme en cama con Rafael.

Ya no resistía que me tocase.

Pero Salvador tranquilizó a la mujer, le dio unas indicaciones, le recetó no sé qué cosa.

Mientras le oía hablar por teléfono, pensé en Gloria, y me entraron ganas de llorar.

36

Estaban en la puerta cuando sonó el timbre del teléfono.

—No lo cojas, vámonos de una vez —pidió Encarna.

Sixto vaciló una simple fracción de segundo. Luego regresó al interior del apartamento y descolgó el auricular mientras le dirigía a ella una rápida mirada de disculpa. Encarna se quedó en la puerta, sin llegar a abrirla. Vio cómo él cruzaba los dedos índice y medio de su mano libre.

—¿Sí?

—Soy yo, papá —escuchó la voz de Guillermo.

—¡Ah, hola hijo! —descruzó los dedos y plegó los labios con resignación al volver a mirar a Encarna. Se le notó la desilusión y el fastidio por ello—. Iba a salir ya, ¿sabes? Me has pillado en la puerta.

—No quiero ir al Tibidabo —le soltó su hijo con determinación, ignorando su comentario—. Quiero ir a Montjuich.

—Pues iremos a Montjuich, naturalmente.

—Hay menos cosas, pero dice Marta que son más fuertes —insistió el niño.

—Lo que tú quieras, el sábado que viene...

—¿Sabes si hay montañas rusas en Montjuich, papá?

—No, Guillermo, no lo sé, pero puedo averiguarlo y te llamo mañana, ¿de acuerdo?

—Bueno —pareció concederle como final de su conversación.

—Buen chico —inició la despedida su padre.

No pudo concluir sus palabras. La voz de Sole apareció de pronto en la línea, cortando el suave viento infantil para convertirlo en una oleada de huracanada animadversión.

Empezó a pensar que la llamada de Guilermo solo había sido una excusa.

—Oye, Sixto, aún no hemos hablado de las vacaciones y están a la vuelta de la esquina, porque yo tengo ya mis planes, ¿sabes?

—Sole —su tono, agotado, y el nombre de su ex mujer, hicieron que Encarna se apoyara en la pared, como si alguien la hubiera empujado, cruzándose de brazos y resoplando con fastidio—, ¿hemos de hablar de eso ahora?

—¿Cuándo quieres hablarlo, eh? Si te llamo al despacho, estás liado, y en ese lugar en el que vives ahora, como está ella... Mira, solo quiero que sepas que yo, desde luego, prefiero julio, porque en agosto todo está imposible.

Si crees que me gusta llamarte y "molestarte" —lo dijo con mucha intención—, vas dado. No te llamaba de casada, menos voy a hacerlo ahora. Pero el tema...

—Sole, por favor, iba a salir, Mañana, ¿de acuerdo?

—No, si por mi parte ya está todo dicho. Quiero irme en julio y ya está. Tú haces lo que quieras luego, en agosto. Y si no tienes vacaciones o habías hecho otros planes, es tu problema, por no haberlo resuelto antes. Como comprenderás...

—Sole, vete a la mierda, ¿quieres?

Colgó el aparato y trató de no mirar a Encarna, pero la inmovilidad de ella era tan evidente y omnipresente como su propia rabia y su fatiga mental y anímica, así que acabó levantando la cabeza para enfrentarse a sus ojos.

No encontró en ellos ninguna emoción.

Nada.

Salvo, quizá, indiferencia.

—¿Nos vamos ya? —fue lo único que su nueva compañera le dijo.

Sixto

Lo entendía, lo comprendía: Encarna trataba de mantenerse al margen, no estar en medio, ser neutral o cuanto menos permitir que yo arreglara mi vida pasada, para empezar lo más limpiamente el presente y el futuro. No siempre lo conseguía, no siempre callaba, no siempre evitaba abordar el tema, pero en esta ocasión lo hizo. Se limitó a sostener mi mirada, y tras ello, reaccionó, me dijo aquello de irse y abrió la puerta.

Me hubiera gustado decirle que nos quedábamos. En ese instante el cansancio por los recientes escarceos sexuales se agolpó en mis músculos y en mi mente, y otro cansancio aún mayor, indefinible, imposible de explicar, me aplastó contra el suelo. ¿Para qué iba a salir, si todo cuanto quería o necesitaba estaba allí?

Al diablo el mundo entero, la agencia, Salvador y Rafael con sus respectivas. Al diablo todo.

Encarna y yo, solos.

Pero la seguí, en silencio, callado, agradeciendo que no hablara, que no dijera nada en ningún sentido, ni a favor ni en contra. Una vez, un mes antes, me había dicho que Sole era una pesada insoportable, una histérica y una borde, pero también me dijo que no por eso yo tenía que pasarme, y que no cometiera ninguna tontería o un día me arrepentiría de lo que había hecho y me daría cuenta de que había perdido a mis hijos. Sus palabras me dieron de lleno. Encarna dice que bastante daño hará Sole con ellos, hasta conseguir que me odien, y que solo el tiempo hará que yo les demuestre que les quiero, y con ello lograré recuperarles, y algo más, volverme a ganar su respeto. Y tiene razón.

Pero a veces lo que deseaba era romper con el pasado de una vez, como si este no hubiera existido jamás.

Romperlo del todo.

Y al diablo Sole. Domingo y Marta eran mayores, podía hablar con ellos y punto. Lo malo era Guilermo.

¿Por qué habían tenido a Guillermo?

Si además, en aquellos días estaba teniendo un lío con la ex-secretaria de Marcelino Escobar y a Sole casi ni la tocaba.

37

Fue Paz la que abrió la puerta de la habitación de Vanessa para despedirse.

—Nos vamos, hija.

—Eso, los padres de juerga mientras los hijos se preparan para el relevo —bromeó no sin cierta acidez la niña.

Estaba estudiando, con la cabeza hundida entre las manos y la música relativamente alta a menos de dos palmos de ella. Se levantó y empezó a repartir besos y abrazos.

—Coman y diviértanse por mi —pidió con falsa lástima.

—En julio y agosto te pediré que te bañes en la playa por mi —le recordó su padre.

—Haga el favor de irse, padre vengativo —dramatizó Vanessa—. ¿Acaso no sabe que el futuro no existe, y que solo cuenta el presente y el ahora?

Los abrazos, las sonrisas, los besos, concluyeron cuando ella les empujó con suavidad fuera de su habitación. Los cuatro se dirigieron a la puerta del piso definitivamente, y en esta oportunidad la traspusieron sin más demoras. El ascensor subió a por ellos desde la planta baja al ser llamado por Paz.

—Es encantadora —mencionó Natalia refiriendose a Vanessa.

—Las hijas son más comunicativas y abiertas —comentó su madre.

—Y maduran antes. Bueno —Natalia puso cara de interrogación—, al menos eso es lo que dicen, porque lo que es yo...

—Tendrías que ir a por la pareja —dijo Salvador.

—Oye, tú, si quieres más clientela vete al Africa —le espetó Rafael.

—¿Qué te pasa, ya tienes problemas de próstata? Puedo echarte un vistazo si quieres.

—¡Anda ya, coño! —Rafael extendió el dedo índice y el meñique de su mano derecha y buscó algo de madera. Encontró la barandilla en el momento en que el ascensor se detenía en el rellano.

—Por cierto, he de hablarte de Gloria, Salvador —recordó Natalia—. Me parece que necesita...

—¿Ah, pero hay por aquí un médico? —la detuvo él mirando alrededor suyo.

—Si es que no está fina, y creo que con unas vitaminas... —continuó Natalia como si tal cosa.

—¡Si vuelves a hablarme de trabajo me meto en casa! —amenazó Salvador sin entrar en el ascensor, ya ocupado por los otros tres.

—Venga, que ya se ha hecho bastante tarde —pidió Paz echando un vistazo a su reloj.

Ninguno de los cuatro abrió la boca en el trayecto de descenso, y salieron a la calle recibiendo con gratitud el tibio aire de la suave noche primaveral. Nada más hacerlo, se encontraron con el coche de Rafael, aparcado sobre la acera justo encima del paso de peatones. Fue Paz la que primero reaccionó.

—¡Pero... cómo eres, Rafa! ¿Es que no tienes sentido cívico?

—Es de noche, mujer.

—¿Y qué, a esta hora la gente no usa los pasos de peatones?

—Pero si lo he hecho para que no tuvierais que andar.

—Di que no —se metió Natalia—, que siempre lo hace.

—Y además encima del vado para inválidos —continuó Paz—. El día que vayas en silla de ruedas te lo recordaré.

—¡Joder, qué noche me estáis dando! —rezongó Rafael volviendo a extender el dedo índice y el meñique de su mano derecha, aunque en esta ocasión no encontró nada de madera a su alcance y acabó dándose con ellos ligeros golpes en su cabeza—. ¿Queréis coger un taxi o qué?

Les abrió las puertas del coche, y entraron dentro de forma maquinal, ellas detrás y ellos delante. Luego conectó el encendido y maniobró para salir de su privilegiado aparcamiento, tratando de bajar de la acera sin brusquedad. En cuanto enfiló la calle pisó el acelerador por primera vez.

—Eso, y ahora a cien por hora —protestó envuelta en un suspiro de insatisfacción Natalia.

38

Rebasó un semáforo en ámbar, y pisó el acelerador a fondo para intentar superar el del siguiente cruce todavía en verde, aunque ya a mitad del tramo de calle este también se puso en ámbar.

Encarna llevó su mano derecha al asidero superior de su lado por mero instinto.

—Oye, que...

El semáforo cambió de ámbar a rojo cuando él todavía no se hallaba en el paso de peatones. No hubo ningún frenado, al contrario, la aceleración fue mayor, brusca, con el pié al máximo en el pedal del gas.

El coche atravesó el cruce como una exhalación.

No había ninguno en sentido perpendicular.

—¿Estás loco? —gritó Encarna—. Ya sé que es tarde, pero ¿a qué vienen ahora estas prisas?

—Tranquila, mujer —dijo Sixto.

—¡Oh, sí, yo muy tranquila! Si soy la que te lleva flores lo estaré más, pero como la que pringue sea yo...

—Nunca he tenido un accidente, en la vida —le recordó él.

—¿Sabes la de muertos e inválidos que solo han tenido uno y ha bastado? —continuó ella, enfadada.

—Cómo eres.

—Como me da la gana, y haz el favor de no pasarte.

—Está bien. ¿Mejor así?

Aminoró la velocidad, hasta convertirla casi en algo ridículo, y frenó el coche a unos diez metros del siguiente semáforo, en cuanto este parpadeó para situarse en ámbar.

—Anda que llevas una noche fina —suspiró Encarna.

—Es que antes no has acabado de dejarme satisfecho —bromeó Sixto.

—¿Y qué quieres, una felación aquí mismo, porque no es mi estilo, sabes?

—Pues no estaría mal —intentó cogerla por el cuello, pero la mujer se resistió renovando sus protestas.

Un coche se detuvo junto al suyo. Se oyó un bocinazo.

Sixto giró la cabeza, a la izquierda, abandonando el contacto femenino. Vio a cuatro chicos en un coche barato pero peleón, de esos con la palabra TURBO escrita en la trasera, las ventanillas abiertas y la música a toda mecha, aunque en esta ocasión no hubiera música, solo sus cuatro sonrisas estúpidas.

—¡Eh, colega! —le gritó el más próximo—. ¡Si se te resiste podemos echarte una mano!

—Serán hijos de puta... —murmuró Sixto.

—No les hagas caso —oyó decir a Encarna.

—¡Si es que a las rubias no les van los pichas frías! —exclamó el que estaba sentado detrás del que había hablado en primer lugar.

—¡Ya, por eso vosotros vais cuatro tíos, so maricones! —dijo Sixto.

—¿Qué pasa, que vas buscando una polla para tu culo, cabrón? —hizo ademán de ir a abrir la puerta del coche.

—¡Sixto, por Dios, arranca! —pidió Encarna.

—¡Vamos, capullo! ¿No querrás quedar como un cagado delante de tu nena, verdad?

123

La puerta ya estaba abierta. El semáforo parpadeó dispuesto a iluminar su círculo verde y abrir el paso. Sixto aferró el volante con ambas manos. Sentía la de Encarna en su brazo. Tuvo una amarga sensación, de fracaso e impotencia, como por la tarde, al enfrentarse al problema de la crisis con las manos desnudas.

El primero de los chicos había bajado del coche.

—Pedazo cabrones... —fue lo último que dijo antes de obedecer a su instinto por encima de su ira y volver a pisar el pedal del gas, con la primera vibrando a toda potencia por la brusquedad de su arranque y el eco de la risa de los cuatro gamberros aleteándole por atrás.

39

El aparcamiento abierto al aire libre al pié del funicular del Tibidabo estaba ya abarrotado de coches. Rafael llegó hasta el restaurante, situado casi al extremo de la placita, por su parte izquierda, y viendo el panorama les dijo:

—Bajaos. Yo voy a aparcar. Así no os tendréis que pegar la caminata de subida, porque ya habéis visto que la cosa empieza desde bastante abajo.

Paz y Natalia le obedecieron sin decir nada. Salvador no.

—Te acompaño —dijo a su amigo.

Las dos mujeres se quedaron solas, mientras Rafael maniobraba con dificultad para dar la vuelta. Dada la anarquía de los coches aparcados no era sencillo.

Desde el mismo momento de quedarse solas, Paz miró a Natalia a los ojos. Solo tuvo que forzarla un poco.

—Vamos, ¿qué te sucede?

No hubo rebeldía, ni falsa seguridad ni tampoco rechazo. Fue más bien un abandono suave, agradecido. Una libertad castigada tan solo por la pesada carga interior.

—Rafa tiene un lío —dijo brevemente.

—¿Qué?

Hubiera jurado que se trataba de algo así, pero la sorpresa no fue menor.

—Simple, ¿no? Hay alguien más.

—¿Cómo lo sabes?

—Lo sé. Son muchos años —hizo un gesto de seguridad y miró hacia lo lejos, hacia Barcelona, extendida como una alfombra luminosa a sus piés—. La mujer que no se de cuenta es que es tonta.

—¿Quién es ella? ¿La conoces?

—No, no tengo ni idea de quién pueda ser.

—Pero, ¿les has visto juntos? ¿Sabes...?

Movió la cabeza horizontalmente, en gestos secos y rápidos. Se esforzaba en no llorar, para no arruinar su maquillaje.

—Entonces puede que no sea nada, una amiga... no sé, y si lo es, tal vez sea algo pasajero, una tontería —buscó la forma de contemporizar Paz.

—Sí, como Sixto —espetó Natalia.

—Sixto siempre fue un calavera y hasta Sole lo sabía —comprendió que no la estaba ayudando y le hizo la pregunta que quizá ella esperaba—. ¿Y qué vas a hacer?

Ahora Natalia volvió a enfrentarse a su mirada.

—No lo sé, Paz. Supongo que... dejarle si es que va en serio. Estoy muy aturdida. No quiero que sea él quien encima me dé la patada.

—¿Has hablado con él?

—No, no —hizo un gesto de incomodidad—. ¿Para qué? Supongo que lo negaría, o diría que estoy neurasténica.

—O aprovecharía para contarte la verdad y entonces... sería el fin, ¿no es eso?

—Tal vez.

—Sea como sea, tendrás que tomar una decisión. Por lo que me estás diciendo...

—Quería dejar pasar el verano, ver cómo se desarrollaba todo, por si es lo que tú dices, una simple aventura. Pero aunque sea eso... a mi me ha hecho polvo. Gloria es tan pequeña. Siempre dije que podía perdonarlo todo menos el engaño, la mentira, la traición. Y ya ves. Ahora he de decidir qué es más importante, si mi orgullo, mi hija, mi matrimonio...

Las primeras lágrimas afloraron en sus ojos. Fue inevitable. Paz se dio cuenta de ello y tomó la decisión, antes de que llegaran Salvador y Rafael. El momento de la confesión, de todas formas, había sido inoportuno.

—Vamos dentro —dijo tomándola del brazo—. Será mejor que vayas al lavabo antes de que vuelvan ellos.

Paz

Puede que lo intuyera, puede que un sexto sentido me estuviese avisando de lo que pasaba, pero no por ello me sentí mejor. Mi perspicacia no era más que una proyección de mis propias inseguridades, porque mientras oía hablar a Natalia, en quien realmente estaba pensando era en mí. En mí y en Salvador, y cómo me sentiría yo si la escena fuese al revés.

Por mucho que estuviese segura de que a mí no me sucedería, porque Salvador no era ni Sixto ni Rafael, afortunadamente.

Podía poner la mano en el fuego.

Podía...

No, tal vez no. Nadie puede poner la mano en el fuego por nadie, porque todas y todos somos diferentes, y a lo largo de una vida se cambia de manera constante, a veces rápida, a veces lenta, a veces impredecible, pero se cambia, y es difícil notarlo aunque sea con quienes están a nuestro lado, compartiendo la vida. ¿Cuánto hacía que Salvador y yo no hablabamos? ¿Cuánto hacía desde nuestro último contacto íntimo? ¿Cuánto hacía que el manto transparente de la normalidad nos había envuelto sin apenas darnos cuenta? Salvador se iba cada día temprano, y regresaba tarde por la noche. Nada más. Nada menos.

No, no sospechaba de él, ni remotamente, pero mi estado me hacía temer por el futuro. Mis cambios me hacían sentir débil. Y cuando ves que el mundo se desmorona a tu alrededor, el miedo te sube por las piernas, despacio, hasta amenazar con devorarte y sumergirte en él. Sole, Natalia, y no solo ellas. ¿Era una plaga? Como decía Vanessa, en su colegio las hijas de separados eran ya mayoría. ¿Qué estaba sucediendo? En los años 80 había un vértigo, la novedad del divorcio salvador para muchas parejas, pero en los 90 el vértigo estaba dejando paso a la locura, las separaciones por cansancio, aburrimiento, cambio de pareja. La gente se sumergía en una desesperanza absurda.

Desesperanza. ¿Era esa la palabra?

La búsqueda de ese algo más, que rompiera la rutina, el fracaso, la crisis, todas las crisis, personales y sociales.

Natalia no quiso que la acompañara al lavabo, y me senté en la mesa reservada para nosotros, mientras la cabeza me daba vueltas. Luego dejé de pensar en mí, y en la trascendencia obligada de mis sentimientos, y pensé en ella, porque si lo de Sole había sido traumático, lo de Natalia podía ser peor, y yo estaría en medio, y sola.

Natalia se esforzaba en estar guapa, en cuidarse, y aún así... Rafael era muy capaz de hacerle la jugada. Rafael estaba cambiando, se había vuelto más cínico, más hipócrita, más frío. Tiempos duros.

127

Personas.

Tuve la sensación de que la noche iba a ser peor de lo que me esperaba y traté de prepararme para ello.

40

Al cerrar las puertas traseras del coche, con Salvador inmóvil a su lado, Rafael inició la maniobra para dar la vuelta y retroceder por donde habían venido, a la caza y captura de un hueco donde aparcar. Un hueco lo bastante grande para su vehículo, por supuesto. Mientras ponía la primera y la marcha atrás, de forma alternativa, una pareja pasó por delante de ellos, riendo, muy abrazados. Ella era una pelirroja impresionante, y él un cruce de playboy y ejecutivo de cabello largo. Los dos lucían palmito, y compañía. El mundo entero parecía de ellos a tenor de sus carcajadas abiertas, la forma de caminar y cruzar la calzada, sin siquiera mirar a derecha o izquierda. Y tanto Rafael como Salvador, se quedaron mirándola los segundos suficientes, hasta que se perdieron por detrás de un coche situado a su derecha.

—¡Joder! —exclamó Rafael—. ¡Hay que ver cómo están ahora!

—Siempre han estado buenas, hombre —aclaró el médico.

—Ya, pero antes eran estrechas.

—Y nosotros tímidos.

—¡La madre que las parió! —volvió a rezongar Rafael—. Hoy, soltero y con pasta, te comes el mundo.

—¿Y la edad?

—¡Anda ya, no me seas carroza! ¿Qué tiene que ver la edad con esto? Mira Sixto.

—Es más joven que tú y que yo.

—¡Coño, es UN AÑO más joven que yo! Y se lo ha montado de puta madre, pasando de todo.

—¿Estás seguro? —dudó Salvador—. Ha liado una buena, y con tres hijos. Pasar, ha pasado, pero les ha costado a los dos sangre sudor y lágrimas. Y espérate, que aún no ha terminado.

—¿Y qué? Si se casa con la rubia, volverá a empezar, que es cojonudo, y si vuelve con Sole, se habrá pasado por la piedra a una tía y encima será la mar de bueno por haber regresado al seno familiar, ¡no te jode! —cambió de tema súbitamente al preguntar—: ¿Y tú qué tal con las mamás de tus pacientes? Porque a la consulta sólo vienen madres, claro, y con hijos pequeños, la mayoría estarán buenísimas, y algunas separadas y divorciadas.

—No seas bruto, hombre. ¿Crees que soy ginecólogo y se me abren de piernas para que les haga un examen?

—Es que tú siempre has sido un inocente, Salva, joder. ¿Cuánto llevas casado?

—Veintitrés años.

—¿Veintitrés? ¿Ya? —estuvo a punto de pisar el pedal del freno a causa de la impresión, aunque circulaban muy despacio por la avenida en sentido descendente—. ¡Yo llevo catorce y es como si me hubiese pasado la vida con Natalia!

—¿Qué te pasa? —Salvador le miró con el ceño fruncido—. No me digas que también tú estás aburrido.

—¿Pasar? No, no me pasa nada —echó con rapidez la pelota fuera, aunque sin perder su tono crítico—. Pero, bueno... Natalia ha cambiado mucho desde que tuvo a la niña.

—Todas cambian —dijo Salvador—. Y nosotros también.

—No, tu mujer y tú estáis unidos, se os nota. Hechos el uno para el otro. Además, siempre has sido conservador en eso, tienes tu trabajo, tus fondos de inversión, tu seguridad, estás estabilizado.

—O sea que estoy muerto —apostilló Salvador.

No hubiera sabido qué contestar después de dejarse llevar por su énfasis, así que agradeció ver que, a su derecha, un automóvil encendía las luces para iniciar la maniobra de desaparcamiento.

—¡Por fin! —gritó—. Anda, bájate y guíame, que no sé si entraré del todo bien.

Rafael

No era mi noche. Primero le pedía dinero de la forma más estúpida, y tenía que soportar que me dijera que no y que me arrojara su falsa superioridad de médico. Segundo, la escenita de Natalia antes de irnos, muy extraña en ella. Ahora, además de echarle en cara lo de sus "fondos de inversión", que era tanto como recordarle que no había querido invertir en mi negocio, le daba pistas en torno a mi mismo y mi estado. Salvador hablaría con Paz, porque seguro que ellos eran de los que hablaban y se lo contaban todo, y Paz se lo diría a Natalia. Y como Natalia...

De todas formas el problema no era ese, sino que yo decidiera qué hacer con Mercedes, y ¿cómo podía pensar en Mercedes cuando mi tinglado se estaba yendo a la mierda?

¿Cómo podía... cuando en realidad lo que estaba haciendo era pensar en ella, desde que se había ido de mi despacho, furiosa y vengativa?

En momentos como ese hubiera enviado todo a la puta mierda para estar con ella y solo con ella. Estaba seguro de que pasaba de que yo tuviera una empresa y la llevara a sitios elegantes y todo ese rollo. Segurísimo. Si quería una decisión por mi parte, era porque, en el fondo, era como la de Sixto, como todas. Quería casarse.

Iba a ser un verano duro pero... esclarecedor. Si Natalia se iba con Gloria a la playa julio y agosto, yo estaría solo con Mercedes, aunque algún fin de semana tendría que escaquearme para...

Eso si no perdía el negocio.

El lunes tal vez fuera el comienzo del fin.

Estaba aparcando, con Salvador haciéndome señas, y deseé acelerar y pisarle. Fue un acceso de furia que naturalmente dominé, pero en mi mente la escena siguió adelante. Y resultó maravillosa. Salvador y su seguridad, su estancamiento, su apolillada manera de ver las cosas, pensando ya en el mañana cuando lo importante era vivir el futuro. ¿De qué le iba a servir los millones que guardara cuando fuera viejo? Igual se moría y serían el melenas de su hijo y la boba de su hija los que se aprovecharan. El dinero era para tenerlo y gastarlo de joven, y eso incluía los cuarenta, y los cincuenta. Bueno, mientras el cuerpo aguante. A veces casi ni reconocía ya al Salvador de los tiempos difíciles, al rebelde, al anarco, al que iba para líder. Una extraordinaria mutación. ¿Era eso la madurez, la estabilidad? ¡Pues al diablo con ello! Salvador tendría siempre clientes, y dinero, y ningún problema, y encima con hijos ya mayores, no como yo, teniendo que pensar en Gloria, pero él nunca se tiraría a una Mercedes, ni a una Encarna.

Salvador estaba ya muerto y no lo sabía, como él acababa de decir, exactamente.

Y yo estaba vivo y tenía que ver a Mercedes, o hablar con ella, para saber si estaba enfadada de verdad o simplemente...

Tomé la decisión, y empecé a no sentirme en paz, aunque la noche no hubiera hecho más que dar sus primeros giros.

41

Vieron a Paz sentada en una mesa exterior, circular, a la derecha, y se dirigieron a ella. Salvador ocupó la silla contigua a la de su mujer. Rafael hizo lo propio al otro lado.

—¿Y Natalia? —preguntó.

—Ha ido al lavabo —le informó Paz.

Ningún camarero se les acercó de momento, ante la evidencia de que faltaban la mitad de los comensales de la mesa, y mantuvieron silencio a lo largo de casi un minuto. Paz tenía la mirada extraviada; Salvador los ojos fijos en la puerta de entrada, como si esperara ver aparecer por ella a Sixto y a Encarna en cualquier momento; Rafael, por contra, describió un arco con los suyos, observando a la gente que le rodeaba. Nunca se sabía si podía encontrarse con alguien de manera inesperada, un cliente, un amigo olvidado. Si algo había aprendido comiendo y cenando fuera de casa, era que las oportunidades no llovían del cielo, pero a veces se presentaban lo mismo que una lluvia de primavera, con suficiente capacidad como para refrescar el ambiente. Su examen fue fugaz, y solo se detuvo en una mujer de cabello negro, madura pero exuberante, que comía con clase cerca de él mientras escuchaba lo que le decía un hombre sentado frente a ella. Un hombre mayor, pero con carisma. Cualquiera lo podía notar.

—¿Le ocurría algo a Natalia? —se interesó finalmente, acabado su recorrido visual y ante la tardanza de su mujer.

—No, estará retocándose —aventuró Paz.

Natalia hizo acto de presencia en ese instante, sin restos de humedad en los ojos ni el aspecto de frustración con el que se había ido. Caminó hacia ellos atravesando la parte interior del restaurante, y Paz comentó lo que de verdad sentía, mirando de reojo a Rafael.

—Que mujer tienes —dijo—. Está guapísima.

No hubo ningún comentario, pero sí el dibujo de sus mandíbulas, apretadas de golpe, a ambos lados del rostro. En cambio oyó la voz de su propio marido comentando:

—Se cuida.

No le miró. Sintió la punzada de la flecha, imprevista o tal vez intencionada. Prefirió no saberlo. Natalia llegó hasta ellos y se sentó al lado de Rafael. Los dos asiento libres eran ahora obvios, uno a la izquierda de Salvador, presumiblemente para Encarna, y otro a la derecha de Natalia, casi con toda seguridad para Sixto, a menos que los recién llegados cambiaran la relación hombre-mujer. Por la misma razón, Encarna iba a quedar situada frente a Rafael.

—Esos son capaces de tardar todavía una hora —protestó Rafael.

Como si le hubiera oído, un camarero se acercó a la mesa iluminado por una sonrisa de bienvenida.

—¿Los señores prefieren esperar o tomarán un aperitivo? —se interesó.

—Yo quiero un whisky —pidió Rafael sin aguardar a los demás ni ceder el turno a Paz o a su mujer.

—Por Dios, Rafa —se quejó Natalia—. ¡Vamos a cenar!

—¿Qué pasa? —se enfadó él—. Tengo sed y no me apetece ninguna mariconada de esas. ¿O es que no puedo beberme un whisky?

—Sí, hijo, sí, por mí... Pero luego lleva el coche Salvador, ¿eh? Además, sabes que te sienta mal —miró a Salvador—. Dile que le sienta mal. Tú eres médico.

—Te sienta mal. Yo soy médico —dijo Salvador.

La cara del camarero seguía cincelada en piedra.

42

—Venga, hombre, que no eran más que cuatro gilipollas —dijo Encarna acariciándole la nuca.

—No me extraña que haya accidentes —rezongó Sixto todavía furioso—. Si dejan un coche en manos de cuatro niñatos de mierda, que ya van colocados y pidiendo guerra a esta hora... Esos mañana salen en el periódico, carbonizados en pleno Cinturón del Litoral.

—¡Calla, hombre! —se estremeció ella.

—¿Qué te crees, que no se lo tendrían merecido? Si llego a bajar se arma, porque encima necesitan ser cuatro contra uno. Y menos mal que nos han dejado en paz y no se han puesto a seguirnos.

—Porque no buscaban pelea, solo hacían el capullito. Ven a una tía rubia en un coche y ya se las dan de algo.

—Si llego a llevar una pistola en el coche, hubieras visto tú como se cagaban encima.

—O sea, que se la hubieras pasado por las narices.

—¡Tú dirás!

—¿Y te extraña que luego haya muertos y desgracias por tonterías así?

—¿Y cómo quieres pararles los piés a esos imbéciles, eh? ¿Quieres decírmelo? Lo que me extraña es que les vea la policía y no les detenga, porque se nota que van pidiendo guerra, que están dispuestos a armar el taco.

—Bueno, vale ya, ¿o vas a seguir dando la vara toda la noche?

Detuvo el coche en un nuevo semáforo, el del final de la calle Balmes. Puso el freno de mano, en lugar de mantener la primera y equilibrar el automóvil con el embrague y el gas, y llevó su mano derecha hasta la nuca de ella.

—Vamos, ven aquí.

Le obedeció, sumisa, aunque antes de producirse el beso dijo:

—Cuando aparques vas a dejar que me arregle, ¿vale? No me vengas con prisas.

Se besaron, sin brevedad ni cortedad, dejando que todo el placer emergiera de sí mismos para conectar a través de los labios y la humedad de sus bocas. Cuando se separaron, el semáforo ya debía llevar un buen rato en verde, aunque a su lado hubiera otro conductor parado, mirándoles con una sonrisa estúpida en el rostro.

Arrancó, y ya no hubo ninguna otra demora en la subida por la vieja avenida del Tranvía Azul, hasta llegar a los primeros coches aparcados al pié del funicular del Tibidabo.

—Vaya, cómo está esto —lamentó.

No llegó hasta arriba. Sabía que luego le tocaría bajar. Buscó un hueco por allí mismo y lo encontró a su izquierda.

—Podías haberme dejado arriba, ¿no? Ahora hemos de caminar un buen trecho —protestó Encarna.

—¿No querías arreglarte?

Lo hizo, nada más cerrar Sixto el encendido. Abrió su bolso, bajó el protector de la parte superior del automóvil, lo ubicó de forma que el espejito le diera de lleno en el rostro, y sacando un pintalabios procedió a retocarse la boca con pulcro esmero, sin prisas.

—¿Tengo algo yo en la cara? —preguntó él.

Ella le miró.

—Mucha cara es lo que tienes tú.

Volvió a maquillarse, un minuto, dos, hasta que guardó el pintalabios, cerró el bolso y salió por su puerta. Sixto la observó, y no hizo lo mismo hasta que ella estuvo de pié al otro lado, bajándose la corta y apretada falda. Emitió un largo y privado suspiro.

Al cerrar el coche y empezar a subir por la parte final de la avenida, ya no volvieron a hablar. Cada cual se sumergió en sus pensamientos, y continuaron así al llegar a la placita, rebosante de coches y movimiento, para dar los últimos pasos en dirección a La Venta.

Al entrar en el restaurante les vieron inmediatamente, y los cuatro que les esperaban también.

Los seis sonrieron a la vez.

Sixto

Lo comprendí en ese instante, al verles.

Fue... una sensación, una verdad, la realidad que me había negado a ver y entender, y que tal vez Encarna intentó transmitirme pero por prudencia no quiso llevar hasta extremos peligrosos, creyendo que para mí eran algo más.

Y aunque lo fueran, aunque se tratase de mis mejores y más íntimos amigos, que tampoco era eso, ni había para tanto...

Supe que era absurdo estar allí, con ellos y Encarna. Lo supe porque Natalia y Paz representaban a Sole, el pasado, el cansancio, mientras que Salvador y Rafael... Bueno, ellos eran distintos, pero de alguna forma también significaban una barrera, un recelo. Salvador se había convertido en un clásico, mientras que Rafael era un cobarde, ¡como yo mismo antes de conocer a Encarna, sí, es posible!, pero eso no cambiaba los hechos. La manera en que miraba a Encarna, lo que leía en sus ojos, su cinismo en las últimas semanas, era demasiado evidente que en el fondo me envidiaba y querría estar en mi lugar, o suspiraba por echar una cana al aire. ¡Qué coño! ¿Y qué? Podía hacerlo. Probablemente lo hiciera, aunque dudaba que él tuviese el valor que yo había tenido. No es fácil decir "¡basta!", aunque se esté tan harto como lo estaba yo.

Con lo de la agencia pinchándome el alma, comprendí que haber salido a cenar con ellos y ellas, como antes, no había sido más que una estupidez, una prueba de fuego por mi parte, o tal vez de superioridad, por ellas, y por ellos. Una forma de gritarles algo.

Nueva mujer. Nueva vida. Nuevos amigos.

Así sería en el futuro, desde mañana mismo.

No quería nada ni nadie que me recordara el pasado.

Encarna

Entrar en aquel lugar, aunque estuviese abierto al aire libre, fue como entrar en un espacio donde los pensamientos volasen libres a su antojo, y un eco se encargara de diseminarlos de uno a otro lado sin parar. Me bastó con mirarles a los cuatro, ver sus sonrisas, leer en sus ojos. Traté de no dejarme arrastrar ni vencer por ello, pero era difícil. Natalia me estaba llamando puta; Paz hacía de madre mientras pensaba que no era más que una loca, una joven sin nada en la cabeza, una viva la virgen; Rafael se me comía con la mirada y me desnudaba y me follaba con la mente; Salvador ejercía de prior del convento, y su tono era de superioridad.

Algunas cabezas en el restaurante se levantaron al avanzar en dirección a la mesa, así que sonreí aún más. Lo que yo pensaba era: "¡Jodéos, reprimidos! No soy guapa, ni una top, pero resulto y estáis babeando por mí. Muérete, Natalia, y ve a un gimnasio a tratar de arreglarlo porque ya estás perdida, mientras que a mí aún me quedan unos años. Y sé muy bien lo que me hago, Paz, porque quiero a Sixto, y yo no he roto ningún matrimonio. Ya estaba roto cuando recogí los pedazos. En cuanto a ti, Rafael, ya puedes follarme con la mirada, ya, que es lo único que podrás hacer en la vida, como tantos y tantos con imaginación en lugar de realidades. Por último, tú, Padre Reverendo, Don Salvador, no seas tan superior y piensa en lo que te queda, y en lo que vas a hacer para procurar que sea bueno, porque si yo tuviera cuarenta y seis años, y ese aspecto, y todo lo que veo en ti, estaría acojonada".

Entonces me di cuenta que de la misma forma que yo podía oir sus pensamientos y leer en sus ojos, ellos podían escuchar los míos y asomarse a mis pupilas.

Decidí que sería la última noche, que tenía que estar alegre, feliz, como si tal cosa, radiante, simpática con todos, comedida en lo posible, aunque si me pasaba... tampoco importaría demasiado. Mañana le diría a Sixto que se había terminado, que teníamos que empezar de cero, los dos, juntos. Si no lo entendía...

Para sus amigos yo siempre sería "la otra", aunque me casara con Sixto.

Asi que...¡a la mierda con ellos!

Tenía que ser una buena noche, y punto. Pasando de todo.

Natalia

Nada más ver a Encarna... me hundí, toqué fondo, aunque mantuve mi sonrisa, y mi apariencia, y todo lo que se espera de una mujer madura y estable, normal, cenando con amigos un viernes por la noche.

Lo primero que me pregunté fue si ella, la de Rafael, sería igual.

Lo segundo, si realmente lo resistiría. Es decir, si podría quedarme en casa, como Sole, sabiendo que él iba a cenar con ella y la gente que nos conocía.

La humillación se me antojaba superior al mismo engaño.

Me respondí a mí misma. A la primera pregunta, sí, por supuesto, porque ellas siempre son más jóvenes, más atractivas, más fuertes, y detalles puntuales como la inteligencia, la madurez o todo lo demás, no importaban. Para acostarse con alguien solo se necesita un sexo. A la segunda pregunta, la respuesta era que no, que yo no podría resistirlo.

Así que la odié, no por ser joven, y sexy, sino por lo que representaba, a qué y a quién representaba.

Estaba viendo a mi marido y a su querida en el futuro, salvo que yo... luchase, le parase los piés, le pusiera las peras a cuarto, o salvo que yo tragase y esperase a que no fuese más que un accidente, una aventura.

Después de todo, Rafael nunca había sido como Sixto, un putero, un maldito braguetero.

Después de todo...

Fue una larga espera, eterna. Desde que entraron hasta que nos dimos besos y se sentaron, pasó una eternidad. Fue como lo de estar a punto de morir y ver tu vida en un segundo. Exactamente igual. Rafael, Gloria, el pasado, el presente, el futuro.

Me dije que no iban a poder conmigo.

Me dije que plantaría cara.

Comenzando por esa misma noche.

43

—¡Vaya, hombre, ya era hora!

—¡Problemas, problemas! Tú porque eres médico, matas a los que te quedan en la consulta y listos, y tú porque tienes tu negocio, y eres el jefe, pero yo... yo he de aguantar al mío, y tragar con los follones y... ¡para qué os voy a contar!

—¡Menos cuentos, va!

—Hola, querida, ¿cómo estás?

—Sentimos la demora, en serio. Cosas de última hora. ¿Hace mucho que esperáis?

—Estás guapísima. Este vestido te favorece.

—¡No, si nosotros ya hemos cenado!

—¡Venga ya!

—Qué buena noche hace, ¿verdad?

—¿Y los niños, qué tal? Tú hija bien, ¿no? Tú en cambio, como ya los tienes mayores, tranquila.

—Bueno, mi Gloria ha estado un poco pachucha. Nada serio.

—¡Yo ya te llevo un whisky de ventaja!

—¿Queréis dejar de gritar? Parecéis críos con un permiso de la mili.

—¡Uy, sí, todo el mundo nos está mirando, por Dios, que vergüenza!

—Venga, sentémonos.

—¿Dónde vas con corbata, hombre?

—Es que uno es un señor.

—¿Me pongo aquí, al lado de mi médico favorito?

—Chico-chica-chico-chica, ¿eh? No me pongáis al lado de uno de estos.

—Tengo un hambre...

—¡Joder!

—Ya empezamos con el lenguaje fino, coño.

—Bueno, vosotros dos, a ver si os comportáis un poco.

—Tú, que las damas se cabrean.

—Vale, vale.

—¿Los señores querrán pedir ya o prefieren un aperitivo?

Segunda Parte

LOS HECHOS

44

—¿Dónde pensáis ir este verano?

La pregunta de Natalia consiguió captar su atención, tal vez porque la había formulado en un momento de silencio, tal vez porque en ese instante todos y todas estaban degustando las exquisiteces del primer plato, distinto en cada caso. Fue Encarna la primera en dejar el tenedor y responder.

—Sixto y yo habíamos hablado de ir a pasar unos días al Caribe.

—Lo habíamos hablado, tú lo has dicho —intercaló él—. Con publicidad, y poniendo en marcha las campañas de televisión de fines de agosto y primeros de septiembre... nunca se sabe.

—¡Es verdad, tú! —comentó Rafael—. Todos los que hacen fascículos lanzan veinte obras el mismo día, coincidiendo con el final de las vacaciones y la vuelta de todo dios a casa.

—Y lo que no son campañas de fascículos, anda ese —le espetó Sixto.

—¿Y a qué parte del Caribe pensabais ir? —se interesó Paz.

—Eso aún no lo habíamos decidido, como hay tantas islitas preciosas.

—Pero iríais los dos solos, ¿no? —repuso Natalia mirando a Sixto—. Los días en que Sole se quede con los niños.

Encarna bajó los ojos al plato. Fue su compañero el que, con cierta ironía en la voz, respondió:

—¿A ti qué te parece, querida?

—Ah, no sé —se encogió de hombros, como si la cosa no fuera con ella—. Igual querías algo más familiar.

—Tú, Natalia, a la playa como siempre, ¿verdad? —estuvo al quite Paz.

—Sí, a Gloria le encanta, y para qué voy a negártelo: a mí también.

—Y este de Rodriguez aquí —señaló Sixto a Rafael.

—Exacto. Como el negocio va solo.

—Pues nosotros probablemente cojamos el coche y nos vayamos unos días a París —dijo Paz enviando una sonrisa a su marido.

—¡Oh, qué enamorados! —se burló Rafael.

—Pero si París ya no se lleva —manifestó Sixto arrugando la cara—. Es mucho mejor Londres, para salir cada noche y ver espectáculos, y en plan comida y cosa cultural, Italia.

—Déjate estar de tonterías, que Paris aún es París, y ahora me han dicho que está precioso con todo lo que han hecho estos últimos años —insistió Paz.

—Salva, que no dices nada, hombre —Sixto le hizo una seña al médico—. ¿A ti te gusta París, o lo que diga Paz?

—Ya sabéis que prefiero escuchar, y además, esto está buenísimo. Con tanto hablar y hablar no le encontráis el sabor a la comida.

—¡Habló el doctor! —sentenció Sixto.

—Tú si que hablas —protestó Natalia—. No me extraña que estés en lo de la publicidad, engañando a la gente.

—¿Cómo que engañando a la gente? Nosotros no engañamos a nadie. Presentamos un producto glosando sus bondades —y satisfecho de su frase agregó—: Eso.

—Pero creáis necesidad, no me digas que no —no se rindió Natalia.

—¡Ah, si la gente que compra es débil y no sabe resistirse…!

—O sea que, encima, la culpa es nuestra. Serás...

—¿Me pasas el vino? —pidió Rafael.

—Ya no queda —dijo Encarna.

—¿Nos hemos libado la primera botella? ¡Bien!

—Rafa, que luego has de conducir —le recordó su mujer.

No le hizo caso. Tenía ya la mano levantada buscando la presencia del sonriente camarero.

45

—Digan lo que digan, las cosas están mal. Ni reactivación económica ni leches. A lo mejor a las grandes empresas les va de puta madre, pero a la mediana y pequeña empresa... Vamos, que nos están jodiendo vivos.

—Oye, cómo se ha vuelto tu marido de mal hablado —le dijo Paz a Natalia envuelta en una sonrisa.

—Y que lo digas.

—Pues este... —Encarna soltó un bufido de pesar en dirección a Sixto.

Ninguno de los tres hombres les hizo caso.

—Y se nota, ¿eh? Se nota —Sixto puso el dedo índice de su mano derecha sobre la mesa, apuntando hacia abajo para dejar bien sentado su punto de vista—. Pasa lo mismo en la publicidad, aunque os penséis que todo es jauja. Las campañas se ajustan al milímetro, hay una competencia feroz, y las empresas ya no gastan lo de antes.

—Nadie se quejaba cuando hace unos años muchos empezaron a enriquecerse con facilidad —objetó Salvador.

—¡Anda ese! —protestó Sixto—. ¡Acabas de descubrir que la Luna es redonda! ¡Pues claro que nadie se quejaba, para eso estamos, para prosperar y ganar dinero! ¿O no?

—Quiero decir que cualquiera hubiera podido pensar que no siempre iba a seguir siendo igual, y que estando

147

como estaba el mundo, envuelto en una recesión global, lo más lógico era imaginar que nos diera aquí. ¿O es que en los 80 no había paro?

—¡Coño, que si había! —rezongó Sixto—. Ese ha sido el gran fracaso del modelo socialista.

—Qué va, hombre —intervino Rafael—. La crisis era inevitable, mandase quien mandase. ¿O crees que hay algún partido político con una varita mágica? Ninguno la tiene.

—Pero hay modelos económicos que funcionan —apuntó Salvador.

—Aquí. Funcionan aquí —le corrigió Rafael—, porque somos catalanes y sabemos cómo hacer las cosas, pero fuera... ¡Anda, dile tú a otro de cualquier comunidad lo de que primero hay que arrimar el hombro y luego pedir, y verás a dónde te envían!

—Que tampoco es eso, Rafa —objetó Sixto—. El modelo catalán es exportable, pero sin una concienciación nacional...

—¿Qué dices, tú? Si el problema es que fuera nunca van a aceptar que aquí...

—¡Eh, eh! —les detuvo Paz—. Nada de política, que todas sabemos de que pié calza cada uno.

—Vaya, la censura —suspiró Rafael.

—¿De qué vamos a hablar? —puso cara de angustia Sixto—. Los hombres, cuando estamos solos, hablamos de mujeres, pero cuando estamos con mujeres hemos de hablar de política.

—O de fútbol —mencionó Salvador.

—Pero en fútbol estamos los tres de acuerdo, así que no hay polémica.

—O sea que a ti lo que te gusta es discutir —le dijo Natalia a su marido.

—Oye, ¿no es aquél Benigno Pascual, el de la marítima? —cambió de tema Sixto señalando a un grupo de personas que acababa de entrar en el restaurante.

46

—Aquí el que vive mejor es este —Sixto señaló a Salvador—, para que vamos a engañarnos.

—Ya empezamos —se quejó el médico.

—Se lo he dicho antes, mira —asintió Rafael—. Siempre hay niños, y los niños pillan todo eso de la tosferina, el sarampión, las anginas y demás leches, y hay que vacunarlos, revisarlos de tanto en tanto y lo que haga falta para que nosotros, los padres, estemos tranquilos, porque lo que es ellos... ellos ya lo están.

—¡Pero qué bruto eres! —se quejó Natalia.

—A nosotros aún nos criaron con Pelargón y leche en polvo, nada de bistecs. Y cuando era niño, pollo solo por Navidad —se quejó Sixto.

—Antes se morían cientos de niños al nacer, o en los primeros meses y años de vida. Ahora no —apuntó Salvador—. Os recuerdo que yo me hice médico porque vi morir a un hermano pequeño de ocho meses, porque un imbécil pensó que era un dolor de oído, cuando en realidad era algo mucho más grave. Se le perforó el sistema auditivo y el pus llegó al cerebro.

Encarna se estremeció, y Natalia cerró los ojos pensando en Gloria.

—De acuerdo, vale, pero volvemos a lo de qué tú vives bien, no te escaquees ahora —insistió con una sonrisa Sixto.

—Pues no será gracias a las nuevas generaciones —contraatacó Salvador—, porque el índice de natalidad sigue bajando. La gente se casa a los treinta, y de tener hijos... ni hablar. Todo lo más uno, por probar. Aquello de la parejita, se acabó. Aquí está la muestra: Rafa.

—No te metas conmigo, traidor, mal amigo.

—No me meto contigo. Tú si lo has hecho conmigo, pero yo contigo no. Solo constato un hecho. Tuviste a Gloria con treinta y seis años —miró a Encarna, de pronto, y le preguntó—. ¿Tú quieres tener hijos?

—Salvador, haz el favor —le reprochó Paz.

—¿Qué pasa? Le he hecho una pregunta de amigo y médico.

—Sí, quiero tener al menos un hijo —reconoció ella.

Todos miraron casi por instinto a Sixto.

—Bueno, este ya sabe cómo se hace —rio Rafael—, y seguro que no se le ha olvidado.

—¿Lo ves? —siguió Salvador—. Un hijo. Y así la mayoría. Si tuviera que escoger especialidad ahora, no sería pediatría, desde luego. Bueno, ahora ni siquiera se escoge así como así, que vaya como están. Te puede tocar de otorrino en Vigo tanto como de oftalmólogo en Granada. Eso si no es peor y acabas en un pueblo.

—Y lo bien que estarías tú en un pueblo, con la gente dándote gallinas y huevos. ¡Seguro que acabarías siendo alcalde! —dijo Sixto.

—Trincando pasta, como todos —asintió Rafael.

—Venga, no os quejéis, que todos podemos vivir, ¿o no? —objetó Paz—. Mucha crisis, mucha tontería, pero aquí estamos, poniéndonos las botas, un viernes por la noche.

—Sí, y ahora me dirás que hay gente que lo pasa peor —protestó Sixto.

—Pues sí, te lo digo.

—¡Y hay gente que lo pasa mejor, anda esa!

—¡Cómo sois! —Natalia defendió a Paz—. Deberíamos agradecer la suerte que tenemos.

—Hace unos años no hablaban así, ¿recuerdas? —aseveró Paz.

—Hace unos años se podía vivir, querida —dijo Rafael súbitamente serio.

—Y ahora también —no se arredó Paz.

—No, ahora no —dijo Rafael con una sombra de pesar en su rostro—. Tú no estás en la calle, ni lidiando con clientes, bancos y toda esa caterva a la que solo le importa jorobarte. Tú estás en tu casa, y hay diferencia, te lo aseguro. De un tiempo a esta parte la gente se ha vuelto despiadada, insensible, dura y egoísta. El que no está loco es que se hace inmune. No me extraña que a veces uno la emprenda a tiros con la gente. Y va a peor. No sé qué pensaréis vosotros, pero va a peor. ¿O no?

Paz

Veía lo que flotaba en el ambiente, pero hasta ese momento yo estaba tranquila, serena. Mi marido parecía más serio que de costumbre, aunque el habitual atolondramiento vocal de sus dos amigos lograse hacerle arrancar de vez en cuando. Por su parte, Rafa acrecentaba su cinismo habitual y Sixto daba la impresión de querer morder a alguien, revolviéndose inquieto a cada momento, tanto por el diálogo como por cualquier detalle, como pedir más pan o más vino. Natalia salía y entraba de su nube a impulsos, golpes de genio o marismas provocadas por sus decaimientos. Encarna, segura de sí misma en cuanto al shock que nos había provocado con su entrada, pero insegura en relación a miradas y algunas fases de las primeras conversaciones, esperaba los momentos adecuados para hablar, sonreír, callar o hacer lo que fuera. Eso sí, se la notaba suelta, decidida, nada cortada y con una clara predisposición a pasarlo bien. Y he dicho pasarlo bien, no hablo de gustar o de caernos mejor por tratarse de una noche en apariencia decisiva para ella en cuanto a su posible integración.

Veía todo eso y más, pero las palabras de Rafael me golpearon allá donde más daño podía hacerme en mis actuales circunstancias.

El me veía como a una simple ama de casa, aburrida, insulsa, tal vez vacía, despreocupada, exactamente igual que su mujer. Una persona ajena viviendo de espaldas al mundo. Ya sé que Rafael es un maldito machista y yo siempre le he visto como tal, y más desde que Natalia me había dicho lo de sus sospechas, que desde luego apoyaba plenamente porque Rafael y Sixto eran tal para cual. Pero que me dijera allí, en público, justo lo que yo estaba empezando a temer de mi misma, me dolió.

Miré a Salvador, pero su cara era de lo más inexpresiva. No me defendió ni alteró sus facciones. Dio la impresión de volver a estar concentrado en la cena, pasando de lo que se hablara o de las evoluciones anímicas del resto del mundo, comenzando por nosotros.

Estuve a punto de decirle a Rafael que yo había elegido ser madre, y que mi opción fue clara, pero no me atreví. Me pareció una posición extraña en plenos años 90, indefendible. Además, Rafa, o Sixto, no escuchaban nunca. Hablaban de sí mismos o hacia sí mismos, pero no de los demás.

Y entonces, casi como de común acuerdo, nosotras nos pusimos a hablar de otras cosas, pasando de ellos.

47

—¿No has pensado en volver a trabajar?

Paz miró a Natalia un tanto extrañada por su pregunta.

—No, ¿por qué?

—¿Pero porque no te apetece o porque crees que ya no es el momento?

—No sé... Es que ni siquiera se me ha pasado por la cabeza.

—Lo decía porque como ahora ya tienes a tus hijos crecidos...

—¿Y qué quieres que haga yo a mis años?

—Sixto me dijo que antes habías sido enfermera de tu marido? —se apuntó a la conversación Encarna con aplomo.

—Eso fue hace mucho —manifestó Paz.

—Pero podrías volver, ¿no? Se ahorraría un sueldo —dijo Natalia.

—Gemma es muy buena, una gran chica.

—Sí, es cierto —convino Natalia—. Y muy agradable además —miró a Salvador al preguntarle—. ¿Está casada?

—¿Quién? —se interesó él volviendo de allá donde tuviera puesto el pensamiento.

—Tu enfermera.

—¿Gemma? No, no lo está.

—Pues ya es mayor para pillar marido. Vamos, digo yo —apuntó Natalia enviando una subrepticia mirada a Encarna—. Al menos tendrá novio, ¿no?

—Ni idea —continuó Salvador.

—¿Es tu enfermera, te pasas todo el día con ella, y no sabes si tiene novio? —se extrañó Natalia.

—La verdad es que no tenemos mucho tiempo para charlar —aseguró Salvador—. Y su vida privada no es de mi incumbencia.

—Si yo fuera médico tendría una enfermera joven y guapa —bromeó Sixto.

—Ya, que te iba a dejar yo —sentenció Encarna.

—¡Coño! ¿Ya empezamos? Pues si que estamos bien —sonrió Sixto.

—No cagues donde comas —dejó ir Rafael.

—¡Por Dios, Rafa, no seas basto que estamos en la mesa! —protestó su mujer.

—No hacía más que repetir un viejo pero sabio aforismo.

—¿Por qué me has preguntado lo del trabajo? —recuperó Paz el tono inicial de la última parte de la conversación mirando a Natalia con fijeza.

—Es que yo estaba pensando hacerlo. Hoy mismo se lo decía a Rafa.

—Pero si Gloria aún es muy pequeña, y menuda eres tú para dejarla con alguien.

—Era una idea. Tampoco he dicho que fuera a hacerlo mañana mismo.

—Yo creo que es importante que la mujer trabaje —dijo Encarna.

—Yo también, pero hay momentos y momentos —comentó Paz.

—Cualquier momento es bueno —continuó Encarna—. Da una cierta fuerza, seguridad, independencia incluso.

—¡Te has enrollado con una feminista! —cantó Rafael.

Encarna no le miró. Sixto sí, pero sin decirle nada.

—Si yo volviera a trabajar, no lo haría por el dinero, sino por una necesidad propia, ya me entiendes —consideró Paz.

—A eso me refería yo, solo que no me salían las palabras ni he sabido enfocar bien la idea —asintió Natalia—. Yo quiero decir que tu hijo ya es mayor y tu hija prácticamente lo mismo. El se irá a la mili en unos meses y ella el día menos pensado se echará novio y...

—Vanessa quiere estudiar —dijo Paz—. Es de las que dice que si ha de casarse, ya lo hará a los treinta. Y Octavio... va a declararse objetor de conciencia.

—Y mientras en casa, a comer de la sopa boba —suspiró Rafael.

—Eso no significa que tú debas quedarte en casa, solo porque ellos sí lo hagan —insistió Natalia.

—Bueno, no sé... —vaciló Paz.

—Te ha dado fuerte hoy con lo de trabajar, ¿eh? —rezongó Rafael.

—Oye, es mi vida, ¿vale? De momento solo lo estoy pensando. ¡A ver si habrá que pedir permiso para todo a estas alturas!

—No, pedir permiso, no, pero hay decisiones que afectan a la estructura familiar y hay que considerarlas como Dios manda —espetó su marido.

—Ya, como Dios manda, y por supuesto tú eres su portavoz único.

—Eso es algo que solo le compite a ella —la defendió Paz.

—¡Joder! —protestó Sixto—. ¿Qué pasa hoy? Estáis combativas.

—Mira, guapo —le soltó Natalia—, es que cada vez hay más mujeres que se quedan solas, cargadas de hijos y sin saber hacer nada, porque han perdido la vida, así que... ya me dirás, ¿vale?

48

Sixto sostuvo la andanada, aunque a base de congelar una estática sonrisa en sus labios. El único que pareció contemplar la escena con un toque divertido fue Salvador, que dejó de masticar y enmarcó las cejas. Fueron apenas unos segundos, no más de tres.

Hasta que, curiosamente, la que rompió el silencio fue Encarna.

—Estoy de acuerdo contigo —apoyó a Natalia.

—Pues menos mal, hija. Porque lo que es estos... —se relajó Natalia.

—Yo ya se lo he dicho a Sixto —continuó la rubia—. No por casarnos voy a dejar de trabajar, y cuando tenga un hijo... los cuatro meses de rigor no me los quita nadie, pero después...

—¿No te va a dar pena dejarlo, tan pequeño? —musitó Paz.

—Supongo que sí, pero es que se trata de mi vida, y no voy a perderla por ese hijo o esa hija. No quiero llegar a mayor y sentirme frustrada —no lo dijo con intención, se notó, pero aún así se dio cuenta de lo que acababa de decir y buscó la forma de rectificarlo de alguna manera—. Y no estoy diciendo que todas las mujeres casadas y con hijos que están en casa lo sean, que conste, porque ahí está vuestro caso: tú te sientes muy a gusto con tu hija aunque ya te replanteas lo de volver a trabajar, y tú estás en las mismas, porque dejaste la consulta de tu marido para educar a tus hijos y ejercer de madre. Fue tu opción.

—Nunca me he arrepentido de ello, y estoy orgullosa de mis hijos —dijo Paz.

—Perfecto. Pero yo tengo veintinueve años, y aún suponiendo que Sixto y yo nos casemos a finales de éste o a lo largo del próximo, antes de otro año, o quizá dos, no voy a dar a luz, con lo cual ya estoy en los treinta y uno o treinta y dos, sino más. Si me quedo en casa a ejercer de madre, a mí se me pasa el tiempo en un abrir y cerrar de ojos, me pongo casi en los cuarenta y... Tal y como está el mercado laboral es un suicidio.

—Díselo a ella —comentó Rafael señalando a su mujer—. Piensa que eso de encontrar trabajo es como antes.

—¡Pero, bueno! —se enfadó Natalia—. ¿Es que he dicho que vaya a buscarlo mañana mismo? Me parece que solo he hecho un comentario, ¿no? Nada más. Lo he comentado y le he preguntado a Paz, porque está en las mismas.

—Tampoco lo tenéis tan mal —sonrió Encarna con valor dado el acaloramiento de Natalia—. Salvador te emplea a ti como enfermera y Rafael emplea a Paz como secretaria en su negocio. Así no hay intereses creados.

—¿Cuánto gana una enfermera? —preguntó al momento Rafael.

—La mitad que una secretaria de dirección —se apresuró a señalar Salvador.

—Entonces ni hablar —concluyó su amigo. Y mirando a Sixto agregó—: Oye, genio, ¿y en publicidad qué tal? ¿No tendrías nada para ellas? A fin de cuentas los anuncios de detergentes y todo ese rollo los hacen señoras de su casa, normales y corrientes, no esas chicas de plástico que dan saltitos en bolas para anunciar colonias y jabones del Caribe, ¿verdad?

Tuvo que ser Encarna la que le diera un golpecito en el brazo, porque él llevaba ya unos segundos en silencio y tan alejado de la conversación como lo acababa de estar Salvador.

Sixto

Oyendo hablar a Encarna de matrimonio, de hijos, de años... sentí un nudo en la boca del estómago. Con Sole nunca habíamos hablado de eso al comienzo, y acabamos casándonos jóvenes, y liándonos con Domingo y Marta a las primeras de cambio. Y así nos ha ido, contando con el remate final de Guillermo. Pero eso fue cuando a mí aún no me habían destetado, o sea, que pagamos bien el pato. Ahora era todo lo contrario, sabía muy bien lo que costaba el pato. Estaba arruinado por culpa de ese precio, y lo que se me venía encima no era como para echarse a cantar, y menos pensar en hijos. El divorcio, el dinero que le pasaba y tendría que pasarle a Sole, los negros nubarrones de la agencia con lo de Roberto Estrada...

Me jodió mucho que Encarna hablara de aquella forma, dando por sentadas muchas cosas, demasiadas. No habíamos hablado para nada de cuándo nos íbamos a casar, y mucho menos de tener hijos. ¿Veintinueve, treinta, treinta y un años? ¿Y qué? Una amiga de mi ex había sido madre a los cuarenta y dos, y una prima mía a los treinta y siete. ¿A qué tanta prisa?

¿O es que Encarna se casaba conmigo para utilizarme de semental?

Trataba de olvidar lo de la campaña, pero no podía, y encima Encarna con su rollo maternal, por si no fuera poco lo excitada que estaba Natalia y lo extraños que parecían Rafael y Salvador.

En ese momento yo no estaba seguro de nada, salvo que tenía que hablar con Encarna y que a Rafael y Salvador no les llamaría en un tiempo, bastante tiempo.

Aunque de momento ahí estábamos todos, cenando y tratando de montárnoslo lo mejor posible en una noche de viernes.

Pasando, pasando y pasando.

Aunque ninguno, ni yo, habíamos cambiado tanto como para eso.

49

Natalia apartó el plato haciendo un gesto de agotamiento.

—¡Uf! —dijo—. Ya no puedo más.

—No me digas que vas a dejarte esto, con lo bueno que está —se interesó Rafael.

—Pues para ti, ¡hala! No sé dónde lo metes —le acercó su plato.

—Yo también estoy a tope —Reconoció Encarna—. No sé ni si voy a tomar postre.

—¿Haces algún tipo de régimen para estar así? —preguntó Paz.

—No, ninguno —hubo cierto orgullo en la voz de la rubia.

—¡Pues qué suerte tienes, hija! —comentó Natalia.

—¿Es que ya no te acuerdas de cómo estábamos tú y yo a los treinta? —le recordó Paz—. Y además, tú no te quejes, que estás muy bien. ¡Yo sí que tengo excesos por todas partes!

—Mis sacrificios me cuesta —se autoreconoció Natalia.

—Pero vale la pena —dijo Encarna—. El aspecto físico es importante. Te da cierta... reafirmación personal, y seguridad.

—En eso estoy de acuerdo —convino Paz—, pero la mayoría de mujeres lo que hacen es dejarse deslumbrar por las de los anuncios, que son simples quinceañeras, lo cual por otra parte es una vergüenza porque ya me dirás como va a tener mal el cutis, o celulitis o exceso de peso una adolescente de las que salen en esos anuncios. A mí eso me parece aberrante, incluso contranatura, porque cada cual es como es, para empezar, y luego está la edad y el hecho de ser lógico con ella.

—Ya, pero si no nos cuidáramos... —objetó Natalia.

—Yo me niego a ser un objeto traumado por esa locura de las modas y las estéticas —insistió Paz.

Se fijó en Salvador. Parecía de nuevo ausente, jugando con el tenedor y unos restos de comida náufragos en su plato.

—Así que nunca te harías una liposucción o un lifting —insistió Natalia.

—¿Yo? ¡No! Me da pánico un quirófano así que encima...

—Yo de momento aún no lo necesito —aclaró Natalia—, pero a los cincuenta años ya te lo diré. Dicen que lo de la edad es un estado mental, pero pienso que lo que ves en el espejo ayuda, qué quieres que te diga. Y tal y como está la medicina hoy en día... —recordó algo, de pronto, y miró a Salvador, sentado delante de ella al otro lado de la mesa circular—. Por cierto, ¿cuándo quieres que te traiga a Gloria para que la examines?

—¿Qué? ¡Ah!, ¿tu hija? Cuando quieras. Llama a Gemma.

—Yo creo que con unas vitaminas... Es que no me come nada, ¿sabes?

—A Gloria vitaminas no sé, pero a ti un antineuras...

Natalia fulminó a su marido con los ojos.

—Si te preocuparas una décima parte de tu hija de lo que te preocupas por el negocio.

—Mi hija está muy bien, el negocio necesita sangre cada día —no quiso ser tan explícito, y evadió cruzar su mirada con la de Salvador. Acabó apostillando—: Pero todo sea para que este tenga la consulta llena.

—Hoy he tenido a un niño con sida —dijo de pronto el médico.

—¡Por Dios, calla, que me vas a dar la cena! —protestó Natalia.

—¿Un caso terminal?

Salvador miró a Encarna. Estaba impresionada.

—Sí, por cuanto ya se le ha manifestado. Como puedes imaginar... ojalá todo fuera recetar vitaminas a niñas sanas.

—¿Qué sientes cuando ves algo así, y has de decírselo? —se interesó Encarna.

—Vaya, ¡les ha dado gusto! —volvió a protestar Natalia en solitario.

—Un enorme vacío —reconoció el médico—. Aunque no creas que es más fuerte que decírselo a un adulto. Es distinto, pero no peor.

—Sí, pero un adulto sabe de qué va la cosa —reflexionó Sixto.

—Por eso te digo que es distinto.

—Cada caso tiene su propia problemática, personal, económica, incluso social —comentó Paz. Y cambiando el tono de su voz, dijo—: Sin ir más lejos, ¿sabéis quién tiene cáncer de pecho? Carmen. ¿Os acordáis de Carmen?

Rafael

Carmen.

¿Que si nos acordábamos de ella?

Los demás, menos Encarna, no sé, pero estaba por decir que sí, que todos la teníamos en la memoria, en mayor o menor grado. Y en mi caso... el grado era superlativo, máximo.

Carmen había sido uno de mis grandes amores, sino el que más.

En aquellos años en los que empezábamos a descubrir la vida, el sexo, la libertad, sin inhibiciones, sin tabús.

A veces aún me preguntaba por qué no me casé con ella.

Había sido antes de conocer a Natalia, mucho antes, aunque el tiempo ya se distorsionaba en mi memoria. Carmen era una absoluta tempestad de la naturaleza, con todos los elementos pugnando por estallar en su alma y dispararse hacia afuera. Eso era parte de su encanto, pero también lo que la hacía imprevisible. Cada vez que creías tenerla, se te escapaba como se escapa el agua por entre los dedos de la mano. No quería comprometerse, probablemente porque ya estaba comprometida con la vida. Si se sentía atrapada, se evadía, huía hacia cualquier parte. Si se había acostado tres veces seguidas contigo, cualquier día podía enrollarse con el primero con el que tropezaba, solo para no sentirse prisionera, y para que tú supieras que eso no significaba nada. Cuántas veces la odiabas, otras tantas la perdonabas, y pese a todo... sí, me hubiera casado con ella, porque sabía que una vez dicho el sí, comprometida, hubiera respetado su palabra, su renuncia a todo lo demás para consagrarse a ti, aunque en reciprocidad habría exigido lo mismo de uno. Y por su forma de entender la vida, de amarla, de querer existir, y ser hasta el máximo, hasta el límite de los límites, sé que con Carmen habría sido feliz, más de lo que lo soy con Natalia.

Una felicidad sin descanso, a cien por hora por la autopista de la existencia.

Y ahora, ¿cuánto hacía que no sabía de ella?

Una eternidad, desde que la negué en mis recuerdos para no hacerme daño, no sentirme ridículo. Porque en el fondo, si no me casé con ella, fue por miedo, porque quería algo como lo que encontré en Natalia.

Ni siquiera sé si me habría aceptado, aunque creo que sí, porque a veces me lo decía:

—Rafa, tú y yo estamos hechos de la misma pasta, y somos tal para cual. Si nada nos cambia, podríamos hacer grandes cosas.

Carmen.

Después de tanto tiempo, allí, en la cena, y para algo tan escabroso como aquello, porque lo del cáncer me cogió...

50

—No sabía que le seguías la pista —mencionó Salvador.

—Bueno, no es que la vea ni nada de eso, pero Amparo sigue siendo amiga de Luisa, y Luisa era vecina de los padres de Carmen y aún tiene contacto con ellos.

—¿No fue novia tuya? —preguntó Sixto dirigiéndose a Rafael.

—Salimos juntos —su voz era opaca—. En aquellos días lo de los "noviazgos" ya no se llevaba.

—Pero estabais muy unidos. Ahora recuerdo...

—Sixto, no seas cotilla —le reprimió Encarna mirando a Natalia.

—No, tranquila —ella lo notó y se dirigió a la rubia sin ambages, aunque con cierta sequedad en su tono—, conozco muy bien todas las juerguecitas de este. Me informé antes de decirle que sí.

—Más bien yo te lo conté —dijo Rafael.

—Por si las moscas, por precaución, no fueras a encontrarte a todas tus ex después de liarte conmigo.

—¡Joder! Si me lo hubiera callado, porque me lo callo, y si se lo conté, porque se lo conté. El caso es hablar.

—¡Qué va! —Natalia volvió a mostrar su lado más combativo y sarcástico—. ¡Lo bien que me fue que te desfogaras de soltero! Mira luego lo tranquilito que te quedaste.

—¡Coño, Rafa! —Sixto casi se atragantó al estar bebiendo—. No sabía yo que hubieras llegado agotado al matrimonio. Ahora entiendo que tardaras tanto en recuperarte y no la embarazaras hasta los treinta y pico.

—Tú no hables que te agotaste lo mismo pero con una sola, en plan legal y dejando visibles "huellas" —le endilgó Rafael.

—Balas de plomo —silbó Salvador.

—Pero bueno —estuvo al quite Encarna—, y lo de esa tal Carmen, ¿qué? Lo del cáncer de pecho es...

—No lo sé —reconoció Paz—. Creo que van a extirpárselo y luego... ya se sabe, hay que esperar. Si en cinco años no le rebrota...

—¿Se casó? —preguntó Sixto apartando los ojos de Rafael por primera vez desde su último comentario.

—No, Carmen no era de esas. Tenía demasiada... vida.

—Y algo más, por lo que me han contado —mencionó Natalia.

—Eso no significa nada —manifestó Rafael.

—Depende. Según tú, fumaba como un carretero, bebía como una esponja, y se lo hizo con un montón de hombres. Si eso no... agota, no sé qué va a hacerlo.

—Es que estaba muy buena —advirtió Sixto—, y si aún se conserva, pese a lo que digas tú, Natalia, seguirá de buen ver, así que lo del pecho la va a hundir. Disfrutaba mucho de la vida.

Por inercia miraron a Rafael, pero éste ya no dijo nada más. Sus ojos acababan de encontrarse con los de Salvador, por encima del bien y del mal, en un extraño silencio que ambos compartieron sin saber el motivo, oculto en el interior de cada cual.

Salvador

Solo me he acostado con mi mujer.

Es algo que... no sé explicar, no puedo explicar. De joven tenía muchos sueños, quería vivir la vida, pero la carrera, la represión, la timidez frente a las chicas, y luego, casi inmediatamente, el hecho de enamorarme de Paz y dedicarme solo a ella... Durante mucho tiempo no me importó, pero ahora pienso en ello, y me pregunto si no me perdí algo importante, si no dejé de vivir una porción básica de mi propia existencia.

A veces me pregunto cómo serán otras mujeres, otras sensaciones. Cuando oigo hablar a los demás de sus conquistas, sus ex-lo-que-sea, sus devaneos amorosos, de soltero o de casado, siento un raro vacío. Una vez dije que yo había sido fiel a mi esposa y no me creyeron, se pensaron que iba de santo, a contracorriente. Eso me hizo sentir como un bicho raro. Sixto y Rafael han tenido experiencias diversas, y se les nota, en su desparpajo, en su manera de ser, aunque no puedo decir que me parezca bien, porque eso va a carácteres. Yo no podría abandonar a Paz por otra y hacerle el daño que Sixto ha hecho a Sole, ni tener una aventura, consciente, fija, porque ello me haría sentir culpable, traidor, sucio. Será que soy así, y así me acepto, pero ello no significa que no piense, y cada vez más. ¿Soy un santo o un idiota?

Todos envidiamos lo que no tenemos.

Y mis preguntas, mis dudas, me han asaltado ahora, precisamente ahora, cuando denoto la pérdida de interés por parte de Paz, la rutina en la que ha caído. Amar a alguien y no poder sentir lo que un hombre desea y necesita, es muy duro. ¿Por qué hay quien piensa que la pasión es solo cosa de la juventud? Al contrario. Pienso que la pasión es cosa de madurez. En la juventud los sentimientos están a flor de piel, desnudos, pero en la madurez están tan profundamente arraigados, que la pasión los hace brotar aún más fuertes y densos.

En aquel momento de la cena, me sentí bastante ridículo. Sixto con su despampanante rubia, Rafael hablando sin pudor de una ex-novia, y yo con mi imagen de santo, de hombre estable y feliz.

Desde luego, todos envidiamos lo que no tenemos.

Y hay momentos en los que es muy difícil mantener un equilibrio.

51

Pidieron los postres, discutiendo sobre cada detalle, preguntándole al camarero el sabor de tal o la clase de cual especie de nombre fantasioso. Solo Encarna optó por no tomar postre. Los otros cinco lo hicieron. Tarta de queso, profiteroles con nata, crema catalana... Al retirarse el muchacho con la nota, fue la rubia la que hizo la pregunta.

—¿Adónde iremos ahora?

Se miraron unos a otros, esperando que alguien hablara y tomara la iniciativa. Ni Salvador ni Paz parecieron dispuestos a hacerlo. Natalia vaciló y finalmente fue Sixto el que, con toda naturalidad, propuso:

—Vamos a tomar una copa, ¿no?

—¿Quieres ir a sentarte a otro lado? —protestó Encarna.

—Sugiere entonces algo tú.

—Podríamos ir a bailar.

—A mi no me lleváis a una discoteca —saltó rápido Salvador.

—Vamos, hombre, cualquiera diría —objetó su mujer.

—Que no, que a una de esas cosas infernales con la música a toda mecha y una panda de locos brincando en la pista no voy —insistió él.

—Menudo carroza estás hecho —se burló Rafael.

—¿Y tú eras el que de joven no paraba? —le apoyó Sixto.

—Era distinto —puntualizó Salvador—. Entonces la música era música, se reconocía, tenía un ritmo y una melodía. Ahora solo es ruido.

—Máquina —dijo Sixto.

—Pues eso —asintió Salvador.

—¿Y tú cómo lo sabes? ¿Cuánto hace que no pisas una discoteca? —le pinchó Paz.

—Vaya, ¿te pones de su parte? —se molestó el médico.

—No, pero por una noche que vayamos de "marcha", como se dice, no pasa nada.

—Tampoco hace falta que vayamos a una discoteca —mencionó Rafael—. Hay bailes que están entre lo uno y lo otro.

—Lo que pasa es que aún es temprano —dijo Sixto—. Lo bueno empieza a partir de la una o las dos. Yo primero iría a tomar esa copa, para bajar la cena, ¿qué decís?

—Yo hace mucho que no voy a bailar —suspiró Natalia.

Salvador miró a Paz. Su esposa tenía una sonrisa de media luna, suave y tierna, iluminándole la cara. Un momento antes pensaba en la rutina, la falta de motivaciones. Natalia tenía razón. ¿Cuánto tiempo hacía que no bailaban? Desde la boda de Paco, y de eso hacía...

Y tampoco era lo mismo.

—Está bien, lo que digáis —concedió—, no quiero que me colguéis el muerto.

—Pues venga, en cuanto traigan los postres pedimos la cuenta, vamos a tomar algo y decidimos qué hacemos y lo que haga falta —concluyó el tema Sixto.

52

El camarero dejó la nota junto a Sixto, que era el que la había pedido. La tomó, la abrió, le echó un rápido vistazo y dijo:

—Ocho mil por pareja.

Salvador fue el primero en sacar la cartera y buscar un billete de cinco mil, uno de dos mil y otro de mil pesetas. Las dejó sobre la mesa y Paz se las pasó a Sixto. Rafael extrajo un billete de diez mil.

—Dame dos —pidió.

Se guardó el cambio. Sixto hizo lo mismo con el dinero, y a continuación extrajo su tarjeta VISA oro. La depositó con la cuenta en la bandejita y luego esperó a que el camarero lo viera y pasara a recogerlo todo. Cuando el muchacho lo hubo hecho, buscó algunas monedas en un bolsillo de la parte frontal del pantalón.

—¿Quieres suelto? —se ofreció Salvador.

—No, tranquilo. Eran ocho mil con propina incluida.

—Oye, a ti no te desgravan las comidas, ¿verdad? —preguntó Rafael.

—No, qué más quisiera yo —respondió Sixto.

—Pues a mí sí, así que... pásame la cuenta.

—¡Cómo eres! —se burló Sixto.

—¡Qué coño, cómo está el fisco, tú!

—Di que sí —le apoyó Paz.

—Bueno, igual a ti también te desgrava... —Rafael miró a Salvador.

—No, tranquilo.

—¿Adónde vamos a tomar esa copa? —quiso saber Natalia, que daba la impresión de haberse animado inesperadamente.

—Conozco un lugar muy divertido, que está muy bien y es tranquilo... —empezó a decir Encarna.

—Al Dos Torres —la interrumpió Sixto.

—Caramba, déjame hablar al menos, ¿no?

—No, que sé de qué van tus lugares "divertidos y tranquilos" —se mostró inflexible su compañero.

—Tú sí, pero ellos no —abarcó a los otros cuatro con la mano—. Esto es una democracia.

—Todavía —intercaló Rafael curvando sus labios hacia arriba.

Sixto pareció súbitamente irritado. Hubo algo especial en su mirada a Encarna.

—He dicho que vamos al Dos Torres y punto —dijo a modo de sentencia final—. Ese sí es un lugar tranquilo, divertido, fresco y normal.

No dejó lugar a dudas. Su tono incluso impidió que Rafael hiciera cualquier otro comentario. Encarna buscó el apoyo de Paz o Natalia, pero sólo se encontró con su indiferencia. Ni siquiera la miraban.

El camarero llegó con la tarjeta de crédito y el resguardo de la VISA para que Sixto lo firmara.

Encarna

Me sentí muy irritada.

No era la primera vez que Sixto me hacía algo así, pero sí era la primera vez que me dejaba en ridículo delante de sus amigos, como si fuera mi padre, tratándome como una niña tonta. Y lo que acabó de ponerme a cien fue que ninguna de ellas, por lo menos ellas, Paz o Natalia, se pusieran de mi parte, me defendieran, por simple feminidad o causa común o lo que fuera. Habían estado amables, incluso estaba por decir que afectuosas, y casi lograron engañarme, pero de pronto se me antojó que todo aquello no era más que un paripé de lo más vulgar. "¡Qué vestido más bonito!",

"¡Hola, cariño! ¿Qué tal estás?"... y hablando de hijos, de matrimonio, de las habituales tonterías de parejas maduras saliendo a cenar...

¿Susceptible? Tal vez, pero decidí estar en guardia, y luego me dije que de guardia nada, que lo mejor era ir a saco, pasarlo bien, olvidarme de ellas. Y si Sixto se ponía borde, tendría una charla con él. Sabía cómo domesticarlo, pero a solas, no con ellos delante. Estaban listos si creían que iban a poder conmigo. No me conocían.

Claro que sabía la razón del comportamiento de Sixto. Vaya si la sabía. Cada vez que íbamos a uno de los lugares que yo había frecuentado habitualmente antes de conocerle, me encontraba a tres o cuatro de mis amigos. Por lo general solo eran eso, amigos, pero Sixto les miraba de arriba abajo, pensando, imaginando, y luego... se ponía como una moto, me preguntaba quiénes eran, dónde les conocí, si había salido alguna vez con ellos... Y lo que en el fondo quería saber era si me había acostado con ellos. Así de sencillo. Se lo dije un día:

—¿Por qué no preguntas directamente si me lo he hecho con él?

Se enfadó mucho, dijo que yo era una mal pensada, que no iba por ahí... y luego reconoció que sí, que se sentía celoso, que solo quería imaginarse a él conmigo, porque estaba loco por mí. A una mujer le gusta que le digan eso, así que zanjé el tema. Pero desde ese día ya no habíamos vuelto a esos sitios, los eludía con cualquier excusa, aunque ahora se le acababa de ver el plumero.

Cuando Quique y yo cortamos estuve muy desorientada. Fueron dos años de búsqueda, no de un nuevo amor, sino de mí misma. Y pensara lo que pensara Sixto, en ese tiempo solo me acosté con tres hombres, y ninguno fue importante.

Tendría que aclarar todo eso antes de casarnos.

No quería volver a tropezar.

Una cosa más que hacer.

Natalia

Al salir del restaurante y dirigirnos a los coches, había tensión. Solo faltó que Sixto le dijera a Rafael que él iría delante, que le siguiera, para que mi marido le soltara:

—Ni hablar, que luego empiezas a correr como si fueras en un Formula 1 y a mi no me da la gana de jugarme el físico saltándome semáforos en rojo para no perderte de vista. Además, ya sé dónde está ese sitio, ¿qué te crees, que solo tú eres un mundano? Está arriba de todo de la Vía Augusta, ¿no?

A lo que Sixto le respondió a Rafa:

—Yo no me salto semáforos, antiguo, que eres un antiguo. Lo que pasa es que aún vas con el coche de hace cinco años, y claro, ya no tiene "trempera". Está como el Gobierno, que necesita un cambio.

Era una forma de devolverle la pelota por el comentario de la cena, lo de la democracia. El "todavía" de Rafa, dirigido al creciente tono facha de Sixto, le había molestado. Si les conoceré yo. Aunque mucho ruido y pocas nueces. Se habían pasado la vida tirándose pullas con más o menos mala uva. A veces no entendía cómo eran amigos. Tal vez se complementasen, se necesitasen, fuesen la respectiva voz de sus conciencias dormidas.

Pero con todo esto, lo que a mí me resultaba más evidente era que Rafa estaba inquieto, irascible, a la que saltaba, y no podía entender la razón ya que en apariencia la cena estaba resultando más relajada de lo previsto. La chica, Encarna, trataba de adaptarse, la pobre, y estaba bastante en su sitio. Incluso había dicho alguna cosa coherente, o sea que no era una jovencita idiota, una de tantas teñidas de rubio, tonta de capirote. Me daba la sensación de que era una mujer, bastante más mujer de lo que en un principio nos pareció a todos cuando la conocimos, el día que Sixto nos la presentó. Eso aún me producía más extrañeza, porque enamorarse de Sixto ya era tener ganas. Y con nosotras aún se la notaba en guardia.

Me despreocupé de Encarna para ver qué le pasaba a Rafa, pero no logré nada, y entonces recordé que la que tenía que estar de uñas era yo con él.

Y es que durante unos minutos había olvidado mi problema, por extraño que pareciera.

Rafael

Me dio por comparar a Encarna con Mercedes.

La furia que sentía acerca de Sixto, imparable y cada vez más convertida en...¿odio?, me estaba haciendo parecer idiota, no a los ojos de los demás, sino a los míos. Si encima se metía conmigo por ser socialista, empleando la prepotencia ostentosa de los fachas, ibamos a terminar mal. Pero la verdad es que siempre habíamos discutido de política, sin llegar a extremos de agresión verbal, y esta noche... todo se me antojaba distinto.

Nos estaba restregando a su rubia por las narices.

Nos estaba gritando: "¿Lo veis, so mierdas? Yo lo he hecho, tengo un conejo nuevo y joven. Vosotros aguantaréis a vuestras santas hasta que la muerte os separe". Me habría gustado decirle que yo también tenía un conejo joven, y mucho más joven que el suyo además. Cuatro años más joven que el suyo.

Tal vez por eso Mercedes era más dura, más terca, más radical, y me estaba llevando por la calle de la amargura con sus presiones y sus "por aquí no paso".

¿Y había comparación? Pues en algunas cosas sí y en otras no. Por ejemplo, Encarna era más mujer que Mercedes, pero por la misma razón, Mercedes era más chispeante, vital, exuberante que Encarna, aunque no fuese rubia. El cuerpo de Mercedes era superior al de Encarna, y el físico... probablemente muy y muy superior. Pero Encarna tenía un morbo que Mercedes no tenía. Esa clase de morbo que los tíos captamos en seguida, y que es lo que más nos pierde. A Mercedes había tenido que enseñárselo todo en la cama, porque pese a ir de moderna, estaba en bragas, es decir, muchos líos y amantes de pacotilla, pero malos, de los que solo van a lo suyo y ni enseñan ni piden, solo toman. Yo la estaba refinando, le decía por dónde ir y qué hacer. Encarna en cambio daba la impresión de saber latín, de convertir el sexo en una sublimación de los sentidos. A Sixto se le notaba en la cara. Toda aquella prepotencia, todo aquel pisar fuerte, era nuevo. Antes siempre fue chulillo, pero no tanto. Si actuaba como actuaba, era por tenerla a ella al lado. Y encima la trataba como quería. Ordeno y mando.

Mercedes en cambio era la que hacía y deshacía conmigo.

Me puse de muy mala hostia.

Tenía que coger a Mercedes y decirle que o blanco o negro, que no me presionara, que necesitaba tiempo, y si no... puerta.

Aunque la idea de perderla y volverme a quedar solo me aterrase tanto como la de enviar mi matrimonio a la mierda.

¿Por qué las mujeres, antes o después, te exigen un compromiso?

53

Puso en marcha el coche, haciendo tronar el motor, y ella ni siquiera esperó a que estuviesen rodando por la avenida para decírselo.

—Oye, ya sé que es tu gente, pero precisamente por esta razón te lo advierto: no te pases.

—¿Qué? —vaciló Sixto más pendiente de la maniobra que de aquellas repentinas palabras.

—Ya sabes a qué me refiero —continuó Encarna—. Si querías ir al Dos Torres, no tenías más que decirlo y punto. No hacía falta dejarme en ridículo.

—Pero, ¿de qué estás hablando? ¿Quién te ha dejado en ridículo?

—Tú, me has dejado en ridículo —apostilló ella incidiendo en la primera palabra, aunque sin gritar ni elevar el tono de voz.

—No es verdad.

—Es verdad, y no lo niegues, porque será peor. Si lo niegas es que ni tan solo te has dado cuenta y entonces resulta más humillante. Quiere decir que vas a tratarme igual en el futuro, y ese no es mi estilo, tenlo en cuenta.

—¡Coño, no jodas! ¿Qué he dicho? Solo que no quería ir a...

—Mira, tengamos la fiesta en paz, no quiero entrar en el juego del "yo he dicho"-"tú has dicho" —le cortó Encarna—. Bastante estoy aguantando a ese par de damas.

Sixto aprovechó la salida facilitada por ella.

—Yo no he notado nada —dijo.

—¡Oh, claro! Son muy sutiles ellas. Hablan de sus maridos, de sus hijos, y te están restregando por las narices con cada silencio y cada mirada que tú eres "la otra". Y no digamos ellos. Bueno, el médico aún, pero lo que es tu amigo Rafa... Aún tengo sus ojos hundidos en mis tetas.

—Ya te he dicho que este vestido...

—¿Qué pasa con mi vestido, eh? —por primera vez levantó la voz—. !Vamos, hombre, a ver si encima...! Si es un reprimido o va corto, que envíe a su mujer a hacer un cursillo de socorrismo.

Sixto lanzó una carcajada.

—Eso ha estado bien, aunque no me imagino a Natalia... Bueno, a Natalia no me la imagino haciendo nada. Paz es de otra pasta. Seguro que tiene golpes ocultos. Si no, no me explico como Salva ha sido tan buen chico todo este tiempo.

—Está enamorado de su mujer, eso no es ser buen chico.

—Eres una psicóloga. A lo mejor ves más en un par de segundos desde fuera que yo en estos años.

—Lo único que veo es a dos matrimonios que no tienen nada que ver con nosotros, y que raramente van a tenerlo, así que... vete pensándolo. Y en cuanto a ti, estás muy distinto cuando te ves con ellos.

—No es verdad.

—Vale, pues no.

—Pero, ¿cómo voy a ser distinto? Soy el que soy, y ya está.

—Sí, hijo, sí.

—Mira, oye, cambiemos el rollo, ¿quieres? Solo faltas tú dándome la vara con todo lo que tengo en la cabeza.

Si esperaba una respuesta contundente de ella, esta no se produjo.

Se detuvo en el semáforo, maniobrando para situarse junto al coche de Rafael que le precedía, y los seis intercambiaron una mirada de vehículo a vehículo. Seis sonrisas cómplices, abiertas, esquemáticas.

Un grupo de chicos, armados con sus litronas, pasó por delante de los dos coches sin prestarles la menor atención.

54

Salvador fue el único que siguió el paso cansino, ritual, como si no fueran a ninguna parte ni importara de dónde venían, del grupo de muchachos, concretamente cinco, cabello largo, vaqueros ajustados, camisetas por fuera de los pantalones, cazadoras colgando indolentes de los hombros.

Fotocopias exactas de Octavio.

—Fijaos en lo que os digo —rompió el silencio Natalia—: Esos no llegan a casarse.

—¿Por qué? —secundó su inicio de conversación Paz.

—Pues... no sé, llámalo intuición, eso que no se ve pero está ahí, o lo que sea. Pero no les veo yo como para casarse y todo eso.

—Ella parece muy normal —dijo Salvador apartando definitivamente su mirada del grupo de jóvenes que ya se perdía caminando por la acera, a su derecha.

—Será para ti —repuso Natalia.

—Venga ya, mujer, que tú le tienes manía porque le ha quitado el sitio a Sole —exclamó Rafael.

—Eso no tiene nada que ver —protestó Natalia buscando el soporte de Paz.

—Yo entiendo a Natalia, Rafa —manifestó ella—. Lo que pasa es que Sixto ha perdido el trasero, como todos los tíos de mediana edad que se lían con chicas más jóvenes, y ella no es precisamente una niña. Va a lo que va, quiere casarse, y cuanto Sixto se vea el lazo en el cuello por segunda vez... a lo peor comprende que no lo tiene tan claro.

—Ya la habéis oído —siguió Paz—. Quiere hijos y todo eso. Y cuando tenga el primer hijo y se ponga gorda y fofa, como todas, Sixto...

—Ha dicho que quería un hijo, no lo compliquéis —aclaró Salvador.

—Tu marido la defiende —expuso Natalia haciendo un gesto de evidencia en dirección a Paz—. Le cae bien.

—Bueno —Paz se inclinó hacia adelante hasta acariciar el hombro de él—, lo cierto es que a Salva le cae bien todo el mundo, y eso no es malo.

—Gracias, cielo. Celebro que se me reconozcan los méritos —dijo Salvador rodeado de falsa discreción.

—Yo solo digo que Sixto es un inmaduro —insistió Natalia—. Y no hablo por Sole, que conste.

—No, que va, no hablas por Sole —bufó Rafael—. Vosotras solo queréis ver una parte del asunto.

—¿Una parte? —Natalia se puso rígida—. Sixto planta a su mujer y a sus tres hijos por una chica a la que lleva trece años, ¿y dices que eso es solo una parte?

—Mira, Nati, que todos conocemos a Sole.

—¡Y a Sixto, anda ese con lo que me sale! Los hijos no los tuvo ella sola, y si se casaron jóvenes no fue porque Sole le pusiera una pistola en el pecho. Hay que estar a las duras y a las maduras, mira lo que te digo.

—Vamos, Rafa, que todos sabemos que Sixto ha tenido otros líos —citó Paz.

—¡Jo! —Rafael las miró a través del espejo retrovisor interior—. ¡No me hagáis hablar!, ¿eh? ¡No me hagáis hablar, que Sole será amiga vuestra, y también mía, pero...! —acabó haciendo un gesto de fastidio y agregó—: ¿Vamos a estar hablando de eso toda la noche? —luego lanzó otra mirada a Salvador—. Cuenta algo, tú, aunque sea de una lobotomía o similar.

—Ya, cuando a ti no te interesa algo... —espetó Natalia.

—Como tu puedes comprender, a mi me la trae al fresco lo que acabe haciendo Sixto —aseguró Rafael—. Yo soy de los que piensa que cuando un matrimonio rompe, es por algo, y ese algo atañe siempre a los dos.

—Pero es triste que la que siempre pague el pato, por lo general, sea la mujer —dijo Paz.

—Será que no hay mujeres que le dan la patada a los tíos —indicó Rafael—. Y cada vez más.

—¡Solo faltaría que no pudiéramos defendernos! —saltó Natalia.

—Menuda noche —suspiró su marido de nuevo.

—Es que me revienta que estés aquí, tan pancho, hablando de Sole como si... bueno, como si ella fuese la culpable y Sixto un santo.

—Sixto es un cabrón, ¿te parece? Y lo digo en serio: lo es. Vale. Pero Sole estos últimos años se ha convertido en un drama, y no lo digo porque haya engordado ni esté horrible ni nada de todo eso, que no quiero herir vuestra suscep-tibilidad. Lo digo porque estaba insoportable e inaguantable. Ya está, ya me habéis hecho hablar —levantó su mirada al techo del coche y gimió—: ¡Ahora la guerra!

—Cuando una pareja se quiere —dijo Paz despacio—, nada importa, ni los años ni los cambios. Y amar significa también respetar. Sole no tiene la culpa de todo, y a lo peor tampoco Sixto, pero en lugar de hablarlo, de probar lo que fuera... han estado callando, callando, consumiéndose, y ahora él ha terminado haciendo lo que todos, lo más vulgar, lo fácil, porque para un hombre esa es la solución fácil, Rafa, no te quepa duda. Y creo que eso es lo que intenta decirte Natalia, ¿verdad Natalia?

La miró a ella, pero con lo que se encontró fue con los ojos apagados y tristes de Salvador.

Paz

Yo hablaba por Natalia, trataba de apoyarla y defenderla a ella, porque de lo que ella estaba hablando no era de Sixto y de Sole, sino de sí misma y de su marido. Sin embargo, en ese momento me di cuenta de que Salvador no lo sabía, y podía interpretar que ese era mi pensamiento, mi visión del tema.

Lo cual no era verdad.

Es decir... en parte no, aunque también hubiera una parte...

Yo no le había dicho a mi marido que no me venía el período, que temía estar menopáusica, que me sentía distinta, quizá mayor, y que no sabía si él aún me quería, porque hacía días, semanas, meses... años, que no me lo decía.

Tal vez hubiera algo de Sole en todas nosotras, el ejército de mujeres maduras de la faz de la tierra.

La pregunta del millón de dolares era saber si ante eso, todos los hombres eran Sixtos.

Quise hacer un alto, parar el coche, decirle a Salvador que le quería, por encima de todo, de la edad, del tiempo, de nosotros mismos, de Octavio y Vanessa. Decírselo y pedirle perdón por no haber confiado en él, o por haber desconfiado de mi. Sentí la necesidad, pero... fue tan solo eso, una sensación, un grito espontáneo que nació y murió en mi pecho. Pensé que, después de todo, no venía de unas horas, y que al llegar a casa lo haría, le hablaría. Si de algo podía estar segura era de él.

Salvador era mi propia sangre.

Nunca se sabe cuándo unas horas pueden ser siglos, o un "demasiado tarde" irremediable.

A veces hay que hacer lo que se siente cuando se siente y donde se siente, pasando de que haya gente delante o de si estás en un sitio absurdo o de las circunstancias.

Puede que no haya una segunda oportunidad.

Salvador

A veces cerraba los ojos y veía a Paz en el pasado, cuando nos conocimos, cuando nos enamoramos. Recordaba todas las primeras veces, la primera salida, el primer beso, la primera película, la primera canción, la primera noche íntima... Y al abrir los ojos y verla ahora, trataba de establecer una relación, buscar el eslabón perdido. Era como asomarme a un comienzo y un final, pasado y presente, sin ningún estadio intermedio. Llevábamos juntos veinticinco años, pero si alguien me preguntase cómo era ella al cabo de diez, de quince, o de veinte años después de ese comienzo, no habría sabido decirlo. Habría necesitado echar mano de las fotografías hechas en los veranos, las bodas, las comuniones, las fiestas y todo eso. Así que en mi mente había una Paz mágica y una Paz actual, y en medio, una gran distancia.

Me preguntaba también si para ella sería lo mismo, porque yo tampoco era ya el joven estudiante de medicina del comienzo.

¿Y si nos queríamos ya únicamente por continuidad, por inercia, porque estábamos acostumbrados a estar juntos y no sabíamos hacer otra cosa salvo seguir?

La idea me aterró, y supongo que seguía aterrado por ella cuando llegamos a nuestro destino y bajamos del coche, porque no me di cuenta de nada hasta que entramos en ese lugar, el Dos Torres, y me vi allí. Por un lado me daba cuenta de que necesitaba la seguridad que Paz me daba, al margen de la pasión. Pero por el otro, se me encogía el alma al imaginarme otros veinticinco años no ya peor, sino simplemente igual. Y tras oírla hablando como lo hizo, defendiendo a Sole y su derecho de cambio y ... ¿Cuál era la palabra?

Resignación.

Resignación era la palabra.

La verdadera cárcel del amor, de la vida, de la esperanza, del futuro, de todo.

Miré a mi alrededor, y me encontré en un lugar extraño, poblado por gente extraña, habitantes de la noche, topos apartados de la vida durante el día, rostros vacuos, hombres y mujeres que hablaban y bebían, charlaban y reían. Parecían como yo, pero no eran como yo. Había otros mundos más allá del mío.

Era tan sorprendente como los pensamientos que aquella tarde había tenido en torno a Gemma.

El lunes le preguntaría más. Le preguntaría si ella, por ejemplo, conocía ese sitio en el que estaba, el Dos Torres.

Aunque antes quería hablar con Paz, era importante.

No quería ser Rafael ni Sixto, ni que ella fuese Sole o Natalia.

Ojalá me hubiera decidido en ese momento, sin esperar nada más.

55

—No hay ninguna mesa donde quepamos los seis —dijo Rafael.

—Dentro...

—No, dentro hará calor, y es más incómodo —objetó Encarna cortando la sugerencia de Natalia.

—¿Qué queréis, llegar y que todo esté a punto? —manifestó Sixto mirando hacia todas partes a la búsqueda de algún indicio de que una mesa fuera a desalojarse.

—Tranquilo sí es, y parece agradable —mencionó Paz.

—¿Tranquilo? —Encarna se estremeció—. Más bien un poco rollo.

—Mejor que una discoteca, seguro —apuntó Salvador.

Encarna se le colgó del brazo.

—¡Ay, doctor, que si pudiera aún te enseñaría un poco de qué va todo lo de los 90!

—¿Quieres reciclarme? —se interesó él.

—Eres una persona encantadora, no necesitarías mucho, solo una puesta a punto.

—Sí, la de los cien mil kilómetros: motor nuevo.

Encarna se echó a reír, sin abandonar el contacto de su brazo. Natalia miró a Paz, pero no encontró ningún eco en sus ojos. Su amiga sonreía.

—Tú no te fíes de él —le advirtió Sixto a su novia—. Con eso de ser médico y un hombre respetable... es de los que las mata callando.

—Apuesto a que sí —Encarna le guiñó un ojo.

—¿Por qué te crees que me hice pediatra y dejé de operar? —bromeó Salvador—. Mataba a todos los maridos de mis amigas.

—Y te descubrieron —le siguió el juego la rubia.

—No, mis amigas se enamoraban de otros hombres y no de mí, así que al final me cansé. Ahora les doy vitaminas a sus hijos.

Encarna echó hacia atrás su melena rubia al romper en una nueva carcajada. Su estridencia casi ahogó la voz de Natalia al protestar:

—Vaya, gracias, eso debe ir por mi.

—No, mujer —la calmó Salvador—. A tu marido aún no le he operado.

—Pues mira, me habrías quitado un muerto de encima.

—A veces eres... —Rafael puso cara de asco, pero autentico.

—¡Mira, allí se va esa pareja! —saltó Encarna de pronto, separándose de Salvador para encaminarse hacia una mesa situada en un ángulo del espacio abierto al exterior, bajo la tranquila noche.

—Yo creo que habríamos estado mejor en el Puerto Olímpico —repuso Paz, cogiendo a Natalia por el brazo para apartarla de su marido.

Salvador, Rafael y Sixto llegaron los últimos. La mesa quedaba libre, pero solo disponía de dos sillas. Esperaron al camarero, que no tardó en aterrizar junto a ellos.

—¿No prefieren los señores pasar dentro? Arriba hay...

—Queremos esta —Encarna se sentó en una de las dos sillas.

—Bien, enseguida les traigo... —el camarero buscó sillas libres en las restantes mesas—. Un segundo, por favor.

Sixto le puso las dos manos en los hombros por detrás a su novia.

—Es todo un carácter —silbó en dirección a Salvador y Rafael.

—No lo sabes tú bastante bien —asintió Encarna.

—Pero voy aprendiendo, ¿eh?

Y en ese instante se inclinó sobre ella y le mordió el cuello, o lo fingió, aunque para el resultado fue lo mismo. La rubia se puso a gritar y a reír, sin ninguna manía. Una docena de rostros anónimos y miradas mitad perdidas mitad indiferentes se concentró en ambos por espacio de unos pocos segundos.

Natalia y Paz también se miraron, pero de forma más acusada, y seguían haciéndolo cuando los demás volvieron a sus respectivos asuntos y se olvidaron de ellos.

56

—¡Jesús! —Paz contempló su copa, como si en lugar de aquel líquido de color indefinible tirando a rosa, contuviera oro—. ¡Seis mil pesetas por seis brebajes!

—Pero son seis brebajes modernos, mujer —le dijo su marido con tanta seriedad que cualquiera hubiera creído que hablaba en serio, salvo ella, que sabía que sí hablaba en serio—. Además, fíjate tú dónde tienes puesto el trasero. Esto no es el bar de la esquina.

—¿Y toda esta gente? —comentó Natalia—. Desde luego...

—¡Cómo sois, por Dios! —protestó Sixto—. Hay que estar al día.

—Hombre, antes íbamos a cenar y ya está, pero ahora, con esto de la modernidad —insistió Salvador.

—Pero que modernidad ni que niño muerto —se quejó Sixto—. Hay cientos de locales como este, y ahora aún es temprano. La marcha empieza mucho más tarde.

—Sí, pero yo... no sé, me parecen todos tan ociosos —comentó Paz—. Es como si ninguno tuviera que madrugar mañana ni ningún día, porque ya sé que mañana es sábado. Dan la impresión de estar aquí como en plan fijo, ¿me explico? Forman parte del decorado, el ambiente.

—¡Qué tonterías dices, Paz, por favor! —la hizo callar Sixto—. La gente está todo el día con lo suyo, y al llegar la noche se pone guapa y se mueve, salen con los amigos, charlan, ven lo que hay, van de un lugar a otro.

—Y se acuestan cuando sale el sol —finalizó Salvador.

—Hombre, por supuesto. La noche hay que vivirla.

—Habló el experto —sonrió Encarna—. Cuando le conocí no era tan "progre".

—¿Quieres una medalla? —le propuso él.

—Yo entiendo a Salva —dijo Rafael interviniendo en el dialogo—. Lo que resulta asombroso es que la gente pague mil pesetas por una copa aquí cuando en otra parte vale lo que vale.

—Claro. Se paga el sitio, el marco —le secundó Natalia.

—No, se paga la distinción, saber que aquí solo va a venir un tipo de gente, que no vas a encontrarte con "lolailos", por ejemplo—rectificó Sixto—.

¿Y no me digáis que esto no tiene sentido?

—Sí, el sentido es que la gente cada día es más clasista y racista —dijo Salvador.

—¡Coño, que no! —saltó Sixto.

—Ah, pues será eso —convino Salvador demostrando sus nulas ganas de discutir.

—Si estáis tan mal nos vamos —propuso Encarna.

—No, ¿qué dices? —se sintió afectada Paz—. Solo eran comentarios.

—Después de pagar seis mil pelas por esto, de aquí no me mueven hasta que haya pelado el asiento a la silla —aseguró Rafael.

—Fijaos en esa preciosidad —señaló Natalia de pronto en dirección a la puerta del local.

Todos lo hicieron, sin disimulo, en silencio, para encontrarse con la imagen de una más que segura modelo publicitaria, alta, bellísima, muy joven, de rostro puro y cuerpo moldeado por algún extraño dios, tal vez de gimnasio o puede que incluso celestial. Estaban tan pendientes de ella que ni siquiera repararon en su acompañante, un hombre de unos treinta años, igualmente atractivo.

Salvo Sixto.

Aunque naturalmente solo él pudiera reconocer en el recién llegado a su compañero, rival y enemigo Roberto Estrada.

Sixto

Hice lo posible para que no me viera, pero por un lado, era difícil apartar los ojos de aquella niña, y por otro, Roberto actuaba como lo habría hecho yo de ir acompañado por ella, asegurándose que todo Dios mirara en su dirección. Era un lujo, un absoluto lujo. Tendría diecinueve o veinte años, pero eso lo sabía yo porque trabajaba en publicidad. Para cualquiera era una mujer, y qué mujer, metro ochenta, un cuerpo perfecto, sin un átomo de más, piernas muy largas, pechos muy precisos, cintura muy estrecha, manos de seda, uñas cuidadas, cabello suelto y como recién salido de la peluquería, ojos verdes, labios sensuales. La gente cree que las chicas de los anuncios son de plástico, o artificiales, o tontas, o que están tan preocupadas de sí mismas que no hacen otra cosa que cuidarse para lucir. ¡Y una mierda! Follan como cualquiera, solo que no es cualquiera el que folla con ellas. O tienes pasta o poder o simplemente se encaprichan de ti porque les vas.

Roberto Estrada aún no tenía excesiva pasta, pese a que se lo gastara todo en sí mismo y con generosidad, como autopromoción, y tampoco tenía poder, de momento, así que debía ser por el físico, a no ser que ella tuviera mucha vista, intuición, y supiera que iba a tener también lo otro. Que estaba en camino.

Hace diez años, cuando yo estaba como él, matando por una campaña y por llegar arriba, no había chicas como aquella, y si las había... ¡mierda!, sí debía haberlas, pero yo estaba casado, muy casado.

Quise matar a Roberto Estrada, destrozarle, verle sufrir y llorar. Pero en ese momento el que lucía un traje de Armani y un Rolex mejor que el mío era él. Yo ganaba el doble o el triple y estaba pasando apuros, con la pensión de Sole y los niños y lo de empezar de nuevo con Encarna. El en cambio vivía al día, y utilizaba la vieja norma de la seducción: dinero llama a dinero, poder llama a poder. Cualquiera que le viera le daría una palmada en el hombro. Ya iba de triunfador.

Por eso tenía una niña como aquella.

El muy hijo de puta.

Me vio. Y aunque hubiera estado de espaldas, o escondido debajo de la mesa, me habría visto igual.

Cinceló una sonrisa en technicolor en su estúpida cara y echó a andar hacia nosotros, hacia mí.

Así que me puse en pié y le corté el avance, impidiéndole llegar a nuestra mesa.

57

—Hombre, Planas, que sorpresa. ¿Qué haces tú por aquí?

¿Y por qué coño le llamaba Planas en lugar de Sixto?

—Nada, ya ves, tomando una copa antes de empezar la noche.

—Mira, te presento a Nadia —le pasó un brazo por los hombros a la modelo, no por formar parte de la presentación, sino como exclusivo signo de propiedad—. Nadia, este es Sixto Planas, uno de los mejores publicistas de este país. Está en mi agencia.

Realmente dijo lo de "mi agencia" como si fuera suya.

—Hola —dijo ella con voz cadenciosa y un cierto tono anglosajón, o nórdico—, me alegra conocerte.

No se alegraba en absoluto, salvo que pudiera darle una campaña millonaria o convertirla en la nueva imagen de una marca de primera o algo parecido, y eso no entraba en sus funciones, ni en las de Roberto Estrada. Ellos solo ideaban campañas, frases, slogans. Pero sabía quedar bien, sonreír para dejarle hecho una mierda, mostrar todo su ángel. De cerca aún era más hermosa, como si fuera imposible que hubiera caras y cuerpos así sobre la faz de la tierra. Sus ojos eran inmensos, y sus labios un deseo. La simple idea de tenerla desnuda en los brazos le produjo un estremecimiento.

Pero se la imaginó así, desnuda, en sus brazos, por una fracción de segundo, a la siguiente fracción él era un simple testigo de la escena y el que la tenía era Roberto Estrada.

—Nadia está haciendo una película en Castelldefels —le informó—. Una coproducción italo-franco-española. A lo mejor podríamos emplearla en la campaña de Aura —cambió de pronto el enfoque de la conversación e hizo un movimiento en dirección a la mesa para agregar acto seguido—: Salida de matrimonios, ¿eh?

—¿Tienes alguna idea para la campaña? —preguntó Sixto obviando su último comentario.

—Bueno... —por un momento no pareció muy seguro de lo que iba a decir—, la verdad es que he estado trabajando en ello por mi cuenta. Puede ser una gran oportunidad, pero por supuesto lo consideraremos todo en equipo, ¿verdad? Pienso que tengo algunas ideas que... en fin, valen la pena. Cuando empieces la campaña están a tu disposición.

—La vas a llevar tú solo, Estrada —mencionó él.

El otro no pudo reprimir un destello en la mirada.

—No entiendo —dijo—. El señor Escobar me sugirió que pensara... Y ayer mismo le comenté...

—El lunes será oficial.

—¿De verdad? —los ojos se dilataron del todo. Aún en su seguridad, la noticia le golpeó de lleno—. ¿Pero cómo...?

—Estoy en la ejecutiva, ¿recuerdas? —Sixto logró sonreír y todo—. Yo también tengo mi voto.

Mantuvo la sonrisa, y su aire de nueva superioridad, aunque por dentro se iniciaba la tormenta.

¿Qué estaba haciendo? ¿Le doraba la píldora? ¿Le hacía la rosca? ¿Por qué le hacía la noche aún más agradable? Se sintió como si dentro suyo actuaran dos fuerzas opuestas, la del odio y la de la inteligencia por encima de todo. La fuerza de los auténticos líderes. Recordó la frase pronunciada por un auténtico Maquiavelo: "Si no puedes vencerles, únete a ellos". Claro que había otras, como ganarse la confianza del enemigo, engañarle, buscar una proximidad para poder después hundir mejor el cuchillo en la espalda, o en la yugular, para que no gritara.

La modelo parecía aburrida en mitad de la conversación. Pasaba de ellos, de los dos. Miraba a su alrededor para reafirmarse en si misma viendo como todo el mundo la miraba. A pesar de todo, se colgó del brazo de Roberto Estrada.

—No lo olvidaré, Planas... Sixto —había logrado desestabilizarle, aunque fuera a base de darle el éxito, lo que más quería. A lo peor aquella noche no se le levantaba a causa de ello—. Te juro que... bueno, esto es lo más grande que me ha...

—Te veré el lunes, aunque por supuesto... tú no sabes nada. A mi ni me nombres —le dio un golpe en el hombro—. Deja que sea Marcelino el que te dé la noticia.

—Claro, claro.

—Adiós, Nadia.

Se acercó a ella y le dio un beso en la mejilla. Olía de muerte. Un segundo más y hubiera tenido una erección.

Luego regresó a su mesa, mitad orgulloso de sí mismo y mitad asesino, por la chica, por su enemigo, por la campaña, por la necesidad de montar números como el que acababa de montar, tragándose su orgullo y con solo una remota, muy remota esperanza, de que todo saliera bien.

Lo cual incluía ver pasar el cadáver de Estrada por delante de la puerta de su casa en un plano no demasiado largo de tiempo.

58

Al sentarse en su sitio, Rafael fue el primero en hablar.

—¡Joder, Sixto! ¿De qué conoces tú a un bombón así?

—Yo no la conozco a ella, sino a él. Trabaja en mi agencia.

—Será el director, ¿no?, porque con esa nena...

—Se te cae la baba, cielo —le endilgó Natalia poniendo voz de burlona ironía no exenta de cierta ira.

—No, no es el director —Sixto miró a Encarna—. Es uno que se llama Roberto Estrada y al que van a dar una campaña muy importante, de unos preservativos.

—¡Claro, los está probando! —soltó una risotada Rafael.

—¡Qué basto eres! —volvió a atacarle Natalia.

—Oye, para ya, ¿quieres? —Rafael la fulminó con ojos cargados de furia.

Encarna movió la cabeza para buscar a la pareja, tras captar la intención acorralada de las palabras de Sixto. Vio como se sentaban en una mesa al otro lado de dónde ellos se encontraban, lateralmente a la posición que ocupaban ella y Sixto. Los dos, además de Rafael, eran los que podían verles mejor, sin esfuerzo. Tal vez por esa razón Rafael aún seguía pendiente de la escultural modelo.

—Desde luego es guapísima —comentó Paz—, aunque Dios sabe lo que le debe de costar mantenerse así.

—A su edad no cuesta, querida —mencionó Natalia con pesar.

—Pues yo creo que sí. Esas chicas han de cuidarse mucho, y su carrera dura muy pocos años. Te apuesto lo que quieras a que se pasa medio día en el gimnasio para mantenerse en forma.

—Es lo que digo yo —la atacó Rafael—: vas poco a tu gimnasio. Con una hora al día no tienes suficiente.

—¡Mira es que... !

—Rafa, no te pases —le pidió Paz en un tono agotado antes de que ella completara su estallido.

—Me callo, me callo —manifestó él reclinándose en su asiento.

Volvió a mirarla a ella, sin ambages.

Sixto aún lo estaba haciendo.

—Tendrán unos hijos sanos —apuntó Salvador, y su voz pareció salir de otro mundo, distante.

—Ya estás pensando en el negocio —le reconvino Encarna.

—¿No decíais antes que venían madres guapísimas con niños y niñas desnutridos a mi consulta? Bueno, pues a ver si viene esa.

—Esas no tienen hijos —aseguró Natalia—. Se estropean. Los hijos los tenemos las tontas como nosotras —miró a Paz.

—Yo creo que una chica así —señaló a la modelo y al ejecutivo—, no puede ser feliz. Es demasiado guapa. Eso tiene que ser... no sé, un trauma, una carga, con todos los hombres buscando siempre lo mismo, y ella con la necesidad de casarse con alguien que esté a su altura.

—¿A su altura? Esas solo buscan dinero, mujer —afirmó Natalia—. Dinero y coleccionar amantes o maridos.

—Pues por eso mismo: no son felices. El don que tienen es también su carga más pesada.

—No estoy de acuerdo —dijo Encarna—. Lo que dices me suena a excusa, o incluso a defensa. Esa chica puede ser tan feliz como tú o como yo si tiene las ideas claras.

—¿Crees que una mujer puede tener las ideas claras cuando a los catorce o quince años ya eres guapísima y todo el mundo te lo dice, y los hombres de cuarenta años con dinero te van detrás?

Natalia y Encarna respondieron al mismo tiempo a las palabras de Paz, una a favor y otra en contra, y las tres iniciaron una profunda discusión en torno a la belleza, los hombres, la vida y otros aspectos que en los minutos siguientes acabó derivando hacia el sexo y las relaciones de pareja. Solo Salvador las miraba a ellas, especialmente a su mujer.

Sixto y Rafael seguían pendientes de la modelo y de Roberto Estrada, que en ese momento y tras pedir sus bebidas, estaban besándose sin ningún tipo de prevención.

59

—Es un hijo de puta —suspiró Sixto.

—¿Por qué? ¿Por qué la tiene a ella? —dijo Rafael.

—No —manifestó el publicista—. Lo es porque lo es y nada más.

—Los nuevos lobos suben empujando fuerte, ¿eh?

Sixto apartó por un momento la mirada de la pareja y la depositó en su amigo, que no había hecho lo mismo con la suya y seguía pendiente de ella.

—Tú eres empresario. Sabes de qué va la película —dijo.

—Te diré una cosa: pienso que había más ética en nuestro tiempo, cuando empezábamos. Ahora la sensación de selva es más fuerte. No hay piedad. Comenzando por los políticos y acabando por la gente de la calle, cada cual no solo va a lo suyo, sino a joder al de enfrente, por si acaso. Antes pegabas si te pegaban, por un mecanismo de defensa. Ahora pegas antes de que te peguen, sin siquiera saber si el que te viene de cara va a hacerlo o te dará la mano.

—Acabas de definir la cultura de los noventa —asintió Sixto.

—La hostia —suspiró Rafael—. ¿Te acuerdas de cuando éramos *hippies*?

—Nunca fuimos *hippies*.

—Ya, pero creíamos que sí, y cuando veíamos que no era verdad, queríamos serlo. El 68, las comunas, los porros, el amor libre...

—Eso era fuera de España, hombre. Aquí nada de nada. Nos enteramos de todo cuando hubo pasado.

—Sí —el tono de Rafael era pesaroso—, nos lo perdimos entonces, y nos lo perdemos ahora —señaló a Roberto Estrada y a su chica—. Hemos sido la generación "bocadillo".

—Tú has sido la generación "bocadillo" —rectificó Sixto—. Yo acabo de tirar el pan y me estoy comiendo el jamón.

Los dos miraron instintivamente a Encarna, que defendía con cierta exaltación su punto de vista en torno al papel que la belleza y la libertad obraban en las mujeres actuales.

—No eres el único —dijo Rafael.

Se encontró con los ojos de su amigo, pero no hubo ningún intercambio de intenciones, ni siquiera un destello de inteligencia en ese contacto visual. La modelo se había puesto en pié y caminaba hacia el edificio principal de la señorial torre reconvertida en bar de moda. La mayor parte de hombres y, en consonancia, sus mujeres o parejas, siguió ese movimiento estudiado y preciso, a cuya espalda quedó Roberto Estrada entre el orgullo y la falsa indiferencia. La sangre, bombeada por varios pulsos acelerados, disparó la adrenalina en un buen número de testigos de la escena.

Cuando ella desapareció, Rafael y Sixto vieron que Salvador era uno de los que había seguido sus pasos, girando la cabeza, como si la estuviese observando por un ojo situado en la nuca.

—Creo que toda mujer que se precie, debe ser fiel a sí misma —estaba diciendo en este momento Paz—. Si todo ha de basarse en complacer a la pareja, estar guapa para él y sacrificarlo todo como si con ello se le quisiera retener, como si se tuviera miedo, para mí no sirve, es un planteamiento falso. Y pobre del hombre que exija eso o de la mujer que se traicione a sí misma viviendo así, porque no van a funcionar demasiado tiempo.

Rafael

Aquel pedazo de mujer me acabó de poner al límite. Por un lado oía como de fondo el parloteo de nuestras respectivas, sobre todo Natalia y Paz, jugando a ser maduras con dignidad; por el otro, la veía a ella, inmensa, una hembra por la que valía la pena darlo todo; y finalmente, estaba mi inquietud, la zozobra que se mantenía en torno al hecho de no saber dónde coño podría estar Mercedes. Me repetía que en su casa, sin haber cumplido su amenaza, pero era una voz desesperada, falsa, sin consistencia.

La voz de una conciencia culpable y temerosa.

Y la única forma de saber la verdad era haciendo algo.

La decisión fue inmediata, por una parte harto ya de la noche, y por otra dispuesto a todo para actuar de una maldita vez, pasara lo que pasara. Me dije que quizá tuviera que provocar yo mismo los acontecimientos, sin esperar a que ellos llegaran por sí solos y acabaran jodiéndome al no darme posibilidad de reacción.

Me puse en pié.

60

—Voy a comprar tabaco —dijo Rafael.

—Toma del mío, hombre —Sixto le tendió su paquete.

—No, déjalo. Si no compro voy a estar toda la noche pidiéndote.

—Pues dile al camarero que te lo traiga y no...

—Coño, que de paso voy a mear, ¿vale? —le cortó terminante Rafael.

Fue su pequeña pero controlada explosión, unida a su taco y a su expresión escatológica, lo que hizo que Natalia mirara hacia él.

—¡Por Dios, Rafa, qué noche llevas! —le riñó—. ¡Vas a hacer que se me caiga la cara de vergüenza!

—Mientras no se te caiga el culo.

Quería herirla, más aún que hacerla callar. Por si no tuviera bastante con todo, Natalia estaba... peor que nunca. Así que no esperó su reacción. Apartó la silla y echó a andar en dirección a la casa, atravesando el patio arbolado y los núcleos de mesas habitadas por su flora y fauna nocturna. La ira inicial, tras el breve intercambio de improperios con su mujer, dio paso a una creciente preocupación. ¿Y si le veían llamar por teléfono? ¿A quién podía decir que telefoneaba a esa hora? ¿Y si...?

No, la autentica razón era no saber qué encontraría al otro lado del hilo telefónico.

Llegó al edificio, entró dentro, se orientó y optó por acudir a la barra. No disponía de demasiado tiempo.

—¿Tienen teléfono?

—Ahí a la vuelta, señor.

—¿Y tabaco?

—Tiene la máquina detrás suyo.

—Gracias.

Iba a retirarse cuando el camarero, servicial, se lo impidió.

—El señor dispone de monedas.

Se detuvo, echó mano al bolsillito del suelto y lo comprobó. No era suficiente para el tabaco y una llamada urbana. Levantó la cabeza y el camarero le hizo una inmediata seña de comprensión. Mientras él iba a la caja Rafael extrajo un billete de mil pesetas. El camarero, experto en el tema, regresó con una moneda de quinientas pesetas y cinco de cien.

—Gracias —dijo Rafael.

—No hay de qué, señor.

Se olvidó del tabaco y buscó el teléfono. Introdujo una moneda de cien pesetas y marcó el número del apartamento de Mercedes. Examinó la hora y suspiró. Si estaba viendo una película, ningún problema. Además, le daría una excusa y en paz. Pero si estaba durmiendo... Ella notaría que solo llamaba para ver si estaba en casa, y quizá fuera peor.

Tenía aquel maldito genio de mil pares de demonios, aquel carácter, aquella dichosa...

Dejó de pensar en excusas y estupideces cuando tras la quinta señal se dio cuenta de que al otro lado no había nadie.

Mercedes no estaba en casa.

Natalia

Rafael llevaba tabaco en el coche, estaba segura. Siempre metía uno o dos paquetes en la guantera, para casos como aquel, cuando se quedaba sin cigarrillos inesperadamente. Podía haberlo cogido al bajar, o tomar uno del paquete de Sixto, como él le había ofrecido, para no tener que levantarse. Más aún: con lo cómodo que es, aquello era demasiado evidente. Su frase favorita en casa solía ser: "Natalia, tú que estás de pié, ¿podrías traerme...?"

Nunca movía el trasero para nada.

Busqué a la chica de película que conocía Sixto, y no la vi con el hombre con el que había entrado.

Eso me hizo sentir rabia y frustración, más aún después de la escenita que acababa de montarme a pesar de que Paz me había dicho al oído que yo estaba muy nerviosa y que se me notaba demasiado, que me controlara o acabaría provocando una pelea.

La mujer de bandera tardó en reaparecer, exactamente lo mismo que mi marido, y cuando ella volvió al jardín, moviéndose como una diosa bajo la mirada de sus acólitos, Rafael apareció justo detrás, disimulando, fingiendo mirar al suelo, como si estuviese preocupado por algo, envuelto en sus pensamientos. Era tan absurdo que no la mirase en ese momento, cuando la tenía delante solo para sus ojos, como absurdo y violento, era para mí el número que se había montado para espiarla.

Ya no solo era cosa de que tuviera una amante, un lío, lo que fuera. Se trataba de algo peor. Iba salido. Estaba en ese punto en el que cualquier mujer es mejor que la propia, y en el que los hombres en lo único que piensan es en que entre las piernas todas tienen un agujero.

Sentí asco además de impotencia, por eso, sin hacer caso de Paz, cuando llegó a la mesa le pregunté con el ánimo encendido:

61

—¿Has comprado tabaco?

Rafael tuvo una primera reacción de pánico. Se envaró, volvió a la realidad de la que había estado ausente y giró la cabeza como si buscara algo perdido tras de sí. En total no tardó más allá de dos segundos en responder, aunque lo hizo cogido a contrapié.

—No tenían del mío —dijo buscando una aparente tranquilidad—. Ya compraré luego —y dirigiéndose a Sixto agregó—: ¿Me das uno?

—Sí, hombre, claro.

Le echó el paquete, cogió un cigarrillo y lo encendió, aspirando el humo profundamente. Hizo un esfuerzo por reintegrarse al grupo, a la conversación o lo que fuera que sucediera en ese instante, pero le costó en exceso. Tuvo que dar una segunda chupada al pitillo para calmarse, y no consiguió mucho más. En lo único que podía pensar era en que Mercedes no estaba en su piso, que había cumplido su amenaza, y que desde luego no había ido al cine o a cenar sola.

Incluso creía saber dónde estaba. Era una chica de criterios bastante fijos y de tendencias constantes.

Se encontró con una glacial mirada de Natalia.

Encima ella. Algo le sucedía. Tenía una noche de perros.

—Tengo sed —dijo—. Voy a tomarte otra cosa de esas.

Buscó al camarero, pero de nuevo Natalia se lo impidió.

—Ya has bebido bastante, Rafa —su tono fue conminante—. Recuerda que tú llevas el coche.

Esta vez no le contestó, ni tampoco despreció su orden para insistir en su reclamo del camarero. Había algo en la voz, pero más aún en los ojos de ella, que le hizo temer por el delicado equilibrio de la noche. La conocía bien, raramente se ponía al límite, pero cuando lo hacía... era temible, porque perdía los estribos, se ponía histérica. Conocía aquel temblor en la comisura del labio, aquella mirada.

Tal vez fuese Encarna. Seguro. Encarna la ponía fuera de sí. Seguía apegada a Sole, y la amante de Sixto era tan...

diferente, abierta, distendida. Paz disimulaba mejor, se comportaba, pero Natalia...

Salvador y Sixto hablaban de la televisión. Genial. Un gran tema.

Paz y Encarna aún discutían de hombres y mujeres.

Pensó que tenía que hacer algo para ponerla de nuevo de su lado, aunque solo fuera para tranquilizarla.

—La mujer no se arregla para que el hombre se sienta orgulloso de ella —decía en ese instante la rubia—, sino para gustarse a sí misma.

—Vamos, querida —insistió Paz—. Sabes muy bien que muchas mujeres pasarían del tema, pero por miedo a quedarse atrás, van a gimnasios, se cuidan y hacen lo imposible para mantenerse jóvenes, y su único objetivo es evitar que el marido mire a otras o algo peor.

—Bueno, y aunque sea así, ¿qué hay de malo en estar guapa para él, y exigir que él se cuide lo mismo para ella? El amor también es físico. No puede pretenderse que por llegar a los cincuenta, los sesenta o los setenta, ya no haya contacto y todo se limite a "ser amigos". Existe un compromiso.

—Pero es difícil mantenerlo —dijo de pronto Rafael—. Mira tu caso. Te enamoraste de Sixto y aunque su mujer hubiera sido... qué sé yo, una ex-Miss, él se habría ido contigo igualmente, porque supiste conquistarle, así que lo de mantenerse o no, es relativo si no hay algo mucho más profundo, ¿verdad?

Encarna

Era un imbécil. Salvador me caía bien, pero Rafael... cuando no me miraba las tetas o las piernas, meaba fuera de tiesto. ¿A qué venía aquello? ¡Por Dios! ¿A qué venía? Ni siquiera le entendí demasiado bien, porque me pilló, como suele decirse, en bragas. Sin embargo sé que no fue afortunado, porque Paz se lo quedó mirando boquiabierta, y su misma mujer puso una cara... Encima él se quedó tan ancho, y buscando una reafirmación de su parida, le pasó un brazo por encima de los hombros a ella. El súbito silencio hizo que Sixto y Salvador dejaran de hablar y nos miraran. Menos mal que Sixto no lo había oído, porque a lo peor, y estando tenso como estaba por lo de la campaña de los preservativos y por la mala suerte de ir a encontrarse a su rival en el Dos Torres, le hubiera soltado una fresca, o algo peor.

Aunque bien mirado, hubiera sido una forma de acabar del todo y por la vía rápida con aquello.

Cada vez me preguntaba más qué estaba haciendo yo allí con ellos.

Traté de conservar mi equilibrio, una vez más, pero sin renunciar a ser yo misma. Estaba dispuesta a acabar la noche demostrándoles que no iban a poder conmigo, y eso pasaba por no seguir allí, bebiendo y hablando de estupideces en las que no podíamos estar de acuerdo porque pertenecíamos a generaciones diferentes. El Dos Torres era un muermo, un cementerio de elefantes, o de aburridos, que para el caso era lo mismo.

Había que animar aquello.

Coger a Salvador y meterle un poco de marcha en el cuerpo, porque en este caso el que no quería mover el trasero era él. Ellas dirían que sí, si Salvador decía que sí, y Rafael diría que sí en cuanto su mujer abriera la boca, porque no era más que un cretino. De Sixto me ocupaba yo.

Superé el shock motivado por el comentario de Rafael y de nuevo le cogí el brazo al médico. Natalia me habría sacado los ojos si le hago eso a su idiota, pero por mí, podía quedarse con el idiota, que se lo tenía bien ganado. Paz era distinta, sabía diferenciar una intención de un gesto amistoso.

—Venga, doctor —le dije—. Esto es un muermo y vamos a dormirnos todos. ¿Qué tal un bailecito?

Repitió lo de que él no entraba en una discoteca ni muerto, y pese a lo de caerme bien, le habría arrancado los ojos. Empleé toda mi paciencia, y mis dotes de seducción para contrarrestar su negativa, mientras él repetía que nosotros podíamos ir a dónde quisiéramos, que él se metía en un taxi y a casa. Yo le dije que habíamos salido los seis, y los seis acabaríamos con la noche, no ella con nosotros. Entonces sugerí que nos fuéramos al Sutton como mal menor.

62

—¿Qué es eso? —preguntó dudoso Salvador.

—Un baile para carrozas, en Tuset —dijo Sixto.

—No es cierto —lo defendió Encarna.

—No, es verdad —apuntó Rafael—. Es algo más que para carrozas. Van todas las solteras granadas ávidas de marcha y los solteros pasados a la caza y captura de un buen chasis de segunda mano.

—No estás tú muy al día —le corrigió Sixto—. Ahora es más bien un paraíso de separados y divorciados con el "libre" en la frente, y su equivalente en damas abandonadas o vi-ce-ver-sa —empleó un tono sarcástico para decir esto último mientras paseaba una mirada preventiva por las tres mujeres.

—¡Ala, tú arreglalo! —protestó Encarna.

—¿Y para qué queremos ir a un sitio así? —puso cara de asco Natalia.

—Puede ser divertido —comentó Rafael animándose.

—Un momento —Encarna extendió las dos manos frente a ella, muy abiertas, para apoyar la fuerza y la convicción de sus palabras—. En primer lugar el Sutton no es un baile de carrozas, sino un baile, y punto. Lo de ser o no ser carroza depende de cada cual. En segundo lugar, no es una discoteca, hay una orquesta, tocan de todo, y se puede bailar, charlar, tomar una copa o simplemente oir la música, porque los músicos son buenos. En tercer lugar, he ido varias veces, con amigas, y ni ellas eran separadas ni estábamos buscando nada ni se nos acercaron una docena de tíos buscando guerra.

—¿No se os acercó nadie? —dudó Sixto—. Irías con esas momias de Ana y Sonia.

—¡No seas burro, haz el favor! Claro que vino alguno a pedirnos un baile, pero eso es normal, ¿o no? —buscó el apoyo del médico—. Entiendo que Salvador no quiera volverse loco en una discoteca, pero el Sutton es una sala de fiestas, y además, elegante.

—Yo, lo que decida la mayoría —dijo Sixto.

—Yo me apunto —reiteró Rafael.

—Ya somos tres —dijo Encarna—. ¡Venga, un voto más! Si no te gusta nos vamos, hombre —le hizo un arrumaco a Salvador—. Que no pasa nada.

—Venga, mujer —Paz le dio un codazo a Natalia—. Anímate.

—No, si por mí... —se encogió de hombros, nada predispuesta—, lo que digáis.

—¡Mayoría! —cantó Encarna triunfal, y de nuevo abocó sus encantos en el médico—. ¡Solo faltas tú, Salva! Y aunque seamos cinco, si has de poner cara de funeral... no vale la pena. ¿Te animas? ¡Vamos!, ¿cuánto tiempo hace que no bailas con tu mujer? Yo te prometo un tango, o un lo que sea. Bailo muy bien, ¿sabes?

Salvador empezó a sonreír.

Salvador

Es curioso, aquella fuerza de la naturaleza había formulado la misma pregunta que yo me había hecho no mucho antes: "¿Cuánto tiempo hacía que no bailaba con Paz?". Fue eso lo que me hizo sonreír, no mi decisión, porque ya la había tomado desde que me vi en aquel bar rodeado de modernos y modernas de diseño, o lo que fueran, porque a lo peor resultaba que allí todos iban de normales y la auténtica modernidad estaba en otra parte.

Habíamos salido a cenar y pasar un rato, ¿no? Pues adelante. Si no teníamos que ir a una discoteca ruidosa, ¿qué más podía objetar? No quería ser el aguafiestas. Y a Paz la idea parecía gustarle. Se la veía animada, aunque a veces, al hablarle a Natalia, o al mirarla, o al oírla, cambiaba, mostraba su lado más extraño y preocupante. Natalia estaba muy rara. Me pregunté si no era a causa de lo que Rafael me había dicho en casa, lo de invertir en el negocio. Tal vez las cosas les fueran peor de lo que pensaba. Había una crispación...

Lo de ese lugar, el Sutton, sonaba bien. Podía ser interesante.

Dije que sí.

Antes solía investigar la naturaleza humana, contactar con la gente, hablar, escuchar. Ya sé que eran "otros tiempos", y que incluso yo disponía de más de ese tiempo, pero el cambio radical, hasta mi soledad en el presente, resultaba muy fuerte, excesivo. Bailara o no bailara, ver a la gente siempre era fascinante. En mi consulta solo veía pasar madres preocupadas y niños y niñas repetidos y repetidas como clones. Siempre iguales en todo, en sus reacciones, sus lágrimas, sus risas, sus caras...

Dije que sí.

Convencido, animado.

Encarna se puso muy contenta. Empezó a batir palmas, a dar pequeños gritos de energía, y dijo que yo era un tío legal. Eso me hizo pensar en mi hijo. Parecía su vocabulario.

Un tío legal.

Seguía colgada de mi brazo cuando nos fuimos del Dos Torres.

Olía muy bien. Solo puedo decir eso.

63

Se separaron en el exterior, para dirigirse a sus respectivos coches con la misma división establecida desde el inicio de la noche. De nuevo fue al entrar Paz, Natalia, Salvador y Rafael en el coche de este último, cuando se inició el dialogo, contenido a lo largo del breve trayecto desde el local.

Y fue Natalia la que rompió el fuego.

—Caramba, Salva, estás desconocido.

—¿Por qué?

—Tú yendo a un antro nocturno.

—Mujer, que tampoco es un antro —protestó Paz—. Además, puede estar bien. Seguro que pasamos un buen rato.

—Mejor que ahí sentados, seguro —opinó Rafael.

—Ya, lo que ocurre es que como esa lagarta le ha puesto ojitos tiernos... —siguió Natalia—. ¡Todos sois iguales!

—Débiles —asintió Salvador, que había recuperado su aspecto serio y casi distante.

—Pues mira, sí —Natalia miró a Paz—. Yo es que no he visto nada igual, vamos, colgada de su brazo y poniéndole caritas. Y Sixto, como va de moderno, pues nada, pasando, pero tú hija...

—¿Yo qué? —sonrió divertida Paz.

—Sí, encima ríete. Te manosean al marido y como si nada.

—Debo de estar haciéndome muy viejo —suspiró Salvador—. Por lo visto acaban de manosearme y yo sin enterarme. ¡Mecachis!

—¡Qué exagerada eres, Nati! —volvió a reír Paz—. O sea que si yo me cuelgo del brazo de Rafa y le digo algo afectuoso, es que me lo estoy ligando.

—Es diferente —objetó Natalia.

—Claro —masculló Rafael—. Encarna es rubia y joven. ¡Es peligrosa!

—Eso, todos contra mí —los ojos de Natalia centellearon, se cruzó de brazos y amenazó con no volver a abrir la boca, por lo menos en los minutos siguientes.

—Venga, mujer —contemporizó Paz—. Visto desde fuera somos tres parejas que han salido a pasar la noche. Puede que Encarna sea algo coqueta, pero...

—¿Bastante? Es una palabra que no le hace justicia. Esa es de las que se hace notar vaya a dónde vaya y esté con quien esté.

—Pero es inofensiva —concluyó Paz.

—No debe serlo tanto cuando se ha cargado un matrimonio.

—Natalia, el matrimonio de Sixto y Sole estaba ya cargado cuando él y Encarna... —quiso hablar Salvador.

—¿Y tú cómo lo sabes? —saltó de nuevo excitada ella—. Que una pareja tenga problemas y atraviese una crisis, no significa que ya esté tocada y hundida. Apareció ella y él perdió la chaveta, como un imbécil.

—No la harás cambiar de opinión —dijo Rafael—. Se ha vuelto feminista radical.

—¡Tú será mejor que...! —empezó a gritar Natalia.

—Natalia —la contuvo Salvador girando el cuerpo desde el asiento de delante para cogerle una mano—, ¿por qué no me pones ojitos tiernos y me manoseas un poco? Te prometo que la semana que viene le daré a Gloria las vitaminas que me pidas.

—¡Anda ya! —se soltó la mujer de su amigo haciendo un gesto irritado y despectivo—. ¡Tomaoslo a broma!

Las manos de Rafael estaban engarfiadas en el volante. Miró a la parte trasera del coche por el espejo retrovisor interior, buscando a su mujer con las mandíbulas apretadas, pero se encontró con los ojos de Paz.

64

—Estás tú muy lanzada esta noche —comentó Sixto mirándola de reojo con una media sonrisa colgada de lo labios.

—Anda ya, que no me has visto tú lanzada a mí.

—No, si no digo nada.

—Faltaría más —espetó Encarna—. Y alguien tiene que estarlo, porque anda que el grupo...

—¡Bah! No son mala gente.

—No quiero hablar.

—Tienen sus rollos y todo eso.

—No quiero hablar.

—Vale, pues no hables —se encogió de hombros Sixto.

—Es que si hablo vamos a tenerla.

—¿Ah, sí? ¿Por qué? —se extrañó él.

—No quiero hablar.

—¡Coño, para ya con eso y habla! ¡Di lo que sea!

No fue una exclamación de enfado, sino un grito intermedio. Todavía estaba demasiado lleno de la imagen de Roberto Estrada y su compañía como para tentar al diablo enfadándose con Encarna. No esa noche. Así que le mostró de nuevo su sonrisa al mirarla.

—Solo quería decirte que mi gente tampoco es mala gente, así que no me vengas con excusas cuando te diga que salimos con ellos.

—Me parece que esta conversación ya la hemos tenido antes —musitó Sixto.

—Más o menos. Y sueles ponerte un poco histérico.

—Vale, ya empezamos —rezongó él.

—Has sido tú el que me ha dicho que estoy "muy lanzada". ¿Es que te molesta que le ponga ojitos al médico?

—¿A Salvador? ¡No, por Dios! ¡Pobre Salva! Con Rafa sería distinto.

—A Rafa ni se me ocurriría tocarle. Vamos, ni le miro —se estremeció Encarna—. Entre él que es un baboso y la parienta, que no sé qué se cree que es y que tiene... Esta noche tu médico va a rejuvenecer diez años, como me llamo Encarna, vas a ver tú. De los tres es el único con el que se puede hablar, porque entre el Rafa que es un cretino y tú que estás un poco borde...

—¿Que yo qué? —ésta vez si se enfadó.

—Que no digo nada, que ya sé que encontrarte a ese gilipuertas y encima con esa nena te ha puesto a tope —contemporizó ella.

—Yo no estoy borde —se defendió Sixto.

—Oye, que te entiendo, no quiero que...

—Yo no estoy borde —repitió Sixto—, y no me des tú la noche ahora, joder.

—¿Yo? Esta sí que es buena —exhaló Encarna—. Yo lo único que quiero es divertirme y pasarlo bien, porque es viernes noche, ¿te enteras? Me siento como si fuera la única que lo sabe. ¡Es viernes noche! —se lo

gritó al aire a través de la ventanilla abierta del coche—:
¡Es viernes noche y quiero marcha!

El semáforo iba a cambiar a rojo y Sixto, inesperadamente, con rabia, pisó el pedal del gas a fondo, rebasándolo en el último momento.

65

Rafael hizo una primera intención de seguirle, aunque el semáforo ya lo tenía en rojo en ese instante. Su gesto quizá hubiera muerto por propia inercia, dado el exceso de tráfico pese a la hora, pero de cualquier manera también frenó debido a que, desde atrás, Natalia, que parecía estar en todo, le soltó un grito obligándole a hacerlo.

—¡Para, para, deja que se vaya! ¡Ya les llevaremos flores al hospital!

Vieron alejarse el coche de Sixto y Encarna en silencio, el mismo silencio que les había acompañado en los últimos dos o tres minutos, como si de repente se hubieran quedado sin nada que decir.

Los cuatro, aunque cada cual con sus propios pensamientos bulléndoles en la mente, vieron el deambular de una nueva partida de chicos y chicas, habitantes irredentos de la noche, moviéndose, caminando, hablando o esperando el paso del tiempo bajo las estrellas, envolviendo un bar, pródigamente poblado, situado en la esquina. La mayoría tenía un vaso o una botella en la mano.

Hasta ellos llegaron las voces de los que reían, despreocupados, como si el día fuese tan solo una quimera en la distancia. Hasta ellos llegaron las imágenes de los cuerpos jóvenes y frescos, livianos de ropa, ellas con el cabello largo, tops que solo ceñían sus pechos, pantalones informales, y ellos con sus cabellos cortos y sus camisetas abultadas por la plenitud de sus torsos. Hasta ellos llegó el humo de la nube formada por sus cigarrillos, porque todos y todas, en abrumadora mayoría, fumaban casi con el desafío de la inconsciencia. Hasta ellos llegó el resplandor del beso de la pareja sentada en la moto, rodeada por la indiferencia de las demás, y la fusión casi etérea de sus labios unida a la voluptuosidad del contacto físico en el que, lentamente y llevados por la pasión, iban cayendo uno y otra. Hasta ellos llegó la indiferencia, la libertad, el desafío.

Un mundo atrapado en otro mundo.

Rafael pensó de nuevo en Mercedes, y en lo lejos que estaba él de todo aquello, y del pasado que pudo ser y no fue, y del futuro, plagado por la incertidumbre arrastrada desde el presente. Y miró a las chicas de pechos generosos, labios de seda, desparpajo rebosando en sus ojos y toda la energía que parecían poseer en exclusiva, sintiendo un vacío que se le extendía por el estómago lo mismo que un agujero negro por el que se devoraba todo su ser.

Natalia pensó en la inutilidad de la lucha si Rafael tenía una Encarna en su presente, o una de aquellas prodigiosas criaturas recién torneadas por la vida y la juventud. Y se sintió débil, perdida, fracasada. Intentó por lo menos sentirse digna, pero lo mismo que el Titanic, el iceberg de la realidad le golpeó de lleno bajo la linea de flotación, provocando el absoluto hundimiento de su resistencia. Tal vez por ello fue la única de los cuatro que cerró los ojos.

Paz pensó en sí misma, en aquellas fotografías del pasado que le gritaban lo que fue y ya no era, y en lo que podía hacer para no sentir el peso del abismo que temía ver formarse a sus piés. Quizá la palabra fuera comprensión, entereza, y devorar con el mismo placer las migajas de la felicidad presente aunque en otro tiempo pareciese que todo fueran atracones. Tenía algo que ya no tenían Sole ni Natalia: un marido. Un buen hombre de verdad.

Salvador pensó en Octavio, atrapado por el efecto de aquellas imágenes que veía como si estuviese asomado a un circo. En lugar de leones y tigres, enanos y payasos, veía aquellas hordas de adolescentes aparentemente sin rumbo, perdidos, ociosos, de espaldas a todo lo que no fuera su breve realidad, mientras los padres dormían o, como él, participaban del ritual bajo otras normas, otros cánones. Su hijo podía estar allí, o muy cerca, o al otro lado de Barcelona, y podía estar sobrio o borracho, con una chica o un chico, sereno o colgado de un porro, porque no sabía nada de él y por contra lo sospechaba todo. Y en sus visiones tampoco había nada de bueno, todo era malo.

La pareja de la moto ya no se besaba, daba más bien la impresión de querer fusionarse. Habían caído sobre el sillín, ella encima de él, y el volcán de su fuego se confundió finalmente con el semáforo cambiando a verde.

Rafael arrancó demasiado abruptamente.

Aún así, no consiguió superar el siguiente semáforo.

—¡Joder! —protestó golpeando el volante con la mano abierta—. ¡Todo va al revés!

Rafael

En ese momento ya lo tenía decidido. Teníamos que pasar muy cerca, y casi podía apostar que Mercedes no era ni siquiera tan lista como para haberse inventado otra cosa. ¿Una salida? Siempre iba al mismo lugar, para moverse en su ambiente. Además, si lo que quería era fastidiarme, darme con un canto en los dientes, lo más lógico era aquello, que fuera a un sitio donde quedara constancia de su acto, por si luego yo no la creía.

Lo que ella jamás habría imaginado es que yo diera

aquel paso, con mi mujer en el coche, jugándome...

El enjambre de chicos y chicas viviendo la noche me hizo asumir el riesgo final.

Sabía que estaría allí.

Lo sabía.

Paz

Rafael, no sé si picado por Sixto o porque los semáforos se le ponían en rojo nada más acercarse él, conducía con bastante nervio y brusquedad, lleno de violencias. Temía sin embargo que fuese a causa de Natalia y su comportamiento a lo largo de la noche. Puro acoso y derribo. Tenía que decirle a ella que si quería conservar, o recuperar a su marido, aquel no era el sistema. Una guerra nunca apacigua otra guerra. Pero eso ya no sería hasta el día siguiente, por teléfono, o a lo largo de la semana, en persona. Difícilmente iba a estar el suficiente tiempo con ella a solas como para hablarle de todo eso en el rato que nos quedara de estar juntas. Y en su estado, tal vez fuera capaz de todo. Solo yo me daba cuenta de lo tensa que estaba.

Salvador en cambio... a pesar de su distancia, de su grave seriedad, había ido entonándose. Daba la impresión de sentirse más relajado, y pese a lo que dijera Natalia, sabía que no era a causa de las sonrisas de Encarna. A pesar de ello, cuando un momento antes nos paramos en aquel semáforo, con toda aquella multitud de gente joven cerca...

Le vi el rostro, su gravedad, y supe que tenía a Octavio en el centro de la mente y de su ansiedad.

Entonces...

Fue en el cruce de Plaza Molina con Balmes donde vimos el accidente.

El coche estaba volcado y empotrado contra otros dos aparcados a la derecha, panza arriba y sin restos visibles de sus primitivas formas, así que no se intuía en su estado la marca o el modelo que unos minutos antes pudiera lucir con orgullo. La moto aparecía caída de lado, a unos diez metros, convertida así mismo en un amasijo de hierros a causa del impacto, que con toda probabilidad había sido frontal. La policía, que trataba de poner orden y canalizar el tráfico, apartaba a los curiosos que se acercaban a pié de forma enérgica, desviando a la vez los automóviles que transitaban en ambos sentidos para que éstos no pasaran por encima de la zona del siniestro. El pequeño colapso tenía tintes de tragedia, de drama, porque a un lado del automóvil vimos a otro grupo de personas que daba la impresión de rodear a las presuntas víctimas.

Eso hizo que Salvador le dijera a Rafael que parase el coche.

66

Un policía se acercó con rapidez y malos modos, agitando los brazos, gritando algo que no entendieron porque en el momento de bajar Rafael del vehículo cesó en sus aspavientos, imaginando con lógica que si hacían aquello sería por alguna razón. Luego, Salvador no le dio tiempo a hablar.

—Soy médico —le informó con rapidez—. ¿Puedo ayudar en algo?

—Oh —la actitud del agente cambió—, no, gracias. Ya se los han llevado hace un momento, en una ambulancia.

El grupo que parecía rodear a unas presuntas victimas se reveló como una simple aglomeración de personas en torno a alguien que había confundido el coche con el de un conocido. Empezaron a dispersarse lo mismo que una nube de humo barrida por el viento de la noche, y la causante de la confusión, una mujer joven que vestía una breve minifalda, hizo lo mismo con su compañero, riendo nerviosamente.

—¿Ha sido grave? —preguntó Salvador.

—Nunca se sabe, así, a primera vista —el policía se encogió de hombros—. A veces los sacamos que dan pena y no tienen nada, algunos cortes y contusiones, y otras parecen estar bien y resulta que por dentro... Pero que voy a decirle que usted no sepa, doctor.

—¿Cuántos han sido? —continuó él, incapaz de moverse de la escena del accidente.

—En la moto iba uno, que es el que ha salido peor parado, y en el coche dos chicos y dos chicas. Parece ser que el de la moto se ha saltado el semáforo, el muy... A estas horas y a toda pastilla, hay que estar loco.

—Sí, claro.

—Y no escarmientan, ¿sabe? —el policía se había animado inesperadamente—. Le juro que a buenas horas le compraría una moto o un coche a un hijo mío, ¡ni aunque pudiera!. Y si es cosa de él, pues mire, cuando tuviera los veintiuno y viviera solo, porque si está en mi casa... tampoco, ¡vamos!. Todo esto —señaló el coche siniestrado y la moto—, es culpa de los padres. ¡Que tanta permisividad ni que niño muerto, toda la noche fuera de casa haciendo el burro!. ¿Para eso quieren ser libres e independientes? ¡Pagando papá es muy fácil! El entierro también lo pagan los padres, ¿no cree usted?

Salvador no le respondió. No hizo falta. Un policía con aspecto de ser alguien de mayor judicatura en el escalafón, le llamó en ese momento, y tras saludarle con la mano, a modo de gesto instintivo, se encaminó hacia su superior.

—¡Venga, circulen, circulen! —gritó otro agente muy cerca de dónde ellos tenían detenido el coche.

Salvador

La gente habla mucho.

Todo el mundo habla mucho.

Y hablan de lo que no saben, de lo que ignoran, de lo que harían y nunca hacen o de lo que piensan y nunca tienen oportunidad de ejercer.

Todo el mundo que no tiene hijos te dice como educar a los tuyos, y te aseguran que él, o ella, no les permitirían hacer esto y aquello y lo de más allá. Te lo dicen a la cara, con una seguridad pasmosa, dándolo por sentado. Te hablan de mano dura, de inflexibilidad, de educación, de respeto, de normas. ¡Jesús!, como si fuera tan sencillo.

Lo ignoran todo, porque solo cuando se tiene un hijo o una hija, se entienden muchas cosas, y no ya de ellos, sino de ti mismo. Los que hablan y hablan no saben que cada nuevo ser lleva impreso el carácter en la mente desde el mismo instante de ser alumbrado, y que hagas lo que hagas tú, acertada o equivocadamente, no altera en exceso la forma de ser de esos hijos. Naturalmente hablo en un plano genérico. Si un padre viola a su hija sí la está marcando, o si una madre es una borracha o una drogadicta, lo mismo.

Luego, si por una casualidad, tienen ese hijo o esa hija... cambian, lo reconocen o lo aceptan. A veces se ríen y te dicen: "¡Vaya por Dios, yo que creía...! ¿Recuerdas cuando te decía...?". Y tú piensas: "Serás hijo de mala madre, claro que lo recuerdo. ¡Menudo coñazo me dabas hablándome de MIS defectos mientras me ensalzabas TUS inexistentes pero convincentes virtudes!"

Fuere como fuere, aquello me afectó. Mi hijo podía ser uno de los cuatro ocupantes del coche, y yo estar allí, sin saberlo, tan confiado como pudiera estarlo en mi perenne inquietud, cada viernes y cada sábado por la noche, tratando de imaginármelo en cualquier lugar de Barcelona. Me afectó porque me sentí impotente, como padre y como ser humano. Octavio ya no era mi hijo, era su propia responsabilidad, aunque como acababa de decir el policía, el entierro también lo pagaban los padres.

Y el dolor que nunca muere y te acompaña hasta el fin.

Volví a caer en las riberas de mi depresión, pero no le dije nada a Paz, que pensaba que me había ido animando.

La noche estaba rota, pero todavía viva.

A veces las cosas son tan... imprevisibles.

67

—¿Les ves?

Sixto volvió a centrar sus ojos en el retrovisor interior y luego en el exterior. Fue suficiente para que moviera la cabeza negativamente.

—No. Estos se han perdido.

—Bueno, da lo mismo, ¿no? Saben dónde es.

—Sí, y hasta por la forma en que ha hablado del lugar Rafa... diría que lo conoce. El muy...

—Pues no habrá ido con la mojigata de su mujer —espetó Encarna.

—Tú y yo solo hemos estado un par de veces, mujer. Aquel lunes, viendo a los Mustang, y la noche del cumpleaños de esa amiga tuya, Tere.

Encarna pareció recordar algo de pronto. Chasqueó los dedos pulgar y medio de su mano derecha.

—Casi lo había olvidado —dijo—. La semana próxima...

—¡Ah, ah! —la detuvo él sin dejarla acabar—. La semana próxima recuerda que tengo a mis hijos.

Encarna cerró los ojos, como si la noticia, por inesperada, o por sabida pero no presente, la hubiera hecho polvo.

—¡Jo! —fue lo único que logró decir.

—Lo siento —se excusó Sixto—. Creí que te acordabas.

—Bastante hago con acordarme de lo mío, para encima saber de memoria todos los pre-acuerdos sellados con tu mujer.

No le gustaba que hablase de Sole refiriendose a ella como "su mujer", pero en esta ocasión no la reconvino. Captaba su pesar, y también algo más: su desfallecimiento.

—¿Qué querías hacer?

—Lo haré igual —le aseguró Encarna—. Sin ti, pero lo haré.

—¿Qué es?

—Mi primo Alberto y su mujer se van a Andorra, y me han dicho si queríamos subir con ellos. La casa es grande y habría sido perfecto.

—¿Y qué harás tú sola con ellos? —dijo Sixto—. ¿Por qué no te vienes conmigo y mis...?

—No —fue terminante—, lo siento. Cuando las cosas hayan ido a más, y se hayan acostumbrado a mi, y yo a ellos, y estemos casados... en fin, que será distinto, pero ahora... A Guillermo aún, porque es un crío, pero a Marta no sé que decirle, y reconoce que ella tampoco ayuda mucho.

—Es la que peor lo lleva, ya te lo he dicho antes otra vez.

—Vale, pues me parece bien. Hay que darnos tiempo, a unos y a otros, y en eso estoy, pero no me fuerces. Cuando estoy con ellos se nota que sobro. ¡Y me caen bien!, no lo saques de contexto. Es solo que...

Sixto no dio muestras de estar enfadado, y Encarna se relajó. Pensó que en el fondo, incluso debía aceptarlo como algo positivo, y real. Tuvo la certeza cuando él comentó:

—Encima solo falta Guillermo haciéndote preguntas de las suyas.

—¡Oh, sí, qué bicho el tío! —se alegró Encarna de que la conversación siguiera aquel derrotero.

—Es igual que yo —Sixto se rodeó de introspección, mirando hacia su interior más que hacia fuera—, mientras que Marta es como su madre. Y Domingo... no sé, Dios, ha crecido tan rápido.

Se detuvo en un nuevo semáforo, y en ese momento ella se acercó a él y le besó en los labios, obligándole a girar la cabeza hacia la derecha.

Sixto se dejó llevar por aquel beso, cerró los ojos, pero no dejó de pensar en el cúmulo de sensaciones que acababan de aparecer en su mente.

Sixto

Lo comprendí como nunca lo había comprendido antes. Lo vi tan claro que hasta me hizo daño. Fue lo mismo que pasar unas horas a oscuras y, de pronto, verte deslumbrado por la súbita potencia de los rayos solares. Y el beso de Encarna, dulce, cálido, no me hizo cambiar de idea, al contrario, me sembró de miedos al alma hasta el punto de reforzarme todavía más en mi decisión.

No quería tener más hijos.

Ni siquiera sabía si quería volver a casarme.

La amaba, claro, eso ni siquiera entraba en el juego de mis disquisiciones, pero tampoco tenía nada que ver. La amaba porque era parte de mi en mi nuevo presente, pero... eso era todo.

Ya tenía una ex-esposa.

Y tres ex-hijos, porque pese a los arreglos, visitas, protocolos, cánones, pactos y demás historias, y aunque siempre, siempre, fuesen mis hijos, para lo bueno y para lo malo, se habían convertido en "ex".

Una etiqueta, un símbolo demasiado fuerte como para ignorarlo.

Sole se encargaría de ello, por si no fuera suficiente.

Miré a Encarna, como si desde este instante ya sintiese que empezaba a perderla, y no me consoló saber que había muchas chicas de treinta años, y de treinta y cinco, o de veinticinco, dispuestas a llenar su hueco. No me consoló porque me di cuenta de que ese amor era auténtico, y mis sentimientos una fuente de vida, de resistencia en mi caso. Solo la tenía a ella.

Dios... la quería, sí, pero aquella convicción fue tan fuerte.

No traería a ningún otro hijo para que viera la tristeza que ahora nos estaba matando a Sole y a mí.

Tal vez si Encarna pudiera entenderlo, comprenderme.

Tal vez.

—¿Qué pasa? —me preguntó ella en ese instante al darse cuenta de mi obnubilación.

—Vuelve a besarme —le pedí yo.

—El semáforo va a ponerse en verde.

—Me importa un pito, y si hay alguien detrás, que se joda.

Sonrió, se acercó a mi, me pasó el brazo izquierdo por encima de los hombros y con la mano derecha aprisionó mi cara, proyectando mis labios hacia adelante. Luego vi su boca, abierta y húmeda, volando a su encuentro.

Cerré los ojos.

No debía de haber nadie detrás nuestro, jodiéndose, porque no sonó ningún claxon en los dos o tres o diez o mil minutos siguientes.

68

Paz le acarició la nuca cuando se sentó de nuevo en el coche. Sabía que sus cervicales podían ponerse tensas en un instante, y ahora lo estaban, lo notó al presionarlas suavemente con las yemas de sus dedos.

—¿Estás bien?

—Sí.

—¿En serio?

—Que sí, de verdad.

Natalia aún miraba el coche siniestrado con expresión extraviada.

—Podemos coger un taxi e irnos a casa —sugirió Paz—. Sixto y su novia lo entenderán.

—No seas tonta, no ha habido ningún muerto, ¿vale? —le reconvino él.

—Pero estas cosas te afectan.

—Venga, hombre, que accidentes así los hay cada fin de semana —dijo Rafael maniobrado para alejarse del tumulto creado por el accidente—. Si estuvieras en un hospital acabarías harto. Tienes suerte de ser pediatra y no tragar toda esa mierda.

Salvador le miró con acritud, pero sin decir nada.

Paz sí lo hizo.

—A veces, Rafa, si no te conociera diría que te has vuelto insensible.

—¿Insensible yo? —se ofendió el conductor del coche—. Lo que pasa es que hay mucho pirado suelto, y no me da la gana de sentir pena por ellos. ¡Encima!

—¿Qué culpan tenían los de ese automóvil de que el de la moto se les echara encima? —preguntó Paz.

—Tú me estás hablando de un accidente. Yo te hablo del de la moto.

—Es lo mismo. En este momento los cinco están en un

hospital jugando a la lotería de la vida y la muerte.

—Ya le estás dando la vuelta al tema —protestó Rafael—. Si vamos a generalizar... Yo solo te digo que los fines de semana, entre los borrachos, los drogatas y los que van a lo que van, es lógico que haya cosas como esa.

—Mira quien habla —resopló Natalia—: el abstemio.

—Oye, que yo controlo, ¿eh? Y aguanto lo que sea.

Salvador apoyó la cabeza en el respaldo del asiento. Otra vez la palabreja. Controlar. Octavio redivivo.

—Me gustaría que te pararan y te hicieran soplar —refunfuñó Natalia.

—Voy a parar en esta esquina —anunció Rafael mirando a derecha e izquierda de pronto, pasando de las palabras de su mujer—. Me parece que ahí cerca hay un bar o un sitio donde venden tabaco.

69

No hizo el menor caso de las reconvenciones de Natalia. Ni siquiera la permitió actuar o moverse. Salió del coche, tras apagar el motor, y lo dejó mitad sobre la acera mitad en la calzada y con los cuatro pilotos conectados para alertar de su presencia allí. Luego echó a correr por la calle lateral hacia las luces del club que se divisaban a una decena de metros. En la puerta también había un grupo de hombres y mujeres. Había sido lo suficientemente astuto como para no aparcar el vehículo a la vista de todo ello.

Entró directamente, y al abrir la puerta, una oleada de calor, humo y música no precisamente estridente le golpeó de lleno en el rostro. Tuvo que esforzarse, en la nueva penumbra ambiental que le rodeaba, para mirar a su alrededor y buscar a quien no deseaba encontrar.

Nadie le prestó la menor atención.

Se movió despacio, primero por los alrededores de la entrada, densos y abigarrados de personal, pasando a través de cuerpos y presencias, rostros anónimos de mujer y sus equivalentes masculinos. La primera vez también había sido así. Entró por casualidad, intentó comprar tabaco, y se encontró con ella. Toda una sorpresa. La magia de lo inesperado que se convierte en realidad. En esta ocasión se abrió paso despacio, pidiendo perdón o empujando sin más, hasta llegar a las inmediaciones de la barra, donde la búsqueda fue más lenta porque había dos y hasta tres filas de bebedores y habladores pegados a ella. Cuando también superó este obstáculo, solo le quedó el fondo del club, y eso fue más sencillo. La gente hablaba, de pie, porque no había dónde sentarse, rodeando las columnas en cuyo entorno había diminutas repisas circulares. Al terminar su inspección suspiró más tranquilo.

Después de todo, solo la había telefoneado una vez, desde el Dos Torres, y no volvió a insistir. A lo mejor estaba ya en casa, había ido a cenar realmente con una amiga o algo así. O quizá, sabiendo que era él, no descolgó el auricular, para ponerle nervioso.

Rafael suspiró con cierto alivio.

Tenía que comprar tabaco o de lo contrario Natalia...

Inició el regreso a la salida, dónde estaba la máquina, y fue entonces cuando la vio, saliendo del lavabo del club.

Mercedes.

70

Llevaba una blusa suelta de mangas, pero muy ceñida de senos y escotada, de tul casi transparente, porque las dos manchas oscuras de los pezones se adivinaban con meridiana claridad coronándolos. Bajo el pecho la tela caía igualmente libre por encima de unos pantaloncitos cortos y apretados, de color negro en contraste con la blancura de la blusa. Brillaban debido al tono reluciente de su textura, lo mismo que las botas, informales y aparatosas, pero de diseño, como ella le había dicho el día que las estrenó. Lo peor sin embargo no era su imagen, ni siquiera su sonrisa abierta y diáfana, desafiante, sino el hecho de que esperándola frente a la puerta del lavabo estuviera un hombre joven como ella, sosteniendo dos vasos. Le entregó uno cuando se paró frente a él.

Mercedes bebió un breve sorbo, y luego se le acercó, le dijo algo al oído, y los dos se echaron a reír con fuerza.

Hubiera podido salir sin que ella le viera, pero no pudo, aún comprendiendo que estaba haciendo el ridículo. Una oleada de furia le invadió de la cabeza a los piés y le hizo cruzar el umbral de su equilibrio. Tampoco tenía tiempo, con su mujer y los otros dos esperándole en el coche. Llegó hasta su amante y se detuvo a menos de dos pasos. Mercedes continuaba riendo y hablando, y el pavo que la acompañaba bebía y asentía con la cabeza.

Cuando la mujer apartó momentáneamente la mirada para ver la figura del hombre que parecía haberse materializado delante de ambos y le reconoció, ni siquiera pestañeó o se alarmó. Solo dejó de hablar un segundo, acentuó la sonrisa, aunque había más malicia que sorpresa en ella, y enmarcó la ceja izquierda.

—Hola, Rafa —fue la primera en hablar—. ¿Ya has librado?

Obvió su comentario. Tenía los puños apretados. El acompañante de Mercedes le miraba como quien mira a un negro en una convención del Ku Klux Klan.

—¿Qué estás haciendo? —preguntó él.

—Ya ves —Mercedes se encogió de hombros—, tomar una copa y pasar el rato.

—Te he llamado.

—No tenías porque haberlo hecho, ya te dije que saldría. ¿Conoces a Pepe?

¿Pepe? Ni idea. Ni siquiera le dijo nada. Le ignoró.

—¿Podemos hablar?

—Claro, en cinco minutos...

—Ahora.

—¿Por qué tanta prisa?

—He de irme.

—¿No te quedas? —el rostro de Mercedes cambió de nuevo.

—No, no puedo. Solo...

—Te esperan en el coche, claro —asintió su amante con cara de fastidio, no de enfado o irritación—. Y has venido hasta aquí con...

—¿Qué querías que hiciera?

—Tal vez fuera interesante salir y verla, ¿no? Hacerme una idea.

—Vamos, Mercedes, por favor.

—Oye, tranquilo, que no pasa nada —aseguró terminante—. Si yo te entiendo. Me molesta pero te entiendo. Lo que no comprendo es porque no lo entiendes tú. ¿A qué has venido? ¿A verme? Pues ya me ves. Te dije que saldría y es lo que he hecho. No quería quedarme sola en casa y punto. Y no pasa nada.

Hablaba en serio. Ahí estaba el quid de la cuestión: que hablaba en serio. Ella podía pasar sin él, por más que le gustase o lo que fuera. Podía pasar. Rafael en cambio sentía una especie de locura interior. Un deseo incontrolable de asesinarla por un lado y cogerla de la mano y salir a la calle con ella por el otro, para plantarse delante de su coche y decirle a Natalia que la amaba, que le estaba volviendo a hacer sentir...

—No eres justa, ¿sabes? —dijo con la pesada carga de su resentimiento.

—¿Qué yo no soy justa? —se movió, pasó junto a Pepe, que ya estaba fuera de su tiempo, y se plantó frente a él—. El que se ha de aclarar eres tú, chato. Yo ya lo tengo claro, te lo he dicho antes en tu despacho.

—¡Pero es que no ves que esto es de locos!

—Esto es lo que es, y nada más. Yo no puedo hacer nada, porque la decisión es tuya. ¿Qué quieres que te diga?

Rafael se movió nervioso. Llevaba allí demasiado rato. Salvador podía entrar a buscarle, a instancias de Natalia. Toda la tensión de la tarde a causa del tema del dinero, y de la noche a causa de su mujer, le estalló entre las manos. Quería quedarse y no podía. Tenía que irse y no quería.

—He de irme —se rindió—. Mañana te llamaré o... pasaré un momento.

—¿Diez minutos? —continuó atacándole ella—. ¿La excusa de ir a comprar el periódico o la de dejar a tu hija en el parque y subir a hacérmelo en un visto y no visto?

—¡Coño, Mercedes!

Ella se le acercó, le dio un beso en la comisura de los labios y luego se apartó sonriendo con una mezcla de ternura y dominio, amor y poder.

—Anda, vete —le dijo en un tono neutro—. Y llámame mañana, ¿vale?

Todo estaba dicho.

71

Subieron por la calle Tuset, despacio, mirando a derecha e izquierda a la busca de un sitio donde aparcar, aunque ya había más de un vehículo en doble fila dada la hora y la irreductible desfachatez de los propietarios. Al pasar por delante del Sutton se encontraron con la animación fluyendo del interior.

—Déjalo en el parking —dijo Encarna.

—Odio los parkings, ya lo sabes —manifestó él con desprecio—. Son cuevas de ladrones. Pasan cinco minutos y te cobran la hora igual. Cada vez que entro en uno se me revuelven las tripas y por lo general acabo pegándome con el encargado o el que sea.

—Es que eres muy chulo tú —se burló Encarna—. Cualquier día te lo van a robar o a rayar o a abollar, y ya verás la gracia que te hará entonces no haberlo dejado en un parking.

—¡Es en los parkings donde se rayan y abollan más coches! —saltó Sixto—. No ves que hacen las plazas estrechas para que entren más paganos, que es la hostia de complicado hacer las maniobras, y más con coches grandes como este.

—Yo solo sé que un poco rata si te estás volviendo, cariño —le punzó la rubia—. ¡Que es un BMW, hombre!

—Como si fuera un Porsche.

Habían rebasado ya el final de Tuset, y solo quedaba girar a la derecha, por Travesera, en dirección a Balmes, o subir recto por la calle frontal. Escogió esto último, rodando a la misma velocidad de crucero sin dejar de buscar un hueco salvador. Cada vez que creía encontrar uno, se topaba con un vado. Hasta pensó en aparcar en uno de ellos, porque a semejante hora... pero no quiso arriesgarse a tener que ir a buscarlo al depósito. Más que los parkings, odiaba las grúas.

La calle se hacía larga e interminable.

—¡Podías haberme dejado en el Sutton! —protestó Encarna—. ¡Vaya caminata vas a darme, rico!

—Lo siento.

—Y mira que está solitaria esta calle.

—No te preocupes. Si nos violan, relájate y goza.

Llevaban recorridos casi cien metros, con las calles transversales tan a rebosar como la que transitaban, cuando de pronto se encontraron con otro hueco a la izquierda. Sixto enmarcó las cejas al comprobar que era enorme, ideal para su coche, y que encima no pertenecía a ningún vado.

—¿Lo ves? —cantó triunfal—. ¡La recompensa de los elegidos! ¡El que la sigue la consigue!

Encarna no dijo nada. Seguía mirando lo vacía y solitaria que estaba la calle, y en determinados tramos, también escasamente iluminada a su juicio.

72

Rafael abrió la portezuela del coche correspondiente a su lado y nada más dejarse caer en el asiento se puso a protestar y gritar.

—¡Cagüen Dios...! ¡A tope, a rebosar, como si regalaran las copas, y encima cuando consigo abrirme paso me dicen que la máquina está estropeada y que no hay tabaco! ¡Para morirse!

—Ya iba a venir a buscarte —dijo Salvador—. Pensaba que habías ligado con alguna pelirroja.

—¡Sí, hombre, las ganas! —le miró irritado por el comentario, y dio otro golpe con la mano abierta sobre el volante—. ¡Es que, mira... hay cosas que me sacan de quicio!

—Sí, se te nota —comentó su amigo.

El cuerpo de Natalia pasó entre los dos, proveniente de la parte de atrás del vehículo, y sin decir nada logró que su mano llegara hasta la guantera, situada frente a Salvador. Pese a la dificultad del gesto y la distancia, consiguió su objetivo. Al abrirla, pudo verse en el interior un paquete de tabaco encima de los documentos del coche, unos planos y una linterna.

—¡Sopla! —dijo Rafael.

—¡Vaya por Dios! —suspiró Salvador.

No quería mirar a su mujer, pero fue inevitable. Era necesario si quería saber...

Los ojos de Natalia le mostraron una tensa dureza.

—No entiendo... —trató de decir algo.

—Siempre llevas ahí, querido —comentó ella secamente—. No sé cómo no has mirado primero.

—Estaba seguro de haber cogido el último ayer o esta mañana.

—Pues si hubieras mirado...

—¡Coño, no lo he hecho, vale! ¿Y tú por qué no lo decías antes? ¿O te crees que me gusta meterme en un bar de esos como si fuera un drogata con mono?

—No sé, tú sabrás.

La ira de Rafael se desbordó. Con las manos engarfiadas en el volante y el rostro rojo por la saturación de sentimientos, se giró de forma violenta para enfrentarse a su esposa, que parecía esperarle como un boxeador en el ring. Fue la misma congestión la que retardó el tropel de sus palabras.

—Bueno, arranca de una vez, va —dijo en el momento justo Paz—, porque a este paso aquellos se van a creer que nos ha pasado algo.

—Y además te voy a estrenar el paquete —la ayudó Salvador, tomando la cajetilla de la guantera abierta del coche.

Logró que todas las miradas convergieran en él, una a una.

—Coño, pero si tú no fumas, Salva —exclamó Rafael arrancado de su conato de explosión.

Natalia

Fue Paz, y luego Salvador. Los dos impidieron lo inevitable. Me pregunté si mi marido estaba irritado debido a mi continuo malestar a lo largo de la noche, o si lo estaba yo por su actitud y mis sentimientos hacia él. Fuere como fuere, la situación estaba ya en un punto límite. Cuando llegáramos a casa, o en el transcurso del fin de semana...

No habría un verano de por medio, ninguna espera. Empezaba a darme cuenta de que no podía seguir callada, porque ni era tan fuerte ni tan cínica.

Rafael sabía que llevaba ese paquete de tabaco en la guantera.

En el Dos Torres pensaba que fue a espiar a la modelo, pero ahora...

¿Una llamada telefónica?

Se me ocurrió que la que no tenía ganas de ir al lugar donde íbamos era yo, pero la idea de volver a casa, y precipitarlo todo, aún me daba más miedo, me aterrorizaba. Así que estaba acorralada.

Paz me cogió la mano en silencio. Recibí su ánimo y su apoyo a través de ese contacto, y también su claro mensaje. Me estaba diciendo: "No te precipites, juega tus cartas, mantén la calma".

Traté de relajarme, me hundí en el asiento del coche, cerré los ojos.

Era más negra mi noche interior que la exterior envolviéndome con su vida trepidante.

Todo el mundo parecía estar en la calle, yendo de un lado a otro.

73

—Cuánto tardan, ¿no? —se extrañó Encarna—. ¿Y si ya están dentro?

—No pueden haber llegado, y mucho menos haber entrado sin más —le justificó Sixto observando como un hombre aseguraba una imponente Kawasaki con la que acababa de aterrizar haciendo un gran alarde de poder y ruido—. Rafa ya iba un poco cargado y su mujer le habrá dicho que vaya despacio.

—Quién habla de ir cargado —le endilgó ella—. Y te recuerdo que has ido a aparcar al quinto pino.

—Vale, vale.

El de la moto subía hacia el Drugstore David, con paso vivo y flexible, dominador. Sixto esperó a que se hubiera metido dentro para acercarse a la impresionante máquina, una 750 nacarada en rojo. Prefería los coches, pero reconocía que una bestia como aquella era fascinante y hermosa. Durante unos segundos, mientras observaba cada detalle, se olvidó de Encarna, quieta en mitad de la entrada del Sutton.

Sola.

No se dio cuenta de la entrada del guaperas, también solo. Ella sí. Pareció emerger de la nada, materializado de entre las personas que en número cercano a la docena y media hablaban esperando entrar o marcharse del baile. Tendría unos treinta y cinco años, buena planta, cabello correcto por encima de un rostro anguloso y moreno, bien tostado por el sol. Vestía un traje claro, sin corbata, impecable, y sonreía como si acabaran de tocarle un par de millones, en un sorteo inesperado.

Pese a todo, a Encarna le bastó un vistazo para saber lo más esencial: que era un imbécil de la noche.

El guaperas acentuó su sonrisa al verla y se le paró delante, sin ningún corte, prevención o respeto. Ella no apartó la mirada, al contrario, la sostuvo, sin alterar para nada las facciones. La sonrisa del recién llegado se congeló por espacio de dos segundos, quizá tres.

—Hola —dijo con mucha entonación y jovialidad.

Encarna miró a Sixto, que seguía encandilado con la moto. Suspiró y se retiró lo justo para apartarse de la frontal del guaperas. Este no se movió, pero no dejó de observarla. Debió creer que era un juego.

Y jugó.

Dio el paso que le separaba de ella en el instante en que Sixto buscaba a su novia con la mirada. El guaperas fue lacónico:

—Estaré dentro, ¿vale?

Y se fue, caminando como si lo hiciera por encima de una alfombra puesta a sus piés, sin mirar atrás, tan seguro de sí mismo como de que la noche seguía al día.

Desapareció coincidiendo con el momento en que Sixto tomó su lugar frente a Encarna.

—¿Quién era ese? —quiso saber.

—Uno con ojos en la cara —pasó la rubia.

—Ya, y tú que te dejas ver —dijo él.

—¿Qué quieres que haga? —se puso en guardia Encarna—. Me dejas sola y la gente va a lo que va. ¿O no te has enterado de que hay mucho tío suelto y con hambre? Y además, ¿a mí que me cuentas, oye? Si estamos aquí de plantón no es por mi culpa, y si estás de mal humor pasa ya de una vez y no la pagues conmigo.

—Yo no la pago contigo —Sixto había endurecido sus facciones.

—No, es un anuncio —se cruzó de brazos ella.

—A veces...

—A veces, ¿qué?

Quizá se lo hubiera dicho.

La aparición del coche de Rafael se lo impidió.

Encarna

Me sentí muy incómoda, más de lo que hubiera estado a lo largo de la noche. Ya en casa, al salir, cuando me dijo que iba demasiado llamativa, me hizo sentir mal, porque es mi estilo y me encanta, y ya he dicho antes que me gusta gustar. Ni casado conmigo tendría derecho a decirme que iba de tal o cual manera, al contrario. El amor se manifiesta de muchas formas, y la mejor, la más esencial, es la de la confianza y la libertad. Ninguna cadena puede unir más que eso, y ningún recelo acerca sino que separa.

No provoco, nunca he actuado como reclamo, pero sé que gusto, y no es mi problema, es problema de los depredadores que se acercan o de los que revolotean babeando o con los ojos cayéndoseles de las órbitas, como si nunca hubiesen visto a una mujer. ¿O no tenemos derecho a lucir nuestros encantos? Yo paso de machismos y feminismos. Soy yo y nada más que yo. Intento ser agradable y cordial, puedo coquetear cuando puedo y cuanto puedo, a mi aire, sabiendo el momento. No se me iba a ocurrir hacerlo estando Sixto delante. Hay otra palabra que valoro mucho: respeto.

O sea que Sixto no tenía porque ponerse así.

Encima.

Hubiera discutido con él, en defensa de mis derechos, pero la aparición de los otros cuatro lo evitó. Paz y Natalia se acercaban caminando. Salvador observaba la maniobra de Rafael.

Estaba aparcando a menos de diez metros del Sutton.

74

Paz y Natalia llegaron hasta Encarna. Sixto por el contrario caminó por la acera, alejándose de ellas, hasta situarse junto a Salvador.

—¡Tendrá potra el tío! —protestó—. ¡Yo he tenido que aparcar en el quinto pino!

—Ibamos a dejarlo en el parking, pero se ha ido uno y...

—Ya no me acordaba que Rafa va de empresario y lo mete en el parking —continuó rezongando Sixto—. A mi el sueldo no me llega para tanto.

—Anda ya —se burló Salvador.

Rafael completó la maniobra, bajó del coche y le dio un vistazo final para comprobar que estuviese correctamente situado.

—Espero que no se ponga nadie en doble fila y me tapen —dudó.

—Eso, encima quéjate —dijo Sixto—. Puedes quedarte aquí controlando.

—¿Qué pasa, hemos tardado mucho? —captó el tono punzante de Sixto—. Hemos visto un accidente y luego he parado a comprar tabaco y...

—¿Un accidente?

—Un coche y una moto —le informó Salvador.

—¿Sangre y todo eso? —empleó un tono de sarcasmo al decirlo.

—Sangre sí, lo otro no sé —dijo el médico.

—¿Vamos? —inquirió Rafael.

Caminaron hasta el vestíbulo del baile, amplio y luminoso, y se reunieron con sus respectivas parejas reanudando el paso de dos en dos. Un cartel, a la derecha, anunciaba el nombre de la orquesta. No se detuvieron hasta la zona de pago, a la izquierda, en la que un letrero indicaba el precio de la entrada.

—¡Coño, dos mil doscientas por barba! —se quejó Rafael en voz baja al verlo—. ¿Dan champán con la entrada o es que luego actúan los Beatles?

232

—Calla, palizas —le dijo Sixto—. Este es un lugar fino.

—¡Ya!

Cada cual pagó dos entradas y al trasponer la barrera se encontraron en otro vestíbulo, el guardarropa a la izquierda y diversos cuadros colgados de las paredes a ambos lados. Otro cartel anunciaba el nombre del artista que exponía en ese espacio.

—¡Qué cosas! —continuó Rafael—. ¡Arte y marcha! ¡Si es que ya no saben que inventar!

—Bueno, como en el Piscolabis —dijo Paz—, y allí es arte y bocadillos y ensaladas y batidos.

—Ese es bonito —Natalia señaló un cuadro.

—¡La madre que los... ! —suspiró en plena escalada Rafael.

—¡Pero quieres callarte! —protestó Sixto.

La música llegó hasta ellos, pegadiza, contagiosa, al abrirse la puerta que conducía finalmente a la sala. Encarna fue la primera en empezar a moverse, dejándose llevar por el ritmo.

75

Primero, les envolvió la penumbra característica de los lugares íntimos, con la música actuando de acompañante lo mismo que la moqueta acolchaba su paso. A continuación, pasearon sus miradas por el entorno vibrante y alegre de aquel espacio contaminado por la sensación de alegría y fuerza. A la izquierda pasaron por delante de las puertas acristaladas de un pequeño bar cerrado, una especie de zona privada para poder tomar una copa y charlar sin la descarga decibélica de la música que llenaba el resto. Rebasado el mismo se encontraron en la sala, con un amplio bar a la derecha, otro más pequeño a la izquierda, mesas, un pasillo circular al frente, y otra zona circular de mesas rodeando la pista de baile que también quedaba a la izquierda, al pié del escenario, en el que una docena y media de músicos atacaba en este momento, con toda energía, una samba al cien por cien de ritmo.

—¡Uau! —cantó Encarna entrando rápidamente en situación.

No parecía caber un alma. La pista estaba abarrotada por un ejército de saltarines y saltarinas, enlazados dos a dos o moviéndose en solitario, por puro placer individual. Las mesas se hallaban igualmente llenas, o con restos y presencias de su ocupación en forma de vasos o residuos agotados que parecían ser los danzantes retirados o aún no estrenados.

—Luego dicen que hay crisis —comentó Sixto.

—¿Qué? —preguntó Salvador.

—¡Nada!

—Ya —asintió con la cabeza—. Luego dicen que hay crisis.

Sixto le miró sin aclarar el cruce de ideas. Un camarero llegó hasta ellos, ya que no sabían muy bien a donde dirigirse de momento. Le bastó una mirada inteligente para ver su número y les hizo una seña para que le acompañaran. Lo hicieron, y el hombre se internó por el pasillo circular, tan lleno de hombres y mujeres de pié como el resto. Al llegar al otro lado descubrieron otra amplia zona de mesas, apartadas del núcleo principal, y en la que aún quedaban una o dos libres. El camarero les instaló en una y pese a que desde allí no veían bien a la orquesta no objetaron nada. Salvador fue el primero en sentarse. Después lo hicieron Paz y Natalia.

—¿Qué van a tomar? —preguntó el empleado del local extendiendo su mano derecha.

Le entregaron las seis entradas que daban derecho a una consumición.

Paz

Me di cuenta de que, pese a todo, Salvador y yo estábamos allí como peces fuera del agua. Y probablemente también Natalia y Rafa. Cuando éramos solteros, íbamos a bailar, y frecuéntabamos discotecas, claro. Pero de eso parecía hacer una eternidad. Además, aquello era distinto, un cruce de sala de fiestas y baile selecto. La gente iba a bailar, a tomar una copa, a charlar, y nosotros...

La noche cada vez era más rara.

El ambiente más extraño.

Tras el último conato de pelea de Natalia y su marido, de lo único que tenía ganas era de llegar a casa, y si querían matarse, que lo hicieran en la suya y en privado. Sabía reconocer una causa perdida, y aquella lo era.

Probablemente por esta razón le cogí la mano a Salvador, y se la apreté con fuerza.

¿Qué hacía una pareja como nosotros en un lugar como este?

Salvador

Me sorprendió el lugar, el ambiente. Lo encontré curioso y agradable, diferente a como lo hubiera imaginado. Desde luego no era una discoteca llena de locas y locos pegando brincos al ritmo de la estúpida música de ahora. Aquello tenía un cierto sentido, gente como nosotros, más joven y también más vieja, pasando un buen rato con música en vivo, buena música en vivo, porque la orquesta le pegaba fuerte y con sentido del ritmo.

Lo primero que pensé fue que Paz y yo tendríamos que dejarnos caer algún otro día por allí, pero solos los dos.

Estaba descubriendo algo nuevo, no esencialmente un nuevo mundo, pero sí algo diferente, demostrativo de que al otro lado de mi consulta existían aún las mismas cosas de

235

antes, y de siempre, solo que al estilo del presente, de los 90, y para gente como nosotros, como Paz y como yo, que también éramos de los 90. No otros 90. Los mismos 90 de Octavio y Vanessa y... Cosas para que la gente viva un poco.

Me gustaba.

En cuanto tocaran algo apropiado me dije que iba a sacar a bailar a Paz.

Rafael

Aquello era una mierda.

No exactamente el lugar, la música, el ambiente... sino más bien la situación, con la escena de Mercedes aún viva en mi mente y el deseo que había tenido de ahogar a Natalia aún fresco en mi ánimo alterado y nervioso. De haber podido, me habría ido a casa.

No, miento. De haber podido me habría ido a buscar a Mercedes, le habría pedido perdón, y luego...

Ver a Sixto y a Encarna me dolía casi más que el mismo futuro de mi empresa. Ellos eran como la burla, o la esencia de lo que yo tal vez quisiera y no podía tener. A mí todo se me complicaba. Una mujer histérica, una hija pequeña, una amante capaz de lo mejor, pero también de pasar de todo.

Mercedes era fuerte.

Yo no.

Yo también era un mierda.

Pedí una cerveza, ignoré la mirada de mi mujer, a vueltas con lo de que ya estaba bastante cargado, y envuelto, o mejor dicho, aplastado por el peso de mis pensamientos, me dispuse a soportar el tiempo que tuviéramos que pasar allí.

Y la de tías buenas que había por el lugar.

Natalia

Empecé a mirar a las mujeres, y vi que la mayoría tenía mi edad, en torno a la cuarentena, aunque también las había como Encarna, de treinta. Salvo una o dos, me pareció que todas eran mucho más guapas, que tenían mejores cuerpos, y sus formas de sonreír, de moverse, de bailar, de fumar, de beber, eran seducciones puras, como si los hombres no fuesen sus maridos o sus novios, sino sus amantes. Me imaginé a un ejército de mujeres casadas en casa, mientras ellos estaban allí, con las otras.

Y eso me hizo polvo.

Fue como una fiebre, de esas que te provoca delirios, y sabes que lo son, pero no desaparecen a pesar de ello.

La gente se divertía, y yo estaba verdaderamente hecha polvo.

O sea que encima la cosa tenía visos de burla.

Rafael se bebió su cerveza de dos tragos, y sentí asco.

Sixto

Estábamos allí por Encarna, había sido idea suya, pero la verdad es que no me apetecía bailar ni beber ni...

No con Paz y con Natalia, con Salvador y Rafael.

Ya no teníamos nada en común, estaban muertos. Muertos en vida. Yo en cambio había vuelto a vivir.

Fue una revelación absoluta, viéndoles sentados en el baile, mirando a sus mujeres, y especialmente viendo a Encarna, joven, rubia, sexy, llena de intensidad. Estaba picado con ella, a veces me entraban ganas de..., pero era la tensión lógica del cambio, sumada a los problemas en la agencia. A veces llegaba a "culparla" de lo que me sucedía con mis hijos, de haberme quedado sin casa, sin apenas dinero.

En otras, hubiera querido hacer el amor con ella y cerrar los ojos y olvidarme y tirar la llave y...

Acabé pidiendo una cerveza, como Rafa, y me la bebí exactamente como lo hizo él, de dos tragos. Puro reflejo.

Iba a sacar a bailar a Encarna, a pesar de todo, para no quedarme allí sentado como un idiota con aquellas momias, pero ella se me adelantó.

Encarna

A la mierda con todos ellos.

Incluso Sixto, por cuya culpa me estaba tragando la peor de las noches, la más aburrida y estúpida. Lo tenía tan claro, que hasta me sentía impaciente, porque no quería calmarme ni reflexionar. De haber podido, se lo hubiera dicho allí mismo, pero era absurdo, así que decidí hacerlo en casa, al día siguiente, cuando nos levantáramos, o incluso aquella misma noche, al llegar, si me veía con ganas de pelea más que de sueño. Se lo iba a plantear abierta y directamente. Yo no estaba dispuesta a casarme con su familia, sus ex-lo-que-fuera o sus amigos y amigas. Me casaba con él, y por amor. Una cosa era aguantar hijos, que eso, si bien me parecía cada vez más duro, era inevitable, y otra aguantar aquella especie de juicio perenne.

Nunca me aceptarían.

Rafael y Sixto bebieron cervezas, como si no llevaran ya bastante encima. Ellas, unas pijadas clásicas de frutitas y cosas así. Salvador y yo nos contentamos con dos refrescos. Precisamente Salvador era el que daba la impresión de estar más animado en ese momento. Lo miraba todo con más curiosidad que expectación, y movía los piés. Una media sonrisa le aleteaba en los labios. Ya he dicho antes que me parecía el menos muermo en el sentido de que era el más persona del grupo, así que como yo quería bailar, me levanté, me planté delante de él, sacudí las caderas y le dije que nos íbamos a mover el esqueleto.

76

—Venga, vamos a bailar, doc.

—¿Yo?

Sonrió con más aire de picardía que de sorpresa, y aunque lo quería, por mero instinto miró a su mujer, indeciso. Fue Paz la que le empujó sin disimulo con ambas manos.

—Vamos, que te están invitando, ¿a qué esperas?

Encarna dirigió sus ojos a ella.

—¿Puedo, no?

—¡Sí, hija, sí, a ver si me lo agotas un poco!

—No estoy yo para muchos bailes —se quejó Salvador.

—¡Qué me lo voy a creer! —espetó Encarna.

Le cogió de la mano y abrió la marcha hacia la pista de baile. La orquesta atacaba con ferocidad un viejo tema de los mismísimos Beatles, Ob-la-di, ob-la-da, en versión sui generis. De hecho hizo el breve recorrido bailando, moviendo las caderas por delante de Salvador, que acabó suspirando y rindiéndose a los acontecimientos.

Por detrás, los otros cuatro les miraron hasta que vieron cómo se sumergían en el trepidante océano humano acotado en la pista. No pudieron penetrar hasta su corazón y se quedaron en la periferia, iniciando el ritual rítmico, Encarna rápidamente lanzada, brazos en alto, oscilando igual que un nervio al compás de la música, y Salvador con la patosidad propia de todos los que un día intentan recordar mejores momentos.

En la mesa, Natalia fue la primera en hablar.

—Menudo carácter —dijo. Y dirigiéndose a Sixto agregó—: Estarás animado con ella.

—Más que con mi ex, te aseguro que sí.

—Bueno, hombre —Natalia captó el tono cortante de su respuesta—, no te pongas así. No lo decía por eso.

—Mejor.

—Deberías casarte cuánto antes con ella —intervino Paz.

—¿Por qué? —a Sixto le extrañó el comentario.

—La perderás si no lo haces.

—¿Cómo lo sabes?

—Lo sé.

—Vale, pues todo el mundo parece saber más que yo —rezongó él.

—Vosotras y vuestro sexto sentido —se burló Rafael.

—Está claro que a su edad lo que ya no quiere es jugar —apuntó Natalia.

—Yo no lo decía por eso —aseguró Paz.

—Mira, me precipité una vez, y no quiero volver a hacerlo, ¿sabes? —dijo Sixto—De momento vivimos juntos y estamos bien.

—Y tú aún tienes todo el lío del divorcio —continuó insidiosa Natalia.

Sixto pasó de mirarla. Sus ojos quedaron unidos a los de Paz, como si entre ambos se estableciera una comunicación más abierta que la de las palabras. El puente de aquella luz solo quedó roto cuando, diez segundos después, Rafael comentó:

—Fijaos en ellos. Parecen haber estado de fiesta toda la vida.

77

Salvador le iba cogiendo el ritmo a la música y al baile. No era tan complicado. Bastaba con dejarse llevar, pasar de todo, sumergirse en la marea de cuerpos y sentir el baño de la suave lluvia decibélica. Por si ello fuera poco, Encarna se movía como una diosa delante de él, ondulante, con la generosidad de su escote y la brevedad de su vestido haciendole resaltar las formas, y el cabello rubio actuando como una llama amarilla que cambiaba de tonalidades bajo el continuo alud de los focos del techo. Se la notaba libre, feliz, como si por fin, realmente ahora, estuviese en su mundo, en su ambiente.

Empezó a comprenderla, mejor de lo que pudiera haberlo hecho a lo largo de la noche.

Encarna se dio cuenta de ese detalle, y se acercó a él para decirle:

—¡Bailas bien!

—Si tuviera a mano un poco de Tres en Uno lo haría mejor.

—¡No seas tonto! ¡Estás en plena forma, aunque algo apalancado!

Volvieron a separarse, no demasiado, porque no había espacio suficiente, hasta que la orquesta cambió de canción y atacó con renovada ferocidad rítmica otro tema aún más pegadizo. Algunas de las parejas se rindieron y se retiraron en busca de lugares más seguros. Los que siguieron en la pista se esponjaron un poco.

Encarna le vio entonces.

El mismo guaperas creído y estúpido de la entrada, bailando a menos de un metro de ella, con su sonrisa cretina y estúpida, segura y dominante.

Le dio rabia, y le dio pena. La noche estaba llena de personajes como él, y ni siquiera entendía cómo ligaban si es que llegaban a hacerlo. ¿Nadie le había dicho que era ridículo?

El guaperas acentuó su pose de castigador y su sonrisa de duro de pacotilla.

Le guiñó un ojo.

Encarna se rio, no pudo evitarlo. La suya fue una sonrisa socarrona. El otro en cambio pareció interpretarla de otra forma. Dio un paso en dirección a ella.

Encarna giró el cuerpo, sin dejar de bailar, dándole la espalda.

Luego se aproximó a Salvador y le dijo:

—¡Vamos a por los otros, o van a dormirse! ¡Creía que se animarían al vernos pero...!

Y salieron de la pista.

78

Salvador cogió de la mano a Paz, sin dejar de moverse al ritmo de la música. Su mujer estalló en una carcajada, pero no pudo negarse. Se rindió ante él y se puso en pié. Fue la primera. Encarna ya hacía lo mismo con Sixto, que daba la impresión de estar absorto con sus movimientos, como si la viera así por primera vez. Se habrían ido los cuatro de no ser porque Paz se apartó un momento de su marido y cogió a Natalia y a Rafael.

—No, no.. —protestó débilmente ella.

—¡No seas boba, mujer!

Tiró de ellos y logró su objetivo, arrancarles de los asientos. Luego les empujó hacia la pista de baile, tras los pasos de Encarna y Sixto que iban por delante.

Los seis entraron en su círculo mágico.

Encarna se disparó de nuevo, al instante, agitándose igual que una coctelera bajo la sabia mano de un barman experimentado. La siguió en la cadencia rítmica Salvador, todavía motivado por la sensación precedente, y luego Sixto, envuelto por el halo de Encarna. Paz obligó a Natalia, que se movía igual que un pato mareado. Rafael, con cara de fastidio, fue el último.

Uno a uno acabaron capturados por la música y la

sensación de libertad.

Uno a uno, cerraron los ojos y se olvidaron de que al otro lado de la pista la vida les esperaba.

Uno a uno, a lo largo de los minutos siguientes, cinco, diez, tal vez incluso quince.

Salvador

Fueron los últimos minutos de paz, los recuerdo bien. De pronto me sentí diferente, ligeramente más jovial, tranquilo. Abría los ojos y veía a Paz bailando con una expresión alegre. Volvía a abrirlos y miraba a Encarna, turbadora en sus movimientos, pero sin sentir ninguna necesidad, nada especial. Tal vez solo fueran sensaciones.

Finalmente parecíamos lo que se suponía que éramos: tres parejas divirtiéndose un viernes por la noche.

Seis personas adultas y maduras, inofensivas.

Sixto

Estábamos bailando, los seis, increíble.

El único instante de la noche en el que nadie le ponía mala cara a nadie, y todos sonreíamos, hasta Rafael.

Pensé que, desde luego, Encarna era genial.

Algún día mis hijos lo entenderían, y si no...

Era mi vida, qué diablos.

Natalia

Me hubiera gustado detener el tiempo, paralizarlo. Me había enamorado de mi marido por su fuerza, su carácter, su convicción al hacer las cosas y la seguridad que me daba. La seguridad de la que yo carecía. Y bailando pensé que había sido hermoso, y que era una pena que todo se destruyera.

¿Por qué las personas cambian?

Fue una sensación distinta, en el momento que podría denominar álgido de la noche.

Paz

Por televisión, parece que todo el mundo sea joven y tenga menos de veinte o treinta años. Incluso en las series, las mujeres de cincuenta o sesenta aparentan cuarenta. Yo a veces me sentía "abuela" comparándome con ellas.

Pero allí, bailando, fue distinto. Las mujeres que me rodeaban eran como yo, mejores o peores, pero ni más ni menos que yo. Y Salvador aún lo hacía bien.

Quizá hubiéramos perdido algún tiempo, solo eso.

Rafael

Por unos segundos, o unos minutos, casi me olvidé de Mercedes y de la empresa y de todo lo demás. Hasta Natalia estaba más atractiva bajo la luz de los focos y moviéndose al compás de la música.

Pero no dejaron de ser unos segundos, apenas un soplo de tiempo.

Fui el primero en retirarse de la pista de baile, mitad cansado mitad ridículo, y Sixto me siguió. Cuando llegamos a la mesa pedimos otras dos cervezas, pasando de todo. Salvador aguantó el tipo un poco más, con ellas tres. Luego Natalia se rindió, y arrastró en su huida a Paz.

Salvador siguió a su mujer.

Y Encarna se quedó sola.

Encarna

Me quedé sola, pero no me preocupé demasiado por ello. Supongo que en otro tiempo, en los bailes el concepto de "pareja" era mucho más rígido. En las discotecas de las dos o tres últimas décadas, la libertad permitía disfrutar sin complejos y sin ataduras.

Y yo necesitaba moverme, liberar energías, saltar, expulsar fuera los demonios, aunque aquella no resultase la mejor música para hacerlo. Sonaba un tanto añeja, ligeramente carroza, aunque esta sea una palabra que no me gusta emplear y que más bien odio.

Cerré los ojos otra vez, y tardé en abrirlos.

Cuando lo hice él estaba allí.

79

Lo tenía a un metro escaso, con la misma sonrisa, el mismo estilo, el mismo porte de dominio trasnochado, la misma convicción y seguridad en su talante conquistador.

El guaperas.

Encarna se sintió molesta, irritada, no por su presencia, que podía obviar dándole la espalda una vez más, sino por su persecución, su estupidez congénita. Cualquiera puede entender...

Cualquiera menos aquel imbécil y toda la cohorte de imbéciles nocturnos incapaces de ver la realidad, su situación en completo fuera de juego.

Porque no era más que un desgraciado.

Encarna sonrió.

Lo hizo con malicia, aposta. Una cosa era ser coqueta, y otra poner a cien a un retrasado mental como aquel. ¿Quería marcha? Se sintió perversa. Llegó a imaginárselo machacándosela en el coche o en plena calle. La imagen le produjo una honda satisfacción.

El guaperas dio una vuelta completa sobre si mismo, imitando al Travolta de los años 70. Encarna contuvo la risa. Levantó los brazos, como más le gustaba, al estilo Madonna, y se movió con mayor intensidad y convicción. Además, puso cara de "mala chica", ojos semicerrados, labios proyectados hacia afuera, y con la cabeza oscilando de lado a lado, para que su cabellera rubia se diseminara a su alrededor.

Incluso asomó una punta de lengua sonrosada por entre los dientes.

El guaperas se puso a cien.

Cerró los ojos, apretó los puños, echó la cabeza hacia atrás, recrudeció el movimiento sincopado de sus piés.

Encarna le miró con desprecio.

Y le dejó con su fiebre en mitad de la pista.

Era el momento.

80

Creyeron que caminaba en dirección a la mesa, pero ella se desvió antes de enfilar hasta el grupo. Tomó el pasillito levemente ascendente de su derecha y la vieron dirigirse hacia la parte de atrás del local.

—¿Adónde va? —preguntó Rafael.

—Al lavabo —dijo Sixto—. Están ahí detrás.

Su imagen quedó borrada en parte por la gente que iba y venía, y en parte porque desapareció casi al instante, al doblar la corta separación que protegía la escalera que conducía a los servicios, ubicados en un nivel inferior de la sala de baile.

No volvieron a hablar. De hecho ninguno había vuelto a hablar desde su regreso de la pista.

Se contentaron con mirar a la gente, como espectadores de privilegio de la Gran Comedia Humana.

81

Encarna salió del lavabo de mujeres y pese a haberse arreglado frente al espejo interior, volvió a examinar su aspecto en el exterior. La zona era amplia, ya que la escalinata de mármol claro desembocaba en un vestíbulo espacioso y confortable, con un puesto de bombones y caramelos a la derecha y las dos puertas de los servicios, el femenino y el masculino, flanqueando un sofá y unas butacas a la izquierda. El flujo de cuerpos entrando y saliendo de allí a través de la escalera era constante. Tanto como impersonal, pese a las miradas masculinas en dirección a las mujeres, y las de ellas dirigidas a sus homónimos masculinos cuando el caso lo merecía, lo cual era menos constante que a la inversa.

Concluyó su examen y llegó hasta la escalera, que empezó a subir sin preocuparse por la cortedad de su falda y lo difícil que era elevar las piernas sin que ésta ascendiera por la parte alta de sus muslos. Cuando llegó arriba, justo al girar el cuerpo para dirigirse a la zona donde estaban los demás, se lo encontró de cara, cortándole el paso.

—Hola —dijo él empleando un tono presuntamente cantarín.

Encarna se detuvo.

Los había conocido estúpidos, retrasados mentales, idiotas, pero aquel se llevaba la palma.

Era de los que no se enteraba.

Hizo ademán de pasar por su lado, ignorándolo, pero el guaperas lo evitó moviéndose para impedirlo. Su sonrisa seguía actuando como bandera de su seguridad y aplomo.

—Vamos, mujer, ya está bien. ¿Cómo te llamas?

—No estoy sola —le advirtió Encarna.

—Claro que no lo estás —convino él—. Estás conmigo.

—Déjame pasar.

—No seas así, chica, que estoy en racha.

—Por favor —Encarna miró en dirección a la mesa, visible desde su posición—. No quiero líos, y ...

Como si le hablara a una tapia.

—En media hora estamos en la Costa Brava, ¿te hace? O si lo prefieres, llegamos a Valencia. Pura marcha. No te arrepentirás, venga.

Le puso la mano encima, en el brazo, por la parte de arriba.

Encarna se lo apartó de un manotazo.

—¡Bien, guerrera! —exclamó el guaperas.

82

Fue Rafael el que llamó la atención de Sixto.

—Creo que tu chica ha encontrado un amigo.

Sixto siguió la dirección de su mirada, y también Paz, Natalia y Salvador, alertados por las palabras de Rafael.

No era un amigo, lo advirtió inmediatamente. Le bastó con ver la cara de la rubia, la forma en que el otro le bloqueaba el paso.

Pero aún antes de que pudiera reaccionar, el hombre le puso la mano encima, y Encarna se la apartó de manera harto brusca.

—¡Cagüen la madre que lo... ! —gritó Sixto poniéndose en pié.

—¡Ay Dios! —gimió Natalia.

—¡Oye, espera! —trató de detenerle Rafael.

No lo evitó. Sixto ya corría en dirección a la pareja.

—Vamos, ¡vamos! —dijo Salvador apremiando a Rafael para que le siguiera.

83

Encarna estaba demasiado pendiente ahora del conquistador como para ver otra cosa que no fuera sus manos.

—¡Déjame pasar, imbécil! —le gritó furiosa.

—¡Huy, huy, huy, que modales!

Su sonrisa se congeló de repente, cuando Sixto irrumpió entre él y ella de forma brusca y no precisamente amigable o contemporizadora.

—¿Qué coño...? —fue lo primero que dijo el aparecido.

—¡Nada, Sixto! —trató de detenerle Encarna—. Un malentendido...

Sixto miraba al guaperas. No le gustó lo que vio. A pesar de todo, el tipo seguía sonriendo.

—¿Quién es ese? —preguntó Sixto encendido, con los puños apretados.

—Nadie. Anda, vamos a...

Por primera vez Encarna notó el exceso de alcohol, el brillo rojizo y difuso de los ojos de su pareja. Demasiado cargado para escucharla. Y demasiada ira para ser detenida.

El guaperas puso su grano de arena en el desenlace de la escena.

—¿Es tu papá? —dijo graciosamente.

Sixto saltó encima de él. Lo hizo en el momento preciso en que Salvador y Rafael llegaban por detrás. El primero logró detenerle el puño. El segundo, aunque precariamente, evitó que todos cayeran al suelo. Los cuatro hombres, en confuso pelotón, se movieron hacia un lado.

Cuando Sixto consiguió desembarazarse de la mano de Salvador, logró estampillarle el puño en la cara del guaperas. El grito del agredido, que finalmente había dejado de sonreír, se confundió con el de Encarna y también con el gemido de Rafael, que resbaló hasta dar con sus huesos en el suelo. Paz y Natalia se incorporaron al grupo en ese instante.

—¡Sixto, no!

—!Salvador, cuidado!

—¡Rafael!

La confusión se hizo general al sumarse más hombres al tumulto y más mujeres a la barrera de escandalizadas espectadoras.

Paz

Un par de empleados del local les separaron, sin muchos miramientos, en unión de algunos hombres más, de esos que se meten sin saber de qué va la cosa. Había bastante nerviosismo, porque en una pelea nunca se sabe quién tiene razón, pero bastó una mirada y algunas palabras para que los empleados se hicieran cargo de la situación. La mirada se la dirigieron a Encarna, y las palabras a Sixto. El ligón, con la nariz convertida en una fuente de sangre, no paraba de chillar que quería un médico, y que viniera la policía. Uno de los empleados fue contundente. Le gritó que si continuaba armándola iban a echarle por la puerta de atrás y la huella de un pié en el trasero. El pobre infeliz se calló al momento

A Sixto se lo llevaron al pequeño espacio acristalado de la entrada, todo palmadas en la espalda, todo excusas, todo palabras de aliento tipo "no ha pasado nada", "lo sentimos, señor" y "usted y sus amigos están invitados por la casa", aunque lo que menos necesitábamos en ese momento era seguir bebiendo, y menos quedarnos allí.

Natalia

No se puede ir como iba Encarna sin que pasen ese tipo de cosas, ¡por Dios! Iba pidiendo guerra, y la había encontrado, o más bien decir que la había desencadenado. Sixto estaba fuera de sí, y Rafael, como si aquello fuera con él o como si... no sé, como si la subida de la adrenalina general le hubiera disparado por dentro, estaba igual de encendido. De hecho era el que más gritaba, diciendo que la gente normal no estaba tranquila ni en un lugar como aquel.

Ni siquiera supe por qué estaba así.

Pero desde luego decidimos irnos.

Salvador

No bebimos nada más. Los del club insistieron, pero ya no era el momento. Un hombre muy educado y respetuoso insistió en que lamentaba las molestias, y que seríamos bien recibidos otra vez, y gratis. Invitados por la casa. Sixto se agitaba hecho un nervio, mirando a todas partes, como si aún buscara al causante de todo aquel lío.

Cada vez que sus ojos se encontraban con los de Encarna, se endurecían, y los de ella también. Era un mudo dialogo, o mejor dicho, una encarnizada disputa.

No sé, puede que ese fuera el detonante, la crispación final, pero aún pienso que las cosas venían de antes, es decir, que cada cual llevaba algo...

No somos violentos.

Fue...

Rafael

Fue la suma de muchas pequeñas cosas, casualidades. Ni siquiera entonces, pese a lo excitados que nos sentíamos a causa del incidente, creo que fuéramos diferentes a cualquiera de los que pasaban por la calle. O sea que lo mismo les pudo suceder a ellos.

¡Coño, nunca he hecho daño a nadie!

Encarna

La confusión era demasiado ostensible, y pese a que me sentía furiosa, decidí que lo mejor era callar. No hubiera servido de nada que le dijese a Sixto que se había pasado, que yo ya era mayorcita para defenderme sola, que no era una cría ni una mujer dependiente de un marido solícito y protector, como las mujeres de sus amigos. No habría servido de nada, salvo para pelearnos, porque encima Sixto estaba absolutamente ido, y cuando me miraba... era como si me acusase a mí por lo sucedido. ¡A mí!

¿Qué clase de mierda era aquella?

Lo único que sé es que salimos a la calle, envueltos en una turbulencia feroz que el aire fresco de la noche se encargó de apaciguar y aminorar. Salvador callaba, Paz trataba de calmar a Natalia, que protestaba lo mismo que si el acoso sexual se lo hubiesen hecho a ella. Probablemente de eso se quejaba. Rafael y Sixto eran los más virulentos, pero fuera del Sutton, en mitad de la calle Tuset y su público nocturno, no tenía sentido gritar o prolongar la excitación.

Parecíamos seis victimas de un bombardeo nuclear, perdidos en ninguna parte.

Salvador estuvo al quite. Intentó arreglarlo.

84

—Bueno, vamos a tomar algo fresco y sano que nos ponga el cuerpo a tono, ¿de acuerdo?

—Yo me voy a casa —dijo Natalia.

—¡Eh! —la cortó el mismo Salvador—. Tú vas a hacer caso del médico, o a tu hija Gloria la próxima semana la llevas al oftalmólogo.

—¿Adónde quieres ir ahora? —preguntó dudoso Rafael.

—Al Puerto Olímpico, a tomarnos un zumo de frutas de lo más sano. Invito yo.

—No creo yo que... —objetó Sixto.

—¿Quieres irte ahora, tan enfadado? —Paz le cogió del brazo, en clara señal de apoyo a su marido—. Has sido todo un caballero, y lo que necesitas es relajarte.

—¿En serio queréis ir ahora al Puerto Olímpico? —vaciló Rafael.

Miraron a Encarna, como si la clave la tuviera ella, pero la rubia evadió sus miradas bajo una evidente crispación que interpretaron al revés.

—Claro que sí —insistió Paz—. Después del sofoco que le ha dado ese borracho...

—Está decidido —lo dejó sentado Salvador—. No vamos a separarnos ahora como si nada, cuando lo estábamos pasando bien.

—Bueno —claudicó Natalia—. Un zumo de frutas me sentaría bien, desde luego.

Sixto asintió con la cabeza.

—Tengo el coche... —empezó a decir.

—Te espero aquí, con ellos —le indicó Encarna—. No quiero darme la caminata por esa calle solitaria.

Sixto

Me hubiera gustado hablar con ella en ese breve trayecto, aunque si he de decir la verdad... no sé de qué. Creo que me sentía demasiado furioso por lo sucedido, y por el hecho de que Salvador, Rafael, Paz y Natalia hubieran sido testigos de todo. Estaba seguro de que ahora dirían que Encarna...

Todo había sucedido muy rápido, pero de haber sabido que lo peor estaba por llegar, esperándome como quien dice a la vuelta de la esquina... supongo que no lo hubiera creído.

¿Qué otra cosa podía pasarnos?

A veces los acontecimientos se encadenan de una forma extraña. Y dices aquello de que "has pisado mierda".

253

Nosotros la llevábamos encima, desde que habíamos salido de casa.

Dejé a Encarna con ellos, para ir a por mi coche, dar la vuelta y recogerla. Subí el breve tramo final de Tuset, crucé la Travesera de Gracia y enfilé la calle que seguía a continuación. Ni siquiera recuerdo su nombre. A cada paso que daba, me sumergía más en mi furia por lo sucedido, y me decía que tal vez aquello no fuese más que un anticipo de lo que me esperaba, porque Encarna era una mujer llamativa, de las que pide guerra, o lo parece. Yo mismo me había acercado a ella el primer día excitado por su visión, así que el idiota del Sutton en el fondo no era más que una proyección de mí mismo.

Pensé que el coche estaba más cerca de Tuset, el trayecto se me hizo insoportablemente largo.

Por fin lo vi, desaceleré el paso, saqué las llaves...

Y entonces apareció él.

85

—¡Eh, tú!

Levantó la cabeza, porque estaba casi encima suyo, y no tuvo más remedio que detenerse, con las llaves del coche en la mano derecha. Debió de quedarse pálido al instante, porque notó la huida de la sangre, el embotamiento de los sentidos, el frio interior recorriéndole la espalda, de arriba abajo. Y aunque se fijó en él, en su aspecto irreal, cabello muy largo, ojos perdidos, camiseta y vaqueros, zapatillas deportivas y una cazadora tejana por encima, en lo único que reparó fue en el cuchillo.

Lo sostenía con una mano y era una navaja de buen filo.

Le apuntaba con ella directamente al pecho.

—Tío, dame lo que lleves, venga.

—Por favor...

—¡Vamos! —gritó, movió la navaja, la acercó a menos de un centímetro de su cuello y tembló victima de un espasmo—. Tengo el mono, ¿sabes? No quiero hacerte daño pero... estoy muy nervioso, ¿sabes? Así que dámelo y no te pincharé. Solo quiero... —le sobrevino un segundo espasmo—, la pasta.

Sixto no se atrevió a moverse, pero por encima del miedo miró más allá de su agresor, por si aparecía alguien.

La calle estaba solitaria.

—Mira, chico... —trató de hablar.

—¡No me llames chico, so mierda!

Esta vez el cuchillo llegó hasta la piel y la carne, le hizo daño. Solo fue lo que él había anunciado, un pinchazo, pero le dolió, y acabó de asustarlo del todo.

—Sí... sí, espera, por Dios, espera... tranquilo.

—Vamos, vamos —le apremió el drogadicto.

Extrajo la cartera de su chaqueta, casi como en las películas, despacio y empleando los movimientos precisos. Se le ocurrió que podía darle el dinero, y recuperar así la documentación, las tarjetas de crédito..., pero el ladrón se la arrebató de la mano con una sacudida.

Pensó que iba a echar a correr.

—El reloj —le pidió—.Dame el reloj.

—No... —vaciló Sixto.

—¡El reloj, maricón!

—Es un... Rolex, por Dios...

—¡Mecagüen tu puta madre, dámelo!

Sixto sintió el corte, en el cuello, bajo la oreja, y también la primera presencia líquida y caliente de unas gotas de sangre resbalando por él hasta la camisa. Sintió un tremendo dolor de estómago, y estuvo casi a punto de hacérselo todo encima. Se sintió ridículo y lo evitó mientras se quitaba el reloj, que desapareció de su mano igual que la cartera para ir a parar al fondo de un bolsillo del muchacho.

Porque no era más que un crío, dieciocho, diecinueve años.

—Y ahora las llaves...

Su BMW. Su maravilloso coche. Si aquel desgraciado se lo robaba... se mataría con él, y desde luego le importaba muy poco lo que le pasara al drogadicto, pero a su coche...

Esta vez no dijo nada, ya no. Le entregó las llaves.

Pero el chico no las utilizó para lo que creía. Se separó de él apenas un par de pasos, hacia atrás, y luego las arrojó a una alcantarilla.

Después le dio la espalda y echó a correr.

86

—La verdad es que no sé porque tenía que montar el número —se quejó Encarna—. Babosos como ese los hay en todas partes, y si una mujer no sabe cuidarse sola... vale más que no salga de casa.

—Pero te ha defendido —manifestó Natalia—. Es lo que haría cualquier hombre.

—No, lo que ha hecho ha sido liar la cosa —la rectificó ella—. Yo, dándole una bofetada, lo habría arreglado todo.

—¿Y si él te hubiera agredido a ti? —continuó Natalia.

—Mira, querida —apareció una sonrisa sarcástica en sus labios—. Hay algo contra lo que ningún tío puede luchar, ¿y sabes qué es? Pues una buena patada entre las piernas. Te aseguro que se quedan más quietos y más finos que nada.

—¿Has dado muchas? —preguntó con una sonrisa Rafael.

—Más de una y más de dos, sí.

—Claro, en según que ambientes... —consideró Natalia.

—En plena Plaza de Catalunya, a las doce del mediodía, por si te sirve de consuelo —quiso puntualizar Encarna.

—Tiene razón —contemporizó Paz—. A mi prima Berta la asaltaron en pleno día en la calle Pelayo, y nadie acudió en su ayuda. Te puede pasar cualquier cosa en cualquier momento y a cualquier hora y lugar.

—A tu prima Berta también la habría asaltado yo —dijo Rafael, y en esta oportunidad un par de palabras le resbalaron de los labios—. Parece una joyería ambulante.

—Ya sabes que estás bebido, ¿no? —le espetó su mujer con sequedad—. Yo contigo no subo al coche, ¿eh? Será mejor que conduzca...

—¿No es ese... Sixto? —vaciló de pronto Salvador señalando hacia la parte superior de la calle.

Era él. Corría de una forma desmadejada, y a la máxima velocidad que le permitían sus piernas, aprovechando el suave desnivel favorable de la calle. Por su forma de hacerlo, se le notaba que algo sucedía, y a medida que se aproximo más y le vieron los rasgos, entendieron que así era. Los cinco salieron a su encuentro, caminando hacia arriba. El encuentro se produjo en menos de tres segundos.

—¡Me han...ro...bado...! —el jadeo de Sixto impidió una claridad inmediata—. ¡Un...un...joder...un...!

—¡Tienes sangre aquí! —se espantó Encarna.

—¡Virgen Santísima! —exclamó Natalia.

—¡Coño que... no es nada! —consiguió articular Sixto—¡Me ha qui...me ha quitado la cartera y el re...reloj! ¡Y ha tirado las lla...llaves del...!

—¿Quién? —le detuvo Rafael.

—¡Un drogata! ¡Un maldito...drogata! ¡Dios! —y agregó empujándoles hacia abajo, en dirección al coche de Rafael—: ¡Vamos, vamos! ¡No puede estar lejos!

—¿Pero que...? —intentó preguntar Salvador.

—¡Me ha tirado las llaves de mi coche a la alcantarilla! —insistió Sixto, con el fuelle más recuperado y un mejor dominio de su ánimo—. ¡El no sabe que podemos seguirle! ¿No lo entiendes? ¡Ese cabrón ha echado a correr, pero en su estado no habrá ido muy lejos! ¡Con un poco de suerte tal vez podamos...! ¡Se ha llevado mi Rolex y mis tarjetas, joder! ¡Vamos!

Llegaron al coche de Rafael, y él mismo se sentó al volante, con Sixto a su lado. Detrás, casi de cualquier forma, entraron Salvador y las tres mujeres. Todavía no se habían acomodado cuando Rafael inició la maniobra para desaparcar.

Lo único que se oía además del motor del automóvil eran las continuas palabras de Sixto, fuera de sí.

—¡Vamos! ¡Vamos! ¡Ese hijo de puta...! ¡Como le coja le...! ¡Cabrón de mierda, peludo!

El coche salió zumbando a toda velocidad Tuset arriba.

Salvador

Fue el inicio de la locura.

Nos vimos metidos en el coche de Rafael, con él al volante, Sixto a su lado obrando igual que un émbolo a presión, las tres mujeres demasiado asustadas para decir algo con sentido y yo...

¿Como estaba yo?

No lo recuerdo. No puedo recordarlo. Era parte de la comedia pero no me sentía dentro de ella, ni involucrado. Fue a partir de este momento cuando mi mente empezó a quedarse en blanco, o tal vez sea que con lo que pasó después... Cuando te dan un puñetazo, los recuerdos anteriores se te borran. Es una defensa del propio organismo. Y desde luego lo que sucedió fue peor que un puñetazo.

Mucho peor.

Paz

Tuve miedo, es lo único que puedo decir, que tuve miedo. Era una mezcla de inseguridad y ansiedad, algo muy extraño. Era como ir en un avión con problemas. Tu estás dentro, y no puedes hacer nada para cambiar las cosas.

Me cogí a Salvador, y al mirarle, me di cuenta de que estaba pálido.

Eso aún me asustó más.

Salvador siempre ha sido esa clase de persona capaz de mantener la sangre fría en los momentos más difíciles.

Natalia

Fue un vértigo.

En un momento estábamos hablando en la calle, aún no recuperados de la escena del Sutton, y al siguiente volábamos como locos persiguiendo aún no sé qué. Y detrás, apenas si podíamos movernos, aunque con los bandazos que daba el coche...

Yo soy de naturaleza asustadiza, así que estaba asustada, muy asustada.

Encarna

Rafael se puso a conducir como si él fuera un campeón de la Formula 1 y Sixto su copiloto, aunque no sé cual de los dos estaba más excitado. Subió por Tuset, se pasó el semáforo prácticamente en rojo porque cambió en ese momento, y enfiló la calle frontal a toda pastilla, al menos en sus primeros cien metros. Luego Sixto le dijo que su coche estaba ahí y que el robo había sido al lado y que el ladrón se había ido corriendo para arriba y que...

Frenaron en las bocacalles, mirando a uno y otro lado, rezongando, mascullando insultos y palabrotas. Se les veía muy lanzados, a mil, a tope. No me hubieran escuchado.

Pero en el fondo yo era la primera en querer coger al maldito ladrón. No estaba el horno para bollos, con la de problemas que tenía Sixto, laborales, personales y económicos. Y además los nuestros.

Aquel hijo de puta podía hacer algo más que haberse llevado el reloj y la cartera.

Rafael

La noche se había roto, pero no lo lamentaba. No era a mí a quien habían limpiado, y en cambio sentía la necesidad de atrapar al tío como fuera, y hacerle pagar...

A veces estás hasta los huevos de tanto cabrón suelto.

Nunca había conducido como lo hice en esos instantes, ni me había sentido igual. Era una sensación diferente a todas.

Y estaba lo de la sangre.

Coño... no sé, la sangre te produce una cosa aquí dentro que...

Sixto se llevó una mano al cuello para ver como estaba su herida.

87

—¡El muy cabrón...! ¡Si no llego a apartarme!

—¿Iba a por ti?

—¿Qué te crees que es esto, una rascada?

—¡Por Dios, Rafa, ten cuidado! —chilló Natalia.

—¡Callate, coño, hay que cogerle y punto!

—¡Pero será peligroso!

—¡Espera, ahí...! ¡No, nada, sigue! ¡Maldita sea! —masculló Sixto.

—¿Cómo era? —preguntó Salvador.

—Pues... joven, uno de esos capullos con el pelo largo, un pasota, y con síndrome de abstinencia, o sea que estaba...

—¡Cuidado! —advirtió Paz viendo unas luces en el siguiente cruce.

Rafael hizo sonar el claxon e hizo ráfagas con las luces largas. Volvió a detenerse para que Sixto mirara a ambos lados.

—¡Nada, mierda, sigue!

Las ruedas chirriaron. Alguien, en el coche parado en el cruce, sacó la cabeza por la ventanilla y les dijo algo que no entendieron.

—Deberíamos ir a la policía, Sixto —dijo Encarna.

Sixto

No pensaba en nada, solo en cogerle.

No me importaba nada, solo cogerle.

No quería nada, solo cogerle.

Jamás había sentido tanto odio junto en la vida. Era la espuma rebosando por el vaso de mi paciencia, de mi equilibrio.

Aquel maldito cabrón, hijo de puta...

Por esta razón, al verle, medio oculto en un portal, registrando mi cartera con movimientos nerviosos, echando al suelo lo que no le interesaba o...que se yo, sentí una llamarada en mi pecho.

Un golpe en mitad del cerebro.

El salvaje placer de una alegría llevada al máximo de la pasión.

88

—¡Ahí está! —gritó Sixto de pronto señalando a su derecha—. ¡Para, para!

—¿Dónde...?

—¡Para, coño! —ordenó—. ¡Córtale la retirada por arriba!

—¡Sixto! —quiso evitar que se bajara Encarna.

No lo consiguió. Él abrió la portezuela del coche de golpe y saltó fuera sin esperar. Aún antes de que Rafael volviera a poner la primera, ya estaba corriendo hacia el ladrón, ajeno a lo que sucedía a su alrededor.

—¡La hostia! —rezongó Rafael.

Le pisó a fondo, hasta rebasar al muchacho, y se precipitó sobre la acera apenas tres metros más allá, metiendo el morro en un vado. Ni siquiera paró el motor. El vehículo aún se movía, por efecto de la frenada, cuando él ya corría lo mismo que Sixto solo que por la parte de arriba de la calle.

—¡Rafael! —aulló Natalia.

—¡Ay Dios mío! —gimió Paz.

Fue el grito de Natalia el que provocó que el muchacho levantara la cabeza, alertado definitivamente del peligro que corría.

Pero ya era tarde para él.

Sixto le cayó encima en el mismo instante, y cuando los dos se vencían hacia el suelo, Rafael le pegó la primera patada en el cuerpo.

Salvador

Todo...sucedió muy rápido.

89

—¡Hijoputa!

El puño de Sixto impactó en su rostro, cegándole.

Escuchó un gemido. Le sonó a música.

Paz

Era un chico joven, pude verlo por entre el amasijo de pies y manos. Tan joven como Octavio, y con su mismo aspecto.

Me detuve a dos o tres metros, sin poder moverme.

Rafael

Yo solo trataba de ayudar a Sixto...

90

—¡Dale, Rafael, dale! —gritó Natalia—. ¡Así!

Casi golpeó a Sixto. Su nueva patada pasó cerca de él, al revolverse ambos en el suelo. Su pié se hundió en el estómago del ladrón. Optó por inclinarse y tratar de cogerle por los pelos.

Lo consiguió.

Entonces le dio un puñetazo, beneficiándose de que él estuviera completamente desguarnecido.

—¡Déjamelo a mi! ¡Déjamelo a mi! —bramó Sixto.

Natalia

Yo apenas podía moverme.

Encarna

Aunque hubiera querido evitarlo, era demasiado tarde.

91

—¡Mátale, Sixto, mátale!

Encarna tenía los puños apretados, el rostro desencajado.

Intentó aproximarse al grupo.

—¡Natalia, ven aquí! —ordenó Paz—. ¿Qué estás haciendo?

Sixto aplastó la cabeza del muchacho contra la acera. Se escuchó un sordo eco.

Luego apareció la sangre.

Sixto

Se revolvía, quería defenderse, sacar de nuevo el cuchillo, que no sé ni dónde podía estar. No hacíamos más que actuar en defensa propia...

92

—¡Dios mío, Dios mío! ¡Vais a matarle! —chilló Paz.

Fue su grito aterrorizado el que alertó a Salvador.

—¡Basta ya! ¿Qué estáis haciendo?

Salvador

Fue una especie de fogonazo. De pronto el chico levantó la cabeza, buscando un respiro, aire, o el fin de la lluvia de puñetazos y patadas, y me miró, o yo pensé que me miraba, porque tenía la expresión ida y los ojos vidriosos. Le manaba la sangre por la nariz y la boca.

Aún así tardé en reaccionar, porque estaba paralizado.

Estaba viendo a mi hijo Octavio.

Y todo el odio que sentía, porque aunque estuviese quieto, la profundidad de ese sentimiento me había alcanzado, se desvaneció lo mismo que una nube batida por el viento.

93

Se interpuso entre ellos. Primero separó a Rafael, que estaba congestionado, fuera de sí, y después sujetó a Sixto, que todavía descargaba puñetazo tras puñetazo sobre el cuerpo caído e inmóvil.

—¡Suéltame! ¡Suéltame, coño!

—¡Ya está bien, por Dios!

—¡Déjame que acabe con ese hijoputa!

Logró empujarle, contra la pared. Fue un grito de Paz el que le alertó de nuevo. Se giró a tiempo de ver como Rafael iba a darle una última patada al desguarnecido rostro del muchacho.

—¡No!

Natalia

Cogí a mi marido, y solté la tensión. Me puse a llorar.

Encarna

Recogí la cartera de Sixto, todo lo que estaba por el suelo, sus tarjetas de crédito, la foto de sus hijos...

Sixto

Me aparté de Salvador. Lo único que me interesaba era recuperar mi reloj. Estaba más calmado, de verdad. Todo había pasado.

Rafael

Abracé a Natalia, y me olvidé del chico. Había sido una explosión, pero había cesado.

Paz

No sé por qué lo hizo. Tal vez fuera un gesto reflejo, o una autodefensa, temeroso de que volvieran a hacerle daño. Salvador estaba de espaldas a él, observando a Sixto y a Rafael.

Probablemente iba a ayudarle, claro. Es médico. Tenía que examinar los golpes, las heridas...

Así que no sé por qué lo hizo.

94

El drogadicto quiso levantarse, como lo hubiera hecho un muñeco con las piernas rotas y sin apenas un átomo de alma. Buscó el amparo de la pared, se movió.

Su mano derecha voló de pronto al encuentro de su pierna.

Y en ella apareció el cuchillo.

—¡Cuidado! —chilló Encarna.

95

El grito alertó a Salvador, demasiado cerca. Al girarse se encontró con el centelleo del cuchillo, y con el muchacho tratando de incorporarse, asustado, con la sangre cayéndole por la cara, sobre el pecho. Tenía un ojo cerrado, el cabello convertido en una pasta rojiza y un diente suspendido de la comisura de sus labios.

El cuchillo se convirtió en el centro de todas sus miradas.

Salvador reaccionó tarde, pero reaccionó. Sujetó la mano armada, aunque ni siquiera era consciente de si ella iba a atacarle o no. Después, cuando la empujó hacia atrás y hacia abajo, se sorprendió de su escasa fuerza, de la nula oposición. Fue como vencer a un niño de pecho en un juego.

Y el cuchillo se hundió mansa y blandamente en el cuerpo.

96

El muchacho tuvo un estremecimiento

Miró a Salvador con su único ojo relativamente sano.

Luego, un invisible y transparente tul le arrebató la visión y la vida.

Paz

Cayó de lado, escurriéndose hacia el suelo tan y tan despacio que pareció como si el mundo entero se hubiese detenido.

Natalia

Creo que se agitó, no sé... como si tuviera una descarga eléctrica, una sacudida...

Sixto

Hasta que se quedó inmóvil.

Rafael

Empezó a formarse una enorme mancha de sangre bajo él.

Encarna

Continuábamos muy quietos, como si aquello no estuviera sucediendo.

El silencio era tan ensordecedor como el aullido de un estadio repleto de fanáticos.

Salvador

Soy médico.

Pero no pude ni reaccionar.

Soy médico.

Así que sabía que estaba muerto.

97

—¡Está muerto!

—¡Oh, no, no!

—¡Dios mío, Salvador! ¿Qué has hecho?

Levantó la cabeza. Las voces sonaban como avispas

pasando cerca de su ánimo, pero era incapaz de reconocerlas. Se miró las manos, y recordó a modo de flash otro momento, otro lugar, muchos años antes. Eran las mismas manos, y también era él, cuando pensó que un día sanarían vidas, y sería un héroe.

El mejor cirujano del mundo.

Lo último que hizo fue enfrentarse a Paz.

Su mujer le miraba aterrorizada, con la boca abierta.

—Yo no... —trató de decir él.

Sus palabras murieron, victimas de un agotamiento súbito, pero la escena cobró vida de nuevo, al reaccionar prácticamente al unisono Sixto y Rafael.

—¡Rápido, vámonos! —ordenó el primero.

—¡Sí, venga, hay que largarse de aquí! —dijo el segundo.

Salvador consiguió apartar los ojos de los de su mujer. El movimiento de los otros dos le devolvió a la realidad.

—¿Qué estáis diciendo?

—¡Hay que salir zumbando, hombre! —fue el primero en empujarle Sixto.

—¡Cuanto antes! —insistió Rafael mirando arriba y abajo de la vacía y solitaria calle—. ¡Joder, aún estamos de suerte!

—No podemos... irnos —balbuceó Salvador.

—¿Estás loco? —el grito de Sixto fue ahora menos evidente, más contenido, para no sonar demasiado fuerte—. ¿No vas a quedarte aquí?

—Pero es que hay que avisar a...

Le empujaban en dirección al coche, sin darle la menor oportunidad. Encarna hizo lo mismo con Natalia y ella con Paz. Salvador aún trataba de girar la cabeza para ver el cuerpo caído del muchacho.

—¡Nadie le echará de menos, hombre! —manifestó Rafael.

—¡No era más que un drogata de mierda! —le recordó Sixto.

—¡Y ha sido en defensa propia! ¡No seas burro! —siguió Rafael.

—¡Aun así, ya sabes cómo es la policía! ¡Nos van a tocar los huevos como si la cosa fuera al revés! —insistió Sixto—. ¡Hijos de puta, si trincaran a todos estos mierdas de la calle...!

Al entrar en el coche, Paz empezó a llorar.

Salvador intentó resistirse por última vez.

Sixto lo evitó, lo empujó dentro. Encarna y Natalia ya estaban atrás, abrazando a Paz. Salvador buscó una mano de su mujer, giró la cabeza. Le sobresaltó el ruido de las portezuelas cerrándose, una a una, en extraña cadencia.

Después, Rafael puso la marcha atrás

—¡Ahora, dale caña! —dijo Sixto.

Y se la dio, hasta la primera esquina, por la cual doblaron para alejarse cuanto antes y lo más rápido posible de la escena del crimen.

Epílogo
LAS VÍCTIMAS

Rafael

Dejé a Salvador y a su mujer en casa los primeros, y tras asegurarnos de que estaban bien, nos fuimos nosotros cuatro. Bueno, lo de que estaban bien era relativo. Pero pensamos que unas horas de reposo nos vendrían bien a todos. Lo importante era mantener la calma, no dejarse llevar por los nervios. Sixto y yo pensamos que por la mañana, lo veríamos todo más claro.

No éramos culpables de nada, salvo de un infortunio accidentado. Había sido aquel infeliz el que se lo había buscado todo, y solito.

Un desgraciado, un pobre desgraciado.

Si no hubiera muerto esa noche, lo habría hecho a la siguiente o a la otra, de la misma forma, o robando un banco, o de una sobredosis.

Quiero decir que... bueno, hay un tipo de gente sin esperanza, ¿no?. Condenada de antemano. Los demás, los normales, hemos de defendernos, y mantenernos firmes.

¿De qué habría servido quedarnos?

Sí, ¿de qué?

Los fantasmas no aparecieron hasta el día siguiente, ¿entiende? Y aún entonces...

Dejamos a Sixto y a Encarna en su piso, y nos fuimos al nuestro. Yo aún tuve que llevar a la canguro a su casa. Eso me ayudó a despejarme un poco más, porque si me hubiera quedado solo con Natalia... Cuando regresé ella se había tomado un par de valiums y ya estaba con los ojos semicerrados. Apenas si me dijo nada. No podía. Pero había llorado lo suyo.

Al día siguiente, es decir, ayer, me levanté tarde y tras haber tenido pesadillas continuadas. Natalia ya estaba en pie, con Gloria. Me dijo que había telefoneado a Paz pero que tenían puesto el automático.

Tras esto... sí, me fui a ver a Mercedes. Le dije a Natalia que necesitaba aire fresco, recapacitar, reflexionar, y me largué de casa cuanto antes. No podía seguir allí. Todo se me caía encima.

No le dije nada a ella, ni siquiera discutí por lo de nuestra pelea y su salida en solitario. Hicimos el amor. A fin de cuentas era lo único que yo quería y necesitaba.

Le prometí hablar con Natalia, pero mentía.

Justamente ahora no podía hacerlo.

Cuando regresé a mi casa, Natalia ya no volvió a mentarme el tema. Era como una autista cerrando su mente a lo desagradable.

Así que vivimos engañados todo el día, en un silencio constante, hasta esta mañana, cuando ha llamado Salvador para decirnos que...

De acuerdo, lo sé.

Uno no puede escapar de sí mismo.

Natalia

Me refugié en Gloria.

Me pasé todo el día con ella, jugando, haciendo lo que fuera para no parar y pensar. Si cuando llamé por teléfono a Paz se hubiera puesto al aparato... no sé, puede que al escuchar su voz...

Pero no fue así, y luego Rafael me dejó sola, no regresó hasta la hora de comer, y estando Gloria presente... Nos comportamos como autómatas.

Una fría, cortés y glacial mentira.

Y cuando al cerrar los ojos, veía al chico muerto, o escuchaba el eco de mi voz, me decía que eso no había sucedido en realidad, que era una película, una película vívida y fuerte, de esas que te impactan, pero nada más.

Nadie tenía porque hablar. Nadie tenía porque sospechar de nosotros, seis personas normales y corrientes. Nadie.

Ayer por la noche, al acostarnos, al ver a Rafael a mi lado, aún en su silencio, me dio por pensar que tal vez aquello volviera a unirnos. Ahora ya no solo era un matrimonio. Teníamos también un secreto.

Deseé irme de vacaciones, que ya fuera verano, marcharme de Barcelona cuanto antes.

De no haber sido por la llamada de Salvador esta mañana...

Sixto

Anduve preocupado, por si me había dejado algo personal allí, en la escena del crimen, y registré una y otra vez mi cartera y lo que Encarna había recogido del suelo. Parecía no faltar nada, pero reconozco que no pegué ojo en toda la noche, y Encarna lo mismo. Dimos vueltas y más vueltas, de forma agitada, hasta que por la mañana me telefoneó mi hijo Guillermo. Dios... era justo cuando acababa de adormilarme un poco, y eso me volvió a desvelar. Y sé que fue su madre. Sole es ideal como torturadora. Sabe cuándo y cómo joder la marrana.

Hablé con Guillermo, y después me levanté y me vestí. Con las llaves de repuesto del coche fui a por él. Lo tenía aparcado cerca del sitio donde sucedió todo pero lo suficientemente lejos como para que nadie me viera ni pasara nada. De las llaves arrojadas a la alcantarilla, mejor olvidarme. Aunque alguien las encontrara en el subsuelo, no había en ellas ningún indicio... ¿o sí? ¿Y el número de...? Pero eso no significaba nada, por supuesto. Con decir que se me habían caído un día, semanas atrás, al ir a meterme en el coche, arreglado.

Subí a mi BMW, salí, y al enfilar calle arriba... no pude evitarlo.

Pasé por el lugar.

No había nadie, como la noche pasada, así que casi me dio por pensar que el cuerpo del drogadicto aún estaría allí. Pero ya se lo habían llevado. En el suelo solo quedaba la constancia de la sangre en forma de mancha oscura recubierta de serrín.

Eso era todo.

Respiré a fondo, y volví a casa. Encarna me preguntó que tal y lo único que le dije fue que lo olvidara. Luego la abracé y, como otras veces, solo con tenerla y aspirar su perfume me volví loco y empecé a desnudarla. Me dijo que no, que estaba nerviosa, que esto y aquello, pero... lo hicimos igual. Bueno, lo hice. Ella no se corrió. Al terminar telefoneé a Salvador, pero nadie contestó. Imaginé que se había ido a alguna parte.

En lo que menos pensé fue en que él no lo soportara.

De hecho, por la noche, el que empezó a no soportarlo fui yo.

Esta mañana me sentía bastante mal, muy mal.

De hecho, al verles me he sentido liberado.

Encarna

Había sido Salvador, no nosotros. Habían sido ellos, no nosotros. Había sido la sociedad, no nosotros.

Y desde luego, la que no había sido era yo.

Yo no.

Me lo repetí, una y otra vez, sin parar, a lo largo del día. Y me miré al espejo, fijamente, para insistir en ello y metérmelo en la cabeza. Cada vez que, a traición, como si se tratara de un fantasma, un eco o un acto reflejo, la cara del chico o la escena reaparecía en mí, la apartaba violentamente, la negaba.

Creí que con eso bastaría. Eso y aspirinas. Eso y tiempo. Tiempo.

No le dije nada a Sixto de lo que pensaba, de sus amigos, de la necesidad de aislarnos y olvidar cuanto nos atara al pasado, para empezar de cero, los dos juntos y solos. Comprendí que no era el momento.

Pero evidentemente era absurdo volver a verles. Siempre que lo hiciéramos tendríamos en la memoria, presente como una pesada losa de plomo, aquel infeliz.

Podía haber matado a Sixto, o a Salvador, o a mí.

Podía.

Esta mañana, Sixto y yo nos hemos mirado en silencio, y ha sido como si lo viéramos todo claro de pronto. De hecho ya sabíamos que acabaría así. Por ello, al sonar el teléfono y oir la voz de Salvador...

Paz

No podía quitarme de la cabeza aquella explosión de violencia.

Veía a Sixto y a Rafael golpeando a aquel chico, veía la sangre, y sobre todo veía sus ojos, sus manos, su débil resistencia quebrándose como una simple caña bajo el pié de un gigante llamado desesperación.

Luego veía a Natalia y a Encarna, gritando antes de darse cuenta de lo que estaban haciendo, y veía a Salvador, quieto, horrorizado, con aquella expresión de absoluto asombro.

Pobre Salvador.

Ni siquiera puedo decir que fuera él.

Ni tampoco la mala suerte.

Fue la noche, Sixto y Rafael, nosotros, todos, el antes y el entonces y el después. Demasiado para unas gentes normales, sencillas, pero capaces de convertirse en asesinas.

O en víctimas.

Cuando nos dejaron en casa y subimos, Vanessa se había quedado dormida sobre los libros, así que la acostamos. Al cerrar la puerta de se habitación, Salvador se echó a llorar, y yo le abracé con todas mis fuerzas. Le dije que había sido un accidente.

Y él solo repetía un nombre: Octavio.

Hasta que dijo aquello.

—Le vi a él, y quise pegarle como hacían Sixto y Rafa, y cuando se hundió el cuchillo en su cuerpo... desperté.

Creí que se volvía loco. Creí que se arrojaba por una ventana. Nunca le recuerdo igual. Abrió la puerta de la habitación de nuestro hijo, que como es natural aún no había llegado, y le pidió a Dios que volviera.

Era como si le hubiera matado a él, ¿entiende?

Cuando llegó Octavio, a las seis y pico de la mañana, nos encontró despiertos y con demasiadas evidencias de que algo muy grave nos había sucedido. Fui yo la que se lo conté, y mientras lo hacía, apareció Vanessa, arrancada de su sueño por la misma excitación y el nerviosismo de su estado en etapa de exámenes. Al comienzo, mi hija se puso a llorar, porque yo lo hice, pero Octavio mantuvo la calma.

Tal vez tenga tan solo dieciocho años, pero es un hombre, de los piés a la cabeza, y también una gran persona, un buen ser humano, no sé si me explico. Quiero decir que es honesto, honrado, y pese a su imagen o lo que Salvador siempre creyera, también tiene carácter.

Fue Octavio el que le dijo a su padre que les llamara.

Dijo que de todas formas lo haría.

Octavio supo que no podríamos vivir con lo sucedido sobre nuestras conciencias.

Fue un largo, muy largo día, hasta esta mañana.

Salvador

Primero telefoneé a Sixto y a Rafael, para decirles que pensaba hacerlo, que iba a entregarme.

Apenas hubo protestas. De hecho estaban de acuerdo.

Después, al llamarles a ustedes...

—¿Está seguro de que no hubo protestas por parte del señor Planas y el señor Martí?

¿Protestas?

¡Dios... ni siquiera recuerdo...!

¿Qué puedo decir, que Sixto y Rafael no querían dar la cara? ¿Que me dijeron que estaba loco, que se pusieron histéricos? O tal vez deba decir que... me recordaron que había sido yo y solo yo.

Fuimos todos, los seis.

Todos.

Y a mi me tocó empujar el cuchillo.

—Señor Marcos, ¿se encuentra bien?

—Sí, sí, disculpe... Llevo todo este tiempo sin dormir y...

—¿Quiere descansar?

—No.

—¿De verdad?

—Quiero soltarlo todo, y acabar cuanto antes. Me quema, ¿sabe usted? Me quema por dentro.

El hombre sostuvo su mirada. Luego le vio cerrar los ojos, respirar profundamente, y al volver a abrirlos el tono vidrioso de las pupilas se hizo aún más evidente.

—Ese chico... —musitó Salvador—. ¿Se sabe ya quién era?

—Sí.

—¿Puede...?

El hombre dirigió una mirada al otro hombre, el que estaba de pié detrás de Salvador. Fue un puente silencioso entre ambos.

—Se llamaba Fermín García Fernández, diecinueve años, padre en la cárcel y madre dedicada a trabajos hogareños. Tiene una hermana mayor, prostituta, y dos hermanos más pequeños, uno en un correccional. Era un drogadicto.

Sixto y Rafael lo dijeron: un don nadie, un desgraciado.

¿Valía la pena...?

Sixto y Rafael.

¿Qué más daba quién fuera el muchacho? Yo hice el juramento hipocrático.

—Yo hice el juramento hipocrático —susurró Salvador en voz alta.

—¿Qué? —preguntó el hombre.

—Creo que mi cliente necesita descansar, inspector —dijo el hombre situado a espaldas de Salvador.

Este levantó una mano.

—No, no... —objetó.

El policía se acodó sobre la mesa.

—Han declarado ya todos, señor Marcos —dijo—. Pero su testimonio es el más importante, ¿se da cuenta?

—Claro.

—¿De verdad los señores Martí y Planas han estado de acuerdo esta mañana en que usted nos llamara para contarlo todo? —insistió—. Es importante, ¿me comprende, doctor?

¿Y Paz? ¿Dónde está Paz? Necesito a Paz.

—No queríamos matar a ese chico, ¿entiende, inspector? Fue...un lamentable accidente. El maldito epílogo de una maldita noche de perros. No somos más que... gente, personas vulgares y corrientes. Eso es. Sucedió y...

Comenzó a llorar, débilmente, arrastrado y empujado por cuanto le surgía del interior. Su abogado le puso ambas manos en los hombros, y miró con firmeza al inspector de policía.

—Ya tiene lo que quería —manifestó—, y le recuerdo que el señor Salvador Marcos ha venido voluntariamente después de haberles llamado por teléfono para ponerles en antecedentes.

El inspector de policía miró al detenido, y después asintió con la cabeza. Dos agentes, situados junto a la puerta, avanzaron hasta colocarse uno a cada lado del médico. No le forzaron a incorporarse, tan solo le ayudaron a hacerlo, con cierta delicadeza. El abogado no hizo ni dijo nada más.

Fue al dar el tercer paso, cuando Salvador giró la cabeza por última vez.

—Quisiera...

—Esté tranquilo, doctor Marcos —asintió el policía.

—Gracias —dijo él.

Después salieron todos del despacho.

98

El inspector de policía tardó todavía un poco en levantarse. Cuando lo hizo apartó los seis expedientes apilados sobre la mesa, sin querer dirigirles ninguna mirada, y caminó en dirección a la ventana del despacho, desde la que se asomó a la calle.

Domingo.

Apenas si había nadie en ninguna parte, salvo allí.

Levantó los ojos, siguió el perfil de las casas frontales, buscó la línea del cielo, y finalmente pareció abarcar Barcelona entera, a pesar de que desde allí no veía más que una minúscula porción de la ciudad.

La ciudad.

Tardó un par de minutos largos en apartarse de la

ventana, pero no volvió a ocupar su butaca frente a la mesa. Ahora paseó la mirada por ella, se detuvo en el portarretratos ubicado en un ángulo y sus pupilas titilaron un instante al reconocer la familiaridad de aquella imagen, una mujer sonriente, un muchacho adolescente con el cabello largo y aspecto informal, una chica igualmente adolescente con ojos pícaros y retadores, y un niño pequeño, de cara redonda y pelo corto.

Al pié del portarretratos estaba el periódico, abierto, doblado por la página de sucesos. El titular era visible:

"JOVEN DROGADICTO APUÑALADO".

Debajo, en letras más pequeñas pero igualmente destacadas, se ampliaba el detalle:

"Muerte en la madrugada" - "Historia de un fin anunciado" - "Fermín García Fernández encontró un cuchillo mientras buscaba drogas en la madrugada del viernes".

El inspector de policía miró la puerta por la que había salido el último de los interrogados, que también había sido el primero.

Sonó el teléfono.

Pero no lo cogió.

Sabía que era su mujer, para preguntarle por qué, en Domingo, llevaba ya tantas horas fuera de casa.

Barcelona, La Habana, Varadero y Vallirana.
Junio y julio de 1994.

Trilogía de la ciudad

LOS ESPEJOS DE LA NOCHE (AMIGOS)

AGUAS AZULES PARA UNA BATALLA (FAMILIA)

LOS VACIOS DE LA SOLEDAD (DESCONOCIDOS)

Made in the USA
Las Vegas, NV
20 July 2023

75023550R00173